A COMPLICATED WOMAN

Sheelagh Kelly was born in York in 1948, but now lives with her husband in sub-tropical Queensland. She attended Knavesmire Secondary School for Girls, left at the age of 15 and went to work as a book-keeper. She has written for pleasure since she was a small child, but not until 1980 were the seeds for her first novel, *A Long Way from Heaven*, sown when she developed an interest in genealogy and local history and decided to trace her ancestors' story, thereby acquiring an abiding fascination with the quirks of human nature. *A Long Way from Heaven* was followed by *For My Brother's Sins*, *Erin's Child*, *My Father, My Son*, *Dickie* and *Shoddy Prince*, all of which were bestsellers.

SHEELAGH KELLY

A Complicated Woman

HarperCollins*Publishers*

This novel is entirely a work of fiction. The names, characters and
incidents portrayed in it are the work of the author's imagination.
Any resemblance to actual persons, living or dead,
events or localities is entirely coincidental.

HarperCollins*Publishers*
77–85 Fulham Palace Road,
Hammersmith, London W6 8JB

This paperback edition 1998
2

First published in Great Britain by
HarperCollins*Publishers* 1997

Copyright © Sheelagh Kelly 1997

The Author asserts the moral right to
be identified as the author of this work

9780007630387

Set in PostScript Linotype Sabon by
Rowland Phototypesetting Ltd,
Bury St Edmunds, Suffolk

Printed and bound in Great Britain by
Clays Ltd, St Ives plc

With thanks to Kate Graham
for her invaluable help

1

13 November 1918

Tension threatened to ruin what should have been a joyful reunion for two of the people in the ornate Yorkshire parlour; a mood dictated by the third, an attractive young woman. The middle-aged lovers shared a helpless quizzical glance. How long could this discord between father and daughter prevail? Why couldn't she be happy that her parents had found each other again after all these years? The hostilities were over. Outside, a state of jubilation reigned, but in here the tick of the mantel clock marked an air of cool antipathy.

The war might be over, but for Oriel Maguire the enemy remained in their midst: the man who had deserted them. Oriel allowed him only a cursory glance from beneath her black fringe as, with awkward excuse, he rose and left the room to answer the call of nature.

Even in his absence she felt unable to relax. A war still raged within her, pitting head against heart, compassion against bitter memory. Such irony that, with thousands of bereaved women keening for the menfolk they would never see again, she was wishing hers elsewhere. Inherent kindness dictated that she should forgive him – she *had* forgiven him two days ago, until she had learned that he was intent on dragging her beloved mother away from her, twelve thousand miles to Australia. Then all the bile she had stored during his twenty-two-year absence had been regurgitated.

Oh, he had asked her to come too, but she knew that it was only said out of duty. He did not really want her along to sour his plans. Yet if she did not go, how would she survive the loneliness? There had only ever been the two of them in this family: mother and daughter. Before Oriel had swapped her cloistered education within these walls for the more gregarious life of a secretarial college she had rarely even played with girls her own age, apart from the brief encounters during the Sunday walks to church. True, she had friends now but none of them close. That was not Mother's doing. Bright Maguire had been just as much a prisoner of her past as had Oriel – more so, for as the mother of this illegitimate daughter she had lived in constant fear of the workhouse. Until this moment Oriel had always felt it her job to protect this dear woman, and now here was her wretch of a father trying to usurp that role. She hoped her attitude had let him know just how much she resented this intrusion.

In the whitewashed quiet of the outside closet Nathaniel Prince lowered his buttocks gingerly on to the cold seat. He might have known that Oriel would not make it easy for him, sitting there all through dinner with her maungy face. Sighing, he hunched over, nursing his wound, a wound ironically not meted during the hostilities but in the throes of peace celebrations. A few hours ago this dark, introspective man had been in hospital, until his dearest Bright had fetched him to her home for the midday meal that they had just eaten. How conspicuous he had felt sitting up to that pristine tablecloth in this bloodstained attire, but his hostess had maintained a lack of concern about his appearance, happy only to have him here. It did not escape his notice that Oriel offered no such palliative.

Tugging the chain, he returned to the warmth of Bright's narrow scullery, glancing around him as he went. Built during the long reign of Queen Victoria the house and its clutter represented that era and all that was bad about it. Nat would have felt rather hemmed in here had he not had Oriel's open hostility to distract him.

A mahogany-framed glass reflected his pallor; it was

immediately obvious that he had only been released from gaol two days ago, the sentence meted out for the crime of grievous bodily harm. Since then he had not had the chance to attend to his usual scrupulous toilet before this latest mishap had occurred. Thank goodness he had managed to procure a razor in the hospital or he would have looked a complete tramp. Yet, he remained ill at ease as he re-entered the front parlour with its elegant occupants in their smart woollen costumes, the gleam on their shoes competing with the highly polished fender whilst his own had seen only a cursory rub with a handkerchief this morning. Nat had always detested slovenliness, never more so than now at this most important of reunions.

Still trying to acclimatize himself to being his own master again he dithered between the jambs, waiting for some higher authority to command his next movement. Bright helped his decision by patting the sofa. In the same instant that he flopped back on to the cushions beside the love of his life the younger woman jumped up and moved to leave the room. Nat appeared alarmed and blurted in his Yorkshire accent, 'Where you off?'

Oriel gave him a deliberate stare. Though she too had been born in York her speech was less accented than his. 'Well, I'm sure you two have plenty to discuss so I'm going for a bicycle ride – with your permission, of course.'

Nat looked at first chastened, then rather offended. Anyone witnessing the exchange would not believe that they were father and daughter the way she treated him – the way he allowed her to do so.

'Ye don't have to go on our account.' Bright's own accent emerged as a hybrid mix. Born in York of Irish parentage, she had adopted idiosyncrasies of both influences. Her overt cheerfulness was just slightly manufactured, an attempt to keep the peace between the two most important people in her life.

'I know I don't have to.' Oriel finished buttoning her

3

coat and drew on a plum velvet beret over her glossy bob. 'I'm only going to escape the washing up.'

Her father was an instant volunteer.

'It was a joke.' The young woman's face with its luminous blue eyes, domed white cheeks and full lips had the appearance of a benevolent moonbeam, until it looked upon him; now its expression was withering. The wretch had only been here a few hours and already he had got his feet under the table.

'Well, I wasn't joking.' Nat fidgeted self-consciously with the blood-daubed rent in his jacket where the knife had penetrated. 'I don't mind doing 'em. It were a grand meal.'

'Don't waste your compliment on me, Mother cooked it.' On this abrupt note Oriel departed.

'Watch the road!' warned Bright. 'It's slippy out there.'

'And try not to mow down any innocent bystanders,' Nat muttered as his daughter left.

Upon hearing the back door close he explained, 'I weren't trying to play the heavy-handed father. It's just –' He broke off with an embarrassed grimace. 'I thought she was off to the closet an' I've made the most horrendous stink out there. It must be summat I ate in that blasted hospital.'

Bright threw back her head and laughed; displaying the mole beneath her chin that had fascinated Nat as a child. 'If that's the best ye can do in the way of romantic conversation after twenty years!'

All apologies, he grabbed her hand and squeezed it, trying to ignore the jolt to his bandaged breast. The knife had incised only muscle but was nevertheless incredibly painful. She returned the fond squeeze of his hand. Then both fell silent, content in each other's company. They had waited for this moment for over two decades – had not expected it ever to happen. Here they were, together at last.

In the small rear garden Oriel, hearing her mother's

laughter, had the suspicion that her father had made some clever comment at her expense. Her breath emerged in angry little gasps on the damp November air as she struggled with her bicycle to the gate and into the lane, bashing her shin and getting oil on her stocking in the process. With a curse she mounted and, forcing all her anger and self-pity into her actions, pedalled off without knowing where.

Fulford Road was greasy with fallen leaves, but pink of cheek and oblivious to skidding tyres, Oriel forged on towards a city emblazoned in a triumphant flutter of Union Jacks, its streets alive with children who had been granted a holiday from school to mark the Armistice: little girls with red-white-and-blue ribbons in their plaits, boys marching in proud imitation of their soldier fathers who would soon be home, and hundred upon hundred of gaunt-faced women who would never see their menfolk again.

She pedalled across an elaborate iron bridge, towards Knavesmire and open countryside where, eventually, exhaustion forced her to turn back. Cycling more casually now, she returned to the city boundary and there dismounted to rest a while upon a stone bench, pondering on what course her life would take hereafter. Her anger dissipated by the action of pedalling, she scolded herself for such childish behaviour. Was not this what she had always longed for? To be like normal people with two parents. Alas, the fact that her father had been reunited with her mother did not really alter things for Oriel, whose illegitimacy would remain a constant slur.

Had she possessed an ounce of objectivity Oriel would have recognized that her life had been privileged in comparison to her mother's. The only detriment she had suffered, if that were not too strong a word, was to be rejected by the nursing profession. But utmost in her mind was that telling omission on her birth certificate: the column reserved for the name of the child's father

5

bore only a dash. This could never be remedied, and the anticipated embarrassment it would cause in years to come was what made it so hard to forgive.

She tilted her face up towards the sky and the welter of bare branches overhead. The last of the damp brown leaves floated down to add to the soggy mattress on the verge around her. Oriel closed her eyes and breathed deeply, inhaling this much-loved scent of late autumn. If she decided to accompany her parents to Australia there were many things like this she would miss. As if to compensate, she filled her lungs to bursting.

'Caught you!'

Oriel jumped and exhaled noisily, her whole skin prickling, as a Union Jack was fluttered under her nose and a familiar grinning face intruded upon her meditation.

The young woman laughed apologetically and, gesturing for her companions to go on without her, perched on the edge of the bench. 'I didn't mean to make you wet your knickers.'

Oriel laughed with relief and dealt a playful shove to her erstwhile college friend. 'Angela Bell, I almost had kittens – oh, it's lovely to see you! I tried to get in touch when it was my twenty-first but no one knew where you were.'

'No, I've moved. My, you're looking wonderful – but then you always did put the rest of us in the shade.'

Oriel gave a self-deprecatory laugh and changed the subject to the Armistice. 'Can you believe this war's really over after all these years?'

The other beamed and fluttered the Union Jack again. 'Marvellous, isn't it? I dare say there'll be a huge party when all this rationing is over – oh, you and I will have to meet and arrange something, all the old college friends.'

'I'd love to but I might not be here much longer.' When the other's face turned quizzical, Oriel added, 'I might be in Australia.' She regretted saying it almost immediately.

'Goodness! But what, I mean, who – but why? I

presume it's your mother's idea. You obviously can't be going alone – unless you've found a husband, of course!' Angela's face lit up in expectation.

Feeling cornered Oriel shook her head with an awkward laugh. How could she say: no, actually my father has returned to marry my mother? She had always allowed the girls at college to believe her father was dead. 'Nothing's definite,' she blurted, but this did not deter the grilling from Angela, who asked when she had decided. 'I haven't actually decided –'

'I mean, it'll be awfully sad to leave the rest of your family.'

Oriel, thinking of the Maguires, shrugged. 'We haven't any real family.'

'What about your grandparents? Aunts, uncles even?' Angela realized that she knew little of the other's background, but then why should she? They were only acquainted through college, and all their other friends agreed that Oriel had always been somewhat of an enigmatic creature, not one ready to share real intimacies – though they all liked her.

Face thoughtful, Oriel shook her head. 'I've only ever met one of my mother's relatives and I've no wish to meet the rest. There was a family disagreement years ago and it left a lot of bad feeling. So, there's no one really to miss.' Catching the look of intrigue on Angela's face, the question forming on her lips, she rushed to forestall it. 'My father was an orphan so there never was any family on his side.'

This appeared to suffice. 'Well, I'm sure we'll all miss you if you decide to go but I wish you good luck and you must promise to get in touch before you leave.' Glancing over her shoulder Angela saw that her family had put quite a distance between them. 'I'd better be going myself. Don't sit too long on that cold slab, you'll get –'

'Piles!' Oriel beamed. 'I know, my mother says that too. I've never found out what they are. When I asked

7

she'd only say, "Well, if you keep sitting on that cold step you're sure to find out."'

Angela frowned. 'I never found out either – I'll go and demand to be told immediately. Tootle-oo!'

'Pip, pip!' Oriel watched the flag-bearer perform a hurried skitter along the greasy pavement to catch up with her family, and decided that it was time for her to do the same. Yet reluctant to go home and play gooseberry, she browsed for a while on the previous dialogue. The lack of kin had never unduly concerned her before and, as had been uttered truthfully to Angela, she had no wish to meet them now. Though she had experienced curiosity over her paternal forebears there was never any sense of being deprived – but now, upon her contemplated departure to an unknown country from which there might be no return, she underwent a change of opinion, was prodded by a desire to know her background.

Once planted, the idea had to be acted upon, for Oriel had never been one to wait until the morrow. Where did she begin? At birth, of course. A child's birth certificate said everything about one. She of all people should know that. It crossed her mind as odd that during all her previous ferreting amongst her father's private documents she had never once bothered to search for his birth certificate – did not even know if he had one – but she would find out now.

Checking that she had brought her keys, she remounted her bicycle and instead of going home headed through town towards the quiet Georgian terrace where her father lived. She could, of course, have asked her mother and had the information readily supplied, but Bright would relay the request to him and then he might get it into his head that Oriel was interested when she wasn't in the least. All she wanted to know was where she really came from.

With the twist of a key and a cast-iron knob beneath an elegant fanlight, she was inside his house. The search was easier than she had anticipated. The copy of her father's birth certificate over which she pored now was dated quite recently – he must have had to acquire it for some official reason. However, Oriel was unconcerned about that, her eyes going directly to the column reserved for the name of the father. It was entered with a dash, the same as her own. This was a bit of a letdown but no surprise. He had flung evidence of his own illegitimacy at her in an argument. Starting at the beginning of the certificate she read that the child had been born in York Workhouse. His name was Nathaniel and his mother's name was Maria Smellie. Oriel touched her lips in sympathy. Poor little child, to be saddled with that! Occupation of the father was, of course, again vacant. The informant had been the Master of the Workhouse. And that was the sum of the information.

Disappointed, she ruminated for a while over Maria Smellie. There must be some other way to find out about her. All she knew was that Nat's mother had abandoned him when he was about eleven years old. Her own mother had told her this. What sort of woman looked after a child for that long and then abandoned him? Oriel could not help but be intrigued. After all, this was her grandmother, whose blood ran through her own veins. Perhaps the workhouse records might shed light on the matter. Her curiosity demanded instant action. She consulted her watch to find that the afternoon was still young. Locking the door of her father's house behind her she pedalled off, undeterred at having no idea where the workhouse was.

Eventually locating the building, Oriel postponed her entrance for a moment, daunted by the greyness of it all. If she, as a mere visitor, experienced such apprehension how must it feel for those who were forced to enter by dire need? She who had never wanted in her life now began to understand her mother's fear of the place. Checking that her skirts were not rucked up, she went

9

up the path where an elderly man was occupied in clearing leaves. He stood aside in an attitude of subservience and waited for her to pass. She thanked him, went on to the entrance and, assuming a look of confidence, approached the desk. During her journey she had concocted a variety of pretences as to why she might want to consult the workhouse records, but in the end had decided to keep as near to the truth as possible. Her first story about Maria benefiting from a will might have all sorts of repercussions – York was a small place, perhaps her grandmother might hear of the fictitious bequest and come to claim it! Oriel could not have that. She addressed the rumpled-looking individual in his mid-fifties who sat behind the desk and now looked up in startlement.

'Excuse me, I wonder if you might help me? I'm trying to assist my employer in the search for his mother, who I'm given to understand was once an inmate of your establishment. I have the details from a birth certificate. It's almost forty years ago, I know it will be extremely difficult, but I'd be awfully grateful.'

The Armistice had instilled a spirit of amiability even in those who might otherwise have proved unresponsive. The grey-haired man with the smudged collar and skewed tie performed a quick assessment of this attractive and well-dressed young woman and formed his lips into an obsequious beam – there might be reward in it for him. 'I shall certainly try me best to help you.'

'I have the exact date when she was in residence,' provided Oriel.

'Oh well, then it'll be no difficulty at all!' Given the relevant month and year, the man responded with a courteous 'Excuse me' and clip-clopped off along a corridor.

In his absence the old pauper who had been sweeping up the leaves shuffled in, rubbing his hands. Oriel glanced at him but he kept his eyes lowered as he attempted to get warm against a radiator. She looked away, trying to avoid inhaling the smell of poverty and disinfectant.

Within five minutes the other man returned with dust on his sleeves and a ledger in his hands, frowning at the unfortunate individual by the radiator but withholding any recrimination, speaking only to Oriel, who decided she did not like him. This was irrational for he was quite charming in his attention towards her. 'There now!' He smiled, displaying a dimple. 'No trouble at all, was it? Shouldn't take two minutes to find them. Now, what was the name of the person?'

'Maria Smellie,' provided Oriel.

Septimus Kendrew coped well with the shock of hearing his wife's name and barely glanced up from his book, flicking through its pages and tutting. 'Dear, dear, an unfortunate moniker. Ah! Quicker than I thought. Maria Smellie, aged fourteen, occupation –'

'Fourteen?' Oriel was shocked. This was even younger than her own mother had been. The poor child! 'Are you sure?'

The man scrutinized the page, brushing away imaginary marks that might obscure the details though they were quite legible, the action merely lending him time to think. 'Aye, that's right, fourteen. Her occupation's listed as a washerwoman. There's a few more notes on her an' all. It seems the Master tried to persuade her to have the bairn adopted but she wouldn't have that and ran away before it were a fortnight old.'

This was all the more perplexing. If Maria had so desperately wanted to keep her baby then, what made her change her mind ten years later?

'Is that baby the man you work for?'

'What?' Thoughts interrupted, Oriel looked confused. 'Oh yes, it must be him. Does the record say where she might have gone?'

'No, but I ought to be able to help you more than this.' The man affected a keen interest. 'If I could discover her whereabouts how can I find you? Should I tell her somebody's looking for her?'

This was the last thing Oriel wanted. 'Oh, don't put yourself to any trouble! I can enquire elsewhere.' She attempted to extricate herself from his company but Kendrew was adept at cajolery, coming out from behind the desk to charm her.

'It's no trouble, honestly! It'd be an awful shame not to bring mother and son together, wouldn't it? If he's that desperate to find her – and he must be keen if he's set you the task. You never know she might've been searching for him all these years. There are so many thousands of mothers'll never see their sons again after this war. It seems criminal not to reunite these two.'

Gulled into thinking that naught would come of this, Oriel scribbled her name and address on the pad that he put before her. Kendrew glanced at it. This name also jogged his memory but for the moment he was too busy attending to his prey to dally over its relevance.

As Oriel passed the old man by the radiator the latter exclaimed, 'I know somebody called Smellie!' She froze but the desk attendant quickly forestalled any conversation. 'No you don't! Get back to work and keep your neb out. He's a bit daft,' he told the young woman, who smiled and left with the feeling she had had a lucky escape.

Only when she had gone did Kendrew realize the connection. Hadn't his stepson Nat once known people called Maguire? But then the young lady who had just left could not be related to them judging by her clothes and demeanour. After another few moments of pondering, Sep came to a conclusion: the young woman was Nat's daughter – she did have a look of Maria, that was what had confounded him when first setting eyes on her. Of course, it might be just a flight of fancy, but whether Nat was her father or merely her employer one thing was certain: he had money. If he was searching for his mother then Septimus Kendrew was the man who could help him.

*   *   *

In his daughter's absence Nat felt easier but still retained the quiet air of disbelief over his sudden reunion with Bright. Laconic by nature, he rarely indulged in conversation except with people he knew well – a contrast to his garrulous partner. However, neither saw any need to voice their pleasure at being reunited, this fact being quite evident in the turned up corners of their mouths.

Nat couldn't stop looking at her: looked at her face edged in tawny kiss curls, her neck draped in the cream waterfall revers of her blouse, her breasts, her wrists, her ankles revealed by the calf-length skirt. Bright had been aptly named as a child. With her freckled nose, the alert brown eyes and spindly legs she had always reminded him of a baby thrush and there was still a resemblance, but the years had been emotionally cruel and the scars were evident in the lines on her face – though when she had laughed a moment ago her treacle-coloured eyes still bubbled in the manner that had first attracted him. Materially, both she and Nat had prospered, though at great price.

'Have they held the funeral yet?' His query emerged completely out of the blue.

Bright flinched and the gleam went out of her eye. Even with no name mentioned she knew that he referred to their old friend Noel Scaum who had died from the Spanish influenza. 'No, it's on Friday afternoon. Will you be off?'

He gave an abstracted nod, rubbing his thumb along the tips of her fingers. 'Why d'you think he did it to us, Bright?' Prior to his stabbing by person unknown, Nat had discovered that the man whom he and Bright had both viewed as their friend had been instrumental in keeping the lovers apart – and this had only come to light when they had found out that their daughter had been deceiving them too! 'It's frightening. You think you know somebody and . . .' He finished with a helpless shrug, trying to put voice to that which plagued both their minds.

His words though far from eloquent were delivered without the glottal harshness often used by local men. 'I keep thinking ... we've just got together after all these years an' it'll be just my luck to get this dago flu. If anything happened to you now I don't think I could go on.'

'Nothing's going to happen!' Bright fought the panic that was never far away at the best of times. 'Except that we're going to make a new life in Australia.'

His blue eyes held a touch of despair. 'They probably have it there an' all. It's all over the world. So,' he shuffled his buttocks round and faced her squarely, his face adopting earnestness, 'I have to tell you now before we go any further just how sorry I am about everything before it's too late. I really am.' He flung his arms around her and she returned his embrace with a desperation born of the knowledge that even if the Spanish influenza did not claim them, time together could be limited for these middle-aged lovers.

A year spent in prison would have been sufficient cause for any man to react as Nat did now, but he and this woman he loved had been decades apart. His face buried in soft wool-clad flesh, he filled his nostrils with the scent of her, before sweeping his lips from neck to cheek to mouth. A flustered Bright gasped under his passionate massage of her body, and though the smell and the taste of him were intoxicating she managed to push him off with a breathless but firm, 'No! Not until we're married.' It sounded ridiculous when they had a twenty-two-year-old daughter, but Nat instinctively knew what she meant.

His eyes were still dark with passion yet his face was chastened as she held him at arms' length. 'You think I'm gonna run off and leave you again.'

Bright did not want to be hurtful, even though he had deeply hurt her in the past. 'I just want to be ... to feel right in myself.' Cheeks flushed, she pulled her clothes straight.

Nat took a few deep breaths to compose himself. With

his ardour contained the wound in his breast began to make itself felt once more and he winced as he raised an arm to shove the dark hair from his brow. 'I don't blame you for not trusting me. I don't trust meself.' He smiled to reassure her as she shot him a look of alarm. 'I mean I don't trust meself to be a gentleman until we're married. I've waited a long time for you – all me own fault, I know.'

'Not entirely.' Bright privately chastised herself. She had fully intended to be honest and tell him how much damage he had done. Don't let him off the hook, Oriel would say, but Oriel did not have to suffer the risk of losing him.

She told him then how her family had thrown her out. Nat appeared to listen, though his mind kept wandering; her face was still pink from their brief but passionate entanglement and it would take very little encouragement from those glittering eyes to induce him to try again.

'It was awful, terrible. But 'tis all a long time ago. Wounds heal – what the devil am I talking about, of course they don't. I can't forgive any of them for abandoning me like that, my mother especially. How could she do that?' There was intense pain in Bright's voice and she could not withhold the tears. Nat made to offer her his handkerchief then stalled on remembering he had used it to clean his boots. Finding her own scrap of linen, she blew into it. 'I'd never ever do it to Oriel, whatever she'd done.'

These words stirred a hurtful memory that he had tried for years to repress: the image of his mother walking away and leaving him. He paused in contemplation, a worried look in his eye. 'If you can't forgive them –'

'Then how can I forgive you? If you're asking if I have, then yes.'

Nat had never been good at voicing his feelings. He crossed one leg over the other and constantly tapped his foot at the air in agitation whilst seeking the right response. However sincere he might try to be, in his opinion the words always sounded contrived and so he had kept his thoughts and feelings to himself. He had never told her how much he had valued her friendship as a child, how she was the only one ever to kindle a spark of warmth in his barren heart. His attempt to tell her now sounded as ham-handed as ever but he said it all the same. 'You're a lovely person.'

Bright's response rather spoiled the effort. 'Or a bloody eejit. That's what people would say, y'know.' Yet she herself was blessed with more insight than many, saw another side to Nat than the view he presented to the myopic outside world – cold, unfeeling, detached. She knew that there was warmth in that soul for those with enough patience to coax it out. 'But I'm past caring what others think. You did come back to me, I love you and that's that – though I'm not saying there weren't times when I could've killed ye.'

'Obviously you're not the only one to have felt like that.' He tapped his chest and winced.

'Oh God, I'm sorry. I forgot all about your wound!' Bright raised her back from the sofa and made as if to touch his chest but stopped short of doing so. 'Ye don't moan much, do ye? If it were me I'd make sure everyone heard about it. I always was a bad patient. Ye said ye never saw who did it?'

'No, I thought I'd just been punched.' Asked if his assailant had robbed him too Nat shook his head. 'Didn't take a penny. It seemed to be done just for the hell of it.'

'God, that's dreadful! If he wanted to stab people he should've joined the army. Any idea who it might have been?'

'Well, I did reckon our Oriel could've had a hand in it.' It was uttered with a wry grin. He raised a hand to stroke his nose. All Nat's movements were slow and deliberate as if he were paying great thought to how he was perceived by others. Superficially, he portrayed a man who was utterly relaxed, but the gravity of his eye betrayed a mind in constant turmoil, always ready to believe that his world was at an end. At her scolding, he played with the rent in his jacket. 'Sorry. It were probably just some loony. We'll never know.'

Bright frowned. 'Is this why you're going to Australia?'

'No, no, I'd already made me mind up before that happened. I can't stand this place any longer. I've nowt to contribute to a country where they stick you in gaol just because of your beliefs.'

She was perplexed. 'I didn't know you were a conscientious objector.'

'Not a conscientious objector, an abject coward.' This was slight exaggeration and just another display of Nat's dry sense of humour. Then he contradicted himself. 'No, not abject – angry. Why should I risk me life for a society that's never had owt good to say for me just 'cause I didn't have a dad?'

'Still got that chip on your shoulder,' she observed with a half-smile. 'Does it never occur to you what that attitude of yours has put others through, Nat?'

Her disloyal observation shocked him. She was speaking as if she had forgotten his mother's abandonment of him.

'I know you don't like to hear the truth, people never do, but we've got to talk about it sometime and it might as well be now so you know exactly how I felt when you deserted me.'

Nat jumped up and paced to the window, his back to her. Beyond the lace curtains the skies were granite but the mood of passers-by was one of euphoria after four years of war. A moment ago he had been close to euphoria himself until her ill-chosen words had bludgeoned him.

Bright knew she was risking everything, yet it had to be said. 'There's no other word for it, Nat. I understand why you did what you did. I know you were frightened

17

– well, so was I! Bloody terrified. Especially when they put me in the lunatic asylum.'

He turned to her, aghast that only two minutes ago he had used the word loony.

'Don't worry, I won't leap up and murder ye.'

Immediately he wanted to comfort her and took a step forward, hands outstretched. 'I wasn't thinking that!'

'Yes, you were! I can see it from your face. God knows I've seen it enough times. I was fifteen, I was terrified beyond any nightmare you'd care to invent, I was all alone –'

'But I had no idea!' Nat's dreams were crashing around his ankles.

'Of course you hadn't, you weren't there.' Bright felt her insides quivering at the awful memory.

He was subdued, his face deeply troubled as he stared with unfocused eyes at the carpet. After a heavy pause he asked in the manner of a very small boy, 'D'you want me to go?'

A surge of panic. 'Bless your heart, no! I've only just found you again.' She jumped up and tottered across the room on raised-heeled shoes that she was obviously unaccustomed to wearing, for she stumbled before linking her arm with his and guiding him back to the sofa. 'I'm not laying the blame, I just want ye to know what it was like so we can start our new life knowing all about each other.'

Deeply affected by her revelation, he allowed himself to be led. 'If it's any comfort, I never had it easy by running away, you know,' he muttered as they lowered themselves on to the cushions simultaneously. 'I aren't gonna palm you off with any excuses. I couldn't think of owt else to do but run. I mean, what sort of a father would I have made at fifteen – even now come to that? I never had a family like yours.'

Bright's lips adopted an ironic twist. 'Neither did I when I needed them.'

His face collapsed, his blue eyes grave as he reached for her hand. 'I did try to see you but your brothers gave me a good clattering.'

'Aw!' She touched his arm in sympathy.

'No, I deserved it.' He waited. 'You can argue with me if you like.' When she merely smiled at his joke he went on, 'After that, I just decided to get on with me life. Bugger her, I thought.' His lips formed a tight, unhappy grin; he was still hurt from her accusations even though he knew them to be justified. 'If she won't let me make it up to her then she can go and sing for it.'

She lowered her eyes to the navy-blue wool of her lap where their hands lay intertwined. 'When ye came storming round here the other day, accusing me of sending Oriel to destroy you –'

'Aw look, I'm sorry. That was ludicrous!' He had the grace to blush, and covered his eyes with his free hand. 'That's what comes of a bloke living on his own for all these years with nobody to talk sense into him. I know you'd never bring her up to hate me.' He raked his hand up into his hair. 'But she hates me all the same.'

'She doesn't. If you knew her – I'm sorry, that wasn't meant as an accusation, honestly!' Bright could not help but interpret his look of indignation. 'But once you get to know her properly you'll find out that Oriel isn't capable of such hate. She was just hitting back at you for not loving her.'

'I do!' He couldn't actually say, I do love her. His feelings about Oriel were complex. Yes, he did love her but he also found her behaviour towards him infuriating. 'You don't know what it's been like for me having her working in my house and not being able to treat her like a proper daughter – and all the time she knew who I was, the little devil. I don't know how you can say she's not capable of hate. She was prepared to see me ruined.'

'Try looking at it from her point of view, Nat. She felt abandoned.'

Still he kept his gaze averted whilst the conversation dwelled upon his irresponsibility. 'Happen you did too, but you didn't try to ruin me.'

'What good would that have done? If I was a bitter person I'd be long dead by now.'

Nat silently disagreed. Often his bitterness had been the only thing that had kept him going.

Bright lay back on the sofa, entwined her arm around his, snuggled up and asked to be told what had happened to him since they had last been together. He glanced at the clock and sighed, dreading that Oriel would return to interrupt this intimacy, but related all he could remember whilst she hung on his words, unconsciously stroking the light covering of hair on the back of his hand.

At the close he gave a painful heave and said, 'So there, after all that's happened I've come full circle, still collecting scrap, the only thing I've ever been good at. Shoddy Nat the ragman – that's what the kids call me, anyroad.' He squeezed her hand and turned to look at her, his expression giving a hint that he enjoyed this little piece of celebrity.

Bright endeavoured to be as brief and unemotional as possible in filling in the details of her own life. 'After I'd had Oriel and tried to kill myself –'

'Oh Christ!' Nat portrayed horror, staring at her.

Bright gave a humourless laugh. 'Well, if we're going to spend our lives together it's only right that you know what you're living with.' She could not summon the courage to admit the whole story, how the voice in her head told her to kill her baby, how her frantic struggle to disobey that order had taken her to the point of death. 'I was up before the beak who very kindly said I must be crazy so he wouldn't put me in prison but I could have a little rest in the madhouse if I promised to be a good girl and not do it again. After that I never saw much of Mam. I might still have been in there if the old woman who owned this place, Miss Bytheway, hadn't taken me in as a servant. I've lived and worked here ever since. God, did I work.' She rolled her eyes and tossed her hair, appearing blithe but feeling physically sick at the memory. 'A year or two ago I did get to thinking I should try and see Mam. She must be getting old and I felt like putting things straight before . . . well, you know. It took me ages to pluck up the courage to go and when I did the house was gone, and a few other places with it, to make way for a new road. York's changing, isn't it?'

'Not enough for my liking,' muttered Nat. 'I thought I saw – in fact I'm bloody sure I saw 'em knocking the Industrial School down but it must've been wishful thinking 'cause it's still standing. They must've just demolished some of the surrounding buildings. I were hoping a Zep would get it but – eh dear!' He broke off with an incredulous shake of head. 'I don't know how you can even want me after all I've put you through. I suppose our Oriel thinks that too.'

'She'll come round in time. It's like I said to her, if you love someone you love them no matter how much they hurt you.' Bright gazed at him and waited.

Nat had never known any tenderness except for that which this woman had shown towards him. Even before his mother had left him she had never been the demonstrative kind. He had never told anyone he loved them until he had muttered it into Bright's ear on the night that their child had been conceived. On that occasion he had had an ulterior motive. Today the sentiment was genuine. 'I know we've sort of taken it for granted but I haven't asked formally. Will you marry me?'

She nodded and smiled, her eyes misting over.

'When – tomorrow?'

She chuckled and wiped away her tears. 'I think it would be more decent to wait until after Noel's funeral.'

Nat winced. 'I'm so happy I forgot about him.' He hoped this admission would not diminish him further in her eyes. 'All right then, it's the Register Office on

Monday – oh, but you might want to get married in a church. Do you still go?'

She laughed. 'Oh yes. Conscience would never allow me to stay away.' She had gone this morning to give thanks for the end of the war and for Nat being returned to her. 'But you'd have to become a Catholic for them to marry us and quite frankly none of that's important.' This was not said without a great deal of thought having gone beforehand, but Bright had decided God wasn't vindictive, unlike some of His clergy. He would allow her back into His house to pray even if the church didn't recognize the marriage. 'I just want to be with you.'

They embraced and kissed again, hugged and sighed and inhaled each other's scent. Then there came the click of the back door and Nat sprang away, wincing at the pain in his shoulder and brushing frantically at his clothes.

'She doesn't seem to have been gone five minutes! I wanted to ask before she got back ... would it be all right for me to stay here?' At the look of embarrassment on Bright's face he rushed to explain whilst the rustle of Oriel's clothing grew ever closer. 'I mean if you've got a spare room. I'm scared if I walk out of that door I'll get flattened by a tram and never see you again. Besides, it's funny after you've been in prison, you get a bit –' He struggled for the right word.

'Of course you can stay,' Bright told him just as Oriel entered, and she threw a radiant smile at her daughter. 'We've plenty of room, haven't we, dear?'

Still pondering on the discovery that her grandmother had been a fourteen-year-old washerwoman when she had given birth, Oriel wrenched off her velvet beret and smoothed her hair, nose pink from the cycle ride. She noticed that her mother's nose was pink too, but not from cold. It was always a giveaway sign that she had been crying, though the look on her face was far from sad at this moment. 'Yes, we could put up an army.' A forced smile hid resentment. It was her house, after all, left to her by Miss Bytheway. If anyone were to issue invitations it should be Oriel. However she had no wish to spoil her mother's obvious happiness, especially when Bright divulged that they were going to be married on Monday.

They're so full of themselves, thought Oriel, making their plans, neither of them cares what happens to me. The look on her father's face when she had entered made her feel like an intruder in her own home. She managed to make her congratulations sound genuine and in part they were, but what a jumbled up bag of emotions went with them.

'It doesn't give us much time to buy new outfits though,' she told them before sloughing her coat and going to hang it up.

'I'm sure you both look lovely as you are,' offered Nat as she disappeared, and in her absence he reserved his compliments for the mother, remarking on her shoes.

Bright lifted one of her feet, rotating her ankle to display a black pointed-toed shoe which had a neat little curved heel. 'Yes, they're new. Oriel persuaded me to buy them. I'm not really used to wearing anything so elegant.'

'They show off your slim ankles,' said Nat, moving his eyes to her dark-stockinged calves. 'I like these new shorter skirts an' all. If you have good legs, you ought to show 'em off.'

The latter was pure flattery and Bright was well aware of it. 'What these? They're like sticks of liquorice – thank you very much though,' she added hastily, and gave a little chuckle just in case her ingratitude had offended him.

As Oriel reappeared her father was looking down ruefully at his own garb. 'I'll have to smarten meself up a bit before Monday. Do you fancy a wander to my house to collect some things?' This was directed at Bright.

'All right!' She sprang up. 'Oh, I forgot the pots. That gravy must have set like cement.'

'I'll do them,' said Oriel.

'Ooh, thanks. I can't wait to see where your father lives – or where he used to live I should say.' The animated face beamed at Nat, who had been instinctively comparing the two women; Oriel had a better figure than her mother, more rounded at the breast and hip and narrower in the waist – but then she was much younger. He flashed a smile at Bright before she tottered off to get her coat.

'Wrap up, it's a raw wind,' instructed Oriel as her mother passed her. 'You'll be frozen in those shoes.' Then she turned her face to Nat with a look of defiance. Don't think I'm entirely pleased about this, her eyes told him, eyes that were the same blue as his own and had the ability to appear as cold.

He remembered the very first time he had seen this extremely pretty girl skipping along the road, and she had turned her face towards him, giving a brief but striking impersonation of his mother. In retrospect he had come to decide that this had been founded more on sentiment than on fact; his mother's eyes had been brown and she had lacked the kind of spontaneous vivacity possessed by Oriel, who had inherited it from her own mother. Even if it was very tightly controlled in her father's presence he had, occasionally, been privileged to see her face light up in a way his mother's never had, knew that behind that wall all manner of emotions seethed. Despite his previous declaration to Bright that Oriel hated him he did not want to believe it even in the face of such open hostility. The one trait that Oriel did share with Maria was that in this unsmiling mood she had the knack of making him feel like a little boy again. He had only just begun to realize that he was being asked to understand a very complicated young woman and did not know if he could stay the distance.

Oriel averted her eyes from the man whose attitude towards her had always seemed distant. Even his attempts to forge a bond between them had not appeared quite genuine when compared to her mother's. She knew without being told that her mother loved her. Apart from the day when Nat's dog had been killed Oriel had rarely been permitted to glimpse inside her father's heart, could not really believe that he possessed such depth of feeling as she had witnessed then. Even allowing for the fact that it had not been a mere aberration, all it had told her was how much he had felt for the dog, not for her.

The awkward silence was interrupted. On Bright's return she had exchanged the shoes for cloth-topped boots and was wearing a high-collared tweed coat and a blue felt hat trimmed with a rosette of ribbon, her kiss curls peeping from its turned up brim. She carried Nat's overcoat upon her arm, examining the rent in its shoulder. 'I don't think I'm clever enough to mend this, it needs a specialist.'

'Nay, don't trouble yourself.' He divested her of the garment and with stiff movements put it on. 'I'll chuck it out. I doubt I'll need a coat where we're going.'

Bright tittered. 'Oh yes! Won't it be strange?' Then she looked at Oriel, rather beseechingly. 'Have you decided whether –'

'Not yet.'

Bright did not press the matter. Her daughter could never be coerced into anything. She would make the decision whether or not to emigrate with her parents in her own time. 'Where's your hat, by the way?' She turned back to Nat. 'I never noticed it when you came in.'

'No, I lost it somewhere last night.' He smoothed his hair, feeling half dressed and vulnerable without the headgear. 'Never mind, I've plenty at home. Away, let's be off.'

As Bright moved past, her daughter laid a delaying hand on her shoulder. 'Hang on! I haven't really given proper congratulations. I hope you'll be very happy.' And with tears in her eyes Oriel planted her full lips on her mother's cheek, thereby confounding her father even more. Would he ever have her weighed up?

Envious, Nat opened the door and moved along the hall towards the front vestibule, not wanting to give the impression that he expected similar treatment. His daughter had never kissed him.

'Ooh, your nose is like a block of ice!' exclaimed Bright, and, patting her daughter's cheek, followed Nat to the outer door. 'And it's not really the done thing to congratulate the bride – but thank you anyway, love.'

Closing the door after them, Oriel allowed her smile to sag, then went to do the washing up.

2

As on every previous release from incarceration, Nat felt oppressed by the surge of people and traffic in the city. To compensate, he was unusually loquacious, exclaiming as they alighted from the tram at the Coach and Horses public house in Nessgate, 'Three ha'pence! I can't get over it. Threepence for two seats that'd double for prison benches.' He noticed Bright's flush of embarrassment and read it correctly; what if anyone should overhear his knowledgeable reference to prison? Urging himself to be more careful, he babbled on, 'How long's it been that much?'

Perched on the kerb, Bright awaited a gap in the stream of traffic. 'I can't remember. It's three ha'pence even if you only want to go one stop, so we did pretty well.'

'And so did the tram company – a fifty per cent rise!' He caught her smirk. 'You think I'm tight, don't you?' She denied it with a little laugh. 'You do. I'm sorry if I'm going on about it, it's just that I can't stand being robbed.'

'No, I don't honestly. I think you're right, it is highway robbery. I'll get the fares on the way home.'

'You won't, you know! I'll harness t'horse up – if the army hasn't snaffled him while I've been away.' Nat hopped impatiently from one foot to the other as motor cars, bicycles, military vehicles and the occasional horse and cart kept appearing from around the bend, many bedecked with red, white and blue ribbons. A man and woman came to stand beside him at the kerb and with a thought as to the influenza epidemic he moved sideways to avoid possible contamination. 'Once we get across I'll just nip into that tobacconist over there.'

'I didn't know you smoked.' He had shown no inclination to light up at all whilst in her house.

'Oh, not regular, like. I just fancy one now and again.' When the outside world made him anxious as it did right now. 'I can take 'em or leave 'em really.'

She was peering at the sign in the tobacconist's window that appeared between gaps in the procession. 'Napoo – they haven't got any.'

He moaned and threw his gaze upwards to the cat's cradle of tramwires above the street, but then with a lull in the traffic he tightened his grip on her arm and, along with the knot of people who had gathered, they hurried across the granite setts and tramlines, dodging the odd pile of horse dung.

A group of pedestrians was crossing from the other side and there was a moment of near collision in the middle of the road. A man apologized to Bright. She smiled and was about to forgive him when she saw that he was looking at Nat with an expression of genuine fear. He cringed as if awaiting retribution. When none came he hurried on his way, head down, leaving the couple to proceed to their own destination.

'Who was that?' From the safety of the pavement she glanced over her shoulder, her breath visible on the cold damp air.

'Who?' Without looking at her, Nat led the way up High Ousegate.

'The man who almost bumped into us. He obviously knew you.' Bright guessed she must sound suspicious and instead of looking at him she gazed casually at the Art-Nouveau façade of Harding's drapery, its windows arrayed in white linen.

'Did he?' Nat appeared to be unaffected by the encounter as they wandered up the street, each shop window displaying some red, white and blue token of victory.

Though he had indeed recognized the man, a fleeting look of menace had been sufficient to convey his feelings to the errant debtor. Today he was too happy to concern himself with such lowlife. 'Probably somebody who owes me money and thinks he's got away with it while I've been on holiday.'

Bright immediately turned to look at him. 'How d'you mean, owes you money?'

Nat realized with some disconcertment that she would be ignorant of his methods of earning his living. 'Well, I give loans to people and sometimes they don't want to pay them back – but that's just one of the services I provide.' He had never cared about the reputation that accompanied this type of business, but now it panicked him to think he might lose her because of it. 'I have houses to let as well but mainly I still rely on the scrap collection business. If I banked on the folk who rent my houses I'd go bust. The state some of them leave the places in – an animal wouldn't be as dirty. And some of the excuses they give you for not paying their dues – huh!' He shook his head.

Bright pondered on his explanation. So, that would account for the look of fear she had witnessed just a moment ago. She tilted her face to examine her husband-to-be through an outsider's eyes. How very little she knew about Nat the man. Without a smile and cast in the gloomy half-light of this November afternoon she supposed he did look rather intimidating. Only those like herself who had known him since boyhood could detect the vulnerability in his eyes.

'Did you see that?' He felt unnerved by her scrutiny and sought to distract her. 'Those darkies there.' He pointed to two black men in uniform. 'They just saluted that officer and he looked right through 'em as if they didn't exist. Ignorant pig! And they wonder why people are reluctant to join t'army.'

Bright allowed her abstracted gaze to follow his

pointing finger across the road, offering sympathy for the soldiers' denigration, but privately wondering over what had gone before.

Their feet carried them along the street's humpback, in a direct line past All Saints Church with its octagonal lantern tower, and the men's underground conveniences where the smell of disinfectant and urine wafted up the steps.

York was a small overpopulated city of narrow streets where churches and public houses abounded. Its buildings ranged from medieval hovels to symmetrical Georgian façades adorned with plaster swags; a patchwork of red brick, white stone and dirt-engrimed stucco, each edifice boasted some manner of ornament from Greek gods and goddesses to scarlet fork-tailed devils. The roofline undulated with jettied gables, cupolas, medieval spires and towers, the Minster dominating all. Glad to be leaving soon and blinkered by his new-found love, Nat paid little heed to his surroundings, but Bright's eyes were rather wistful as they took in every detail, though her mood was induced by sentimentality. Only the fact that she would never look upon these landmarks again rendered them significant today.

They left the main street and wandered along a quiet backwater. Then abruptly Nat stopped outside one of the elegant dwellings and announced, 'Well, this is it!'

It was a disquieting experience for Bright, stepping into a house in which Nat had lived for years: tricked into a sense of *déjà vu* by furnishings that were impregnated with the scent of its owner whom she knew well, yet at the same time totally ignorant of its history. 'It's lovely,' she murmured. For one with such a lowly upbringing Nat had impeccable taste both in furnishings and clothes.

'Aye, it's not bad.' He looked round. There were ashes in the grate and the temperature of the house was not much warmer than outside. 'I won't offer to take your

30

coat. I can't even offer you a cup of tea – cupboard's bare.'

A rush of love propelled him forward and he took her cheeks in his hands to kiss her, knocking her hat askew in the process. Bright allowed it to perch on the back of her head, ignoring the painful drag of her hatpin, hugging him close and running her gloved hands over his back. Then, afraid that she was about to be overtaken by all the years of repressed emotion she tore herself away with a laugh and straightened her hat. 'I think we'd better get packing!'

Blood pumping, Nat uttered a moan of disappointment, but managed to smile again. 'Will you give us a minute to change? Have a look around if you want.' And he went upstairs leaving her in the front room where Oriel had once worked.

In the quiet wake of his departure she wandered through each of the rooms, studying pictures, admiring and touching furniture, until a call from the landing summoned her aloft. She paused for a moment at the foot of the stairs, looking up at him, conjuring a scene in her mind in which Nat dragged her on to his bed and forced himself on her despite her entreaties.

'What's wrong?' He saw the hesitation on her face.

'Oh nothing!' She came straight up to meet him then, scolding herself for her wild imagination; weren't there going to be enough difficulties without her inventing them?

He watched her coming up the stairs towards him, imagining that kiss-curled face without its hat, her hair tumbling round naked shoulders. Oh, if only she knew how much he wanted to throw her on to the bed right this minute and plunge himself into her – maybe she did know. Maybe that was why she looked so apprehensive. The perfect gentleman, he escorted her into his room without touching so much as her elbow, whilst his body strained to do otherwise.

If it had been an odd experience for Bright to enter his house then it was even stranger to be here in his bedroom, going through his wardrobe and cupboards, and the feeling showed in her movements. Nat felt a great deal more comfortable after his change of clothing, though occasionally as they took it in turns to lay items into a suitcase he would catch her gazing wistfully into midair and it worried him that the discovery of his financial dealings might have changed her view of him. 'You're not having second thoughts about coming with me, are you? I know it's a big step but –'

Bright, who had been imagining herself in that bed with her lover, looked startled, then turned dancing brown eyes on him. 'No! I'm never letting you out of my sight again.' She stroked the shirt that lay folded over her arm. 'Yes, it is a big step, but if that's where you're going, so am I.'

He looked relieved and continued packing. 'I'd like to be off as soon as possible. The only delay will be in selling this place and the business. I'll keep the rented properties. It'll be something to fall back on if I fail over there.' Scolded for his lack of optimism, he replied, 'Now when have I ever been an optimist?' He shared yet another grin with her, thinking that he had never smiled so much in all his life as in these last few hours. The unused face muscles ached from it. 'The rents'll provide a regular income – and I don't want to put Spud out of a job at a time like this. He collects them and other debts.' There followed a short explanation of how he and his boyhood pal had formed this business alliance. 'He has a family and not much brains. Christ, even the army didn't want him for cannon fodder so there's not much chance of anyone else employing him.' He tucked a pair of shiny boots down the side of the case and looked around the room in search of other items he might need.

'D'you reckon Oriel will change her mind about going with us?'

Bright looked exasperated and anxious. 'I wish I knew.'

'If she intends to stay in England, I could sign the business over to her.' Nat was amazed by how little it meant to him now that he had Bright. 'She's been nigh on running it herself this past year anyway.'

'That's very generous!'

'No it's not, she's me daughter.' There was a trace of impatience in his response which he quickly replaced with warmth. 'I need to make things up to her. Now then, what else will I need?'

'You'd better bring your ration card,' suggested Bright.

'Oh aye, that's in me pocket. I meant in the way of clothes.'

She cocked her head. 'D'ye think the sun really does shine all the time in Australia?' He said it had better do if he was going all that way on the strength of it. 'Well then, it's no good us going dressed like this. We'll have to buy some lightweight clothes.' She caught his grimace. 'If you don't like shopping you can give me a list and I'll do it for you.'

His eyes stopped flitting around the room and settled on her freckled nose, his look betraying a need to confide. 'It's not so much the shopping, it's the people. I always get like this after a spell o' being locked up. I can't really explain it.'

Bright nodded. 'You get all chewed up inside, feel that people are crowding in on you, you're just frightened and want to run.'

He nodded, amazed at her intuition. 'You're sure you haven't done a stretch yourself?'

Bright made a joke of her own insecurities. 'I served a good few years under Miss Bytheway – she could match any prison governor.' She patted him tenderly. 'Let's not dwell on it. All I'm saying is, when you think you're alone in your fear, you're not.'

His eyes showed gratitude before turning thoughtful. 'Do you want to visit your family before you go?'

'They might as well have been miles away for years for all I've seen of them.' She returned to bustling around, pretending to look unconcerned but failing. 'No, I don't think so. Anyway, Mother . . .' She gave up the pretence and turned to look Nat in the eye, hugging a bundle of his clothes to her chest. 'I think she's dead. Don't ask me how I know, I haven't seen it in the paper or anything. I just felt her go . . . slip away.'

Nat was unaccomplished in responding to such raw emotion, and on the premise that Bright was only saying that her mother was dead in an effort to deny the woman's rejection of her – which was the way he himself had coped with such loss – he answered quietly, 'Aye well, it's easier to tell folk she's dead, then they don't keep pestering you with questions.'

But she replied calmly, 'I'm not just saying it, Nat. I can feel it. You know when your mother's dead. You just know.'

The look on her face was one of such distress that he changed the subject, as much for his own sake as for hers. 'By, it's nippy in here, isn't it? I've just thought, there's a load o' coal in t'cellar. At least there is if nobody's helped themselves in my absence. I'm not going to need it here now so I'll get a lad to cart it round to your house.'

Bright was dogged. 'I've wanted to ask all day but I didn't like . . . did you ever find out what happened to your own mam?'

He shook his head and tried to appear busy.

'Didn't you ever wonder?'

'Nope.'

'Do you want me to shut up?'

'Aye.' He could never envisage a time when he would be able to talk about that pain even to Bright. 'Away then!' He patted her, shut the suitcase, fastened its catches and hefted it to the floor. 'I'll just grab some money out of t'safe and find out if I'm still the owner of a horse,

34

then we'll go home and see whether that lass of ours has made her mind up about coming with us.'

Oriel had been doing a lot of thinking while her parents were out, envisaged herself in this tall spacious house alone when her mother had left. How could Bright do this to the child she had prized above all else? The act of rolling this thought around her mind over and over again invoked a mood of depression and when her parents returned at six o'clock they found Oriel brooding in the dark.

'Oh, you are in here!' Bright peered through the dinge at the figure reclined by the fire and went immediately to light a gaslamp on the wall.

'Curtains,' said Oriel absent-mindedly, remaining seated.

It'll be curtains for you if you speak to your mother like that, thought Nat darkly, but he sufficed with a tight-lipped scowl that his daughter could not fail to notice as the light came on.

'The war's over,' Bright reminded her, appearing not to notice what Nat had considered to be Oriel's rudeness, though she had. 'We don't need the blackouts. It's like fairyland out there.' After years of stumbling along darkened wartime roads they had just returned via town where not only were the street beacons in full complement but the shop window displays shone out like fairy grottoes with their shimmering array of glass and china and silver. 'I'm going to rip these down tomorrow. In fact the whole place needs a good bottoming. Especially if we need to sell it.' She looked hopefully at Oriel. 'Have you thought any more about coming to Australia with us? I'm not pushing you, but Nat –' here she looked at Nat and corrected herself for the umpteenth time, 'your father says if ye choose to stay here then he'll give you the business.'

'What would I want with that?' Oriel ejected herself

from the chair and went to ignite the other gaslamps. Did he imagine he could buy her?

'It would be just as easy to decline politely,' reproved her mother, finally drawing the curtains. 'I think it's a very generous offer.'

Oriel snorted as she replaced a globe over the yellow flame. 'If there's any generosity involved it's on my part. Without me that business would have collapsed a year ago when he was in gaol.'

Nat's anger was controlled. 'If you looked after it for a year there must've been good reason.' The only response was a look of haughtiness.

Bright should have raised her voice then, should have scolded her daughter for such lack of respect. But as terrified as she was that Oriel's bitterness might drive Nat away she was also sensitive to the emotion that lay behind the hauteur and could not bring herself to add to the girl's misery with a maternal rebuke. So, saddened and unnerved by the animosity, she merely went off to the kitchen muttering, 'I'll go and get us some tea.'

Nat glared at his daughter. 'You could have done that while we were out to save your mother a job.'

She glared back and left without a word. How dare he remind her of her duty! What about the duty he had owed her mother these last twenty-two years?

'Will ham and eggs be all right?' Almost colliding with her daughter, Bright came back to poke her head around the door, receiving the answer that this would be most welcome. 'I'm afraid there's only one egg each,' she apologized and sighed. 'You'd think the hens had all been away fighting in the war, wouldn't ye? And the ham's not the size of a threepenny bit.'

'I never have more than one egg,' lied Nat with a smile. 'Besides I'm still full up after that dinner you cooked us. I'm just happy to be here.' I just wish others felt the same, came his thought as his daughter swanned in and flung the cloth over the table with a defiant flourish.

Oriel smoothed the linen, wheeled around, then saw her mother's downcast expression and immediately berated herself. Stop behaving like this! You're only hurting Mother. I know but I can't help it. It's all his fault. No it isn't! How could he help being abandoned by his mother? No, but he knows what it's like to be abandoned yet he did the same thing to me!

Another glance at her mother's face coaxed her into making amends. 'Shall I show Father to his room?'

Nat flinched visibly at the use of this personal term. Though well aware that it had not been intended as any endearment, the sound of his daughter calling him Father melted his resentment completely. She had every right to be angry at him. What had he ever done for her? Very little. Now was his chance of restitution. Just allow her to vent her spleen, he told himself. You have no right to expect anything of her – though he did.

Bright cheered up. 'Oh, good lass. I'll see if I can resurrect this fire.' Oriel apologized for allowing it to get so low. Her mother said it couldn't be helped. 'Nat's having the coal in his cellar brought round here so it should see us over Christmas. They say supplies will be back to normal by then. Oh, by the way!' She halted Oriel's exit. 'D'you know what's happened to your father's horse?' Finding the stable bare they had been forced to return by cab.

'Charlie from the yard is looking after it.' Oriel directed her answer at Nat. 'He had to stable it nearer to his home. He's been doing your rounds for you as well.'

Nat enjoyed a twinge of satisfaction that so many people had been looking after his interests in his absence, but his response displayed ingratitude. 'I wonder how much that'll cost me.' Picking up his suitcase he followed her upstairs, grunting at the strain which the heavy baggage placed on his wound. Arriving at his room he swung the case on to the bed and looked around.

'Will you need any help in unpacking?' enquired Oriel,

but as her offer seemed half-hearted Nat said he would do it himself. 'I'll go and assist Mother with the meal then.' She left him.

Later in the evening, Oriel sat with her parents by the fire, her mother providing most of the dialogue. Reading Nat's mind, Oriel knew he felt as encumbered as she did, wanted her to go to bed so that he could have her mother to himself, but she stubbornly refused to be the first to crumble. This was her house.

By ten he gave a yawn of capitulation, apologized and prised himself from the chair. 'I'm sorry, if I sit here any longer I'll be dropping off. I didn't get much sleep in hospital.'

'Aw, off you go then, love.' Bright had changed back into the shoes he had admired earlier and in the quiet moments prior to his announcement had been admiring them herself discreetly. 'Hang on, I'll give you a jug of hot water to take up with you.'

He followed her into the kitchen in the expectations of a good-night kiss and watched as she filled a jug from the kettle. 'There'll be enough for a bath tomorrow morning if you want one.'

'Stink that bad, do I?' he grinned.

'No! I just meant what with you being in hospital. We'll bring one up before breakfast.'

'You haven't got a bathroom, then?'

She gasped a laugh. 'Listen to Lord Muck!'

Nat feigned arrogance, licked his middle finger and dabbed it behind each ear as if applying perfume. 'Oh, I have all the modern amenities at home, you know.'

'Well, you won't have them here! It's a privilege for you that I'm offering you a bath in your bedroom. I haven't carried water up those stairs since Miss Bytheway popped her clogs. Oriel and me take ours in the kitchen.'

At the sound of her name Oriel's ears pricked, trying to hear what they were saying about her, and gritting her teeth at the murmurs of canoodling laughter.

'Eh, I'm not having you lugging water all that way up there! A tub in t'kitchen'll do me – if you promise not to look.'

'Get away with ye!' Bright handed him the jug of hot water and accepted the kiss he gave in exchange, patting his arm fondly. 'Good night, dear. Oh, it's been a lovely day.'

It's been the happiest day of my life, thought Nat, but was too inhibited to voice it. Hoping that it showed in his smile, he turned away.

Her warm eyes followed him from the room with longing, then she went to sit down again with Oriel, both of them staring into the dying embers. With another in the house, this might be the last opportunity she got to speak to her daughter alone. Anguish over the enforced parting induced such terrible nausea. There were important things to say, but how could one start?

'Your father's going to put his house up for sale tomorrow.'

'Is he?' Oriel continued to stare into the fire. Normally, she would be as talkative as her mother but a visitation of melancholy such as she was experiencing right now would always render her dumb.

Bright was persistent. 'I think you ought to give him an answer about the business so's he can put that up for sale at the same time if needs be.'

'I thought I'd made it clear, I don't want it.'

'When are you going to stop this?' came her mother's sudden demand.

'Stop what?' Oriel detested herself for being so silly, but could not restrain the impulse.

'I feel like I'm tearing myself in half between the two of you.'

'I don't want to prevent you going anywhere you want

to go,' muttered Oriel. 'But you surely don't expect me to be happy when my mother's leaving me?'

Bright was hurt and angry. Why in the midst of all this happiness should she feel that her heart would break? 'Don't you think I'll miss you dreadfully? But for heaven's sake, you're not a child, you're twenty-two years old!'

Oriel was shocked to tears – as if that made a difference!

'Now I've said you're quite welcome to come with us if you wish. We both want ye to come, but if you choose not to then that's your decision. I'm not going to let you make me feel guilty.'

But she would, of course. She prayed desperately that her words of bravado would have an effect and Oriel would come too, for without her daughter Bright's happiness would remain incomplete. She told this to the other, who was sobbing now.

'You know how much I love you. But I love your father too and if push comes to shove . . . well, don't ask me to choose between you, that's all.' The girl's tearful face spun on her but she forestalled the accusation. 'I know what you're going to say – your father left me once. But he won't do it again. I know he won't. But you will. You've your own life to live and I don't want to end up alone.'

'What life?' A deeply confused Oriel reviewed the past two decades. 'What is there for me? Who is there for me?'

In a spirit of wretchedness Bright lurched over to hug and soothe her daughter. 'Oh, don't! I can't go when you're like this.'

'I'm not trying to stop you, honestly I'm not!' wept Oriel. 'I have considered going with you, I've been sitting here all night thinking about it, trying to imagine what I might do over there.'

'Why, you could do anything you wanted! What about

your ambition to go into nursing? Attitudes might be different in Australia.'

Here we go again, thought Oriel. Why did her mother insist on exhuming what to her had only ever been a childhood desire? Any lingering significance was only because that wish had been denied. It could have been any profession, she would still have felt the same. 'I'd never have made a nurse.'

'You've got a very caring nature, darlin', and if I'm honest I think you're wasted on this secretarial work.'

The young woman managed a quip. 'Oh thanks, that's nice after I've single-handedly saved your prospective husband from bankruptcy while he's been in gaol.'

Bright tapped her lightly in reproof. 'I mean you care about human suffering.' Her daughter was always deeply affected by newspaper reports of someone else's misfortune. 'Well, now ye might have a chance to do something about it.'

'I claim to care but what have I achieved? Nothing.'

'I think most of us would claim to care but there's little we can do about a worldful of suffering. It's always been with us and always will be. No matter how many heroes and heroines risk their lives to stop one tribe's inhumanity to another it's a waste of time. The highest most of us can hope for is to live our own lives as best we can and hope we don't harm too many people along the way.'

Oriel collapsed at this cynical philosophy that only served to emphasize her own hopelessness. 'But then what is it all for?' she wailed. 'What's the blessed point of any of it?'

Bright had no answer. 'God only knows. I'm making a pig's ear out of this. What I was trying to say in my clumsy fashion was that if you're expecting yourself to help every single person in the world then you're always going to feel like a failure. You're young, you've plenty

41

of years ahead in which to do all this soul-searching. If you must nail your banner to a mast just concentrate on one cause and stick to that. I know you'd like to help everyone but that's impossible.'

'But I haven't helped anyone at all!'

Trying to alleviate the mood she had created Bright exclaimed, 'You have! You were a companion for a lonely old lady and you brought me and your father together after all these years. In my eyes you couldn't have achieved anything better.'

'Let's not make me into Saint Joan.' Oriel had recovered from her tears and now sat quite composedly, with the occasional sniff. 'That happened by fluke. I was trying to get back at him for all the pain he'd caused.'

'Well, some might say the end justified the means.' Bright watched her daughter for a while before continuing, 'Aren't ye just a bit glad that we've found each other?'

'Oh yes, of course!' The pretty face depicted anguish. 'If that's what you want. I just can't understand how –' She made a futile gesture at the air.

'I love your father, Oriel, but I don't expect you to swallow that when you obviously despise him so much.'

'But I love him too! I know, it's madness, isn't it?' Oriel clasped handfuls of her black hair. 'One day I want to ruin him, the next I feel deeply sorry for him, and the day after that I want to kill him again. I don't understand it myself.'

She shook her head, glowering as if she were suffering a violent headache. 'As much as I wanted to be there in his house to discover what kind of a man could do this to us – to me – I never came close to finding an answer. He was always lovely to me, and with every thought I had against him another part of me would be crying out for him to know I was his daughter – because I wasn't aware that he already knew.' She sighed. The harsh lines on her brow melted away and she looked dazed. 'He gave me a locket for my twenty-first birthday. All the time I was cursing him in my mind, saying that he was trying to buy me, I couldn't bear to throw it away. It's in the cellar.'

'May I see it?' asked her mother.

Oriel's dark eyebrows expressed surprise. Nevertheless she wandered off to fetch the locket, returning with a velvet box from which she brushed away the salt that had trickled on to it from the damp brickwork below ground. 'It's gone mouldy.'

Her mother opened the box and examined the gold locket. 'It's lovely.' The brown eyes swam with fresh tears. 'He really does love you, ye know.'

Oriel could not bring herself to acknowledge this. How could you abandon your child, then purport to love her? Yet even as her mind continued to argue she knew that what her mother said was true. He did love her. At least he would do if she herself would allow it, which for the moment she could not. The wall of hostility would remain.

Bright gave her daughter one last hug. 'Come on, let's go to bed. I'm worn out with all this excitement. And no laying awake all night trying to make your mind up about going to Australia. It's not as if we'll be going right away.'

'My mind was made up for me two days ago,' confessed Oriel. 'Whether I like it or not, I'm going with you.'

Her mother let out a little cry and slumped in relief. 'Oh, I'm so glad, darlin'!'

'I'm dreading leaving,' squeaked Oriel. York had been her world. She had never been anywhere else.

'So am I! But I was dreading leaving you more. Oh, I can't tell you –' Bright put her arms round her daughter again, then drew away with another teary exclamation. 'You little monkey, you knew what you were going to do and you kept me in suspense all this time! Well then, we really had better get to bed, what with all the work in front of us. Though God knows how I'll sleep. Oh!' She hoisted her shoulders in the gleeful manner of an infant. 'I've never had such an adventure in all me life!'

3

The next morning when Oriel came down, it was apparent that her mother had informed Nat that their daughter would be emigrating with them. As was his nature, he was uneffusive in manner but said by way of endorsement as she joined them at the table, 'Looks like there'll be two houses to put on the market instead of one, then.'

Still muzzy and pale from sleep, totally overwhelmed by the upheaval that lay ahead and the thoughts of her fourteen-year-old grandmother that had kept her awake, Oriel merely raised her dark eyebrows. 'I suppose so. I'll need the cash to buy a house over there.'

At her daughter's entry Bright had immediately risen to fetch her a dish, which annoyed Nat though he made no comment and proceeded to eat his own meal. 'Oh, you'll be coming to live with us surely?' she urged anxiously, delivering the porridge and sitting down again to her own. 'I mean, it's a strange country.'

Oriel looked at her father, eyes still bleary and conveying an expression that said, but does he want me?

'Suits me,' said Nat, but could not help feeling a twinge of unease at what he might be letting himself in for. 'So this place is all yours, is it?'

Bright answered for her. 'Oh yes, didn't ye know? I haven't a penny to me name. So if you were only after my money be warned, you're marrying a pauper.'

This was met by a deadpan offer. 'I reckon I could lend you sixpence till this aft. Mindst, I'd have to charge interest.'

Oriel allowed her mother a few seconds of mirth, then,

45

untutored in such matters, asked, 'How do I go about selling it?' For one who appeared so confident she was somewhat afraid of officialdom, dreaded ridicule.

'Your father would be better able to help you with that. I've never had anything to sell, wouldn't know where to start.'

Nat continued with his breakfast, waiting for Oriel to ask him and knowing how much it would irk her to have to do so.

'Would you mind?' his daughter's moonbeam face enquired.

'My pleasure.' He scraped his bowl clean, laid down the spoon and immediately reached for some toast. 'We'll advertise in the Press for a few days and see what response we get. If we don't ask a daft price we might be able to sell within the month. There's bound to be army personnel being relocated. What about your furniture?' He spread margarine on his toast. 'We won't need two lots.' Upon receiving the friendly advice that he would probably get a better price for his, he looked awkward and paused to drink from his teacup before replying, 'I don't really like yours – I mean it's not as if you chose it!' he added hastily at her look of indignation. 'It belonged to t'old lass, didn't it?'

Bright had to agree that it was rather old-fashioned.

'I want to take that if nothing else.' Oriel indicated the ruby glass centrepiece with its tinkling icicles. 'It reminds me of when I was little.' But you wouldn't know about that; her eyes transmitted the silent accusation to Nat, who was quick to take note.

'Will selling your business be difficult?' Reflecting his every move, Bright drank the last of her tea, a hint of worry in the eyes that looked at him over the rim of her cup.

'No, I can always start up again over there.' Nat found he could say this quite truthfully. Now that he had a family the fruits of commerce were not of such great

46

significance in his life. Used to taking care of himself, he lifted the teapot and refilled his cup.

Make yourself at home, thought Oriel.

'I'll need some help in winding up my accounts, though,' he added, and flashed a shifty glance at his daughter who, out of mischief forced him to ask outright, 'Could I beg your assistance? I just need to have all the books in order to show the tax man – and t'person who buys t'business. It's just that with being away for a year I'm not quite sure what's what. I noticed that money was still in t'safe but I weren't sure about – you know.'

Oriel looked disapproving. It was her father's custom to keep some of his transactions secret from the Inland Revenue. 'I don't want to know about the money in the safe. As far as I'm concerned whilst I've been running the show everything's gone through the books.' Though having no wish to incriminate him she herself was entirely scrupulous. 'I'll go over everything with you later. I think you'll find it's in order.'

Nat gave half-hearted thanks, then took a bite of toast, munched and swallowed. 'Right, well, let's get down to brass tacks. How much d'you want to ask for the house? Will six hundred do you?'

Both women said they had no idea, and this subject occupied the next half an hour. The rest of the day was given to perusing the account books, placing advertisements in the newspaper, corresponding with the relevant authorities over their emigration, a trip to the barber for Nat and the purchase of suitable attire for their new life – and the most important purchase of all, a wedding ring.

The excitement was interrupted by mourning on Friday when Noel's funeral took place. Even in death there was little peace to be had in York Cemetery these days. Such was the effect of the influenza epidemic that soldiers had been drafted in to assist in the excavation of graves and as inconspicuous as they might assume themselves to be, their occasional sniggers of laughter at some joke were carried by the November breeze across the sepulchral acres to disrupt this private moment of grief.

Over the weekend there were more preparations to be made, both for the voyage ahead and for Nat and Bright's wedding. During the snatches of intimate conversation they had enjoyed during Oriel's all-too-brief absences, Nat professed to Bright again and again how deeply he loved her, stole kisses, made confessions, discussed who they would invite to witness their marriage. Their daughter was an obvious candidate but who else did either of them know?

'What about Spud?' queried Bright.

Nat gasped, hating the idea of guilt by association. 'That dope? The registrar might get the impression he's a friend o' mine.' At the cry of denunciation from his partner he relented but only through sheer expedience. 'Oh well, I suppose I could pretend I've just dragged him in off t'street. Only thing is, we'll have to invite Mrs Spud too.'

She laughed at his nickname. 'Aw! Don't be mean.'

'You haven't seen her.' Nat's expression was serious. 'She's really rough and smokes a pipe. She'll probably organize a spitting contest as entertainment. Listen, I've been thinking. I know we'll be off to Australia in a few weeks but –' He winced and squirmed like an adolescent. 'I'll just feel awkward with Oriel in t'house on our wedding night.'

Bright thought she understood and agreed to his suggestion that they have a couple of days away.

'I could telephone the Grand Hotel at Scarborough,' Nat suggested.

She sucked in her breath. 'We can't go there!' When he demanded to know why she explained, 'It's too posh. I mean, I've never been but I've heard of it.'

He insisted she deserved the best and, with Bright's permission to use her telephone, he went to the hall. When he returned it was with the information that he had booked three nights in the Grand's best suite with a sea view. 'I don't think they could believe that anyone was mad enough to go to Scarborough in winter. They gave me a reduction. Mindst, we'll probably die of pneumonia.'

'Oh, don't joke about that.' Bright shivered.

He had momentarily forgotten the flu epidemic. 'Sorry. I didn't mean – I think we'd've had it by now if we were going to catch it off Noel.'

She gave a nod of acceptance, eyes glazing over as she remembered the young doctor's last afternoon with her. This was such a conflicting time of joy and grief and excitement and regret. 'Probably.' Then she turned her worried gaze on Nat. 'D'you still get bronchitis every year?'

'Usually. I've escaped this year so far, though.' It was rather ironic when people were dropping like flies that his puny lungs should remain uncongested. 'I never had it at all while I was in Canada, so I should be fine once we get away from this damned place. Don't worry.'

At this point Oriel returned from her trip to town and Nat had never been so glad to see her, for her breezy parcel-laden entry steered the atmosphere away from the brink of melancholy. However, he was not so pleased when she ignored his smile and directed her greeting to her mother only. It's as if I'm not here, he thought angrily.

Bright could not wait to tell her daughter about their honeymoon destination. 'Aren't we posh? Only for three nights, mindst. Sorry I'm so full of myself. Will you be all right on your own?'

If you're not then too bad, Nat warned his daughter mentally. I'm not having you on my honeymoon.

But Oriel looked relieved as she dropped her parcels on the table. 'Of course I'll be fine!' For once she did not feel as if she were intruding; her father had actually smiled a welcome.

On Sunday when his beloved announced she was going to Mass, Nat said he would take this opportunity to call on Spud.

'Aren't you going with your mother, Oriel?'

'Oh no, I hardly ever go to church,' she answered. 'I'll do some more clearing out upstairs.' And after her parents had gone she donned a pinafore and set to examining the dust-covered collection on the top of her wardrobe.

When the doorknocker rapped she ignored it, too involved in her work, but then when it went again she crossed to the window and tried to see who it was, though it was not until the caller was on his way through the gate that she recognized the man from the workhouse. Her flesh crawled – thank goodness her parents had been out! Peeping from behind the curtain, she clicked her tongue in annoyance, having assumed when she had given her address that he would have contacted her by letter and not in person. Immensely glad that she had not answered his knock – for she had sufficient information on her grandmother and had no wish to pursue the search – she hoped this futile venture had doused his enthusiasm and he would not call again. After waiting to see that he had really gone, she went back to her work.

Whilst his old enemy was knocking on his door, Nat was rapping on that of his debt-collector.

'Nat! I didn't know you were out o' gaol!' The big, dim-witted face lit up and its owner gestured for his employer to enter his home.

'Why don't you take out an advertisement in t'paper?' Before entering, Nat glanced around to see if anyone had overheard, then added at the look of incomprehension, 'Never mind, I just came to see if you want to come to me wedding, you and your missus.'

Spud showed astonishment. 'Wedding? I thought you'd

come to see where your rent money's got to. Who're you marrying then?'

'Bright. You remember her, don't you?' Nat fought exasperation. Spud had always irritated him. 'You know!'

'Oh aye! That lass –'

'Aye, well we're getting wed tomorrow.' Nat spoke in clipped sentences. 'And then we're off to Australia – not right away!' He forestalled any interruption. 'But soon. So I thought it right and proper that you know I'll be selling t'business. I'm keeping t'houses so you'll be all right. I don't think there's owt else I have to tell you –'

'Will you gimme first refusal?'

Nat stared at the other. 'You're not on about the business?'

'Aye!' The lumpen face showed enthusiasm. 'I couldn't buy it outright but –'

'Spud, you've never done owt like this before.' Nat showed unusual philanthropism. 'I can't let you throw your money away.'

'I handle your debt-collecting all right, don't I? And there can't be much to running a scrap yard.'

Nat suffered an instant change of mood, offended that this idiot could assume himself on a par with his employer. 'Do you know what happens to that scrap when it passes through them gates? Do you know how to grade it, who to sell it to, what foreign parts each commodity goes to?'

'No, but the lads who work there do. I'd keep them on.'

'There's the shop an' all, don't forget, and the loans. Think you could manage all them accounts, do you?'

'I aren't daft! If I buy the business I'd be buying the contacts. And as for the books, well, what about Oriel?'

'Ah.' Nat cleared his throat. 'As a matter o' fact, she'll be coming to Australia with us an' all. Oh, I might as well tell you: she's me daughter. There, so now you know.

51

If you don't want to come to me wedding that's up to you, but t'offer's there.'

'Well, I know that!' Spud beheld the other as if he were the idiot.

Nat was astounded. 'How do you know?'

'It's been common gossip for years that you'd got somebody in the pudding club when you were a –'

'Eh! I want none o' that kind o' talk at my wedding.'

'Sorry. We all just took it for granted that you'd given her a job 'cause she were your lass.'

'All?' Nat frowned. 'How many people know?'

'Well, all them as work for you – but don't worry, they'd never look down on you! And me and the missus'd be honoured to come to your wedding – even if it is a bit late!' He guffawed and nudged Nat, who beat a hurried departure, telling Spud to broadcast the invitation to his other employees.

'God I wish I'd never opened me mouth about inviting any of 'em!' he wailed at Bright, having made his confession that everyone apparently knew Oriel was his daughter. 'Sorry if I've embarrassed you.'

Bright, preparing dinner, said it couldn't be helped, though she looked concerned. 'But will they be expecting a meal? It'll be hopeless trying to organize –'

'Oh, I aren't inviting them here!' He beheld her as if this were a ridiculous suggestion. 'They're only employees.'

'You can't expect them to get dressed up for a wedding and not feed them! No, no, I'm not being shown up like that.'

'Sorry, I've made a mess of it, haven't I? I were only trying to make it a day to remember for you.' Nat offered a lame suggestion. 'You could give them a bit o' cake and wine.'

She lifted a joint from the oven, looking flustered as she tried to get the dinner ready. 'I haven't got a cake! It'd take a miracle to get hold of the ingredients and anyway it'd be no good making it today, it would crumble to bits. Ye have to let it stand for weeks before ye can cut into it.'

'I can't really go and uninvite 'em now,' he mumbled.

'Oh – just go in there and let me get on with this dinner! We'll discuss it later.' After he had slunk from the kitchen Bright realized to her horror that they had been together for only five days and already she had started to treat him as if they had been married for years. It was only because she felt so comfortable with him – but would Nat understand that? What if he should leave her before the wedding? What if he were on his way to the front door right now? Her stomach churned as she carried the meat dish to the table and, after gaining only slight relief that he had not left immediately, she began to carve.

'I'll do that,' mumbled Nat, and made to divest her of the carving knife and fork. If she says no I'll kill her, he swore to himself.

Bright glanced up at him and it suddenly occurred to her through the haze of confusion that this was another mistake she had made; it was always the man of the house who carved the joint. So accustomed was she to being in charge that she had insulted him a second time in five minutes.

Handing over the implements she seated herself dutifully to receive a plate of meat, waiting until he and Oriel had their own portions in front of them.

The meal that followed was rather strained. Nat hardly tasted the precious rations that had been so difficult to acquire, her sharp words tainting every mouthful, making it almost impossible for him to swallow. Why had she turned on him like that? His eyes were intent on his meal but saw instead the retreating back of his mother as he called out her name in vain.

Nat would have continued to suffer in silence but Bright with her open nature could not allow the meal to proceed any longer without apologizing, laying down her knife and fork to do so. 'Forgive me for snapping at you, Nat. 'Twas just that ye caught me on the hop.'

His frozen expression immediately thawed. 'It were my fault.'

'No, no.' Hands in lap, she shook her head, one tawny kiss curl blowing in the draught that came from under the door. 'You were just trying to make it a nice day for us and I've been racking my brain to think how to solve the problem.'

'May I ask what problem?' Oriel stabbed a sprout with her fork and put it into her mouth. There had been no raised voices but only an idiot would be unaware of the atmosphere between her parents.

When her mother related Nat's impulsive actions Oriel pondered for a while as she continued eating. 'We could bring them back here, give them a drink of sherry – I'll see what I can get tomorrow morning in the village – then we give each of them a little purse of sovereigns to show their employer's appreciation for all the hard work they've done for him over the years.' This submission ended with a triumphant flourish and it appeared to win favour with her mother, which had been her intention, for if she were going to migrate with her parents then she certainly must make an effort to get on with her father.

Nat chewed on a mouthful of meat. During the war he had been hoarding gold in the hope that it would appreciate in value. He was none too keen to part with it. 'It'll mean getting a lot of purses. How about a nice new five-pound note each?'

Oriel shrugged. 'I suppose that would do.'

'Aye, that's not a bad idea of yours,' complimented her father, pausing to dab his lips on a napkin. 'It'll make a nice sweetener before I have to deliver the bad news that they'll soon have a new boss.'

'What makes you think it'll come as bad news to them?' smirked Oriel. During the time she had worked for her father they had often undergone cryptic exchanges like this, and it had become a kind of game between them, but Bright was not to know this.

'I'm just sick of this rudeness towards your father!' Once more she deposited her knife and fork on to the plate with a loud clatter, shocking the other occupants of the table.

'I didn't mean –' Oriel began.

'I don't care what ye meant! I haven't brought you up to be contemptuous of others and you'll apologize at once.'

Oriel showed astonishment. In her view she had been much ruder to her father than this but it had until now passed without comment from her mother.

With the two women intent on each other Nat was made to feel like an interloper, a feeling he detested, but nevertheless he watched closely for now he was presented with a different Oriel to the one he had sparred with on the work front. He had viewed his daughter as independent, headstrong, now he learned that one word of admonishment from her mother could reduce her to a tearful child. Without apology she rose and dashed upstairs to her room.

'I don't think she meant owt,' he offered in the awkward silence that followed.

Bright clicked her tongue. She had abandoned her meal altogether now. 'I just don't like to hear her talk to you like that!'

He made light of the matter. 'Nay, I'm used to it.'

'Yes, I forgot she's been working for you. I'm surprised you didn't sack her.' The spot between Bright's eyebrows maintained its V of annoyance as she leaned her elbows on the table, wringing her hands. 'I would've done if I'd been her boss.'

'I've never seen her like that before.' Unable to continue his meal, Nat also laid down his cutlery.

'Oh well, I dare say you'll get used to that too.' Bright jumped up and began to side the dishes, feeling very foolish that she had overreacted out of her own self-recrimination. 'She's quick to tears. I've gone and done it now – we won't see her for the rest of the afternoon.'

'We'll have to put her absence to good use then, won't we?' He gave a crafty smile.

'Yes, ye can help me wash the dishes,' she announced with a laugh, her outward appearance lending the impression that she was back to her old self now, though her stomach still churned.

Outsmarted, he shoved back his chair and rose. 'Ooh, Mrs Prince, you're a hard woman.'

His comment stopped Bright in her tracks. She put down the plates and covered her mouth with her fingers, her words emerging through them. 'That was something I've been meaning to ask you about.' The hesitance of her tone conveyed the delicacy of the question.

'You can stop worrying about being called Mrs Smellie. I changed me name officially years ago.'

'I wasn't worried!'

'Yes you were!' he laughingly accused. 'And you've every right to be. Nobody should be lumbered with a name like that. It should be mentioned in the Cruelty to Children Act. Away, let's get these pots done, then.'

'No, sit down, I was only kidding.' She resumed her task.

'Bright, I don't need a slave. I've been looking after meself for years.' He insisted on helping.

'Sorry, I didn't mean to be bossy.' Her words were flung over her shoulder as they moved to the scullery. 'I've just got used to running around after Miss Bytheway for twenty years.'

'And that one up there.' He cocked his head at the ceiling to indicate his daughter's bedroom.

'Oh no, Oriel's always helped me.'

Nat was about to say that he hadn't noticed a lot of that going on in his presence, but he had no wish to argue the point and changed the subject as he made ready with a tea towel. 'Don't suppose she'll want to take my name.'

'Ah yes, there's that to consider too. Well, I don't see why she wouldn't want to make her name the same as ours. If she kept Maguire it'd be a bit awkward for her to explain to all these new people she's bound to meet over there why her name's different to her parents' – especially if she meets someone she wants to marry. We'll ask her when she comes down, shall we?'

It was growing dark before Oriel eventually crept out from her self-imposed exile, and though she didn't apologize she made a great effort to invite favour by offering to make tea. Bright knew better than to mention the disagreement – it would only have her daughter fleeing tearfully back upstairs for another four or five hours – but Nat was perplexed at the lack of reference to the incident. It was as if nothing had happened.

'Your father and I were discussing your name,' began her mother.

'You mean that I was named after a window.' Oriel was unusually merry for someone who had been in the depths of despair a few hours ago, thought Nat, and looked to Bright for explanation.

'It's been a standing joke for years,' she told him, feigning weariness. 'I spelled Oriel's name wrongly and I've been teased about it ever since.'

Nat had never heard of an oriel window and so did not grasp the connotation but, not wishing to appear ignorant, pretended that he understood with a sapient nod.

'Anyway,' Bright went on, addressing her daughter, 'I didn't mean that. We thought that as I'll soon be taking your father's surname, you might like to change yours too.'

Immediately the name Smellie sprang to Oriel's mind – the last name on earth anyone would choose to adopt. But if she raised the question of its legality they would know she had been snooping so instead she replied in breezy manner, 'Oh it really doesn't matter to me now.' Though deep down it did matter, this response was designed to wound her father. 'I can't alter my birth certificate so there doesn't seem much point pretending – but of course I'll give it some thought.' The hasty addendum was to prove to her mother that she was not being unreasonable. 'Now what delicacy can I prepare for your tea?'

That night, their last night of loneliness, each of them lay in their respective beds, immune to slumber. Wide awake and trembling with excitement, Bright rehearsed tomorrow's events from beginning to end, pictured herself with her beloved groom. Oh, how she ached for him, felt his warm palms running up under her nightgown . . . but no, those were her own hands that explored that yearning body, offering not satisfaction but a deep and overwhelming frustration. Enveloped thus, Bright was attacked by the neurotic idea that something was going to prevent this wedding, envisioned a tiny accidental flame burgeoning into a raging inferno that trapped her here in this room whilst the burning house crashed down on top of her before she ever had the chance to be Nat's wife. Heart thudding in her chest, she tried to hang on to reality, breathing the frigid air in rapid little gulps, trying desperately to think of other things whilst her whole being threatened to explode.

Nat, too, was kept awake by the memory of that last night they had lain together, reacquainted with the great burden of guilt over the way he had forced himself on Bright when she was but a child. He could admit that now. He *had* forced her. She had not protested but he had taken advantage of the affection of a little girl. The perspective of his thirty-eight years blinded him to the fact that they had *both* been children. All he saw now was his own abuse and betrayal of a child who had loved him. Handicapped by this image he remained sentient, his mind invaded by maggots of self-loathing. He should be happy, tomorrow was his wedding day – he *was* happy; just the very thought of Bright caused his body to react instinctively. But would his happiness be for ever tainted by this guilt?

The third occupant of the house lay awake too, staring into a darkness that reflected the vision she had of her future. For Oriel, tomorrow would mean that she had two parents at last, but perversity had dubbed this the beginning of loneliness for her, for those two parents were totally bound up in each other.

On Monday afternoon, after futile attempts to keep out of each other's way that came close to turning the whole day into a farce, the union that both had long ago abandoned to their dreams became reality: Bright and Nat were married at last.

Oriel wept through the entire ceremony, deeply moved by the way her parents offered their vows, yet even more acutely aware of her own exclusion. In three more hours her mother would be gone. She would be completely alone. It was the greatest ordeal she had ever had to face but she did her utmost not to show it and so ruin her mother's elation. Hence, it was a gay and munificent moonbeam who presided over the ensuing reception, delighting the guests with her attention to their needs.

The modest nuptials exceeded all hopes. Bright was relieved to find out that the description of Spud's wife had been just another of Nat's jokes; she was really quite pleasant, as were all the members of his workforce, and she felt glad that Nat had decided to accept Spud's offer, thus safeguarding the others' jobs.

Their future was the last thing on Nat's mind. With the nerve-racking ceremony over he was engulfed by relief that manifested itself as nonstop banter, amazing and entertaining his employees, who had never heard him utter more than half a dozen words at one go – and they were even more astonished to receive the monetary gifts from one who was usually so parsimonious. Nat beamed as they toasted his health, amused at how easy it was to please simpletons. If only they knew, he thought, how I can't wait to get rid of them, but he played the perfect host, wanting this to be a day to remember for his bride, until a respectable time lapse would allow him and Bright to escape to the railway station.

Towards the end of the afternoon the groom displayed a reluctant smile and said he and his wife would have to depart, and so the guests filed out. As her parents, too, made for the door Oriel followed them to the threshold, wishing them a safe journey. Then, after kissing her mother, much to Nat's surprise, she leaned over and kissed her father on the cheek and muttered a genuine, 'Good luck.'

Deeply touched, he planted a quick peck on his daughter's cheek, breathing in the clean fresh smell of her, then hurried outside to the waiting cab before his burning eyes gave him away.

Oriel closed the door and wept. Alone in the house and feeling miserable, she was at a loss as to what to do. Thoughts of her coming migration spurred a series of telephone calls to friends, which resulted in talk of farewell parties.

'Oh, I don't know if I'll have time for that,' she laughed. 'We've so much to do – but of course I'll nip and see you before we go.' But in reality her heart balked at the thought of saying so many goodbyes and she knew that she would be unable to fulfil her promise.

A look at the clock told of a long night ahead and so, having changed out of her wedding costume, she plodded to the top of the house and began to sort out the attic in preparation for departure.

The east coast in winter was an ill-chosen spot for a honeymoon, the effect of the wind on one's ears an assault from a thousand knives. Waves reared and crashed against the wind like gunfire as the newly-weds arrived at their hotel, an Italian-style, wildly ornamental building that dominated St Nicholas Cliff. Yet once inside the foyer of the aptly named Grand the weather was of little consequence to the nervous bride, who was daunted even by the efficient staff who fussed over their luggage, and whispered that she felt everyone was looking at her.

'They are – you look lovely.' Nat smiled and squeezed her arm to reassure her as they followed the uniformed youth to their suite.

The Grand had suffered from German bombardment during the war but no one would know it from these luxurious amenities. Even after the porter had left, the couple retained their awkward stance for a while, both apparently awed by the sumptuous décor and the vast perimeters.

'We'll need to catch a tram to get from one side of the room to t'other.' Nat went to the window to check that he had acquired a sea view and, contented, remained there for a while looking out at the rough grey waves.

'I hope Oriel's all right. She's never been on her own before.'

'There's good locks on t'doors and we won't be away long.'

Bright gave an intuitive smile at his back. 'You think I mollycoddle her, don't you?'

'No! Well, I'm selfish, I suppose. I enjoy having you to meself.'

Unsure of herself, Bright suddenly decided, 'I'd better unpack.' She began by removing her hat and looked for a place to deposit it, finally laying it on the quilted satin counterpane.

Grappling with his desires, but not wishing to crowd her, Nat merely turned his head and smiled, then looked out to sea again, listening to the rustle of her clothing as she moved back and forth between portmanteau and wardrobe.

Why isn't he hugging me, kissing me? Bright affected to busy herself with garments whilst her mind argued that she should not be wasting her time hanging them up but taking them off. Why doesn't he hold me, caress me, love me? Perhaps he thinks I'm too old. Am I too old? Maybe it's abnormal to have the sort of thoughts I've been having. In such mind, an air of anticlimax was to hamper the rest of her task.

As she neared the end of her unpacking Nat turned and studied his own case. 'Well, I suppose I'd best do mine.' His voice was half-hearted as he watched her rear view move across to the wardrobe with the last item of clothing, longing to grab her and take her to bed, and the mere thought of it making him hard. No, he must go about this carefully. He couldn't scare her, couldn't risk losing her for ever. Bright appeared to have lost her chirpiness. Though she smiled when he announced his intention to unpack there was a faint air of disappointment in her attitude. Had he failed her in some way? What did she want of him, for God's sake?

She clasped her hands and looked around as if deciding what to do next. The gleam of the polished dressing table caught her eye and she went to sit before it, examining the duchesse set that she had laid upon its monogrammed runner. She picked up a hairbrush and ran her thumb over the bristles, deep in thought.

'Can I do that?'

Her head came up and her reflection looked at Nat in surprise. 'If you like.' Beaming, she watched his approach through the mirror, simultaneously removing the pins that fastened her hair to her crown, along with the tortoiseshell comb.

Taking up the brush he hesitated as if somehow afraid, then began to run it gently over her hair sending a little shiver through her body. At once he was back in the hovel where he had been born, running the brush through his mother's dark tresses, asking her as he had asked so many times how she could have deserted her little boy. He brushed and stroked with a featherlight touch, remembering . . .

Mesmerized by his repeated caress, Bright closed her eyes and drifted into a trance, feeling his touch not just at the point of contact but throughout her entire body. Each nerve-ending tingled. Her head lolled back in ecstasy and suddenly, presented with the dark mole under her chin Nat became aware that it was Bright's tawny hair that he was stroking and the image of his mother evaporated. Feeling a new tenderness in his strokes, she opened languorous eyes to gaze at his reflection and was overwhelmed with such intense love and longing that unable to restrain herself she spun around on the stool, wrapped her arms around his hips and clung to him, pressing her cheek into his belly. Nat dropped the brush, then wrapped his arms around her head and shoulders almost suffocating her as he covered her skull with kisses. Neither of them said it'll be better this time, for there was no need to voice it. Not a word was uttered as they fumbled and ripped at buttons and laces as if groping for their last chance of life, their naked bodies finally colliding, fusing skin and flesh and spirit and memory and pain and joy. And, thus entwined, Nat and the woman he loved consummated their twenty years of loneliness at last.

Besieged by solitude in her parents' absence, Oriel had hardly sat still for ten minutes, sorting and tidying and packing. Even now on the day of their expected homecoming she could not allow herself to relax and bustled about checking that she had enough bread and milk in the pantry. Uninformed as to the actual time of their arrival she was too on edge to sit and wait, every time she did so remembering some other task that required attention. Hence, when her parents arrived they caught her by surprise.

Nat dumped the suitcase in the hallway and barged straight into the front room. 'My God! What you burning in here? Smells like –'

Before he could utter another word, Oriel, who had dropped the poker in her shock, elbowed past him, wearing a crimson scowl. 'Why don't you try knocking?' she blurted, and ran upstairs.

'Welcome home.' Nat exchanged glances with his wife.

Bright wandered over to the fireplace and immediately looked embarrassed. 'Oh, I see.' She nibbled her thumbnail and could not meet her husband's eye. 'You came in at the wrong time. I'm afraid we're not used to having a man in the house.'

He was thoroughly perplexed at his wife's coy behaviour and came to peer into the hearth. 'Women's things,' Bright told him, and moved away. He frowned, still ignorant of his crime. 'You know! Women's monthly things!' Her cheeks resembled two beetroots.

'Oh!' Nat blushed too and immediately came away from the fireplace. 'Oh well, I'll just take these cases upstairs.' He made for the stairs, clearing his throat.

'I'll come up too and say hello to Oriel.' Bright followed him.

Nat spent a respectable time unpacking his case and when he went downstairs his wife had managed to coax Oriel out of her room. She reddened again as he entered. So too did Nat but he asked quickly, 'I hope you didn't miss your mother too much?'

'I did,' confessed his daughter, jabbering to cover her embarrassment. 'I couldn't live here on my own. I've done loads of sorting out to keep me occupied – oh, and somebody came to view the house while you were away. A Lieutenant-Colonel Somebody and his wife. They seemed very keen.'

'Let's hope he has the cash then.' Nat rubbed his hands. 'We might be away sooner than we thought.'

It was fortunate that Oriel had done so much cleaning whilst her parents were away, for both their houses were sold within the next three weeks. Come the day after tomorrow, their possessions would be loaded on to a lorry and taken south to be transferred to a cargo vessel. With Nat's business transferred to Spud's name there was little else to be attended to on this Sunday afternoon, apart from the huge stack of unwanted household goods and clothes, which Bright surveyed now with uncertainty.

'I intended to telephone some charity tomorrow and give them all this, but I just keep thinking it would be mean not to offer it to our Eileen or one of the others. Pat and Eugene both left widows and young children. I'm just a bit wary o' going round there and having it thrown in me face.'

'I'd offer to do it,' said Nat, 'but I've had enough clatterings from that family. I could ask Charlie to take it on t'cart – if his new master'll let him.'

'Would you go, darling?' Bright asked Oriel, who was reading an article in the newspaper and did not seem keen on the idea. 'Just to explain what's going on. It'd be pointless to have Charlie drag all this stuff round there only to have them say they don't want it.'

'Of course they'll want it!' scoffed Oriel. 'Though why you'd want to give it to them – oh, all right I'll go.' She abandoned the newspaper. 'In fact I might as well go now.'

Collecting her hat and coat she returned to improve on her offer: 'Do you want me to go to Charlie's as well and arrange for him to pick this up?'

Bright accepted. 'That'd be a great help. I'm worn out. I think I'll make a cup of tea.'

'Right, where does this sister of yours live then?' Receiving the details, Oriel collected her bicycle and ped-alled off towards Walmgate.

'I'll get the kettle on,' said Bright.

Nat portrayed disappointment. 'Oh, and here's me thinking that when you said we were having a cup of tea it were a secret code for summat else.'

'And you not long back from your honeymoon!' laughed his wife. 'You are incorrigible.' But just the same she came over to indulge in a fervent embrace, until the loud rap of the doorknocker caused them to pull apart like guilty children, Bright leaping from his knee.

'Bloody hellfire!' Nat sighed and got to his feet. 'Looks like it's tea after all. You go put kettle on I'll answer t'door.'

At the opening of the front door there was astonishment from both Nat and the caller. For Nat, it was as if all the experience of the past three decades had been stripped away. He was a small boy again, unsure how to act.

Kendrew was the first to recover, delighted that upon his third visit he had finally struck gold. 'Nat? By, I'd hardly've recognized you!' After touching the brim of his bowler he shoved his hands into the pockets of his shabby overcoat.

'What do you want?' The clipped retort belied Nat's total confusion. All the dreadful memories came rushing back.

The hands came out of the pockets, entreating. 'Don't you know me? It's Sep!' A row of uneven teeth coaxed response.

'Aye, I remember you.' Nat's voice was as cold as the afternoon. 'I asked what you wanted.'

Kendrew gave an awkward cough but maintained his smile and shoved his hands back into his pockets. 'I heard you're looking for your mother – well I might be able to help.'

There was a look of derision and swift retort. 'Go to hell!' Nat was about to slam the door but Kendrew's scuffed brown boot prevented it.

'Hang on! Don't be like that, I'm trying to help you.'

Nat could hardly suppress his fury, was all at once thankful for this intervention. For almost thirty years he had been denied one of his greatest wishes and now here it was handed to him on a plate. The boy reclaimed his manhood. His wound nicely healed, there was barely a twinge as he drew back his left arm and aimed a blow at the reviled face of the man who had stolen his mother, catching it on the mouth and sending Kendrew tumbling on to the path.

Hearing the commotion Bright came running wide-eyed, saw that her husband was unhurt and stood behind him gripping his arm. 'Who is it? What's going on?'

Kendrew pressed a handkerchief to his throbbing lips and heaved himself up to issue a muffled retort. 'Well, you're never gonna find her now!'

'I don't want to find her!' The whites of Nat's eyes had turned pink. 'I've no bloody interest in her whatso-ever.'

'Just as well 'cause she's dead!' Kendrew flourished a blood-drenched handkerchief at his attacker. He had been hoping to postpone this news until he had gained financial reward, but it seemed that was not to be and so he resorted to spite. 'She's been dead for years!'

'Good!' Rage sent a glob of spittle on to Nat's chin.

Seeing that Nat was about to shut the door Kendrew yelled, 'Well, that lass o' yours is interested! Aye, thought that'd change your tune.' He gave a painful laugh as Nat stopped to stare at him, blood oozing from his gash. 'She came to t'workhouse to ask about Maria and had the spiffing good luck to find me in charge – fancy that! I told her I'd do what I could to help. Can't let her down, can I? Have to tell her all I know about her grandmother.' Oriel's relation to Nat had all been pure guesswork but by the look on Nat's face he was not far off the mark, and his mouth formed a bloody grin emphasizing the dimple that the other had always loathed as a child.

'Don't!' Bright grabbed her husband's arm, knowing the man's identity now. 'The neighbours'll be calling the police if they haven't already. Just give him what he wants, Nat, please. I don't want Oriel involved.'

Swallowing his detestation, Nat urged her to go inside, then approached a wary Kendrew. It was only for her sake he was doing this. 'How much?'

There was no prevarication. 'Two hundred.'

Nat snorted in disgust, but surprised Kendrew with his lack of argument. 'Right, and then it's finished. Don't think you're coming back for more. I know blokes who'd break your arms for half a crown.' Reaching into his pocket he began to scribble a cheque.

Suspecting trickery, Kendrew's swollen mouth refused it. 'I'd prefer cash.'

'In that case you'll have to wait.' Nat looked grim. 'Come back on Thursday afternoon.'

Kendrew studied the other closely for a moment, then gave his mouth one last dab and examined the handkerchief before nodding. 'Some of us have to work. I'll come on Thursday night.'

Nat, watching him turn towards the gate, wanted desperately to ask, did she ever try to find me? But the words were too painful, and he was too proud. However, he did manage to blurt a question before the man's departure: 'Were you telling truth about her being dead?'

Kendrew turned, his lip swollen almost to the size of a ping-pong ball now. He nodded again. From his expression Nat knew his affirmation to be genuine. 'Aye, she died, ooh, about fifteen year ago. I miss t'lass, you know. We'd been wed a fair while, never had any kids. Anyroad, I came back to –' He got no further. Nat had slammed the door.

Bright was gentle on his return. 'I'm so sorry about your mam, darling. Maybe he was lying.'

Expressionless, Nat shook his head. 'Doesn't make no

difference whether he was or not, she's always been dead to me.'

She sympathized, then, with thoughts as to her daughter's wellbeing, enquired, 'What did you have to pay him to keep quiet?'

'Nowt – oh, I promised him two hundred but he won't get it. When he comes to collect we'll be gone.' He rubbed his red knuckles, sighed and sat down with Bright beside him, his face abstracted. 'Funny, you know, I've wanted to do that for years but I didn't get as much satisfaction out of it as I'd hoped. Still, it's better than nowt. The only other bit of pleasure I'll have is the thought of his face when he turns up to get his two hundred and finds us gone.' And if he could find the time to arrange it he would hire one of Spud's henchmen to deliver more fitting reprisal. He urged his thoughts back to the present, his voice exasperated. 'What made her go and do this? Here's us trying to start a new life and our Oriel has to go digging up past.'

Bright made allowances, twiddling her finger through a buttonhole of her cardigan. 'Well, I can understand it in a way. Most people know where they've come from, she never did. I think it's the thought of leaving York and not having another chance to find out that's sparked it off.'

'At least we've saved her discovering t'worst of it,' sighed Nat. 'I'd hate her to know any o' that stuff.'

'Well, I'm not going to tell her.' Bright echoed his sigh. 'Roll on Tuesday. I can't wait to get away from here myself now.'

Oriel turned in to the dingy terraced street where her Aunt Eilleen lived and sallied along the row of houses on her bicycle, looking for the number. Upon finding it she dismounted, leaned her bicycle against the soot-engrimed wall, inhaled, and knocked.

There was a moment of waiting, then she heard footsteps coming down the passageway and within seconds was looking into the face of an emaciated and world-weary woman.

'Hello, I'm Oriel. Bright's daughter.' She did not smile.

'Yes, yes! I remember you.' Only half recovered from her astonishment, Eilleen smoothed her grey hair and offered a pleasant invitation. 'Won't you come in?'

There was quick and not so polite refusal, 'No, I only came to deliver a message. My mother and I are emigrating and –'

'Oh! Where will ye be going?' Eilleen showed genuine interest.

'Australia.'

'Just the two of yese?' The question was filled with amazement.

'No, as a matter of fact my mother has just got married.'

'Fancy that! Aw, well you can give her my congratulations and tell her I hope she'll be happy.' Eilleen plucked at her limp blouse. 'What a pity Mother's not alive to see it. Did Bright hear she left us?'

'How would she know if no one told her?' Oriel felt no sense of loss herself.

Eilleen flushed. 'I would've come but I was half dead myself – the flu. Nearly all of us got it. Mary lost her husband. Have you and your mother been well?' When the other nodded she went on, 'Good, I'm glad – and isn't your mother the lucky one that somebody's taken her after all these years? And he's accepted you too, has he?'

Oriel felt herself redden with anger. 'That's just the kind of ignorant comment I'd expect from the likes of you!' She reached for the handlebars of her bicycle, giving Eilleen no time to respond. 'No wonder Mother couldn't bear to come. Well, I'll deliver her message as she asked me to though God knows you don't deserve it. We've had a clear-out of clothes and furniture. Mother thought you or other members of your family might be in need –'

'I'll bet your mother didn't put it like that!' Eilleen bridled, her own cheeks as red as Oriel's. 'Whatever Bright's crimes she's never donned airs and graces, pretending she's better than anyone else – not like some.'

For years Oriel had wanted to tell the Maguires what she thought of their cruelty. Grabbing this last opportunity she retorted, 'I don't need to pretend I'm better than you. I know I am. I'd never abandon anyone who needed me.'

'Huh! That's a good one,' cried Eilleen, coming to the edge of the pavement as Oriel clambered on to her bicycle. 'You trying to teach me a lesson in morals, the sort o' stock your father came from. You want to try asking him what his mother did for a liv–'

'There's nothing shameful about being a washer-woman!' Oriel forestalled her.

Eilleen gave a nasty laugh. 'Sure, and is that what they're calling it these days?' She grappled with the handlebars of Oriel's bicycle, preventing her from moving off. 'Well, let me put you straight. It might be called washerwoman now but in my day it was called prostitute. There! See how you like that!' Then with a triumphant nod of spite she crossed her arms and watched the news move across her niece's features.

At the sound of that word every drop of Oriel's blood seemed to rush up to her face. It was a term she had once read in the newspaper and had asked her mother what it meant, and her mother had blushed and told her it was a name for a woman who was not very nice but if she really wanted to know she should look it up in the dictionary, and Oriel had looked it up and found all sorts of other words relating to the term – debased, corrupt, las-civious, debauched – and though she still did not fully know what the act of prostitution entailed she knew that it was reserved for the most degraded of creatures, and now this woman here was telling her . . . she was telling Oriel that her grandmother was a harlot.

Watching that stricken face, Eilleen regretted her impulsiveness and parted her lips to emit apology, but her niece had already launched into motion and was cycling away as fast as she could up the street.

Oriel lunged at the pedals, throwing all her weight against them, forcing every ounce of energy into the motion in an attempt to rid herself of the squalid feeling that invaded her. The shame! How many others knew? Why had her mother never warned her? There was no reluctance to leave York now. Oriel could not wait to get away, fearing that every person whom she passed on the street was laughing at her.

By the time she arrived home the initial shock had been wiped from her face though it still invaded every pore of her body. However, she must have hidden it well for her parents did not appear to notice anything amiss. When her mother asked if the offer had been well received Oriel replied that it had, omitting to mention that she had told Charlie to ignore any other instructions and transport the goods to the Salvation Army. Be damned to the Maguires!

4

With their finances in order and their possessions loaded
on board a cargo vessel, the Prince family spent two days
in the capital, enjoying the numerous landmarks and dis-
bursing a great deal of money in swish departmental
stores. This was their final night in London before embar-
kation and Nat was feeling particularly satisfied over his
achievements. This afternoon, having made a secret telephone call to York from the hotel foyer, he had been
given the information that the hospital bed that had been
reserved for his mother's former pimp was now occupied.
He smiled down at his wife, who smiled back.

Bright felt utterly untrammelled as she sauntered down
the busy illuminated road between the two people she
loved. They had just emerged from the cinema – her first
ever visit – after viewing *Shoulder Arms*.

She laughed. 'When my grandchildren ask me to recall
my last memory of England I'll be able to tell them –
Charlie Chaplin!'

'Who's going to provide you with these grandchildren?'
asked Oriel, dressed in the cream trenchcoat she had purchased that day. 'I hope you're not looking at me.'

'Well, maybe not today,' smiled Bright.

'Not ever.' The young woman was emphatic.

'Then what did you pack all those toys for?' demanded
her mother.

'For me! I'm attached to them.'

'Sentimental.' Bright felt a pang of disappointment that
Oriel had no wish for children. Perhaps she would change
her mind. A placard giving news of the impending general
election caught her eye and she laughed again. 'It couldn't

be anything so momentous as that for my last memory of England, no it had to be Charlie Chaplin! Makes you sick, doesn't it? I've just been granted the vote and I won't even be here to use it. They could've brought it forward a few weeks.'

Oriel pictured her own lasting memory of England: the spiteful look on Eilleen's face as she informed Oriel of her grandmother's profession. Shoving this aside she responded to her mother with a teasing smile as they made their way along the cosmopolitan thoroughfare to their hotel. 'Since when were you at the forefront of suffrage? I never saw you chained to any railings.'

Her mother gasped. 'No, I was always too busy chained to Miss Bytheway's kitchen sink! Anyway, you're only jealous 'cause you're too young.' She smirked.

Nat invited assault. 'Women shouldn't be allowed to vote, anyroad.' He snatched an amused glance at Oriel but she did not appear to appreciate that he had been joking and he sighed inwardly. He never knew where he was with his daughter. She had been quite affable once all the pressure of selling up and packing was over, but now it was as if she had decided she had been far too nice to him for too long and had abruptly taken herself in order. He tried to make amends. 'Oh well, you never know, they might let you vote over there.'

Obviously not regarding this as a prime issue, his wife's mind had hopped on to another subject. 'I wonder what our Eilleen thought to that stuff I sent. I might've expected a note of acknowledgement.'

Oriel balked, but chose not to confess that the goods had gone to the Salvation Army.

'At least it didn't get sent back,' added Bright.

Oriel was scathing. 'Of course it didn't! It was good stuff. They know when they're well off.'

'I wouldn't exactly say that,' returned her mother. 'I'm the lucky one.'

'It wasn't always so,' retorted Oriel, who could not

possibly imagine how bad it was to be thrown out on the streets as her mother had been, but nevertheless felt intense bitterness towards the Maguires. 'They don't deserve anything after treating you so badly.' And me, she thought.

Bright was not so vindictive, she just did not feel close to her family any more. Still, the news of her mother's death had brought floods of tears and they were not far away now. In answer to Oriel's observation she merely shrugged.

'You've got to stop looking backwards,' announced her daughter. 'Look ahead,' and instantaneously she collided with a lamppost, which made them all roar with laughter as they continued to their hotel.

As the moment to depart grew nearer Oriel and Bright became quiet and reflective, thinking of the old city where both had been born and which they were now leaving behind. In contrast Nat, with not one qualm in his heart, gave the impression of a pent-up greyhound straining to be released from its trap. His excitement at finally boarding the liner, however, was dampened somewhat when he discovered that most of his fellow passengers were homegoing Australian troops, and he guarded Bright jealously as they made their way to their cabins.

'I didn't spend the best part of a hundred and fifty quid for us to travel on a troopship!'

'Ssh! They'll hear you,' whispered his wife, as much alarmed by the look of excitement that had taken over Oriel's face. Her daughter had always shown an inordinate interest in the opposite sex – perhaps because of a lack of male company in her childhood – and now here was a whole boatload of men. However would Bright prevent one of them from taking advantage of her?

'What do I care? They needn't think they're making that racket all the way to Melbourne.'

'Don't make a fuss, please,' she begged him.

Oriel, enraptured by the multitude of khaki, agreed

with her mother. 'They have been fighting for us,' she reminded Nat, who was immediately standoffish and did not speak again for some moments except to complain.

'They've given us the wrong cabin an' all!' Upon investigating all aspects of the journey he had found out that the northerly cabins would be cooler. 'Right! Well, they needn't think they're fobbing us off with this.'

Oriel felt he was showing off and with a grimace at her mother she went to examine her own cabin.

Unused to making complaints to those in authority Bright offered a tentative suggestion. 'It looks quite comfortable to me. Oh, look it's got –'

'It might look comfy now but you won't think so when we get out to Egypt. It'll be like an oven. I haven't paid all that brass for the three of us to arrive like Christmas turkeys. Don't unpack, I won't be long – and look after that case!' All his money was in it.

Complaint did not work, though a bribe did. By the time the ship cast off from London bound for Marseilles, Nat, his wife and daughter had exchanged their cabins for superior quarters.

Now up on deck, the waving crowd on the quay getting further away, Bright lifted misty eyes from the oil-streaked water, trying to take her mind off the parting from her homeland. Worrying over her daughter's barely concealed interest in the soldiers, she indicated another young woman of similar age who was travelling with her parents, and suggested Oriel make friends. 'That girl'd be better company for you than your father and me.' She would also act as a chaperone.

Oriel was busy enjoying the soldiers' tomfoolery and hardly glanced at the subject of her mother's attention, whose bearing spoke authority, a feature that both attracted and repelled Oriel at the same time. She declined the recommendation. 'She looks too bossy. I hate people who try to push you around. I'll have a look for someone friendlier.'

'Aye well, just be careful who you choose.' Bright observed the soldiers with a mother's dread.

The distance between ship and land widened until England finally melted into the horizon, and tears could no longer be held at bay. With his money locked in the ship's safe, Nat could concentrate more fully now and tried to bolster them with talk of all the exciting things that lay ahead, and for a time his enthusiasm managed to restore their spirit of adventure – until the band played 'Land of Hope and Glory' at the evening concert, plunging them into tearfulness again. This fluctuation of emotions was to be maintained for some time. One minute Oriel and her mother were throwing themselves wholeheartedly into all the fun and games that the liner had to offer, and the next were throwing up their lunch as a gale buffeted the ship across the Bay of Biscay. Even in moments of relative calm Bright was particularly affected, groaning, 'Oh God, how am I going to stand a month of this?'

With their only view grey open sea, Nat tried his best to soothe her. 'The trick is not to regard it in them terms,' he advised the women who huddled beside him in deck chairs, their only reason for being out here in the cold was the hope that the fresh air would blow away their nausea.

'Just try to live life in an everyday fashion as you would at home.'

'I don't fancy doing the washing up after a few thousand people,' came the wan attempt at humour.

'I mean, don't concentrate on ticking the days off, it'll drag like mad. Just try to forget you're on board ship and find something to occupy yourself. That goes for you too,' Nat added to his daughter.

Oriel felt as bad as her mother. 'When I try to do that you both harp on about my being molested by soldiers.' Her face was even paler than usual.

Not the best of sailors himself, Nat got up and looked around in desperation for someone to take her off his hands. 'I'm sure there must be female company for you.'

'I apologize for being a nuisance to you.' Oriel's brain was rocking inside her skull.

'I didn't say you were a nuisance!' He steadied himself as the deck heaved beneath his feet. 'I'm just trying to take your mind off this blasted ship plunging up and down.'

Bright dry-retched, clamped her hand over her mouth and staggered to her feet. 'I'm going to have to lie down.'

'Aye, go on, love – d'you want me to come with you?' When she shook her head Nat was relieved, having no wish to be cooped up below deck unless the captain gave a specific order. 'I'll come and check up on you before dinnertime.' At his wife's expression of disgust, he sighed. 'Eh, I don't know, all this free food and none of us are fit to eat it.'

Bright managed to mutter before departing, 'Keep an eye on her.'

Nat suggested that Oriel lie down too. She shook her head, exasperating him. Now he would have to entertain her. 'I won't be much company for you.' He looked round and spotted a tall well-dressed girl in obvious distress, leaning over the rail some yards away. 'That lass doesn't look too good. Go and see how she is.'

Oriel glanced to her left and saw the bossy girl whom her mother had pointed out when they had first embarked. 'You go.' She hunched into her cream woollen collar, feeling wretched.

'I can't go! She'll think I'm trying to proposition her. Oh look, she's just thrown up.'

'Charming.' Oriel turned her face away. Then at her father's insistence, she sighed, rose and wobbled off to enquire as to the young woman's health.

Nat heaved, more from a sense of relief than sickness and leaned over the rail, presenting his face to the salt-laden wind.

'Are you all right?' Oriel placed a solicitous hand on

78

the young woman's arm. Up and down, up and down went the deck.

The other swayed. 'Not really.' Braving ridicule, she turned to display the vomit spattered down the front of her dress. The circulating breeze carried the smell past Oriel's nostrils and she covered her mouth to contain her own nausea. 'I tried to lean over the side but the wind blew it back at me.'

Despite her revulsion Oriel giggled. The other pulled a face, holding a drenched handkerchief between her fingertips. 'I need to get down to my cabin but I daren't pass the boys.' She gestured with her head along the deck at a group of soldiers. 'If I'd bothered to put my coat on I would've been sick on that, then I could've taken it off and folded it up, but I only came up for a breath of air. I know it's a lot to ask but could you perhaps lend me yours to cover this?'

Amusement wiped from her face, Oriel looked tormented, but the expression of rejection on the other's face was sufficient to propel her into action and notwithstanding her distaste she unfastened the belt of her brand-new garment, whipped it off and put it around the other's shoulders. 'Sorry it doesn't fit.' The invalid was a good two sizes larger. 'But at least it hides the mess.'

The recipient showed gratitude. 'It's so good of you. If you come with me to my cabin you can have it straight back.' At the other's expression she managed a laugh. 'What am I thinking of! I'll obviously have it cleaned for you as soon as I can. But would you mind accompanying me anyway? I still feel bilious.'

Oriel said of course she wouldn't and began to walk towards the group of soldiers, hoping that the girl would not be sick just as they reached them.

Introductions were performed. Coincidence had it that Dorothy Ratcliffe was the same age and travelling with her parents. 'It really cramps one's style, doesn't it? Especially with all these good-looking men around.'

Dorothy checked to make sure that the coat was hiding her soiled dress as they drew nearer to the group. 'As if that isn't bad enough I've got my younger brother with me too. One of the soldiers asked if he was my husband!'

'You've spoken to them?' It was uttered in wonder.

Dorothy looked at her askance. 'Yes, it's hard to avoid them, isn't it – even supposing that one wants to?' She smiled, then grimaced. 'Of course, it'll just be my luck for them to have seen me throw up.'

Oriel smiled as they neared the group of men and, taking Dorothy's lead, replied to their friendly hellos.

Nat glanced up to check on his daughter's whereabouts and noticed to his concern that she and the other girl were approaching a group of soldiers. However, when the females passed by without incident he allowed his eyes to be dragged back to the waves. The sea had always had this effect upon him. The more he gazed upon it the emptier he became until he was sucked towards the edge of melancholy. Hitherto he had been travelling under the assumption that the reunion with his lover would conquer all previous woe, but now under the spell of these cold grey waves he came to realize that the bouts of despair that had often plagued him were simply a part of his character, with which he was doomed to live. He had in some foolish way equated Bright with his mother – with their reunion it would be as if Maria had never left him – but however much Bright may pamper and cosset him the treachery of his real mother would remain as acutely raw as the day it had been inflicted.

The dreadful revelation brought desperate thoughts. If this was an indication of things to come why not end it now? He could jump over the side and by the time the ship had turned around to search for him he would be gone. Hypnotized by the waves he was dragged further and further into despair. Only with the greatest effort did he strive to rip himself away from the rail, stagger like a marionette down to his cabin and burst in upon his wife.

'Oh!' Bright was ejected by shock from her reclining position on to the edge of the bunk, pressing her hand to her chest. 'You scared the living daylights out o' me!'

Solicitations rolling from his tongue, Nat came to crouch down beside her, taking her in his arms with no sign of his inner turmoil on his face. 'Sorry, I just came to see how you are.'

'Dead from shock – no, I'm a lot better. I had some ginger.' She smiled and certainly her complexion had improved. 'I was just thinking of coming up to join you. Where's Oriel? Oh, you haven't left her on her own, have ye?'

'Don't worry, she's made pals with that big lass.' Though still trembling, Nat prevented his wife from rising. 'Stay here. I'll join you instead.' He began to take off his clothes.

Bright gave a soft anxious laugh. 'What if she comes back?'

Half out of his jacket he sighed and went to lock the door. 'She'll get a shock, won't she?' With that he finished undressing and proceeded to help his wife to disrobe.

The brief ferocity of his lovemaking took her by surprise but she accepted him, uncomplaining, as he plunged into her as if his life depended on it. When it was over he lay there heaving on top of her – it's all right, everything's going to be all right, you've found her, you love her, she's all that matters – and eventually the panic abated, he lifted his face and gazed into Bright's loving eyes, and the grey tide receded.

Calm restored, Dorothy, too, had recovered from her *mal de mer* and was now changed and back on a more stable deck with her new friend, who had found another coat to wear.

'You really must be hard up for company,' she laughed, linking Oriel's arm with her own, 'if you're prepared to allow your best coat to be covered in vomit.'

Oriel gave a laugh of disgust. The instant they had

spoken, she had liked Dorothy, discovering that any hint of bossiness was only superficial. In repose her eyes and mouth were inclined to turn down at the outer edges, lending her a misleadingly serious look, but her laughter had since given lie to this. Oriel felt happier than she had done for weeks or even months as she sauntered arm in arm along the deck, luring the attention of male eyes, even if it were Dorothy they were admiring.

'You're a true friend. Anything I can do in return you only have to name it.'

'Er, let me see,' Oriel mused, her face tilted at the sky. 'You can introduce me to those soldiers.'

'Which ones?'

'The ones who can't take their eyes off you.'

Dorothy laughed. 'They're more likely to be staring at you. You're the pretty one.' She was kind enough not to comment on the other's blush.

Oriel returned the scrutiny with a knowing smile. Her friend must be quite unaware of her powers of attraction. There was no prettiness, that was true, but Dorothy was . . . how could she describe her? Quietly majestic. She was one of those extra clean-looking people who make you feel inferior just by their very existence, with cheeks that appeared to have been scrubbed, not one glossy hair escaped from its chignon. Her tall figure, was – well, matronly was hardly a flattering description but it was the only one which sprang to mind right now and it made Oriel feel girlish in comparison. She was quite certain that it was her friend who attracted all the male attention, but was happy if some of it rubbed off on her.

'You said you'd spoken to them. It's more than I've done.'

'It was rather that they spoke to me – and Father doesn't know about it. He'd have piglets if he did. Mother too.'

'Oh, yours are like that too, are they?' The breeze whipped short tendrils of dark hair around Oriel's cheeks.

'The way my father talks you'd think they were the Hun instead of our own heroes.'

Dorothy adopted a conspiratorial air. 'Maybe if we chaperoned each other they wouldn't be so suspicious. Come on, we'll go and find out.'

Oriel showed gleeful acquiescence and said the voyage wasn't going to be as boring as she feared.

After being introduced to her new acquaintance, Dorothy's parents were quite happy for the girls to keep their own company. Before embarking on the mile-long promenade around the ship, Oriel looked for her own mother and father but could not find them, and was rather relieved. Her father was not very friendly towards strangers.

'Hullo, girls!' A cheeky uniformed figure blocked their path, his grinning friends in tow. 'We was just discussing whether you two were sisters.' At their looks of disparagement he tried another tack. 'Aw, stay a while and comfort a poor old soldier.'

Dorothy exchanged a smile with her companion. 'I don't think our parents would approve.'

The man in the slouch hat jutted his chin. 'Disapprove of you helping a poor wounded veteran?'

'You don't look wounded.' Dorothy's reply was suspicious. Oriel remained quiet, seeking protection in her friend's authoritative shadow and hoping they would not speak directly to her. If there had been only one man it would not have been so bad but they were now surrounded by a crowd of khaki hats, each with the brim pinned up on one side in a devil-may-care attitude, and inside every one a tanned grinning face. Though all were friendly, and much as she had fervently desired male company, she felt slightly intimidated by their number, and looked for a gap to squeeze through but found none.

'Appearances can be so deceptive, eh?' said the ringleader. Then he turned to Oriel, leaning so close she could smell the caramel toffee he had just eaten. 'Give us a few minutes o' yer time, miss?'

Oriel flushed, dropped her gaze to his chin strap then glanced nervously at Dorothy. 'Oh, I don't know.'

'Fair goes. Few words from those pretty lips'd bring real pleasure after what we've been through, wouldn't it, mates?'

His friends agreed.

Oriel was completely at a loss as to what to say. It showed in her manner.

'Come on!' he coaxed. 'Tell us what yer did in the war.'

Invaded by the smell and the nearness of male bodies, she felt embarrassed that she hadn't really done anything to tell. Whilst these men were defending the Empire, her war had been spent in wreaking vengeance on the father who had deserted her in babyhood. 'Much the same as anyone else at home,' she replied, twisting her embroidered bag. Her gaze flitted from face to face, resting nowhere but taking in all, from the apple-cheeked clerk with his downy moustache to the leathery jackeroo burned by thirty-five summers, all with eyes as old as the hills upon which their comrades had bled. She felt very small and childish.

Dorothy saw that her friend was in difficulties and sought to take the attention on herself. 'I was a land girl.'

'With hands like these?' Another of the soldiers grabbed her fingers and stroked them. 'They're more fitted to tinkling the ivories than pulling veggies.' There was a private joke at the rear that Oriel did not catch but it appeared to cause great merriment amongst the Anzacs. 'Shut up, you blokes! I'll bet yer do play the piano, don't yer?'

'As a matter of fact I do.'

'Knew it,' nodded the soldier. 'Will yer give us a tune?' He indicated the concert room.

'I can't right now, we have things to do.' Parting the

group with a majestic hand, Dorothy began to forge a casual passage. 'But maybe later.'

'Yer hangin' on tight to that bag!' A lanky digger grabbed Oriel's handbag and ran up some stairs to another level. 'What've yer got in here? Trying to smuggle the crown jewels out?'

'Give me that back!' Summoning bravery, Oriel put her hands on her hips and glared up at him whilst he made great play of throwing her bag over the side. She wagged a finger. 'Just you dare and I'll toss you off.'

There was smothered laughter as the soldier returned the bag to her with a muttered, 'Half me luck,' to his pals.

Dorothy, face crimson and mouth agape, hurried away with Oriel after her. 'For heaven's sake, are you trying to get yourself into trouble?' she hissed at her friend as they left group laughter in their wake.

Exhilarated by the episode, Oriel looked baffled. 'Why, what did I say?'

The large figure was almost convulsed with merriment. 'I forgot, you don't have a disgusting brother like mine – don't look back!'

'God, you were so cool with them,' breathed Oriel, then frowned at the other. 'What's the matter? Why are you laughing?'

'Nothing. Oh well, it's just that I never dared introduce myself to you before today because I thought you were really sophisticated, with your hair and your clothes. When all the time you're more innocent than me.' She laughed and shook her head.

Feeling gauche, Oriel tutted and said nothing.

'Sorry, I didn't mean to mock.' Dorothy grabbed her friend's arm. 'Talking to them doesn't bother me, I suppose because I have a brother. What really does worry me is that they're going to take me at my word about playing the piano for them. I can't play a ruddy note.'

* * *

By the time the ship docked in Marseilles Nat and Bright had met Oriel's new friend, whom they took to immediately. Oriel wanted to venture into town with Dorothy for souvenirs but neither set of parents was keen to subject their daughter to the attentions of greasy foreigners and so the girls were forced to part company for a while. However, when Oriel and her parents visited a small restaurant before embarking she spotted her friend, who waved a welcome.

'Look, Mr and Mrs Ratcliffe are asking us to go and sit with them.'

Nat preferred not to socialize and tarried by the door. 'Nay, this table'll do us here.'

Bright, who was nervous enough already at being in these unfamiliar climes, tried to hide her embarrassment whilst returning the Ratcliffes' smiles and gestures. 'It'll look rude if we ignore them,' she muttered.

A waiter had come to stand in their path. '*Bonsoir, monsieur, madame, mademoiselle!*' Receiving only blank looks he exclaimed, '*Ah, pardonnez-moi*, you are foreigners?'

Oriel showed slight offence. 'Oh no, we're English,' came her emphatic retort. 'And we'd like to sit with our friends over there.' She set off towards the Ratcliffes' table, followed by her mother. Nat was obliged to follow too or look foolish.

As he brought up the rear, Oriel, having already met Dorothy's family, was about to perform introductions. 'Mr and Mrs Ratcliffe, these are –' On the brink of announcing her own parents the reality hit her. How could she explain the discrepancy? For the first time she recognized that her pig-headed refusal to change her name would cause great embarrassment to her mother. The only thing for it was not to mention names but simply say, 'This is my mother and my father.'

The couple also had an eighteen-year-old son, who after shaking hands made little impression as he was too consumed with interest for the *patron*'s daughter, whom he watched with hooded eyes whilst pretending to read the menu. Nat pulled out a chair for his wife to sit next to Mrs Ratcliffe, a jolly, large-boned, dark-haired woman. The two were instantly attracted and set up a conversation, leaving the men to their own devices. Nat studied the menu from which Mr Ratcliffe had just made a selection, seeing no need to utter anything more than a thank you as the other man handed it over. His attempts at conversation answered in the briefest manner, Mr Ratcliffe soon fell back to await his meal. Oriel felt shown up by her father's rudeness and, burying her head in the menu, wished she had pretended not to notice the Ratcliffes' gestures now.

'Oriel tells us you're from York,' Mrs Ratcliffe was saying to Bright, who was trying in vain to select a meal from the unintelligible list. 'It's a small world, isn't it? We used to live there ourselves a long time ago. We've been in the Midlands for about fifteen years now. The company Robert worked for has gone into liquidation so he's having to go further afield. May I enquire what you do, Mr Maguire?'

Nat looked up frowning from his menu to correct the surname, but his wife looked so uncomfortable that he simply replied without elaboration, 'I run me own business.' Then he lowered his eyes to the menu again. Oriel felt sick with embarrassment.

'And you're going to the capital – any particular reason why you chose Melbourne?' asked Mr Ratcliffe.

'No. Just off on spec.'

'How very brave!' Mrs Ratcliffe smiled her admiration. 'Robert has a post lined up for him. And we have friends there who've found us a place to live. I'm afraid we're not as intrepid as you. Oriel tells us you have no close relatives to leave behind, but still the wrench must be awful.'

Bright issued mental thanks to her daughter for saving

on explanations. 'There are things I'll miss but, well, it's an adventure, isn't it?'

'It certainly is! More so for you, I imagine, with no people out there. Oriel's told us you don't know anyone at all in Melbourne. Well, I'll give you our address.' She delved into her handbag, scribbled on a small notepad, ripped out the page and with a plump hand gave it to Bright. 'You must keep in touch. It'll be so lonely for you at first, you must have someone from home to talk to.'

Bright gave genuine thanks and tapped Nat's knee beneath the table. He gave an unequivocal nod.

'I'm sorry, you're trying to decide upon a meal,' said Dorothy's mother, noticing that his concentration was more for the menu. 'I'll stop chattering and leave you in peace for five minutes.' Though she exchanged glances with her husband that said she considered Oriel's father to be less than sociable.

'Actually I can't read a word of it,' confessed Bright, an admittance her husband would never have made, nor Oriel neither. 'Could you?'

'Glad to be of use,' replied Dorothy's mother.

Bright thanked her. 'What a good job we met you – isn't it, Nat?'

After the meal, to Nat's disgruntlement, they were forced to return to the ship in the Ratcliffes' company, but once they had gone to their cabin he felt free to complain to his wife. 'Oriel told us this, Oriel told us that – what else has she told them? And I knew her not changing her name'd cause bother. Mr Maguire indeed! God, I thought the woman'd never shut up.'

'Aw, I thought she was lovely.' Bright slipped off her coat.

'You would,' teased Nat. 'She yammers as good as you do. Surprised she didn't get cramp in her tongue.'

She punched him. 'I'll be glad of her when we arrive! It's a bit frightening not to know another soul.'

'You know me, don't you?'

She laughed. 'You've never set foot in the place. Mrs Ratcliffe has friends who know the ropes. I'll be glad of any advice they can give – or aren't I allowed to go visiting?'

He performed a theatrical heave of breast. 'Eh, I suppose so. Just so long as you don't expect me to put up with any more nights like tonight.'

'Oh, I'm sure you'll get used to Dorothy's parents after you've spent Christmas and New Year with them as well,' Bright laughed, and fell into his embrace.

The festive season was spent under the Mediterranean sun. It didn't feel at all like Christmas despite the crew's efforts to organize carol singing and pantomimes, and the exchange of gifts that Nat and his wife and daughter had purchased in London. He was surprised to receive a present from Oriel, even though he had bought her one. Though he was intelligent enough to realize that she was the type of person who would buy her worst enemy a gift so as not to make him feel left out, and he attached no great meaning to the shaving mug with the picture of St Paul's Cathedral on it.

After a morning service on deck held by the Commander, Christmas Day was a round of eating and drinking, and in the evening a concert was given by some of the bolder passengers. On Boxing Day there was an afternoon of games and a fancy-dress party to look forward to later, for which Oriel and her friend plundered the ship of its brass curtain rings, pennants, sou'westers and even a crutch from the sickbay to concoct an impersonation of Long John Silver.

'Nay, I can't be doing with daft games,' said Nat when asked what he would be going as, and despite his wife's participation refused to budge. Chess tournaments, tugs of war and relay races – throughout all he remained aloof in his deck chair, though Bright and Oriel noticed to their amusement that he could not retain a straight face at the ridiculous concert performed by the Australian soldiers dressed up as women.

Bright failed to understand why he refused to participate when he was obviously so bored. 'After what you said to us when we set sail about taking your mind off the journey, you're a fine one to talk.'

'I'm happy enough to sit here and think.' He gazed out upon turquoise waters and gave a sound of disbelief. 'Look at the colour of that sea! I wonder what that land is?'

Oriel viewed the horizon. 'I think it could be Crete.'

'We passed Crete days ago,' said her father.

'I don't think so.'

'We did.' Nat was adamant.

'I didn't notice it.' Oriel had inherited her father's annoying trait of being convinced that the other person was wrong.

'You always want the last bloody word, you do.'

'No, I don't.'

Nat sighed and looked at his watch. There was another five hours before they could dress for dinner. He really looked forward to the evening when there would be dancing, one of the rare activities in which he took part so long as he did not have to dance with anyone but his wife.

'Why don't you go and see if you can find Dorothy?' suggested Bright. 'Have a game of deck tennis or whatever.'

'She's having her hair done like mine,' replied her daughter with a look at her own watch. 'But she might be finished by now. I'll go see.'

Throughout her daughter's absence Bright's anxious eyes would sporadically flick up from the book she was purporting to read, lest Oriel had been waylaid by a member of the military. Beside her in his deck chair, Nat had his eye on the soldiers too.

His wife squinted at him. 'You can't help worrying, can you?'

'What? Oh! Aye, sorry. I'm not just keeping me eye on them for that reason. Their uniforms have given me an idea for a little business venture. The army's going to have a lot of surplus equipment now this war's over. I might take it off their hands.'

'But who'd want stuff like that?'

'You'd be surprised. There's a buyer for everything.'

'Oh well, I know nothing about business.' His wife smiled and tried to reimmerse herself in the printed page but his agitated foot-tapping made this impossible. Eventually, she closed the volume and stretched in her deck chair. For a time she reclined, face directed at the sky, eyes closed. Then she turned to him with an exclamation.

'D'you remember when –' She broke off with a smile. 'I forgot, we weren't together then.'

His tanned face was moved to recognition. 'That's what I find myself doing too! It's hard to believe that we were ever apart. I couldn't survive on me own now.'

'Well, you don't have to.' She leaned towards him in an affectionate manner.

Oriel, unable to find Dorothy, had wandered all the way around the ship without being accosted by soldiers and now approached the place where she had left her parents. Seeing their heads close together, how intimately her mother was talking, her cheek almost touching Nat's, who was hanging on her every word, Oriel faltered. It happened every time. Every time she left them to their own devices and then returned she felt this awful sense of exclusion. Instead of joining them she remained where she was and leaned on the rail, snatching the occasional sideways glance to await the wave of her mother's hand that would invite her into their company. But she might as well have been invisible.

Suddenly two hands grabbed her around the waist and,

taken off guard she turned angrily on her tormentor, Dorothy, who had sneaked up behind her and now stood grinning.

'Bet you hoped it was a soldier!'

'What a stupid thing to do! You could've pushed me overboard – not to mention what damage you might have done to my giblets.' The injured party rubbed her waist and glared with tears of rage in her eyes, confusing the joker with her hostility. 'You big stupid devil!'

'Gosh, I'm sorry. I didn't mean to hurt you.' Dorothy lost her smile, though did not go into a huff as Oriel herself would have done if called stupid. Instead she looked rather timid and chastened, awaiting the explanation which was to come after a short bad-tempered hiatus.

'Oh . . . it's all right. I'm sorry too. You just made me jump.' Oriel turned her head to blink away the tears. 'It's not you. It's them.' She blew her nose and indicated her parents who were still in their own private world.

Dorothy came closer and leaned over the rail next to her friend. 'Why, what have they said to you?'

'Nothing, that's the trouble. I always feel as if I'm intruding, as if they don't really want me along.'

'But why would they not want their daughter?'

'Oh, it's just me being silly,' blurted Oriel. 'I shouldn't have said anything.' She glanced at Dorothy and was about to change the subject but the integrity of the other's face caused her to have second thoughts. She had never really had a friend in whom she could confide. This privilege had always been reserved for her mother – but how could she divulge these thoughts to her, who was partly responsible for them? The patient kindness in Dorothy's eyes urged her to risk a confidence. 'It's a bit embarrassing. If I tell you –'

'I won't tell a soul,' came the promise, and Oriel knew this person could be trusted.

'They were only married a few weeks ago.'

'Who, your parents?' Dorothy gave a scandalized titter and covered her mouth, looking over her shoulder to make sure they weren't being overheard before continuing. 'Sorry, I didn't mean to treat it lightly but . . . d'you mean that they weren't married when you were born?'

Oriel nodded and kept a lookout for eavesdroppers too, her expression betraying that her illegitimacy had caused all sorts of problems. 'He ran off when he found out that Mother was expecting me. She was left to rely on charity in order to bring me up.'

Dorothy was intrigued. 'So, how did you meet up again?'

'I found out where he was about three or four years ago. There was an awful row between us.'

The larger girl craned her neck to study Nat and Bright, then smiled. 'It must have cleared the air.'

'Yes. I suppose you could say everything turned out all right in the end.' If you were one of those dolts who voiced such platitudes, thought Oriel.

'You don't sound as if you're too pleased at them getting back together.'

'Oh, I am – well, I am and I'm not – oh, I don't know what I mean. I wish I hadn't told you now.' Oriel thought she must sound ridiculous.

'I'm glad you did. It's really interesting, isn't it?'

'Oh, very.' Oriel looked cynical. 'I like your hair, by the way.'

Dorothy's long fingers primped at her new bob before swiftly returning to the topic. 'Thank you – and so romantic. After all those years apart. Your mother must love him very much.' At the sight of tears welling in her friend's eyes the onlooker guessed that this was the problem. 'But she must love you very much too or she wouldn't have cared for you all these years – and even if your father did run away he's come back so he must love you too.' Receiving a shrug, she felt such great sympathy for the other that she was inspired to utter a promise. 'I'll never tell anyone. If ever you feel sad or just want to talk then you can confide in me and I'll always be here.'

Moved by this declaration of friendship, Oriel responded to it with a teary grasp of Dorothy's arm. 'So, you won't lose touch after we arrive in Australia?'

'Are you joking? How many friends have I got over there?'

Oriel smiled back then gave a hesitant wince. 'Could you think of some way to tell your parents that mine aren't called Maguire without giving the whole game away? That was Mother's maiden name. I suppose I should've changed mine when they got married but I didn't give much thought to the embarrassment it'd cause – such as the other evening. It was my fault, I know, for simply introducing them as my parents but it wasn't my place to explain. Father's name is Prince.'

'You know what the easy answer is, of course,' replied Dorothy. 'Find a nice man and get married! I can't wait to meet someone and change my name. Don't worry, I'll say you're adopted or something. Come on, let's go and interrupt your mother and father. It isn't decent for old people to be so lovey-dovey.' She grinned. 'Can't you tell I'm deeply jealous?'

Later, Oriel thought it best to inform her mother that she had disclosed the family secret in order to explain the difference in name. Bright looked devastated. 'I hope you won't see the need to do it with everyone!' After years of being regarded as a fallen woman, her recent marriage had just brought with it a degree of respectability. What was the point of that if Oriel was to go around advertising the fact that she herself was illegitimate?

'Of course I won't! I just had to explain about the difference in our names if we're going to keep seeing them. It's only Dot who knows. She's going to make up some story for her parents.'

'Well, find out what she's told them or things could get really complicated.'

This had been Dorothy's experience on trying to explain about the discrepancy in names, at first telling her parents that Oriel was adopted. Her mother had not believed her. 'She can't be, she looks just like a mixture of both of them! Come on, child, spill the beans.'

'Oh well . . .' Dorothy was not as strong as her appearance would suggest and under her mother's forceful demand caved in without further argument. 'I promised I wouldn't tell but – I know you're very tolerant!' She lowered her voice. 'Actually Oriel was born out of wedlock.'

Mrs Ratcliffe hid a smirk behind her hand. 'I'd never have thought it about Mrs Prince; she doesn't seem vulgar at all.'

Mr Ratcliffe agreed but from then on vowed to pay keener interest to the scarlet woman and her daughter.

'You won't say anything?' Dorothy looked concerned.

'Of course not!' Her mother was genuine. 'I like them – well, I like her, he's morose – but I wouldn't hold it against anybody for one indiscretion.'

On next meeting the Ratcliffes Bright watched their eyes closely for signs that they knew about her past but they treated her no differently than before so it appeared her secret was safe. Mrs Ratcliffe was to reiterate her opinion that the two families should keep in touch and Bright said they would for they were the only people she knew in Australia, which sounded a bit insulting in Oriel's opinion but Mrs Ratcliffe took it the right way and a firm friendship was established.

The weather grew increasingly warm. They had shed their coats weeks ago but even their summer attire felt as heavy as bearskin as they cruised into Port Said. The entrance to the Suez Canal was crammed with shipping – coal barges, fishing boats and another troopship bound in the opposite direction. There was a great roar and a scurry of khaki as thousands of soldiers flocked to the rail and a lot of barracking and hurling of missiles took place as the ships glided past each other. Oriel shared a smile with Dorothy. Over the weeks many of the faces had become familiar to them and they often chatted to the soldiers, though the liaisons were purely platonic. Despite the girls' best efforts, neither had found romance.

With aching slowness, the vessel bearing Oriel and her family was lined up behind three large steamers, all ready to make their voyage down the waterway. The area around Port Said was flat, with little activity to be seen on the concrete jetties but there was exotic-looking architecture – domes and turrets – upon which to feast their fascinated eyes. After an interminable wait their liner joined the procession along the Canal, a journey of around a hundred miles, taking the jaded passengers deeper into the heat and dust and smells of Egypt.

After several hours of monotony the artificial cutting opened on to the deeper waters of a lake where lay the midway station of Ismailia. Soon afterwards, though, the canal became so narrow that Bright was fearful that their huge ship was going to become wedged. There was little to thrill the eye now. The sandy banks that sloped gently to either side were decorated only with sparse shrubby growth and the odd dhow undergoing repair.

From time to time there would be villages where small dark-skinned boys would run alongside the liner, waving and flashing their white charming smiles shouting, 'Baksheesh! Baksheesh!'

Seated in her deck chair, parents by her side, Oriel tweaked at the front of her embroidered cream blouse and shook it, attempting to create a draught. 'I wonder what they're saying?' She hardly had the energy to cock her ear.

Even in the buff lightweight flannel suit Nat felt as if his head were about to explode into flames, and he fanned himself with his panama. It was hard to believe that this was winter. 'I don't know, but if they don't shurrup I'm gonna start legging a few bricks at 'em.' His foot twitched like an angry cat's tail, displaying incongruously garish socks above the Oxford-style lace-ups, Nat's one concession to flamboyance. 'I can't stick this much longer. I think I'll go and lie down, are you two coming?'

Whilst Oriel said she would go and look for Dorothy, her parents peeled themselves from their deck chairs and wandered lethargically below deck.

Oriel approached another flight of steps that led towards Dorothy's cabin. She was about to go down them when she saw ascending towards her one of the diggers whose face she had come to know well. Head down, his first sight of Oriel was her pretty ankles upon which his eyes lingered before he glanced up and smiled a greeting, touching his slouch hat as he drew level with her. There were few other people on deck and no one at all in this vicinity. Feeling bolder than if she had encountered him in a group, Oriel paused with her hand on the rail, showing an eagerness to chat.

She and Dorothy had already divulged their names, but the soldiers had hitherto remained an anonymous mass. Today, however, the young digger revealed his appellation. Without the company of his mates, he was less impudent, though his eyes showed that he found her very attractive. The feeling was reciprocated. Without a hint of romance, Oriel experienced a thrill in her abdomen as his smooth-skinned face bent near to hers to share one of the less risqué jokes he had learned on his travels. She responded with amusement. Sunshine percolated the tiny holes in her straw hat, casting spangles of light to dance upon her nose. Presented with this laughing vision the digger had but one option. He kissed her.

It lasted three seconds but to Oriel, who had never known such contact, it was a transportation to heaven. She closed her eyes, experienced every contour of those warm young lips, would remember the taste of them for ever.

Strolling, cane in hand, along the deck towards the

steps that led to his cabin, Mr Ratcliffe faltered as he saw his daughter's friend tilt back her head to receive the soldier's kiss. Pricked by a long-forgotten excitation, he rested the cane upon his shoulder to watch in envy.

The young digger pulled away, issued a triumphant grin, then with a flick of his hat allowed his ecstatic victim to go on her way. Alas, her exhilarated descent of the stairs was abruptly halted by the sight of Mr Ratcliffe who had obviously been watching her for the expression he wore was all-knowing. Blushing furiously, she gave a self-conscious smile and not waiting for him to catch up hurried on her way, praying that he would not be so unkind as to tell her parents.

Throughout the afternoon and evening she squirmed, waiting for Dorothy's father to betray her, but the treachery failed to take place. In the confidence that it never would, Oriel ceased to fear every encounter with Mr Ratcliffe, even going so far as to share the secret winks he would throw at her in passing, and feeling nothing but gratitude towards this fellow conspirator.

In spite of Dorothy's envious yearning to reproduce her friend's experience, the kiss was to remain an isolated event, though its mental repetition served to occupy Oriel for the remainder of the voyage through Egypt.

Twelve hours after squeezing its way into the Canal the vessel emerged from the last narrow section of cutting and stopped in order to take on fresh food.

Oriel was eager for a chance to explore the dramatic landscape with Dorothy, to gasp at the superb views of mountains and rivers that were hitherto only names in the Bible, but her mother was afraid that she would be captured by white slavers and her father was concerned for his money, and so she was condemned to a boring wait until the ship was moving again, nosing its way through the biblical landscape into the simmering heat of the Red Sea Passage.

Wilting under the sun, the passengers were less energetic now. Even dressing for dinner was too much of an effort, yet out of habit, Nat donned his swallow-tailed dress coat and braided trousers, a white waistcoat, white piqué bow tie, starched wing collar and cuffs, and patent leather shoes, whilst Bright draped herself in a creation of salmon-pink chiffon and silk, laden with fringing and beads.

Red-faced, she wafted herself. 'God, this weather really gets my back up! I'm mafted now but I know I'm going to be freezing by the end of the evening.' The nights had been very cold. 'I hope it isn't as hot as this in Australia. I've had to take my corset off – do I look too lumpy?' When Nat berated her with his eyes she came up behind him to try to catch her reflection in the mirror. 'I shouldn't have worn this colour, I look like a boiled shrimp. I wonder if we'll be invited to sit at the Commander's table tonight.' All the paying passengers seemed to have had this honour but them and the Ratcliffes.

'I wouldn't count on it. If you were married to a civil servant or a general then maybe.' Nat gave a last tweak of his bow tie and moved away from the mirror. 'I couldn't give a monkey's.'

He went to answer the knock at the door. It was Oriel, clinging with crêpe georgette and a beaded headband. At the sight of her parents she gave a flattering exclamation. 'Oh very swanky!'

Bright wafted the ostrich feather fan, a recent purchase, and said in a worried tone, 'You don't want to wear that headband in this weather, it'll cut your circulation off.'

Oriel's heart sank. 'It feels all right.' She had at least expected a compliment in return. Mother was a paradox in that she had always brought her child up to believe that she could do anything she wanted if she put her mind to it, that she was as good as anyone else, but she also had the knack of eradicating all this support by one derogatory, if unintentional, comment to paralyse Oriel's confidence. Her father, she had learned, would give a compliment even though he might not mean it, just to make a person feel better, but Bright would speak her mind if not granted time to ponder on her response first.

'You look lovely,' said her father.

'Well, she knows that!' Bright laughed. 'She doesn't need telling.'

I do, thought Oriel.

'You go on ahead, love,' ordered her mother. 'I'm not quite ready and there's hardly enough air in this cupboard for two, let alone three.'

Having an aversion to entering the dining area alone, Oriel said, 'I'll go and see what Ratty's doing then.'

On her way along the corridor she met Mr Ratcliffe, who cried out with admiration, 'My, what a bobby-dazzler!' The young woman grinned as his appraising eyes ran up and down her. 'Oh dear, we're going to have to squeeze past each other, I'm afraid.'

A trolley was parked outside one of the cabins, narrowing the passage. Oriel did not consider it that much of a restriction and it certainly did not warrant the type of pressure that Mr Ratcliffe was bestowing upon her body. The contact was unwelcome and had it been a younger man she would have been suspicious, but Dorothy's father was older than hers so there could not possibly be anything untoward in his actions. Thus, not wishing to offend the man who had been so nice to her, she gave a polite giggle as, with great leisure, he dragged his belly over hers.

At that moment Bright and Nat emerged into the corridor, saw their daughter's giggling encounter and stopped dead.

'Oriel!'

At Bright's horrified admonishment Mr Ratcliffe offered a blustering apology – 'They should move the blessed trolley out of the way. Somebody'll be tripping over it!' – and beat a hasty retreat into his own cabin.

Oriel stared at the disgusted faces of her parents, wondering what on earth she had done. Her mother was quick to tell her.

'I'm sure I didn't bring you up to behave like that!'

'What do you mean?' She looked bewildered. 'Mr Ratcliffe was just trying to squeeze –'

'We saw what he was trying to squeeze!' Nat was furious. 'And you didn't look as if you were doing much to deter him.'

Belatedly, Oriel deciphered the accusation and reflected their horror with scorn. 'But he's old!'

'Oh, so it'd make a difference if he was young, would it?' demanded her father. 'Showing us up like that. Acting like a trollop.'

Only now did it really dawn on Oriel what they were accusing her of – and totally unjustly. Her stomach was seized in a cramp-like grip, her flesh prickled and tears sprang to her eyes. She tried to barge past them to her cabin but was waylaid.

'I don't know how I'm ever going to show my face!' accused Bright. 'I never thought you capable of such behaviour.'

'Well, what do you expect of me with a prostitute for a grandmother?' Oriel shrieked at them both with tears of injustice streaming down her face – just as the assembled Ratcliffe family opened their cabin door to go for dinner.

Everyone aghast, the door was hurriedly closed and so were Bright's eyes. 'Oh, Oriel, how could you?' When her daughter took off she pursued her into the cabin leaving Nat standing shocked and wan.

'I haven't done anything!' Oriel felt corrupted by the man whom she had only regarded in avuncular fashion, but the lack of trust from her own mother was what hurt most. She plumped herself down on the bunk and hunched over, sobbing.

'I don't mean that, I was just angry because I thought –'

'I didn't do anything to encourage him!' Oriel hid her face in a handkerchief.

'I know!' Her mother was contrite now and sat down to put a comforting arm around her. 'I meant . . . oh God, ye shouldn't have said that to your poor father.'

Oriel's distorted face came up. 'Oh, I'm to blame for that as well, am I?'

'No, no!' Bright's mind was in a whirl. Would the past ever stop returning to haunt her? 'I'm not blaming you for anything. Really, I'm not.' After a few trying moments, she stroked her daughter's back and asked, 'How did ye find out? I suppose it was that man ye went to see – he came to the house.'

Oriel shook her head, blew her nose and wiped her eyes, unable to look her mother in the eye after such an accusation. 'From your sister.'

Bright frowned. 'Eileen. God, the bitch. When?' At her daughter's explanation she was even more angry. 'I wish I'd never sent her that furniture and stuff now. I hope it's got woodworm in it.'

'She didn't get it. I sent it to the Sally Army.' Oriel's eyes were still downcast.

'Good! Aw, I'm sorry I accused you before, darling, I was just so shocked. The dirty old – I wonder if his wife knows about him? Well, that's it! We can't see the Ratcliffes after this voyage is over.'

'But I like Dot.' Oriel sniffed and shuddered.

'Yes, I like her mother too, though I don't know how I'm ever going to face her. God, and here's me worried about them knowing you're illegitimate! Well, never mind that for the moment. Tell me how ye found Sep Kendrew.'

When the explanation was given, Bright marvelled over the sheer coincidence that had brought them together, and went on to answer Oriel's questions as to his identity with the revelation that ostensibly he had been Maria's husband but in reality her pimp.

She sighed. 'He must've thought all his birthdays had

come at once when you walked in that door.' Contributing a final motherly pat, she rose. 'Well, that's enough talk about him. I'll have to go tend your father.'

She found a pensive Nat in their cabin and, though he did not ask, gave him the explanation that Oriel had given her. 'I don't feel like going to dinner now, d'you? We'll send for something in our cabin. That takes care of tonight, but I don't know how we're going to avoid the Ratcliffes for the rest of the voyage.'

'We're not going to avoid 'em,' came her husband's grim announcement. 'We've nowt to be ashamed of. Anyroad, I reckon it'll be that Ratcliffe bloke trying to avoid us. I've a good mind to thump him.' At his wife's objection that this would only draw more attention, he agreed to restrain himself.

'Away, let's go to dinner. If we don't brazen it out now we never will.'

Unable to persuade Oriel to come with them, they went to the dining room alone. To Bright's disconcertment her husband, fighting his nature and wearing a determined smile, made straight for the Ratcliffes' table. Seeing the combined look of horror spread over their faces as they recognized his intention, she hung back, awaiting rebuff. However, when she and Nat reached them, Mrs Ratcliffe's voice and expression held nothing but welcome. She even went so far as to exchange seats with her husband in order to sit next to Bright. The evening passed without incident and by the time they excused themselves Nat's wife was glad that she had let him persuade her.

Unconsciously employing one of her father's expressions, she murmured when they were out of earshot, 'God, the English are a funny lot. Not so much as a wink that they heard what Oriel said, and I know they must have.' She cheered up. 'Maybe she will be able to keep up her friendship with Dorothy after all. She doesn't go to their house without one of us being there, though. I'm not having that old lecher trying his hand again.'

Mrs Ratcliffe watched the couple retreat and gave an admiring smile. 'Well, I never thought they'd show their faces, did you?'

Her husband looked uncomfortable – had felt this way all through dinner, wondering whether Prince was going to inform his wife what had sparked the argument that so amused her. He wouldn't try that again in a hurry. The girl was obviously not as loose as he thought.

'Poor Oriel,' said Dorothy. 'She must be so embarrassed over what she said. I wonder what the row was about? I think I'll just go –'

'Sit down.' Her mother caught her elbow.

'But you said it wouldn't make any difference to our friendship, said you liked her.'

'I might be liberal-minded, and yes I do like Oriel, I'd never shun her like some, but I'd rather you were in the company of others when you meet her in future. You never know what bad ways she might've picked up and I don't want you exposed to them.'

'I'll look after Sis,' offered her brother nonchalantly.

'I'm sure you would, dear.' His mother patted his hand knowingly. 'I'm sure you would. But we don't want to lead you into temptation, do we? No, I think it's best that we keep an eye on you both for the rest of the voyage.'

Holding its middle course, the ship continued more swiftly now on its route towards the coaling station at Aden. Woken during the night by the rumble of fuel being loaded from the wharves, and unable to get back to sleep, Oriel lay there picturing herself telling the whole world that her grandmother had been a prostitute. Dorothy had been understanding as usual, had whispered that one could not help what one's ancestors had done, that it made no difference to their friendship, and Oriel believed her, thanked God for Dorothy's alliance, for there was no such trust from others.

Dawn broke upon the British Colony that, to this despairing young woman, presented itself as a lifeless peninsula of volcanic precipitous rocks. Later in the day, however, when Nat bowed to pressure from his wife and took them on shore, Oriel was to be pleasantly surprised. Beyond the scorched red rocks, in the hill gorges just above the town around the water tanks from where the ship replenished supplies, there was dense and beautiful tropical vegetation, grapevines, date palms and other unfamiliar trees with a delicious heady scent.

The walk had made them thirsty and Nat allowed the women to sit for a while glugging from water bottles as they surveyed the biblical landscape, whilst he himself kept watch for robbers. Spotting movement, he viewed the interloper with suspicion, but it was only an old man leading a donkey. The animal was grossly overburdened, tottering under a great mound of sacks, its head hanging.

Anger sprang to Nat's lips. 'You want to try carrying some o' that yourself, pal!'

The weatherbeaten old man merely smiled and looked straight ahead as he prodded the donkey on its way, leaving Nat feeling impotent at not being able to communicate his disgust. 'Cruel bugger.'

'Shush,' urged his wife. 'He might come back and attack us.'

'Think I'm frightened of a bloke in a dress?'

Uncomfortable at his open hostility, Bright watched the man's retreating back for a while, thoughts drifting.

'I wonder if Jesus sat here,' she mused, after slaking her parched throat for the last time before replacing the cap on the bottle.

'Or Mary Magdalene.' Oriel wondered whether her allusion to that other fallen woman would be understood. Under the quick examining glance of her father she looked away and wiped her brow with her sodden handkerchief.

Nat hung his head and sat in silence for a while in the balmy afternoon. 'I'm sorry you had to find out about your grandmother like you did,' he muttered eventually. 'I'd never've inflicted that on you. I know what it's like. But I can't help having the mother I had. So . . . now you know.'

Oriel picked at her handkerchief. 'But I don't really.'

'You know as much as I do. You'll learn nowt else and neither will I. She's dead.' His voice belied the pain he felt. 'I'm not gonna talk about her ever again.'

At his daughter's nod of acceptance, he rose abruptly, helping both women to their feet. 'Away, we'd best be getting back to t'ship or they'll be going without us.'

Her despondence unassuaged, Oriel allowed herself to be chaperoned, but said as they walked, 'Is this what it's going to be like for the rest of the voyage? Me being treated like a naughty child, never let out of your sight? Because if it is I'm turning round now and going back. I mean it.'

Bright exchanged glances with her husband. 'Well, I suppose we are being a bit overzealous. It's just that we worry about you, darling.' She squeezed Oriel's arm. 'We'll try not to smother ye so much when we get back on board.' Though she could not help thinking that with more than halfway yet to go to Australia she was going to suffer an awful lot more anxiety over her daughter.

With the proviso that she would get back on board only if both parents swore to respect her freedom, Oriel accompanied them to the ship.

Restocked with coal, food and water the liner departed for Bombay, then beyond there the even more devastating heat of Colombo. From here only the Indian Ocean lay between the Prince family and their destination.

5

A cloudless sky, brass bands, flags, banners and jubilation awaited them on the afternoon of their arrival in Melbourne. Sounding its horn on a burst of steam, the liner, carrying its cheering diggers, forged up the bay towards a wharf that was crawling with excitement. Yachts and coal barges, mail ships, timber vessels, all gave answer, the bay resounding to honks and toots and whistles and sirens. Weary from her twelve-thousand-mile voyage, the liner finally edged her flank against the Old Railway Pier, ropes cascaded through the air and another volley of cheers went up.

'By, I didn't know they'd be this pleased to see us.' Shouting above the fanfare, Nat leaned on the rail and studied the delirious throng on the wharf below.

'I rather think they've come to welcome the soldiers.' Oriel tutted at his cryptic comment, but was nevertheless enraptured by the vastness of the sky, its diverse shades of blue.

Her mother's excited brown eyes danced from scene to scene. She gasped. 'Oh my God, look at those girls wearing make-up!'

'I wear make-up,' pointed out Oriel, unable to see the subject of her mother's scandalized gestures.

'Yes, but theirs is an inch thick and they can't be more than twelve! Look, look, there! What can their mothers be thinking of?' Bright hoped this wasn't an indication of Australian youth in general.

'Listen to you complaining already and we haven't even got off the ship.' Her husband nudged her.

'Oh, I'm not!' His wife grabbed his arm and hugged

it, her eyes ignoring the industrial outline of Hobson's Bay – bone mills, candleworks, tanning and meat preserving. Even the smoking kiln chimneys seemed robbed of ugliness against the brilliance of the sky. 'I think it's wonderful. I didn't expect Melbourne to be on the seaside. I've always dreamed of a house by the sea – though we've been so long on board I'll feel a bit funny leaving it.'

'I wain't!' replied Nat. 'But I think we have to hang on for them quarantine blokes to see if any of us have the dreaded flu. Anyroad, we're better off staying where we are for a while, we'll get crushed to death with that lot down there.'

Hours of frustration were to follow whilst the ship was cleared by quarantine and customs. Oriel and Dorothy passed the time by going around the ship saying goodbye to the soldiers and wishing them well in their civilian life. Today there was no sauciness, the diggers too anxious to be reunited with their families, who formed the crowd on the wharf below and entertained themselves during the long wait with a patriotic medley of song.

The sun got lower and lower in the sky, yet the late afternoon still retained its devastating heat. At last it was time to disembark. A great roar went up as the married men pounded down the gangway to be hauled into the crush and reunited with their families. Oriel waved to those she had come to know, but their eyes were for others. Bright cried, watching them – though she was soon to reissue her shocked disparagements as the single men loped down the ramp to be pawed and embraced by the girls in the heavy make-up.

Thereafter, the troops were transported into Melbourne by a stream of cars from the Royal Automobile Club of Victoria, who had volunteered to help throughout the war.

When it was time for the other passengers to disembark, Oriel accepted a kiss on the cheek from Dorothy and arranged to send an address as soon as they had one. Bright vowed to contact Mrs Ratcliffe too, though privately doubted that the friendship could be preserved after what had occurred on the ship. Nat merely nodded and gave his tight smile, then suggested to his wife and daughter that they make a move to find an hotel before everywhere was full.

There were quarantine officers at the foot of the gangplank making random checks of people's bags for fruit. Once they were past this obstacle Nat hailed a wharf labourer to help collect their baggage, then began to fight his way along the pier, midst people and exhaust fumes. Bright tottered alongside, exclaiming that her legs felt like rubber, both she and Nat made nervous by this unfamiliar country and its crowds.

After watching Dorothy go her own way with the people who had come to meet them, Oriel struggled after her parents beneath the fluttering banners – 'Well Done, Boys!' 'South Melbourne Welcomes You Home.' The sun was very low now, but there was no alleviation of the heat. As in Colombo, it was almost palpable. It crept up her nose and into her ears, the sweat trickling inside her clothes. Telling herself that she would never be able to stand this, she tagged on to her parents.

There was not a taxi to be had, but luckily there was an hotel not too far away. On the way, however, they passed a pub that had obviously done great business, for there were inebriated men laughing and singing and one even vomiting on the pavement. Projecting contempt, Nat ordered his companions to avert their eyes but he was too late to spare Oriel, who showed aversion and was still grumbling about it as they approached the reception desk of their hotel.

'Shush, there's nothing we can do about it,' scolded Bright, then explained to the proprietress, Mrs Churchill, 'I'm sorry, there were some dreadful men outside who –'

'Don't tell me, my dear!' The well-spoken woman held up an elegant hand, an expression of disgust on her face.

'Our guests have to suffer it every evening. I refuse to serve alcohol here but one cannot temper the habits of others. I have tried to speak to the publican but to no avail. It's a product of our licensing laws, I'm afraid. Some men feel the need to get as much down their throats as they can before closing time. What is vulgarly termed the six o'clock swill. You would be well advised to avoid the streets at this time of the evening. I myself have received dreadful threats. The war seems to have lowered everyone's standards. It was much nicer in the old days.' Mrs Churchill came from a privileged background and there was an air of resentment in her manner that gave the impression she did not have the respect she deserved. 'Now, let me find you a room – for how long?'

'Just a couple of nights.' Nat spoke up. 'Till we find somewhere more permanent.'

Mrs Churchill said she could accommodate them. 'And how are things at home? You must have had a dreadful time for the past four years.'

Bright nodded, assuming that the woman was an immigrant too. 'Did you come here before the war?'

'Oh no, I was born here – but I intend to go home some day. Please do sit down whilst I organize someone to take you to your room.'

'Is it always this hot?' Bright sank into one of the nearby armchairs, portraying relief. Oriel and Nat remained standing to catch the draught from the ceiling fan.

'Goodness me no, we're in the grip of a heatwave. We've had some dreadful bushfires. No, it certainly isn't normal for this time of year – but then I'm afraid you'll find that there is no normality in Melbourne, where the weather is concerned at least. You can get four seasons in one day.'

Bright smiled up at her husband. 'A bit like York then.'

'Heaven forbid,' muttered Nat. He leaned on the pile of suitcases, his eyes touring the foyer that abounded with pictures of royalty.

'Oh, do excuse me!' Mrs Churchill detached herself with an aloof smile to attend another guest of oriental appearance. 'Your key, Mr Kamio – good, thank you!'

When the smiling Japanese man had gone she turned her artificial smile on Bright again, murmuring through her teeth, 'I'm so sorry, we don't really encourage those types here but the war has robbed us of a lot of our clientele and I suppose they were our allies so we have to make allowances. He's very quiet. I don't think he'll disturb you.'

Bright rummaged in her bag for the piece of paper which bore the Ratcliffes' new address. 'You might be able to help us in our search for a house. Some friends of ours are staying in a place called Brighton and we'd like to be near them.'

'Which particular part of Brighton would that be?' When handed the scrap of paper the proprietress looked short-sightedly at it, then handed it back with a faintly contemptuous smile. 'I think you will find they do not actually live in Brighton at all, my dear. They would not even squeeze into North Brighton. This street is on the Gardenvale side of North Road. It's a failing of some, I fear, to tell little white lies to make them appear more affluent than they actually are. However, if you wish to live near them, then Brighton proper would not be too far away.' The implication was that friends such as these were hardly worth knowing.

Her face already flushed with the heat, Bright's embarrassment was not so obvious, but she was glad that at this point a porter arrived to escort them to their rooms.

'She's very posh, isn't she?' opined Oriel, referring to Mrs Churchill. 'More English than the English.'

'I think she's the sort you have to keep on the right side of,' agreed her mother, then spread her arms to receive the cooling draught of the ceiling fan and looked amazed. 'I can't believe we're really here at last, can you?'

*   *   *

The next day at breakfast, all of them laughed at the way their beds had seemed to go up and down all night, so accustomed were their brains to being on a ship. Bright said it made her feel quite sick and hoped the illusion would not last too long for the heat in itself was enough to contend with. After breakfast, she sorted out a pile of their clothes that required cleaning and pressing after the long voyage, then all went out to explore the metropolis. Thankfully, the temperature was not quite as intense as it was yesterday, but the thermometer in the foyer showed it was already eighty degrees. Unable to believe that they would not need more protection than their dresses in January, the women took their lightweight coats with them in case it rained, but were forced to carry them over their arms and thus were soon imbued with a sensation of leadenness. Despite being dressed immaculately as usual, in a gleaming white shirt, buff suit and panama, Nat felt grubby already as the dust of the city clung to his perspiring brow.

Coming from war-weary Britain they felt as if they had entered another world, and not simply because of the heat. The city of Melbourne was such a contrast to the antiquity of York, with magnificent, cloud-touching architecture, square blocks and wide streets which its half a million residents shared with brown-and-cream cabletrams, hansom cabs, bicycles and automobiles, and even an incongruous team of bullocks hauling a dray. Although the streets might be straight, the land upon which they were built was undulating, creating vistas and valleys. There was a bank on every corner and all manner of building styles in between, some wildly ornamental, others sober and craggy, and others which Nat thought reminiscent of the kind he had seen in Canadian cities. There was also resemblance to the flickering motion pictures he had seen of America, saloon bars with Irish names, verandahs, skyscrapers.

Yet despite all this there was an air of conservatism,

the odd glimpse of the old world in a narrow dingy lane where a dray horse shifted his weight from one hock to the other, blinking lazy lashes above the nosebag containing his lunch.

Urging his wife and daughter to proceed slowly, Nat made use of a cast-iron urinal before rejoining them. Oriel and her mother were flabbergasted at the luxury of the shopping arcades, one with caged birds and a hall of mirrors. It was all too much to take in at once. They gazed into window after window – many with 'LATE AIF' emblazoned across them to indicate the shop was run by a returned hero and so encourage profit – and were amazed at how much food was offered for sale. In the end it made Bright so dizzy that she announced she could not stand to be in the hustle and bustle for much longer and asked if they might take a sandwich lunch in the beautiful gardens by the river.

Swapping the stench of exhaust fumes for the industrial effluence of the Yarra, they found respite from the fierce midday sun beneath the shade of thick foliage, yet still the perspiration bulged from every pore, trickled in rivulets between breasts, dripped from nose and chin, making their once crisp outfits feel like damp rags. Barely rejuvenated, it was some ordeal to follow their intended proposal and investigate the bayside suburb of Brighton.

Having gained directions from Mrs Churchill before leaving the hotel that morning they knew this involved a journey of about seven miles by train, a common form of transport in the big city. Even so, Nat had to ask for directions to the station and felt conspicuous when his Yorkshire accent drew a gawping response. On the way, they caught sight of a poster advertising a Charlie Chaplin film and nudged each other, Bright laughing, 'He's everywhere, isn't he?'

Reaching an intersection, they faced a scene of havoc, the two orderly streams of traffic thrown into sudden chaos by train passengers pouring out of Flinders Street

Station and wandering willy-nilly across the road, ignoring honking horns. Unsure when to cross, Nat dithered – then grabbed Bright and Oriel's arms and made a dash for the other side.

With several suburbs in between it took them about half an hour to reach North Brighton, though they did not alight, for Mrs Churchill had advised them to proceed to Brighton Beach. The journey was worth the wait. At the southerly end of the track they disembarked to an air of sedate conservatism, acres of park and farmland with few public houses, and the smell of the sea where handsome mansions and villas abounded along the foreshore. The moment she saw the area Bright overcame her heat exhaustion to exclaim that she had to live here, and when they discovered that some of the upper storeys were available for rent they immediately made a booking.

'I really must find a church too,' she added. 'I haven't been in weeks – a real one, I mean.' There had been a Sunday service aboard the liner but to a lifelong Catholic that did not count.

Nat had other priorities. The train journey giving some hint of the metropolitan vastness, its suburbs sprawled over miles to all points of the compass, his first necessity must be personal transport. Though he had hitherto favoured a horse-drawn vehicle and was not mechanically inclined, he accepted that the world was changing and so, after they went back to their hotel he made enquiries as to where he could purchase a car. Driving, he announced, did not look difficult; he'd soon pick it up. A few days later, after a great deal of red-faced cranking and muttering and struggling with luggage, they were on their erratic way back to Brighton to be shown around their new seafront residence by the very genteel middle-aged couple who owned it, Major and Mrs Johnson.

The hallway was huge, leading on to a dome of mosaic tiles. Bright's eyes scanned the high ceilings with their elegant cornices as she, Nat and Oriel took the staircase to the upper floor. She had thought her previous home to be grand but this far surpassed it.

The journey up the staircase was retarded; the Major had a limp.

'Came through the war unscathed, did you?' he asked his tenant as they reached the upper landing. Nat nodded. 'Lucky. Got through the first two years myself, then copped this.' He tapped his right leg which issued a different-sounding response than flesh. Then he looked at Nat with suspicion. 'Weren't a conscript by any chance, were you?'

Nat replied truthfully, 'No.'

'Good! I'd have to reconsider our arrangement if you were.'

Mrs Johnson explained. 'He can't abide anyone who didn't volunteer. We didn't need conscription here, you see. All our boys went voluntarily.'

More fool them, thought Nat, and glanced at Bright and Oriel who were both rather flushed. His wife took a paper fan from her bag.

'Where were you stationed?' asked the Major.

Bright tensed and began to fan herself rapidly.

'I was a prisoner for most of the last year,' replied Nat, hoping to save his wife's blushes, though he did not care at all what these people thought of him.

'Really – in Germany?'

'Oh, this is wonderful!' Oriel seeking to alleviate her mother's discomfort swept out on to the balcony that overlooked Port Phillip Bay. 'Come and look, Mother!'

Distracted, the Major and his wife forgot about Nat and joined the two women on the balcony.

'Yes, it's a pleasure to sit here and sip long cold drinks and watch the sun go down,' smiled Mrs Johnson. 'I'm sure you'll be most comfortable. Well, we must leave you to settle in. Do call if you require anything.'

When the Major and his wife had gone, Bright

performed an exuberant twirl. 'I'd love to buy a house like this.'

Nat did not know if he could bear to look out over the sea every day but said, 'We'll see what we can do.'

However, upon investigation he was to discover that the cost of these residences was prohibitive.

'There's nowt much here under two thousand quid – not of the sort that you like.'

Bright and Oriel gasped – this was over three times as much as they had got for their house.

'We'd only be paying for the view. I feel rotten having to disappoint you,' he told his wife, 'but if we put all our money into one of these houses we'll have nowt left for me to start a business without borrowing any. If you really love the sea that much I can at least buy you one o' them bathing boxes so you can say you've got a little house on t'beach, then we'll buy a place elsewhere.'

Oriel shrank from offering her inheritance to a father who had abandoned her, but to grant her mother's wish, said, 'Well, I suppose I could pitch in. I can't see me needing my cash just yet.' Despite the imitations of Englishness that she had witnessed since arriving, Australia was very foreign in some ways and faced with her own inexperience she was rather glad to be living with her parents.

Her mother refused the offer, saying Oriel would need it when she got married. So too did her father.

'Nay.' Straight of face, he held up his hand to quell any argument. 'You keep it – but don't stick it all in the bank. I've been studying house and land prices in general. They're quite low at the moment. Buy yourself a place whether you want to live in it or not, then rent it out. By the time you need it it'll hopefully have made a nice profit.' He made a suggestion to both women. 'We haven't looked around t'other parts of Brighton. Shall we go and have a look tomorrow?'

'I can't tomorrow, I have something important on.'

Bright watched her husband's face drop, and laughed. 'Your birthday. You'd completely forgotten, hadn't you?'

'So I had! It's this weather that puts you out of kelter.' When asked if he would like to do anything special, he was at a loss. 'I suppose we could always cut up some dead wasps. That used to be a lark.'

Oriel blurted a laugh. 'What?'

'It's what your father and me used to do for enjoyment when we were ten years old,' explained her mother. 'Now there's a thing I haven't seen here, wabbies.'

'I don't bloody want to neither,' muttered Nat. 'There's enough to contend with with flies that nip like crocodiles. I'm covered in lumps.' He scratched his leg to endorse this.

'What weird children you must've been,' opined Oriel.

'Aye, we were nobbut strange,' agreed her father, still raking at his flesh.

'Getting back to the subject of your birthday,' Bright directed herself to Nat, 'we could have a little celebration and invite the Ratcliffes.'

She had not forgotten the episode with Dorothy's father, but as it had never been repeated she had decided to give him a second chance, if only because his wife was the only female she knew here and Oriel had no one but Dorothy.

'It's a lot o' bother for nowt,' replied Nat. 'All that work preparing food and all folk do is shove it down their necks, then go home and leave you with the washing up.'

'Oh, suit yourself!' She lashed out playfully. 'We'll go and look at houses instead – but don't say I didn't offer.'

A wide tour of the bayside suburb the next day told just how large an area it was. With so much farmland and market garden between structures the roads were much longer than those in York and even by noon they had barely seen half it had to offer. Throats dry, they retired to the Brighton Coffee Palace, a local temperance hotel. After lunch they collated the details they had taken from For Sale boards and went to enquire at the real estate office for further information on the properties that had caught their eye, but these too turned out to be very expensive. There were much cheaper dwellings, but feeling it a bit of a comedown Nat refused these. The agent asked if perhaps they might like to see something completely different, a very special property, and upon receiving details they accepted his offer to take them there.

In vacant possession, its elderly owner having died, the rambling old single-storey farmhouse was in need of a few repairs but even so its shabby gentility took their breath away. Built in wood except for two brick chimneys and an iron roof, it was like nothing they had seen at home, with wide verandahs all around, each bordered by intricate iron lacework. It was as if someone had bisected delicate lace doilies and pinned each half to the top of every verandah post. There was a peeling front door with a window to either side. Inside was a central hall with rooms off. Bright made allocations as they toured – one for dining, one for sitting, two good-sized bedrooms and two smaller ones, one of which Oriel designated as an office, whilst Nat said the other would make a bathroom. The kitchen and laundry were at the rear of the building and part of the back verandah had been boxed in to form a long and narrow sleepout.

Emerging from the back door they discovered that the lavatory was in a separate outhouse away from the main building.

Becoming irritated by the agent's descriptions, Nat demanded some time to think, and the man went to sit in his car, leaving the three to their discussion. Bright thought the place was glorious – so too did Oriel, but not without a reservation. 'I don't know if I could live in a house without an upstairs.'

Her mother retorted, 'You didn't have to run up and down four flights of stairs carrying buckets of coal and water for twenty-odd years! It'll suit me fine. And I don't have far to go to church either.' On their drive along North Road she had noticed the sandstone edifice of St James.

Nat's concentration was more on the land that went with the house, almost ten acres in all. It would make a good investment. On top of this, there were paddocks everywhere. 'It's like being in t'country with all these cows around, in't it?'

'Yes! Don't ye just love the smell of cow muck?' exclaimed Bright quite seriously.

'Personally I reckon it's crap.' Nat remained deadpan.

She cuffed him. 'And there's another lovely smell –'

'I think it's those.' Oriel pointed at the numerous eucalypts. 'Aren't they an unusual shape?'

Showing curiosity, her mother approached one of the trees and picked at some peeling bark. 'Oh Jesus!' She leaped back, clutching at Nat. 'Will you look at the size o' that spider? It's like a carthorse.'

Her husband seized a fallen branch and dealt the arachnid a hefty whack. 'Not now, it's not. So, what d'you think to the place then? Handy for shops and everything. There's a lot of warehouses just around t'corner on that main road. I might be able to get me hands on one. I noticed a printer's round there an' all. I could have some leaflets done and shove 'em in folk's letter boxes, see if I can get a scrap business going again. I haven't noticed anybody else having one round here. Would you mind helping me?'

'So, you're forgetting about army disposal?' Oriel squinted at him through the sunshine.

'Oh nay! I'm doing the lot. I noticed in the paper this morning they're asking for tenders for a load of army tents. I'm gonna put my bid in – but there's no saying I'll get it and scrap has always been good to me.'

'Well, we don't mind helping you deliver the leaflets,' responded Bright.

'I were rather hoping you'd consent to doing my books again once I get going.' Nat hardly dared look at his daughter, anticipating a negative response.

But Oriel was quite amenable. 'Well, I've nothing much else to do, have I?'

'Good! So are we all agreed on t'house?'

After gaining approval of the purchase Nat went along the driveway to make his offer to the real estate agent, returning with the news that the house was not in Brighton at all but in Gardenvale, being on the 'wrong' side of North Road. So if either his wife or daughter were bothered by the snobbery of the likes of Mrs Churchill they should speak now or for ever hold their peace. With much laughter at being regarded as the poor neighbours they made their purchase, then returned to their lodgings for a celebration of this and Nat's birthday.

During the next few weeks of January they alternately sweltered and shivered in the unpredictable climate, waiting for the cargo vessel bearing their furniture to dock, whilst the farmhouse received quick improvements, the addition of electricity, new copper fly-wire and a few coats of paint. Nat made frequent visits to the site to check that the workmen were not slacking, though he was unable to keep watch for long as there were other demands on his time.

Never one to let his money sit idle, he toured the city looking for investment properties, and with his usual flair for supply and demand he decided almost immediately on two buildings in an industrial inner suburb where there would be a ready supply of rent-payers. Conveniently, the houses were already filled with tenants so he would be assured of an instant return on his purchase. The sale took place within a matter of days, depleting his liquid assets, but that was no sacrifice. To one with an eye for business there was definite indication that the property market was about to boom.

Eventually, by the end of the month, they were able to move into their new home. Farmhouse it might once have been, but with its decorative fireplaces, pressed metal ceilings and other intricate features, it provided a suitable background for Nat's elegant furniture.

It was very different indeed to the houses they had previously owned. Accustomed to city living, each of them liked it for the reason that even though it was not far from convenient industries – garages, smiths and coach-builders, shops and a railway station – it appeared to be out in the middle of nowhere, set back as it was from the road amid all these gumtrees. How wonderful it was to relax on the verandah after a hard day's unpacking and look out over these rangy-limbed trees, senses overwhelmed by the scent of eucalyptus and the call of magpies, their fluid toodle-oodle-oo so much easier on the ear than the raucous cackle of their British counterpart. Nat felt a great sense of exhilaration and achievement – there was so much to build on here. Oriel, too, felt happy with her lot, sharing her father's urge for discovery.

Alas, by four o'clock clouds of voracious mosquitoes drove them indoors, and a mere three hours later, as if by the flick of a switch, darkness fell, cutting off any expectation of the sun-kissed evenings they had enjoyed in the gardens of the Northern Hemisphere. Yet all agreed that the magical light of the day, the vastness of the sky and the wonderful feeling of space were fair compensation, erasing for Nat all memory of that claustrophobic greyness of home.

After they had gone to bed that first night, they were alarmed to hear thuds in the roof which sounded like a man walking up and down. Surmising that one of the workmen had hidden up there with the intention of creeping out in the night and robbing them, Nat grabbed a hurricane lamp and made purposefully for the loft, Bright pleading for him to be careful. Tentatively he pushed open the hatch to the roof space and shone his lamp inside – then cried out, and came skimming down the ladder.

'It's a beast! I can just see its big eyes glaring at me. Well, I'm not tacklin' that. We'll have to shut it in t'loft till we can get somebody to get rid of it.'

Though relieved to find the intruder was not human Bright remained jumpy. 'I'll never dare sleep with it thudding around in there.'

'Don't worry, it can't get out. I've bolted the door.'

'Well, how has it got in?' Attired in her nightdress and feeling clammy, Oriel had come to investigate the noise and stood scratching furiously at the red lumps on her arms.

They all looked at each other. 'Maybe under the eaves,' tendered Nat. 'It can't be that big then. Away, we'll have to go to bed – though I doubt I'll get back to sleep in this heat.'

As a man who liked anonymity, Nat abhorred any dependence on neighbours, but the next morning was compelled to visit the nearest house for assistance, apologizing for calling so early on a Sunday.

'No trouble at all!' The gnarled old man came out on to his porch, hands on hips. 'Been up for three hours, went for a stroll to the beach, got me feet wet, came back for –'

I don't want to know your bloody life story, thought Nat, interrupting the slow drawl. 'I've got this animal in the loft and I'm wondering who to call on to get it disposed of.'

The old man frowned and stroked his pitted chin, then gave an exclamation. 'Oh! That'll only be the possums. They've been living there for years – got 'em in me own roof.' When Nat asked what they were the man beheld him as if he were stupid. 'I just said! Possums. They won't do much harm. Course, I'll come and have a look at 'em for you if you want rid of 'em.'

'Are they dangerous?' Nat had never been famed for his bravery.

'Nah! Nice little blokes – well, some not so little, but they won't harm yer, long as yer don't upset 'em. Haven't got any electric wires in yer loft, have yer? You have? Better make sure they're protected then.' He obviously wanted to stand and talk but Nat was already turning for home.

'Thank you! Sorry to have bothered you.'

'She'll be apples – call again any time!'

Apples? thought Nat. What's he on about now?

'"Possums," he kept saying, like I'd know what one o' them is!' Nat complained when Bright returned from Mass. 'Silly old – I wouldn't know a possum from a rhinoceros.'

'Well, as long as it's not dangerous I don't mind it being there.' His wife removed her straw hat. 'I'd just like to know what one looked like.'

She was to discover this sooner than expected that evening when, after a hard day organizing the house, she went to take some rubbish outside and one of the bulging-eyed marsupials hissed at her as she came too near its fruit tree. At her scream Nat came running along with Oriel but upon re-examination they found the possums were 'nice little blokes' and decided to let the one in the roof remain.

'I can't kill a furry little thing like that,' said Bright. 'I just wish he'd take his boots off when he comes in my house.'

If it were not the possums and the heat and the magpies that were keeping them awake it was the traffic. Halcyon impressions were dashed by Monday morning when they were woken by the squeaking and grinding of cartwheels against the tramlines on Point Nepean Road, metal upon metal carrying for miles.

Bright was still half asleep as she ate breakfast. 'I thought it would be like living in the country round here but I can't believe the noise – and that's from someone who's used to living on a main road. I don't think I'm going to last till ten o'clock tonight and there's still so much to do.'

'What we need is a domestic help,' announced Oriel. 'To live in. I mean, I don't mind helping you, of course, but it might be an idea.'

Bright's face portrayed doubt. Nat, too, abhorred the idea of a stranger in his house, saying he had never needed a servant before.

Picturing herself running about after him, Oriel persisted. 'You've only ever had yourself to think about until now. It's a large house, the maid wouldn't be under your feet, you'd hardly have to see her.'

Giving in, Nat seized the morning paper. 'Let's have a look if there's anybody in here wants a job then.' His eyes perused the columns of newsprint. 'God, I think I'm suffering from double vision. Mabel Normand, Mabel Normand – I get the impression that Mabel Normand might be on at the Majestic Theatre but then again I could have misread it. Where the hell are the jobs? I'm up to page eight ... there's a whole page and a half advertising summer sales. Oh, here it is.' He scrutinized the situations wanted on page ten. '"A woman, very capable –" Capable of what? "Charwoman, cook, general."'

'Don't strain your eyes,' smiled Bright, raising her cup of tea. 'I'll go to the shop later and put a card in the window.'

'I can do it,' offered Oriel. 'I have to go to the shop myself – well, I don't have to but I fancy some sweets.' And a sly reconnoitre of the area for eligible bachelors, came her private thought.

'We'll go together, then,' replied Bright. She saw the look her daughter passed her. 'I'm not checking up on you!'

Oriel grinned. 'I didn't say you were.' Her parents had become more reasonable in granting her privacy, the outburst over Mr Ratcliffe totally forgiven. 'But I can get whatever you want. Save us both getting sunstroke.' The temperature had risen to a hundred degrees yesterday noon, confining them to the house. Today looked like being the same. Inside, the ceiling fans provided relief but there would be none out there.

Bright insisted she did not mind.

'I'll mow that grass before it gets too hot then,' announced Nat.

'It doesn't need cutting!' The grass was parched and hadn't grown due to the lack of rain.

'Yes, it does. There's long stalks all over the place. I can't stand stalks. It'll give me summat to do while you're away.'

Although he had acquired a warehouse the sale had not yet gone through, so there was little point in starting up a rag-and-bone collection. Not to mention that the army tents were piled in several rooms of the house. The horse he had bought stood idle in a paddock and the leaflets he had arranged with the printers had not been delivered. As someone who found it hard to relax he was at a loose end. 'You're sure you don't want me to come?'

Bright laughed. 'I'm going a few hundred yards, not to Timbuktu.'

Nat had the feeling that he wasn't allowing his wife any time to herself. He just could not stand the thought of being away from her. 'All right then, but don't spend too long in there. You might breathe in some flu germs.' The epidemic had arrived in Australia with the returning soldiers.

'I'll hold my breath,' she teasingly reassured him, then leaving the cooling draught of the ceiling fan she donned a straw hat and the flimsiest of gloves and made ready to leave with Oriel.

The act of going outside was like opening the door to an oven, hot air rushing in to envelop them. There had been a wartime embargo on the use of tar and the roads were cracked and dusty, coating their shoes. Oriel observed that it was a good job they did not have far to go, for already the bare skin of her arms felt as if exposed to fire. Her bicycle had been transported from England but as yet she did not feel confident enough to use it on these roads.

In passing, she glanced at a young man who raised his hat at both women. Bright noticed his eyes flit up and down her daughter's dress and his mouth turn up at the edges – in fact she had been forced to admit that Oriel had this effect on many of the opposite sex. Frowning, she prayed that her daughter would reach marriage unmolested. But, as Oriel had complained, she was a grown woman who must take care of herself, and there were other things to worry about now.

At the corner shop she told her daughter to take charge of the advertisement while she herself went on a different errand. 'There's just something I need to get. I'll meet you back at the house.'

'Hang on, I'll come with you.' Oriel was reluctant to go into the shop without moral support. As soon as she opened her mouth in front of the locals she felt conspicuous.

'You're as bad as your father!' scolded Bright. 'There's just something I want to do – on my own.'

Oriel allowed her mother to go, then waited behind a group of women in the shop, occasionally fanning her face with her purse. When her turn came she made her own purchase of lollies – having learned not to ask for sweets for this would attract a gormless expression – and, after buying her mother's requirements, asked for the card to be put in the window. This was done immediately. Oriel left the store, hovered a moment beneath the shade of the canopy, looking up and down the street and wafting at flies, then braved the fierce sun and made for home, still alert for masculinity.

She had not gone far before a female voice accosted her.

'S'cuse me, miss!'

Oriel turned, becoming slightly discountenanced by the heavily pregnant figure who approached her, face gleaming with perspiration.

'Is it you who needs the live-in help?'

Oriel hesitated, gaping at the burgeoning front of the summer dress before replying, 'Yes, do you know of someone?'

'Yeah, me – wait, don't say anything till I've said me piece!'

'I wasn't going to,' replied Oriel, and waited. Once again the heat began to sear her bare arms. To date the only Australians with whom she had shared more than two words – Mrs Churchill and the Johnsons – could have been from England, but here was an entirely different accent.

'I'm not pretending I'll be able to do the job as good as somebody slimmer but as you can see I need the money desperate. I'm having to fend for meself since my bloke went on the lam when he found out about the reason for me putting weight on. I've never seen him for five months and my family can't help me. I'm really desperate, miss.' The latter emotion showed in the speaker's eyes as she waited for a response.

Oriel required little time to think. Besides any notion of charity it was far too hot to linger. 'Come along then.' And she turned on her heel.

'What – you'll gimme it?' The girl sounded flabbergasted at the efficacy of her own persuasion. Oriel had to laugh, and kept walking with the other in tow. Her companion stopped abruptly and turned hostile. 'If you're stringing me along –'

'Of course not!' Oriel had not realized how her reaction

would have affected this desperate young woman. She paused briefly. 'I wouldn't do that. I mean it, you can have the job.'

'Aw, bonzer!' The applicant, though still hardly able to believe her luck, saw that Oriel was genuine, and sought to offer a word of caution as she hurried in the other's wake.

'I'll do me best for as long as I can but you realize –'

'I understand completely.' Oriel prevented further explanation. 'And I assure you that you won't be over-worked, and once you've recovered from the birth your job will still be open.'

'I'm not having it adopted!' warned the other, clutching her side.

'No one would expect you to.' Oriel's buckskin shoes created little clouds of dust as she crossed the road. 'Your child will be quite welcome to stay.'

This was more than the girl could have hoped for. 'You're an angel!'

Face shaded by the brim of her hat, Oriel smiled to herself and imagined that her father would have a differ-ent term of endearment for her. 'I haven't asked your name.'

'Melinda Elliot. Most folk call me Mel.' She was begin-ning to see that the other young woman's sophisticated air that had almost prevented her from asking for help did in fact mask a kind and friendly character.

Oriel held out a white-gloved hand as they walked. 'I'm Oriel Maguire. How do you do?'

'Bit crook at the moment.' Melinda summoned a grin as she touched the extended glove briefly and tried to keep up. 'Sorry, but could I ask you not to walk so fast? I've got this awful stitch and the heat is killing me.'

Oriel had been preoccupied with what her father's reac-tion would be. She apologized and at a more leisurely saunter took the new maid home to meet the master of the house, during the journey making casual enquiries.

'Do you live around here?'

'No! I'm from the bush. I come to Melbourne about five months back thinking it'd be easier to find a job and somewhere to live but I don't like it.'

'Are you living in the city now?' asked Oriel, pulling the damp armpit of her dress away from her skin.

'Yeah, a place in Fitzroy.'

'Oh I think my father's just bought property there.' At his suggestion, Oriel herself had purchased land in North Brighton. She frowned. 'But that's miles away.' Fitzroy was on the northerly side of the city. 'What are you doing all the way down here?'

'Well, I was living there until this morning.' Melinda looked sheepish. 'Since I lost me job a few weeks ago I can't afford the rent. Worked in a shoe factory but they couldn't help noticing I was getting fat and that was it – I got the boot! Anyway I couldn't keep working forty-four hours a week. Been all over the place looking, spent a fortune on trams but haven't done no good. So anyway, this morning I saw a job advertised in Brighton with a room to go with it. I rings up, the woman says yeah come over. I can just about scrape the tram fare together, come all this way, she takes one look at me and says she doesn't want my sort.' There was a hint of angry tears in Melinda's eyes. 'I was just trailing back along the road wondering what I was gonna do when I stopped to look at the cards in that shop window, seen her pinning yours up. Still can't believe me luck.'

Oriel sounded stern. 'You really shouldn't be working at all in your condition. Isn't the father supposed to pay maintenance?'

'Yeah, if they can find him.'

Oriel nodded. 'Do you need to go and collect your belongings from your old lodgings?'

Melinda decided to be honest. 'I daren't. I crept out this morning with me nightie and toothbrush.' She held up a brown paper bag. 'I owe two weeks' rent – almost a quid.'

'I could lend you it if you want to retrieve your belongings.'

'Aw, God bless yer but they're not worth two bob!' Melinda looked down at her swollen ankles, then snatched a glance at her benefactor. 'Bet you're wondering how I got meself like this.'

'It's really none of my business. Of course, if you want to tell me . . .'

'I've known Dan since we were kids but he's changed since he came back from the war. He'd never've done this to me before – run away, I mean.'

Oriel made a quick calculation. 'But if he's just returned from the war –'

'Oh no, he's been back about eighteen months,' replied Melinda. 'He was wounded in France and got sent home. I only found out 'cause me letters were returned unanswered. I had to go looking for him. I think he felt a bit funny about me seeing him like that. But I thought it was quite romantic, being able to nurse him and that.'

'Was he badly wounded?'

Melinda nodded. 'Copped a piece of shrapnel in his head. It's still there. Not doing any harm, the doctors said, so they left it there. Not doing any harm! I could tell 'em different. He never would've run off 'n' left me like this in the old days. And he got so bad-tempered whenever I said something that he thought was silly. Sometimes I think I'm better off without him. Who am I kidding? Any bloke is preferable to being in this mess.'

'Well, you don't have to worry now.' Oriel's attempts to soothe were genuinely felt. 'We'll help in any way we can.'

'Can I ask why you are helping me like this? Not that I'm ungrateful, but, well, I have to admit that you're not gonna get much work out of me until after I've had the bub – not that I'd expect paying. I'm happy enough to have somewhere to sleep.'

'You don't have to tell me the difficulty you're facing.'

Melinda thought she detected a note of authority in the reply. 'You mean you've been in a similar mess?'

Oriel looked horrified. 'Oh no! Not personally, but . . . oh, I might as well tell you as we've got different names and it's going to get complicated.' If Melinda were to call Nat Mr Maguire it wouldn't bode well for her situation. 'My parents are called Prince, they weren't married until after I was born. My mother had me alone. That's why I know she'll help you.'

'Yeah, but what about your dad?'

'Of course he'll help too,' emerged the confident reply.

After mowing the area at the front of the house, Nat was now relaxing in shirtsleeves under the ceiling fan with a cold drink to the sound of his wife's gramophone records. Rarely had he been granted time to enjoy such leisure in the old days but on introduction it had not taken him long to acquire a taste for Bright's collection of music.

Eyes closed, his free hand brushed the air in gentle rhythm to the strings, until he heard the outer door being opened and shouted, 'Brush that grass off your feet. I'm not having anybody mucking up my clean carpet!' The joke died on his lips when he saw the stranger accompanying Oriel. 'Sorry, I thought your mother was with you!' He stood.

Confronted with the two young women his first impression was of how alike they were in feature – dark hair, blue eyes, round face – but each presented a totally different visage. Melinda wore the eager entreating smile of a Labrador dog whilst Oriel appeared vague and aloof with her dreamy faraway gaze.

Relieving her perspiring skull of the hat, she put it on to a chair, tossed her hair and stripped off her gloves. 'Father, I put the card in the window but Melinda's already available for work so I thought she might as well start now.' The look in her eye dared Nat to complain.

However, Nat was neither intimidated nor embarrassed to speak out in front of the girl. He was vexed at Oriel's presumptuousness in taking over the role that he as head of the house should be doing. 'Look at the size of her. How's she going to be able to work in that condition?'

Afraid that she was about to be thrown out the girl forestalled Oriel's objection by piping up, 'I'm as fit as a mallee bull, sir. Please gimme a chance. I've got nowhere else to go.'

'Where've you been living till now then?' Nat went to turn off the gramophone.

'A house in Fitzroy but she can't afford the rent,' provided a businesslike Oriel. 'So I told –'

'I thought there were places that'll help girls in your predicament?' Ignoring his daughter Nat continued to direct his questions at Melinda.

'Father!' Then Oriel frowned, a sudden thought coming to her. 'Hang on, what was the address of the place you've just left, Melinda?' Upon being told, she noticed the look of recognition on her father's face and at once she seized the advantage. 'That's one of your new places, isn't it?' she demanded of him.

There was not the slightest hint of guilt on Nat's face. 'I think you owe me a fortnight's rent.' At his daughter's gasp of disgust he retorted, 'I could've thrown all them tenants out when I took over the place, still could do, but I didn't. If folk are fair with me I'm fair with them, but I'm not running a charity.'

'I'll throw her out then, will I?' came Oriel's icy enquiry.

Even Nat was not so callous as to throw the girl back out on to the streets in this predicament, but his reply came on a gasp of exasperation. 'Oh . . . go on then! I suppose you can stay till we get another maid. There's a room right at back of t'house. Go stick your belongings in that.' He had forgotten it was full of army tents.

Taking a dislike to the man but too afraid to show open hostility Melinda spread one empty hand and another bearing the brown paper bag, trying to display pathos. 'I haven't got any belongings, only this.'

'Well, just go and have a look at the room and see if it's to your satisfaction.' It was a command rather than an invitation. The girl left father and daughter to argue in private.

When Melinda had gone, Nat confronted Oriel. 'How long did it take you to find her?'

She guessed his meaning immediately and although it had been mere accident that had brought the girl to her she was annoyed at Nat for thinking her action was deliberate and so let him continue to think this. 'Not long. It seems there's as much abandonment over here as there is in England.'

'Is this the only reason you came to Australia with us?' Nat sounded hurt.

'To help the unfortunate? How could I have known before I came here that I'd find the same problems as in England?'

'You know what I mean, Oriel. Your mother and me are here to start a new life and I won't have you spoiling it.'

'I'm not the one who ruined my mother's life!'

'I don't need to have a constant reminder from you what harm I did. You think I can't see through this little act of charity of yours?'

'You're saying I'd use Melinda just to get back at you?' exclaimed Oriel. 'It seems to me she's been used enough already. And if I were just using her then we know who to thank for that family trait, don't we?'

'Oh, I can see there's no point in talking to you!' blurted Nat. 'But think on.' He wagged a finger, his eyes turning dark. 'You're not filling my house with more like Melinda –'

'Who's Melinda?' Bright put down her shopping and stood framed in the doorway.

'You may well ask!'

'I am asking.' She smiled from one to the other, noting the air of tension.

'Go on, tell her!' Nat ordered Oriel.

'I've hired a maid,' she announced.

Bright removed her wide-brimmed hat. 'So what's –'

'A maid who's a fortnight off having a bairn!' cut in Nat. 'What the hell use is she going to be?'

A sound in the hall caused Bright to turn. She could see Melinda hanging back but her husband could not. As Nat continued ranting Bright held up her hand to stop him and called cheerily to their new employee, 'Hello! I'm Mrs Prince. You must be Melinda.' At the girl's awkward pose she added, 'Could you go make a pot of tea? I'm parched. The kitchen's through there.' She pointed and waited for Melinda to close the door after her before turning back to the two intransigent faces in the drawing room.

'My father doesn't like the idea of having an illegitimate child in his house.'

'Oriel!' Bright was angry. Nat turned away in despair. 'You can stop that right now!' She glared at them both. 'Melinda is well aware of your feelings. She's just overheard you shouting.'

Her husband groaned. 'I didn't mean – I've got nowt against the girl nor helping her through her predicament, it's just this one who got me mad!' He gestured at his daughter. 'You realize she only brought Melinda here to spite me. Go on, tell your mother!' he urged a tight-lipped Oriel. 'Tell her how you didn't really come with us to make her happy but to make me miserable! She's using that lass to prick my conscience – as if I don't feel guilty enough already.'

Bright put a hand to her sweating brow and wandered further into the room, dropping her hat on a chair. 'Oriel.'

'Oh yes, believe him rather than me!' Her daughter's cheeks were pink, not just from the heat but with anger and betrayal.

'It's not a case of –'

'I couldn't just be doing Melinda a good turn because her family threw her out. I thought you of all people –'

'You have nothing to teach me on that score,' came her mother's brisk issue.

'And I know how much you suffered and I want to prevent it happening to other girls!' objected Oriel. 'That's my only purpose. And what he isn't telling you is that he owns the building she can no longer afford to live in, that's why I think he has a responsibility. For heaven's sake, you'd think it was a sin to help people. I couldn't be a nurse because his name wasn't on my birth certificate and now when I'm trying to do my bit in other ways he wants to ruin that too!'

Nat walked out. The front door slammed. Afraid that she was going to lose him again Bright rushed to the window, but her husband went no further than the perimeter fence where he lit a cigarette and proceeded to take several drags. After watching him for a moment Bright turned back to Oriel.

'Look, I know your intentions were genuine.' She probed deep into her daughter's eyes. Both women knew that Nat had been correct in his accusation; it was not just out of charity that Oriel had brought the girl here, though neither would admit it. 'But you have to think how it would look to your father, how Melinda and her bulge would present him with his guilt day after day. I mean, what's she going to do after she's had the baby?'

Oriel did not foresee a problem. 'She'll continue to work here. That's what I hired her for, to help us.'

The lines on Bright's face deepened and she looked at the carpet. 'Yes, well, we may need more help than you imagine with two babies in the house.' She peered from under her eyelashes at Oriel's face.

At first there was disbelief. 'You mean – you?'

Her mother nodded and was pained to see a look of disgust appear around her daughter's mouth. It lasted only two seconds, but Bright felt as though she had been stabbed. Tears welled in her eyes.

Oriel, not knowing how she had presented herself, mis-evaluated the sorrow. 'You haven't told him because you think he'll leave you.'

Her mother was indignant and blinked away the tears. 'I haven't told Nat because I've just this minute found out. I went to see a doctor while you were at the shop.' There was, however, an element of truth in what her daughter had said: she was afraid of Nat's reaction.

Oriel appeared deeply thoughtful.

Bright waited, wanting to ask, 'Aren't you the least bit pleased for me?' but not daring to risk an unsatisfactory response. She glanced out of the window. Nat was still there, puffing less feverishly now, bending over something in the garden. How she loved him.

'It's going to be difficult at your age,' pronounced Oriel.

Bright took offence. 'I'm not that old!'

'I wasn't being rude.'

'Well, that's what it sounded like. It'll be no more difficult at this age than at fifteen. I coped then and I'll cope now – and at least this time I'll have some support. At least I hope I will.'

Oriel knew that her mother was not referring to Nat, but to her daughter. 'I'll do anything I can to help. It must have been a shock.'

Bright gave an inward sigh at her daughter's lack of intuition. 'A nice one, though.'

Oriel nodded, still stunned and embarrassed. So embarrassed that she felt unable to remain in the same room as her mother.

'Well, I'd better go and fix things up with Melinda. If she overheard our argument I wouldn't want her to think she's unwelcome. She is welcome, isn't she?'

Bright nodded. 'Didn't I say so?'

'I meant with my father. I don't want there to be an atmosphere.'

'He doesn't bear Melinda any grudge. Tell her it's nothing personal. She's bound to feel awkward not knowing the reason behind all the hostility.'

'She does know actually,' replied Oriel. 'On the way here I told her you'd understand what she's going through.'

'You've told a stranger our family business?'

'Not in detail! I just said that you'd been in a similar situation when you had me.'

Bright gasped. 'Well, thank you for nothing!' Red of face, she looked around her, headed for the sideboard, dragged out a writing pad and scrawled something on it. 'There! I'm just going to stick this on the front gate.' She held the paper out for Oriel to read: 'Scarlet Woman – Apply Within.' 'Well, I might as well! It'll save you advertising it to everyone. Be as charitable as you like but don't lay the blame at my door!'

Oriel was horrified that her motives had been misunderstood. 'I'm not blaming you! I'm just giving a reason.'

'It's enough that you brought her here, you don't need to dangle all the family skeletons before her. I warned you about that when you told Dorothy. We've come to start a new life. I'd hoped to leave all that prejudice behind. Anyway, I'm not going to stand here arguing, I want to speak to your father.' Bright hurried to the door. 'He should have been the first to know.' She was annoyed at Oriel for making her mad enough to blurt it out.

'I hope he's pleased,' called Oriel.

Bright stopped in her tracks, and revolved to gauge if the sentiment was genuine. From the expression in the blue eyes it appeared to be.

When she had gone Oriel let out a sigh and pressed her hands to her stomach, feeling nauseated. All kinds of thoughts and emotions whirled around her head. The child, this sister or brother, would be twenty-three years her junior, what would they have in common except their parents? She was gripped by childish jealousy. For over two decades she had had her mother to herself and now not only did the man who deserted them insinuate himself back into Bright's heart, but he had inflicted upon Oriel yet another rival for her mother's affection. The hate she felt at this moment was so overwhelming that it almost made her faint. How could Mother bring a child into the world at her age? It was disgusting.

'Tea's made.'

She turned to find Melinda with a tray balanced on her protuberance. 'You'd better just leave it there,' she muttered. 'Mother'll be back in a moment.'

'He didn't mean it about wanting the two weeks' rent, did he?'

When Melinda's benefactor murmured a negative reply, she looked relieved and added, 'Sorry if I've caused any trouble.'

'You haven't!' Not wishing to talk, Oriel made for the door.

Alone in the big room Melinda put down the tray, shrugged and lumbered over to the window, at a loss as to what to do.

Nat had finished his cigarette and now ground the tab under his heel into the path. Bright wandered along the dusty driveway to stand beside him as he crouched over an inch-long ant, which reared up at his intrusion into its territory. She picked up the cigarette stub and threw it under a wattle bush, out of sight. 'I swept a dozen of these up last night.' Tobacco was a lot easier to come by than in England.

His blue eyes squinted up at her, ready to issue apology but she was smiling. He thought how lovely she looked today in the sunshine. Bright, ever bright.

'Stop tormenting it, you'll get bitten!' she scolded as

he relentlessly poked his toe at the bull ant. 'Come away to the house, we're going to get sunstroke.'

He refused to go back inside for another altercation.

'Well, at least come to the verandah. This sun's blinding me and I want to talk to you.'

He straightened and followed her along the drive to the shade of the verandah where they fell upon wicker chairs, both dripping copious amounts of perspiration. 'What did she have to say for herself then?'

Bright in turn was reproachful, ineffectively wafting her face with a handkerchief. Flies had begun to gather round them. 'You're being a bit unfair on Oriel. She has a genuine desire to help the girl.'

He dealt her a glance that said I knew you'd side with her.

'I'm not,' said Bright quietly.

'Not what?'

'You think I'm just saying it because she's my daughter. She does care greatly for people's welfare.'

'Well, happen she does, she's got a lot of her mother in her. But she's also got a side of me in her, a side I can read very well, and however much you defend her and say she wants to help I still say there was another reason she brought that girl here and that was to spite me – and she'll do it again. Whatsername, Belinda, won't be the last. Our Oriel's found her vocation in life and it pays the dividend of enabling her to get even with her rat of a father.'

Bright stopped wafting the handkerchief, face creased in pain. 'Why do you do that? Say that she gets all her good points from me and her bad points from you? It's not true. You've got good traits.'

'Name one.'

Bright was stuck for words.

Nat gave a sardonic laugh and reached over to pat her hand. 'The list is endless.'

'Behave!' She stuffed the piece of damp linen back into

her pocket. 'I don't need a list of pros and cons, I just love you and I wouldn't love anybody who's as black as you like to paint yourself.'

'It's not me who's the Van Dyck. Ask any of that lot who tried to make me into an upright citizen. They can't all be wrong.' He flicked a bush fly off his cheek.

'Probably not. You probably did let a lot of good people down. I don't know why you did it – I have an idea, but I'm not inside your brain and I don't know what makes you hate yourself.'

'Eh, I'm not that bad!' quipped Nat, trying to swat the persistent insect.

Bright remained serious, knocking the fly from her own face. 'I don't think it's your fault at all. I think your mother's to blame.' She felt the sudden change in atmosphere but proceeded on her theme. 'What woman would abandon a child she'd looked after for ten years?'

Frowning, Nat reached into his pocket for another cigarette. 'Apparently men do it all the time.'

'It wasn't a dig at you. I've told you I'll never ever use that against you. Anyway, you weren't a man when you fathered Oriel, you were little more than a boy.' She sighed and rubbed the back of her hand, the one he had let drop a moment ago under the guise of lighting his cigarette but, out of anger, had continued to neglect. 'I came out here to tell you something and I got sidetracked.'

Nat was relieved to escape from the subject of his mother. 'Oh aye, Belinda.'

'Melinda,' she corrected.

'I'll put it right – though I can't say I'll enjoy having a stranger living with us.' It was bad enough having Oriel here. 'I'd hoped it would be just you and me . . . and Oriel, of course.' Noting that his wife looked rather worried, he added, 'I promise I won't be rotten to her.'

'I'm having a baby.'

He was in the act of inhaling and almost choked. 'Christ!' A conflict of emotions erupted. He detested the idea of sharing her with anyone else but was simultaneously overjoyed at the concept of this new bond between them.

Bright waited anxiously for him to recover. He could think of nothing to say, just threw his cigarette down and enveloped her in a fiercely enthusiastic hug.

She chuckled over his shoulder as he embraced her. Flies settled, but were ignored. 'I wasn't sure how you'd take it.'

'Aw!' He squeezed her even more tightly. 'It's . . . champion!' Here, now, was the chance to make up for all his wrongs. 'I don't know what to say. I never gave it a thought.' No, you never did last time either, taunted his conscience. But Bright did not participate in the condemnation, just laughed her delight, looking radiant. 'How d'you feel then?'

'I've felt a bit sick now and then but nothing like the last time.' The responding look in his eye made her gloss over this quickly – would he never stop feeling guilt? 'I didn't say anything before I'd had a chance to ask a doctor. That's where I've been just now. I thought it might be . . . but, well, at my age you can't be sure.'

'Eh, it's gonna be murder with two bairns in t'house!' But Nat was laughing as he pulled away, setting the flies buzzing again. 'I'll bet Melinda didn't realize what she was starting.'

'I don't think we can blame her,' joked his wife. 'It must've happened on our wedding night.' Bright's fertility amazed her. Here she was, thirty-eight years old, up until and including that wedding night she had only ever made love twice and both times she had become pregnant. 'And there was me putting it down to seasickness. It's due in late summer. No, I'm forgetting, it's not summer, it's winter here – whatever, it'll be around the end of August, or the beginning of September.'

'Be nice if she arrived on your birthday,' opined Nat. 'You were a lovely little lass.'

'What if it's a boy?' Bright began to fend off the insects again, using both hands.

'I'll send it back. We're not having any lads in this house.'

'Aw, I'd quite like a little boy.'

'Sorry.' He was adamant. 'I've already booked a girl.'

She opened her mouth to say, don't fathers usually want a son to carry on the family name, but just in time she remembered that Nat had no such family tradition. 'Oh, whatever it is I don't care as long as it's all right.'

'She'll be right, mate.' Nat tried to mimic the vernacular but failed to impress, and laughed. 'God that were pathetic, weren't it? Eh, she'll be an Australian! What better way to start a new life in a new country?' There was one small seed of concern and it showed on his face. 'I wonder what madam'll say?'

Bright flushed with guilt and tried to divert from her discomposure with another bout of semaphore. 'She already knows – I'm sorry, I meant to tell you first but it was just the way she was carrying on in there made me let slip.' She bit her lip. 'I don't think she's too pleased.'

Nat was sick of trying to make amends to his capricious daughter, and was rather hurt that Oriel had known this important news before himself. 'She'll have to lump it then, 'cause I'm chuffed to bits and nothing and no one's gonna spoil it. Eh, it's a shame we've nobody else to share it with. I'm dying to tell somebody.' A moment of sadness ensued as both thought of their dead friend Noel, and others who might as well be dead.

Bright was first to rally. 'You can write and tell Spud.'

'Aye! He was always bragging about his kids. I could never retaliate and say I had a daughter without giving the game away to Oriel – like an idiot not realizing that she and everybody else already knew!' He laughed. 'Eh dear, what a palaver. Anyway, I can have a free hand with this bairn. Oh!' He hugged his wife again. Bright had never seen him so animated, so happy. 'And what

I'm going to give her is no one's business! She'll want for nowt, specially not a father. What're we gonna call her?'

'Or him.'

'I've told you, no lads!' He pondered over a suitable name for this child. 'We need summat that'll match our new life. I know – Victoria!' His wife pulled a face and said it was a bit old-fashioned. 'Nay, I weren't meaning after t'old Queen! I meant the lovely country our bairn'll be born into – what'd be more fitting?'

'Well, if you think of it like that it's not so bad, I suppose.' Bright still didn't like the name. 'Victoria Prince. It does have a noble ring to it.'

'Oh aye, very aristossic,' Nat mispronounced. 'Victoria Prince. Nobody's gonna take her for a ragman's kid, are they?'

His wife smiled and said of course they wouldn't, and wondered if Nat would carry this insecurity for the rest of his life. As they went inside to toast Victoria Prince she prayed that he would not be too bitterly disappointed if the child were male.

6

As Nat had feared Melinda was turning out to be more of a liability than an asset. Not only had Bright wasted good money on a pram and baby clothes for the maid, but also refused to let her do any heavy work nor even anything as strenuous as ironing.

'We can't let her stand ironing in her condition!' she had said, as if he had asked the maid to dig a trench.

'Then what use is she?' he'd demanded.

'Very useful, as a matter of fact.'

'Aye, about as much use as a chocolate parasol. She plays on your good nature, moaning and groaning till you let her off.'

'No! She's only been here a couple of days and she's taught me all sorts of things about life in Australia. For instance, you know how the food's been going off so quickly? Melinda says there's a man who comes round selling ice. That tree out the back, the one I've been flummoxed over, that's a pepper tree. The thing that makes that awful shrill noise then stops when you look for it, that's a cicada – d'you want to know any more?'

'Very informative,' came Nat's droll reply. 'But does this walking encyclopaedia have a W section for work?'

'I don't know what you're crowing about, you're not even paying her.'

'Not until she does some proper work, I'm not.'

'I would've thought it would be worth half a crown at least for introducing us to the pleasures of roast pumpkin.'

'Ooh good, is that what we're having tonight?'

'Not if you don't behave. Now it won't be long before

she can do the work. How much do we pay her then? I thought about ten shillings.'

'Ten bob! Half o' that'd be too much.'

'Oh, get away with ye!' Bright had scolded, then she had gone to the kitchen, grabbed three bowls and put them on the table, then she, Oriel and the maid had launched into a pile of vegetables, talking almost nonstop whilst he, the master of the house, had been forced to stand there watching from the doorway like a spare part. In the end he had wandered outside to the garden where he stood now, feeling jealous and left out whilst the women continued to talk and laugh inside.

After a while Bright went to get some water, spotted him through the window and mopped her glowing brow. 'Well, I think I've done enough. Oriel, don't let Melinda be carrying those heavy pans to the stove now.'

'I won't.' Oriel, dark hair sticking to her neck, carried on scraping and peeling. Did this heat never ease? It was bad enough for her, what must Melinda feel like, having to carry that lump around with her? During the short lull in the conversation after Bright's departure she took to wondering about Melinda's baby, where its father was, feeling a kind of affinity with the unborn child. Though curious, she felt it would be an intrusion to ask the maid to elaborate and so made other enquiries about this strange country.

'Are women allowed to vote here, Melinda?' She was pleased to receive the answer that they could, plus a short explanation that there were two seats of government to vote for, state and federal. 'What party d'you vote for?'

'I just pick the same as me dad,' the maid told her, adding darkly, 'don't know if I will since he's thrown me out, though.'

Oriel thought this rather feeble but did not say so. 'Has your family been over here for a long time?'

'Dad's parents came over from England, Newcastle, in

the gold rush. Me mum's lot are Irish. I don't know when they came.'

'My mother's family were Irish too,' murmured Oriel.

'She's the real dinky-di, your mum,' smiled Melinda. 'Is it right she's gonna have a bub too?'

Oriel flinched and delivered a look that told the maid she was getting above her station.

The culprit didn't seem too perturbed. 'Sorry, I didn't mean to be a sticky beak. You can't help overhearing when you live in the same house.'

'I suppose not.' Her companion remained tight-lipped. Unlike Dorothy, Melinda was not the type with whom to share intimacies.

'Must be funny having a little brother or sister at your age,' ventured Melinda, her knife going tap, tap, tap on the chopping board.

'Quite hilarious,' muttered Oriel. When asked if she was not pleased, she added, 'Would you be?'

'Well, I dunno.' Melinda stopped to muse over the growing pile of carrots, her fingers orange. 'Reckon there's not much you can do about it now it's on its way.'

Oriel was not about to confide the true depth of her feelings, felt disloyal even over this brief discussion. She changed the subject. If Melinda was rude enough to mention her mother's pregnancy then she would reciprocate. 'Have you any idea where your baby's father is?'

There came a bitter laugh. 'Still on the lam if he knows what's good for him, the mongrel.'

Oriel looked puzzled. 'You've said that before, what d'you mean?'

'On the run. Me dad'll bash his brains out if he catches him.' Asked if she felt the same way, she responded, 'Well, I'm mad, I reckon, but it's more . . . aw, I never thought Dan'd let me down like that otherwise I wouldn'ta let him. But you know what it's like when a bloke gets intent on having his way. You've the devil's own job to stop him. Specially when he's a wounded hero.' It emerged as a sigh. Melinda's face turned dreamy.

Oriel had inherited the part of her father's character that prevented any admission of ignorance. Hence she gave a sapient nod, though she who had never even been properly kissed had no inkling of what was involved in a man having his way with a woman. The knowledge that her grandmother had been involved in prostitution had, for her, no equation with the secrets of the marital bed. To her they were two separate acts and she had no education in either. The extent of her knowledge was that it involved the lower body regions but as for the mechanical aspect she was totally in the dark and had absolutely no idea of what a naked man looked like; the nearest she had come to this was the exhibits in the public art gallery which could hardly be paid the sort of scrutiny that Oriel would have liked. But she assumed a matter-of-fact air whilst her ears pricked assiduously for information on this taboo subject.

But none was to come. 'You reckon I'm mad, I suppose.' Melinda's blue eyes oozed tears, which she fought to control. 'Aw, why'd he have to go and leave me for? It wasn't as if we'd never talked about getting married. Thought I had it all worked out, nice house, four kids . . . I wonder what he's doing now.'

'Maybe he will come back.' It was said out of kindness.

The injured party lost her dreamy expression and sliced into another vegetable. 'Well, if he does I'll bloody kill him.'

'I think we've done enough of these,' announced Oriel, collecting the peelings and pods together. 'Only the pumpkin to do now.'

Melinda performed a little whine. 'D'yer think you could do it? I can't seem to get the leverage on the knife these days. Aw, good on yer,' she praised the other's efforts. 'Yer know, I can't win. If I stand up me ankles puff up and if I sit down this gets in the way.' She patted her abdomen. 'I can't wait to get rid of it. Even though I'm terrified. They say it really hurts.'

Hacking her way through the tough skin of the pumpkin Oriel tried to reassure her. 'Well, it can't be that bad or people wouldn't go on having them, would they?' Nevertheless, she balked at the thought of a baby being extracted from her own navel.

'No. I suppose not. I'd love to be able to go to a dance.'

'Oh, I would,' agreed Oriel. 'But it doesn't matter whether or not you're in that condition, you still wouldn't be able to go, everywhere's closed.' Due to the surge in influenza cases she had been unable to visit many of Melbourne's public amenities but had confined her excursions to the beach and open spaces. 'Father's always going on about me bringing this wretched flu home – but as soon as the epidemic's over I promise we'll go to a dance.'

Melinda looked wan. 'I haven't even got the price of a tram fare.'

'Don't worry, I'll pay for us both.'

'Oh, you're a real pal,' grinned Melinda, then glanced up as Mr and Mrs Prince came in, and tried to make herself look busy.

'It must be your father's lucky day!' Bright made room on a bench for Nat to deposit the large parcel. 'His leaflets have just arrived and there was a letter in the post saying he can take over the warehouse from tomorrow. Thank God, we'll be rid of those blessed tents.'

Nat showed uncharacteristic enthusiasm as he ripped open the packaging. 'I can be up and working within a week! Does anybody fancy helping me deliver some leaflets – oh, don't worry, I don't mean thee!' He saw Melinda's face drop.

Both his wife and daughter offered to help. 'You don't mind putting the dinner on, d'you?' Oriel looked at Melinda, who shook her head.

'Are you sure ye'll be all right on your own?' Bright looked anxious, but at Nat's expression she was forced to put on her hat and gloves and, each of them carrying a wad of leaflets, the family embarked upon the streets of Brighton to inform its residents of the new entrepreneur in their midst.

A week later Nat, equipped with horse and cart, was able to revisit these streets and reap the fruits of his enterprise. It was a good haul, Bright agreed with him when the cart rolled up outside their front door that evening.

'Aye, there's some grand stuff here.' He collected a bundle of items in his arms and started to come towards the house. 'Can you take these, they're not heavy.'

'I thought that's what you got the warehouse for?' Though puzzled, she accepted the bundle.

'Well, I've nobody to help me there. These need to be graded and rather than ask you to come to the yard I thought we could all do it in t'house. You don't mind, d'you?'

Bright said of course she didn't and began to help carry the clothes indoors. Seeing this, Oriel assisted too.

Melinda stood watching, rubbing her back. Bright spotted her discomfort and paused to ask, 'Oh no, have ye started?'

The maid grimaced. 'Dunno. But I've had awful backache all afternoon.'

'Oh, you have started.' Bright glanced at her husband, who was carrying another pile of clothes in. 'Melinda's in labour, Nat.'

He did not falter in his task. 'She isn't going to have it right now, is she?'

'Oh no, I should think it'll be hours.' But his wife retained her look of concern.

'Well then, we'll be long finished with this.' With everything transferred from the cart to the drawing room, Nat disappeared for a while to tend the horse. When he came back his wife was trying on a coat. 'Eh! If there's any money in them pockets it's mine.' He bent over and started to divide the clothes into two separate piles, hurling them expertly with both hands. 'Now then, that's your lot,' he instructed his three helpers and pointed to the clothes unfit for resale. Seizing his own selection of garments he added, 'You can get cracking on them while I go take this good stuff to t'warehouse.' These would be resold, not at a shop like before but at the market stall he had acquired.

'But what d'you want us to do?' asked his wife. 'Melinda –'

'Don't worry, it's nowt strenuous!' Nat paused to explain. 'All I want you to do is cut every button off. I think even she can manage to do that.' His eyes abraded Melinda. 'It'll take your mind off things.'

Muttering over his insensitivity, Bright tried to make the girl as comfortable as possible. 'Just do it for as long as you feel able – and you will tell us when it gets too bad, won't ye?'

Melinda passed a fearful look at Oriel, then reached over her straining abdomen for a garment and all three women set upon their task.

Later that evening, after a tinful of buttons had been removed and Oriel had helped Melinda to her room, Bright dispatched Nat to fetch the midwife.

'Why didn't you send for her earlier?' He had been about to get ready for bed.

'Melinda wasn't far enough gone.'

'No, but we could've got them buttons removed a damned sight quicker with five of us on t'job.'

Hours after the household had retired to bed, the groans from the sleepout rose to yells, which burgeoned to screams as if Melinda were being tortured with hot irons. Startled awake, Oriel was riven with horror and wished she could go out for a walk but it was the middle of the night. Instead she rammed her pillow over her head, squeezing it against her ears. Never, never would she submit herself to this violation and indignity.

Eventually, there came one more frightful scream, then gasps of relief and a baby's cry. She must have fallen asleep then for she did not hear the midwife leave. Everyone slept late in the morning. When Oriel went to breakfast her parents had not been up long judging by their puffy faces. Bright announced that Melinda had given birth to a daughter, Alice.

'I suppose I'd better go and see it,' sighed Oriel.

'Aw, don't refer to her like that,' scolded Bright. 'She's a canny little thing.'

'Well, I'll have breakfast first.' Oriel rubbed her head. 'My God, I just had this awful nightmare that I was cutting buttons off a pile of dead fish.'

Bright laughed. 'Probably the smell of these kippers piercing your sleep – would you like some?'

Oriel declined, making do with toast and tea. Fifteen minutes later, carrying the tray her mother had prepared, she opened the door of the sleepout and was presented with the mother feeding her baby. 'Sorry! I'll come back.'

'No, yer right! Come in and see her.' Melinda grinned a welcome and fortunately for Oriel's sensitivity closed the bodice of her nightgown. 'Ooh, good on yer, brekkie! I'm famished. What d'you think to her?'

Oriel considered the baby to be a maggoty little creature but naturally kept her opinion to herself. 'She's lovely.'

'I'm surprised you can see her from there,' laughed Melinda. 'Come and sit on the bed and I'll tell you all about it.'

Oriel grimaced. 'I heard enough last night.'

'Oh, I thought I was gonna be ripped apart, I really did. My bum's all split.'

Shock rippled Oriel's breast and she was unable to prevent herself blurting in ignorance, 'But it doesn't come out of there!'

Melinda was jolly. 'Tell that to Alice! The front door wasn't big enough for her, she had to use the back as well – ooh, I am sore. Never again! Do you want to hold her?'

Oriel, absorbed by the obstetrical information said quickly, 'No, it's all right,' and she changed the subject, oblivious to how this might hurt the new mother's feelings. 'Wouldn't you like to contact your family or anyone?'

Melinda winced. 'If you're game enough to have 'em come stormin' down here to gimme the rounds of the kitchen. Oh, I suppose I could write to 'em – dunno what they'll say, but.'

As it turned out, the Elliot family gave a very different reception to the news than Melinda had feared. On receipt of the letter, her father travelled the fifty miles from his home to welcome her back into the fold. At first sight, Oriel and her mother had shared private giggles over the countryman with his big wide-brimmed hat pulled down over his eyes and the old-fashioned clothes, but were glad when after this initial visit Mrs Elliot and the rest of the clan came too.

Nat complained at the intrusion, of course. 'But at least we can look forward to getting the pair of them off our hands,' he told Bright.

Alas, they seemed content – nay delighted – that she had found such a nice place to live and work, and were content to leave her in Mr Prince's service.

'Work?' he barked when his wife reported this. 'We haven't had a stroke out of her and now she's gonna be stuck in bed for two weeks!'

If Nat was none too pleased to have his maid bedridden then neither was Melinda herself. 'I'm really fed up,' she wept to her friend. 'I feel rotten stuck in here with nuthin' to look at.'

Oriel tried to cheer her. 'Mother says you can get up tomorrow.'

'Yeah, but that's not much to look forward to either,

is it? When bub's been giving yer larry-dooley all night yer don't feel much like doing housework. It's me birthday next week an' all.'

'Oh, then we'll have to do something special! I'm not sure if it'll be a dance, though, they're few and far between.'

However, when she mentioned this later to her mother Bright thought she might be able to help. With the recent fall in influenza figures some places of recreation had reopened their doors. 'I'm sure I saw one advertised in the paper.' She went to sort through a stack of newspapers, chose one and riffled the pages for a moment. 'Yes, here it is. Next Saturday at St Kilda Town Hall.'

'She's hardly out o' bed and you want to take her gallivanting,' said Nat. 'Is she ever gonna be allowed to do some bloody work? Anyroad, there's still lots of this flu about.'

Bright had grown used to the threat and was no longer quite so hysterical about her daughter going out. 'If she's going to get it she can catch it at the shops.'

'I weren't thinking of her! If I cop it with my chest I'm a goner. And who's gonna look after t'babby?'

Oriel looked glum.

'I will, of course!' exclaimed Bright. Receiving a frown from Nat she explained, 'It'll be good practice for me. I'm a bit rusty after twenty-three years. Not that I was very good at it then.'

'Well, that's marvellous, that is!' he exclaimed after Oriel went to tell Melinda. 'We hire a maid to take the work off your shoulders. Not only do you end up doing twice the work but looking after her bairn an' all.'

'You should get some practice too,' she told him, then had a sudden thought. 'Oh, I'll bet poor Mel has nothing to wear!'

Nat provided a dry riposte: 'Don't worry, I'll run her up a tutu next week.'

* * *

Bright was correct in her assumption, but with a week in which to make preparations Oriel managed to find one of her own frocks that was rather too big and after the side seams were let out it was perfect for Melinda. At the fashion parade the donor, clad in beaded apricot, put on an envious expression and demanded of her mother, 'How come it always made me washed out and she looks radiant in it when we're the same colouring?'

'Well, Melinda has just had a baby,' replied Bright.

The young mother smoothed the pale green satin over her hips and asked anxiously, 'It's not too tight over here, is it?'

'We've already given too many compliments,' teased Oriel. 'Here, open this.' She handed over a small gift.

'What is it?' Melinda fingered the present.

'If I'd wanted to tell you what it was I wouldn't have wrapped it up!'

'Aw, that's really kind of you.' Having ripped off the paper Melinda took the top off the box to reveal a brooch. 'That's gorgeous! Thanks.' She pinned it on her dress and looked in the mirror.

'Happy birthday,' smiled Oriel. 'Now come on, let's go.'

Her mother gave a last-minute instruction. 'Home before midnight, please – and aren't you going to take a jacket? It's chilly on a night now.'

Oriel grabbed two light garments from her wardrobe and dashed out with Melinda in tow. Watching them from the window, Nat tutted. 'These modern lasses, going out with hardly owt on. She's sure to catch summat.'

Taking a train from Gardenvale Station to St Kilda, the young women did not have far to walk before the classical columns of the town hall came into view. After handing over the entrance fee and discarding their jackets at the cloakroom they followed the sound of music and entered the dance hall, hiding behind their handbags and flitting self-conscious looks around them. There was a good crowd here, half of it made up of demobbed soldiers, all injected by a frantic impulsion to enjoy themselves as if it were their last night on earth, the band on the stage stirring them to greater efforts.

Despite the activity, both girls felt as if all eyes were on them.

'I feel really fat beside you,' bemoaned Melinda.

Oriel reassured her, then overheard two girls sniggering about the diamanté on her headband and shoe buckles – who does she think she is, the dog's breakfast? – and the entire night was spoiled before it began. Vexed, she spotted a pair of vacant seats along the edge of the room and suggested they head for them.

'Hey, I haven't come to sit like a shag on a rock, I've come to dance!' objected Melinda, but followed Oriel, both weaving their way in and out of the dancers.

Almost immediately they had sat down an unattractive youth with pimples approached Oriel and asked if he could have this dance. Still smarting from the criticism, she opened her mouth to give polite refusal, when Melinda chimed up, 'Yeah, you go! I'll hold your bag. Don't worry about me, I'll be right.'

Without wanting to appear rude Oriel was forced to accept the young man's clammy hand in hers. Despite having visited classes at home she was not very adept at dances that required a lot of co-ordination with one's partner, and obviously neither was he, but during one awkward twirl Oriel was able to spot Melinda being whisked from her chair with no prompting whatsoever by an extremely good-looking chap.

Her charitable nature sorely taxed, she prayed for the tune to end. When it did she hoped Melinda would return to her seat, giving her the excuse to say, 'I'm sorry I can't leave my friend on her own.' Unfortunately other young men appeared to be bowled over by the fluffy and frivolous Melinda and were queuing up to dance with her. Therefore when Arthur asked eagerly if he could have this next dance too, and Oriel's anxious eyes searched the room for a saviour, there were no candidates and she was obliged to undergo further torment.

She glared at Melinda. Look at her! You wouldn't think she was the mother of a three-week-old baby the way she disported herself. Melinda caught her eye and winked and grinned. Oriel responded with a sickly smile, then cringed as Arthur's clammy hand burned through the apricot satin into the small of her back. When the music ended and Arthur opened his mouth with hope in his eye she forestalled him with as much kindness as she could muster. 'Thank you very much! I think I'll sit the next one out. I'm a little thirsty.'

'I'll get you a drink!' Arthur was not the kind to take a hint. He escorted her back to her seat, disappearing only to visit the upstairs room where beverages were served. Oriel tried to catch Melinda's eye and having done so made gestures.

'Come and rescue me!' she mouthed.

'What?' came the frowning response.

'Come and – oh, thank you, that's very kind!' Oriel tried to convey warmth as the young man handed her a glass of lemonade. Her heart sank when he sat down beside her and tried to instigate conversation, asking whereabouts she lived and for how long. 'We only arrived from England in January.' Oriel hoped he would not ask for her address and began to invent one just in case.

Arthur nodded in recognition. 'I thought I hadn't seen you before. I know all the pretty girls who come here.'

What a dreadful smile, thought Oriel, attempting to be nice. She looked round at all the other men in the room. Please, at least one of you take pity.

Arthur edged slightly closer. 'As you're new to the area you might find getting home a problem. Maybe I could –'

'Oh, no! It's no problem at all.' Oriel looked frantic and cursed Melinda.

The message finally got through. A breathless Melinda,

swinging Oriel's handbag on her wrist, returned to hover over Arthur, who was forced to give up his seat. She planted her buttocks.

'Cripes, I'm worn out.'

'I'm not surprised,' muttered Oriel, and snatched a gulp of lemonade.

'Could do with a drink.' Melinda handed over her friend's bag and looked beseechingly at Arthur, who offered in a reluctant tone to get her one.

The moment he had gone Oriel turned on her friend. 'Thank you very much for landing me with that troll!'

The answer was simple to the other girl. 'Well, why didn't you dance with someone else?'

'They were all too busy dancing with you! Anyway, I couldn't be mean. Who else would dance with him?'

Melinda recognized the problem. 'None of the other blokes dared ask you, you're too pretty.'

Oriel blushed. 'That didn't seem to inhibit Arthur.'

'The ugly ones don't realize they're ugly.'

'Never mind all that, just help me escape before he comes back!'

Melinda rose. 'Come to the dunny with me. I have to – aw, look!' She gawped at the small damp patches on the bodice of her dress. 'How long have I been sitting there like this? How will I get across the room?'

Oriel, trying not to show her distaste, offered her handkerchief. 'Pretend you're blowing your nose and cover the damp patches with your forearms.' She rose and was about to follow the other when her suitor reappeared with the glass of lemonade. 'Excuse us, Arthur, we just have to visit the cloakroom.'

He nodded and sat down.

By the time they reached the lavatory Melinda's damp patches had spread and Oriel could hear groans coming from the cubicle. 'Aw, bloody hell, I'm leaking both ends!' After much swearing and sighing the cistern flushed and a miserable face emerged. 'Sorry, but I'm gonna have to go home – and just when I was really enjoying meself.'

'Don't worry about it. I don't mind at all. There must be a side exit, we'll just sneak out.'

'What about your friend Arthur?'

'He's not my friend! I just said we were going to the cloakroom. I didn't say we were coming back, did I?'

Melinda grinned. 'Good while it lasted though, weren't it? I feel heaps better. Shows I can still attract the fellas and I haven't even got my figure back properly yet.'

'You look lovely,' said Oriel, checking her dark bob in the mirror. Maybe the diamanté headband was a little too showy after all. 'If Dan had been there he would've been really jealous to see all those men dancing with you.'

'Too right! Did you see the last young bloke I was with, the one with the fair hair? I could really go for him. If I hadn't had to visit the dunny he might've taken me home.'

'Thank heavens for weak bladders,' murmured Oriel, 'or I would've been stuck with Arthur.'

'Yeah, he is a bit spotty, isn't he?' Melinda wrinkled her nose. 'Plenny o' money, but. Yer could tell by his clothes.'

'Don't kid me you would've gone home with him. I wouldn't believe you.'

'Least he's better than one who runs orf and leaves yer.'

Oriel opened the door, then closed it again quickly. 'He's out there!' When asked who she hissed, 'Arthur! He's virtually waiting outside the door.'

Melinda saw no obstacle. 'Well, just tell him I've got to go home.'

'He might ask me to stay – come on, we'll have to climb out of the window.' Oriel's teenage years had been spent in single-minded revenge against the father who had deserted her; she had never involved herself in such childish pranks as this. But the near annihilation of her own generation had infected her and other young things with a sense of urgency. She was now determined not to waste another minute.

They ran back into the lavatory. Giggling, Melinda hoisted her dress and, with Oriel pushing from behind, clambered up on to the sill and after much grunting and laughing squeezed through the small sash. Dress round her thighs, Oriel followed, banged her head, complaining and laughing at the same time, then jumped down – almost on top of a couple involved in some lewd activity in the bushes. She stood to goggle, feeling thrilled and shocked and disgusted at the sight of the man's brown fingers on the white fleshy thighs and the girl hurriedly trying to pull down her skirt over her stocking tops. Melinda grabbed Oriel's arm and they hurried away tittering out of the gardens and onwards towards the station, past houses and shop fronts, around a corner – right into the arms of two soldiers.

Before Oriel had the chance to object she was grabbed by the upper arms and found herself sandwiched between a hard body and a plate-glass window to receive a passionate kiss. Fired by the sight she had just witnessed, she made no attempt to pull away but responded in kind, grinding her lips against the soldier's, experiencing a burning heat in the cleft of her thighs as he pushed himself against her, harder and harder – then suddenly there was an enormous crack as the window gave way to their compression. Jolted by panic, the vacuum between Oriel and the soldier was broken. Men and girls scattered in opposite directions, Oriel and her friend making a breathless escape, laughing deliriously as they pelted to the station.

'You'll have the traps after us!' accused Melinda as they jumped aboard the rattler, then teased, 'Cripes, you're a bit of a doer on the sly!'

Her companion looked guilty as the train pulled away. 'Don't you dare say anything to Mother!' Feverish of eye, heart still thudding, she settled back into the seat, wondering what might have occurred had the window not given way.

A week after Oriel had been to the dance she and her mother went on a shopping expedition to the city to buy, amongst other things, a layette for the Prince baby. Its birth might be six months away but the expectant mother's enthusiasm held no bounds. Whilst hitching his horse that morning, Nat had teased that Bright was wasting his money, he could find her decent enough baby clothing on his rounds, but she knew him well enough now to realize that he would never allow a child of his to wear castoffs. He had, though, donated several tiny garments from his collection to Alice, and Melinda had been delighted with them.

With the flu again gaining rampancy, many shops were closed and the streets were less hectic than usual. It was pleasant not to be bumping into people all the time, as often happened. Many folk wore protective gauze masks which Bright thought they should adopt but her daughter was not keen to look so outlandish, more intent on plundering the light and airy shopping arcades.

Whilst they were in a department store, with metal tubes whizzing overhead, to and from the central cash system, her mother picked up a little dress. 'Wouldn't Alice look pretty in this? I'd like to buy it but your father'll think I'm mad. Still, folk've been saying that for years so why should I care. I'll take it.' She handed it to the saleswoman to be wrapped, along with the dozens of other small items. 'It's a real pleasure. I never had any o' this with you. All I got was a few things from the nuns, and Miss Bytheway paid for the rest o' your stuff. I'm going to enjoy having this baby – not that I didn't enjoy having you, love!' She caught Oriel's hand and squeezed. 'It's just that I never had the chance to have you to myself, what with people interfering.'

When the items were packed, Oriel handed over a purchase of her own. 'Will this fit?'

'Aw, that's lovely.' Bright held up the lacy bonnet. 'You're a good lass.'

Oriel felt guilty. She didn't feel good – felt selfish for not looking forward to this baby as much as her mother was.

They left the shop and, after visiting others, were walking through Coles Arcade towards the cool repose of the fernery where they would find a seat, when they encountered Mrs Ratcliffe and Dorothy. Framed in her amethyst basin-like hat, Oriel's face lit up in pleasure.

'Ratty, it's been weeks! You said you'd keep in touch. I sent you my new address and telephone number – didn't you get it?'

The tall majestic figure looked equally delighted to see her friend. 'Sorry! I've been meaning to ring, it's just that we've been so busy arranging our move. We've got a new house in Elsternwick, near the park.'

'Oh, I know, it's dreadful trying to organize things,' agreed Oriel.

Bright and Mrs Ratcliffe looked at each other and smiled knowingly as their daughters twittered like the caged finches.

'And Father's so concerned about this flu epidemic.'

'Mine too! He's hardly let me out of the house.'

Bright objected, 'That's not true!'

'I did manage to go to a dance at St Kilda last week but we didn't stay that long. I went with Melinda – she works for us – but she had a bit of an accident so we had to leave, thank God. Oh, let's get a cup of tea and I'll tell you all about it. Have you time?'

Mrs Ratcliffe asked if they would mind risking their necks to cross the street to Buckley's where she had discovered their Elizabethan Tea Room, which had become her regular watering place in the city. As they struggled across Bourke Street, Oriel described the embroidered silk kimona gown she had just purchased in Buckley's sale.

Her friend exclaimed, 'I bought one of those a fortnight ago! Oh, don't tell me, I'll bet you got yours half-price.'

One eye on the traffic, Oriel delved into a brown paper bag to look at the price tag. 'Five guineas.'

Dorothy guffawed as they stepped on to the kerb. 'Oh, I didn't do too badly then – mine was eight and eleven!' Safely on the pavement, she and her mother spent a moment peeking into the bag to admire the silk gown, then made for the second-floor tea room.

Here in the quiet dignity of their surroundings, Mrs Ratcliffe watched her friend trying to decide what to do with the large parcel she was carrying. 'You look like a native bearer. Put it on this spare chair.' The waitress came to take their orders. Whilst they waited, Mrs Ratcliffe eyed the large parcel again. 'Bought anything else nice?'

'Oh, er,' Bright flushed, 'they're baby clothes.' Immediately she noted that both pairs of eyes went towards Oriel and announced swiftly, 'Nat and I are expecting an addition to the family in September.'

'How wonderful!' Both Mrs Ratcliffe and Dorothy agreed.

'I know I must seem terribly old to –'

'Not at all!' Mrs Ratcliffe patted her kindly and grinned. 'It's not as if you're an old crone like me.' There was six years' difference between the women.

After the interruption by the waitress who delivered tea, Dorothy's mother continued, 'Oriel, this must be a thrill for you. Do you want a brother or a sister?'

'Oh, I don't mind.' Oriel smiled and raised her cup, responding silently, I'd prefer to be an only child. 'As long as it's all right.'

'Quite.' Mrs Ratcliffe leaned her hefty shoulder towards Bright, and fingered her pearls in a manner that told the younger women they were about to indulge in intimacies.

Dorothy set up a quiet conversation with Oriel, telling her that she had found herself an office job which she would be starting on Monday and she hoped to meet lots of new people. Oriel replied that she was doing similar work for her father and had met no one, apart from Melinda. Dorothy asked had she not met anyone nice at the dance?

'Far from it. I spent the entire evening trying to escape some hobgoblin.'

Bright overheard and made an admonishment with her eyes whilst still nodding at Mrs Ratcliffe's conversation.

'The first dance I've been to over here and I had to be lumbered with him.'

The dark sloping eyes held sympathetic laughter. 'I haven't fared quite so badly. The people we've been staying with have a daughter and she has plenty of friends, so I wasn't being quite truthful before. I have been busy with our move but I've also been dragged all over Melbourne.'

Oriel huffed. 'The only place we've been lately is Brighton library and all they have there is romantic trash.'

Dorothy looked embarrassed at having to confess, 'I like romantic stories.'

'So do I but you wouldn't like these, believe me.'

'I'm going to another dance in the city this Saturday, would you like to come?' Dorothy knew that her mother was not keen for her to go out with Oriel alone but there was safety in numbers. 'There'll be about half a dozen of us but I'm sure the others wouldn't mind and they're good company. We're meeting at my house, then going down to the station – here, I'll write the address and telephone number down.' She took a notebook from her bag and scribbled on it.

'Thanks!' Oriel had a thought. 'Could I bring Melinda along? She doesn't get out even as much as I do.' In a low murmur she told Dorothy about how she had saved their domestic help from being cast out on the streets and how she had been abandoned by the child's father. 'I feel really sorry for her – though I don't know why, she was hogging all the decent men at the last dance whilst I was stuck with the hobgoblin with a face like a plate of tripe. He looked as if he'd been put together with all the bits God had left over.'

Laughter shone in her friend's eyes. 'You are awful! Yes, you can bring her.'

'Good, I think you'll like her.'

But when Oriel and Melinda arrived at her friend's house – Oriel avoiding any private encounter with Mr Ratcliffe, as she had been instructed by her mother – she could see that notwithstanding Dorothy's smile she had taken an instant dislike to Melinda and wondered why, for their companion was quite personable. Thinking perhaps that Dorothy was in a bad mood she set off with the other seven girls to catch the train. But later her suspicion was confirmed when she took an interval from the dancing to rest in a corner and her friend launched into a critique of Melinda.

'Look at her, isn't she a dreadful flirt?' Prior to this, Dorothy had felt herself to be Oriel's only friend and was now experiencing jealousy, though Melinda's type would have inspired her disapproval at any time. Whilst the morals of Oriel's ancestors might be in question this did not reveal itself in her behaviour. 'There's no wonder she got herself into trouble.' At the heavy silence Dorothy realized her gaffe. 'God, how stupid of me!' Her voice rose above the band. 'I didn't mean to imply that your mother's a flirt. She's lovely – I'm sure none of it was her fault.'

'I know you didn't intend anything.' Oriel smiled forgiveness and tapped her foot to the music.

'But that one's a different kettle of fish. I can't imagine your mother behaving like that. Is that your dress she's got on? I thought I recognized it. Well, it's far too tight. She'll split the seams if she isn't careful.'

Oriel was worried about this too, but reminded Dorothy, 'She has just had a baby – and we didn't have time to let it out. Actually, I did think it was a bit too small but she didn't want to wear the same one as last time.'

'You're too generous!'

'Not really.' Oriel recalled that her mother had warned her of this too when she said she was taking Melinda out again: don't throw your money around, it might not always be there.

'I shouldn't think the men care very much what she's wearing, the way she clings to them. You can only see daylight between her and that one because he's got a concave chest.'

Oriel laughed but wondered what Dorothy would have said had she known about her own rude entanglement with the soldier last week. Thankful that she had not mentioned it, she defended the other girl. 'I think she's just desperate to find a husband, that's all.'

'So am I but I wouldn't lower myself to her antics, and neither would you,' said Dorothy. 'I mean, I'm not a prude – I like to dance close to my partner – but she's almost wearing his suit. Oh look, someone's coming over. He's going to ask you to dance!'

Oriel tweaked at her diaphanous bodice and pretended not to watch the young man's approach. 'He can't be, he's too good-looking.' Even though she had enjoyed more dances than on the last occasion, none of her partners had been to her liking.

'He is!' Dorothy growled into her chest.

The young man in the sharply tailored suit came to a halt before Oriel and asked her to dance. 'Well, I don't like to leave my friend on her own . . .' She saw to her horror that he was about to take this as a rebuff. 'But if she doesn't mind!'

'Of course I don't.' Dorothy granted permission and flashed her a look of envy.

Oriel could not believe her luck. With his dark wavy hair and classical features her partner had to be the best-looking bachelor in the room. The instant attraction she felt was obviously shared, for although he didn't say much she could see it in his attitude towards her. Exchanging names, they had three dances together. Even though she was out of breath Oriel wished it would never end. But end it did and after thanking her, Errol made it obvious he expected her to return to her friends and he to his. She could have cried and her disappointment forbade her to dance with anyone else, spending the rest of the evening twiddling with the feathers on her headband until one of them was in danger of coming off in her hand. However, this mood was not to persist for Errol was to revisit her somewhat hesitantly. 'Would you mind dancing with me again?'

'Mind?' Oriel, though feeling awkward in his handsome presence, laughed out loud. 'After I've been sitting here like a wallflower half the night?' Catching sight of the bedraggled feather that dangled over her brow she puffed at it, then ripped it off.

He laughed too, and for the first time she noticed there was an abnormally large gap between his two front teeth, detracting from his perfect looks. 'I thought you might want to dance with other people. I didn't want to appear pushy.'

Informed by Oriel that she had no wish to dance with anyone else, he held her closer this time and when both were worn out he did not desert her but led her to as private a corner as he could find. She pressed herself into her seat, hoping that no one else would accost her whilst Errol had gone to fetch them drinks. How very typical that someone did.

At the same time that she spotted Errol returning with the filled glasses a voice said, 'Hullo, Oriel!' and she looked up to see Arthur, who, in his futile search for love, was a regular participant in all the Melbourne balls.

'Oh, hello.' She gave a half-smile and turned away.

'What happened to you last week? You didn't come back.'

She tried to peer around him but he was blocking her view. 'My friend was taken ill so we had to leave quickly.'

'Doesn't look too ill tonight.' Arthur formed his dreadful smile and turned to watch Melinda on the dance floor with her tenth man of the evening. 'Can I sit down?'

'No!' Oriel felt a lurch of pity for the look on his face. 'No, I'm sorry but I'm with someone. He's just here now.'

To her relief she saw Errol a few yards away. He was obviously hesitant to approach but when she smiled eagerly at him he proceeded.

Arthur looked around at his rival and, with a defeated expression, backed away with an apology.

'Wasn't sure if I was interrupting,' said Errol. 'Thought maybe he was a friend of yours.'

'No! I don't know him. He just asked me to dance.'

Errol revealed the gap in his teeth and sat down, placing one of the glasses before her. 'Lucky for me he didn't ask earlier in the evening.' After a moment's silence as both sipped their drinks Errol asked, 'Where are you from originally?' When told, he looked amazed. 'Well, I'll be – I'm from Tadcaster!'

'You don't sound as if you are.' Oriel retained her self-conscious air.

'No, well, I was only born there. We lived in Bath before we came over here.'

'You came with your family?'

'Yeah, twelve years ago.' His face clouded and he rubbed his hands up and down his tailored thighs. 'My father's since died, last month from the flu. This is the first time I've been out. I feel a bit guilty leaving Mum tonight but she insisted I come, and I'm glad I did.'

She blushed, watching his hands move over his legs,

imagining her own hands doing it. 'I'm sorry about your father. It's a dreadful thing, this flu. A close friend of ours died from it before we left England. We seemed to have arrived in the thick of it here. Do you have any brothers or sisters?' When he shook his head Oriel added, 'Me neither. I know Mother worries about me going out in case I catch it but, well, you can't stay in for ever, can you?'

Errol agreed. 'It'll be just my luck to come through all that fighting and die from the flu.'

'Where were you?'

'You name it, I was there. Egypt was the worst. Not for the fighting but the water. We all got dysentery. Sorry, it's not the sort o' thing you tell a lady.'

'Did you lose many friends?'

He nodded and took a long drink. There was an awkward pause, then Errol announced, 'Would you excuse me just for a minute? I won't be long.' He rose and made off in the direction of the cloakrooms.

In his absence Oriel flicked an apprehensive gaze around the room, afraid that the predatory Arthur would reappear, but when she spotted him he turned his face away. Instead, it was Dorothy who was to mar the evening. She approached, smiling, with most of the girls they had arrived with – though Melinda was still dancing. 'Sorry to spoil your obvious fun. You make a wonderful couple, but it's time for us to go.'

Oriel showed alarm. 'I can't! Errol's just gone to the whatsit. I can't just walk out on him.'

'You did with Arthur,' teased Dorothy.

The reply was blunt. 'That's entirely different. He was a cretin.'

The responding expression clearly said, that's a bit nasty, though it was not voiced.

'Errol's just special,' Oriel mumbled.

Her friend was accommodating. 'Well, we can wait a few minutes. It looks as if we'll have to use stain remover to get Melinda off that chap. The flapper. And the way she calls you Orrie! Doesn't it annoy you? Well, it would me. And if she refers to me as Ratty once more –'

Oriel was concerned. 'Sorry, I call you Ratty. I never thought you might not like it.'

'That's different. You're my friend. She gets my back up – and she knows it. She's doing it on purpose.' The usually placid Dorothy was heated. 'Anyway I think we'll wait outside. I don't want people seeing her with us and thinking we're all the same. We'll get your jacket for you. Come and join us when your friend appears – and try to remove Melinda from that man.'

Whilst awaiting Errol's return Oriel hurried across the dance floor to where Melinda and her partner were locked in a sensual embrace. The young woman frowned at the tug on her elbow but seeing who it was she reluctantly obeyed the command and took her smiling leave of the man.

'You certainly know how to spoil a girl's fun.'

Oriel apologized and said she'd stay if she could but Dorothy and the others were waiting.

'Huh, that wowser! She doesn't like me either.'

Oriel knew that Dorothy would never openly voice her disdain to Melinda. 'What gave you that idea?'

'The way she looks down her nose at me, that's what.' Melinda smoothed the wrinkles from her dress, which kept riding up around the heavy thighs.

Oriel tried to mediate. 'I think it's only the way her face is made. I thought she was that way too before I met her but she's really nice.'

'Not to me,' growled her companion. 'I'm only having a little fun. I think I deserve it after being left with a baby and deserted by a rat.'

Oriel's expression showed she was in agreement but soon her gaze was absent as she searched the room for Errol.

'Well, are we going or not?'

'I have to wait for somebody to tell him I'm leaving.'
I'll just die if I never see him again, thought Oriel.

'Nice is he?'

'Gorgeous. Didn't you see him?'

Melinda shook her head. 'I was too busy enjoying meself. What's his name?'

'Errol. I don't know his second name.'

The other was frowning. 'Didn't you have two feathers in that headband when you came out?'

'Yes, I'm moulting.'

'Come on, you two!' Dorothy had re-entered and hailed them urgently from the doorway. Others were leaving too. 'We're going to miss the rattler!'

'Where's he gone, the dunny?' Melinda asked.

Oriel nodded anxiously and stood her ground as the large figure carved her way back through the exiting dancegoers in order to thrust their jackets at them and push them towards the door. 'Come on!'

Melinda tutted and muttered aside, 'Bossy cow.'

Oriel moved but kept looking over her shoulder and when she reached the door she prevented herself from being ejected by holding on to a jamb. 'Wait! I can see him.'

Errol had begun to return to his seat, had seen her empty chair and now looked perplexed. 'Errol!' She used his name self-consciously. The fringing on her dress trembled with her furious attempts to attract him. Her frantic oscillations rather than her voice caught his eye and he saw that she did not go voluntarily. 'I have to leave!' she mouthed. 'Sorry.'

He tried to approach but people blocked his way. 'Can I see y'again?' At her eager affirmation he added, 'Meet me under the clocks next Friday at half past seven!'

'What clocks?'

But Oriel did not hear the answer as Dorothy finally succeeded in dragging her out of the hall.

She was almost deranged with her friend as they hurried through the garden. 'I don't know which clock!'

'*The* clocks,' said Dorothy, obviously conversant with the landmark, and explained briskly as they ran for the train, 'you know, the row of clocks at Flinders Street Station. Now come on! I'll kill you if we miss this train.'

They did not miss it. Breathless, Oriel fell back into her seat, unheeding of everything and everyone around her, her mind filled with thoughts of him.

After parting company with the rest Melinda was more talkative. 'Getting really cool on a night now, isn't it?' She shivered and quickened her step along the wide dark road. Autumn colours glowed under the lamplight. 'Thanks for taking me out with you, Orrie. I've had a lovely time. I hope bub's behaving herself. It was really good of your mum to look after her again.'

Oriel barely heard her partner's chatter, but kept smiling and nodding as they hurried through the cool night air, rehearsing what she would tell her mother about the lovely young man she had met tonight.

The avenue of elms gave way to the silvery limbs of gumtrees that encircled the farmhouse. Glad to be home, Oriel and her friend burst into the hall, giggling and happy . . . to be confronted by a dark and angry Nat.

As the sound of a crying baby filled the house Melinda immediately read his expression. 'Oh strewth, don't tell me, Mr Prince! I'll see to her right away.'

'Do that!' He glowered at Melinda, who was already pelting through the house.

'I don't think there's any need –'

'Shut up! I've had enough o' whining bloody babies without another one trying to rule the roost. You and that . . . blasted trollop gallivanting all over town every five minutes.'

Oriel swallowed. He must be really angry to use the word trollop. 'It's only the second time she's been –'

'Shut up I said!' He stormed up to her. Oriel shrank.

The quiet man rarely lost control of his temper but when he did it was advisable to lie low. 'And go tell her to shut that bloody baby up an' all or it's going straight out of t'window!'

Oriel was sober, realizing then that Bright had not come running to save her. 'What's wrong? Where's Mother?'

'She's in bed trying to rest with that little sod screaming its arse off. I knew, I bloody knew this'd happen.' Faced with Oriel's horror he calmed only slightly to explain, pressing his hand to his anguished brow. 'Your mother collapsed.'

Oriel gave a little squeak.

'I got the doctor round and he said –' Nat's voice cracked. 'She's got that bloody stinking flu – and it's all your fault, trollopin' round those bloody dancehalls fetching germs home! You couldn't stay at home till the danger was over, could you? No! You put your own selfish enjoyment above everything else including your mother. I could bloody kill you, Oriel!'

Dumbfounded, she just stood there, white-faced and swaying, her bedraggled-looking feather quivering in the draught.

Nat was already showing regret for the pain he had inflicted and took a deep breath before saying more evenly, 'Just go to bed.' He wheeled around and marched towards his own bedroom.

Stupefied, Oriel followed and when he felt her presence and turned, she whispered croakily, 'Can I see her?'

'No! I don't want you going anywhere near her.'

Again he was forced to apply salve to his cruel words. 'I don't want you catching it an' all. You can stand in the doorway and say goodnight to her if you like.' He opened the door, saw that his wife was crying and came immediately to her bedside.

Disobeying his order, his daughter pursued him, shocked by how ill and drawn her mother was. Surely she had not looked like that earlier in the evening or

Oriel would have noticed and cancelled the excursion. Or would she? Had it been her own selfish desire for young company that had blinded her to this illness? Noel sprang to mind – how quickly the disease had overcome him, fine one day, dead the next. She began to cry too.

'Don't fight,' wept the victim from her bed. 'It's not Oriel's fault, Nat, don't blame her. I could've caught it at the shops or anywhere. Please don't shout. I can't bear it.'

He gave profuse apologies, clinging to her hands, kneading them, willing this not to be the dreaded influenza but some harmless ailment.

'Put those masks on that the doctor left.'

Nat refused. 'I'm not wearing that!' He tossed one to Oriel. 'Here, you put one on.'

She picked it up from the end of the bed but merely stood there fingering it and weeping. 'I wouldn't have gone out if I'd known you were ill.'

'That's just it, I didn't feel ill,' said her mother. 'I haven't even had a cold. I just keeled over – but don't worry, I'll be all right, darling.' She held out her hand. 'It's not a bad dose. I'm just feeling a bit weak that's all.' An attempt to smile made her simply pathetic. 'Go on, go to bed. Did you have a good night, by the way?'

Oriel nodded tearfully, feeling guilty at being so happy a moment ago. Images of herself and Errol dancing were replaced by her mother collapsing over and over again.

'Good – and Melinda?'

Nat clenched his teeth.

Oriel nodded again and made as if to come and kiss her mother but Nat held up a warning hand.

Bright whispered, 'Best not. I'll be all right in a few days, you see.'

Mouth turned down in woe, Oriel continued to stare for a while through the dingy glow of the electric globe, watching the shadow of the ceiling fan play upon the sheet that covered her mother. Then she turned and went to her room, closing the door behind her.

The sufferer could not maintain her smile and reached for Nat's hand but her grip was weak. 'I love you.'

'I love you too.' Hanging on to her hand with both of his he bent to kiss it.

'I'm going to say something now.'

'No, just rest,' he insisted.

'If I should – if I don't recover –'

'Oh, shush!'

'No, Nat, promise you won't do anything.'

He was almost frantic. 'You're going to get better. It's only a slight dose you've caught, you said yourself.'

'Whatever it is I don't want you to catch it so put that mask on right now. Go on.'

Reluctantly he did so and Bright continued though she felt dreadful. 'Now, promise me you'll go on living.' She could not bring herself to say, Don't kill yourself, but they both remembered that he had told her he would never be able to live without her.

Nat knew exactly what she meant and did not answer.

'Oh no, don't, don't.' With agonized expression she chided him.

To pacify her he mumbled a promise from behind the gauze mask. 'I won't. Just concentrate on –'

'Stop fobbing me off. Just think of Oriel. Swear to me now you won't –'

'All right!' He was forced to make a promise he did not know whether he could keep. But with luck the flu would probably get him as well. 'I swear it. Now shush and just try to sleep.'

His wife closed her eyes and very soon drifted off. Once she was in a state of unawareness Nat ripped off his mask and threw it to the floor.

Oriel had not undressed but sat for ages on the edge of the bed staring through the lamplight. At least Melinda had managed to pacify baby Alice. The house was quiet now. Quiet as death. No – Mother wouldn't die! Of course she wouldn't. It happened to other people but not to Mother. Eventually she took off her clothes, got into bed and closed her eyes. Mother would be fine by morning.

7

After her employer's dreadful outburst Melinda thought it best to go straight to bed and so did not find out the reason for it until she met him the next morning in the kitchen during his brief excursion from the sickroom.

She was preparing the usual Sunday breakfast of bacon and eggs when Nat came in to refill an enamel bowl with cold water and muttered, 'I suppose Oriel told you Mrs Prince has the flu?'

She gasped and looked fearful.

Oriel had entered only seconds after him. 'No, I didn't get the chance. How is Mother?'

'Badly.' Nat turned off the tap and, towel over his arm, began to carry his bowl to the door, then paused. 'I forgot to mention last night. There's some blokes coming to fumigate the place. House has been put under quarantine so none of us is allowed out.'

Oriel's heart lurched. 'How long will it last?' She felt incredibly selfish for even thinking about her arranged rendezvous with Errol but as anxious as she was over her mother's health she could not bear the thought that she would be prevented from seeing him.

Nat had barely slept and it showed. 'Till we're all dead or cured.' He moved off.

She cringed at his brutality. Her mind began a series of images: Bright in her coffin with Oriel weeping beside it; Oriel in her own coffin, never having known the love of a man; Errol waiting in vain under the clocks for someone who would never arrive. Desperate as the situation was she must get word to him.

'Can I telephone Dorothy?' she called after him, 'to let her know about Mother.'

Nat gave a dispassionate grunt and returned to his wife.

Oriel hesitated, wondering how to convey her message without her father overhearing. What kind of monster would he think she was then?

Melinda hefted the frying pan. 'Will there only be me and you eating this bacon then?'

Oriel said she did not feel like any. Clutching her address book, she approached the telephone in the hall, paused and thought of what to say before picking the receiver off the hook and acquiring the number. She waited. Luckily it was Dorothy who answered straight away.

'Oh hello, Oriel! Or Orrie, should I say?' She sniggered. 'Now, about this Friday–'

'Dot, Mother's got the flu,' came the interjection.

'My God, that's dreadful!' Dorothy was genuinely concerned. 'Oh, Oriel, I don't know what to say. Is she . . . is she very bad?'

The responding voice was kept lowered. 'She's really ill. The house has been put under quarantine. We have to swear an oath that we won't have anyone coming in or going out for four days.'

'Oh dear – ah.' Dorothy read the situation expertly. 'So you need me to get a message to whatsisname?' Oriel did not wish to raise Errol's name in case her father overheard and merely gave a yes. 'Well, I can do that for you. You were meant to be meeting him under the clocks this Friday at what time?'

'Half past seven,' muttered Oriel. 'Of course Mother could be better by then but it wouldn't be right for me to go rushing off. I'd be very grateful, Dot.'

'Don't mention it. Is there anything else I can do – absolutely anything. Your poor mother . . .'

At this last phrase Oriel's eyes filled with tears. 'No, I don't think so, but thanks for offering.'

Dorothy was a practical sort. 'What about groceries?'

'We're going to make arrangements for food to be dropped off at the gate. Thanks for offering, though.'

'I'll be thinking of you.'

'Thanks.' Oriel drew in an emotional breath. 'I'll see you when I can. Bye.'

This done, she went directly to her parents' bedroom but was barred entry.

'Are you daft? You're not coming anywhere near her.' Nat peered round the door. 'I know you think I'm hard but I'm not having you cop it too.'

His daughter looked agitated. 'But you said it wasn't too bad.'

'I didn't, your mother said that.' He sighed heavily. 'It's no good you coming in, she's too poorly to talk.'

Oriel panicked. 'Then we've got to get her into hospital.'

Exasperation on his tired face he came out and closed the door behind him. 'How – with a bloody shoehorn? They're crammed to bursting, if you hadn't noticed.'

Oriel was furious with him, tears bulging. 'You're ready to let her die!'

'You what?' he snarled at her. 'Don't you dare say that to me!'

She blubbered immediately. 'I'm sorry!'

'I love your mother.' Nat almost broke down. 'She is not going into one o' them bloody wooden sheds they call a hospital.' Such buildings had been meant for the military but were now taking the massive overflow from civilian hospitals. 'They can't give her any better nursing than I can, and they won't let me visit her neither. If she should die in there . . .' He tried to shake the awful thought from his mind.

Oriel had rarely seen her father with his sleeves rolled up, he was always so immaculately dressed, but now in his unkempt state she noticed scabs of dried blood upon his arms and wondered over them briefly but was too acutely aware of her own misery to enquire as to their cause.

Nat felt her scrutiny and tried to cover up his arms. The addiction to self-mutilation, a relic of his days at the Industrial School, was never far from his fingertips in times of trauma. In his terror of losing Bright he had been picking and gouging at his flesh all night.

'If you want to help you can fetch and carry stuff, cold water and towels, aspirins, fresh sheets and t'like and leave it outside door. You're coming no closer than you are right now – oh, and the poor hoss!' He told her how to feed and groom it. 'Make sure he's got plenty o' water. Don't suppose that'll break t'rules, you won't be coming into contact with anyone. And keep that bloody bairn quiet an' all.'

'What about you?' Oriel's handkerchief was drenched and did no more than move the tears from one side of her cheek to the other. 'Will you come and have some bacon?' This homely, tantalizing aroma was at odds with the trials being endured here.

'Nay, I couldn't eat a thing.' Nat looked sick. 'I'll never leave her side till she's well.' He backed away into his room.

Oriel caught a glimpse of her sick mother propped up on pillows, complexion like tallow, before the door closed in her face. She ran to her room, shoulders racked with sobs. Please don't let her die! Take Melinda or the baby but don't let it be Mother. If she dies, I'll be left on my own with him.

Nat squeezed out a rag in ice-cold water and laid it across his wife's forehead. There was nothing to show she had felt this attention. Bright was too sick to talk to him, even to know he was there. He sagged over the bed, damning the flock of cockatoos that would periodically rise as one from a gumtree and circle screeching overhead before coming to settle like white washing on a line, only to rise again when the fancy took them.

So utterly agonized was he at the thought of losing Bright that he began to pray even though he had learned from experience that there was no one out there listening, that all torment came to an end eventually – reached a natural conclusion without the intervention of a higher being. People might say that their prayers had been answered but Nat knew that the God to whom they prayed did not care. Nevertheless he set up a pointless chanting: 'Please don't let me lose her when I've just found her again, if somebody has to go let it be the bairn but not her, because if you take her you'd better take me as well.' To this end, he lurched over his wife's recumbent form and pressed his lips to hers, running his tongue along their dry surface, feasting on the virus that was trying to take her from him.

For two days Bright hovered beneath the ever-gyrating ceiling fan on the verge of pneumonia, whilst the other prisoners of the house coped as best they could. In the world outside a flutter of yellow quarantine flags had begun to amass over Melbourne. One by one another school, another church, another public house closed down. In the luckier neighbourhoods teams of ambulances ferried the stricken to ever-burgeoning hospitals. To those less fortunate, the hearse became a regular visitor, quarantine laws preventing family members from attending their loved ones' funerals.

Terrified for her own health and for that of her baby, Melinda was glad to allow Oriel to do all the fetching and carrying to the invalid's room. However, her regular enquiries as to Mrs Prince's health were not entirely selfish and, over morning coffee today, she asked, 'Is there no medicine at all they can give her?'

'Apparently not,' murmured a tired-looking Oriel, elbows on the table, wringing her hands. 'If there was you'd feel as if you were doing something but to have to watch your mother lying there –'

Melinda had been impressed by her employer's devotion. 'Your dad's a real ripper, isn't he? Looking after her like that.'

Oriel simply nodded. His vigilance had not really surprised her. She was well aware that her parents were the two most important people in the world to each other.

'Oriel!'

Her heart leaped at the urgent summons and in her haste to rise she banged the table, tipping coffee from cup to saucer. Ignoring everything and filled with trepidation, she moved through the house, dreading what she might find. The door to the sickroom was no longer closed to her. Having been forbidden to enter for two days, she feared what this might mean. Imagining her mother's waxen face, she hardly dared to peer around the jamb.

Catching a peripheral glimpse of Oriel, Nat said, 'I think she might be on the mend.' He spoke as if hardly able to believe it.

Oriel sagged in relief against the wooden jamb. Christ, you stupid man, I thought she must be dead! But instead of mouthing this she made to enter.

'Don't come in!' The command was not harsh. 'I just left door open to get a draught through, but there might still be danger of you catching it.'

'You haven't.' Tears of relief pricking her eyes, she hovered in the doorway, trying to assess her mother's condition. The sleeping figure did indeed look better.

'No.' Nat's black eyebrows lifted in surprise and he scratched his head. He had done his best to catch it too.

Happiness began to flood through Oriel, procuring sympathy for her father, who looked haggard. 'What can I get you?'

'Oh, some fresh water.' He eased his back and suddenly realized that he was hungry. 'And a cup o' tea and some toast if you don't mind.'

'Of course I don't.'

She turned to go, but as she did so she hesitated and

saw him lift his hand to her mother's cheek and caress the skin with his knuckles. It was an act of such tenderness that Oriel was transfixed. Her father was not a demonstrative man; even though she knew he adored her mother he had always been reticent in allowing others to see it. Aware that he assumed himself to be alone, she backed slowly around the jamb but continued to watch those fingers caress her mother's pale skin – and found herself falling deeply in love with him. Not an innocent kind of love but one that stirred all manner of sexual feelings. Shocked to the core, she tore herself away and rushed to fulfil his request, berating and condemning herself – what sort of person fell in love with their own father? Surely the lowest of the low. The image of a fourteen-year-old prostitute flashed to mind. Blood will out, mocked the phrase. Could it be the influence of her harlot grandmother?

To counter these perverted feelings, on her return Oriel behaved even more coolly towards Nat than she had done before he had married her mother. He was too exhausted to wonder what had occasioned this relapse, his only concern being his wife, who had just opened her eyes. He leaned forward eagerly.

'Did I hear arguing?' Bright licked her dry lips.

'No, you must've been dreaming.' He snuggled up to her fondly. 'By, you've worried me, you have, missus.'

She uttered a dry laugh and accepted the glass of water he put to her lips. 'God didn't want me. I'm a reject from Heaven.' Her gaze, still bloodshot, but quite lucid now, took in the pair of them. 'Am I the only one who's had it?'

' 'Fraid so,' answered Nat. The likelihood that he would contract it now was slight.

'Thank God. I don't remember a thing. Oh, that fan's making me feel dizzy.' She closed her eyes. Nat went to turn it off, it had simply been used to keep her temperature down.

As Bright regained her thought processes her calm demeanour was threatened by another concern. 'What about the baby?'

Nat looked awkward and lowered his voice, feeling embarrassed that his daughter was standing nearby. 'Er, I'm not sure, love. You had a little bit of bleeding last night – nowt heavy. I tried to get t'doctor in to see you but he's gone down with flu as well. They said they'd try and send another chap this morning.'

Their daughter cast her gaze around the room pretending that she had not heard.

Bright tried not to think about losing the baby. 'You look fagged out.'

'I am.' Suddenly overwhelmed by fatigue he turned his heavy-lidded eyes to his daughter. 'I think I'll just get some kip, if you don't mind.'

Overjoyed that her mother was recovered, she stuttered a happy riposte and left the room.

Nat looked fondly down at his wife. 'Is there owt I can get you?'

She offered a lazy smile. 'No, just get in beside me and have a nap.'

'I love you,' he mumbled to her as he dragged his leaden body on to the double bed and relaxed into the mattress.

The nap lasted for ten hours. When he woke in the evening he found his wife refreshed and demanding food, though she was still worried about the baby, and a hasty visit from an overworked doctor the following day did little to reassure her. It was still intact, he said, but she must have bed rest for another week or so to avert the threatened abortion.

'Abortion?' Bright was horrified. 'But I'd never – I want this baby!' She burst into tears, forcing the doctor to explain that he was not casting aspersions on her morality, it was simply a medical term, an accident that had occurred due to her rise in temperature. He felt sure that as the haemorrhage was only slight, she would keep her much-wanted child – so long as she remained in bed.

Bright could not have risen had she wanted to, her legs were too weak, but she was not averse to the pampering bestowed upon her and had no qualms about losing any independence. Nat enjoyed looking after her and after years of drudgery she was happy to let him.

Though Mrs Ratcliffe had been making telephone enquiries throughout, Oriel rang Dorothy to let her know that her mother was truly mended.

'Oh, that's wonderful!' cried her friend. 'I can't tell you how relieved I am. I didn't like to say before but you know those two rosy-cheeked sisters who went out with us – Mary and Jean? They're dead. Yes, the flu. They came home from the dance and were dead in a few days!'

'But they looked the picture of health!'

'I know! But we went to their funeral so I know it's true. I mean, I hardly knew them but . . . you don't know what to say to their parents, do you? And Anne, that's the girl whose family we lived with when we arrived, she's had lots of friends who've died.'

'Yes, I just keep thinking how lucky we are that none of us has caught it off Mother. There's been a procession of funerals past our house all week.' Without benefit of a newspaper, Oriel could not appreciate the extent of the devastation. In the days of her quarantine the wildfire epidemic had claimed thousands of people, including exhausted medical staff.

'Neither I nor my brother is allowed to go out now – oh, but don't worry I did manage to see Errol in the street before the embargo.' Dorothy laughed at the sound of relief from the other end of the line. 'The object of your affections has given me his number and asked me to ring when the danger's over. He also says he knows how you must be feeling and that he's thinking about you – so there, now you can relax!'

In the knowledge that he would wait for her, Oriel

decided not to go rushing off and abandoning her mother, but stayed in the house for some weeks until Bright was on her feet again, her baby safe, by which time the epidemic was showing signs of being on the wane. Even so, the longing to be with Errol made her vague and Bright sought to alleviate this mood tonight by suggesting she go out and enjoy herself.

'I notice there's a few dances advertised again. It should be safe enough now.'

Receiving only a happy shrug, she made an exclamation. 'Sorry, I'm not tutting at you but meself. I can't possibly want to go again. Excuse me.' And she traipsed wearily off to the closet.

Never knowing what mood his daughter was going to be in – one minute warm to him, the next like an iceberg – Nat had reserved his conversation lately, but offered tentatively now, 'Don't mind me, you know.'

Oriel was thinking of Errol and did not respond to her father for a moment. He took her thoughtful expression as a form of reluctance. 'What I said about you bringing the flu home, I was just . . . well, you know.' He couldn't bring himself to say scared out of my bloody wits. 'Here.' Adopting a conspiratorial air he reached for his wallet and handed over a note. It was the only way he could show his fondness for her. 'Quick, before your mother gets back,' he said, as if it were some sort of crime. 'Get yourself a new frock.'

Oriel was touched, but out of fear of invoking perverted feelings, could not allow herself to display the newly found affection she felt for him. 'Thanks, I will.'

She reached to take it but at the last minute he flicked his hand away. 'On one condition, that you don't take that lass with you and leave us with that bloody baby.' At Oriel's expression he said, 'Oh, go on then, take her if you must – but I aren't buying her a new frock, mind.'

She grinned and accepted the offer. 'I feel sorry for

Mel. She doesn't get much chance of enjoyment and she's such a good laugh.'

'Aye, at my expense.' He had finally been coaxed into paying wages, though not the full request. 'Seven and six for a bit of cooking, all her food and board and she acts as if she's hard done by. Why don't you stick with that other lass?'

'Dorothy? Oh, Dot's my best friend. She's good fun too, but she and Mel don't get on.'

Oriel pondered on how two such conflicting personalities could both be her friends. She supposed it was because she was attracted to different qualities in each of them. Whereas Melinda could bring out the impulsive side of Oriel's nature, Dorothy was for more meaningful and serious conversation. Oriel could never convey to Melinda just how lonely and abandoned she sometimes felt but dear steadfast Dorothy was always there to listen.

'The last time we all went out together –' She broke off, remembering that it was the night that her mother had been stricken with influenza. 'Well, they're so different.'

'Aye, I'd noticed,' commented Nat. 'That one in there, she's too fond. Dorothy's more your down-to-earth type.'

'Oh, Mel's down-to-earth too,' countered Oriel.

'When I say down-to-earth I don't mean that far down. She's a bit too straightforward for my liking, not to mention she's always on t'scrounge for handouts. Anyway, take whoever you like and have a good time.' He went back to his paper. 'I might buy you a few more dresses if these house prices keep going up like they have been.' Similar properties to the ones he had bought were now fetching up to fifty pounds more than they had three months ago. 'That land you bought's gone up too.'

Too busy making plans, his daughter merely nodded. Melinda would be disappointed at not being invited to go out with her but Dorothy was the one who had the important telephone number, and so it was that Oriel contacted the latter and asked her to arrange a rendezvous with Errol. She balked at telling Melinda that she would not be able to go, but luckily there was no need to, for her parents announced that they would be visiting the Ratcliffes on the same evening so Melinda was obliged to stay in and tend her child.

As they were all headed for the same destination Nat gave his daughter a lift in his motorcar. He was more used to driving now, and there was less grinding and clanking, but Oriel noticed that his knuckles were white on the steering wheel as he reached the busier roads. Her own knuckles were white on the handle of her bag as she thought of the liaison ahead. When Nat also offered to run her and Dorothy into town to save them catching the train, she was quick to refuse. Bright was not impervious to the nervous air of her daughter, but made no comment, smiling contentedly behind the mesh veil on her sage-green hat, guessing that Oriel must be going to enjoy more than a dance.

Mrs Ratcliffe, too, noted the air of preoccupation as she and her friend waved the girls off at the gate. 'Are you meeting someone nice?' She still held the concern that Oriel's background might make her a bad influence, but Dorothy had cajoled her into letting the pair go out.

Her daughter grinned. 'Not me, I'm afraid, but this lucky girl is.'

'I sincerely hope he isn't a soldier,' opined Mrs Ratcliffe. Much unrest had been stirred by the Returned Soldiers League's fight to gain preference in employment for their members. This bitter issue between them and trade unionists had even caused pitched battles with police up in Brisbane.

'No!' Oriel did not consider it a lie – Errol was no longer a soldier. She squirmed self-consciously and hardly dared look at her mother. 'I would have told you about him before but never seemed to get the chance.'

Bright saw from her daughter's expression that she set

great store by this man. 'Well, have a lovely time, and take care.'

'Yes, and just remember,' Mrs Ratcliffe advised both girls, 'keep your hand on your ha'penny.'

Misconstruing the adage Oriel patted her handbag. 'We will.' And linking arms they departed for their rendezvous, leaving a smiling Mrs Ratcliffe to quash her previous assessment of Dorothy's friend.

The same time and meeting place had been arranged. The girls arrived early at the copper-domed station, Oriel feeling particularly nervous as she waited on the Swanston Street steps beneath the row of train time indicators, listening to the trams go clanging back and forth across the wide intersection. She found that she could not recall what Errol looked like but had only an image of handsomeness in her mind. She was afraid that absence may have exaggerated his attraction but when he arrived on time, as virile as she remembered, her heart burgeoned with joy.

Dorothy was very discreet and, not short of dance partners, left them to their own company all evening. Oriel and Errol found out more about each other – surnames, birthdays, ambitions and desires. Unlike many returned soldiers Errol had found work straight away in the office of an insurance firm in Collins Street, but his hope was to be a professional artist. He had done many sketches during his wartime service and was now in the process of turning them into works of art.

'You'll have to come and see them when they're finished,' he told her as they danced.

Oriel replied that she would love to. 'And in five years' time I can tell everyone I saw Errol Windross's work before he became famous.' And she danced until she felt her heart would burst, so thankful was she to be alive, and that her mother was alive, and to be held in this intimate manner.

Inebriated by happiness, she was nevertheless silent on

the way home, not wanting to talk but to think only of this desirable man. Oriel and Errol. Errol and Oriel. If only he were called something different – the combined names made such a mouthful. The train swayed and rattled, jerking her body from side to side, but her mind was faraway. Suddenly conscious of Dorothy by her side she sought to issue profuse thanks to her friend.

'Sorry I'm not much company, Ratty, it's just –'

'I know, you're madly in love with him.' Dorothy's eyes stroked her like velvet.

Oriel blushed and turned to study her reflection in the darkened train window. 'I wouldn't know about that.'

'You are! And he is with you.'

Oriel turned back to her friend. 'D'you think so?'

'Of course. He's gorgeous, isn't he?' Dorothy's grinning face swayed from side to side.

Oriel shared a conspiratorial giggle. Was she in love with Errol? She truly did not know what falling in love meant. But if it meant that she felt a squirming in her belly when his eyes flickered over her, that she experienced all manner of unmentionable thoughts that she did not understand, then yes she was in love with him.

'Are you going to see him again?' asked Dorothy.

'He's asked me to go to the beach tomorrow afternoon at two. Hey, and d'you know he lives in Middle Brighton? Not sure where, though. He said he'd bring a friend so you won't be bored – we're meeting at Tommy Bent's statue.'

Her friend looked concerned. 'Sorry, I can't come! I said I'd help Helen to make a dress. I'd break it if I could but I promised.'

Oriel bit her lip. 'I can't go on my own to meet two men. Maybe I could take Mel.'

There came a scathing laugh. 'Are you mad? Remember what she's like. What if she takes a fancy to Errol?'

Oriel laughed to negate this. 'She won't – and I felt awful leaving her behind tonight. I feel as if she's expecting me to take her every time that I go out and I just can't. Tomorrow might be a good idea.'

'What about the baby?'

'It'll be a treat for Alice too.'

'Oriel, you can't do that! What will his friend think to her being an unmarried mother? He'll think you're the same as her.' Dorothy clamped a hand over her mouth. 'I've gone and done it again, haven't I? I just mean that if you really like him it would be a bit risky.'

Oriel fell mute, knowing exactly what was meant but feeling angry too, for the comment reflected on her own mother. Once she could forgive but these slips of Dorothy's were becoming rather too common. Why didn't she think before she opened her mouth?

'Well, I've no one else so I'll have to take her. Maybe Mother will look after Alice for a few hours.'

'How can you even ask her in her condition?' Apart from the fatigue caused by her pregnancy Bright was still suffering the aftereffects of the flu.

Oriel felt annoyed that Dorothy's nature was more thoughtful than her own and tried to brush the matter aside. 'Oh well, I'll decide what to do later.'

Her infatuation taking precedence over all else, Oriel spent the next morning trying on different outfits. But the tussle over whether or not to ask her mother to look after Alice, and risk her father's wrath, still preoccupied her. Dorothy was right – it wasn't really fair. Dot was also right about the sort of impression that would be created by Melinda turning up with her baby. Oriel sighed and glared at what, to her, was an unattractive reflection in the mirror. Attempting to pull the ill-fitting dress over her head, she discovered she had forgotten to undo the buttons. The frantic struggle to extricate herself sent her into a rage which ended with her ripping the garment and hurling it to the floor with a 'Sod it!'

Every skirt she tried on seemed too tight. In the end

she was forced to decide on one of them but chose a long-line jumper to cover imagined bulges. Eventually, too, she came up with a plan which might, with Melinda's co-operation, solve her dilemma.

After inviting the girl to join her on the date she added, 'I have to ask you to do something, Mel. This is just for my sake. You'll probably think I'm awful for asking but it's going to create lots of problems and this man is very important to me.'

In high spirits at the thought of going out, Melinda clapped her hands together, sending a cloud of flour into the air. 'Tell me about him! Has he got pots of money?'

'I couldn't say but he's really good-looking. I mean really.'

'Hoho! Well, watch your step.' The young woman picked up a rolling pin and wagged it at her friend, then went back to shaping the pastry.

Oriel crossed her arms, watching the other's competent little hands roll the pin back and forth, noting the white dust that had settled in her fluffy black hair. 'He thinks he's bringing his friend for Dorothy but she can't come.'

'And you imagine his mate'll be disappointed? She's built like a footy player! He'll have a better time with me.' The maid began to cut the pastry into shapes. 'I hope he's as handsome as yours. Pass me that baking tin, will yer? So what's this other favour I have to do for you?'

Oriel obeyed the command. 'You can borrow anything out of my wardrobe you want . . . but would you mind pretending you're a widow? I know you'll think I'm awful –'

'Course I don't.' Melinda seemed unoffended, deftly inserting the circles of pastry into each hollow. 'I'll be in it. So long as you tell your dad that me having the after- noon off is your idea. He thinks I'm enough of a bludger as it is. And I'll expect to get some bathing togs out of it – unless you want me to swim in me birthday suit.' She uttered a gay laugh, wiped her hands on a cloth and told

Oriel, 'Here, shove some jam in these while I go and have a gander in your wardrobe.'

When the two attractive young women approached Sir Thomas Bent's statue, which stood at the apex of three roads, Errol was leaning over the nearby marble drinking fountain and did not see them at first. As he looked up, wiping his mouth and saw that Oriel's companion had a pram, he nudged his friend and both looked askance.

There was swift explanation. 'I'm afraid Dorothy couldn't make it! I knew how disappointed your friend would be so I invited Melinda along. She's a widow, her husband was killed in the war.'

Melinda, sporting a temporary wedding ring bought by Oriel, gave her lively smile and introduced the baby. 'This is Alice. Had to bring her, hope you don't mind.'

'My troubles!' David, Errol's friend, was charming and stooped over the pram to tickle Alice's ribs with a digit. 'I can't kid on I know much about babies but she's very pretty like her mother.'

'I like him,' grinned Melinda to her friend.

Oriel smiled shyly at Errol, performing a quick examination of his wide cream flannels. Under his own admiring stare at her pleated skirt and hip-hugging jumper she found she did not know where to look and, lifting her eyes to the outstretched arm of the statue, saw that some wag had placed a beer bottle in Sir Thomas Bent's bronze hand. She laughed and pointed, diverting attention from herself, and shortly they all moved off along Bay Street.

David was to do most of the talking as they undertook the long trek to the beach. 'Brought your togs, girls?' The autumn days were still occasionally warm enough to bare one's skin.

Oriel replied that they had. 'We can use my mother's bathing box to change.' She turned her blue eyes to the cloudy sky. 'Hope it doesn't rain. It's a bit muggy, isn't it?'

'She'll be right,' Errol assured her, grabbing hold of her hand. 'Nothing's going to spoil my day.'

Be that as it may, something was about to spoil Oriel's. A while later, as they approached the Railway Hotel, a drunken man and woman staggered out on a cloud of beer fumes, and to Oriel's great astonishment the laughing female squatted right in their intended path and proceeded to urinate. Watching it trickle its way to the gutter, she felt her face burn but kept walking, incensed that there were such brutish people in the world. Equally disconcerted, none of her companions said a word as they gave the inebriated couple a wide berth and went on their way to the beach as if nothing had happened.

'Strike!' exclaimed Errol, after a lengthy promenade. 'I wish I had've known your bathing box was right down here before I arranged to see you – it's almost outside my front door.'

Oriel felt silly, apologized and plodded down the sloping path from road to beach where a row of wooden huts nestled below a bank of greenery. Leaving the men in charge of the pram both girls went into the hut to change, emerging in neck-to-knee woollen costumes, rolled-up scarves knotted around their heads. Feeling the male eyes upon her, a self-conscious Oriel kneeled down quickly on her towel and adopted what she hoped was an attractive pose, but feared that she looked as bloated as she felt. Thankfully her friend looked much heftier. The men went off to change then, allowing Melinda to release her stomach muscles with a gasp. 'I don't know how long I'll be able to keep this up!'

The males returned wearing similar garments to the girls and sat beside them. The wind was uncomfortably warm but Oriel only noticed that it carried the pleasant smell of Errol's body under her nose. Dialogue was a little stilted at first, consisting mainly of remarks about the other people on the beach. Bedevilled with the previous distasteful incident, Oriel tried to focus on an innocent group of pigtailed youngsters in sombreros, who were building a sandcastle, and other young couples enjoying their Saturday afternoon off. The sun made a temporary appearance from behind the clouds. She lifted a hand to shield her eyes.

'Your hair's gone a lot lighter since we first met,' observed Melinda, fingering a strand of her own dark mop. 'It's a real plummy colour. Your dad's is the same.'

'Yeah, Dave was just saying to me how nice it looks,' contributed Errol.

Oriel uttered coy thanks and wondered what else they had been saying about her, until to her chagrin she noticed his eyes flitting over Melinda's body.

Totally innocent that she was providing entertainment for her male companions, the other girl stretched her flesh and prostrated herself on the towel to receive the hot rays upon her skin. Oriel flopped over on to her stomach too, tracing her toe in the sand, feeling the heat burn into her calves and listening to the rumble and shush of the tide in the background. Errol lay down beside her. She opened one eye against the glare, smiled, then closed it again, feeling his presence. For a while she lay there imagining herself in his arms, his lips crushing hers – then she leaped up with a yell. 'Blessed March fly!' She rubbed her thigh, making frowning examination and damning the insect that appeared for many more months than its name might suggest.

Her scream woke Alice, who started to cry. The child's mother showed annoyance. 'I'm gonna have to feed her now!' And she wobbled off to the bathing hut.

In her absence, having run out of things to say, the young men raced each other to the sea, plunged in, and after a brief tussle in the water, raced back to Oriel, peppering her with sand on their skidding arrival. Thus roused, they began to wrestle, then performed acrobatics,

David lying on his back whilst Errol balanced upside down atop his knees. Oriel watched and grinned, but then her gaze began to flicker. In this unnatural pose she noticed that their genitalia were more prominent, and though her face turned crimson she nevertheless took sly peeps, trying to make out the various lumps and bumps that jiggled beneath the wet wool costumes, until Melinda's voice made her jump and look away sharply.

Her friend had changed back into her clothes. 'Miss here won't stop crying and I haven't brought anything to soothe her. I'm gonna have to take her for a stroll to send her off otherwise she'll get on everybody's nerves.'

'Half a tick!' David jumped up, unbalancing Errol, who fell to the sand. 'Let me change out o' me bathers and I'll go with you. Don't mind d'you, El?'

And before Oriel had the chance to realize it she and Errol were on their own. He smiled, pulled her to him and delivered a light kiss. 'I've been wanting to do that all afternoon. I never thought I'd be so grateful to a March fly.'

She gazed at him adoringly and enjoyed the feel of his skin against her arm. His own arms were quite tanned and covered in dark hair, though his legs and feet were white.

'I like your friend.' The sun went behind a large bank of cloud and Oriel noticed the same effect on Errol's face. 'It's a damned shame that someone so young's widowed.' His voice was grave. 'But then there are heaps of Melindas left alone with little babies.'

He had told her on their second meeting that he had fought at Gallipoli.

'Did many of your friends die?' she asked softly.

'Dozens – I mean personal mates. There were thousands more, obviously.' His face displayed the horrors he had seen. 'To wake with the knowledge that you could be dead before dinnertime – then just when you think that's all over you come home and there's an epidemic sweeping the country. It makes a bloke look at life differently. I feel as if I haven't lived yet. Know what I mean? What I'm trying to say is, if you think I've been acting too wildly there is a good reason behind it.'

She was quick to soothe, exclaiming that she did not consider him wild at all. Gazing at him now she decided she would prefer his face to be for ever cast in solemnity. Only in laughter was there evidence of imperfection, whence the spell would be momentarily shattered, Oriel suddenly deciding that she was not really attracted to him at all. But then, as if he had guessed, the gap-toothed smile would be wiped away and once more she was entranced.

He continued as if she had not interrupted, his dark eyes smouldering. 'When y'see your mates blown to bits you realize how short life is and you want to live it to the full – even if it does mean acting the lunatic like I was with Dave just now.' He turned sheepish and grinned. 'But if I ever embarrass or upset you –'

'You couldn't,' vouched Oriel.

'You're a good listener.' He leaned over to kiss her again. 'Just what I need after being through that mess.'

'Actually, you have embarrassed me,' blurted Oriel. 'Not with anything you've done but by your openness. You make me feel a fraud. Melinda isn't a widow. She's never been married. I invented the story because I didn't want her situation to reflect on me. I was afraid of losing your friendship.'

The clean-cut face showed bewilderment. 'How can it reflect on you?' Then he laughed kindly and nipped her nose. 'Just because she's got an illegitimate kid doesn't mean I expect you've got one tucked away too. I don't judge people by the company they keep. Anyhow, she's a nice girl – and so are you. I've never met anyone I'd want to court for more than a couple of days but I think you and me stand a good chance.' He kissed her again.

Eyes closed, Oriel pictured herself in six months' time, deeply entrenched in this relationship. She would have to divulge her illegitimacy before committing herself to marriage. Breaking away, she looked into Errol's eyes and decided that she could not bear for it to last so long only to be rebuffed at the last moment. Hence she summoned the bravery to tell him, 'I'm illegitimate too.'

'So? Am I meant to storm off and leave you?'

She searched his face, trying to detect a change in his attitude towards her, but in fact he was more attentive than ever. She smiled her relief as he kissed her, a warmer, more affectionate kiss than before. She wanted to tell him how she felt but did not know how to explain and anyway did not have the time for he had jumped to his feet and was pulling her towards the sea.

She screamed. 'Oh no, Errol, it'll be too cold – and there might be sharks!' But her wriggles to escape his hold were pathetic.

The water was freezing. Bits of seaweed licked at her ankles as she shivered happily beside him, casting the occasional anxious glance at the beach in case Melinda should return and ruin her idyll. Her body had just become acclimatized to the water when there was a sudden cool change in the wind and it began to rain. Oriel squeaked as the heavy drops pounded on her head. She would have made a run for the bathing box but a mischievous Errol grabbed her and held her closely, ducking their shoulders under the water where it seemed warmer all of a sudden. She felt his limbs entangle with hers, felt the mysterious shape of his lower body, the breath from his laughing face.

The rain stopped as quickly as it had begun. They emerged to soggy towels and a beach that looked as if it had been peppered with grapeshot. Oriel, hair and scarf dripping around her happy face, did not want the afternoon to end but other people were making an exodus and her stomach told her it was teatime. 'I suppose I'd better get dressed,' she sighed, breathless after their frolics. At his crestfallen nod she held his eyes for a moment, then jogged off to the bathing box.

She had not removed her costume, but was leaning over, head to one side, making futile attempts to dry her hair with a wet towel, when he came in. Alarmed but excited, her breast rose and fell as he hesitated a moment before moving forward.

'Melinda and Dave might come back.'

'There's no sign of them.' His eyes were dark with an expression she had seen once before on the face of the soldier who had manhandled her. Oriel did not recognize it as lust, for Errol smiled and held her tenderly, brushing his lips over her cheek, neck and shoulders. Naïve in technique she may be, but innocence did not prevent longing. The urges she felt might not be understood, but Oriel felt them all the same. With great gentleness he pulled her closer. A mysterious change had taken place in the anatomy that her eyes had tried to decipher earlier. Something hard was pressing between them. There was a fluttering in the pit of her stomach. His kisses became more desperate and she returned them, feeling a great heat, almost a fire, in her lower belly – and then he touched her, there, right at the seat of the fire and Oriel squirmed away from his hand and wriggled free.

'I can't, it's wrong!'

Errol made one more attempt to pull her against him. She fought him off and he stood there breathing heavily with the front of his bathing costume poking out like a tent. 'You've made it like this and now it won't go down until it's done what it wants to do. It really hurts.' There was reproach in his voice. 'I thought you cared about me.'

'I do!' Oriel clasped her hands protectively over her bosom.

'After all I said this afternoon about the war, and how I felt. I thought you understood. I wouldn't say those things to any other person, Oriel.'

Her heart turned over. Such was the hurt and betrayal in his eyes that she desperately wanted to comfort him in the manner that he sought, but her head still fought the urge to surrender.

'You're so lovely and desirable,' he came forward again murmuring, his tone so seductive.

'I want you too!' she anguished, swaying in her wet costume. 'But you see . . . Mother . . . I don't want to end up with a baby.'

Relief flooded his face. 'If that's all!' With kind little kisses, he coaxed her into another embrace. 'I know how to prevent it happening. Things are different these days, people don't have to worry about that any more. I swear I'd never do anything to hurt you. Trust me.'

'If we were married –'

'I might be dead by next week, I can't wait that long. Feel what you've done to me.'

Her body almost exploded as he pressed against her. Ginger hands began to tweak at the wet straps of her bathing costume, leaving their white mark against her pink, sunburned skin. Once she had permitted this, both he and Oriel knew that she was lost.

When they made their furtive exit from the bathing box she expected all eyes to be on her, but in fact there were few people left on the beach for the sky was overcast and more rain seemed imminent. There was no sign of Melinda either. Oriel brushed at the clothes that were clinging to her still damp body and glanced shyly at Errol. 'I suppose I'd better go home.'

He finished lighting his cigarette, then took her arm. 'I'll take you. I wonder where Mel and Dave got to?'

'They've probably come back and thought we've gone.' Her Cupid lips tweaked.

A puff of cigarette smoke emerged on his smile. Oriel tasted it as he bent to kiss her. Her heart was even now beating rapidly, everything had happened so quickly. The heat of his body remained inside her – though she was still almost ignorant of what he looked like, deeming it impolite to stare.

A shout caused Errol to look up. Dave waved and called down to them from along the road. 'Melinda's gone home!'

'Righto, mate! I'm just taking Oriel home. See you later!' Errol winked at his pal, licked his finger and stroked the air with it, then at Dave's grin he shoved his cigarette between his lips, took Oriel's hand and embarked on the long walk home.

When they finally reached the end of the road where she lived Oriel wondered how she could avoid inviting him in, for her parents would surely guess the change in her and perhaps confront him. However, Errol said that he must go home. Before parting company, he kissed her and arranged to meet her on the ground floor of the Federal Coffee Palace in Collins Street after he left work on Monday evening.

In a state of exhilaration, she skipped indoors to find Melinda had been there for some time. The maid showed relief and said she had returned to find Oriel gone.

'Where've you been? Your mum and dad wanted to know why I got back without yer. I didn't know whether you'd told 'em you were going out with a bloke so I said you'd called at the shop and yer dad done his block wanting to know why I hadn't done the shopping seeing as I was the bloody maid.'

'We were sheltering from the rain.' Oriel's face gave her away.

Melinda had been sweeping haphazardly at the kitchen floor but now stopped and looked worried. 'I wasn't sure whether or not I should leave you on your own with him. Him and his eyes all over the place. You didn't fall for anything, did you?'

'Of course not!' Oriel donned her sophisticated air as she reached for a jar of cold cream to smooth over her burned skin. Who did Melinda think she was, trying to teach her how to behave? She was the one who'd fallen for the baby. 'We're meeting again on Monday night.'

'Oh, I don't know if I'll be able –'

Oriel looked abashed. 'Oh no, when I say we, I mean Errol and I.'

Anxiety turned to sulkiness. 'Served me purpose, have I?'

Oriel laughed warmly as she took off her shoes and went to empty the grains of sand outside. 'Mel, you know I didn't mean that. We just want to be on our own.' Dearest Errol, how would she ever survive until Monday?

Her eagerness to see him again prevented any kind of work that Monday afternoon, though with her father's books up to date there was little to apologize for. Anticipating that the rush-hour traffic might delay her, Oriel decided to go to town much earlier than planned and spend an hour or so looking round the shops rather than be late. Having told her mother that she would have tea in the city, she also had to provide a reason and decided to tell the truth, knowing Bright would be happy for her. Then, all smiles, she caught a train to town.

Today the shops, usually so alluring, held little interest for her, and before long she was standing on the corner of Collins and King Street outside the Federal Coffee Palace – a palace indeed, its seven storeys crowned with a domed tower. Stomach rumbling, she entered the exotic temperance hotel, feeling highly conspicuous as she searched for a quiet corner and slid into the first vacant seat to wait for service which came almost immediately. Provided with coffee, she crouched over her cup in eager anticipation of Errol's face coming through the doorway – though there were still ten minutes yet to wait. Around her, other patrons lounged, dining or smoking, some writing letters or reading, the atmosphere serving to relax some of Oriel's tension.

She sipped her coffee. The allotted time came and went. Fifteen minutes were added, and then ten more. She had been sitting at the table for over half an hour, people around her coming and going, before the cold reality dawned on her that he was not coming. The smell of freshly roasted coffee, the friendly tinkling of teaspoons upon china, the low drone of conversation, all paled into the background as her excitement turned to worry. Perhaps he was ill. Perhaps, God forbid, he had suffered an accident on the way here. He wouldn't have allowed her to sit here feeling abandoned without good reason. Had she made a mistake? Might he have said the first floor? Finishing the last dregs of tepid coffee, she abandoned her cup, looked around for a staircase or lift and finding the latter went up to investigate the first floor.

He was not there. An anxious tour of every nook and cranny of the luxurious palace, a tentative peep into the billiard room, each met with strange faces. Maybe he had been forced to work late. With this her last recourse she left the palatial building and hurried outside to Collins Street where the commuters had all but gone.

Too anxious to stand around waiting for a tram that might spare her legs, Oriel set off on foot, trying to expel the sickening doubt in her mind. In the lull that preceded the next rush of nightlife she headed up Collins Street towards the Treasury and Government offices at the opposite end, a lengthy trek but it was not her feet that suffered. Past solid colonial masonry, slender skyscraper, doctors' grand apartments, newspaper office, bank after bank after bank, a row of hansom cabs, another row of automobiles, her mind took in none, focused only on the building at the Paris end of the street where he had told her he worked. It was dark now. Theatre lights illuminated her way – the nightlife had begun to liven up – but Oriel didn't feel lively, she felt hollow and worried and vulnerable. A musical clock appeared to taunt her. Three, four, five intersections, past the police barracks on the corner of Russell Street . . . another block . . . and then finally she was there.

His workplace was in darkness. Feeling conspicuous just standing there panting, she escaped from under the beam of the elegantly drooping streetlamp and moved into the gloomy pool beneath a tree, where she dithered for a while longer, casting helpless glances along the street, ears humming in tune to the tram cable. A light shone from an upper casement, framing the figure of an artist at work in his studio, but it was not Errol. How foolish of her not to have asked for his telephone number – but Dorothy would still have it. With this in mind and anxiety in her heart, she faced up to the seven-mile journey home.

When she reached the farmhouse there were questions to be dodged. 'I didn't expect you home yet,' observed her mother, needles clicking knit-one-purl-one over the baby's matinée jacket, Nat raising a finger of greeting from the arm of his easy chair.

'He had to leave early.' How wretched Oriel felt now at having divulged that she was going to see Errol. 'Is it all right if I give Ratty a ring?'

At her mother's happy nod she closed the door and picked up the phone. Dorothy sympathized. Then when Oriel asked if her friend still had Errol's telephone number, she said, 'Hang on,' and went to search for it. After what seemed an interminable time she returned to the phone. 'Sorry I was so long. I do have it. Got a pencil?'

Oriel said in a pathetic little whine, 'Could you . . . ?'

'Course! I'll ring you back.' Dorothy's sentence ended with a click.

Oriel poked her head into the living room and warned her parents. 'If the phone rings it's for me. Dot's going to call me back.' Then she returned to pace the hall, grabbing the receiver the moment it rang.

There was to be more disappointment. Dorothy passed on the information that Errol's mother had given her: he was out – perhaps she could ring tomorrow?

Insistent that it must be tonight – for how could she go to bed knowing he might have suffered an accident? – Oriel begged her friend to try again later. Dorothy gave a kind reply and the line was broken, leaving Oriel to bite her nails for another hour.

When the telephone rang again her friend's tone had altered. It was still kind but tinged with a note of compassion. 'I'm sorry, Oriel. He can give no good reason for standing you up.' In fact Dorothy, upon hearing that he had been out with someone else, had had a blazing row with Errol who without any pressure at all had gone on to admit that his mother wouldn't approve of him going out with someone who was illegitimate so it was rather a waste of time. 'So you just left her there waiting, you coward!' she had yelled. 'She thought you'd had an accident!'

'Could you tell her I'm –' he had begun.

'Tell her yourself, snake-face!' Dorothy had bawled before hooking up the phone; but she knew that he was not the type to do this and so tried to break the news as gently as possible to her friend, which was difficult for Oriel was crying. Without mentioning her friend's illegitimacy, she explained, 'I think he's a bit of a mother's boy really. Just get him out of your mind. He isn't worth it.'

The victim sniffed into her handkerchief and, suppressing a feeling of nausea, thanked her friend.

'There's not much to thank me for. I'm only glad you found out about him before it went too far.' By too far, Dorothy did not mean to imply sexual terms but this was

Oriel's inference. Errol might blame his mother but in reality it was he who had lost respect for her. Panic rippled through her entire body. Too far? It had already gone too far.

8

Naïve as she may be, Oriel had learned from her mother that the purpose of menstruation was to show that all was well within, and if 'The Cardinal' did not pay his visit it could be for only one reason: the woman was pregnant. Ergo, instead of being allayed with time, the hurt and fear that stemmed from her liaison with Errol increased as days, then weeks went by and there was no ecclesiastical manifestation.

She could broach her terror to no one, not even Dorothy; particularly now as her friend, thinking she was doing Oriel a service, passed on some gossip about Errol's penchant for confidence trickery. 'You had a lucky escape – it seems he's a bit of a Lothario. Once he's had his way with a girl he drops her.'

Oriel blushed. Did it not occur to her friend that this was what had happened to her, knowing what she did about her grandmother's profession? But no, Dorothy was genuinely taken in, still believing the reason for his abandonment to be Oriel's illegitimacy.

The reason was of no importance to Oriel when, shortly afterwards, she bumped into Errol at a local dance, canoodling with a girl. The shock of coming face to face with his callous disregard was like being poleaxed. When he granted her the briefest unashamed hello she could not respond but hovered there like a gooseberry watching him waltz his new victim around the floor whilst Dorothy, trying to alleviate her misery, labelled him worthless. 'Forget him, he's nothing but a lecher!'

Melinda, too, seemed well informed. 'I could've told you that,' she announced now to Oriel upon the divulgence as to why there would be no more afternoons on the beach with Errol and David. 'But I thought you already knew, you being much more travelled than me. Thought that was what attracted yer. Never trust a city type, that's what I say. Never trust a boy from the bush neither, come to think of it.' She grimaced and patted her stomach. 'They're all after one thing. You didn't give it to him, did you?'

'Of course not! What d'you think I am?' Oriel made a great show of offence to put Melinda in her place, even though the lie robbed her of a chance to ask for help from one who had been in this dilemma – for she could not possibly tell her mother. There was no alternative but to visit a doctor, though she balked at the imagined reaction to her unmarried status. Her eyes fell on Melinda's hands as they cleaned the table and a flash of inspiration occurred. The maid still wore the wedding ring which Oriel had bought for her.

Without asking for its return, for this would invite suspicion, she instead went to purchase a ring for herself and slipped it on to her wedding finger before at last going to consult a physician, choosing one in the city to avoid any embarrassing encounters.

Seated in the waiting room, she tried to fight her terrible nausea at the smell of ether. Others who waited were reading magazines, but Oriel was too terrified to absorb the printed word, too dizzy even to take in pictures. An eternity passed, during which her bowels threatened to explode every time the doctor opened his door to invite another patient in. Acquainted now with the terrible decision that her mother had had to face, she tried to adopt the same maternal feelings, imagined herself with a tiny human being to care for, and found herself lacking. There was no question that, unlike her own mother, she would get support from her family. But did she want it? Should she instead pretend to go away on a holiday and have the baby adopted? No, she could not do that either, could not live with the hurt this would inflict on those who loved her.

'Mrs Maguire!'

Oriel's innards leaped as the doctor finally summoned her. Twisting her wedding ring she sat at his desk and explained her reason for consulting him, all the while dreading that she was going to be sick any moment.

Noting her nervousness, the doctor responded with a kindly, calming air, asking her several questions, such as what was the date of her last menstruation.

Blushing, Oriel told him it had been about seven weeks ago.

'Ah, then it may still be a little early to tell,' came the thoughtful reply. 'Is there anything else that leads you to the expectation that you might be pregnant? Any tenderness of the body? Any sickness?'

Oriel did feel sick, but answered, 'I'm . . . not sure.'

'Well let's just have a look at you anyway.' The doctor invited her to go behind a screen, remove her clothing and get up on a bed.

Bashful and vulnerable, Oriel lay there for what seemed like another eternity and when he did not come called in a reedy voice, 'I'm ready, Doctor.'

He appeared, rubbing his hands which he applied to Oriel's body. She flinched and lay there deeply humbled whilst he performed his examination.

He left her to dress then. When her pink face appeared at his desk he pointed to a chair and told her, 'As I said, it's a little early to tell with any surety, but I would doubt very much indeed that you are pregnant, Mrs Maguire.'

Oriel broke down in tears of relief.

'I'm so sorry to disappoint you.' The doctor leaned over to pat her shoulder. 'But you can't have been married long?' In answer he received only a tearful shake of head. 'No, well, given time it'll happen. You seem very highly strung. I can only surmise that the delay in menstruation is due to anxiety. I'll give you a tonic, and if nothing happens after a couple of weeks come back – but I am sure it will.'

Oriel issued nasal thanks, blew her nose and hurried from the consulting room, deeply relieved.

There was, however, no escape from the hurt and deception inflicted by a man who, she now recognized, had simply duped her in order to satisfy his appetite. Slipping the wedding ring from her finger and into her bag, Oriel determined never to be so taken in again, vowed to amend her ignorance without delay. There must be literature that could enlighten her.

After treating her dry mouth to a glass of lime juice she went directly to a large book arcade where she first perused the novel section and slowly worked her way around the shop, her darting eyes searching every shelf. She was in the store for so long, flicking nervous glances around her that she aroused the suspicions of the assistant, who to her horror came over to offer help.

'I'm a nurse!' Oriel hoped her blush would not convict her. 'I'm looking for the medical section.' The assistant nodded and escorted her to a short row of books. She thanked him and began to browse a copy of *The Modern Physician*, her manner confident until she came to a graphic illustration and hurriedly replaced the tome on the shelf. She picked up another, equally descriptive and crouched over it lest anyone should see over her shoulder. Under the persistent scrutiny of the assistant she put it back and eventually found one entitled *Married Love*, which she hoped might be enlightening. It was, and another, called *Wise Parenthood*, provided all the knowledge she required, but she was too embarrassed to purchase it on its own and so took three other textbooks with it to the counter, the resulting bill leaving her with only enough money to get the train home.

Most of the books turned out to be fascinating in one way or another. How she wished she had been in possession of them before, but however engrossing, the pages led her thoughts back to Errol's duplicity and despite the relief that she did not carry his child, her melancholy was to remain.

'What's up with that lass?' Nat demanded of his wife that evening when his daughter remained closeted in her room. Normally if he made some remark that she did not care for she would return his fire, but lately she had been most lethargic.

Obviously her mother had noticed this too and guessed that it had something to do with the young man whom her daughter no longer went to meet. She feared it might be something more than a broken love affair, but for Nat she played dumb. It was no good the two of them worrying until there was something to worry about. 'Why do you ask?'

'She's been stuck in her room all afternoon – not to mention she's hardly said half a dozen words all week.'

'I think as she gets older she's getting more like you in that respect. She used to be such a chatterbox.' A fond smile played at her lips as she recalled Oriel as a little girl.

'There's more to it than that. She can still yammer on if she wants to.' He worried about his daughter, recognizing his own black moods from the expression on her face, hating to think of her suffering in that manner. 'Is there summat you're not telling me?'

'No! Go and ask her, if it'll put your mind at rest.'

'She won't welcome my interference. You go – go on, you can't kid me you're not worried.'

So Bright was pushed into a task that she ought to have done long before. Knocking on her daughter's bedroom door, she opened it straight away and poked her head in.

With no time to hide the book, Oriel's fumblings sent it to the floor. She snatched it up, but not before her mother had seen that it contained obstetrical diagrams.

'You're not ill, are you?' Bright's face portrayed shock.

'No!' Oriel tried to lay the book nonchalantly aside

but her mother came to look at it. 'I was just considering whether or not to try my hand at nursing again.'

Bright sensed the lie and her heart wept for it. 'Your father's worried that you don't seem very happy – I mean, we both are. It's nothing to do with that young man, is it? You'd tell me, wouldn't you? You're not –' She broke off and stood there, anxiously awaiting the words she was dreading.

Oriel was experienced enough now to grasp Bright's meaning. 'No, no.' She shook her head, looked back at her mother, whom she had rarely burdened with her problems, then sighed. 'Have you ever bitten into a sugared almond to find the kernel is rotten? Well, that's what happened to me. That's all.'

Bright rested her hands on her abdomen, feeling the child move beneath. 'He wasn't as nice as you thought?' When her daughter merely nodded, obviously unwilling to discuss the matter, she nodded too and looked thoughtfully upon the book. 'Well ... as long as you're all right.'

'Yes, I'm fine, honestly.' Oriel could say this with surety now. The Cardinal had appeared at last, without her barely having sipped the doctor's tonic. 'I'll come and join you in a minute.'

And this was the answer that Bright took back to her husband. 'She's just been let down by somebody. The pig, I could kill him. The look on her face.'

'You don't mean –'

'No, she says not.'

'Is there nowt we can do to cheer her up?'

His wife shook her head. 'We'll have to let her get over it in her own way. You know what she's like, least said soonest mended.' She picked up her knitting, noticing the thoughtful look on his face. 'And don't be feeling guilty that you're happy and she isn't. I know you.'

He was amused that she read him so well. 'Aye, but contentment has its price – look at this!' He patted his stomach. 'What with all this good food I'm like an old porker.'

'You know just what to say to make me feel rotten, don't you?' she laughed, indicating her own plump figure.

'Nay, you've got an excuse, I haven't. I'll have to get some exercise.'

'Why don't you take up gardening?' Oriel had entered in ghost-like fashion making her parents start.

Glad that she had chosen to join them Nat was overly cheerful. 'Aye! Not a bad idea, we could grow our own veg at back there. I don't know if I feel like tackling it at moment, though. D'you know what I've often fancied doing? Painting.'

'There's plenty of painting round here to do,' said Bright. 'Excuse me, I'll have to go again.' She hurried off to the lavatory.

'Painting pictures, I mean,' called Nat, and heard an exclamation to show that she'd heard.

Oriel displayed an interest she did not feel, asking why didn't he buy some art equipment.

'I'd feel daft. Still, I might just give it a bash – you might fancy it an' all.' He tried to raise her spirits.

'It's not really my forte.' Her brain saw not oils and canvas but the interior of a bathing hut with two writhing bodies.

Melinda's baby started to wail. Nat threw up his eyes, but then his wife distracted him with an excited call from the back yard. 'Come outside and have a look at this!'

'His master's voice,' announced Nat, and pushed himself from the chair.

Oriel was listless but, at her father's prompting, followed him out into the darkness where the gumtrees loomed in the moonlight, their rustling leaves touching the air with the faint scent of eucalyptus. It was cold and she wrapped her arms around herself as her mother pointed triumphantly skywards.

'I rather think it's the moon,' Nat said drily.

'Dozy! Look at it carefully. This man in the moon has a different face from the one at home. A squat little face! Not like ours. I mean not like an English moon. That's because it's upside down. Turn your head like this.' Nat and Oriel copied Bright as she leaned to her left, her head on one side.

'Oh aye!' From his contorted position Nat could make out a more familiar visage now. 'Well, I'll be blowed.'

All three of them hung virtually upside down for another few seconds until Bright groaned and held her side. 'I shouldn't be doing this.' She straightened, then something caught her eye and she peered into the dinge. 'What's that moving out there?' Unnerved, she grabbed Nat's arm. 'There! It's some sort of animal.'

Nat tilted forward. 'Soft bugger, it's a paper bag.' He went to pick it up and shoved it into the dustbin. Then, still intrigued by the night-time sky, gazed up again to study all the millions of stars – many more than at home, it seemed. 'I wonder if all them constellations are upside down an' all?' murmured Nat. 'I'm not very well acquainted with heavenly bodies.'

'I hope that isn't another dig at my physique,' puffed his wife, holding her thick waist. 'You made me like this.'

Nat saw Oriel flinch and was abashed that his wife should make such a quip in front of their daughter. In some matters she could be almost prudish, then at other times she would come out with a most inappropriate comment like this. To detract from his blush he made an exclamation. 'You've just solved a problem. Summat's been throwing me since we got here. When I'm out for a walk I've been really disorientated, never seem to know what time o' day it is without looking at me watch. That's 'cause sun's in a different position in t'sky. Wait for me to come home from me rounds tomorrow and I'll show you. Away now, it's too cold stood out here.' Grabbing another mallee root for the fire, he led the way back.

Just before entering, however, he gave a shout. 'Whoa,

look out!' He shielded his wife from some imaginary terror. 'Mind that paper bag.'

Even Oriel had to laugh as her mother pushed and pummelled him indoors.

The next day when he came home with the artist's equipment that he had bought whilst on his scrap-collecting round, Nat proceeded with his theory to his wife and daughter.

'Look! Normally at this time the sun would be some-where over there. Everything in this country is back to front or upside down. It really throws me.'

'Oh, that's it then, we'll have to go home,' teased Bright.

'It'll take more than t'moon being upside down and t'water going wrong road down t'plughole to get me back there.'

She laughed. 'You love it here, don't you?'

'Aye, as long as Spud keeps sending me money orders every couple o' months I won't be going back to England.' He turned to her. 'Why, don't you like it, then?'

'Oh yes! It's just some days, I miss the old streets. The bar walls.' She paused in the driveway to look back beyond the perimeter fence at the avenue of elms. No matter how the settlers had tried to make their parks and towns a corner of England they could do nothing about the seasons. When Bright thought of April she pictured daffodils and sticky buds but here in front of her was the bronze tinge of autumn. 'Isn't there anything you miss?'

'Nowt.' Then Nat pondered. 'Aye there is – fish and chips. Fish they have here tastes like a monkey's bum looks.' Despite his protestations his wife insisted on hav-ing it every Friday.

'Oh, and I miss my *Evening Press* – and my Sunday paper too,' added Bright. There was no sabbath publi-cation here. 'What about you, Oriel, do you miss anything?'

Thinking of Errol, the young woman shook her head.

'Nothing springs to mind. What I do find strange about here is, the people refer to England as home when some of them have never even been there.'

Nat knew what she meant. 'Aye, they'd get a shock if they did. The poms treat their own like muck so God knows what they think to colonials – except when there's a war on, of course.'

'Listen to him – poms!' laughed Bright.

'Oh, I'm a dinkum Aussie now you know.' He became alert and frowned. 'Eh, there's some little buggers larking in our field. They'd better not be harming my hoss. Oy!' Face enraged, he laid his parcel of paints on the ground and set off across the grass.

Bright looked concerned as he descended with menace upon the culprits, managing to deal each of them one hard punch to the head as they ran in terror.

'Nat, they're only boys!' She threw a quick glance at Melinda, who had come to see what the noise was all about, and lowered her voice: 'God, I've never seen him like that before,' she breathed to her daughter.

'I have,' murmured Oriel, her own anxiety turning to relief as her father strode back to the house, face like thunder. The maid beat a hasty retreat. Bright looked at Oriel quizzically. Yes I've witnessed another side of him that you haven't seen, thought Oriel with some satisfaction. 'He can't stand boys. I'm only glad he never got hold of them. He would've murdered them.'

Bright touched her lips thoughtfully, but with Nat's approach she attempted to soothe his ruffled temper. 'Don't let them get you so worked up. That animal would make mincemeat out of them.' She was rather afraid of Nat's horse, who was not averse to nipping anyone given the chance. 'Come on, I'll make a pot of tea.' She fought for something that would wipe the harried look from her husband's face. 'Why don't you set your easel up and have a bash at your painting?'

'Oh, I've things to see to at t'yard.'

'Go on! I'll bring your lunch out here.'

Nat's face remained dark, but as her suggestion sank in his mood gradually lifted. Fetching a chair from the house, he began to set everything in order. Bright watched him through the window and smiled at her daughter. 'Here, take him these sandwiches and we'll leave him to it.'

Towards the end of the afternoon, his wife and daughter wandered up behind him and exclaimed over his almost completed landscape.

'Ooh, that's really good, is that!' said Bright. 'Isn't it, Oriel?'

Whilst her husband continued to work, she studied his brush strokes with great attention, comparing the picture with the actual scene in front of them, cocking her head and frowning.

'D'you mind me saying, you just haven't got that tree quite right there. If you alter that it'll be perfect.'

Oriel, standing at her father's side noticed his smile wither. Though he maintained his artistic position he was deeply hurt, she could tell.

'Are you going to put it in a frame?' It was Bright again.

'Ah, I don't see no point,' muttered her husband. 'I'm only a fifth-rate artist. Nobody'd want that on their wall.'

'But it's not as if you want to sell it or anything, is it? You're doing it for your own enjoyment.' She patted him.

He glanced up briefly from his canvas. 'Yellow Peril's here.'

Distracted, Bright observed Mr Kee, the Chinese vegetable merchant, trundling slowly along the road on a cart painted with dragons, and cabbages dangling round its sides.

'I'll get Melinda to deal with him. He makes me nervous – never looks you in the eye.'

As soon as she had gone into the house Nat began to wipe his brushes off and laid them in their box, folding up the easel and packing everything away, totally disenchanted by the fact that his wife had not disagreed with him about being a fifth-rate artist.

His wife may not have seen his hurt but Oriel had and now tried to make him feel better. 'She can sometimes be a bit blunt, can Mother.' Her eyes followed Melinda, who went running down the drive to catch the vegetable seller. 'She didn't mean to. It would kill her if she thought she'd hurt your feelings.' How often had she herself been stung by one of her mother's thoughtless remarks?

Nat was about to retort that he wasn't bothered in the slightest but when he caught the look of genuine compassion on his daughter's face he merely gave a little smile and nodded. 'Happen she's right anyway. I just thought I'd try me hand, that's all.' He put the paints away knowing he would never take them from the box again.

Whilst her father packed up, Oriel went into the kitchen where Bright was preparing a joint of meat for the oven. She did not tell her mother how much pain her flippant remark had caused. However, the culprit had had time to ponder on her own thoughtlessness and drew her daughter aside with a cringing whisper.

'I've said the wrong thing again, haven't I?' At Oriel's nod she bit her lip. 'I didn't mean to. I tend to forget how sensitive he is. I think his picture's really good. I just wanted it to be perfect for him.' She left the subject abruptly as Melinda came in, muttering that the Chinese would be taking over the place soon if the Government didn't do something about so many of them creeping in. She was followed almost immediately by Nat, who attempted to get his landscape past the gathering as unobtrusively as possible. Melinda spotted it.

'Aw, that's ripper!' Depositing her vegetables on the table, she went to examine the picture more closely whilst Nat tried to escape. 'Are you gonna sell it?'

'Nay. Hold on, it's still wet.' At Melinda's flow of compliments he muttered, 'You can have it if you like it that much. Don't suppose anybody else'll want it. Shall I stick it in your room?'

'I doubt it'll dry in there, it's too cold.'

'Sorry, Mel, you should've said.' Bright looked concerned.

'Oh, I wasn't meaning to whinge. Just saying that the painting might get spoiled. There's loads o' slaters in there too – you don't want them paddling all over it and making a pattern.'

'What the hell are slaters?' Nat frowned.

'Yer know! Those flat little armoured things that you find where it's damp.' Melinda thought she might as well hammer her point home.

'You mean woodlice!' exclaimed Nat.

'No, slaters.'

'Well, we call 'em woodlice.'

Bright jumped in. 'You should've mentioned it before, Mel. We can't have Alice getting a chill. We'll get you a little kerosene heater. I'm sorry, I never thought it'd get as cool as it does.' Her expectations of perpetual sunshine had been quickly disillusioned by the morning mists that had lately begun to swirl over the paddocks. 'D'you think winter's going to be as bad as the ones we got at home?'

'I hope not.' Nat tried to fake cheerfulness as he went to dispose of his painting. 'I'd reckoned on saying goodbye to my bronchitis.'

It was thus that winter caught them off guard. Whilst there might not be blizzards to contend with they found that the overcoats they had thought to discard were once again necessary as protection against the frost. Even in the house there was little escape, for the draught percolated its wooden boards, attacking knee and ankle joints. Having been spared his annual bout of bronchitis earlier in the year by favour of glorious sunshine, it was all the more dispiriting for Nat when, in the grip of the cold damp air, his jaded lungs were revisited by this ailment, his racking cough keeping the household awake throughout most of July. Whilst others might grumble, Bright said kindly that it was a change for him to keep her awake instead of the other way around – her increasing size made it difficult for her to get comfortable when lying down – but the constant interruption of sleep made them both rather irritable.

With her parents so indisposed Oriel did not deem it right to enjoy herself at the peace celebrations held in the city that month, contenting herself with festooning the house in paper decorations, and thus avoided her own personal injury. The festival, which began so well, developed into a riot by returned soldiers aggrieved at their treatment, and many were arrested. Demanding their release, a mob stormed the state offices, resulting in a bloody head for the Victorian Premier, Mr Lawson, who was struck by a flying inkstand.

'I've never known a place where they fight so much,' sighed a corpulent Bright when her daughter read her the account from the newspaper. There had been nothing but social unrest throughout the country since they had arrived. 'Peace Day – hah! Isn't it enough that they've been fighting Germans for four years without fighting each other?'

Now that the birth was approaching she grew increasingly uneasy but did not know why. True, she was fearful of the pain, and nervous of being responsible for a tiny individual again, but that was not the whole of it. Sometimes she felt a kind of panic. Even in the confidence that Nat would never leave her this time her brain would begin to race for no sensible reason and then her heart would pound and she would have to make excuses for herself all the time.

As one who lived in perpetual bafflement over the female psyche, Nat was again bewildered by her need for constant reassurance but gave it gladly, answering her anxious queries with the promise that he would love their child whatever its sex. Nevertheless, having witnessed his hatred of boys, Bright was relieved and happy in the safe arrival of their second daughter.

Victoria Prince was born amid a downpour on the first of September, two weeks before her mother's birthday, spring instead of autumn, an unremarkable child, except to her parents.

Oriel, still in the grip of rejection by her lover, felt even more wretched as she watched them dote over the new arrival. It was ridiculously childish, she knew, but that knowledge could not prevent this awful feeling of loneliness. Life seemed to revolve around Victoria. Even Melinda, usually such good company, was full of baby-talk, saying her own child looked so grown up beside the newborn. From a maggoty creature Alice had developed into a golden-haired cherub, but neither infant held any attraction for Oriel. And the spring rains did naught to lift her mood.

Bright sensed that her elder daughter felt left out and tried her best to include her, especially when organizing the christening at the local Catholic church, but when all was said and done, she told Nat, she was an adult. Besides, Bright had other worries on her mind.

Nat always knew when his wife was ill for she made him aware in no uncertain terms by her moaning. As she herself admitted, she was a very demanding patient. However, the type of affliction from which she was suffering now did not bear advertisement. Only when Nat and Oriel went out for half an hour to the warehouse and returned to find Melinda trying to calm a screaming baby, several pans boiling over on the stove and his wife nowhere in sight did Nat begin to suspect that all was not well.

'What's all this to-do? Where's me wife?'

'She's in the bath!' Melinda shoved his new daughter at him. 'The bub wants feeding and I can't get any sense outta Mrs Prince. Here, I'll have to go see to those sauce-pans or they'll boil dry.'

Anxious over his wife, Nat handed the screaming baby to Oriel, who drew back. 'I don't know what to do with it!' To her the human infant was synonymous with a kitten, so lightly clad in flesh that its bones threatened to bend under the lightest touch. She had only ever held it once, the mere thought of damaging their precious bundle invoking panic.

'You're a woman, aren't you?' At her continued reticence, Nat gasped in exasperation and carried the purple-faced infant to the newly installed bathroom where he found his wife up to her shoulders in the tub, teeth chattering.

'Bairn's screaming to be fed!' When she did not greet him, he came forward looking perplexed, and dipped one hand into the water. 'It's stone cold! Has hot tap run out?'

Bright shivered, as much from terror as from cold. 'I . . . feel funny in the head.'

After a second's vacillation he dumped the squirming baby on the linoleum and came to comfort its mother, wrapping his arm round her quaking shoulders and drenching the sleeve of his jacket. 'How d'you mean, love?'

She could not bring herself to say what horrors were in her brain. The knives and the blood and the voices. How could she feel like this at a time of such happiness?

Nat coaxed her from the bath and helped to towel her dry. 'D'you think you can manage to feed t'bairn? Here, I'll help you.' He patted her shivering skin, then noticed Oriel's worried face in the gap between door and jamb and called for her to fetch him a blanket.

With anxious face, she hurried to the cupboard, grabbed a blanket and inserted it tentatively through the gap, not wishing to intrude, trying not to eavesdrop on the intimate endearments. She took a sharp step backwards as her parents emerged, her father cuddling both the wide-eyed woman and the screaming infant. Clasping her hands over her bosom, Oriel watched them go into their own room, whence the door was closed to her, swamping her with emptiness.

In a while, when Nat had managed to soothe his wife and sat cuddling her in their room whilst their infant drew from her breast, Bright regained her normal rate of breathing and, though still quivering, murmured, 'I'm all right now.' After a few heaving exhalations she added, 'It comes and goes. In the hospital they told us it's not good for the brain to be overheated and gave us cold baths.'

'Does it work?' he asked hopefully.

Despite her torment, she laughed, albeit nervously. 'Well, the shock of it takes your mind off things for a while.'

'I'll go and make a cup o' tea.' He began to rise.

'Don't leave me!' Her eyes were wide again. Dislodged, the baby started to complain.

He embraced her. 'It's all right! I'm here. I'll always be here.' He assisted her with the infant, who calmed immediately that her mouth was full. After a moment of rocking and comforting, he suggested, 'Might be an idea to go see t'doctor.'

'No!' Bright became frantic. 'They'll stick me in the madhouse again! I might never get out.'

'You know I'd never allow that!' Nat tried to reassure her but felt ill-equipped, not knowing what it was that instilled such terror. 'I'll be with you every minute o' the day if you want me to.'

'I'm sorry for being such a nuisance to you,' came his wife's agonized groan. 'I've been nothing but a pest since we got married, what with the flu and now this. You must find it hard to understand – God knows, I do meself.'

After Oriel's birth there had been an excuse for the hysteria – she had been cast out of her home with a tiny baby to care for, no money, no friends – but now she had a husband who loved her, two beautiful daughters and a wonderful new life. Why had this insanity come crawling back into her brain like a malevolent slug? She curled protective arms around the infant, shielding it from its own mother.

'You're not a nuisance!' Though frightened himself, he maintained his reassuring stance.

'I'll bet Melinda thinks I'm loony, doesn't she? Ye can't hide anything from that one. I've seen her looking.'

'She's said nowt to me and if she did she'd be straight through that door. Just let me be the one to worry about that.'

And he did worry. The pressure on Nat was greater than he had ever experienced before. Never in his life had he been called upon to care for anyone, but during his brief marriage he had succeeded in nursing his wife through the scourge of influenza and now had to fend off her madness as well. It was all too much. He could not eat and the flesh began to fall from him. In his desperation, he sought Oriel's help, choosing the only time when Bright permitted him to leave her – when she visited the lavatory.

'I don't know what to do,' he anguished to his daughter. 'D'you reckon I'm doing t'right thing by not calling a doctor? Your mam says they'll put her away and I'd never allow that, but I just don't know if I'm making her worse.'

Oriel abandoned her secretarial work for the moment and shuffled round in her chair to look at him, twiddling her pen. Flattered at being consulted she tried to reassure, even though she felt far from happy about her mother's illness herself. 'It's frightening, I know, but it eventually goes away.' As all pain does. She realized that she had not thought so much of Errol lately.

'You've seen her like this before?' Nat remained standing in the doorway of the small room they had assigned as an office.

His daughter gave a sombre nod. 'Mother never said anything to me but when I was little I recall her being a bit like she is now. And from time to time as I grew up she'd act strangely.' Oriel had almost become used to it.

'She's worried that lass'll think she's crackers.' Melinda was out of earshot. 'Has owt been said to you?'

His daughter shook her head. Though she had seen the look of wariness in Melinda's eyes her friend had betrayed nothing.

'I need to go and get me rents but she won't let me leave her.' Nat's horse had been standing idle for over a week. His daughter had been feeding and grooming it.

'I'd offer to stay with Mother but I know she'd prefer to have you here.' This was not just an indication of self-pity. Oriel knew that by volunteering to remain she might be asked to handle the baby and this was only something she would do if forced. 'But I'll go and collect your rents.'

'Nay, it's not an area I'd like you to go. You've got enough to do with your bookwork.'

'If Melinda once lived there it can't be that bad.' She was used to travelling around other parts of Melbourne now. 'And I'm almost done here. Just give me five minutes.'

He nodded, then took on an expression of concern. 'Your mother's been a long time. I think I'll just go and look for her.'

Oriel turned back to her desk to finish off her secretarial work. After completing it, she donned a beret and her trenchcoat, then searched for her father to tell him she was ready to leave, finding him sitting at the dining table, head in hands. A dart of anxiety stabbed her breast. 'Where's Mother?'

He jabbed a finger at the table, a look of defeat upon his face. Perplexed, Oriel stood there for a moment trying to gauge his meaning, then spotted beneath the edge of the chenille tablecloth a pair of feet and the folds of her mother's skirt.

Slowly emerging from her maelstrom, Bright's mind returned to focus. In the gap of light twixt tablecloth and floor she saw two pairs of shoes. No one spoke, but she felt the silent conversation that passed between her husband and daughter.

'You go,' she heard Nat murmur. 'I'll look after her.'

The owner of the other pair of pointed-toed shoes hesitated, then came towards the table and lifted the edge of the cloth. Shame-faced, Bright looked into her daughter's kindly expression.

'I'm just going out, Mother, is there anything you want?'

'Are you going past the ham and beef?' Though subdued, Bright sounded quite normal.

'Can do.'

'I fancy some German sausage.'

'I'll get it on the way back – tootle-oo!' Oriel dropped the cloth, straightened her beret and left as if everything were as it should be, though once out of the room she allowed her true concern to show. Please God, make her better soon.

Catching a train to the city, Oriel then strode to Bourke Street where she jumped on a tram. Handing her fare to the conductor whose bell-punch rang to indicate that she had paid, she sat back on the wooden seat and at a pace of ten miles per hour glided off towards the inner suburb of Fitzroy.

She discovered an area that was more industrial in nature, more densely populated than her own, many of its tiny crumbling cottages undergoing demolition and others awaiting the same fate, like sheep outside an abattoir. There were larger houses too. The two which her father owned had apparently been subdivided as he had informed her that there would be four lots of rent to collect from each building.

'I want nine bob off each of them,' he had told her. 'Make sure you don't take any sob stories or they'll be away without paying next time you go.' His tenants mainly transient workers, he had always made sure they paid in advance.

Oriel wandered slowly down each street looking for the addresses. The large brick and stone terraces had once been occupied by middle-class folk, but as the population of the city increased these had moved ever outwards to the more genteel areas such as the one where Oriel herself lived, and the only people she encountered now were obviously of lesser means. When the workers had taken over the area industrialists had followed, erecting their shoe and clothing factories, foundries and brush works to draw from the ready supply of labour. In the shadow of these were narrow cobbled lanes where the very poor resided. Oriel faltered at the sight of a small barefooted girl with a shaved head, dragging her even tinier brother by the hand, his soiled nappy swinging round his dirty knees.

Dismayed, she proceeded and eventually found the right street, hovering on the litter-strewn footpath to check the address on her bit of paper before entering.

Her first vision was of a lavatory tucked away at the end of a linoleumed hall, its door left open to display its stained, decrepit furniture. There was a hint of urine in the air.

Turning away she knocked at the nearest door. A hard-looking woman answered and, when Oriel asked for the rent, gave a wheedling response.

'Me man's laid off. Yer couldn't wait till next week, could yer?'

Oriel's heart sank. Were all the tenants going to be so difficult? She appraised the woman a moment. Her father had warned that they might try it on. 'I'm afraid not,' she answered firmly, whilst preparing for another excuse. The woman did not seem perturbed but went into the room, collected some silver off a table and thrust it at Oriel before closing the door.

Pleased with herself, she knocked at the room next door and waited, wondering over the low whirring vibrations from within. The tenant appeared. Oriel gaped past the young Indian man to the scene inside, counting nine more dark-skinned people there, most of them bent over sewing machines.

'I've come for the rent,' she murmured. He nodded and delved into his pocket. 'Do all these people live here?' Oriel could not help but ask.

The man was polite. 'Yes, that is correct.' He mirrored her frown. 'There is a problem?'

'Oh no! Thank you.' She pocketed the money and left to visit the upstairs rooms, which might have fewer occupants but were nonetheless equally cramped as the others.

The next building was of a similar pattern. Oriel knocked at the first door and asked the tenant for her rent.

The young woman's face dropped. The small child she carried was yelling, two rivers of mucus running from his nose. She hefted him on to her other arm, looking harassed. 'I'm sorry but I just haven't got it. My husband's been rushed to hospital so he hasn't had any wages.'

Oriel looked past her into the room. Its few items of furniture were very poor, and there was another small child running around with no knickers on. She turned her eyes back to the woman whom she was certain was not lying. 'I'm sorry about your husband. I'm sure we can wait for the rent until next week.'

'I have to be truthful, I might not be able to manage it then. He's lost his foot in a machine so they might not take him back at the factory. I don't know what I'm going to do.'

She jiggled the child but only succeeded in making him scream louder.

Irritated by its noise, and feeling desperately sorry for

its mother, Oriel terminated the discussion. 'All right, I'll let you off this week and I'll explain to Mr Prince. I'm sure he'll be patient.'

'Huh! You can't know him very well – but thanks for your understanding.'

The woman was about to close the door when Oriel fumbled in her purse and said: 'Here! That should tide you over until your husband gets back on his fee– I mean gets well.' Blushing over her gaffe, she handed over a five-pound note, then hurried upstairs to the next apartment, taking nine shillings out of her purse and dropping it into the bag reserved for the rent money. Father need never know.

Succeeding in gathering the rest of the rents, Oriel asked the last occupant, 'Where is your lavatory?' When told it was downstairs, she gaped. 'You mean that has to serve all of you?' Receiving a nod, she asked, 'Is there no bathroom?' This drew amusement. Feeling rather stupid, she hurried downstairs and paid a tentative visit to the lavatory, trying to avoid her cream trenchcoat coming into contact with the walls. How could she have been feeling so sorry for herself when people had to live like this? Much humbled by the experience and disgusted with her father, she embarked on her journey home, where it was some relief to see that her mother was seated in a normal position on the sofa.

Nat was delighted that his daughter had not been taken in. 'You got it all? Good on yer!' He put the rent money in his safe, then came back to sit next to his wife.

'I don't feel good.' Oriel's face was stern.

'You didn't have any trouble, did you?' Bright showed anxiety.

'No!' Oriel was quick to allay worry and patted her bag. 'I got your German sausage.' Then she turned to her father. 'Are you aware of how many Indian people are living in one of those rooms? Ten!'

'Oh, I'm not putting up with that, they'll be damaging

t'place,' returned Nat, shaking his head. 'If they're going to be playing them tricks I'll start charging 'em more rent.'

'I was thinking of their welfare!'

'Nay, that won't bother 'em – they're used to living in large communities.'

He patted his wife's knee reassuringly. She did not appear to be listening to the interplay but had drifted off again and had adopted that fearful expression that he had come to dread. He could not bear the torture in her eyes, felt sometimes that he was going mad himself. Hence, he only attended Oriel's grumblings with half an ear.

'Even so, I would've thought nine shillings is rather extortionate considering what they're getting,' argued Oriel.

'Nobody's forcing them to pay it.' However, Nat had taken advantage of the fact that people were prepared to pay high rents to be near work if they would soon be moving on. His anxious eyes watched his wife get up and leave the room.

Oriel did not seem to notice. 'There's one lavatory between twenty-five people and no bathroom.'

'Nay, you'll be wanting a roof on next.'

'You wouldn't care to live like that.'

'That's heaven compared to some of the places I've had to live! They're near to their work, food markets, hospitals – excuse me if I don't share your sympathies but mine are concentrated a bit nearer home.' He made an abrupt move to check on his wife's whereabouts.

Oriel felt guilty then, and evicted those unfortunate people from her mind in favour of concern for her mother. 'How's she been?'

He paused, puffed out his cheeks and shook his head. 'I just keep worrying she isn't going to get better.'

'Oh, she will!'

He sounded so pathetic that Oriel was moved to

comfort him, coming forward and touching his arm, her eyes abrim with compassion. He seemed to appreciate the gesture, returning her touch and holding her gaze with sad affection. They stood for a moment thus, patting and comforting like friends. Then, after long hesitant moments, Oriel summoned enough courage to take the risk she had avoided for so long. She laid her head upon his breast, and to her vast relief experienced not the unnatural feelings she had dreaded but those of a daughter for her father. Her father. Warmth flooded through her as, with equal hesitancy, his arms enfolded her. Without passion, they stood embracing for some seconds, and when they drew apart a new understanding had been forged.

Fighting tears, she urged him, 'Don't try to do it all on your own. I'm here too, you know.'

Nat's anxious blue gaze probed her face. 'We've been neglecting you lately, haven't we?'

Berating her own selfishness, Oriel reddened. 'Oh, I'm all right.' She sought to relax his tension with a smile. 'Really I am – and don't worry, Mother will be too.'

9

Oriel's advice appeared to be well founded, for by the first anniversary of the Armistice, Bright had regained enough lucidity to remind other members of her household to observe the two minutes' silence that fell upon the nation. Though still anxious, her cringing episodes under the table were fewer, and for Nat's sake she felt daring enough to risk a timorous trip across the main highway to Landcox Park to celebrate their own first wedding anniversary with an outdoor performance of music from *Madame Butterfly* by the Orchestral Society, fighting any threatened twinge of panic by sinking her fingernails into her palms. By the time summer came and Victoria was three months old Bright was exhibiting signs of being her old self again; in fact she had even taken up Mrs Ratcliffe's invitation to join her bowling club, leaving Melinda to look after Vicky. Being involved with his work and so not at home to miss her, Nat had no objection, though he was glad that she continued to reserve her weekends for him. His paints relegated to a cupboard, Nat himself had taken up his daughter's suggestion that he try his hand at gardening and Bright discovered that she thoroughly enjoyed it too, finding it deeply therapeutic.

If her illness had had one good effect it was that the concern Oriel had felt over her mother helped to force the memory of Errol's treachery into the background. Occasionally she would see him in the street but would make a sudden detour if she could. It was harder to avoid him at dances, but Dorothy was a godsend here, making such derogatory comments about him that it was impossible not to collapse in laughter.

Despite having recovered from her bruising experience, Oriel had decided to concentrate her efforts on other things for a while, work being one of them, balancing her father's accounts and typing the occasional business letter – although she had never offered to collect the rents again. Unwilling to upset the new-found intimacy with her father she had not known how to correct the poverty she had seen, and so she had done nothing, had tried to pretend those people did not exist, just as she tried to deny the existence of her sister.

Victoria was a well-behaved infant, though nothing could endear her to her elder sibling. Oriel showed little interest unless prompted, preferring to spend her leisure time in tennis or cycle riding with Dorothy, or anything that did not involve babies – which was all that people in this house ever seemed to talk about. This did not go unnoticed with her parents.

'I know she's acting a bit immaturely for her age,' she overheard her mother say one evening, assuming her daughter to be safely in bed when in fact Oriel had been about to return to the kitchen to collect some forgotten item. 'But I feel sorry for her all the same. It can't be much fun for her to see Vicky getting all the attention that she missed as a child.'

Though peeved, Oriel continued to eavesdrop and heard her father reply: 'What's she going to be like if we have any more? It could happen, you know.'

There was a note of dread in her mother's response when, after a pause, Bright murmured, 'I don't think I can go through that again, Nat. If I'm going to be like it every time I have a baby –'

'We won't have any more then.' He was adamant. 'There's nothing so important to me as you.'

'I don't see how we can prevent them. I couldn't bear for us not to . . . you know. I just love ye. I couldn't stand it.'

There had been silence then and Oriel had hurried away

to avoid sounds of further intimacy. But she carried with her an idea: instead of hiding *Wise Parenthood* away in her cupboard she would leave it for her mother to find and hope that she would be game enough to sneak a look inside its cover. By this action she knew that she risked a detrimental effect upon her own privacy, but better that than a houseful of siblings.

The next morning being washing day, Bright went to strip the beds and in Oriel's room found the book just as her daughter had intended. Intrigued by the title, she dropped the bundle of sheets on the floor and after a surreptitious lifting of the cover, recoiled in shock as she realized its topic. Her first thought being for Oriel's chastity, she covered her mouth and sat on the edge of the bed for a moment, before picking up the book and gawping over its diagrams. She was still here fifteen minutes later when Nat poked his head in.

'I'm off to t'yard!'

'Oh Jesus!' Bright leaped up. 'I thought it was – Look at this!' Pulling the book from behind her back she showed it to him. 'I don't know what to do, what to say to her. I hope she's not going to get herself into trouble!' Her husband's mother came to mind. What if Oriel turned out like her?

Nat took the book from his wife and stared at it. He was not a great reader but could not fail to interpret its contents. Stunned, he made no suggestion, but darted anxious glances over his shoulder between snatching at words.

'Maybe we ought to confiscate it.'

Nat found his voice. 'We can't do that! She'll go mad if she thinks we've been spying on her.'

Bright agreed. 'Well, I don't suppose there's much we can do – apart from encouraging her to find a nice man to marry. I'd better put it back where I found it.'

'Aye.' Nat seemed reluctant to part with it. 'But mebbe we'd just better check it over a bit more first.'

Oriel could not tell if the book had been touched for it was still there when she returned to her room, but from the number of hints her mother kept making about marriage, she rather suspected it had. Fielding the questions, she replied that she had no intention of getting married just yet, and changed the subject.

'Do you want me to help with the garden tomorrow?' Her parents were together landscaping a garden out of an acre of scrubland at the back of the house. They had already planted trees and shrubs and had carved out lawns and flower borders. Even in its infancy the garden looked wonderful and had become so much of a passion between them that they were out there whenever Nat had any spare time.

Giving up on the topic of matrimony, Bright exchanged a look of despair with her husband and replied, 'If you like.'

Thus, on this hot summer's afternoon towards a Christmas that would be their first in Australia, Oriel found herself pulling weeds from the front garden whilst her mother and father were around the back. Despite the new understanding with her father she still sometimes felt as if she were intruding upon her parents' privacy. It could be just a certain look or a mood that she perceived, but she could guess that her company was superfluous and would make herself scarce. Would she be for ever compelled to bear this incredible loneliness?

It was in such a mood that she performed her toil this sabbath afternoon with the sun on her back, tugging haphazardly at weeds, her languid gaze fixed to the task in hand but never actually seeing it, mind far away.

'Hullo there, miss!'

Hearing the Australian accent, Oriel looked up and peered from under her large straw hat to see a wiry, rather impudent-looking man beyond the fence.

'Would you be the lady of the house?'

Trowel poised over another weed, she answered, 'I'm sorry we don't wish to buy anything.'

The man lost his friendly demeanour and looked crushed. 'Aw, fair goes for an old digger, miss! I've only sold one box all day.'

'Oh, you're selling matches.' She rose, almost tripping over the hem of her navy and white dress, and spoke in the bumbling manner of one who is experiencing guilt – after all the times she had condemned her mother for buying unwanted clothespegs from gypsies she was discovering how hard it was to give a direct rebuff. 'Well, actually I do need a box of matches, I'll just get my purse.' She was about to traipse to the house when she saw that he was smiling again. An extremely attractive but mischievous smile.

'Did I say I was selling matches?'

'But –'

'I asked if you were the lady of the house. I'm not selling anything. Course, if you do need some . . .' He took a box of matches from his pocket and rattled them at her, grinning.

In repose beneath the shade of his hat his eyes had held the opaque quality of the muddy Yarra. Now, when he smiled the sun rippled on these waters, bringing them alive with the reflection of greenwood.

'I'm awfully sorry.' Oriel looked chastened and puzzled at the same time, and went across the grass to introduce herself, the fence still between them. 'We don't get many visitors apart from haw– salesmen.'

His clothes were of poor quality but clean. He obviously paid a great deal of attention to his boots. Her father would approve. Her first impression of wiriness had not been mistaken; however, she noticed that his arms and wrists were very solid. She watched as he took off his hat to reveal light brown hair, parts of which had been bleached by the sun to a colour resembling straw, appearing even more vivid against the nutbrown of his skin. Her eyes followed a trickle of moisture down the side of his nose, feeling an immediate jolt of attraction, though the face sported no classical feature. He was not tall but possibly slightly taller than her father. He was saying something to her but Oriel was mesmerized.

Suddenly aware that her mouth was hanging open, she tried to collect her senses and said, 'Er, I'm sorry, I didn't answer your question. No, the house belongs to my parents. I'm Oriel Maguire.'

'Ah, we've got the same name!' he exclaimed, reaching over the fence to shake her hand vigorously.

She raised her eyebrows. 'Maguire?'

'No – Oriel.' He chuckled whilst she, feeling silly, laughed too and realizing that she had been ogling him, removed her fingers from his grip and shoved her hands deep into her big patch pockets out of embarrassment. 'Sorry, it's a very nice name – mine's Daniel Maguire. Doing a good job on the front yard.' He turned admiring eyes on the garden whilst she continued to look at him.

'Thank you.' Oriel had the strange impression that she had known this man for years instead of only minutes and responded to his easy manner by asking, 'Do you like gardening?'

'Nah! Don't do it less I'm forced.' He chatted amiably for a moment longer then took a deep breath. 'Well . . . don't like to trouble yer but I'm looking for Melinda Elliot. I've been to her mum and dad's place and they told me she works for you.'

'Yes, she lives –' With a start Oriel realized that this was Alice's father and the spell was broken. Her whole attitude changed. Melinda said he had been wounded in the war but he looked as fit as a flea. Relinquishing all desires she asked somewhat curtly from beneath her large straw hat, 'May I take a message?'

The abrupt change in mood did not appear to faze Daniel, who stood firm, even seemed amused by her. 'I'd like to convey my intentions to Mel, if that's all right with you.'

'Very well, but I don't know whether or not she'll see you.'

Unsmiling, she removed her gardening gloves, turned on her heel and marched to the house. Once inside she abandoned all decorum, ripping off her hat and pelting through the rooms to where Melinda was breast-feeding Alice.

'He's here! The child's father, he's here – at least I think it's him.'

Ignoring the teeth of the ten-month-old child clamped to an elongated nipple, Melinda dashed through the house to the front window, peeped from behind the curtain and sucked in her breath. 'Aw, it is Dan!'

'D'you want me to give him his marching orders?'

'Get orf with yer – ow!' Melinda jumped as the child bit her, then referred herself to Oriel again. 'Oh, I'll do me block with him all right – but I'm not mad enough to do it till I get the wedding over!' Her face radiated gladness and she cuddled little Alice who, unmoved, still sucked. 'Aw, I knew he'd come back once he'd had time to get over the shock.' She began to retrace her steps to her own room. 'Could yer fetch him in, please, Orrie?'

'Let him in?' Aghast, Oriel pursued her to the sleepout.

'Well, I reckon your dad'd gimme a serve if I was to go out in the front yard like this, don't you?' She flourished the bosom that swelled from the open flaps of her blouse. 'And this is the only bit of private space I've got. Tell him to gimme a minute to get meself decent.' She spoke to the child. 'Make the most of that, miss! Now your dad's back I'm not just a wetnurse any more.'

Oriel sighed and went back through the house and outside. The man whom she had deliberately left beyond the gate had invited himself in and was now seated on the front step of the verandah, fingering the brim of his hat. He rose at her arrival.

'Melinda will see you in a moment.'

There was a chilly interval of twenty seconds. She shoved her hands into her dress pockets and looked around at the fuchsias, oleanders and cotoneasters, snatching occasional glances at him, and noting that despite his devil-may-care attitude a twitching muscle in his jaw betrayed nervousness. The air was still and sweat began to drip off them both. Somewhere in a nearby wattle an insect gave an imitation of someone winding a watch. Daniel, hat in one hand, dashed the back of his wrist across his brow and asked, 'How long've yer been in Australia, Oriel?'

She bridled at this informality. Her tone was cool. 'Almost a year.'

He gave a sage nod and answered, 'Thought you hadn't been here long. Born here meself.' Then he proceeded to donate his family history, though it was apparent she wasn't interested. 'Me grandad jumped ship back in the time o' the gold rush.' He looked down at his clothes and grinned. 'Don't need to ask me if he struck gold, do yer?'

Oriel's moonbeam face dealt him a tight smile, then glanced through the open front door. 'Melinda should be ready now. Would you care to come with me?' Half expecting him to feel awkward at the expensive interior she undertook a swift inspection of his face but he was apparently unimpressed and simply smiled when he caught her looking at him. She marched on through the rambling house towards Melinda's sleepout. As they reached the rear hallway a tired-looking Nat emerged from the back garden and immediately stopped to frown at the visitor, who merely nodded and smiled and issued a 'G'day.'

Nat muttered a hello, then turned to his daughter. 'Who's this?'

'Nobody.' Oriel continued walking.

'Daniel Maguire's the name.' Swapping his hat to his left hand, the visitor offered a quick handshake before seeing that Oriel was not prepared to wait. 'I'm a friend of Melinda's.'

Still frowning, Nat watched the two of them disappear into the sleepout, then rushed back out into the garden where his wife kneeled weeding the flowerbed, Victoria in her pram nearby. 'Our Oriel's just taken a young bloke into Melinda's room.'

Bright suspended her task, wincing as she straightened her back, and peered up from beneath her wide-brimmed hat, looking slightly shocked. 'Who is he?'

Nat lifted his hat, dashed the sweat from his brow, and replaced it. 'Said his name was Daniel Maguire.'

Immediately she thought of her own family. As far as she knew there were no relatives called Daniel. 'I don't think he's one of ours.'

'No, no! He's a friend of Melinda's. The cheeky bugger, acting as if he owned the – eh!' Nat had just spotted Oriel emerging through the back door. 'Come here, you! What d'you think you're larking at, taking him into that lass's bedroom?'

She hurried forward to explain, whispering, 'He's Alice's father!'

Bright was delighted. 'Ooh, he's come back to marry her!'

'I couldn't tell you, I got thrown out before anything interesting was said.' Her daughter looked peeved.

'Get back in there and listen at t'door!' ordered Nat. 'You never know what they might be up to.'

'I'm not doing that!' Oriel feigned outrage. 'I'm going to wait on the front verandah to catch him on the way out. If I happen to overhear anything on the way past Mel's door . . .' She tossed a cheeky grin at her parents before heading back to the house.

Bright stopped her with the hissed question, 'What does he look like?'

Gorgeous! was Oriel's instinctive response, but as he belonged to someone else it was hardly a fitting exclamation. She threw a brief jocular comment over her shoulder. 'He's got a broken nose and a wooden leg.'

Her mother turned to Nat. 'Is she having me on?'

'Well, he's got the twisted conk for sure but he didn't appear to be limping. He looks a right larrikin. Go in and have a look for yourself. Just barge in and pretend you didn't know he was here.'

His wife laughed and bent down to resume her weeding. 'You're terrified we're going to end up with another baby in the house.'

He tutted and strode off. Bright called to ask where he was going. 'If nobody else'll do it I'll have to.' Reaching the rear wall he hovered by Melinda's window, ear cocked whilst his wife gestured forcefully for him to come away.

On the front verandah Oriel waited in the December sunshine, occasionally sighing and pacing the wooden boards until eventually Daniel emerged alone. She probed the virescent eyes enquiringly but the man simply grinned, nodded and replaced his hat, announcing, 'See y'again, Oriel,' before going on his way.

Frustrated, she watched his retreating lope for a second or two before rushing back into the house to accost Melinda. 'Well?'

'We're gonna be married at Christmas!' Melinda almost threw the whining Alice on to the bed and approached her friend with unrestrained excitement. 'And I want you to be my bridesmaid.'

Oriel gasped and sat down on the bed – would have sent Alice bouncing to the floor had the child's mother not made a quick grab to save her.

'Will yer be in it?' Melinda grinned expectantly.

'Of course! That's wonderful, Mel, I'm really happy for you. You're so lucky.' She saw again the impudent grin and chased it from her mind. 'Where's the wedding going to be?'

'Dunno yet! Dan's a mick but he hasn't been to church for years so there'll be no problem. Don't breathe a word to me mum 'n' dad, though – they'd go right orf.'

'I thought you said you'd known each other since you were kids?'

'Yeah, but I didn't mean we come from the same place! We only used to meet at bush concerts an' that. Once the wedding's over they can call him what they like. Not that I have anything against Catholics,' Melinda reassured her friend, then swung the grizzling Alice up in the air. 'Your daddy's come home! I always knew he would. Your mum and dad're invited too, by the way!' This last sentence was for Oriel, who smiled.

'I know they'll be delighted.' She was curious. 'Did he give any indication of what made him come back?'

'Said he'd had time to work things out in his head and knew he never should've went and left me but he just felt he didn't have anything to offer us before.'

Oriel noted that there was no mention of love. 'So, he's got somewhere for you to live?'

'Oh yeah, don't worry, we're not dumping ourselves on you!' Melinda shifted Alice to straddle her hip. 'Danny's got it all worked out. He's applied for the Soldier Settlement Scheme and got a little place in the Mallee – gonna try his hand at farming. They give you six hundred quid and you don't have to pay anything back for three years till yer get going. Aw, what a Chrissy present. It's all happened so fast I feel like I'm dreaming. Whad'yer think to him – isn't he beaut?'

'Very attractive,' agreed Oriel. 'But I must say I expected somebody younger.'

'Cripes, you make him sound like an old bloke! He's only twenny-six!'

'Oh, I didn't mean he looked old! It's just that I was expecting someone immature from what you've told me. Well, I'm really glad for you, Mel. But I'm going to miss you.'

'Oh, me too! But once we're settled you'll have to come for a holiday.'

'I can't wait. In the meantime let's go and tell Mother and Father your good news.'

Melinda sniggered and cast her rapturous gaze to the garden. 'I reckon they already know. Your dad was sticky-beaking under the window, pretending he's weeding the flowerbed.'

'Isn't he the limit!' gasped Oriel, but she laughed and taking her friend's arm went out to share the glad tidings.

Upon Melinda's announcement, Bright made the suggestion that they hold the reception here, it being quite a large house, and despite complaints from Nat she knew that he would do anything to please his dear wife and so the arrangements went ahead. In the city department stores there were incongruous window displays of cotton-wool snow, Santa and reindeers, whilst outside the sun baked everything to a crisp. Bright, Nat and Oriel toured the arcades, having done their own Christmas shopping, now looking for a wedding gift. Nat had complained that he was allowing the girl to keep the painting he had done but his wife had said they should buy her a proper gift as well, so offending him. He had been shirty all morning.

Bright sighed. 'I don't feel at all Christmassy.' Though at least she could face the crowds without fear today.

Oriel admitted she lacked the festive spirit too. 'No, I can't see me ever getting used to it. It spoils things in a way, doesn't it? I mean, what's the point of decorating a tree?' In her memory, Christmas meant snuggling round the fire with roast chestnuts, coming home to a warm bed from Midnight Mass and waking in anticipation of a snowfall.

'And church was half empty on Sunday! It's disgusting. Even folk who aren't regular churchgoers usually make an effort to turn up at this time o' year.'

Nat juggled his parcels in order to open a new packet

of cigarettes. 'They're all on summer holidays.' When his wife looked at him enquiringly he enlarged. 'I've told you, everything's arse road on here –'

'Don't say that in the street!'

'You know how our school kids get their month off in summer? Well, Aussie summer just happens to fall at Christmas.'

'Don't remind me.' Bright fanned her face. 'I certainly don't feel like cooking a huge dinner in this heat. I've decided to get caterers in.'

'Hang on!' he argued. 'Isn't it her parents' job to pay for it?'

'Well, as it's doubling as our Christmas dinner too, I'd feel a bit mean. And there aren't that many coming.' The guest list consisted only of Melinda's parents – Daniel's having refused to come on hearing that he would be marrying a Protestant – grandparents, brothers, sisters and their respective spouses and children, plus a couple of Daniel's friends who had served with him in the army.

'However few there are there'll be too many for me,' said Nat. 'I won't be sorry to see the back of that lass. And while we're on about it there's one thing I do intend to get me own way on. If we get another maid, I do the hiring and she doesn't live in. Think on,' he added for Oriel's benefit.

'Aw, she's a good lass,' replied his wife. 'I'll miss her – but I'm glad he's done right by her.'

'Noble bugger,' muttered Nat. Though secretly empathizing with the young man in one respect, he was annoyed at him too. Daniel had done the right thing by Melinda and it served to remind Nat of his own guilt.

Bright guessed this. 'Well, he's a lot older than you were,' she soothed. 'It's easier to do the right thing when you're set up with your own land and a house for your wife.'

He nodded. 'Maybe – now come on, are we going to

get this blasted present or not? It would've been easier if you'd asked her what she wanted.'

'I did.' His wife steered him into an arcade where a carillon of bells chimed out festive tunes. 'She just said manchester, but I –'

'What, the whole of Manchester? I might've known that greedy little cat'd ask for summat big.'

Bright thumped him, laughing. 'I mean manchester as in bedding and towels! I must admit I've only just found out that that's what it means. Did you know?' she asked her daughter, who nodded as if she had known all along. 'I just thought there were an awful lot of shopkeepers with the name Manchester.'

'So we're getting her a towel?' asked Nat.

'Towels! Plural, you stingy devil. Though I wanted to buy her something a bit more special.'

'Nay, I can't think of anything handier than a towel,' said her husband, with new purpose to his stride, 'specially at moment. The sweat's dripping off me. Away before I drop.'

Watching the bride take her wedding vows in a local church Oriel felt deeply envious of her friend, imagining herself in Melinda's place. She still felt a certain resentment against Daniel for his abandonment of mother and child, but fought to put it aside. After all, if Melinda was happy to take him back it was no concern of hers. Besides, Daniel was far too nice for her to be able to maintain her reproval.

After the ceremony the guests retired to the house that had been suitably decorated for a Christmas wedding, both inside and out, with gum boughs tied to each verandah post, white ribbons and silver bells.

Oriel found herself as maid of honour sitting next to Daniel at the table and as no one else appeared to be making much conversation felt compelled by politeness to say, 'Mel tells me you're a bit of a hero.'

His confused eyes looked at her over the waitress's arm as she reached across to serve him roast potatoes.

Oriel felt silly. 'Weren't you wounded in the war?'

He cracked a grin, his whole face lighting up as he did so. 'Oh yeah, that's right, but I wasn't doing anything heroic. I was loading someone on a stretcher and copped a bit of shrapnel. Sorry, I've no daring tales to tell.'

'You were in the medical corps, then?' Oriel leaned aside to allow the waitress to serve her.

'Yeah, all of us.' He indicated his two groomsmen who were as laconic as all the other menfolk seemed to be, leaving any conversation to the women.

'So was a friend of ours.' She poured gravy on her meal, then reached for the salt cellar. 'I always wanted to be a nurse, but I changed my mind.'

'Good job too. Can't stand nurses, they're too bossy.'

Oriel's lips parted, then at his sudden grin she laughed. 'Just as well I became a secretary then, isn't it? Want some salt?' She jumped at the clatter of metal against china and looked around, clutching her chest. Seated to her right, Jimmy Magee, one of the groomsmen, had dropped his knife and was looking uncomfortable, a spattering of gravy on the white linen.

'He'll try and make music out of anything, won't yer, Jimmy?' announced Daniel, trying to lighten his friend's discomfort, explaining to Oriel, 'He's in a band. Sorry, Jim, yer failed to impress that time.'

Oriel smiled forgiveness at the man, then noticed that his hands were shaking and was too astonished to tear her eyes away. Earlier, she had seen a young good-looking chap with pointed features, dark hair and eyes, but now those eyes were like black swirling pools.

'The Two Mugs, that's what they used to call us in the army!' Daniel appeared to be putting on a show. Realizing that he was trying to distract attention from his friend, Oriel pulled herself together and turned to listen, though sensed the man trembling beside her, his leg vibrating against that of the table, rattling the crocks. 'Magee and Maguire! Always getting us mixed up, they were. And if there was any trouble he'd usually caused it and I'd get the blame.' With grinning face he related a couple of incidents, flicking occasional glances at his friend, who had begun to slide lower and lower in his chair. The day was hot, every face glowed, but this brow was beaded in the sweat of terror.

Despite the patter none of the other guests could fail to notice the man's head descend beneath the table. Fixed smiles held Daniel's face, nodding heads forcing laughter, eyes flickering to the empty chair. Only Oriel appeared not to notice, her own attention concentrated on Daniel, who was the life and soul of the party. Not until he paused for breath did she turn and see the vacant seat and began to look around for Jimmy Magee.

Banter exhausted, Daniel muttered from the side of his mouth, 'He's under the table. Don't make a deal of it.' He smiled for the other guests.

The incident made Bright feel uncomfortable herself, and she took up where Daniel had left off, exhorting the guests to embark on the feast and eat as much as they liked.

'Had we better slip him something under the table?' Used to seeing this kind of behaviour from her own mother Oriel did not share the harassed looks of others.

Daniel shook his head. 'Nah, he'll be right in a minute. Just knock that fork on the floor, help him save face.' He ate a mouthful, then studied her. 'Yer don't seem too put out by it.'

As unobtrusively as she could, Oriel knocked the piece of cutlery off the table, then inclined towards him, murmuring, 'I'm just relieved it isn't Mother under there.'

Daniel gave an acknowledging smile. Melinda had told him about Mrs Prince's funny turns. All at once he seemed to remember that he had a wife and looked away from Oriel to check if Melinda was feeling neglected, but she seemed happy enough. Catching his eyes on her, she grinned affectionately and shared a few words as both continued to eat. When the person on her other side solicited her attention, Daniel turned back to glance at Oriel, and then at Jimmy, who had just emerged with the fork as if nothing had happened – though his face was drained.

Oriel tried to pretend as if Jimmy's behaviour were normal, happy to continue her conversation with his friend. 'It's a pity your parents couldn't come, but it's nice to meet your brothers and sister.'

'Yes, three out of eight isn't bad.' Daniel smiled. 'I come from a family of eleven. Ten boys, one girl.' When Oriel expressed amazement he laughed, then was in turn subdued. 'Three o' me brothers was killed in the war.' He brushed aside her sympathy. 'I expect me Mum 'n' Dad's written me off too. Oh well.'

After a brief shrug, he fell silent to finish his meal, Oriel enjoying the occasional contact with him as their elbows brushed.

During the toasts and the brief halting speech from the other groomsman, Norm, it was agreed that the young couple had been most generously served by Mr and Mrs Prince. To finish, Norman lifted his glass to Oriel and said that she was the best-looking bridesmaid he had ever seen, at which everyone called, 'Hear, hear!'

It was then the groom's turn to make his speech. Oriel lowered her blue eyes to the tablecloth and, wearing a little smile, listened whilst Daniel made his address.

'Ladies and gentlemen – and Norm.' He grinned at the other who, after the effort of speaking, was now guzzling a pot of beer. 'I'll bet some of you thought this day'd never come.' A glance at his grim-faced brother-in-law caused him to wince. 'Well, I'd just like to say I regret all the trouble I've caused, but now I'm here to take care of Melinda and Alice, I've got a good home for them, and I hope you can let bygones be bygones. It's a pity some folk chose to stay away, but there y'are, yer can't please everybody.'

Oriel listened in fascination to the pitch of his voice, as soothing and pleasant as linctus.

'I want to say thanks to Mel's mum and dad for being so reasonable. Don't you worry, I'll take good care of her. And there's just one or two other people to thank. Mr and Mrs Prince for giving us this bonzer spread. I haven't eaten this good since I was in the army. Yes, that was a joke. And a special thanks to Melly's friend Oriel for giving her the support that really should've come from me. So, will yer lift your glasses – to Oriel and Mr and Mrs Prince!'

After the toasts, the male guests retired with refilled tumblers and gathered together in the next room for serious drinking, leaving the women behind. Oriel would have much preferred to integrate and, though ostensibly listening to the bride's chatter, her eyes wavered through the open doorway to where Daniel and his fellows exchanged the odd cryptic comment between supping from their glasses. For once, with no conversation expected of him – the other men as laconic as he was – her father did not appear out of place, and sat in happy ponderance. From time to time Daniel would take the stage and, with just one brief inaudible sentence, induce a loud burst of appreciation, causing Oriel's lips to turn up at the corners though she had not caught the joke.

'Like yer frock, love.' Mrs Elliot had to speak twice before Oriel heard her. The recipient of the compliment looked startled, then smiled her thanks and was forced to attend the countrywoman's slow delivery. 'Yer mum looks a picture too, doesn't she?' The feminine circle murmured accord, some sipping sherry, others beer, but all bestowing admiration upon Bright. 'Never think you were mother and daughter. Lovely slim figure.' She herself was well padded.

Made giddy by compliment and sherry, Bright smoothed her dress and gave self-deprecating comment. 'Just as well it's fashionable to look boyish. I don't know what's happened to me since I had Vicky. My bosoms seem to have disappeared altogether.'

'You'll have to get one o' them brassieres,' suggested a rosy-cheeked grandmother.

'They don't make them for caraway seeds,' replied Bright, drawing loud laughter. Oriel laughed too, but as the dialogue became less entertaining, Melinda telling the others of her domestic plans, her eyes and mind were lured back to Daniel, who was no longer holding court but had given the stage to his friend Jimmy and stood laughing at what was obviously a much more interesting speech than was going on in here. Watching that genial face, she could not help a warm little smile from tweaking her own lips – though when his gaze happened to land on her she was quick to look away, reminded that this was her friend's husband. Concentration diverted, she allowed her mind to return to where it should be. The bride was still babbling on about how she was going to arrange her new house, and Oriel was able to contribute some comment upon this before going on to ask a more pertinent question. 'That friend of Daniel's, Jimmy Magee –'

'Oh strike, wasn't he an embarrassment!' Melinda's look of apology toured the female circle. 'But Dan would insist on having him.' Too late, she remembered Mrs Prince had a slate loose too and tried to inject compassion by lowering her voice. 'Shell shock. He's a real wreck. I'd never met him before today, nor the other one, Norm – he's a good bloke, got a well-paid job too.'

Oriel glanced at Daniel's other friend whom she had privately dubbed Normie No-nose in accordance with the little button of flesh in the middle of his face, a baby's nose. He was a pleasant enough fellow, but she felt his charm was just a little artificial. Of course, her aversion could just be due to the fact that he had a large gap between his teeth which, ever since Errol, she had regarded as synonymous with knavery. In contrast, she felt desperately sorry for the other man. Freed from terror, his face showed a keen intelligence.

'Won't be seeing much of either of 'em after today, though. Norm lives in Carlton and Jimmy's at the Anzac Hostel.' This was the name given to the nearby Red Cross convalescent hospital. 'Been there over a year apparently, and he's just getting used to going out on his own. Still gets scared. 'Sa wonder Dan could persuade him to come out today.' She gave a sound of mild irritation at her husband. 'He only asks if we can take Jimmy to live with us! I wasn't having that. Look at 'em there side by side. He's seen more of Dan today than I have. Anybody'd think they were the married couple.'

Oriel felt a pang of emotion that was almost akin to bereavement. 'Well, you'll have him all to yourself after today. Can I refill anyone's glass?' Several tumblers were immediately extended.

The drink continued to flow in abundance. Nat might grumble over the expense but he was having no one call him miserly. In consequence the guests became increasingly drunk and as the late afternoon brought relief from the sun, Bright steered the party out into the garden where they would cause less damage.

In the dark confines of the lavatory, Oriel could hear male voices nearby, and sat for a while longer than necessary, knickers round ankles, eavesdropping on their conversation. Unaware that they could be overheard, Daniel and his friends had resorted to low speech.

She recognized Norm's ponderous drawl. 'Did yer see the arse on that sheila who dished up the grub?'

A Yorkshire voice offered dour description. 'Here's me head, me arse is coming.'

'Christ, she leaned over to give the next bloke some spuds and stuck it right in me face! I was just gonna tuck in with me knife 'n' fork – no wonder Jim had one of his funny dos.'

There followed all shades of colourful military phrases and rude language that had Oriel doubled over in silent laughter – until someone knocked on the closet door and enquired, 'Anyone in?'

After hurried adjustment of her clothes, she handed over possession of the lavatory to an apologetic man and rejoined the party where very soon the mood was to change.

Somehow, the men's talk had come round to the recent election for the House of Representatives. Having registered too late on the electoral roll Nat had forfeited his franchise this year but, unfamiliar with the political parties and the complicated nature of government he was happy to wait until properly educated. One of the others provided explanation. The end of the war had brought new beginnings for everyone, the old divisions between city and bush, the sense of injustice felt by those who produced the wealth against those who made use of it, had led to the formation of the Country Party led by Earle Page. Conservative in outlook, it had supported the Nationalists, who had recently been returned to government.

Melinda's father had given his vote to the new party. 'I'm sick o' Billy Hughes. He takes the piss out o' the Page bloke but accepts his help when it suits him.'

'Needs all the help he can get,' slurred his son. 'Too busy kowtowing to the army.'

His father made some other comment which inspired drunken retort from Norm. 'Yer don't know what yer talkin' about, yer silly old galah!'

Melinda's brother, who had been waiting for an excuse to punish Daniel for his abandonment of her, started pushing and shoving Norm, then picked on those who came to help, landing such a blow that sent the groom flying across Bright's prized flowerbed, and with that the rest of the Elliot clan pitched in.

'Oh, my kangaroo paws!' Bright wailed. She pushed her way through the scrummage and helped to haul Daniel to his feet, gasping at the flattened border he left behind. 'On your wedding day too. You should be ashamed of yourself!'

'Yes, you should, showing me up!' Melinda was furious.

Oriel tried to calm the situation as the victim mopped at his grazed cheekbone. 'It's not Daniel's fault!' She glared at Melinda's brother, who was being held back by others.

The bride was quick to defend. 'He was only sticking up for his family!'

Oriel tried to gauge how Daniel felt at this lack of loyalty but his face gave nothing away.

'Aye well, I reckon it's time you were off on your travels before it gets dark.' Nat gave an exaggerated look at his watch, bringing the wedding party to an abrupt end.

The bride, the groom and their child were escorted to their old car that Daniel had purchased with money borrowed from the Government and which was laden with gifts and belongings. Before climbing in, Melinda, now all smiles again, clutched Oriel's hand and thanked her for all she had done.

Teary-eyed, Oriel replied with, 'Write soon!' then took a last look at Daniel, who leaned over to murmur: 'Will yer do us a favour? Keep an eye on Jimmy for me. He's a good mate.'

'I will.' She smiled into his eyes, he patted her, then after vociferous farewells and kisses drove out of her life to the clatter of tin cans, leaving behind a mob of waving relatives who very soon departed too.

'What dreadful people!' Bright felt safe to say of the

bride's family after all were gone. 'I've never seen such violence.'

'They remind me of your lot.' Nat relaxed with his feet up, cigarette in mouth.

At first offended, Bright was forced to admit with a laugh, 'I suppose they are – but at least they took Melinda back.' She turned to her daughter. 'You're going to miss her aren't ye?' There was no response. 'Oriel!'

Her thoughts concentrated on the newly married couple in their marriage bed, Oriel blushed and jumped as if caught in the act. 'Oh sorry, yes. Yes, I am.' Yet it was not Melinda who inspired her wistful air. Try as she might not to covet her friend's husband, she found it impossible to erase Daniel's laughing image from her mind.

Having not seen Dorothy since before Melinda's surprise visitor had called, Oriel had plenty to tell her when they met up for a New Year's Eve jaunt to the city.

'He sounds like he's a real rough diamond,' opined the taller girl as she sat and watched her friend apply a line of pencil to her heavily plucked eyebrows.

Oriel's reflection smiled at her from the mirror. 'One might get that impression from the way he's behaved but he didn't offer any retaliation towards Mel's brother – now he is a rough one. No, Daniel's really kind and friendly and good to talk to. I feel as if I've known him all my life. Not to mention he's got the most beautiful eyes.' Her speech was distorted by her efforts to apply crimson lipstick. 'I can see why Mel's attracted to him – and he was very taken with little Alice. I was a bit short with him at first, because of the way he walked out on her – well, you know my circumstances. But he doesn't seem the heartless type at all, and at least he decided to accept his responsibilities before Alice is old enough to be affected by his absence.'

Dot smiled into the mirror. 'D'you think you'll ever forgive your father?'

Oriel wrinkled her painted Cupid's bow lips. 'I think I already have. It's only when something like this arises to remind me that I start moaning about it. I don't harp on too much, do I?'

'No, that's what friends are for, to listen to your moans.'

'Oh no, don't say that! It always seems to be me doing the moaning. I'm sorry, Dot.' Oriel inserted a cigarette into a black holder and lit it. Since before Melinda had left she had been practising the art of smoking but had not wished to display it in public before achieving proficiency. Taking a deep inhalation she blew smoke at the ceiling, then paraded for her friend. 'Do I look all right?' Once she had felt insecure and girlish beside Dorothy, but the new straight silhouette and short skirts did nothing for her friend's ample proportions and now Dorothy was the envious one.

'Gorgeous,' the robust young woman sighed. 'You always look so elegant but even more so tonight. I hope we bump into that Errol Windross just to show him what he's missing.'

'Errol who?'

Dorothy laughed. 'How long have you been smoking? I haven't had one since I was fifteen and nearly choked myself. Can I have a puff?' Having taken a tentative drag she accepted the offer of a whole one and the two went to say goodbye to Oriel's parents.

Bright wished them a good time, then added jovially, 'A bit heavy with the lipstick, dear. You look like one of those dubious ladies on St Kilda Road.'

Oriel flinched. A great cloak of embarrassment settled over the gathering, including Bright.

'Oh you look lovely, though!' she stammered and after a quick apologetic glance at her husband, bent her head over her knitting.

Oriel sighed at Dorothy, who was looking at her feet. 'Come on, let's pull this wishbone before we go out, and see if we can make 1920 a better year than the last. It can't be much worse.'

'Do I get a go?' asked Nat. His daughter said she would make his wish for him. 'I wish them orientals'd sell that land I'm after.' For weeks he had been trying to get his hands on some allotments owned by the Chinese gardeners. 'The only answer I get is nods and smiles and bows. It's true what people say, they are inscrutable.'

'That's a big word to come up with before he's had his supper, isn't it?' His wife tried to sound cheerful when in fact she despaired of her own stupidity. 'What would you like for the New Year, Dorothy?'

'A husband,' came the reply.

So would I, yearned Oriel, but what was the point in wishing when the man with whom she had fallen hopelessly in love was married to someone else?

10

Whilst Nat might have been thwarted in his New Year's ambition, Dorothy's appeared to have been granted for on that very same night she had met her heart's desire. Cuthbert, the young man who escorted her home from the party, had been courting her for several weeks now, thereby robbing Oriel of her friend's company. Only with Cuthbert's sanction were they permitted to socialize.

'Isn't he masterful?' Dorothy had breathed when this tall and brooding young man had announced in impeccable English that henceforth she would dance with no one but him. 'Just like Mr Rochester.'

Oriel considered this to be domineering, but was too kind to wipe the happiness off her friend's face. Hailing from the wealthy residential area of South Yarra, Cuthbert was to all intents and purposes a good catch for any girl. Indeed, he was well groomed, good-looking and appeared to have great command of a situation. But beneath this façade of urbanity Oriel detected a poor brain. Left to his own devices, Cuthbert would never aspire to the position his parents had built for themselves and, to compensate, must for ever surround himself with subordinates.

If Oriel did not like Cuthbert then the feeling was mutual – any girl who wore her skirts so short could not be decent. Considering his opinion of her it was a wonder he even allowed Dorothy to see her friend at all, but when they did meet it would be Cuthbert who dictated at what time they would leave, announcing briskly, 'We're going home now, Dorothy!' And she would meekly comply.

Looking at that robust physique people would never imagine Dorothy to be so pliable but Oriel, who had once been taken in by this authoritative façade, knew that it concealed a placid nature.

Now that the dreaded influenza had faded to a bad memory, nightlife had started to perk up again but, with her friend so absorbed in another, rarely did Oriel have the chance to take full advantage of this. There was, however, a rush of daytime social occasions to entertain the immigrants. In March, she and her mother joined the crowds behind the barricades and the decorated trees on North Road to salute the Prince of Wales, who had come to honour the war-damaged veterans of the Anzac Hostel.

Many of the crowd had been here since noon. By the time Oriel and her mother arrived they found it hard to find a viewpoint, but knew by the excited buzz that something was about to happen. At four fifteen the Prince, a dapper figure in bowler hat, overcoat and spats, came along New Street into North Road towards the iron gates of Anzac Hostel. Flag and paper parasol aloft, Oriel reared above the row of schoolchildren who blocked off the road beyond the entrance to the former mansion, waving and cheering for all she was worth, until the Prince was finally escorted by local dignitaries through the gates, leaving the crowd on tenterhooks for another half-hour until he emerged to more cheers and was on his way to Melbourne.

About to disperse with the rest of the onlookers, Oriel tugged at her mother's sleeve. 'Hang on, that's Jimmy Magee, isn't it?' She pointed to a lone figure inside the gates. 'If I can get through I'll have a word with him.' Her promise to Daniel had gone unfulfilled, for though she passed the gates of the convalescent hospital most days she had seen nothing of his friend. 'I want to ask if he's heard anything from Daniel.'

She had received one letter from Melinda shortly after her arrival in the Mallee but there had been nothing since, and no invitation to visit. Oriel was eager for news.

'They won't let you in,' warned her mother, but followed all the same.

Unable to gain access because of the official visit, Oriel hailed Jimmy from the footpath and he came hesitantly forward.

'Oh, it's Oriel!' On recognizing her he smiled. 'Hello, Mrs Prince. Did you both enjoy the visit?'

'Yes! I was just wondering if you'd heard anything from Daniel?'

'Got a letter a few weeks ago. Seem to be doing all right.' Jimmy tried to remember what was in the letter, relating it to Oriel, who listened assiduously, eyes glittering, in the shade of her parasol. 'It's a good job somebody is. I can't get work for love nor money. Some o' the blokes from the RSL are going on a march next week to talk to Billy Hughes.' He referred to the Prime Minister. 'Reckon the Government should pay some sort of allowance till we find employment.'

'I quite agree,' endorsed Oriel. 'And if there's anything we can do just come and ask. You have our full support, doesn't he, Mother?'

A sudden nervousness came over Jimmy's face. 'Thanks – don't know if I'll be going though.' Oriel asked him what he did before the war. He scratched his head frantically, face confused. 'Oh, er, this and that – look, I'm sorry I'll have to go now – so long!'

The bemused women watched him hurry away, then turned for home. Never a great admirer of the aristocracy, Nat had stayed behind, angry too that the visit had forbidden his cart access to the streets and so robbed him of a day's work – 'Bloody royalty, some of us have to earn a living!' – though his wife and daughter noticed that he was suspiciously close to the perimeter fence.

'You've been sneaking a look!' observed Bright as they met with him. 'And all the time pretending you're not interested.'

He gestured at the pram. 'Nay, I was pushing t'babby round t'garden – she wouldn't stop crying! What would I want to go waving at that funny-looking little bugger for? Bet he doesn't wear socks like these.' He hoisted his trouser leg to display striped hosiery, then beheld her tear-streaked face with mock accusation. 'Anyroad, if he were that good a sight why are you looking so miserable?'

Bright tucked her miniature Union Jack under her arm, blew her nose and wiped her eyes. 'Oh it was lovely to see him!' she said, as if of a favourite relative. 'But it reminded us of home, didn't it?' Her daughter nodded, though her mind had wandered from the Prince of Wales to Daniel, imagining him toiling on his farm.

'Well, I don't need too many reminders, thank you very much,' said Nat. 'Especially ones like this. Look at all that rubbish the mucky buggers have left outside our house! Next time I hear he's coming I'm going to demand they divert the procession past somebody else's front door.'

Oriel twirled her paper parasol, a mischievous look on her face. 'Better get your skates on then, there's another march next week! Oh, don't worry, it's not more royalty.' She grinned at her father. 'I shouldn't laugh really, it's serious. It's a protest march by returned soldiers – Jimmy Magee just told us.'

'Protest? I'll show 'em protest if the bludgers come marching past my front door!' Nat had adopted many Australian words without knowing their true meaning. An elderly passerby gave him a look of disgust which he did not comprehend, ignorant of the fact that in her day bludger had meant pimp. However, he was never one to care what people thought of him and continued blithely, 'Have they got nowt better to do?'

'That's the whole point of the march,' explained his daughter impatiently. 'All these strikes are preventing them from working. They're going to talk to the Prime Minister about it. It's disgusting that these poor men should be treated so shabbily after what they've been through, and I'm going to support them.'

'You're not going – tell her she's not going.' Nat grabbed the handle of the pram and began to move towards the house. 'Wherever there's soldiers there always ends up being trouble.'

Bright tried to mediate. 'He's just worried about you being hurt.'

Oriel acquiesced and, not wishing to upset the happy household, said, 'Oh, all right! I'll just support them in spirit instead – providing!' She hurried after her father. 'Providing you give Jimmy Magee a job.'

'There's not work for two of us at yard!'

'Then why do Mother and I have to cut buttons off till our fingers are raw? I'm sure there's something you can find him to do. He can do the collecting!'

'I like doing that meself.'

'The market stall then!'

'Nay, I didn't really want to start employing folk again. They're more bother than they're worth.'

'I suppose they are when you've got slaves at home.'

'Eh, cheeky monkey!' Nat pointed, but was not really angry.

'He can have Melinda's old room,' suggested Oriel.

'What! We have to put a roof over his head an' all?'

'He can't stay at the convalescent hospital all his life. Oh, please. I promised Daniel I'd look after his friend and so far I've done nothing.' And she did so want to please him.

Nat looked helplessly at his wife. 'You might as well put your two pennorth in about this Jimmy Magee bloke. I can see you're dying to.'

Bright had been nodding in agreement with her daughter but now assumed a theatrical air of indecision. 'Well, I don't know. We've only the one table, I'm not sure we'd both fit underneath. He'd have to take his turn.'

Oriel's look of anxiety crumbled into a giggle.

Nat sniggered too. 'Oh go on then!' He shook his head at being so manipulated.

'Thanks, Father, you're a brick.' Oriel's voice projected real gratitude. She knew how much he hated having strangers in the house.

Nat bent and muttered privately to the baby, 'I hope she said brick.'

Oriel did not hear, chattering to her mother. 'I'll be able to tell Daniel his friend's being looked after the next time I write to Mel. I'll go and let Jimmy know tomorrow.'

Oriel's good intentions were harder to carry out than she had anticipated. Standing in autumn sunshine before the gateway of the convalescent hospital, she balked at the long driveway ahead and the army of chairbound veterans dotted about its lawned acres. Behind her, from the redbrick school of St James came the sound of childish chanting. Nearby, through an open window of the Star of the Sea convent school, a nun's voice demanded obedience from her class. The harsh sound of a rule striking a desk prodded Oriel through the gates and along the driveway. Under the grinning scrutiny of the inmates, she felt extremely uncomfortable and walked with head down as quickly as she could without actually breaking into a run. The mansion seemed miles away from the road, especially with wolf whistles hampering every step.

'Will yer stop 'n' talk to me?'

Barely able to decipher the request, Oriel glanced at the twisted wreck of a man in a wheelchair, saw the great dent in his forehead, the saliva on his chin, and muttered, 'Sorry, I'm in a hurry!'

'Why would she want to talk to a cabbage like you?' The sarcastic response emerged from the shade of oaken branches. Oriel turned to see the man she had come to visit, and at once was deeply embarrassed. Jimmy Magee continued to lean against the expansive trunk, drawing on a cigarette. His black eyes were scathing.

Wondering now what had possessed her to come, she approached the shady spot with caution, holding on to her bag for support. 'Hello. I just came to tell you that my father has a job if you want it. I'm not sure how much he'll pay but you'd get board and lodgings.'

Jimmy did not immediately jump at the offer of work as she might have expected. 'What does it involve?'

'Well, I haven't really discussed it with Father. I don't suppose it will be anything special, just helping him to cut the buttons off garments he collects and –'

'Yer mean even a cripple could do it?'

'I didn't mean that at all!' Oriel showed insult.

'Thanks, but I want a real job, not just charity. Ray might fancy it, though.' He threw away his cigarette and stepped into the sunshine, grabbing the handles of the brain-damaged man's wheelchair. 'What d'yer say, Ray? Think yer can be trusted with a pair o' scissors?'

Humiliated, Oriel stood there watching Ray's tortured mouth form his words, which to her were unintelligible but Jimmy Magee appeared to know what he said.

'Ah, I don't think the lady comes with the job, mate!' With great theatrics, Jimmy turned the wheelchair around, his back to Oriel. 'And I think she's seen enough of an ugly bugger like you for today – back in the cupboard yer go.' With this he left Oriel standing there on the lawn, with only the brim of her straw hat to hide her discomfiture.

Her father was astounded when told that his kind offer had been rebuffed. 'They chunter on about not having jobs and when they're offered one they turn their noses up! And d'you know why? 'Cause they won't have the excuse of going on all these marches and brawls!'

Oriel was subdued. 'I don't think Jimmy's that type,

somehow.' Though his inexplicable resentment at her offer had wounded her deeply.

'He's the same as his mate!'

Her eyes shot up. 'Who, Daniel? It wasn't him who started the fight at the wedding.'

'They're all the same! And just because meladdo's turned the job down don't think it means you can break the bargain and go to this protest march. You watch, there'll be hair and teeth flying all over t'place.'

As it turned out, the newspapers reported comparatively little violence at the march. At the Commonwealth offices the diggers were told that there had to be a limit to the responsibility of the repatriation department. Some of the men had been home for more than two years – it could not be expected they would be insured against any job loss or financial setback which arose from industrial circumstances. There was plenty of forestry work around for those who wanted it. The Government would resist all attempts at intimidation.

Nevertheless, the unrest and protest marches were to continue.

'Is that all they do here, have bloody processions?' exclaimed Nat, when in only a matter of days yet more soldiers were marching in the St Patrick's Day parade – ten thousand of them. Even in York with its large pockets of Catholicism they had never seen the saint so vastly supported. Bright thought it wonderful and, as it was a religious event, felt it would be safe enough for her and Oriel to attend this display, taking Vicky in her pram bedecked with green ribbons. They were also in line to shed a sentimental tear at the Anzac Day commemoration in April when the diggers once again paraded along North Road.

Oriel had not seen Jimmy Magee since the day she had visited Anzac Hostel and was none too pleased to see him today outside the gates, alongside his friend Ray and other men in wheelchairs, Red Cross nurses in attendance, all watching the marching band. She would have pretended not to see him if that had been possible but unfortunately Ray caught sight of her and delivered a lopsided wave. To ignore him would have been an even greater insult to the mutilated soldier than she had delivered previously and so telling her mother that she would just go and share a word, Oriel nipped deftly across the road between the last marching band and the next and found herself standing beside Ray's wheelchair, with Jimmy Magee on her other side. After a few awkward words and grotesque contortions from Ray, she felt she must turn to Jimmy.

'I'm sorry if you were offended by my offer. I really didn't mean to insult you.'

'I know you didn't.' He looked equally uncomfortable. 'You just caught me on a bad day. Sorry for being snaky.' At her smiling acceptance he added, 'Anyway, you must've brought me luck 'cause I've found a job with a room to go with it, so I'll soon be leaving here. Come and stand round my other side!' In characteristic offhand manner, he dragged her to his left, then continued talking as though nothing had happened. Totally confused, but glad of Jimmy's good fortune, Oriel stayed to chat with him for a time, trying to include Ray in her smile.

The next marching band came upon them, forcing her to shout above the blare of brass. 'Have you heard anything more from Daniel?'

He looked down at her and for a second there lingered a knowing smirk upon his lips. But then above the sound of the band he proceeded to shout out the latest news, which she absorbed with a smiling nod, trying to include Ray in the conversation until he accosted another young lady who came to stand beside him and she could safely confine her attention to Magee.

'Daniel said you were in a band!'

The bass drum gave way to the more delicate sound of flutes. Jimmy lowered his head to hers in order to be heard without shouting. 'Not this kind. I play the violin.

Used to be in a quartet before the war.' He offered her a piece of chewing gum which she refused.

'Do you still play in it?'

A shake of head. 'They all got killed.' He looked at her. Oriel felt rather afraid of what was in his eyes.

'I know Dan asked you to keep an eye on me. But I'll be right now I've got this job. You could come and share a few words with Ray and the others if yer get the time though.'

Oriel blushed and tapped her foot. 'I will. I'm sorry I was such a – well, I didn't know what to say to him.'

'Just say the same as yer would to a normal bloke. I know it's hard to tell what he's saying but yer'll get used to it. Just one bit of advice: don't stand to his side, stand right in front of him.'

Oriel took this to mean that it would be easier to decipher his words. 'So I can see his face, read his lips?'

A sudden shriek like an off-key flute caused all heads to turn, catching Ray's arm up the young woman's skirt.

'No, so you can see his hands.' Jimmy gave a reproachful laugh at his friend as the red-faced victim hurried away. 'That's why I told you to move a minute ago.'

Oriel bit her lip to avoid laughing.

Jimmy spoke up above the music for his friend to hear, a note of mockery in his voice. 'He thinks just 'cause he's a cripple he can get away with it – and the rest of 'em are just as bad. You've been warned.'

'Thanks, I'll bear that in mind.' Oriel looked at Ray, who gave her a contorted wink. She laughed out loud at him. Then, more at ease in the men's presence, she continued to stand and watch with them until the final brass band marched by.

After that day, she felt confident enough to stop to chat with the men in wheelchairs whenever she passed those iron gates, often taking them small gifts of cigarettes and chocolate and asking after Jimmy Magee, whom she had never seen since Anzac Day – nor did she expect to, though every time she heard a brass band she thought of him.

But despite her sympathies, jazz bands were to become of more relevance to this vital young woman than military ones. Shortly after Anzac Day, an exciting new sound suddenly burst upon the genteel Melbourne suburb where she lived and Oriel threw herself wholeheartedly into its pursuit. It did not please everyone. Whilst awaiting her turn in the shop or riding on trams, she would overhear grumblings from old folk that the country was going to ruin under these flappers and trade union Bolsheviks and how things were not the same as before the war, but to Oriel, who had been here little more than a year, and for other young Australians, this was a time of optimism, of picture theatres, new music, and outrageous dancing.

On this wintry eve she and her peers had flocked to the local town hall to indulge in the new risqué pursuit. Oriel, having practised with a book of instructions for hours at home to her gramophone records, was able to school others in these gyrations, pleased at the stir she created.

But this kind of music was too frantic to keep up all night for both dancers and musicians, and as the band took a well-earned break she collapsed breathlessly next to Dorothy and the others who had tired two dances before her. For once her friend had been allowed out without Cuthbert, though only because he was working overtime stock-taking. She had been instructed to meet him later.

After catching her breath Oriel turned shining eyes to study her friend, who had a secretive twitch to her lips. 'Just what are you up to, Ratty? You've been treating us to that smug expression all night.'

The brown eyes twinkled as Dorothy enveloped the entire clique in her smile and made a grand announcement. 'I'm getting married in the spring!'

There were squeals, the shimmer of sequins and the trembling of fringed skirts as girls made excited congratulations. 'You little devil, you've really been saving that up for effect, haven't you?' Oriel gripped her friend's long arm and shook it, eyes bright as the diamanté on her headband. 'When did he ask you?' She was told, last night. 'Oh, it's really wonderful news, Dot.' But then the reality dawned on her and she bemoaned the loss of yet another girlfriend. 'Wonderful for you at any rate. I'll have no one to go out dancing with now.' She put a cigarette into a holder and lighted it, her own comment bringing thoughts of Melinda, who had not written in months. Perhaps that was just as well. Oriel would only be reminded of the man she could not have.

'I doubt you need me to hold your hand.' Dorothy looked radiant. 'You've been twirling about like a dervish all night. Anyway, I'm sure the others would enjoy having you along.' She looked at the girls who had accompanied them tonight. One or two of them gave verification to this, but although Oriel nodded she knew she would not take up the offer for she was barely acquainted with them and she would feel as if she were merely tagging along. 'Both my friends married – nobody seems to want me.' She blew a stream of smoke at the glittering globe suspended from the ceiling. Who would risk the embarrassment of marrying someone who was not only born out of wedlock but soiled goods too?

Dorothy spotted Arthur looking hopefully across the dance floor and laughed. 'He wouldn't say no.'

Oriel turned vicious. 'I would, though. I'm not that desperate. How could you wake up to a face like that every day? I hate and loathe having to look at it even in here.'

Her more serene friend batted her eyelids. 'You seem undecided.'

Oriel made a face and took another drag of her cigarette.

After more avid discussion over Dorothy's wedding, one of the group asked, 'How many children do you want, Dot?'

'Cuddy wants two. I think that's enough.'

'I don't want any,' said Oriel firmly. 'A husband will do for me.' Instantly her mind embraced Daniel.

One of the plainer members of the group had taken umbrage against Oriel for her cruel remark about Arthur. 'Why bother getting married if you don't want children!'

Dragged away from her imaginary embrace, she frowned. 'You don't just get married to breed.'

'I thought that was the whole point of it,' retorted the other. 'What do you get married for then?'

Oriel looked away in disgust, unwilling to voice her intimate thoughts to this dunce. To share your life completely with another, she thought silently. To be able to have one special person to whom you can say absolutely anything and know they still love you. Small chance of that for me.

When she got home it was to the sound of her father's racking cough and she sighed, for it had been driving her mad all day. She frowned as her baby sister came crawling gleefully across the carpet at high speed towards her, and took a side step, asking, 'What's she doing up?'

Bright was sitting by the fireplace listening to music and put a finger to her lips. 'The doctor's just in there so don't say anything you'll regret later. I had to call him out. Your father was almost sick with coughing, woke Vicky up. I can't get her back to bed.'

With her elder sister now seated, the nine-month-old baby paused on the carpet like a frog, before targeting Oriel once again, playing with the buckles on her sister's shoes. Wearing a tight smile, Oriel allowed her to continue, then glanced at Bright as another burst of coughing drowned the chamber music.

In the bedroom an exhausted Nat was fastening the buttons of his shirt.

'Queensland,' rasped the doctor in his Scottish brogue.

'King's fishpond,' replied Nat, causing the physician to frown at him. 'Sorry, I thought it was some kind of word game. What d'you mean, Queensland?'

'You'll have to go and live there,' said the doctor as if the patient were an idiot. 'You'll get bronchitis every year if you stay down here.'

'Oh, I don't know about that,' replied Nat, breathing gingerly to avoid a fit of coughing. 'We've just got settled here, we like it – anyway, I've got a good business going.'

'Stay here and die then.' The doctor clicked his bag shut and made for the door.

'D'you mean it?' Bloodshot eyes showed concern.

The man turned a poker face. 'Aye. Your lungs are shot to blazes. Did nobody ever tell you?'

Nat admitted that someone had. 'But I thought if I came to Australia I wouldn't have to face winter.'

'You won't if you go to Queensland. You won't have many to face if you stay here either.'

There was a grimace from Nat who said he knew nothing of the northern state. Having lived in several different towns there himself the doctor devoted a moment to instructing his patient on the diversity of the climate, and said that there was no need to go as far as the tropics, somewhere lower down the coast would be far more comfortable.

Nat nodded acceptance. 'I'll think about it, er, but don't tell my wife. I'll have to break it to her gently. She loves it here.'

When the doctor had gone Nat returned to his family, greeting Oriel with a wheeze. 'Now then, done enough jazzing around for one night, have you?'

'Yes, but I'll be going again next Tuesday.' Her face shone.

'Eh, I don't know how you get the energy.' He eased himself into a chair beside the fire and sat hunched over, his breathing shallow.

'I was just saying to Mother, Dot's getting married in the spring.'

'Is she, by gum?' he ruttled. 'I hope she's picked a good un.' His words erupted on a staccato series of barks, alarming the resident possum in the roof, who showed his annoyance by thudding around. No one commented, they had grown used to his presence by now.

'Did the doctor give you any medicine?' Bright came over with extra cushions to try to make her husband more comfortable.

He pulled out his handkerchief and attempted to stifle the noise. 'Aye, he said it should clear it up in no time.' Nostrils flared and eyes bulging, he continued to cough. Irritated, Oriel wanted to leave the room but felt that would be too blatant.

Suffering with him, Bright sat on the arm of his chair rubbing his heaving back. 'I wish I could make it summer for you all the time.' She sighed. 'I must've been daft to believe those who said there'd be permanent warmth here. Still, I suppose it's the same everywhere, we all have to have our share of winter. And if people had warned me I'd still have come, wouldn't you? I love it here.' The tone of her voice showed sincerity.

'Aye.' Nat had stopped coughing and gazed into space, hating the smell of his own breath. 'Aye, I do.' How could he pass on the doctor's news now?

She delivered a solicitous hug. 'Feeling better?'

'Better?' He shoved his handkerchief away and tried to look alert. 'I'm going jazzing with her next week.'

The following week, however, the local paper announced that the jazz dances were to be discontinued: the town hall was otherwise engaged.

'It's all a ruse by the old fogies who run the committee!' Oriel complained bitterly. 'Do they think that our dancing's going to summon the devil or something?'

Bright shivered. 'Oh, don't talk like that.'

Nat, recovered from the worst of his illness, was more liberal. 'I reckon it's just 'cause these new dances take a bit o' getting used to for old folk.'

'But you're old and you don't complain about them,' said Oriel.

'Eh, not that bloody old! I could keep up with you any time.' To prove this her father put on a gramophone record and started to kick up his heels like he had seen her doing.

'Oh don't, you'll start yourself coughing again!' warned his wife, and so he did, but she had to laugh for it wasn't often that they were treated to such spontaneous displays from Nat. Oriel broke down and giggled along with her mother. He took their amusement in good part, coughing and banging his chest with a fist.

'I don't know what's so funny. Once the powers that be see a respectable chap like me participating they'll realize there's nowt to be worried about.'

'My God, close the curtains, if they see that they'll ban it altogether,' laughed Oriel.

But it turned out that her father was right. As people grew accustomed to the modern ways of young people there were more jazz dances to be enjoyed throughout the year and in early October there was also Dorothy's wedding. Once again Oriel was a bridesmaid. With Cuthbert's family as humourless as its son, it was a rather testing afternoon. Unwilling to question the bride, Oriel could not help but comment upon the strained atmosphere to one of Dorothy's other friends.

'It's almost as bad as a funeral. Don't their families get on with each other?'

The other bridesmaid explained. 'It's the Grand Final and nobody bothered to tell Mr and Mrs Ratcliffe before they arranged everything.' At Oriel's look of incomprehension she hissed, 'Footy! It's Richmond against Collingwood. The last place all these men want to be today is at a wedding!'

Dorothy seemed not to notice the faces as flat as punctured footballs, oblivious to all but her groom, and for this same reason by the beginning of December she and Oriel were seeing rather less of each other. With the newlyweds now living in Middle Brighton one might have expected this proximity to lead to more frequent socializing, yet this was not the case. The bride had fallen pregnant on her honeymoon and Cuthbert was treating her like an invalid, forbidding her to go out on an evening unless accompanied by himself. Dorothy viewed this as an indication of his devotion, but Oriel guessed it was just an excuse to keep her from unsuitable company, and as she did not particularly want him listening in on her conversations she made the decision to visit her friend whenever she had time through the day and he was at work.

When they did eventually meet, shortly before Christmas, her friend appeared thrilled about the baby, exhibiting the layette in front of Oriel, who had to pretend interest.

'Aren't they tiny?' Oriel exclaimed over the collection of doll-like garments.

'A good job, too.' The mother-to-be gave a fearful laugh. 'I hope it's the minutest baby ever born. I'm really dreading it.'

'At least it's a long way off,' comforted Oriel, who could not imagine anything worse.

'It's not just the birth, it's the things they do to you.' Dorothy lowered her voice even though they were the only two in the house. 'I had no idea until I went to the doctor's – they stick their hand inside you!'

Oriel recoiled, her voice aghast. 'That can't be right!' All she herself had suffered under the physician was a prodding of her outer body. 'What for?'

'I don't know – to have a good rummage around. They never tell you what they're doing it for. And someone told me that when you have the baby they spread your legs and put your feet in these stirrups.'

Oriel wished her friend had not told her this. 'That's it, I'm definitely never having any.' She remembered the letter and Christmas card from her other friend that had arrived two days ago, the first in nine months. Aware of Dorothy's aversion, she nevertheless relayed the news.

'Melinda's having another one around May or June. She doesn't sound very happy. I don't think their farming venture is going very well. She did nothing but moan about him.' Oriel imagined herself in the pioneering role with Daniel.

Dorothy shuddered. 'She's probably suffering from morning sickness. It made me feel really down. At least mine's finally gone at last. I feel a bit happier about facing the world now – oh, that's what I wanted to ask you! Cuddy and I are going for a ride to the country on Saturday afternoon. He asked me to invite you to accompany us.'

Astonishment banished all thoughts of Daniel. 'Cuddy did?'

Attempting to strike an alliance between her husband and friend, Dorothy neglected to mention that it had been her own idea that Oriel came and had for once managed to overcome Cuthbert's reservations. 'He has this workmate, Clive, who's just had his engagement broken off and he's feeling a bit battered.'

'And you want me to cheer him up?' Oriel showed some reluctance. 'You're sure this isn't your idea just because you feel sorry for me not having a husband?' She was assured that it wasn't. 'What's he like?'

Dorothy said he was really friendly. 'He's been round here a lot lately, which is nice. Cuddy doesn't seem to have many friends.'

I can't imagine why, thought Oriel. 'I meant what does he look like?'

Dorothy said that he had been at their wedding. He lived in nearby Elsternwick, where she herself had lived before her marriage, although she had not met him until then. She tried to describe him but seeing her friend struggle to remember said, 'He's really good company.'

'I assume there were some who said that about Quasimodo.'

'He's nothing like that! Besides, you shouldn't judge people on their looks. At least go out with him for one afternoon. He's got a lovely car.' Dorothy laughed at herself. 'Listen to me – that's something Melinda would say. Oh, go on, Oriel, it'll be good for you both.'

When Oriel was introduced to Clive she was immediately struck by his eyes, which were an intense blue, almost piercing, and performed a quick look up and down of her as their owner shook her hand. Apart from the eyes, there was no physical attraction for Oriel. Accustomed to her father's dress sense she was highly critical of this young man who wore a jacket and trousers of two different greys that did not match, a fawn waistcoat and brown shoes, and carried in his hand a straw boater. His hair was of the unruly variety and in an attempt to control it he had been rather heavy with the grease.

He felt her criticism and laughingly made a joke of it. 'I know, it looks as if you could fry chips on it. Sorry, it was sticking out like I'd had an electric shock and I got carried away trying to create a good impression.'

Oriel laughed, flattered that he respected her opinion, and decided that she liked Clive, who had a shy but friendly and gentle manner, and who made a jocular companion throughout the afternoon. And she could not fail to be impressed by his automobile, a powerful growling beast of lustrous maroon and brass, totally out of character with its owner.

'So what do you think of him?' whispered Dorothy, when the men and the girls split into pairs of their own gender and walked along the track by a creek.

'Lovely car!' Oriel beamed, but reserved her opinion

of the man, the idle saunter of her legs distorting the pleats in her white skirt.

'Oh, that's a bit mean,' scolded Dorothy. 'I think he's really nice.'

'And so he is.' Oriel lifted the straw pudding-basin hat in order to smooth wisps of hair from her cheeks. 'He's offered to give me driving lessons. I might take him up on it. Father won't let me near his car.'

At the end of the afternoon, after dropping off the married couple, Clive drove his partner home. With the leathercloth hood turned down, Oriel reclined like royalty in the comfortable seats, savoured the smell of leather and polish, the wind in her face, occasionally abandoning her tranquil pose to grab hold of her hat that almost fell victim to the car's sudden bursts of speed. Wondering if this was Clive's attempt to impress her, she decided from the look on his face that he was not of that ilk, was simply enjoying himself and obviously hoping she would too.

Nearer home, she sought to issue directions. Clive slowed and extended his right arm, steered the chugging vehicle into the driveway and up to the house where he allowed it to stand vibrating as he ran around to open the door. Though reluctant to invite him in, in case her parents got the wrong idea, she felt she must return his courtesy.

'Would you care to come in for a cup of tea?' At his smiling acceptance, she added, 'I should tell you that my parents are called Prince, not Maguire. I'll explain why some other time. I just thought I'd better warn you. Father hates to be called Maguire.'

'You don't need to explain, it's none of my business.'

Turning off the engine, Clive tugged his clothes into order and followed her into the house.

As Oriel expected, her father was most put out by this intrusion, presenting the usual morose face he reserved for unexpected company. It was a wonder Clive did not take the hint and leave, but instead he accepted her mother's offer of tea, then made a beeline for the pram in which lay Victoria.

'That's Oriel's sister,' Bright explained rather too hastily. She did not want him to think the child was Oriel's. Though hesitant in his manner, Clive offered a few words to the baby, then turned away from the pram smiling. 'She looks like you, Mr Prince.'

Nat grunted. Oriel wanted to say to the poor man, it's no good trying to flatter my father, you won't get round him. She found herself smiling into his kind blue eyes without the fear of rebuff that she had suffered for so long. Clive was genuine, she could tell. He would never hurt anybody.

Her mother liked him too. 'Did you have a good afternoon, the pair of you?'

'Smashing!' Both answered at once and laughed.

Bright came forward with a tray bearing her best china. 'I think there's more than an ounce of Yorkshire in that accent, Clive, am I right?'

He confirmed this. 'I was born in Rotherham. The family'd been there for generations, until we came over in 1914 before the war. I wasn't in it, I'm afraid, I was turned down – on health grounds.' His explanation seemed to have been given a lot of practice as if he had faced much accusation over his negligence to contribute.

'Oh, so was Mr Prince,' replied Bright, pouring tea.

Nat wanted a cigarette and felt compelled to extend the packet to Oriel's guest. Clive accepted. Bright asked him where he worked.

'I'm a clerk at Myers.' Bright was familiar with the big department store.

Nat frowned over the ignition of his cigarette. 'They must pay good money. That's a grand car you've got out there.' At the sound of a motor approaching down his drive he had looked from the window to see who owned the glossy maroon vehicle.

'It's taken me five years to save for that.' The young

man sounded proud. 'My parents gave me the last few pounds I needed for my twenty-fifth birthday.'

'Oh, did you have a party?' Bright asked out of habit.

His expressive blue eyes smiled through the haze of cigarette smoke. 'Well, just with the family.'

During a short hiatus when all took a sip from their teacups, he tapped his foot wondering how to befriend Oriel's rather stern-looking father. 'Who do you barrack for, Mr Prince?' Nat returned a blank look. 'Footy, I mean.'

'Can't be doing with it.'

'Cricket man, are you?' Clive sipped his tea.

'All sport's a waste o' time in my book.'

'Mine too. I'm more interested in physics and brain surgery meself.' The young man pursed his lips then chuckled to show he was joking, but his laughter petered out in embarrassment as Oriel's father showed he was unimpressed. What a dry stick he was.

Bright, eager for her daughter to find a good husband, asked pleasantly, 'So, what family have you got left in England then, Clive?'

'Not many. One of my grans and an aunt came with us. Then another uncle and aunt and their family came over after the war.' He directed his information only at the two women now and was happy to talk about his family for an hour or so. Oriel said little, but sat on the edge of the conversation and watched as he chatted quite easily to her mother. Finally, he said, 'Well, thanks for the tea, I'd better be off.'

Oriel rose to accompany him to the door.

Her mother followed them. 'We're having some friends around on Saturday, would you like to join us, Clive?'

He glanced at Oriel to see if this met with her favour. She gave an agreeable nod. 'Thanks, I'd love to.'

Her father did not appear to care one way or another for he had already turned his back as Clive departed. 'I didn't know we were having company,' he muttered to Bright when the young man had gone.

'We weren't but I don't seem to have met anyone for ages and that little chat with him whetted my appetite – anyway, it's Christmas, the time of goodwill to those in possession of any.' She turned back to Oriel. 'He's really nice, isn't he?'

'Sarcastic sod, if you ask me.' Nat crossed his legs.

'Stoppit! Where did you meet him, Oriel?'

Her daughter, leafing through the daily newspaper, was only half interested. 'He's a friend of Dorothy's husband.'

'Oh yes, come to think of it I think I remember him from her wedding. Good, then he knows the Ratcliffes already.'

'Marvellous, isn't it?' muttered Nat. 'I come twelve thousand miles to get away from England and every bugger you associate with are poms.'

This reminded Bright of their former maid. 'What about Melinda and her husband, Oriel? Do you think they'd like to come?'

'How about the Poultry, Pigeon and Cat Society?' tendered Nat.

Bright scolded him. 'And you call him sarcastic?'

'Nay, mine's wit.'

Oriel answered her mother's question. 'I could write but I don't know if the letter would arrive in time.' The image of Daniel's smiling face came to mind; was never far away. 'Besides, Ratty and Mel have never got on.' She put down the newspaper and turned to go to her room in order to change.

'I do miss her,' said Bright.

'Aye, we'll have to hire another maid,' agreed Nat. 'You're taking too much on yourself again.'

'I meant I miss her as a person! Honestly, you're dreadful – isn't he, Oriel? Melinda was such good company.' Though it was true Bright had been forced to curtail some of her activities due to losing her babysitter.

'Hire a maid anyway if you're thinking of having a do,' advised Nat. 'Though I don't know why you think you have to bother – he's nowt special to you is he, lass?'

His daughter glanced over her shoulder to deliver a blithe response. 'No, I wasn't really expecting to see him again.'

11

She thought little about Clive through the following week except when she was actually discussing him with Dorothy, who wanted to know what had happened when he had driven her home.

'Mother seemed impressed with him,' Oriel told her. 'She's asked him to a party this Saturday. You're invited too – and your parents.'

Her friend looked pleased. 'Will you go out with him again?'

Oriel had only been dancing a few times since her friend had married, not feeling comfortable tagging along with Dorothy's pals. 'If he asks, I suppose so,' came the barely enthusiastic reply. 'It's better than sitting at home, isn't it?'

At the party, however, she began to take more interest in Clive, admiring his easy manner with the other guests, and found herself laughing at his jokes. At the end of the evening when he asked if, after Christmas, she'd come with him to the pictures she readily agreed. She even allowed him to put his arm around her in the darkened theatre and engage in a kiss. There was no quickening of her heart, but Oriel found herself warming to him by the minute.

Clive was not a man to speak his feelings, but from the way he looked at her she felt he liked her too, and the manner in which he treated her showed a willingness to please. Upon being told that dancing was her favourite pastime, he announced that he would take her to a jazz party on New Year's Eve. This was not a success. Clive, though competent, did not match Oriel's standards as a dancer and although he promised to come with her again she knew that he was only saying it out of kindness, and so she proposed they go somewhere else. If he couldn't dance there would be no point in going anyway. Instead, out of affection, she allowed him to choose the next venue and he took her to meet some of his friends, of whom she discovered there were many. Clive was a very popular young man.

This Saturday afternoon in early January they had been boating on Albert Park Lake with more of his pals. The weather had been perfect and they drove home with the leathercloth hood down, Oriel's dark hair fluttering around the edges of her pudding-basin hat.

She turned a crimson smile to her partner and reminded him, 'You said you'd teach me to drive.'

Immediately, he put on the brakes and began to climb out. 'Come on then, get behind the wheel.'

She gasped, but wasted no time in swapping seats with him. It was harder than it looked and she issued little screams as the vehicle jolted and juddered along the road. But once she got the hang of the gears she became blasé, increasing her speed and leaning back against the leather with a triumphant expression on her face.

'Oh look, they're moving a house!' She lifted a white-gloved hand from the wheel and pointed as a team of six horses came towards them pulling a wagon that bore someone's home.

'Watch the road!' Clive grabbed the walnut dash as she failed to respond, almost lying down in the passenger seat, trying to push at pedals that weren't there. His face was white as he watched the huge load get closer and closer to his precious car. 'Stop!' As Oriel veered further to her right he was forced to grab the wheel and slewed the car off the road before the engine tickered out. Gasping, he waited for the wagon and its house to pass.

She bit her lip in guilty manner. 'Sorry, shall I get out?'

Recovered, now that his car was no longer in danger,

Clive laughed aloud at her performance. 'No, come on, I'll start it up for you again – but for God's sake, keep your eyes on the road, and don't go so fast.'

There were no further mishaps on the way home. Oriel even managed a cheery wave to her friends in the grounds of Anzac Hostel as she drove past.

Clive gave a smiling frown as the men reacted with waves and whistles to his partner, then quickly tore his eyes away to issue instructions to Oriel on how to negotiate the gateway. With his vehicle parked safely outside the door, Oriel was able to announce proudly to her parents that Clive had allowed her to drive him home.

'Well, you're not driving mine,' said her father. 'I'm surprised you let her an' all,' he told the young man. 'After the years it took you to save up.'

'He trusts me more than you do,' retorted Oriel, ripping off her white gloves. She turned to Clive. 'Will you stay for tea?'

'Thanks but I can't. I promised Mother I'd be home – my aunt's coming to visit. When shall I see you again?'

'Whenever you like.' She threw her gloves into her upturned hat. 'Come on, I'll back your car out of the driveway for you.'

Allowing him to crank the vehicle, she jumped into action with the engine and, once he was seated beside her, began to reverse along the drive.

'She's gonna hit that fencepost if she doesn't straighten up,' murmured Nat to his wife. Both had come out to watch.

As Oriel continued to chug merrily backwards, Clive looked worried. 'I think you're going to –' There was a crunch and both were jolted in their seats. 'Hit the fence,' he finished lamely, then jumped out to investigate the damage.

Oriel was enraged. 'Who put that there?' she demanded loudly, glaring at the fence.

'A little man saw you backing the car out and he rushed

out to build it.' Despite his obvious anguish Clive could still manage a joke.

Angry as she was at herself, Oriel had to laugh too, then was once more contrite and tears sprang to her eyes. 'Clive, I'm really sorry. You're so good about it.'

He gave immediate forgiveness. 'It's only a little dent.'

'I wouldn't blame you if you didn't want anything more to do with me.'

His kind blue eyes studied her. 'Would you be sorry if I took you at your word?'

She gazed back at him, her feelings reflecting the warmth in his face. 'Yes, I would.'

'So would I. I'm glad I came on that afternoon out with Dot and Cuddy. I thought they were only fixing me up because . . . oh well, I'm glad I came.'

'Me too.'

He gave her a kiss on the cheek and was about to get into his car, then he turned back. 'I'm afraid it'll be shank's pony till I get the car fixed.'

Now enamoured of Clive for his own sake, Oriel felt rather ashamed that she had given so much priority to the vehicle. 'That's all right. We don't live far from each other – I've got my trusty bicycle.'

He sat behind the wheel and indulged in some afterthought. 'I know I said I have to go home for tea but I don't think I'll be expected to suffer Aunt Rose's yacking all night. Are you fit for the pictures?' With her affirmation, he beeped his horn and began to drive away. 'Good, I'll be back for you at seven!'

The following Saturday saw them still in each other's company. The car under repair in a garage, they were strolling along the foreshore indulging in desultory conversation when Clive noticed that she had turned vague as they passed a row of bathing boxes and asked, 'Are you all right?'

Oriel started, drove the rat who had seduced her from

her mind and laughed. 'I was just remembering something I read in the paper. Someone actually had a glass eye stolen from one of those beach huts. I mean, what could anyone possibly want with a glass eye?'

'What did the paper report say – police are keeping an eye out for it?' Clive pursed his lips.

'Oh that's dreadful!' Oriel nudged him.

'I know, dreadfully old. But I couldn't come up with anything better.'

They continued to laugh and talk about things in the newspapers. 'Did you see in Wednesday's edition, I think it was, the man from Sandringham who got home to find his wife in a torrid embrace with the greengrocer?'

'Ah yes!' Clive had seen it. 'And he took the man's horse and cart to the sea and tipped all the veggies in.' He shook his head. 'I can't understand that, you know. If I came home to find my wife with another man I'd kill 'em both.'

Oriel tried to imagine this placid young man in such a role and could not. She merely grinned at him.

He returned her smile warmly. A rush of love took her by surprise. Not the purely physical kind she had felt for Errol but a deep and genuine urge to be with this man for ever – if he would have her.

Risking rejection, Oriel found herself telling him all about her childhood, her illegitimacy and about her attempts to get revenge on her father who had deserted her in babyhood. Clive showed nothing but sympathy, and gave account of his life, bolstering her into divulging more of her own – sad things, bad things, things that made them laugh. But she did not tell him about her prostitute grandmother and she did not tell him about Errol.

'She's seeing a lot of that Clive bloke,' commented Nat, upon informing Bright that Oriel was getting ready to go out.

His wife had just arrived home from an afternoon's bowling and was still dressed in white from head to toe. With no offer forthcoming from Oriel he had volunteered to babysit, knowing how much his wife enjoyed this social activity. Vicky sat on his knee, practising the words he had been teaching her.

Bright deposited her bag of wooden bowls under a table, then collapsed into a chair and slipped off her white shoes, happy of face. 'It's good to see her smiling. I've been worried about her being lonely, what with both of her friends getting married – not to mention her feeling pushed out by Vicky.' It was obvious that Oriel had still not acquired any sisterly affection.

Nat was thoughtful. 'It's not that I love this un more than Oriel.' His wife said she understood the difficulty. 'It's ... like having a dog right from the puppy stage.'

She laughed, still kneading her feet. 'I don't think Oriel'd appreciate that comparison.'

Nat delivered a lop-sided smile and stood the baby on his knee. 'It's true, though. If you have a dog right from being a puppy you feel safer with him, you know he'll never bite you.'

'Things are all right between you two now, though, aren't they?' There was a note of anxiety in her query.

'Oh aye.' He snuggled the golden-haired baby to his chest, his eyes turning thoughtful again. 'I hope she isn't thinking of marrying this joker.'

'Why ever not?' His remark had taken Bright by surprise. 'If she does I'd be very happy for her.'

'He's not right for her.' Nat was firm. 'Too ordinary. She might just be grabbing him out o' desperation.'

'No! It's more than that. I can tell by the way she smiles at him – and you couldn't ask for a better son-in-law.'

'Oh, got me married off already, have you?' Oriel came in on the tail end of the conversation, obviously attired for an assignation.

Bright flushed at being overheard and took up rubbing her feet again. 'We were just saying how much we like your young man.'

'Yes, he's lovely, isn't he?' Her daughter smiled affectionately and launched into a commendation of him.

Whilst his wife shared their daughter's pleasure, Nat was noncommittal. 'So, your mother's right, you will be marrying this Clive, will you?'

'This Clive?' Oriel fingered her pearl earrings, feigning deep thought. 'Oh no, I might marry another Clive if he's more to your satisfaction – why d'you keep calling him "this Clive"? He's just Clive. And he hasn't asked me to marry him.'

Her father sounded cautious. 'If he did what would you say?'

'He hasn't so it's academic.' Oriel wasn't going to look a fool by pinning her heart to her sleeve only to be rejected again.

'Well, it's not very often I give advice, but if he does ask, say no.'

Both Oriel and her mother gasped. 'And exactly what is wrong with him?' snapped his daughter.

Her raised voice alarmed the baby whose mouth turned down at the corners. Nat patted her reassuringly. 'Nowt's wrong with him, he's a nice enough chap, I suppose.'

'You don't like anybody,' accused Oriel.

'I'm just choosy, that's all.' Her father paused. While he was speaking out, this might be just the right time to break the news he had withheld for seven months. 'Also, I don't want you to get settled here because we might not be here for much longer. I've been told I should move up to Queensland.'

'Queensland!' Both his wife and daughter echoed, frightening Vicky to tears.

Nat stood and paced the room to try to soothe her. 'When t'doctor was here he said if I didn't do owt about this bronchitis o' mine I'd be dead in a few years and I should move up there. Winters down here are no good for me, he said.'

'You never mentioned anything to me!' Bright snatched the baby from him and jiggled her.

'I didn't have the heart! You like it so much here. I've been wanting to tell you for months.'

'Rubbish!' yelled Oriel. 'If you think you're going to drag me thousands of miles up there just to get me away from Clive then you've got another think coming.' Grabbing her bag she left the room. 'I'll wait for him outside!'

Vicky had stopped crying now, her wide blue eyes looking from one parent to the other. Bright sat back on the sofa cuddling her. Finally she spoke to Nat, her face bereft of emotion. 'You're not just making it up, are you?'

'You think I'd uproot us just because I don't want our Oriel to marry Mr Personality?' He sounded hurt and then eventually conceded, flopping down beside her and patting her white pleated lap. 'Aye well, it does sound that way, I know – but honestly I've only waited till now 'cause I didn't have the guts to tell you, and t'doctor did say if I stayed here I'd die. And I don't want to, lass. Not now I've got you. Would it be such a wrench? I mean you left England easy enough.'

'It wasn't easy! Anyway, I had no friends to leave there, no one was speaking to me.' She delivered a petulant kiss to Vicky's golden head.

'But you haven't that many friends here.'

'Thanks for nothing!'

He looked wan and tapped his foot at the air for a while. 'We don't have to go if you don't want to.'

She turned to study him seriously. 'Is that what the doctor really said, that you wouldn't live very much longer if you stayed here? Did he honestly?' When her husband nodded, Bright tilted her jaw and said resolutely, 'Well, then, I don't have much choice, do I? Wherever you go I go. But don't expect Oriel to come too.' Oh dear

God, I'm going to miss her, came the thought! What a dreadful end to a perfect afternoon.

Nat damned himself for letting his daughter get too entrenched in the partnership before divulging his intentions. Had he only succeeded in pushing her into a relationship that, if left, might have run its natural course? Would she consider matrimony just to spite him? He asked his wife, 'D'you think it's wise to leave her behind?'

'Wise or no I don't see as we've much choice. She'll be safe enough with Clive. I'll be glad to see her settled.'

'He's not right for –'

'I know, you've said!'

Following a long silence, Bright gave a big sigh and asked, 'Whereabouts in Queensland are we going?'

'Dunno.'

'You can't just head off without a direction.'

'Why not? That's what I did when I first came here. I didn't know Melbourne from Wetwang. I'm not reckoning on going right up top end. We'll just go as far as we have to, to escape winter. Stick a pin in t'map and see where it takes us.'

Bright marvelled at his sense of adventure, but there was no more arguing. She had come to this country to be with Nat, and be with him she would, whatever the cost.

'My father's talking of going to live in Queensland,' Oriel announced to Clive the moment she got into the car and he commented on her angry expression.

His piercing blue orbs displayed concern. 'I don't want you to go.'

'Don't worry, I won't!' Her face showed resolve. 'I've got money, I'll buy my own house down here. I've already got the land – I'll just build on it. He's not bullying me into anything.'

'I wouldn't let him.' Clive tussled with the gearstick

and set off, looking to right and left before pulling out of the drive and heading for the main highway.

Oriel's tone showed she had been exaggerating. 'Oh, he's not really. The reason he's going, so he says, is to cure his bronchitis. But I'm not going. I'm really not. I want to stay here with you.'

Clive appeared highly pleased at this, but there was concern in his next sentence, which was delivered whilst waiting to pull out on to Point Nepean Road. 'You're probably wondering why I haven't taken you to meet my parents when I've met yours.' When she merely smiled he turned thoughtful eyes on the road. 'I don't know how to put this. Dorothy must have told you I was engaged to Laura for a long time?' When he glanced at her she gave a quick nod. Suddenly jealous, she did not care to be reminded. 'Well, Mother got very close to Laura.'

And I'm not going to measure up, thought Oriel, and looked away as he was finally able to negotiate a right turn.

Clive's face was worried, juddering as the car wheels bumped over the tramlines. 'I have to warn you that she's really soft-hearted and I know she'd get fond of you too, I couldn't bear to see her hurt again. So if you're not serious I'd rather you didn't meet her.'

'I am,' came the instant reply.

His hands were steady on the wheel but his face lacked confidence. 'You're not going to get fed up of me after a few months?'

'No!' She clung to his arm. 'You're more likely to get sick of me.'

'No danger of that.' Clive looked relieved and pleased, then laughed. 'I've no earthly idea where I'm going, I got so preoccupied.' When Oriel gave fond instructions for him to keep driving, for any journey was pleasant in his company, he added, 'I'd better just pull into this garage and fill up then.'

Whilst the car was taking sup from the bowser Oriel

moved away to avoid the unpleasant odour of motor spirit. Clive waited by the car. Returning his warm smile, she was struck by an overwhelming compulsion to utter words which she had never uttered to Errol, and once they were on the move again told him, 'I love you.'

He looked abashed and changed gear. 'You don't have to go that far. You've only known me a month.'

She was deeply wounded, but tried not to show it. How could he be so caring of his mother's feelings and disregard her own?

'I think it's a bit early for us to be talking in those terms,' he added.

What a paradox he was, thought Oriel. On one hand demanding her commitment, but unwilling to reciprocate. Knowing how much he had been hurt by his fiancée's rejection she forgave him, though she was quiet for a time, head nodding as the car tyres encountered a bumpy patch.

'You see, I'm worried things are moving too quickly, that we might be seeing too much of each other,' explained Clive after a while. 'I don't want you to get fed up of me like she did. So, I've been thinking we might cut down the nights when we meet and see more of our friends.' He kept his eyes on the road. 'It's not a good idea to lose touch with them. That happened to me when I was engaged to Laura. When we split up I was left twiddling my thumbs, all my mates had their own interests. Some of them thought I was just using them when I had nothing better to do.'

Even though there was sense in his words Oriel was bitterly disappointed. It seemed to her as if Clive had been drawing her in just to shove her away. 'I've no one I really want to go out with but I suppose I could tag along with Dot's friends next time they go dancing.'

His face dropped and he ceased to concentrate on the road, almost running into a cyclist. 'Dancing? You mean with other men?'

Confronted by this air of jealousy, she said appeasingly, 'I can just dance with one of the girls.'

'Oh, don't let me stop you enjoying yourself! But I was thinking more along the lines of you going round to Dorothy's to keep her company.'

Wanting to please him, she delivered an amicable shrug.

'Tell you what.' He took one hand from the steering wheel and patted her. 'We could arrange to see each other, say, Tuesday and Thursday nights and Saturday afternoon and night.'

'All right.' Regarding this as yet another rejection, she could barely speak for fear of crying but tried to issue the words cheerfully and smiled as Clive put his foot down, accelerating the car towards heaven knew where.

There was even worse to come on Saturday when Clive told her, 'I won't be able to see you next week, I've been asked to go camping with Eddie and Phil. I've managed to get a week off. You don't mind, do you?'

What could Oriel say but no? When she spent the following week alone without giving explanation, Bright was worried and after asking roundabout questions discovered the truth.

'He's just gone on holiday with two pals,' divulged her daughter matter-of-factly. 'He'll be back on Saturday.'

'Holiday, with two blokes?' scoffed Nat. 'If I'd just met a young lass I wouldn't be wasting me time with blokes.'

'He'd already arranged it before we met. Besides, we don't want to spend every hour of the day in each other's pockets.'

It was a miserable week for Oriel, a week in which she wondered just how Clive felt about her. After all she had confided in him, would he be like Errol and not return?

However, he did return, blue-eyed and tanned from his camping trip to Lorne. Overjoyed that he was back, Oriel hung on his every word as he told her all about it, wishing her parents weren't there. Bright did her best to get Nat off to bed but he was having none of it and Clive was forced to leave at eleven, for his parents always worried if he were out late in the car. Bitterly disappointed, Oriel followed him outside to the verandah, closing the outer door behind them.

'I love you,' said Clive.

It was so totally unexpected that Oriel responded with a simple, 'Oh!'

'I didn't really enjoy the holiday. From the very first day I realized I'd rather be with you. I missed you.' He took her in his arms and kissed her fiercely.

Responding, Oriel decided she had never felt so wanted.

He drew away, laughing. 'Eddie forgot to bring his tent so I had to let him sleep with me. I'd rather it had been you.'

Oriel laughed, 'Me too,' and she pressed herself close to him. 'I wish you could stay with me tonight. Oh, do we have to wait till Tuesday before we see each other again?'

Clive shook his head. 'I've just been daft, wanting to spend time with my pals. I've spent enough time with them this week to know that one day out of every seven is quite enough, thank you. If you're not doing anything special tomorrow d'you want to come and meet my parents and have tea with us?'

The question took her by surprise. 'Isn't that a bit short notice for your mother?'

'No, she's always ready for unexpected guests. Besides, she's been nagging me to invite you,' he confessed. 'She's dying to meet you. So is Gran.'

Oriel felt like some exhibit as she entered the Widdowes household, a much smaller residence than her own with old-fashioned trappings. Eight faces turned towards her, seven of them smiling, one remaining blank. Clive introduced her to his parents, George and Daphne; Mrs

Widdowes, his grandmother; Aunt Rose, his father's sister come to visit; his two sisters and their boyfriends who, it turned out, were brothers from the north-eastern suburb of Clifton Hill. Mr and Mrs Widdowes appeared to be a good fifteen years older than Oriel's parents, neither having any outstanding feature except friendliness. Under their cosy patronage she began to feel more at ease, but was soon once again to be put off balance by the aura of dislike that emanated from one of Clive's sisters, Thora, a deceptively mousy creature, and after their initial introduction Oriel took the retaliatory measure of ignoring her. Sister Mabel, though, was welcome personified, as was Mrs Widdowes, who could not do enough for Oriel, giving her the most comfortable chair, fending off silly questions from the old lady and for ever enquiring, over the tea table, if she had enough to eat. Indeed, with the exception of Thora, this seemed a warm, closely knit family.

Clive's grandmother was very attentive throughout the meal, seeking to offer, 'More tea, Laura?'

'It's Oriel, Mother,' corrected Daphne. 'I'm sorry, dear.'

'That's all right.' Oriel kept her polite smile whilst inwardly annoyed. 'No, I've had enough, thank you. It was smashing.'

Now that the excellent meal had been consumed, George Widdowes pushed back his chair and sat like a monarch holding court in his blue serge suit and gold watch chain. 'So, what does your father do, Oriel?'

She had anticipated this question and had rehearsed what to say. 'He deals in textiles, mainly.'

'And do you have a job?' George knew this already for his son had told him all about Oriel, but it helped to break the ice.

'Yes, I look after the family business accounts.'

'Lucky you! I wish my father could find a little job for me to save me going out to work.' The tone of Thora's voice was pleasant enough but Oriel took it as an insult.

Clive saw the look on her face, knew that she was too well brought up to return the rudeness of her host's daughter. 'Oriel's father employs her because she's good at her work. She once ran the business on her own while he was away.'

Thora raised an eyebrow which could have conveyed admiration or contempt. Sensitive to criticism, Oriel interpreted it as the latter, but gave Clive's sister the benefit of the doubt and asked in friendly manner, 'What d'you do, Thora?'

'Oh, I'm just a humble secretary.' She smiled at her fiancé.

'Well, that's what I am really,' conceded Oriel.

Thora laughed. 'Not to my brother. He sees you as some kind of magnate.'

'Magnet?' Grandmother had misheard.

George and Daphne Widdowes chuckled at each other. 'Yes, she is very attractive,' grinned Clive's father. 'He's picked a good un there.'

Oriel blushed with pleasure and smoothed her black shingle self-consciously.

'Robert and I are getting married next month,' said the other sister, Mabel, to whom Oriel had taken a liking. 'Would you like to come?'

'Thank you. I'd love to.'

'Thora's getting married the following week,' said Daphne. 'We thought a double wedding might be nice – two brothers marrying two sisters – but she wanted the day to herself.'

Thora did not like the implication that she was selfish. 'It would've been stupid. Mabel has different taste to me.'

'You mean no taste at all.' It was evident the sisters did not get on. Oriel wondered, therefore, how they had come to meet brothers, and was not surprised to learn that this had been sheer coincidence.

Oriel gave a little laugh and attempted to make greater

contribution to the discussion. 'Well, I trust both your weddings will run more smoothly than my friend Dorothy's. She wasn't to know when she arranged it that it fell on the day of the VFL Grand Final, and the men were all behaving like petulant children because they couldn't attend. Can you imagine anything more childish than spoiling someone's wedding over a silly thing like football?' Noticing the plummet in temperature, the uncomfortable laughs from Rose and Daphne and the glowers from some of the menfolk, she dropped her gaze to the floor in embarrassment and twiddled a strand of hair.

'Clive tells us your parents are going to live in Queensland.' Aunt Rose hurriedly changed the subject. 'Whereabouts?'

'Bundaberg.' Oriel was still playing with her hair.

'Never heard of it. What's there?' asked Rose.

'Bert Hinkler.' Everyone looked at George. 'You know! That young aviator chap. He's from there.' He turned to Oriel with a smile. 'Your dad isn't thinking of taking up flying, is he?'

She laughed. 'I doubt it. He just stuck a pin in the map and that's where it landed.'

'That's a bit of a silly thing to do, isn't it?' opined Rose.

'No sillier than flying,' retorted George. 'If we were meant to have wings God would've given us them.'

Clive's mother, realizing that his sweetheart was probably exhausted by being interrogated, deftly steered the conversation round to family matters. Oriel did not know any of the members of whom Daphne and Aunt Rose spoke, but smiled politely as they included her in the dialogue, though dialogue was rather a misnomer. When Aunt Rose launched into speech it was difficult for anyone else to get a word in edgeways. Oriel herself could be garrulous in familiar company but amongst these strangers this trait receded. It would have been impossible for her to compete with Aunt Rose anyway. She glanced at a movement, caught Daphne making facial contortions behind Rose's back, and averted her face to enjoy a private smile with Clive.

'Well, d'you like my mum?' he asked as he drove her home later. Oriel said that she did. 'Yes, she's nice, isn't she?' He smiled to show he was very close to his mother. 'Everybody likes Mum. I'm sorry about Gran getting your name mixed up. She's old, she didn't mean anything by it, she likes you.'

'Your sister Thora doesn't.'

Clive made a joke of it. 'Well, your father doesn't like me so that makes us even.' There was the slightest hint of pique to his humour.

Oriel was upset that he had been hurt by her father's attitude. 'You're wrong. If he really doesn't like anyone he never talks to them at all. It's just that, well, fathers never approve of the men their daughters choose.'

'Neither do sisters. Don't worry about Thora, she just doesn't want to see me hurt again. D'you think that's why he intends you should go to Queensland, to get you away from me?'

'No! If that was his intention it hasn't worked. I've told you, I'm not going.' She suddenly remembered something. 'Oh, and what on earth did I say wrong about Dorothy's wedding?'

He laughed. 'It wasn't the wedding it was the mention of footy. You broke the golden rule of never discussing religion. My sisters' fiancés are bitter rivals. Rob barracks for Collingwood and Bill supports Carlton. There's been hell on over the seating arrangements at the weddings, trying to keep them apart.'

Oriel remembered that the two men had been seated at opposite sides of the room this afternoon. 'But I thought they were brothers?'

'You never believed that old chestnut about blood being thicker than water, did you?' laughed Clive. 'Their mother almost has to divide the house to keep them from each other's throats. The very mention gets them going – it's a wonder you didn't get them to blows this afternoon.'

Only since Dorothy's wedding had Oriel begun to realize how widespread was this fanaticism. She sighed and wondered how much else there was to learn.

When they reached home she invited Clive in but he hesitated by the front porch, then pulled her out of the beam of the hurricane lamp and kissed her. 'Shall we get married?'

Oriel gasped and said, 'Rather!'

Clive uttered an enthusiastic exclamation and gave her a smacking kiss. 'I suppose I'd better do it properly and ask your dad for your hand. Will they still be up?' When Oriel said she thought so he laughed nervously. 'I'm a bit scared. Can I leave it till tomorrow?'

She replied that of course he could. Receiving a more tender good-night kiss she waved him off, then, trying to withhold her excitement, went indoors.

After greeting both her parents she asked casually of her father, 'Did you mean it about going to Queensland?'

Nat looked up from the hearth and eyed her with interest. 'Aye, we've talked the matter over and we've decided to sell up here, houses, warehouse, everything. I never expected I'd have it to do twice in two years. I'm sorry, it'll mean you're going to lose your job –'

'That won't matter,' said a pink-cheeked Oriel. 'I won't need it. I'm getting married.'

Bright squealed and went to hug her daughter, who responded with delighted laughter. Nat was less effusive but tried to smile. Whilst he lacked confidence in this match he reasoned that it was not as if Clive were an axe murderer and he was obviously fond of Oriel. It was futile to resist once she had made up her mind. 'I wish you both well.' It was said with warmth.

Pleased at this softening, Oriel herself adopted a conciliatory tone, just in case her father might have taken some offence at not being consulted. 'Clive's coming to ask officially tomorrow. He needs to bolster his courage before he faces you. But I couldn't keep it a secret.' Her eyes shone. 'I wonder if Dorothy will still be up?'

'Oh, no don't disturb her in her condition,' cautioned her mother.

Her father was pondering his move to Queensland, envisaging the painful separation ahead. 'Will you be getting wed before we go?'

'Have you heard him? Of course she will!' chaffed Bright. 'You don't think we're missing our own daughter's wedding?'

After a celebratory glass of sherry, all went off to bed. Too excited to sleep Oriel lay awake for hours planning her great day, what sort of dress she would wear, the flowers for her bouquet. But into all this frivolity crept a sombre note. The more she thought of it the more she was riven with guilt over her intimacy with Errol. On their wedding night, would Clive be able to detect that there had been another man before him? If he could and she had not said anything . . .

She could tell no one, not even Dorothy, for her friend had always condemned such loose behaviour. The thought of whether to confess or not nagged at her mind for days, making her irritable and abstracted. Even whilst she was discussing wedding plans with her intended it became obvious to Clive that there was some underlying problem and eventually he begged her to tell him what was wrong. 'There should be no secrets between a man and his wife – or at least we soon will be.' Everyone had been delighted at the news of their whirlwind engagement.

'That's just it,' stuttered Oriel.

He got the wrong idea and his warm coaxing expression turned to one of dismay. 'You've changed your mind.'

'No! I'm just . . . frightened.' She looked pleadingly into his eyes, so kind, so concerned, so loving. She must risk it or never be at peace. 'You might not want me after I tell you but I have to because I'd always feel guilty about it if I didn't. When we met we'd both been let down by people. I used to know this boy called Errol –'

'Don't think that's the only reason I asked you to marry me! Even if Laura walked in that door –'

'I know, and I love you too, that isn't what I mean.' She anguished but finally came right out with it. 'I was intimate with Errol.'

A mixture of emotions flashed across Clive's boyish features. He dropped his hold on her and turned away, looking out over the dark tortuous outlines of the gum-trees. Moths performed a frantic flight around the porchlight and only the chirruping of crickets broke the heavy, eucalyptus-perfumed silence.

'It only happened once.'

He nodded and kept his face averted.

'I wish it had been you,' donated Oriel in a small voice.

'Ah well, it wasn't.' The nastiness was veiled in self-pity, intense jealousy.

She was aching. 'Did you and Laura . . . ?'

He blushed and seemed annoyed that she had even asked. 'That's different, we were engaged to be married.'

'I thought I was going to be married!'

'The bastard,' muttered Clive, but Oriel could not help feeling that he saw Errol's crime against himself rather than her.

She waited for his decision, envisioning herself having to tell her parents that Clive had changed his mind about marrying her – and worst of all the reason.

'I still love you.' Hesitantly, he took her in his arms again, his eyes piercing. 'I hate him, but I love you.'

She swallowed. 'And d'you still want to marry me?'

He nodded, and a relieved Oriel broke down and wept against his chest, hoping that it would never be mentioned again. But something in the tenseness of his body told her that it would always be there between them.

12

Before a date could be set for matrimony, it was essential that a house be erected on the land that Oriel had bought upon first arriving in Melbourne, and if her father was to escape to Queensland before another winter set in this gave the prospective bricklayer only four months. With a building boom in progress, there was a dearth of candidates, but eventually they found a man who, after calculations, informed them that he could provide a single-storey brick residence by autumn and so the wedding was arranged for Empire Day in May, granting Nat sufficient time to escape another maybe fatal bout of bronchitis.

Even so, there was a tremendous sense of rush about the weeks following Clive's proposal. Nat tried to coax his daughter into taking over the farmhouse and so kill two birds with one stone – he would not have to go to the trouble of finding a buyer, nor would she have to worry about having a home built. But Oriel, independent as ever, insisted that she start her married life in a brand-new house with modern amenities.

'Let her do it!' Bright sighed when he tried to enlist her help. 'She wants to be able to show that sister of Clive's how to do things.' She herself had not met Thora but had heard all about her and hated her almost as much as Oriel did. Thora sounded a thorough snob and her own recent wedding had been a display of this with all kinds of pretentious accessories, though again Bright only had her daughter's word for it. At least the other one, Mabel, sounded decent and so did Clive's parents, which was a relief when Bright was leaving her daughter to their mercies.

With such lack of co-operation from his wife and daughter, Nat had been faced with a great deal of work, having three houses to sell and a business to wind up. But these were prosperous times and he did not have far to go to find a buyer. Within no time at all he had sold the land around his farmhouse for development, but in a rare show of sentimentality retained the garden that he and Bright had created, selling this and the house to a couple who were willing to pay a great deal more than he had done. Over the two years since they had arrived they had seen the farmland around Brighton shrink and housing was taking over the paddocks. The Englishness that had helped them to feel at home was quickly being eroded by American-type bungalows. Even a few of the Chinese gardeners had been persuaded to sell up, such were the profits being made. Nat hoped to make similar investments in Queensland.

Though Bright did not share his enthusiasm, she did her best not to mope, especially today on this late summer's afternoon, when she and Nat had been invited for tea at the future in-laws. Dressed in an ivory silk frock, she put the finishing touches to her hair and stood to attention for her husband. 'There, how do I look?'

'Rotten – well, what do you expect me to say?'

'How long have we been married?' scolded his wife, under the gaze of her younger daughter, who sat on the bed watching them dress. 'Not two and a half years. What happened to all those compliments?' Jocular smile fading, she projected her mind to their daughter's coming nuptials and sighed as she lifted Vicky and pulled her frilly dress to order. 'Oh God, this wedding's going to be awful. All I keep thinking about is saying goodbye.' Her eyes misted over and she hugged her small child.

'You're making me feel really good.' Nat gave a last-minute inspection of his reflection.

'I didn't mean to!' She sniffed and tried not to cry.

'Wedding's weeks away – we haven't even met t'in-laws yet.' Though he made light of it he too was feeling the wrench. 'And at this rate we're not going to. Where's Lillian Gish?' He went to call Oriel and, all together, they left for the Widdoweses' residence.

George and Daphne, conversant with Oriel's origins, were intrigued to meet the scarlet woman who had borne her. George was particularly attentive, taking Bright's jacket and ushering her to a comfortable chair. Noting the contrast between the two sets of parents – hers rather youthful and stylish, his old-fashioned – Oriel was nervous, knowing how unsociable her father could be if he did not take to someone.

Following introductions and a brief exchange of words with little Victoria, George Widdowes asked in his cheerful manner, 'So, how long've you been here now? Two years, is it?' He received a nod. 'You fought in the war, I suppose?' A shake of head from Nat. 'No? Reserved occupation then?' Another negative response. George caught a hint that Oriel was uncomfortable and rubbed his blue serged knees. 'Oh well, you managed to avoid it somehow. Good luck to you, I say. I had to come all this way to escape it. I make no bones about it, I saw it coming and I wasn't going to let our Clive get mixed up in it. From what I read in the papers I might even have been called up meself if we'd stayed – at my age! I'm not saying I wouldn't have defended England if she'd been attacked but I wasn't fighting the Frenchies' war.' He shook his head. 'Never get involved in somebody else's business, that's my motto and that's what I've told our Clive.'

When Nat merely responded with a thoughtful smile, Mrs Widdowes asked as if from habit, 'Would you like a cup of tea, Mr Prince?'

'Can do.' Nat sat down in the chair that his hostess had indicated.

Though knowing this was just her husband's way and

he did not intend to be rude, Bright felt embarrassed by his lack of manners and so was overzealous to compensate. 'Oh, that would be lovely!' She bounced Vicky on her knee as much from agitation as to keep the child from wriggling off her lap.

George Widdowes, similarly eager to please, asked Nat, 'Maybe you'd prefer a stronger drink?' And when his guest showed interest he cried, 'Oh well then! Come out here and tell me what you reckon to this 'ere parsnip wine I've made. Away, Clive.' His son followed them out.

Oriel took charge of her sister to allow Bright to drink her tea in comfort, dragging her by the arm with little affection to the gesture. Upon being told that Dorothy would be unable to be matron of honour due to her girth, her mother had suggested that Vicky would make an enchanting flowergirl and of course Oriel could not reject the child, but there remained no sense of kinship in her heart. Vicky was the only one Oriel would not miss when the family went to Queensland.

Daphne gave the little girl a glass of milk then asked, 'Do you take sugar, Mrs Prince?'

'No thank you – and please call me Bright.' When the other commented on this being an unusual name she laughed. 'Actually I was supposed to be called Bridget but my father spelled it wrongly on a census form and everyone liked it so Bright it became.'

'It was a man's name originally,' said Daphne knowledgeably, handing over the cup of tea. 'I had a great uncle of the same name.'

'So I'm not unique after all.' Bright smiled politely over her cup, giving a sideways look at Oriel.

'Have you managed to find a buyer for your house?'

Bright said the deal was all but signed. 'Yes, and the ones in Fitzroy too.'

'Oh, you've got property then?'

'Well, yes – but nothing grand.' Bright wondered why she should feel self-conscious at being thought of as a woman of property. 'The tenants are safe.' She glanced at Oriel, who had insisted that this be taken into account. 'The man who's buying the houses says he was going to rent them out anyway, so that's all right. Nat's winding up his business affairs nicely as well so by the time the wedding comes we should be able to relax – thank goodness!'

'We seem to have had nothing but weddings lately,' smiled Daphne, picking up her own flowery cup and saucer. 'First Mabel, then Thora and now Clive. You're lucky you've got a big gap between your two. You'll have a few more years to save up for that one's wedding.' She looked fondly at the little girl who had managed to wriggle to the floor and now stood playing with the fringing on the chenille tablecloth. 'Don't you mind that Oriel's chosen to get married in our parish?'

'Well, I would've liked to see her married at St James but –'

'You're Roman Catholics, then?' Daphne sipped her tea but it was apparent this had come as a bit of a shock.

'Well, I am.' Bright glanced again at her daughter. They had had a bit of an altercation over this but it was reconciled now. 'It doesn't seem to interest anyone else in the family. If Oriel wants to get married at Clive's church it's not really anything to do with me. I married out of the faith myself. I'm sure my mother would turn in her grave.'

Daphne smiled but veered on to another topic until the teacups were empty, when she said, 'I hope George isn't filling your husband too full of his wine. I know it's home-made but it can be very potent. I hear you like gardening, Bright. Come out and see mine and we can look for the men at the same time.'

Taking hold of infant fingers Daphne led her guests outside and found Nat and George, glassy-eyed, in the shed. Clive was nowhere to be seen. Still holding on to Vicky, Daphne ushered Nat from the shed. 'Your wife's going to look at the garden, Mr Prince, would you like to come?' And when Nat was out of earshot she hissed at her husband, 'He looks kettled! You must've been pouring it down his neck.'

'I had to!' whispered George. 'He just sat there saying nowt, it was embarrassing. We had to have something to do. Lad was right when he said her father was hard-going.'

'Tut! I've just found out they're Catholics as well. I could kill our Clive for not telling me. Where is he? Good job I didn't invite Rose, we'd never have heard the last of it. It was bad enough having to explain why Oriel had a different name. We'll have to make up some story for the rest of the family.' Beholding her son coming from the lavatory she crooked a little hand to summon him.

Nat was weaving his way around the garden after his wife, who occasionally bent over a plant to inspect and sniff. Oriel, seeing that her father's eyes were rather glazed, took his arm to keep him on course.

Nat had made no great play of examining the Widdoweses' modest home though it was evident he had when he leaned towards her and asked confidentially, 'How much money has Clive got?'

She was astounded. 'I don't know!' She did, but it was none of her father's business.

'Don't you think it's about time you found out?'

'I'm not marrying him for his money.' Oriel looked round to see if they'd been overheard.

'No, but it's best to know before you're wed. It wouldn't do if you were the one with all the brass.'

She gasped. 'Was that a consideration when you married Mother?'

'That's different. I wasn't bothered that your mother had nowt.'

'It's not different.' Oriel spoke through her teeth. 'I couldn't give a fig how much Clive has, I'm not marrying him for his money. Everything I have is his. You judge everyone by how much they're worth.'

Nat saw that he had injected deep hurt and reacted awkwardly. 'Nay, I didn't mean owt untoward. I want you to be happy, that's all.'

'I will be!' Prickling with indignation, she left him and went to catch up with her mother, who was admiring the horticulture.

'Look at these kangaroo paws, they're much bigger than mine. I wonder if she feeds them?'

The image of Daniel sprawled in a clump of kangaroo paws jumped into Oriel's mind.

Bright glanced up, saw the sulky mien and asked, 'What's your father done now?'

'He asked me how much Clive was worth!'

Her mother sighed, left Oriel where she stood, arms crossed in an attitude of resentment, and went to remonstrate with her husband.

Nat huffed and pretended to examine the garden. 'She got the wrong end of t'stick as usual.'

'Even so, it's not the sort of question you put to a girl who's in love.'

'Maybe not,' he accepted grudgingly, and offered no more in his defence for it was no use arguing with Bright where her daughter was concerned.

Clive returned to find his fiancée sulking and enquired what was wrong.

'Oh, it's just my father,' she told him. 'I'm sure your parents must think he's the most unsociable man they've ever met.'

Privately Clive agreed, but he laughed. 'Why don't we go out and leave them to it? I'm sure there're better things to do with our time.'

She did not need to see the gleam in his eye to know what he meant. Since her confession about Errol, Clive had obviously considered that she should sleep with him too and now that she was engaged Oriel felt she must.

Although she trusted him implicitly and knew enough now to avoid pregnancy, there was still the fear that he might leave her – leave her if she did sleep with him and leave her if she didn't. It could never be called a grand passion, but she found pleasure in the physical side of their relationship, and now she grinned back at him to show she was in agreement.

'We're just going to eat,' objected Daphne as her son voiced his intention to leave.

Replying that he and Oriel would slake their hunger elsewhere, Clive gave his fiancée a sly wink and went to fetch his car.

When Bright had said goodbye to her daughter and had gone inside with the others, Nat sidled up to Oriel in an attitude of appeasement, handing her a slip of paper as if it were a secret document. 'Put that in your bag.'

She read the cheque. 'Two hundred –'

'Ssh! Just put it away.' He looked uncomfortable. 'It's a wedding present.'

'But you and Mother have already bought us a vacuum cleaner!'

Nat's hand performed a semaphore of disparagement, his face warding off her effusive thanks, and as Clive drove up in the car he strode inside.

Upon being shown the cheque, Oriel's fiancé was sparing with his enthusiasm. 'Doesn't he think I can look after you or something?' Her smile faded and she pointed out that it was a wedding present. He corrected her as he opened the car door. 'The cheque's made out to you.'

Oriel sought to soothe his hurt pride. 'Oh, but that's nothing! It's meant for both of us, he said.' She climbed into the seat, dealt Clive a kiss to bolster his self-esteem, and after some cajolery managed to restore his good mood before they drove away.

Much later, in the dark quietude of the bush, the engaged couple enjoyed a rushed and furtive coupling. Afterwards they reclined in the car, sharing Clive's last cigarette.

Resting her neck against the leather back of the seat, Oriel gazed up at the night sky and pondered dreamily. 'Sometimes, when you read in the paper about all the awful things that happen, you wonder if God really exists. Then you come out to a place like this, and you look up at all those stars and it makes you feel so . . . I suppose spiritual's the word I'm looking for. I feel as if God's so close that I'm holding His hand.'

Clive's hand felt its way through the darkness to pat her thigh. 'I know we're different religions, but I wouldn't object to you going to your own church, you know.'

She felt a rude dampening of spirits, as if he had let her down. What had church to do with what she was saying? She experienced a flash of anger at his stupidity. How frustrating and embarrassing to divulge one's innermost thoughts to have them completely miscon-strued.

When she sighed, Clive turned to examine her, wonder-ing what he had said. Not knowing how else to right things he ground out the butt of his cigarette, leaned over and kissed her.

'I think our mothers liked each other,' came his quiet opinion when their lips parted. 'I'm not sure about the dads.'

Oriel agreed that Nat was a hard man to fathom. She uttered a sound of wonderment. 'To think that he'll be giving me away in a few months' time.'

Again he misinterpreted. 'Well, it might be breaching etiquette but I'm sure no one would blame you if you didn't want him to do it.'

She turned on him. 'Why wouldn't I want him to do it? He's my father – I love him!'

He was utterly confused. 'Sorry, it's just that you keep going on about hating him.' She often spoke of her childhood.

'I said I used to hate him! That was years ago.' Oriel

was exasperated. Clive wasn't a stupid man, and whilst not particularly talented, he was sensitive and thoughtful. Why then could he not grasp the simplest concept? She lifted her wristwatch right up to her face, could not see what time it was but said tersely, 'Come on, we'd better go. It's late.'

By the time they arrived home she had forgiven Clive's misunderstanding. It was wrong of her to decry him for one small fault, and God knew she had plenty of faults herself. He might not be the soul mate she had yearned for, but his kindness and his gentleness and his love was a good enough basis for any marriage.

On the morning of her wedding, however, Oriel awoke to a feeling of apprehension when such episodes came back to haunt her. What if she had made a mistake? What if there were more to marriage than each could provide? He had offered her plenty of chances to withdraw at the beginning of their relationship – why had she not taken them? Whatever her qualms, there could be no backing out at this late stage. It was inconceivable that she would hurt him thus.

But once the ceremony was over, Oriel felt a great wave of relief and elation. When the groom smiled back happily at her as they came down the aisle she knew that everything would be fine. The celebration in the church hall afterwards was an enjoyable occasion, the guests being mostly Clive's relations, for the only family the bride possessed was her parents and sister. Growing up as she had without aunts and uncles and cousins, Oriel found it delightful to be part of such a large clan – even if it did include Thora. That was not quite fair. Thora had done her best to be sociable today – even adding her compliment to the dozens of others Oriel had received on her wedding dress. Perhaps now that she had seen Oriel had no intention of jilting her brother as had Laura, she would be friendlier. The day had been perfect. With

Rob and Bill at separate ends of the table there were no rows about football or anything else.

'What a pity Mel and her husband couldn't come,' said Bright to her daughter, taking a rest from entertaining the guests. 'She would have really enjoyed this dancing.' On receipt of the invitation Melinda had written back to say she was too big with child now and dared not make the trip.

Oriel was smitten with an intense dart of melancholy. Driving away the image of Melinda's husband, she fingered her veil and murmured, 'I suppose it's just as well they're not here. She and Dot aren't the best of pals. There might've been a scrap and I wouldn't want blood all over this dress.' She smiled across the room at Dorothy who, having given birth a few weeks earlier than expected, had been able to attend and had brought along her lace-bedecked son, tiny but perfectly healthy. Then her eyes fell on Clive's father, who was gesturing at her. 'Sorry, I'm being summoned to dance with George.' However warm the relationship, she could not bring herself to call Clive's parents Mother and Father. To her there was only one Mother and Father . . . and in a few hours' time she would be parted from them. She hurried off before they saw the mist in her eyes.

'Somebody else is enjoying t'dancing an' all.' Nat looked pointedly at Mrs Ratcliffe. 'Look at the skirt on it, for God's sake. You can almost see her drawers – and her a grandmother! Your grandma never looked like that.'

Bright laughed tearfully at the thought of Granny Maguire in her little black bonnet.

Yet, there was more reason for her watery eyes than this memory. Their house had been handed to its new owner, the furniture put into storage until a forwarding address had been found and for the last couple of days she and Nat had been staying in an hotel. The parting she had dreaded was here at last. Every time she thought about Oriel leaving for her honeymoon she almost choked with emotion, for she knew that when her daughter returned she herself would be on her way to Queensland and who knew when they would next meet?

Oriel was trying her best not to think of this as she danced first with George then with various admiring uncles before Mabel came to relieve her.

'Is it all right if a sister-in-law gets a look in? These men! Come and sit down, you must be exhausted.' With Oriel at her side a fussy Mabel pulled the bride's veil into order, then said, 'Now, when you come back off honeymoon – I don't mean straight away, I know there'll be things you want to do in the house – but when you feel ready, you'll have to come round one afternoon, to one of my "at homes" as my dear sister calls it.' She chuckled at Thora's attempts to invade the middle-classes. 'She can't really afford that house in Prahran, you know.'

Oriel shared the joke. 'I don't suppose I'll receive such an invitation from her.'

'If you do it'll be something more than I've had.' Mabel's round face creased in jollity. 'You think she doesn't like you? She can't stand me! I'll never forget her face when she found out Bill was my Robert's brother. She makes up for that by letting everybody know Bill's got the better job. It takes her all her time to own up to having Mum and Dad as parents. She thinks we're really common! God knows how Clive won her affection – oh, I shouldn't say that about your husband! He'd win any-body's heart, he's a lovely brother. And it's been a lovely wedding.'

'Thanks – for your present too.'

'Oh, it wasn't much. Well, nothing would be when compared to Thora's.' Mabel's sister had outdone every-body with her own expensive gift. She turned her face and spoke into the bride's white satined shoulder. 'Don't look now but her ladyship's coming over.'

Oriel smiled up at Thora's approach. The smile was

returned but it did not extend to Thora's eyes – though few had ever witnessed any spontaneous sparkle.

'I won't keep you, Oriel, I can see you're being entertained. I just want to say that it's been a lovely afternoon. You must come to one of my at homes some time.'

'Thank you!' Mabel jumped in, beaming, whilst Oriel studied the embroidered cuff of her wedding gown and tried not to laugh.

'I didn't mean you.' Thora kept her attention on the bride. 'And once you get settled in your new home don't hesitate to give me a ring if you need any advice on furnishings.'

Clive wandered up then, smiling at his bride, though it was his sister Thora who took affectionate possession of his arm. 'I don't want to drag you away,' he told Oriel, 'but we should be making a move.'

Her stomach lurched and, unable to look at her mother and father, she merely nodded.

'You're going to miss them, aren't you?' observed Mabel.

'Don't you just love people who state the obvious?' came Thora's sardonic opinion, and for once Oriel had to agree with her.

Mabel tried to make amends. 'But you'll be able to go and visit them.'

'Not every week!' Again Thora belittled her less intelligent sister. 'It would be like travelling from London to Rome. You don't do that every Sunday afternoon. Anyway, she's got Clive now, haven't you?'

Oriel smiled at him and nodded, then took his hand. Delaying the moment of parting for as long as she could, she suggested they both change into their travelling clothes using the small anteroom at the back of the hall. Embroidered satin dress folded carefully away, she wandered around the hall with her groom, shaking hands, kissing cheeks, wondering how she was ever going to keep these tears at bay. After the final group of relatives had been thanked for coming, she murmured to Clive, 'D'you mind if I say my goodbyes in private?'

He understood and made gestures at his wife's parents to follow him and Oriel to the room in which they had just changed. Oriel was rather dismayed to find that Clive remained to share this moment of intimacy. When requesting privacy she had meant to exclude him as well as the guests, but of course he would assume that as her husband he would be included. She stood there awkwardly looking on whilst Clive shook her father's hand and dealt a brief kiss to both her mother's cheek and Vicky's before stepping back to make room for his wife.

Feeling physically sick, Bright could hold back her tears no longer, sobbing noisily as she hugged her elder daughter, patting and squeezing till she thought bones would snap. Nat, holding himself responsible for her distress, hung back in a spirit of wretchedness, gripping the hand of his two-year-old daughter who gazed up at the sobbing women with solemn eyes. But when his wife pulled away to cover her pain with a handkerchief, when Oriel turned her plaintive, tear-stained face towards him, he let go of the tiny hand and launched himself at her in what was more like a physical assault than the show of great affection that it actually symbolized, his palm inflicting resonant thumps to her slender rib cage, squeezing his eyes tightly shut to fight off tears, whilst Clive remained silently in the background.

Quite unable to speak, Oriel finally drew away, dealt a hasty kiss to her sister's beflowered golden head and indicated to Clive that she wished to depart right now. Her eyes remained fixed to the floor in order to avoid her mother's distress as she picked up her bag and hurried ahead of her husband through the congratulatory crush of relatives to the decorated car outside.

Equally desirous of a quick getaway, Nat gave no thought to politeness and made for his own vehicle, unwilling to speak to anyone. Averse to leaving in such rude fashion, Bright reached up to her hat and tugged its veil over her face before going to seek pardon for his haste and exchange sincere thank-yous with the Widdoweses. When the latter glanced in his direction Nat merely raised a cursory finger of acknowledgement as he got into his car, and their eyes soon abandoned this morose man, keener to smile upon the bride and groom as the engine whirred and Clive and his wife climbed aboard.

Nursing an aching heart, Oriel could barely look at her parents again, except to issue a falsely cheerful wave as the car chugged past them. Bereft, her mother and father merely nodded and wept and sniffed, and waved their last goodbyes.

13

The bride and groom spent their honeymoon amongst the fern valleys and lakes of Gippsland. Now that the ordeal of parting with her mother was over Oriel felt somewhat relieved and able to embark on married life with gusto. The land in North Brighton that had been a mere investment was now the grounds of a Queen Anne-style bungalow with terracotta gables and fretwork fringes. It had a central hall from which branched spacious rooms that must be decorated and furnished. It may have been Oriel's inheritance that paid for all these things, for Clive had minimal savings, but once acquired they were put into joint possession along with the remainder of her money. Clive had further to travel to work now, but was happy to fit in with his wife's plans. It was he alone who earned their living, for the departure of Oriel's parents meant the end of her job as her father's secretary and so she was content to play the housewife and let the man of the house have his self-respect.

Oriel enjoyed caring for her husband, washing and ironing his clothes, cooking his meals, and cuddling up to him in bed on the winter nights. In return Clive was a good and responsible partner, selecting just the right present for her birthday – buying her gifts even if there were nothing to celebrate – his only vice being to spend Sunday morning drinking with his pals whilst his wife cooked dinner. Oriel did not complain that this extended the hours of solitude she had endured through the week, for she wanted him to be happy and besides she had every evening in which to enjoy his company.

During those first light-hearted months of their marriage they went out frequently – never dancing, for Oriel had given up that pleasure when they had met – but they would go to the cinema, and at other times to visit family and friends. Apart from Dorothy these were all acquaintances of Clive's – not that they were unpleasant to Oriel, they were most of them extremely amiable. But she began to suspect that she alone was not enough for the gregarious Clive, that he needed more companionship than he was granted at home, and so one night she put this to the test by asking, 'Could we spend an evening on our own sometime? Not go out anywhere, just stay in and talk?'

He gave a pleasant laugh. 'But you don't talk to me!'

'Yes, I do.' She frowned.

'No, you don't, not really.'

Oriel supposed he was right in one respect – they never indulged in any deep conversation – but after her first intimate disclosures had met with incomprehension she had decided not to open her heart again.

Seeing that she looked despondent, he told her fondly, 'It's not that I don't love you. I do. It's just that, well, you know I like to talk and because we're together all the time I suppose we don't have much news to tell each other. That's the only reason I like to go out so much. Anyway, I thought you liked my friends.'

Oriel replied that she did, when in fact she gained little stimulation from them. She, too, craved companionship but the type she desired could not be provided by her husband. However, the fault lay in her, not in him, it must do, for everyone liked him, and Oriel wanted to be a good wife. Hence, for his sake she continued to be dragged around places she would not otherwise have gone.

But then an insidious change occurred. One particular Saturday afternoon Oriel obliged Clive by accepting an invitation to his friends' house for tea. She had not met the friends, Billy and Jean, before and was therefore taken aback when Billy asked Clive to go for a beer and he accepted.

'You girls don't mind if we nick to the pub, d'you? Just for the one.'

So Oriel found herself saddled with Jean, with whom she had absolutely nothing in common and who rambled on all afternoon about her children when she knew very well that Oriel didn't have any.

Had this been an isolated occasion she could have forgiven Clive, but it began to happen quite regularly. After being left in this fashion yet again, Oriel complained to Dorothy on one of her regular visits.

'He's always sloping off and leaving me with some boring woman who harps on about babies all night.'

'Oh, thanks.' Dorothy laughed and patted her own baby's back.

'I didn't mean you! I love coming here, you know that. At least I get a decent conversation, but there hardly seems any point in my going out with Clive if he's going to desert me.'

'I sometimes wish Cuddy would go out more – not that I don't love him.'

In Oriel's opinion this was said rather too quickly but she made no comment.

'He's just a very demanding person to live with.' Dorothy rocked back and forth, more from habit than any attempt to soothe the baby, who was very placid. 'D'you still not want any children?'

Oriel shook her head adamantly. 'Apart from anything else I couldn't stand the pain. I'm a dyed-in-the-wool coward. I haven't even been to the dentist for years.'

'You forget all about it afterwards,' vouched the young mother. She gave a self-mocking chuckle. 'I'm having another one. Yes, already!'

Oriel congratulated her friend but could think of no worse position to be in. 'I'm sure my mother would love a grandchild.'

She went on to tell Dorothy of the letter she had received from her mother shortly after coming back off honeymoon, in which Bright said that they had found a place to settle and were in the process of buying a house. There were pages of detail extolling the virtues of the area and what a wonderful place it was for children, with its animal- and birdlife, which Oriel took to be her mother's way of hinting that perhaps her daughter should start a family.

'But motherhood's not for me,' she finished, then wrung her hands and looked at the floor. 'I'm beginning to think that I'm no use at marriage either. Maybe he's too good for me, Dot. I mean everyone likes Clive – I've never heard a bad word about him – what's wrong with me?' She felt such a failure. 'I know he's right when he complains that I never talk to him and that's why he seeks other company, but I ask you, what's the point in wasting one's breath on someone who could be from another world?'

'But you still love him, don't you?' The dark sloping eyes held anxiety.

'Oh, yes.' Oriel repeated it as if to prove to herself that it were true. 'Yes. But I'm not really happy and I don't know why.'

Perhaps, she thought, it's better if I don't go out with Clive so much, just let him seek the company he desires, then be here for him when he comes home. But when she made this proposal, her husband exclaimed, 'I can't go out on my own!'

'You do on a Sunday.'

'But all the blokes do that! It's different through the week. People'll think I'm neglecting you.'

'No they won't. I don't mind. We can go out together a few evenings but I'm really too tired to go out every night.'

'I'll stay in with you then.' He didn't look too enthusiastic. 'I'd feel too guilty leaving you by yourself.'

For a week or so the arrangement worked satisfactorily, the pair going out one or two evenings and spending the remainder of the week with each other, but in the end Clive simply could not resist the urge to invite company, in the form of a middle-aged bachelor from a neighbouring street, to join them. Clive made friends very easily and Fred, a lonely man, idolized his new pal. When it was mentioned that some alterations needed to be done in the kitchen, Fred was able to reciprocate the hand of friendship by offering to undertake the work.

He would accept no gratuity, saying that the young couple's friendship was enough. If he could have the pleasure of their company from time to time then he was happy.

Things continued quite amicably for a while, with Fred coming round occasionally, and on Sunday after Clive had returned from his grog session he and Oriel would visit his mother and father of whom, in her own parents' absence, she had grown very fond. For the rest of the week Clive would stay in with his wife.

He detested being cooped up in the house, she knew, and she guessed he was only doing so for her sake. When, through a lack of stimulation, he began to fall asleep well before bedtime Oriel recognized that there was no point in this and, with things of her own to do, said he could go out one or two nights on his own if he really wanted to. 'Just because I don't want to go out doesn't mean you can't.'

'But why don't you want to go? Are you ashamed of being seen with me or something?' He sounded peevish.

'Of course not! I just don't feel like going out. But I don't want to stop you enjoying yourself. I don't mind if you go, I really don't.'

'You'll have me thinking you've got somebody else coming round.' He laughed but there was a tinge of insinuation to the remark. 'All right, I'll go if you want to get rid of me.'

The trouble began when Clive's two nights out extended to three and then five, creating a fresh problem for Oriel. Whenever Fred came to call, her husband would be out and she was the one who had to give him a cup of tea and make conversation and apologize to the poor man that Clive was not in yet again. Oriel was annoyed at her husband. It was he who had accepted the man's work for nothing, but she was the one made to feel responsible when Fred's expression showed that he felt he had been used, and he eventually stopped coming.

'I didn't ask him to do all the work,' complained Oriel to Dorothy. 'Clive did. I would've preferred to pay someone to do it. Why then do I feel so humiliated when I see the poor blighter coming down the street and have to cross the road to avoid him even though I know he's seen me? I could kill Clive for making me feel like that. And it doesn't seem to bother him that he's let Fred do all that work for nothing then virtually dumped him. That's what I've noticed about him: he'll see people for six months at a time, then he'll suddenly come home talking about a new lot.' Dorothy said they had not seen much of Clive lately either, forcing Oriel to apologize for him. 'He doesn't appear to have one really good friend like I have you, just loads of acquaintances.' Feeling that she might be complaining too much, she issued a guilty shrug. 'But then if he's happy . . .'

With Clive continuing to rely on these acquaintances to meet his needs, Oriel grew more and more bored and miserable in her marriage. It was of her own making, she realized. She should never have entered matrimony. She wasn't cut out for it. Poor Clive. He was much too good for her. She knew it. Everyone knew it. But if he was everyone's friend why, then, had Oriel become reacquainted with the terrible loneliness that, upon her marriage, she had thought never to see again? Only Dorothy's companionship prevented her from sinking into greater despondency, and the letters from her mother and Melinda – though the latter's correspondence was usually full of grumbles about the hard life Daniel had chosen for them and how Melinda wished she were nearer so she could see Oriel in person. Reading about the dust and the droughts and the plagues of grasshoppers that defied Daniel's best efforts, Oriel had a vivid image of the pioneer, seeing the sweat trickling down his brow as clearly as if he were standing before her.

Overwhelmed by a great inexplicable longing, she wrote a letter of her own, telling Melinda that she too was missing her friend's company and suggesting that perhaps she and Clive could go for a holiday. But months passed and the letter had still not been answered and so the unhappiness of her own life remained.

However, in mid-December amongst the parcels and cards that arrived from Queensland, another letter came. Oriel's heart leaped when she saw that it bore Melinda's writing – perhaps it contained an invitation to visit at Christmas! Already she was laughing at Daniel's jokes – though a glance at the postmark made her frown and she hurried to open the envelope.

'Oh no!' Seated at the breakfast table, she bit her lip and told Clive, 'Their farming venture's collapsed.'

He showed genuine sympathy, but, being forced to leave for work, said she would have to read the rest to him when he came home. He bent to kiss her, receiving only half her attention, then left the house.

Reading on, Oriel learned that Melinda and Daniel, at last considering themselves beaten by the harsh Mallee, had returned to the forested slopes of Melbourne's hinterland and had taken up residence at Yarra Junction to be nearer her family, who lived in a neighbouring stretch of timber country. Daniel had got a job at a sawmill. 'So we'll be a bit nearer now if you and Clive want to visit us,' the letter ended.

Discovering from a map that it was hardly more than forty miles away, Oriel could scarcely contain her delight. Though her responding letter was full of commiserations she wrote of her gladness that her friend was to be within easier access and she could not wait to visit her and Daniel.

Alas, she was to learn from Clive that this must be obliged to wait until the New Year of 1922, for her husband's annual fortnight holiday had already been used up by their honeymoon.

'We could go when you break up for Christmas,' she suggested. It was only a week away. 'I know it'll be a bit rushed but –'

'I think we have enough family to visit then, don't you? We've got Mum and Dad on Christmas Day, then Thora's invited us on Boxing Day, Dorothy and Cuddy – we'd be better waiting a few weeks till I can organize a proper holiday. Tell you what, we'll spend a whole week up there, do some mountain walking. There's a nice hotel at Warburton. It'll do us both good.'

To Oriel, hungry for contact, any wait would be a nightmare, not to mention that she was annoyed with Clive for reminding her that he had a family to visit whilst hers was thousands of miles away. 'Maybe I could go for a quick trip on my own while you're at work,' she suggested.

The look on his face told her otherwise. Clive said he didn't like the idea of her going by herself.

Oriel was about to point out that he went by himself to meet his friends, when he added: 'You might get blokes pestering you on the train – course, you might appreciate that.' He shrugged and tried to sound reasonable. 'But you do what you like.'

Faced with this thinly veiled show of possessiveness, Oriel decided not to force the matter. Feeling her high spirits descending like lead, she replied, 'Oh, it doesn't matter, I can wait until January.'

With Christmas in between there was at least something to look forward to – or so she had hoped. In reality the opening of the presents from her distant parents only served to exacerbate her loneliness, whilst she dreamed of a reunion with the one who was close to her heart.

As the day of her trip grew nearer she became sick and nervous with anticipation, like the child who fears he will get measles on the morning his seaside holiday is due. But at last the day came to pack the car and here she was, driving towards the city and out the other side, heading east, joining the mass weekend exodus from Melbourne in a haze of exhaust fumes, one thought to carry with her all the way – I'm going to see him!

During the forty-mile journey she shared little conversation with the driver of the car, gazing at the undulating scenery but hardly noticing it ... Lilydale ... Seville ... Woori Yallock ... Launching Place – at last they were almost there.

Having agreed to Clive's suggestion that, initially, they drive straight through Yarra Junction and deposit their luggage at the Mountain View Hotel at Warburton, Oriel was forced to satisfy herself with a glimpse of the small but thriving country town where her friends lived. Its roads carved out of a hillside, the buildings were higher on the right than on the left. Railway timber yards flashed past, blacksmiths, farriers, feed merchants, saddle and harness makers, livery stables, their customers in Sunday mode today, tails twitching the bush flies from bay and chestnut flanks, patient Clydesdale, high-stepping mare with her two-wheeled sulky carrying the vicar and his children, lady on a bicycle, her umbrella held aloft against the sun.

Within minutes the town had gone and they were driving through a tortuous stretch of forest, blinking at the intermittent glare of the sun through the trees and coasting the miles to the next small town. Hidden amongst a blanket of trees, trestle bridge spanned forested gorge, the surrounding mountains enlaced by a network of tramways, some wood, others steel, enjoining one timber mill to the next, carrying supplies into the bush and the logs out.

The Wesburn Palais came and went, Millgrove, a post office store and a blacksmith, another stretch of perfumed forest and then at last Warburton.

After lunch at the hotel, Clive suggested that instead of wasting time they make the most of the day by going on a forest walk, and see Melinda and Daniel tomorrow.

But Oriel was eager for a reunion. 'I didn't come to get stuck with a load of tourists, I've come to see Mel. Tell you what, we'll have a picnic made up, then go fetch her and Daniel back here and all go on the walk together.' This agreed, they made the chugging thirty-minute drive back along the forest road to Yarra Junction.

Melinda was as lively as ever, but was embarrassed at Oriel seeing her modest home. 'Look at you in your flash car! All dressed up to go dancing.' Her friend was in a very chic white outfit trimmed with black, and a neat little hat to match. 'I don't know what you must think to us.'

'You both look wonderful.' Oriel kissed her friend, then smiled at Daniel, and had the feeling of being immersed in warm water. 'It's so good to have you back.' An afterthought struck her. 'This is Clive, by the way.'

'I'm only here to carry the luggage.' The remark was issued with a smile but Oriel felt its barb.

Melinda laughed at the joke. 'How yer going, Clive? Meet Dan.' She watched the two men shake hands then, after showing off her little vegetable garden, invited everyone into the weatherboard cottage where two infants played on the rug. 'You know Alice – hasn't she grown? She's nearly three. But you haven't met Angus, have you? He was born around the time of your wedding. You must've been married about eight months now? So, how you enjoying wedded bliss?'

Both smiled and issued little mutterings and gestures that could have meant anything. But Melinda said, 'Yeah, good isn't it?' and linked arms with her own husband.

'What d'you do for a crust, mate?' asked Daniel, his free hand offering the other man a cigarette.

'Oy, I think Oriel smokes too, don't yer?' Melinda instructed her husband as he withdrew the packet.

He apologized and extended the offer to Oriel, who took one with smiling thanks. 'So, where d'you make yer living, Clive?'

'Myers. I've been there nearly seven years.'

Daniel unlinked his arm in order to light their cigarettes and nodded through the eddying smoke. 'Should think that's a safe enough bet. Hang on to it. Reckon you heard about my bit of strife in the back block, did yer?'

Clive looked at the man's wife, whose smile had dimmed. 'Well, er –'

'Ah, don't worry about not wanting to make me look a fool. I've been called it before.' Daniel glanced at Melinda, who put her tongue in her cheek. 'I'm not ashamed to have walked away from it.'

'He never really gave it a chance,' Melinda told Oriel, seeing her husband's failure as her own. 'We hadn't been there two years.'

'However long I'd stayed I would've had Buckley's of making anything out o' that dust bowl. I put some real hard yakker in but it just wasn't to be.'

'We were offered assistance,' said Melinda.

'Yeah, if I'd been prepared to show 'em me grocery lists to justify me need.' The set of his face showed he was not about to suffer that humiliation. 'Anyway, I've borrowed enough – so, I'm back at the sawmill where I should've been all along.'

Melinda gave an embarrassed laugh. 'Don't know what

made him think he could be a cocky anyway. All that money lost.'

Daniel remained firmly patient. 'But we didn't lose the house, did we?'

'For what it's worth.' Melinda turned away from him to explain to their guests. 'Got this bit o' land cheap and we brought the house from the Mallee. Didn't cost us anything, a mate helped us.'

Oriel had gone to the window from where she could view the mountains and the beautiful Yarra Valley where eagles soared. 'You've got a spectacular outlook.'

'Yeah, that's something, I suppose. There's nothing much else to do here – not like when I lived with you and your mum 'n' dad. We had some good times, didn't we? How are they liking it up in a strange country?'

After Oriel had given this information, there was a short pause, then Melinda brought her palms together. 'Righto, I'll get something to eat.'

'No! We've come to take you on a picnic in the forest,' announced her visitor.

Melinda whooped. 'Are we all going in your car? Cripes, I'd better get the kids changed. Er, can I ask what kind o' tucker you've got?' When Oriel told her, she added, 'I'll fetch a few things for the bubs then.' After rushing round collecting a bag of essentials she and Daniel picked up a child each and followed the others beyond the picket fence to the car. 'Can Orrie sit in the back with me?'

'Yes, she can hold this as well.' Cigarette in mouth, Daniel thrust eight-month-old Angus at Oriel, who disposed of her own tab end and accepted him gingerly.

'Orrie doesn't like bubs,' Melinda laughed as her friend remained temporarily hampered. 'Here, Alice can sit between us and I'll take him off your hands.' Planting Alice on the back seat Melinda allowed her immaculately dressed friend to take her place.

'Will it be too draughty for them with the hood down?' asked Clive, ever thoughtful.

'Nah! Tough as dingo pups,' vouched Daniel. 'Come on, Melly, get yer bum in – oh, by the way!' He turned to Oriel. 'Jimmy Magee said I should pass on his regards if I see yer. Told me all about the job you offered him. Thanks for that – even if he did refuse it.'

Oriel noticed Clive's face, knew he wanted to ask who Jimmy Magee was. 'Well, I suppose it was a bit of an insult –'

'No, no, it wasn't that!' Daniel explained. 'He needed a job where he could work on his own, gets a bit funny when he's with other people. Well, you saw him at our wedding, he comes over a bit claustrophobic.'

Oriel nodded. 'He found a job anyway, that's all I was concerned about.'

'Didn't keep it very long though.' Daniel showed a hint of despair. 'Just takes work where he can get it nowadays. Anyway he wanted me to pass on his thanks for your concern for him and the other blokes.'

'My pleasure.' Oriel felt Clive's jealousy. He hated it when she even as much as waved to the soldiers when they drove past the Anzac Hostel. 'Come on then, let's go!'

On the way along the winding dusty road through the forest towards Warburton she sat in the back seat answering Melinda's questions about her domestic affairs, occasionally allowing her eyes to settle on the head of the man in front of her, studying Daniel's tanned neck, the collar of his shirt, his yellow streaked hair fluttering in the draught. When it was her turn to listen she smiled and nodded and took deep inhalations of a breeze laden with eucalyptus, cleansing her senses. By the time they pulled off the road and stopped at the opening to a walking track her brain was purged of any troubles that she might have brought with her.

Spreading their picnic on a flattened rock on the

tranquil bank of Warburton creek, they enjoyed a leisurely half-hour by the gurgling ribbon of water, before entering the forest to wander amongst the filtered sunlight of giant tree ferns. Daniel took the lead, holding Alice's hand, Melinda and the baby behind him. Next in line, Clive reached back to take hold of his wife's hand, but she pointed out, 'The track's too narrow, I'll just walk behind you.' Out of chivalry he took up the rear and so, with him walking behind her, Oriel could pretend that he was not even there. For a time they fell silent, even the children. The air was very still, pierced only by the threatening buzz of an insect, a furtive scuffling in the grass or the peal of a bellbird. Salved by this awesome canopy of green, the soft carpet of the forest floor, the birdsong and the bouquet, she felt a tremendous uplift in her mood.

With infants in tow it was not possible to maintain the trek for long and Daniel suggested they sit down to rest, checking the hollow log and long grass first for snakes. Oriel examined the skewbald bark of the log for dirt and flicked at it reluctantly before sitting down to imbibe the sound of tiny children romping with their father, the creek scrambling over pebbles and the sporadic whiplash call of a bird.

'Hey, Ally!' Melinda called the little girl to her. 'Come and sing your song for Aunt Oriel.'

But Alice seemed reluctant to leave her father, arms around his neck.

'Go on, Ally!' When she refused to move, Daniel changed his expression. 'I can hear a wolf coming. Listen.' And he started to growl and make claws of his fingers. Understanding the game Alice giggled and backed away but not fast enough to escape her father's tickling attack. Screaming with glee she begged him to put her down and promised to do as she was told.

Positioned before the elegantly dressed lady the little girl immediately launched into a well-practised verse, her immature voice wavering occasionally but her blue gaze remaining steady on the woman's face. It was not a particularly sad refrain and Oriel felt foolish that she could not prevent tears from springing to her eyes. When the song came to an abrupt end and the beaming child ran to throw herself upon the lady's lap, Oriel was forced to blink rapidly to clear her vision, then gave Alice a hug, wondering what it was about her that so attracted this small child when she herself had no maternal urges at all.

'She likes you 'cause you're always smiling,' Melinda explained without being asked. Oriel laughed self-consciously.

Daniel agreed and caught his daughter up in a bear hug. 'We'll have to call her Smiler.' Oriel glanced at him to indicate her pleasure but his attention was on Alice.

'He has nicknames for everybody,' said Melinda. 'But I'm not telling you what he calls me.' She grinned and went on to ask her friend for more information about the household appliances she had briefly mentioned before and without wanting to show off, Oriel listed them.

'My oath! I feel really embarrassed at you seeing our place. You must've thought you'd walked into a real humpy.'

'I didn't at all.' Oriel snatched another glance at Daniel, who never seemed to look her in the eye. 'It's a lovely little cottage. You've made it really comfortable.' She hoped it did not sound too patronizing for it was not intended that way.

'Dan's done most of the work.' Melinda smiled at her husband in an attempt to make up for her previous derogatory comments. Daniel returned a look of affection as he hurried to retrieve a venturesome baby from the long grass. It was obvious to Oriel that despite the earlier contretemps they were devoted to each other. How she envied her friend.

Clive spoke. She had forgotten he was even there. 'Anyone want a cigarette?' His offer was accepted. 'I meant to bring the camera but I've left it in the car. Shall we wander back after we've had our fags and take a few snaps?'

Oriel pulled on her cigarette, trying desperately to pretend that she and Daniel were alone. Ash formed, grew to an inch, fell to the ground as she automatically raised and lowered her hand. Eventually, feeling the heat of it against her knuckles, she dropped it to the forest floor.

'You tryin' to fry us alive?' Daniel ground the smouldering tab-end deep into the earth, giving her a look of reproach. But when she offered blushing apology he forgave her with a grin. 'Just don't do it again.'

Grateful for any crumb that he might cast at her, even his rebuke, she smiled and rose, brushed at the seat of her dress and joined the procession back to the car where she posed before the camera alongside Daniel, Melinda and the children.

'Look out – jumping jacks!' Between clicks of the shutter, Daniel grabbed the children and hurried everyone away from the colony of acrobatic ants to a safer spot where a further length of film was exposed.

'Clive, you'd better get your face on one before they're all gone!' Melinda ordered her husband to take over the photography.

Several more ensembles were snapped. Then Daniel inspected the camera. 'One left.'

The owner took repossession. 'Give us it here then, Dan, and you stand between the girls.'

Taking a stance before the giant creamy trunk of a mountain ash that soared three hundred feet to the sky, Oriel felt Daniel's right arm snake round her waist, felt his hip against her middle, his shoulder against her face, the heat and scent of his body . . .

And then it was over. Clive was replacing the Kodak in its case and saying, 'We'd better call it a day before the mozzies come out in force.'

It had been a wonderful Sunday and Oriel did not want

it to end, hoping to extend her time with Daniel by asking if her friends would like to come to dinner at the hotel this evening.

'Don't think we could get a babysitter at such short notice,' was the reply.

'Tomorrow, then,' she persisted.

Melinda looked keen. 'I'm right to go but Dan won't be back till next weekend. S'pose you'll have went by then. It's too far for him to travel to the mill every day so he has to bach up there through the week.'

Oriel's hopes were shattered.

''Sbeen a great day, though, thanks for taking us, mate.' Daniel turned back to include Oriel in his gratitude. 'You too, Smiler. It's good for Mel to have her friend back. She's really missed you.'

Oriel noticed the reflection of her own dazzling smile in the car mirror and marvelled at how she could produce it when feeling so desperately sad inside.

Monday dawned to a feeling of emptiness for Oriel, yesterday's euphoria totally expunged by the thought of having to endure the rest of the week with Clive.

It must have been a difficult week for him too, being presented with her lacklustre expression day after day, for on more than one occasion he suggested that she spend some time alone with her friend if she preferred to, and he would go fishing.

'Clive's a good bloke, isn't he?' said Melinda, whilst the two of them were eating the cakes that Oriel had bought for them that afternoon, two flies zizzing overhead. 'Letting you spend all this time with me. Nice-looking too.'

Oriel raised one eyebrow to denote that she did not consider him to be so.

'Oh, he is. It's a pity he isn't called Maguire, though. I got used to pretending I had a rich sister.' For a period after Melinda's wedding both girls had held the surname

Maguire. 'Mrs Widdowes, eh? Does Mr Widdowes have any faults? He doesn't seem to.'

'Oh, not many.' Oriel felt disloyal mentioning Clive's habits. Even though they annoyed her she blamed her own irritable nature.

'Strewth, Dan's got loads.'

'He seems all right to me.' Oriel used a finger to brush icing sugar from her upper lip, then lashed out at a fly that tried to settle on her cake.

'You want to try living with him – Ally, Angus stop that!' The children were wrestling over a hairbrush.

Embarrassed by her own thoughts, Oriel blushed to the roots of her hair, then covered her discomposure by wafting at her face with a hand. 'God, it's hot today, isn't it?'

'Yeah, I'm sorry we've got no fans – I said, stop fighting!' Melinda leaped up and slapped both children hard, causing them to break into howls.

Even though she had no wish to bear children of her own, Oriel was soft-hearted and tears burned her eyes.

Her friend noticed and looked uncomfortable. 'Sorry, but they're little mongrels when their father isn't around. When you gonna have one, then?' She sat down to finish off her cake.

The blue eyes blinked. 'I don't want any.'

'What about your husband?'

Oriel flinched and shrugged, wiping her hands with a handkerchief.

'You're really lucky to have him, you know,' opined Melinda.

Oriel nodded. Yes, she was lucky having such a generous man. Why, then, did she not feel it?

The remainder of her year was a period of stagnation, the only highlight coming in December with her first chance to vote in a Federal Election. Here, there was echo of Oriel's own discord, the country showing its disapproval of the way the Government had handled all the various disputes since the war and thereby robbing the Nationalist Party of its majority. With the Country Party holding the balance of power, Prime Minister Hughes was now facing a coalition with Earle Page, a man he had so often ridiculed.

Despite not fully understanding the system, Oriel was firm in her views that this present Government was not fulfilling all the promises it had made to returned servicemen, and showed pleasure upon reading the results of the election in the morning newspaper that Clive handed over as he made ready for work.

'I wonder what Daniel thinks. He's a fan of Billy Hughes.'

Clive was tart. 'Well, I for one'll be pleased to see the back of that bloody little dictator. There's more people in this country to consider than soldiers, you know.'

Oriel bit her tongue and changed the subject to discuss the coming Christmas, though her heart was far from merry.

The festive season brought the usual round of parties with Clive's relatives and friends, and a fleeting visit to Yarra Junction, which left Oriel feeling emptier than ever. At the birth of another New Year she pulled the traditional wishbone with Dorothy and made the passionate plea for some miracle to happen that would make her into the kind of wife that Clive desired. It did not work. In February, shortly after the resignation of Prime Minister Hughes in favour of Stanley Melbourne Bruce, Clive's grandmother died.

Oriel had never experienced the embrace of a grandparent, had no inkling of how deep was her husband's bereavement. The commiserations she offered were sincere but lacked real empathy, and Clive reacted accordingly.

'The funeral's on Thursday,' he told her. 'There's no need for you to come if you don't want.'

Oriel interpreted this to mean that he did not need her, an indication of what a sham her marriage was, and so took him at his word. Her absence from the funeral was to reinstate her unpopularity with Thora. Indeed, other members of the family thought she was strange too, though they did not say so to her face. Deeper she descended into misery, existing on sporadic visits to her friends, both of whom seemed to be happy in their marriages. Melinda and her husband came to visit, bringing news that she was expecting a third child.

Clive and Oriel's second wedding anniversary came and went without celebration. The months rolled by into another winter and they began to spend even less time together. Clive had readopted his boyhood habit of attending football matches on a Saturday afternoon just, it seemed, to get away from her, and Oriel did not care.

Today's wintry weekend began the same as any other. Clive made ready to depart for work, dealt a meaningless peck to her cheek and announced, 'I'll be going straight to footy after I finish.'

Oriel would usually have simply nodded but this Saturday morning she blurted from her place at the sink, 'I thought I might go and see Mel, take her a few things. The baby must be almost due.'

From the doorway, he turned an unsmiling face to look at her, and picked his nose, his tone dull. 'If you want. I'll go and have tea at Mum's. What time will you be back?'

'Not sure, but not late.' She continued washing the pots.

'Mm, have a good time – although I suppose you will seeing as I'm not going with you.'

When he had gone Oriel, in buoyant mood, went to change, put on fresh make-up, tucked a few things in a bag then after checking she had enough for the second-class fare, left the quiet house to travel the electrified route to Flinders Street Station, where she would meet the noon connection to Warburton.

On a hiss and a burst of steam the engine shunted into action, squeaking and grinding out of the city, through densely populated suburbs and on towards the fertile flood plains of the Yarra Valley, maintaining its leisurely pace – too leisurely for one whose heart threatened to burst with impatience.

Two and a half hours after boarding, rolling stock appeared on the line bearing vast quantities of timber, and Oriel knew that she had at last reached Yarra Junction. The train jerked to a halt. First to the door, Oriel hardly felt the blast of chilly air and was out of the station in no time, her hurrying legs reflecting the Saturday afternoon activity of the town. Fresh-cheeked boys rushed in and out of stores, delivering boxed orders to the carriages that lined the road. Verandahs heaved with shoppers. Ignoring all, she skipped across the busy road and onwards, glancing at her watch as she hurried up the rise away from the town. Clive would be at footy now. Dismissing him from her mind she smiled in anticipation as Melinda's cottage came into sight through the trees.

On answering her knock Daniel produced a spontaneous grin, but then looked troubled.

'Sorry, have I come at an inconvenient time?' She stood on the tiny verandah clutching her bag before her, her face studying him anxiously. 'I would've phoned but you haven't got one.' She dealt him a fleeting top-to-toe examination then, under his stare, gave an awkward laugh and turned her head to look out over the wintry valley.

Daniel pushed back his hair, still beholding her with concern, his own eyes flitting from her head to her shoes. 'No, no! Well, Melly's in the hospital but there's nothing wrong. She just had the bub a few days earlier than expected – on Thursday.'

Oriel gasped. 'I've come all this way and she's in the city?' There was no hospital out here. 'I would've thought you'd have paid us a visit when you brought her in.' She sounded hurt and pulled the collar of her coat around her neck.

'I was at work. She made her own way into Melbourne. The kids are with their gran.' Suddenly appearing to notice how cold it was, he rubbed his hands down his moleskins and waved her inside. 'I was just having smoke-o, are yer gonna come in and join me?'

Oriel caught the smell of his freshly laundered shirt as she passed, finding it highly erotic. She offered congratulations for the new baby but was consumed by disappointment, for obviously it was impossible for her to stay. Her blank expression toured the tongued and grooved lining boards, the modest but clean and tidy furnishings, the flat iron on the hearth, the row of Daniel's underpants hanging on a rail above the fireplace. 'Oh well, never mind, I'll get the next train, and visit her when I get back.' Her voice held disappointment.

'Next train's not till ten past six.'

'A bus then.'

'Have yer cuppa tea first. Take your coat off and sit down.' Daniel turned to a cupboard and put his hands on his hips.

Watching him as she divested herself of hat and coat, Oriel mistook his attitude for one of confusion. 'Would you like me to make it?'

He revolved the top half of his body to eye her. 'You saying I'm incapable of making a cuppa tea?' When her face dropped his own creased in laughter. 'I'm kidding! It's just that I've tidied all the cupboards while Mel's been away and I've outsmarted meself. Can't remember where I put the tea. Ah, here we are!'

Oriel was amazed. 'Tidied the cupboards?'

'Ah, us army chaps know how to fend for ourselves.' Maintaining his grin, he spooned tea into the pot and lifted a kettle from the fire to add boiling water.

Feeling her heart rate increase, Oriel tore her eyes away

from him and indicated her bag. 'I've brought all this stuff thinking I could cook up a treat for Mel. I've cut a recipe out of a magazine and I thought I'd experiment on her before I cook it for myself.' She laughed aloud at Daniel's contorted face. 'I don't want to lump it all home with me, would you be a guinea pig?'

Rattling a spoon around the pot, he acquiesced. 'All right, Smiler, if you're twisting me arm.'

'Shall I put the meat in your whatsit, Coolgardie?'

'Go for your life. You can see if the drip tray needs emptying while you're there.'

Radiating delight, she went outside to the meat safe and lifting the hessian flaps put the beef into the mesh cupboard. With it safely installed she checked that there was enough water to keep the hessian soaked, then tipped the drip tray on to the garden as she had seen Melinda do in the past. When she went back inside, a cup of tea had been poured for her and whilst they supped Daniel told her all about the new child, Alan, whom he had been to visit that morning. 'I know you're not keen on babies but he's a dear little thing.'

Oriel did not care what the subject matter was, happy just to sit here and listen to his voice and watch his face, be comforted by his presence.

During the consumption of tea they talked about nothing in particular, until in a quiet interval, Oriel bent down and rubbed her cashmered calf in thoughtful manner and said, 'I'd better start the dinner if it's to cook in time. D'you know how to work your oven? I haven't a clue. Mine has numbers on.'

Daniel stacked the primitive stove with wood, then fiddled with it a while. 'Think that's it. I know Melly puts a bit o' butcher's paper in there too. Seen her do it, but don't ask me what for.'

Oriel thought she knew. 'It'll be to see whether it's hot enough. The paper will turn brown. We'll soon find out anyway. I've got that piece I brought the meat in.'

Whilst she prepared their dinner the conversation continued. Oriel asked, 'Do you see much of Jimmy Magee these days?'

'The swaggie?' Daniel grinned. 'That's what he is now.' He told her how Jimmy, unable to stand the pressures of society after returning from war, had taken to living the life of a hermit, built a house of kerosene tins in the mountains, existing on the money he earned from odd jobs when his mental health allowed him to do so. 'That's what Norm told me, anyhow.'

Oriel looked impish. 'Normie No-nose.'

He laughed at her description. 'Yeah, not like this honk. Anyway, he saw Jim on his travels in Melbourne. Haven't seen him meself in ages.'

Oriel offered sympathy for the man, wondering if he ever went to visit the Anzac Hostel, then, hungry for more meaningful discussion, touched hesitantly upon Daniel's contribution to the war. 'I noticed there's an ambulance depot in Yarra Junction. Can I ask why you never thought to go and work there after you did that sort of thing in the army? I'd've thought it would be more worthwhile than the sawmill.'

He held her eyes, seemingly reluctant to explain. 'You would, would yer?'

'Well, all that practice you must have had.'

'I had six years' practice at the sawmill before the war and only three with the medics.'

Oriel shifted her buttocks. 'Yes, but what I'm trying to say is it's a bit of a waste of those three years, isn't it?'

'People need houses, don't they? They need furniture, they need bridges and telegraph poles and fuel for their fires –'swell-paid job, yer know.'

'Point taken. I'm not trying to belittle what you do now. I just wondered when I saw the sign for the ambulance service on my way here.'

Daniel acknowledged this and gave her a direct answer

this time. 'I didn't go to work at the ambulance depot 'cause it's just opened, that's why. Not that I would've joined anyway.'

Oriel was quiet for a while as she mixed the contents of her bowl, but was reluctant to let the subject drop. 'What made you join the medical corps, then?'

'I didn't fancy killing blokes but I wanted to do me bit for the Empire.'

'Clive wasn't in the war,' she murmured, adding her ingredients as she went.

'Don't make the mistake of thinking he got away with it lightly,' replied Daniel, watching her hands work the mixture. 'I don't envy the pressure he would've got from those bitches with their white feathers. I had a few of them meself while I was making up me mind whether or not to go.'

'He did register but he was found to be unfit.'

'That won't've stopped those sheilas, raving on like a bunch o' chooks, not satisfied till they'd sent some poor kid to his death. I can't stand 'em, nor them that go crook about equal rights with men neither. They dunno what the hell they're stirring up, wanting to be equal to a bloke in everything. They'd damn soon moan about it if they got their wish. It's all right not wanting to be chained to the home and kids, I quite agree they shouldn't be treated like slaves. If a woman wants to have a career instead of a family that's all right for me – though I can't see how they can have both, someone's going to suffer. But if you take equality to the limit you'll have women fighting on the battlefield beside fellas and believe me you wouldn't want that.' His bitter expression was wiped away by a sudden grin and he scratched his temple with one finger. 'Sorry, going on a bit, aren't I? Talking meself out of a good dinner too. 'Sjust something that really gives me the . . . thingos.'

'Fair dinkum?' Oriel's eyes gleamed.

He faked astonishment. 'You mean, you guessed? Was

it something I said gave the game away?' Then he chuckled and was pensive for a moment before asking, 'Can you keep a secret?' At her nod he divulged, 'Yer know that farm I walked off? The Government's after me for the money I owe. Got a letter yesterday. Good job it came while Melly was in hospital. She'll do her block.'

'Oh God, what are you going to do?'

'Huh! My troubles. I can't give 'em something I haven't got.'

'I could lend –'

'No! Thank you, but no, I'll have to offer to pay 'em back bit by bit.'

'But it's disgusting treatment of someone who's been through what you have!'

He gave a cynical nod. 'Debt of honour to the conquering heroes? Might've known there was a catch to it. Anyway, keep it to yourself. I don't want to worry Mel.' He started as if remembering something. 'Aw cripes, she asked me to run a message at the shop and I've forgot all about it.'

'I'll come and help,' she offered.

'No! No, it won't take long.' His tone implied that he did not want to be seen with her lest it engendered gossip. 'You've got enough to be going on with there.'

When Daniel returned the meal was well underway. He unloaded his shopping on the table and said it smelled excellent.

'Share a beer?' He held up a bottle. Oriel did not normally consume ale but on impulse got two glasses from the cupboard.

'Don't dob me in to Mel, telling her I've been into the grog while she's laid up in hospital,' he warned her with a grin.

'I won't – cheers.' She tapped her glass to his.

They sat for a while, sipping at their beer. It must have been a potent brew for after only a half a glass she felt giddy and was emboldened to ask, 'Do you have a dream, Daniel?'

He eyed her over his glass. 'Funny sort o' question to ask of a Saturday arvo.'

'Sorry.' Oriel hoped her voice was not as slurred as she imagined. 'Is it too personal?'

He gave a self-conscious chuckle. 'Not really – I'd like to make films.'

'Really?'

'Yeah! I can't get enough o' going to the pictures. Did you see *The Kelly Gang*? No? Aw, pal, it's a real ripper. If you ever get the chance go and see it. I'd love to make a picture like that, only with sound. Now that would be great.' Curbing his effusiveness he laughed at himself. 'Don't suppose I ever will, though.'

'It doesn't matter. Having that dream's the important thing.' She took another gulp of beer.

'And what's yours, Smiler?'

She looked abashed. 'I feel stupid for starting this now.' At his coaxing she finally admitted, 'Oh well, I'd just like to be able to stop people hurting and killing each other. You read such awful things in the paper.'

'Why?' At her look of incomprehension he extended his query. 'Why stop people doing what they do best?' There was a gleam of cynicism to his eye now. Oriel felt uncomfortable under his grilling. 'Is it because you genuinely care or just because yer don't like the way it makes you feel?'

At first offended, she opened her mouth to issue retort, but was unable to justify her claim. She bent her head, an admittance of guilt, saying he could be right.

'Nah! It's just me getting snaky in me old age. Who am I to ruin your dream?'

She shrugged. 'You're more likely to realize yours than I am mine.'

'No, you'll never change human nature that's for sure.' Daniel's mind was in a distant land. 'Life's a fair cow –

sorry, I forgot who I was with for the minute! Thought you were one o' the lads.' He laughed. 'Digging me grave deeper, aren't I? I just meant – aw well, never mind.' He seemed to have become uncomfortable.

Now slightly intoxicated, Oriel felt bold enough to feast her eyes upon him, gazed and gazed until the burning deep within became so unbearable that she feared she must speak of it and to do so was disaster. Instead, she sank her face into her glass, pressing its rim against her cheeks.

Apparently relieved to have her scrutiny removed, Daniel began to jabber, anything to relieve the intensity of the atmosphere. 'Didn't like me much when we first met, did yer?'

Oriel gave a little laugh. 'Oh well, that was before I knew you. It was just the similarity with my own –' She hesitated for a moment and dared to look at him again. 'You know my parents and I have different names but I'm not sure if you're aware of the reason. They weren't married when I was born – in fact my father didn't live with us until just before we emigrated.' From the lack of surprise on Daniel's face, the cognizant nod, she guessed that Melinda had informed him. Of course she would have, thought Oriel. Wives told their husbands everything. At least they should feel able to. She had never volunteered information about her grandmother to anyone at all, but did so now. 'I don't hold that against him any more. He had a dreadful upbringing. His mother had him when she was fourteen. She was a prostitute.' She looked for signs of shock on his face but did not find it and so went on in vague murmur, 'I often find myself wondering about her, putting myself in her place. Funny, isn't it? The ones that fascinate you the most are the ones you so despise.'

'Poor little devil,' murmured Daniel.

The fact that he did not condemn was no surprise to her. Nodding, she buried her face in the glass again. The beer was almost finished. 'Oh dear we're getting maudlin! So – when are you going to collect Belinda and the maybe from hospital?' She burst out laughing.

Daniel recoiled as though she had deafened him. 'Cripes, you sound like a ruddy kookaburra!' But he chuckled with her. 'Smiler's not a good enough name for you, it's Kooka from now on.'

Oriel was convulsed and could barely speak. 'I think I'd better not have any more till we've had dinner.'

Notwithstanding the unsteadiness of her hand, dribbling gravy on the cloth as she doled out the portions, the meal was a success. Afterwards Daniel told her to leave the washing up he would do it later, and they sat down in easy chairs to have another beer.

'You never really told me why you didn't join the Ambulance Service after the war.'

He took a gulp of alcohol and did not respond.

Oriel recalled her friend Noel's sense of disillusionment after the carnage. 'I know it must've been hideous. Our friend who was a doctor was never the same when he came back. But surely it couldn't be as bad in peacetime as in war. I mean I know there are some terrible accidents and everything but the scale of it wouldn't be so huge. Don't you want to use your expertise to help people?'

'Ah, there's enough do-gooders in the world without me sticking me beak in.' Daniel was rubbing the side of his neck furiously as if in discomfort.

She sensed that she had delved too deeply and, not wishing to ruin her own brief spell of happiness, searched for something to restore his equilibrium. No words would come, but the impulsive sense of humour inherited from her mother that had been repressed by marriage to Clive now gained new life. Standing to put her empty glass on the table, she made out as if her legs had turned to rubber, doing the most idiotic walk and hoping it would make him laugh. It did. And he laughed even louder when, continuing her drunken theme, she opened a door and pretended to smash her face into it.

But amid the laughter Oriel caught sight of the clock and a wave of panic rushed through her. Time spent with Daniel went nowhere at all. Oh, how she longed to stay! To press her lips to that laughing mouth . . .

He noticed her concern and said abruptly, 'Well, you must be wanting to make for home.'

I don't, thought Oriel. I never want to go back.

He rose. 'That was a great dinner you cooked for us. I can vouch that it's safe to test on Clive now. We'd better make a start for the train. I don't want to look as if I'm trying to get rid o' you after I've scoffed all yer tucker but I've got a hunting trip to organize.'

Half-heartedly, she put on her hat and coat. 'What d'you hunt?'

'Oh, possums, rabbits –'

'Possums? Oh you cruel devil. I don't think I'll talk to you any more.'

Daniel's face adopted a sudden hard edge and he shrugged. 'Suit yourself.'

Oriel felt as if she had been stabbed, feared she would cry, and turned away in the pretence of looking for her bag. 'I was only joking – where's my bag? I brought some cake for Mel, you might as well take it on your trip. I'll get her some flowers instead.' Without looking up at him she handed over the parcel. 'Oh well, I'd better go. You don't need to come if you're busy.'

'I'm not that busy.' More subdued, Daniel put the wrapped cake on the table and reached for Oriel's bag. 'I'll carry that for you.'

Taking a lantern, he guided her along the darkened slope to the railway station and waited with her until the train arrived. By that time she had composed herself and was able to look into his face as she prepared to get on board. The sight of it made her want to weep again but she managed to ward the feeling off in order to say, 'Well, goodbye, Daniel. I'll go see Mel at the hospital tomorrow and I hope to come and see you both again before too long, look after her.'

'I will. She's a good kid.' Only half-smiling, Daniel saw her on to the train, then stepped back and presented his palm as a form of curt wave.

Oriel waved too, then sat back in her seat feeling swamped by misery.

14

After visiting an innocent Melinda in hospital, Oriel felt a resurgence of anger over the bureaucratic pursuance of the Maguires' debt and despite having sworn not to reveal it to her friend she felt that something had to be done. Hence, she penned a caustic letter to one of the Melbourne newspapers demanding to know if its readers were aware that only three years after the Victorian Government had promised to do all it could to help Australia's returned soldiers it was now harassing these valiant men. Clive disapproved of the stir she created, but Oriel retorted that she did not care. Whether or not the letter would do any good she was unsure, but if getting something done meant writing to the Premier himself then she would.

'I knew this'd get you into trouble,' her husband scolded her when an official-looking letter arrived some days after her own had been published.

Oriel's mouth fell slack as he handed her the missive. Maybe she had been too forthright in her views. Taking a deep breath she opened it and in a relieved tone uttered, 'Oh, it's from the editor of the *Sun News-Pictorial*!' After glancing at the embossed heading she read on, a smile slowly forming on her lips. Upon finishing the document, she handed it over to Clive with a smug expression. 'They want me to submit another article with a view to a regular weekly column.'

He read it with disbelief, then gave a hesitant smile. 'Very good. Will you have time?'

'I'll make time,' replied Oriel, and barely waiting for him to close the front door on his way to work began to clear the table, swapping breakfast pots for writing paper.

Having had success with the theme of returned soldiers, she decided to improvise upon this for her current submission, and taking up her pen poured forth upon the evils of the trade unions whose continual strike action had caused untold discomfort to Australia's heroes.

Clive despaired when, on his return from work that evening, his wife showed him what she had prepared. 'You're going to have stones thrown through our window!'

She was offended that he remarked only upon the detrimental effects of the letter and not upon her erudite composition. 'Well, I'm sending it anyway.'

'Oh, it's a good letter.' Too late he praised her achievement. 'I just don't want you to get into trouble. Don't be too disappointed if they don't publish it, will you?' Tired, he went to wash his hands in preparation for his evening meal, muttering to himself, 'I hope they don't in a way – no good'll come of it.'

Again, Clive was wrong on both counts. Oriel's opinionated submission paved the way for a regular weekly column, whilst the result of her first letter was of great benefit to Daniel, who had lately been informed that his debt had been written off.

'You little bottler!' He heaped praise upon her when next she and Clive visited their friends in Yarra Junction. 'I don't know what you said but you ought to run for Premier the way you've got things done.'

Oriel looked abashed. 'I only wrote to the newspaper.'

'I know you did!' Melinda, arms akimbo, chipped in. 'Had 'em on me doorstep asking what I thought to it all when I hadn't a clue as to what was going on 'cause he never thought it necessary to tell me.'

Oriel apologized for causing discord.

But her friend was laughing. 'Nah, you're right! Fancy, you being the big newspaper journalist. I'll make a cup o' tea and you tell me all about it.'

Oriel tried to catch Daniel on his own, which was difficult as he seemed to be trying to avoid her. 'I know you asked me not to tell Melinda but it was so unjust I had to try and do something. I hope it didn't cause too much trouble.'

Daniel seemed unperturbed, laughing. 'Oh, she was spitting chips till she found out we weren't gonna lose any more money. Don't worry, she's right now – and thanks again for what yer done.' He included Clive in the conversation. 'Mate, yer must be proud of her.'

Clive affected a cheery grin. 'I am.' Only his wife seemed to notice that his enthusiasm did not appear wholly genuine.

Melinda served tea. 'And you say you're gonna be writing every week? How much do they give you?'

From Oriel's expression it was evident that the thought had not crossed her mind. 'I'm not sure.'

'Well, make sure you find out!' urged her friend. 'Don't be letting them use your talents for nothing. What're you gonna write about this week? I'll have to buy a paper if you're in it.'

Oriel smiled and accepted a cup of tea. 'Oh, there are all sorts of things I could cover – but I'd better write to Mother first before news of my fame spreads.' She laughed to show it was a joke. 'I haven't written for ages.'

In fact, she corresponded often with her mother, the letters full of news: news of what she was doing to the house, the cookery classes she had been to, the piano lessons she was taking, news about Dorothy and Melinda and now news of her literary success. Had Bright been able to read between the lines, to read her daughter as well as she read her husband, she would have detected that all was not well with Oriel's marriage.

Apart from an irregular visit to the pictures, the occasions when she and Clive went out together had now been reduced to Sundays when they visited his parents. Even here, though, they were not really together, for after lunch he would fall asleep, leaving his wife to make conversation. When they had first been married the vision of them as old people celebrating their Golden Wedding had brought an affectionate smile to her lips – but now he was acting as if he were an old man already, as if they had been married for years.

It was time for one such visit today. Even feeling as wretched as she did Oriel was never one to neglect her appearance and, wearing a smart new outfit, waited impatiently outside the front porch for Clive to find his car keys.

An old man leading his overweight dog back from a walk paused at the gate and raised his hat. 'What a sight for sore eyes.'

The recipient of the compliment grinned and came down the path to chat over the wire fence. After living in this house for over two years she had come to know her neighbours and they assumed that they knew her too.

Whilst thus engaged she heard the door slam and turned to see Clive's mistrustful face hurrying to intrude on the imagined liaison. She gave an inward sigh. For God's sake, the man must be sixty years old! What possible reason could there be for jealousy here?

'What a lucky fellow you are,' opined Mr Anderssen on the younger man's arrival. 'Not only is your wife good-looking but placid with it. My Doris is always saying to me, we never hear that young couple arguing, they're so well matched.'

Oriel enjoyed an ironic smile that anyone could mistake the lack of argument for compatibility. She bent down to pat the corpulent black and white terrier, then edged towards the car.

'Oh, I daren't argue with her,' joked Clive, only his wife knowing what tension lay beneath his skin. 'She keeps me well under control.'

Mr Anderssen chuckled and made to move on, tugging at the dog's lead. 'Well, we like living next door to you anyhow. I've told you before, if you ever need anything, don't hesitate to call in.'

The car journey was undertaken in silence. On arrival at the senior Widdoweses' residence there was a meal of roast beef to be enjoyed. Alas, it was a mixed pleasure as, besides Mabel and her husband, Thora and Bill were also present. Despite the invitations to her sister-in-law's 'at homes' and the chats they might have, Oriel knew that Thora did not really like her. Mabel might say her sister did not like anyone, but Oriel took the offhand remarks personally and no excuse could convince her otherwise.

By some miracle Clive managed to keep awake this afternoon, though she did not flatter herself that it was her company that provided the stimulus. Thora had just had a baby girl, the first grandchild and the centre of attention. Oriel felt compelled to admire it too, just to keep the peace.

'What've you called her – Angela, isn't it?'

'Angela Rose,' corrected Mabel, tongue in cheek.

Determined not to employ this pretentious appellation, Oriel merely nodded over the pram, then abandoned the inspection, obviously too soon for the baby's mother, who looked hurt at this dismissal. Seeing this, Oriel felt guilty and said, 'That's a nice dress you've got on.'

Her sister-in-law rallied. 'Yes, it's from Bon Marche.' Thora assumed the French name gave its garments class. 'I buy lots of things there.'

'Well, I suppose you've got such a big mortgage,' responded Mabel, causing her sister's nostrils to flare. 'You wouldn't have enough left for clothes – oh, didn't you know?' She added innocently, 'Bon Marche means cheap.'

Oriel listened to them bickering. At least there was some form of entertainment here. At home, little exchange of any kind took place.

*   *   *

She decided there must be some inherent flaw in her character that she could not find contentment. Sinking even lower, she began to harbour the feeling that everything in life had always been her fault. Had she not been born her mother might have been allowed to continue her own childhood, her father would not have felt the need to run away and they might have married at leisure and had children because they wanted them, not because of one foolish mistake.

'There must be something wrong with me,' she sighed to Dorothy on her next regular afternoon visit. 'Everyone else likes him, thinks he's kind, amusing, supportive – and he is. Why don't I love him? I do care about him as a friend. I just feel as if something's missing.' She shrugged, unable to articulate her needs.

Dorothy sympathized but privately felt that Oriel had no right to grumble as she did. 'At least he's not selfish like Cuddy.'

'No, he isn't.' She puffed away on her cigarette. 'Sometimes I wish he was. I don't mean in your context – wanting things all his own way – but I just wish he'd have stronger opinions instead of always fitting in with whatever I want. If I said I was going to jump off a cliff this morning I swear he'd tag along just to be a bloody martyr. Then that makes me feel selfish and I have a sneaking feeling that that was his intention. And he's got so suspicious, as if he thinks I'm having an affair while he's at work. If a delivery man comes to the door he watches him like a hawk, even if he's old and ugly. It's so insulting. He's even got me feeling guilty when he asks what I've been doing through the day.'

'Next time he asks you'll have to make something up to give him food for thought,' advised her friend.

'My God, I don't want him any more jealous than he already is! I just wish he didn't have such a low opinion of me.' Stubbing out her cigarette, she sighed. 'I suppose I'd better go.'

Dread in every footstep, she made the journey home, neglecting any transport in order to delay her arrival. Attacked by all manner of thought, she was in no mood for the sight that greeted her – Mr Anderssen's elderly dog defecating all over the path in front of her house. Fury surged within her breast and she let fly.

'Couldn't you even have the courtesy to drag it into the gutter?'

The alarmed old gentleman offered explanation, tugging on the lead. 'I'm sorry, I didn't have time. He's eaten something that disagreed with him.'

'And that's an excuse, is it? How would you like it if I let my dog shit outside your house?' It was of no consequence that she did not own a dog, her unbound rage making her insensible to the expletive and the frozen smile of horror on the old man's face. 'Well, you can just go get a shovel and clear that up for when I come out!' And picking her way through the mess she stormed off into the house.

When she next emerged the excrement was gone but by that time she had taken stock of her impulsive action and was feeling ashamed and guilty at such behaviour towards a harmless old man. What sort of person was she becoming?

Too embarrassed and immature to go round to her neighbour and apologize, Oriel took to peeping from behind the curtains before an expedition to the shops, waiting for Mr Anderssen to come home with his dog before scurrying down the path like a fugitive. For all that, it was inevitable that she should cross paths with the old man who, ever the gentleman, raised his hat and smiled at her as usual, making her feel a thousand times worse.

Spring rains came, the resulting deluge causing the Yarra to burst its banks, bringing chaos to the city and its suburbs. Oriel compared the scene to her own restrained emotions swollen to the brim of endurance. How she longed to burst free of this prison with its half-hearted conjugal couplings, ached for fulfilment, both physical and spiritual, but felt destined to suffer the attentions of this man whom everyone thought was wonderful, for they could not all be wrong.

In this state of low self-esteem, dreams became her only escape. Under constant suspicion from her husband she determined to give his jealous theory some foundation and began to flirt with men in shops, men on buses, men in the street, men in wheelchairs at the Anzac Hostel. It was only a matter of looks and smiles and hands drawing attention to her hair, but it helped to lift her from her dreary existence, restored a modicum of confidence in the face of marital neglect.

Clive's repertoire of derogatory comments increased. He knew she did not love him but was incapable of confrontation; the stinging utterances were his way of fighting, whilst hers was to retreat into her shell and pretend to the outside world that everything was rosy, taking out her temper on some poor unsuspecting numskull who allowed his dog to defecate outside her house.

Periodically there were twinges of conscience from both. Motivated by one such pang Oriel said this Friday morning over breakfast, 'It's your birthday tomorrow.' It was his twenty-eighth. 'Do you want to go out somewhere nice? Maybe for a meal and then to the theatre. We could invite Dot and Cuddy.' It might help to have friends present.

Clive looked preoccupied, then smiled up from his newspaper. 'Mm, that'd be good. I've arranged to go to the races in the afternoon but you could come if you want, then we could go for a meal in town – sorry, I was just reading this. Looks like the Victoria Police might be going on strike.'

There had been murmurings earlier in the year of this happening but nothing had transpired. She showed disgust. 'My God, if the police go on strike who's it going to be next?'

'Well, I suppose they have got a point.' His eyes were on the print again. 'Says here they get the lowest pay of any force in Australia.'

'I suppose everyone would like more money.' Oriel took a drink of tea.

Clive read on. 'It's more complicated than that. It's about pensions and all sorts. Apparently this new Commissioner's appointed spies to watch how they perform.'

I know how they feel, thought Oriel.

'The blokes at Russell Street refused to go on duty on Wednesday night – I wondered what was going on when I left work! Noticed a lot of 'em congregated round the barracks, some with different badges on their uniforms. They've brought them in from the country but it seems they won't go on duty either! Says here, they were told if they didn't turn up for duty again last night they'd be sacked.' He showed amusement. 'I like the way the newspaper's telling all the crims in Melbourne that there'll be no police force tomorrow.' He put the paper down and made signs of getting ready for work. 'Well, it's not going to spoil my birthday. Do you want to come to the races with us?'

'Who's going?'

'Oh, just Cuddy and a few blokes from work.'

Oriel shook her head. 'I'll meet you in town afterwards – outside Myers. I've still got to buy your present. What would you like?'

'It's a good enough present that you're going out with me.' Deeming this insufficient, Oriel went out that morning and bought him a gift, then spent the rest of the day thinking about her next newspaper article. The editor had recently told her that her writings were getting a little too political and suggested that she might rather submit a short story or her view on the latest fashions, or other women's issues. Though annoyed over this criticism, she saw no point in wasting time in creating something that would not be published and so chose to temper her pen. Alas, Oriel was to discover that she could only write when spurred by injustice. Destitute of inspiration, she had still not written a word when Clive came home.

Over dinner, he told her that the Victoria Police had indeed gone on strike.

'The young blokes were having a field day when I left work, taunting the few coppers I did see. One got all these eggs thrown at him.' He shook in mirth. 'Covered in 'em, he was. Should be back to normal by tomorrow though – they've sworn in all these special constables. So we can still go for our night out.'

On the morning of his birthday Clive opened his gifts and cards, then went off to work. Oriel spent the next hour trailing around the house, picking up all the clothes, shoes and other objects that Clive had left in convenient places – convenient for him, that was – then failing yet again to compose an article for the newspaper, was leaning chin in palm over the table, thinking of Daniel, when the telephone rang. Still preoccupied, she went to answer it and on hearing her husband's voice gave a half-hearted, 'Oh, hello.'

'Yes, it's only me, I'm afraid,' came his pettish retort. 'Sorry to disappoint you.'

She felt the anger surge up in her but managed to restrain it and merely waited.

'Listen, I've just heard from Cuddy that there was more trouble than egg-throwing last night. Apparently some hoodlums beat a group of people up that he knew. I wondered if you want to cancel going out tonight?'

Oriel thought about this. Even though her marriage was in tatters she had been looking forward to going to the theatre. 'Has there been any trouble at the races?'

'Well, no more than there usually is.'

'Is Dorothy still going?'

'Yes, and I've asked another bloke from work and his girl to come too.'

She pondered further. 'It seems a shame to let a few thugs rule our lives.'

'Well, it's up to you. I just thought I'd give you the option.' Clive became businesslike. 'All right then, I'll see you as planned outside Myers. Bye.'

When Oriel went to keep their arrangement, however, she began to doubt her decision. Saturday nights were always lively but this evening the city was swamped by Melbourne Cup visitors. As a rule this traditional race meeting provided an air of jollity and indeed there were many in the throng who were bent on enjoyment, but as Oriel hurried through the fading light towards the Myer Emporium she felt an underlying sense of menace in the absence of a police force and was for once glad to see Clive's face.

The gladness was not to last. Her husband took one look at the outfit she was wearing and, pleasantly sarcastic, said, 'Very nice – still I don't suppose you went to all that trouble just for me.'

She was unable to offer retort as at that juncture the others arrived. She had not met Ethel and Richard before but after introductions, Dorothy said, 'It's a double celebration tonight. Ethel and Richard have just got engaged to be married!'

Made cruel by her anger at Clive she proclaimed to Ethel, 'Huh! Better make the most of it while you still have your freedom then.'

There was an embarrassed silence. Clive turned his grim expression away in order not to explode, muttering, 'Come on, let's go if we're going.'

As they hurried up Bourke Street towards the restaurant, Dorothy attempted to save the evening by quickly telling Ethel about the funny things her children did, her laughter managing to dispel the bad atmosphere. Oriel fell silent as she walked on her own behind them, feeling wretched at upsetting the girl, not knowing why she had done it, only that being with Clive was driving her towards insanity.

No one could quite agree later how the riot started, but as they neared the Swanston Street intersection Oriel saw a man with a brick in his hand, her eyes widened in disbelief as he drew back his arm, took aim and hurled the missile through a jeweller's plate-glass window. This seemed to be the signal for a free-for-all. In an instant those friendly faces in the crowd had scattered in panic, leaving behind a mob bent on pillage, and Oriel and her companions were in the thick of it. Dorothy screamed as a thug almost knocked her off her feet, grabbed at Cuthbert's arm as he made to avenge her. 'Don't, Cuddy! Just let's get home!'

Intimidated by the violence, they dithered, until Clive shouted above the din that they should head back down the street to the lane where he had parked his car. They broke into a trot, but the way was barred by fighting. Hoping to circumnavigate the block and gain entry to the lane from the other end, Clive led the foray into Swanston Street, but there was rioting here too – the entire block surrounded by it – and they were driven back from whence they came, the men weaving a passage through the fracas, dodging flying bottles and almost colliding with the handful of loyal long-service policemen who came running from their barracks in Russell Street to uphold the law as best they could.

The bluejackets had no hope, were overwhelmed as the howling mobsters, men and women, attacked them with sticks, bottles and stones ripped from the road. Window after window was smashed, the air was ripe with the sound of destruction as Oriel and the others scurried like rats over drifts of broken glass, attempting to get to Clive's car.

There was a familiar cry as Dorothy's husband was suddenly floored by a bottle and stumbled, righted himself, then urged the others on, bleeding from a gash to the forehead.

Gangsters swarmed over the shop windows, looting furs and jewellery, clothing, brawling over their spoils – and then a soldier appeared holding a rifle. Someone shouted, 'They brought the troops in!' And a stampede overpowered Oriel and the others carrying them in the opposite direction. As they fought against the tide there came realization that the soldier was alone. The mob turned on him, punched him to the floor and kicked his body without mercy, but there was nothing Oriel could do for at once there was a knot of rioters before her, preventing escape. Trapped, the men hurried their wives into a shop doorway, shielding them with their bodies, lashing out with boots and fists. From her terrified hidey-hole, back pressed into the doorway, clinging to Dorothy's arm, Oriel watched in horror as the Visigoths swarmed over a tram like ants upon a caterpillar, forcing it off its line, crew and passengers trampled in the maniacal lust for plunder.

Praying for deliverance, she heard the urgent clamour of a fire engine's bell as it roared down the street, thanked God as it achieved its objective of scattering the rioters, luring their attention away from Oriel and her companions, allowing them to attempt a getaway. The effect was but temporary. As they crunched over the carpet of glass the mob regrouped and returned to attack the vehicle with missiles. More windows were smashed, dummy figures were flung into grotesque postures on to the street, a sporting depot was looted, its rifles, revolvers and hunting knives distributed amongst the rabble. Oriel screamed as right in front of her a man was pushed through a plate-glass window, ripping his throat wide open, but she like others dashed on, intent on her own salvation – and then it came!

A voice yelled, 'More wallopers!' and fifty volunteer policemen came smashing their way along the street, swinging their pickaxe handles to right and left, hacking a passage through the mob. But in the attempt to break up the riot decent citizens were caught before the vicious batons, herded shoulder to shoulder with gangsters, bashed around the head and body like the rest of the scum. Oriel opened her mouth to protest but was driven and beaten back along the street further than ever now away from the car.

Finding herself becoming parted from her companions she tried to reach for Clive's hand but the crowd carried her along. Up ahead, a reporter had his notebook ripped from his hand and was forcibly hurled over a verandah rail. Terrified, Oriel was propelled onwards, unable even to turn her head to look for the others. She felt herself grabbed – thought perhaps that Clive might have managed to reach her – but a wild glance saw him yards away, still trying to fight his way through the mob. The man who had grabbed her arm pushed her into the first available doorway and shielded her with his body – 'Stay here, you'll be safe!' – and both were left as residue as the flailing machine proceeded down Bourke Street. Clive gestured wildly to her as he was carried away by the panicking crowd. Further and further away.

Heart thudding, Oriel felt the masculine body against hers, smelled his fresh breath, made no effort to escape from his arms even when the danger was past.

Eventually managing to free himself, Clive ran back along the street – and witnessed his wife in the man's embrace. At that same instant Oriel spotted him, saw the anger and disgust in his eyes. He hovered there for only two seconds. Even as she was disentangling herself from the stranger who had rescued her Clive was making a spurt to catch up with the others who were once again heading for the car. She saw Dorothy's anxious enquiring face turn to look for her but Clive pushed her onwards with some exhortation, leaving Oriel behind to rely on the stranger's charity.

Unaware of the private drama, the dark-haired businessman took her arm and with anxious look to right and left said, 'Come on, I'll get you home.'

She could have said, 'My husband's up there!' But she didn't. Instead she allowed the stranger to take her arm and followed his dash along the footpath, dodging verandah posts, swerving around the dozens of bodies that were strewn amongst the broken glass and other debris. One more last obstacle blocked their way. Below the illuminated rainbow of a shopping arcade a man had been knocked to the ground almost at their feet. Oriel pulled up to watch in horror as blows from sticks and fists and boots began to rain down on him. She wanted to cry out and stop this but was too terrified, became transfixed by the awful sight and sound and the bubbling blood until the stranger jerked her from her trance, pushed and pulled her down the street and around a corner, so that they finally reached his car.

The day had been warm and the hood had been left down but now the man wound it up and attached clouded Cellophane windows to guard against missiles. With rapid movements he pushed Oriel in, then cranked the engine and leaped in beside her, asking where she lived. At her instruction he steered a cautious passage out of the alley and into the main street. There was no way out but through the riot. A policeman's helmet fell victim to the car's wheels. Bottles and bricks smashed against the vehicle's chassis. Behind the Cellophane windows Oriel slid right down in the seat, cowering as the maelstrom surged around her, still hearing the terrible sound of the man's head reverberating to his attackers' boots as the car accelerated out of town. Tonight she had witnessed a glimpse of the battlefield and she never wanted to see it again.

*   *   *

By the time she arrived home to suburban calm she had learned her rescuer's name but little else about him for she was too shaken and bruised by the violence to indulge in conversation, and too angry with Clive for leaving her. When she thanked the man and made to get out of the car, he asked, 'Could I see you again?'

She had to smile. 'I don't think my husband would like that – thank you anyway.' Wishing him a safe journey home, she turned towards the house. On her way down the path she saw the curtain move and a fleeting chink of light, but when she entered the living room Clive was sitting in a red moquette armchair, eyes fixed to the wall, no hint of this morning's birthday mood.

'I wasn't expecting to see you home as soon as this. You looked to be having such a good time.'

Oriel gave terse retaliation. 'Well, thank you very much for hanging around to see if I was safe!' She threw her bag on the table so violently that it bounced to the floor.

'That bloke seemed to be doing a good enough job,' he retorted, glaring up at her.

'For God's sake, he was rescuing me!' She fell into a chair, lay back her head and closed her eyes in exasperation.

'I hope he got the reward he was after!'

At her look of contempt his scowl eventually collapsed and he asked in a pathetic, begging manner, 'What's wrong, Oriel?'

'I've just been almost trampled in a riot.' The horrors reformed in her brain, her own bruises making themselves felt now.

Clive had the grace to look guilty. 'I'm sorry. You know I'd never have left you like that normally – but you're pushing me beyond endurance, Oriel.' He sounded weary. 'We have to face this. You're not happy are you? You don't hug me, you don't kiss me . . . is it my fault?'

She shook her head, looking at the floor. Yes, he had abandoned her tonight, but his defence was justified, she had goaded him. Still, she could not bring herself to broach the source of her misery. 'I don't know what it is.'

'You do and you're going to sit there until you tell me – sit there!' She had begun to rise.

Oriel fell back against the cushions, face dismal. Even the drama of a riot paled in comparison to the mental turmoil she was suffering now. Eventually she took a deep breath. 'I just don't love you any more.' She did not look at him but could not miss the hurt in his response.

There was a period of deep thought, but Clive though bitterly wounded was not one to give in so easily. 'Maybe . . . maybe I've been neglecting you. I could try and get some time off work and we could take a holiday, give us a chance to make things how they were before.'

I don't want to be alone with you all day and all night, Oriel's mind screamed. I don't want to spend any time with you at all.

He seemed to read her thoughts. 'Or maybe you'd like to go on your own, have a week at your mother's. Think things over.'

She nodded. Because of the great distance between them, it had been more than two years since she had seen her dear mother, she missed her desperately. How wonderful it would be to see both her parents, especially at such a time of emotional famine. The cloak of despair that had been weighing down her shoulders for months slowly began to lift. Her lips formed tentative comment. 'I'll have to send a telegram and let her know.'

He nodded, sadly thoughtful. 'Will you be coming back?'

Oriel shrugged. 'I don't know.'

In her isolated environment Bright had not yet heard of the Melbourne riots and so, upon receiving the telegram that gave news of her daughter's imminent visit, her only reaction was excitement. 'It's so unexpected! I wonder what's made her come at such short notice? I think she might have something to tell us.' Nat asked what she meant and his wife hoisted her shoulders. 'She's having a baby! I just know she is. She wants to tell us in person. Oh God, I can't wait for her to get here!'

With gangs of hoodlums still roaming the streets and trouble continuing to flare over the weekend, putting hundreds of people in hospital, Oriel deemed it safer to wait until Monday, by which time order had been fully restored with the help of a volunteer force. What a scene of devastation awaited her in the city. Melbourne looked as if it had been ravaged by war, its heart completely ripped out. Paradoxically it looked even worse now that the tons of glass and rubble had been swept up, a sense of utter despair and loneliness about its blinded shop windows. Hurrying from the post office, she caught a passing tram to Spencer Street Station.

Ordinarily, to stand in early summer sunshine with few other people about was a pleasant experience but there was no cheer today, only a nervous wait, none of the travellers quite sure whether those others on the platform were friend or foe.

In a cloud of steam, the train squeaked and ground to a halt alongside the brown and buff platform. Doors opened and slammed. A whistle blew. Leaving behind the boarded up shopfronts Oriel was trundled from city to suburbs and all points north, through parched golden paddocks, sedate country towns and meandering creeks, earth that ranged from rich chocolate to ochre dust. In the foreground of distant mountains, a multitude of woolly backs competed for sparse blades of grass; vast treeless plains divest of any feature save a lonesome windmill, and far away on the horizon a tiny isolated dot betrayed a pocket of civilization.

The train would not take her all the way to Queensland for the line gauges differed between states. Six hours after boarding came the call, 'Albury – all change!' whence she alighted from the train and transferred to another, thankfully with sleeping cars, that would negotiate the track of New South Wales.

Hour after hour she watched the landscape vary between barren scrubland, dramatic, craggy mountains, rolling hills and deep wooded valleys that were vaguely reminiscent of the Lake District at home. Night came, leaving only the view of her own miserable reflection in the darkened window. She tried to sleep but there was too much on her mind. Morning brought another gruelling stretch; there were still hundreds of miles to endure before the livery of this train could be exchanged for that of Queensland, the line from Sydney adopting a tedious indirect route around remote inland townships before arriving at Brisbane.

Another day, another train, another long excursion. Eventually, though, the vegetation underwent a subtle change. Oriel began to see pineapple crops and lush sweeping canefields, hills like folds of green velvet, palm trees and Norfolk Island pine dotted amongst the eucalypts, occasional glimpses of deep rich red soil, bovine herds with attendant flock of egrets, houses on stilts with iron roofs that matched the bloody hue of the earth, and knew from her mother's descriptive letters that she must be close to her destination.

She alighted from the train too late to make the rest of the journey before nightfall. Lodging overnight at an hotel, she enlisted the help of a Good Samaritan with a horse and cart – for again she had remembered from her mother's letters that this was the only mode of transport that would negotiate the often marshy passage.

When she finally arrived she was thoroughly worn out, though happiness lent a spring to her gait and she came bounding through the spindly gums and wattles, up the steps to meet her mother on a verandah bedecked in elk-horn ferns. Though constructed of weatherboard, this house differed slightly from their last by reason of its elevated position. A dozen or more steps had to be climbed to its verandah and some of the windows had panes of coloured glass. Inside, though, it was much the same layout and Oriel found her way around quite easily, which was just as well in her confused state.

Bright was surprised that her daughter had come alone, but Oriel explained it was because Clive could not get any time off work. After hugs were exchanged and a meal devoured she informed them briefly of the police strike and resulting riots but made no mention of her own involvement. At her daughter's yawn, Bright noticing that she was rather subdued, said, 'Well, it's wonderful to see you after two long years but you must be worn out. Did you get much sleep on the way?'

Oriel managed a laugh. 'Not really. I did stay at this quaint hotel last night. Good horsehair mattresses, they advertised outside. I think they must've left the bloody horse in.'

Her parents both showed amusement and Bright opined, 'You'll be comfier in the bed I've prepared for you. And I think you'll like your room. Off you go – unless there's any news you want to tell us that won't wait till morning?'

Reminded of her reason for being here, Oriel lost some of her zest. 'No, it'll wait.' She kissed them both. 'Good night.'

At the breakfast table next morning she gave a half-hearted greeting to her sister, who had been in bed when she had arrived the previous night, and sat at the table gazing blankly as her mother handed the child bread and butter soldiers to dip in her egg. Bright looked up and smiled. 'That's good timing, I've just taken the eggs out. Sorry, there's no bacon. You can't get any decent stuff up here, it's all smoked, but they're our own eggs. Help yourself to toast. Did you sleep well?'

'You're joking.' Oriel appeared to be in a bad mood

as she attacked the eggshell with a spoon. The skin of her cheeks was puffy and creased. 'What the hell does your neighbour find to keep sawing in the middle of the night? I'd just get off to sleep and he'd start again.'

'We haven't got a neighbour. That's why your father chose the place.' Bright frowned, then gave a chuckle of recognition. 'Oh, it'd be a frog croaking.'

'Sounded like someone rasping or sawing wood to me.'

'Well, it was a frog,' insisted her mother. 'Must be going to get some rain.'

'And what's that bird who can't decide whether he wants to sing Gilbert and Sullivan or Beethoven's Fifth?'

'Beethoven's Four and a half,' donated her father.

'What?' Oriel beheld him with irritation.

Bright laughed at her husband's joke and explained, 'It's only Beethoven's Four and a half. He can't quite get the last note. The butcher bird.'

'I feel like butchering him – half past four this morning he started. Not to mention your chickens wittering under the window.' After a cross interlude during which she further attacked her boiled egg, she added, 'The sheets were a bit damp.'

'Yes, they're often like that with the salt in the air.' They lived close to the sea. 'We've got used to it.'

'I wouldn't.' Oriel pushed aside the empty shell and sulked over her cup of tea, blue eyes staring hazily at the tablecloth. 'And I don't know how you stick this humidity. It's like being smothered by a hot wet blanket.'

'It's not usually like this.' Bright remained serene, cradling her teacup in her palms. 'And the evenings are normally lovely and cool. Your father thrives on it, don't you?' She smiled at Nat who nodded. 'And he hasn't had his bronchitis since he left Melbourne.'

'No, but you have to put up with all sorts of other nuisances.'

'Like the one sitting here bending our lugs,' muttered

her father. 'Is there owt else you want to moan about before we send you off home?'

Oriel felt churlish and apologized. 'I just haven't slept very well. It is a lovely place. A lovely house.'

Nat agreed. 'We like it. It was a bit of a fluke we found it really.' Severely tested by the abominable Queensland roads, the car had broken down in Childers. As this was not far from their intended destination, and finding it such a pretty town, Bright had suggested it might be Divine intervention and persuaded him to call a halt to their suffering. They had lodged there for a while – but then he had heard people talking about their vacations on the coast and, knowing how much his wife loved the sea, he had brought her here just for a look. It was the kind of place Nat had always dreamed of, far away from so-called civilization, the days filled with light. There was no outlet for his business acumen here, but with money coming in from his investments and plenty of other things to do besides work, he did not care. 'We get some cold winds in August, but you won't find any snowmen. I've never worn a coat for ages.'

'What are the people like?' asked Oriel.

There was a thoughtful pause. 'Different.'

Her mother laughed at Nat. 'Come on, let's have a walk along the beach. That'll wake you up. Vicky, d'you want to come?'

To Oriel's relief the little girl said she wanted to stay with her father. Leaving Nat to clear the breakfast pots the two women descended into a garden of yellow hibiscus and trembling palm leaves, and onwards to stroll barefooted along the wet sand towards a headland that was miles away. Though it was only just after eight, already they could feel the sun burning through their flowered dresses. Neither spoke for a while, heads hanging limp as the delicate tassels of she-oaks in the still air. The sea was like a millpond. Dragonflies hovered and darted above the barely rippling waters of the bay, the only sound a thousand seashells tumbling in the tide, like the crumpling of a paper bag. Bright felt happy, awaiting her daughter's news.

But Oriel did not know how to approach the matter and instead gazed out to sea asking, 'Aren't you lonely here?'

'At first I was. Your father enjoys isolation, though I can't say I do. I was frightened of the blacks as well. I mean I've seen the odd one before but not up close. Your father never batted an eyelid at them – said they're just like anyone else, which was rather charitable for an unsociable devil like him, I thought. Apparently he met all sorts of people when he lived in Canada – even Red Indians! That's where he learned how to look after animals too – did I tell you we've got a cow as well as the chickens? And he's managed to find a horse that doesn't want to take lumps out o' me.' She lifted her eyes to watch a squadron of pelicans soar overhead. 'And look, there's so many wondrous things here. I've been keeping a journal since we arrived, writing bits and pieces in it every day about the birds and animals and plants. D'you still write articles for that newspaper, by the way?'

Oriel's stomach lurched. In all the upset she had forgotten to tell the editor she would be away. Still, that was the least of her worries. She simply nodded.

'Isn't it funny how we all seem to be picking up the pen? Your father's writing a book – a proper story, I mean, not a journal. It's all about his life.'

Oriel waited for her mother to remark on the oddity of this, but Bright appeared to see no anomaly in someone who was barely literate writing his memoirs. 'Don't mention it, I'm not supposed to tell anyone. He thinks people will regard him as odd. As if they don't already! I'm not allowed to read it till it's finished. If it's like all his other fads it never will be. The gardening's fallen out of favour. And I'm using his paints now – you know the ones he spent so much money on ages ago and he only used once.

They're handy for colouring the pictures in my journal. I'm not very good but I enjoy it. I'll show you later if you promise not to laugh.' However pathetic Bright considered her attempts to be, they certainly illustrated how much she loved this place. 'I don't know how long we'll be staying, though. When Vicky's ready for school it'll be too far to travel. Your father'll probably have got itchy feet by then and we'll be sailing away to India.'

'Can I stay?' blurted Oriel.

'Well, that's what you've come for, isn't it?' The skin around her mother's laughing eyes was creased from squinting against the sun, her face a mass of freckles. 'I've really missed you. How long do you plan to be up here?'

'I meant stay for good.' Oriel had made her decision. 'I don't want to go back.'

Bright was devastated and stopped in her tracks. 'Oh, love –'

'I'm not settled,' rushed Oriel.

'What d'you mean, not settled?'

'I don't think I should've got married.' Out of nowhere, a willy-willy came twirling along the sand, picking up dried leaves and hurling them into a frenzy, whipping up the women's dresses and tousling their hair before spinning on its way. Oriel's eyes followed its passage. The air was suddenly filled with jewels: chattering lorikeets, turquoise butterflies drifting like fallen petals on the breeze.

'But you've got a wonderful life! A kind, considerate husband, a lovely house, a car – what else could you ask for?' Bright didn't see her stance as accusing, merely wanted Oriel to see how fortunate she was. Dragging the tousled strands of hair from her eyes, she thought she detected guilt on her daughter's face. 'There isn't anyone else is there?'

'No.' Oriel wondered why she felt as if she were lying and blushed. There was no one else, no one accessible, just some idea, some longing in her imagination.

Bright felt relieved in a sense. She began to walk again, but there was no lightness in her step now. The heat was like a ton weight upon her shoulders and she had a headache from squinting. 'Well then, don't do anything rash. Have a think about it.'

What else have I been doing in the last six months? thought Oriel, who wished she had never said anything now. Even her mother did not understand.

'Spend a few days with us, then if you still feel the same way . . .' Bright's voice trailed away. 'I won't tell your father yet just in case.' She felt silly and angry that Nat had foreseen that this marriage would not work. But she was damned if she would let it collapse without a fight. 'You won't get anyone better than Clive, you know.'

That was when the young woman realized that she was not going to get the support she had hoped for, was made to feel that she was letting everyone down, that there was no way she would ever be able to leave Clive without hurting her mother. And Oriel could never bring herself to do that.

Nothing further was said about the fact that she had been going to leave her husband. Judging by her father's behaviour towards her he had not been informed; it remained a secret between the two women. Indeed, by the way her mother acted towards her it was as if it had never been spoken of at all, and Oriel was glad to forget. With much news to exchange throughout the day and visits from the wildlife it was comparatively easy to blot out one's troubles.

Alone in one's bed, however, it was harder to ignore. Rain thundered on to the tin roof all night, adding to her insomnia. The few brief hours of oblivion she did enjoy were shortly to be wrecked by kookaburras and magpies feeding their squabbling young, and the crack of the tin roof expanding under the heat of the sun's rays. After lying with eyes closed for a further hour, listening to the creaks and groans and squawks, Oriel dragged herself out of bed much earlier than she normally would at home.

She entered the kitchen to find her parents had only just risen themselves. Bright suggested that Oriel go to keep an eye on her sister in the other room whilst she and Nat made breakfast. Unenthusiastically, Oriel did as she was told. At first she was uncertain how to communicate with the child but smiled in friendly manner when Vicky brought her a toy to examine, and remarked upon its splendour. With such a good reception the little girl decided to bring another toy, and another, and another till Oriel's arms were full and she found herself laughing.

Nat paused at the kitchen door to watch his elder daughter play with her younger sister. Oriel seemed to be paying her more attention than usual, which gratified him. He went about helping his wife in preparing breakfast.

'Well, you've never said owt,' he muttered. 'Is she having one or isn't she?'

Bright shook her head. 'No, it was just me desperate to become a grandmother, imagining things.'

He patted her. 'Bide your time, lass, it'll happen.' Once more he craned his neck to eavesdrop on his daughters.

'You're my sister aren't you?' Vicky was saying. She was thoroughly enjoying making friends.

Oriel smiled. 'Yes, your big sister.'

'Why don't you live with us?'

'Oh, because . . .' Oriel shrugged.

'I like you,' said Vicky.

'Thank you! I like you too.' Oriel was surprised to find that she actually meant it. It was hard to maintain animosity in the face of such charm. Not quite sure what to do she poked a wiggling finger into Vicky's ribs. The child bent over laughing. With the repetition of this act

Vicky wriggled on to the floor where she rolled about like a kitten, Oriel still tickling her, laughing at her giggles and feeling a sudden wave of great emotion that she had never experienced before. The little girl was angelic, anyone would have fallen in love with her, but Oriel's feelings took her off guard. She was overtaken by an urge that had hitherto lain dormant, found her thoughts at odds with everything she had ever declared. She suddenly realized that she wanted a child – more than anything else in the world.

Throughout the day there were sporadic showers but consumed by this new-found desire Oriel made no grumble. At least it eased the unbearable heat, and with enough conversation to last a week she was happy to remain indoors.

In the late afternoon a rainbow appeared over the bay and the family enjoyed a walk on the sands. At their intrusive approach, tiny crabs scurried back to their holes. Vicky clung to her sister's hand, and complained bitterly when either of her parents tried to divest their elder daughter of some childish demand, screaming, 'I want Oriel to do it!'

After dinner, served by her big sister naturally, Vicky continued to cling. Bright told her not to be a nuisance. But Oriel said, 'I'm enjoying myself. Come on, nuisance, let's see if we can count how many baby tree frogs are clinging to the windowpane.' After counting to twenty, she set Vicky on her feet. 'Now, go and fetch one of your books and I'll read you a story before bedtime.' She sat back on the sofa, at ease and smiling. Then she lifted her head to listen. 'What was that?'

Bright was concerned that her elder daughter was perhaps getting too comfortable here. 'Kangaroos,' she muttered, narrowing her eyes to thread a needle.

'How d'you know without looking?' Her sister returned with a book, Oriel dragged the child on to her lap and pressed her lips to the small head.

'Ah well, when you've been here as long as I have . . .' Her mother smiled and tried again to thread the needle. 'No, it's their tails you can hear dragging along the wooden boards.' Sure enough when Oriel, still carrying her sister, peered outside she could see the dark outlines of kangaroo ears between the spindly gums, smelled the musk from their bodies. Chuckling, she pointed them out to Vicky, and paused to stand for a while, breathing in the scent of damp soil and foliage. 'It is a lovely place. It'd be a shame if you had to move.'

'Who said owt about moving?' enquired Nat.

Bright jumped in. 'Oh I just mentioned that there's no school nearby. For Vicky, I mean.'

'Well, what's to stop you teaching her?' asked her husband. 'You did it once.'

'I could but I feel I'd be depriving her of other children's company.'

For once Oriel was allied to her father. 'The lack of peers never did me any harm.'

Didn't it? thought her mother. I often wonder if I'm the one to blame for your wandering restless soul.

Oriel murmured to Vicky, 'You're such a lucky girl to live here. I'd like to come and live here too.'

Bright flicked a worried glance at her husband. How was she ever going to tell him that Oriel wanted to stay?

Her daughter must have sensed this apprehensive air for she sighed and told them, 'But I've asked the man who brought me in the horse and cart to return for me in a week.' Even then she must unconsciously have known that she could not stay.

Nat puffed out his lips. 'He'll probably forget. They're like that up here. Half 'em seem to walk round in a coma. I've lost count of the stuff I've ordered from town and it's never arrived. God help us if we ever need an ambulance. Don't worry, I'll take you. It'll give me chance to give t'hoss some exercise.' Knowing his wife's aversion to being left alone, he told her, 'It'll be a day out for you an' all, throstle face.'

Bright sounded relieved. 'Well, we'll be sorry to say goodbye, but I should think Clive'll be glad to see you. What day's he expecting you back?'

Oriel had turned vague, paying more attention to the little girl in her arms. 'I didn't say for definite. He won't be anxious.'

'Oh well, meladdo's loss is our gain,' announced Nat. 'If you're staying, though, I have to warn you we'll have to cut down on food else we won't have enough to go round till we can get to t'shop. And it'll be your job to cut all t'peas into four.'

'I don't mind,' came the absent reply.

Nat grinned slyly at his wife and shook his head. 'You only have to cut the currants into three. I don't like currants.'

Oriel, coming to her senses, realized he was teasing her and laughed almost gaily – another five whole days before she had to go home.

Clive's wary face beheld her from the door when, after almost a fortnight of living alone, he came home from work to find her in the kitchen. 'I didn't know whether you'd come back,' he mumbled, standing there.

'Well, I did.' She had prepared dinner for him – his favourite dish. Oriel gained little pleasure from food herself but was happy to fulfil this need in others.

He did not kiss her, but asked with a cautious smile, 'Did you have a good time?'

'Yes, it's a lovely place. Very isolated though.'

'I suppose it was really hot, wasn't it?'

'It was on the day I arrived but the rest of the week was quite pleasant. And the temperature drops in the evening. You don't get those unbearably sticky nights like you do down here.'

He lifted his chin in a gesture of acknowledgement, then looked at the table.

'Well, sit down.' She pulled out a chair.

Clive did likewise and gave polite acceptance of the food she spooned on to his plate. 'That looks nice.'

'I thought you might've been at your mother's,' said Oriel, dipping a fork into her meal.

'I went once or twice for my dinner.' He looked to be enjoying his repast. 'I just said you'd gone to visit your parents. There's a pile of letters for you.'

'I know, I've opened them.' She looked rueful. 'One of them was from the newspaper. They must have been trying to telephone me while I've been away. Because I haven't contacted them for a fortnight they've assumed I'm not interested in submitting a weekly article and they've asked someone else to do it. I don't care anyway.' Consumed by her need for a baby, everything else seemed trivial. 'What's the weather been like here?'

'Good. It was great for Cup Day.'

'Did you win anything?'

'Not on the Cup race – the favourite won – but a few quid overall.'

'The city looks a bit tidier. Has there been any more trouble? What about Myers?'

Clive said things were fine now. The dialogue was to proceed like this for the rest of the evening, each moving cautiously around each other like strange dogs, each of them fearful that the other was suddenly going to sink its teeth into its rival's throat.

Only when they went to bed did Clive embark on serious matters. 'I missed you.' His voice wavered. After a moment's silence he reached a tentative hand through the darkness. Oriel allowed him to touch her. Encouraged, his embrace grew bolder and without further preamble he launched himself upon her body, ramming himself home as if punishing her, pausing only to lean on his elbows and scour her face through the darkness. 'When you said you didn't love me –'

'I do love you!' Overwhelmed with compassion at the

tremor in his voice, Oriel hugged him and wept, too immature to recognize that her words came not from genuine love but from pity.

15

Upon receiving a letter from Oriel telling her that everything was all right now, Bright gave thanks to God, and was even more overjoyed when another arrived two months later to say that her daughter was expecting a baby.

No one was more amazed than Clive who had assumed his wife to have no maternal feelings whatsoever and thought that she was joking when first she made her announcement. Even at her laughing insistence he still beheld her as if this were some cruel hoax, making her wonder if that was what he really believed she was capable of. It rather took the shine off her announcement.

Only when she had made her divulgence to others did he actually believe her, but once convinced he was beside himself with joy. 'I really thought you were kidding! When do you have it? How are you feeling? God, I can't believe it!'

Oriel laughed fondly and told him it was due at the end of July, grunting as he hugged her. 'Ouch! I'm feeling a bit sick at the moment.'

'Sorry! God, I can't believe it.' Two months ago his world had been at an end and now he was to be a father. 'I hope it's a boy.'

'Me too,' smiled Oriel.

But as the birth grew closer she found herself regarding the child inside her as female, began to hope desperately that this were so, even though she, like Clive, still referred to the baby as 'him', and they had only ever discussed boys' names. She enjoyed being heavily pregnant, revelled in the status this bestowed upon her, had never felt so wonderful, and for three of those marvellous months had a valid excuse for refusing her husband his conjugal rights.

'I just can't get over how radiant you look,' beamed Dorothy one afternoon in June. 'How long have you got to go now?'

'Six weeks.' Oriel eased her extended abdomen to the other side of the armchair. 'I might look radiant but I feel like a Zeppelin.'

'What're you going to spend your bangle bonus on?'

Oriel had not thought about maternity benefits. 'I'm more bothered about how much it's going to hurt.'

'If you went into hospital they'd give you Twilight Sleep.'

'Oh no, not me!' After hearing all about her friend's humiliating experience in hospital Oriel had plumped for a home delivery.

Dorothy gave a reassuring smile. 'Don't worry too much. They say the first one's the worst but having Terence was a picnic compared to his little brother.' She lifted a hand to scratch her head, the action causing her long sleeve to crease round her elbow.

Oriel remarked upon the purple colour of her friend's arm. 'What a dreadful bruise!'

Dorothy looked abashed and tugged on her cuff. 'Oh, that! I fell down the back step and on to the concrete. So, do you miss not writing your newspaper column?'

'No, I couldn't give a fig. I wouldn't have time to do it when the baby's born anyway.' Distracted from the other's abrasion, Oriel rubbed her huge abdomen, wearing a maternal smile.

Dorothy smiled too. 'I never thought I'd see the day. You're obviously a lot more settled with Clive now, are you?'

Oriel replied evenly, 'Oh yes.'

'Good, I'm glad you're happy,' came her friend's sincere response, and she poured the tea.

*   *   *

Others were to echo Dorothy's sentiment. Shortly before the expected birthdate Nat and his wife travelled down to Melbourne to stay at their daughter's home. It was Bright's intention to look after the house during those last few uncomfortable days, though there were other things to be dealt with too. For months she had been longing to converse with her son-in-law about the previous marital difficulty he had endured, but had been unable to do so. Now, Oriel's incapacity made it possible for her mother to share an intimate chat with Clive whilst they were in the kitchen making tea and Nat was keeping their daughter company. She had felt sorry for the young man, wanted him to know that he had her support.

'I'm glad everything's all right between you two now.' She stood before the grill, waiting for the crumpets to toast. 'I knew it would be. Oriel's very loyal, you know. I think part of the problem of her being . . . well, unsettled as she called it, goes back to her childhood. She's all mixed up about men. It's probably because her father wasn't around when she was a child. Don't mention it to Nat, he'd be terribly hurt, but I'm just telling you so you don't feel as if it was all your fault. There's nothing wrong with you, Clive, and Oriel's obviously come to realize that. I'm really happy for you both.'

'Now then you two, it looks as if there's more than tea brewing in here!' Nat had come in to enquire why things were taking so long, interrupting Clive's show of gratitude.

Bright turned to her husband, wearing a guilty smile, then removed the brown crumpets from under the gas flame. 'Oh, we're just putting the world to rights. Clive's been talking about their new Labor Government in Victoria. He doesn't think they'll last long.'

He took her word but had the niggling idea that his wife was keeping something from him.

'Mother!'

All three heads turned to the room from which the cry

emerged. Juggling the red-hot crumpets, Bright was the first to rush and investigate. Oriel stood there, legs apart and indicating her sodden chair. Her mother took instant charge of her, ordering Clive to telephone the midwife.

It was Oriel's mother, too, who sat beside her throughout the groaning nocturnal hours of agony, her mother who first cradled the newborn infant in her arms at sunrise.

Clive was an easy-going fellow but it was an important occasion in his life and he could not help feeling pushed out by this interference, was acutely jealous as he stood in his own bedroom watching his daughter being held by her grandmother before he himself had even had a chance to see her. It was six o'clock in the morning. Consigned to the sofa he had barely slept. The midwife had just gone, giving the signal for him to go in and meet his child, but others had got there first.

'Isn't she just like your father?' Bright was saying to her daughter, rocking and cooing. 'What're you going to call her?'

'Jennifer Bright,' announced Oriel.

Clive wondered when she had decided this but remained silent in the background.

Aching from her labour, Oriel lifted adoring eyes from her child to behold the men standing behind her mother, and noticed the young father's expression. 'Here, come and hold her.'

'No, no, I'm not bothered.' He pretended not to care and made to leave the room. 'I'm off for something to eat.'

Bright, still smiling at the compliment bestowed upon her, turned and regarded him with hurt surprise on her daughter's behalf. Oriel knew what had provoked his churlishness but was too elated and in love with her child to care.

Nat moved closer to the bed, stopped to examine his granddaughter. 'Mm, I reckon she's like her mother.' He hovered for a respectable length of time then said, 'I'm a bit peckish an' all. I think I'll go and join meladdo.'

Bright offered a tentative question. 'Where will you have her baptized?' When the new mother looked awkward, she said, 'Oh, I didn't think you'd be having her done in a Catholic church! I was just wondering that's all. But, you're right. Better not to rock the boat when things are going so well.' *But I'm sure my mother would never understand,* she sighed inwardly.

Nat found Clive in the kitchen though there was no food being prepared. The look on his son-in-law's face told all. Nat was unsure what to do and so looked out of the window, noting the sparkle of frost on the bare branches. 'By, I'm really feeling the cold down here. Funny, isn't it, what you get used to?' When the other offered a monosyllabic response he changed tack.

'Jennifer, eh? What made you call her that?'

Clive gave a petulant shrug. 'Ask Oriel. It was nothing to do with me.'

Much as Nat did not care for the young man's sarcastic streak he empathized on this occasion, offering awkwardly, 'Eh, women and their babies. Makes you feel a bit like the proverbial at the wedding, doesn't it? Is it all right if I make a pot o' tea?'

'If you like. I'm off to tell Mum and Dad they've got another granddaughter on my way to work.'

'Oh aye, they'll be wanting to come and see her.'

'Yes, if they're allowed anywhere near,' muttered his son-in-law, and departed.

Once Oriel's parents had gone, however, and Clive was able to reclaim his own domain he allowed himself to become enamoured of his daughter. So too did Oriel but alas it was to the exclusion of all others. She adored her baby, had fallen totally in love with her, spent every hour of the day singing to her and cosseting her. At night she was so tired from attending the baby's needs that she went to bed early and was asleep by the time her husband climbed in, so escaping any advances he might make. Feeling excluded he began to go out alone on an evening again.

The emotions Oriel held were conflicting. She did not really miss him, but since Jennifer's birth the euphoria she had felt during her pregnancy had begun to drain away. She was feeling vulnerable and weepy and had no one near at hand to turn to apart from Dorothy, who unfortunately at the moment was on holiday visiting Cuthbert's relatives. Melinda was a two-hour journey away. Besides, Oriel's visits there had tailed off recently. In the recognition that her longing for Daniel could never be assuaged, she had decided not to think about him, to devote all her tenderness to her baby – yet, there were days when she desperately needed contact with another woman, and today was one of them.

Thora was the last person who would normally have fulfilled her requirement, but when Oriel saw this familiar face in town, she gave a friendly smile and parked her pram alongside to chat.

Clive's sister was unusually amicable. 'And how's little Jenny doing? She certainly looks a picture of health. Not like this one.' She pointed to her own pram. 'She's a horrible little wretch, she really is. Won't talk, just points to what she wants. I'll do you a swap if you like.'

'I don't think you'd want her smelling as she does at the moment. She always manages to save it for when we're on the train to town.'

Oriel grinned and felt a new affinity with Thora, an obligation to make an effort to befriend Clive's sister. Now that she was a mother herself she could understand things that had hitherto been a mystery, realized how much she had hurt Thora in the past by not showing any interest in her child. How could she make up for previous antagonism? Everyone had given her baby money. It was the thing people did with children. Feeling warm, she delved impulsively into her purse and handed a coin to Thora with a smile. 'Here, put this in her moneybox.'

It drew an immediate retort. 'I don't want your money!'

Oriel's smile froze. She was so astonished to receive this discourtesy in the face of her friendship that she could think of no response, and tried to muster some chitchat that would help fight the tears that threatened, whilst dropping the coin back in her purse.

Thora, seemingly unaware of her own rudeness, continued blithely, 'Are you going to Mum and Dad's on Sunday?'

'Probably.' Oriel kept her eyes lowered, urging the tears not to spill over whilst tucking her purse under the pram covers. 'Are you?'

'No, we're going to Bill's parents.'

Good, thought Oriel. I hope you have an accident on the way, you and your bloody snotty-nosed little Angela Rose. 'Oh well, I'd better go, I suppose.' Casting a sideways glance at Thora she pushed the pram away.

'Give my love to Clive!'

'I will.' Cow! Oriel found it hard to concentrate on her shopping, Thora's insult ringing in her ears. In her mind she invented all sorts of curt ripostes; why could she think of nothing to say at the time?

And why did the house feel so empty when she got home? She tried to read the newspaper. The year had seen great political change. The Labor ministry had lasted four months and now at its collapse Victoria had its first Country Party Premier – would he, the editorial demanded, be able to remedy the dreadful unemployment figures and industrial disputes? But Oriel's newly maternal eyes saw only the dreadful amount of cruelty and murder in its pages that she broke down sobbing and put the paper under a cushion out of sight. A noise drew her to the window. The local children were home from school and had organized a game of football in the street. Sharing her father's dislike of adolescent boys, she glared at them for a while, then tried to find something to do, but at every shriek of victory she came rushing back to the window to check that they were not about to hurl a ball through her window to injure the sleeping cherub who lay beside it.

That evening during dinner Clive noticed that his wife had eaten hardly anything. 'Are you off colour?'

'What?' Oriel looked dazed. 'Oh, no. I'm just not hungry.'

'You used to eat great piles when you were pregnant.'

'I've never eaten haemorrhoids in my life.' She managed a laugh. 'No, I just feel so run-down. I don't think I've ever felt as good as I did when I was expecting.'

'Well, if you're planning to have another let's discuss it first. Don't just go ahead and do it on your own, so to speak, like you did last time, without any discussion with me as if I don't count.'

She accepted this and said it might be nice to conceive another soon. The children would be more company for each other if they were close together in age. Clive acquiesced, and in no time at all Oriel was once again experiencing the wonderful contentment that pregnancy brought to this marriage. Fifteen months after giving birth to Jennifer, she had a son.

This time there had been discussion over the child's name. Clive had feared she would take over again and christen the boy after her father but no, she was quite amenable to his suggestions and it was eventually agreed that he would be called Dorian.

Once again her parents came down from Queensland to attend the new arrival but were several hours too late for the actual delivery. On this occasion Oriel, feeling guilty after allowing Clive to be so pushed out over his first-born, made sure her mother did not hog the new baby quite so much.

Her father, she noticed, required no such persuasion,

in fact he hardly paid any attention to his grandson at all. Tears pricked her eyes as he gave a cursory grunt at the newborn in its mother's arms, then spun away from the bed to turn his attention back to his younger daughter. 'Where's our little Jenny Wren, then? We've come to play with her, haven't we, Vicky?'

The six-year-old nodded. Educated at home by her mother it was not often she had anyone smaller than herself with whom to play.

Clive saw the sparkle of brine in his wife's eyes and felt intense dislike of this man who, in his opinion, was responsible for Oriel's neuroses. 'My mother's taken her out of the way for a while.'

Nat looked disappointed and found no consolation in his grandson as his wife seemed to do, though Vicky returned to her elder sister's bedside to gaze in fascination at her baby nephew.

Still holding her son, Oriel busied herself with the pile of letters that had been delivered to her bed. 'This one's from Mel! She had another little boy last week. Oh, that's nice, isn't it? They're calling him Albert. We'll have to go and see them when I'm on my feet.'

'That's three lads they've got, isn't it?' Nat rolled his eyes. 'I wouldn't like to be in their shoes. Cooking up a lot o' trouble for theirselves in a few years' time. Spud's daughter keeps churning 'em out like chips, by all accounts.'

This news had accompanied the latest money order from his friend who, to Nat's amazement, had not ruined the business but was doing very well. He cocked his head at the sound of the outside door, summoned Vicky after him and went into the hall to find Clive's mother and his granddaughter. 'Ah, this is who we've really come to see – our little Jenny Wren!'

Bright felt deeply sorry for her daughter but did not want to push those tears over the brim by uttering anything sentimental. Instead she patted Oriel and said, 'I'll give you two a bit of peace and go offer Daphne a cup of tea.'

'Old sod,' muttered Clive, coming to sit on the bed. 'What's he got against lads?'

'He's been one himself, he knows what they're like.' Oriel tried to smile and gazed down upon her son who, having just been fed, looked lazy and contented and wore a trickle of milk on his lower lip. 'But I don't think we need to worry about Dorrie taking after his grandfather – he looks just like you.' She nuzzled the tiny crumpled face, addressing her words to her son. 'And he didn't cause half so much trouble getting here as his sister, no he didn't!' Eager not to exclude the child's father she stopped cooing and kissing and passed her bundle over. 'Here, have a cuddle.'

Clive folded his son in his arms, beaming down at him. 'It's nice to have somebody who'll let me cuddle them.'

Choosing to ignore the double-edged remark, Oriel merely watched the pair and shifted on the mattress, trying to ease the weight on her sore posterior.

The father chuckled as his baby yawned and then stared up at him with navy-blue eyes. 'He's really wide awake, isn't he?'

'Yes, we're both a lot less battered and weary than last time.' Her labour had only lasted four hours in all. 'I felt really close to him straight away.'

He gave a warning smile. 'Don't let the other one hear you say that.'

Oriel heaved a sigh. 'I don't mean I feel closer to him than Jenny, I couldn't feel any closer than I do. All I meant was the birth didn't wear me out so much this time and I was able to take more notice.' Bloody idiot, her mind condemned him, don't you ever listen to anything I say?

Clive's blue eyes turned apprehensive. 'I think he wants changing.'

'Give him back to me then.' She had just taken the

child into her arms when the bedroom door opened and Jennifer appeared around it, closely followed by her grandmother. 'She wanted to come and see her mammy,' explained Bright as the little girl toddled up to the bed arms upstretched and obviously put out by the sight of a usurper in her mother's arms.

Oriel immediately handed the bundle back to her husband and dragged Jennifer on to the bed, smothering her in an affectionate embrace. 'Oh, my big girl!' She kissed and cuddled her then lifted her head to address her mother. 'Dorrie needs his napkin changing, would you mind doing it, please?'

'Of course not, I'm your mother!' Bright held out her arms to Clive, then snatched them back with a look of concern. 'Unless you want to do it?' She had obviously learned from past mistakes.

'Are you joking?' He laughed and handed over his son. 'I don't want anything to do with that end. I'm off for a cup of tea.' He left the women to their business.

Bright grinned at her daughter, then sat in a chair with knees apart, put the baby across her lap and proceeded to strip off the wet napkin. 'Aw look, he's like a little skinned rabbit!' Smearing Vaseline on her grandson, she told Oriel of the dresses she had bought him. 'I looked all over for a present that was made here but could only find foreign rubbish. It's the same with everything you try to buy – American, German, French, Japanese but no Australian. I wouldn't mind if they were cheap but they're not. I finally found something British. At least it'll be properly made.'

She inserted a safety pin through terry towelling, conversation moving to the recent Federal Election which had occurred during Oriel's labour. 'D'you think you'll get into bother for not voting?' An act had made it compulsory to vote in a national poll.

Her daughter laughed. 'What was I supposed to do – have Clive roll me down to the polling station between contractions like a barrel? I hardly think they'd have missed my little vote.' A ninety per cent turnout had returned the Bruce-Page government to office.

'No, don't suppose so. I see they've ripped all the tram-lines up from Point Nepean Road. Every time I come down here there's something different – there! All done and dusted.' Unable to resist the lure of baby flesh Bright hoisted him up to kiss a dimpled knee. 'Couldn't ye just eat him?' she asked her daughter, who gave fond endorsement.

Indeed, Oriel fell deeply in love with her son as she had done with Jennifer before him, cuddling and pampering him. Never were two children so adored. Determined to give them the childhood that had been denied her by means of her mother's drudgery, she abandoned house-work in favour of play, bestowing upon them toys that she herself had loved as a child. In return, and much to her surprise, Dorrie brought a much needed stability to her marriage. She and Clive seemed to have more in common now, liaised quite amicably for the children's sake, and Oriel even felt quite warm towards him. She found that going out together was not such a great ordeal as it once had been, could joke and laugh and share intimate moments as they had done five years ago, and any tribulation that might occur to disrupt this happy family life was shared between them.

Alas, it could not last. For all the family get-togethers and summer holidays, jaunts and picnics, the fact remained that Oriel was living with a man she did not truly love. And Clive knew it. For all she might assent to his physical demands, there was little joy for either of them except in their children.

No one was aware of it except the two of them. Oriel was certain of this by the way her mother greeted Clive so warmly upon their arrival in Queensland that summer.

'Oh, I can see she's looking after you!' Waiting for them at the top of the verandah steps amid abundant foliage, Bright hugged Clive, the first to ascend, and remarked on how plump he had become in the months since they had last met.

Clive returned the warmth. 'Yes, she hasn't thrown me out yet!'

Oriel alone knew it was not simply a joke. Her father did not laugh but then he was unsociable with everyone. Almost everyone. Lower down the staircase and yet to be embraced, she smiled as he swept Jennifer off her feet. But the smile wavered when, after leaning over to kiss his daughter, he totally neglected the four-month-old grandson in her arms and instead marched off down the steps with one little girl in his arms and another at his heels, to show them his new chickens.

Bright herded them inside. 'Come on, lunch is almost done. I'll bet you're ready for it, aren't you?'

Oriel was more hungry for conversation, but replied that she was famished. 'I'll help you. Here, Clive, you hold Dorrie.' Leaving him with their son, she joined her mother in the kitchen.

Later, when all were relaxing after a wonderful meal, Nat perused the newspaper that he had not had time to read that morning and announced, 'Looks like you've come to t'right place, anyroad. I see they've had some pretty bad bushfires down in Vic.'

Along with her mother Oriel was at the table cutting out pictures from magazines and helping the two little girls to stick them in scrapbooks. 'I didn't see anything in our paper. It must've happened whilst we were on the way up here. Whereabouts?'

'Gilderoy, Powelltown – that's up near whosit's place, isn't it?'

Oriel's hand had frozen on the scissors. 'Has anyone been hurt?' Her heart had started to pound.

'Hang on, I'll just read it.' Nat was quiet for a moment

whilst his daughter sat motionless, her mind urging him to hurry. In the tense silence her heart competed with the low rumble of the tide. 'Two men, two women, three children –'

Bright gasped in sympathy, causing her son-in-law to emerge from his doze.

'And twelve horses.'

Abandoning the scissors, Oriel was on her feet, a wild look to her eye. 'We'll have to go.'

Clive looked perplexed. 'What's that?'

His creased and bleary expression annoyed her. ' Didn't you hear? There's been people killed at Powelltown.'

'Does it mention Yarra Junction?' He stretched and yawned.

'No, but – it's near!' And Daniel worked up there. 'We have to go.'

'But we haven't been here two hours!' He turned watery eyes to his father-in-law. 'Does it name the people killed?' The other shook his head. 'Well then, there's not much point us trailing all the way back down there before we're certain. We've hardly recovered from the journey up here. And what makes you think that out of hundreds of people it's Melinda who's the victim?'

Melinda? Oriel reddened and banished the picture of Daniel from her mind. Though sick with worry, she saw the wisdom to his words, and slowly began to resume her task, scissors snipping round the outline of a dog. 'I suppose you're right.'

'Thank heavens!' Nat put down his paper and grabbed his granddaughter as she toddled over to show him her scrapbook. 'I thought I was gonna have to say goodbye to my little Jenny Wren just when she'd got here.' A wail disturbed his concentration. 'Oh, there's that nuisance of a brother of yours! He can go if he likes, tell him.'

'He's hungry,' muttered Oriel and, picking her son from his makeshift bed on the sofa, took him out into a bedroom to feed him, still worrying over the victims of the bushfire.

Even at the end of the holiday this thought was only put aside in order to concentrate on farewells to her parents and sister, who had accompanied them the thirty-five miles to the railway station.

'It's been wonderful to see you all,' Oriel told them tearfully, as she hugged each in turn. 'Oh don't!' she begged her mother, who had broken into sobs. 'We'll try and get up here again next year – if you'll have us?'

Babe in arms, she took a last fond look, then stepped up into the train, Clive following with Jenny, and embarked on the tedious return to Victoria.

During the days that followed there was plenty of time to dwell upon her course of action. However, her plan of visiting Yarra Junction immediately she got home had to be postponed for the train from Albury did not arrive in Melbourne until two-thirty in the afternoon, missing the connection. There was an express at five but no return to the city. Exhausted from the journey and apprehensive over Daniel, Oriel was unable to sleep that night and so overslept the next morning. This did not matter to Clive, who was preparing to enjoy a last leisurely weekend at home before returning to work on Monday and was astonished at her proposal to visit Yarra Junction.

'Aren't you sick of travelling? I thought we'd have a lazy day round at Mum and Dad's.'

'I couldn't sleep another night not knowing.' Her insides still churned with uncertainty.

'Pity they aren't on the telephone.' He sighed but fell in with her plans. 'All right, let's have an early lunch then – but the traffic might be bad at this time of day. I don't know what time we'll get there.'

'Oh, I wasn't meaning that! You go and have a nice afternoon at your mum's. I'll catch the half-past two train if I go straight after lunch.' At breakneck speed she prepared a meal, then afterwards changed her blouse for a fresh white georgette one.

Clive watched her pack a bag with tins of salmon, fruit and jam. 'Sure you're not off on a trip up the Orinoco?'

She laughed. 'I'll be back tonight. But I know Mel will ask me to stay for tea and they haven't much money. Can I leave Jenny with you?'

Still following her with his eyes as she collected napkins and other necessities to pack into the baby's pram, Clive asked, 'How're you going to manage with that thing?'

'I'll shove it in a dog box. I'll have to go – bye!' She pushed the pram to the front door, kissing Jenny on the way.

Skimming over the pavements to the local station, she was lucky enough to find the train already there and people almost boarded. Seeking one of the carriages with wider doors she was just in time to manoeuvre the pram into the carriage before it glided away, and was to enjoy similar luck in catching her connection at Flinders Street. Flushed with anticipation, she heaved a sigh and sat back in her seat for the two-hour journey to Yarra Junction where, to her great joy, she found her friends safe and sound.

'Oh, thank God!' she cried as Melinda, seeing her from the window, came down the sloping path to meet her at the gate, Daniel following. Daniel, dear Daniel! What rapture filled her breast at the sight of him. 'I've been worried out of my mind – almost came down from Queensland.' Overcome by this release of emotion, Oriel dropped her bag and covered her mouth, urging herself not to cry.

Melinda was touched at this concern. 'Aw, you poor thing, having your holiday spoiled like that! Here, let me hold the bub – aw, isn't he sweet?' She picked Dorrie from his pram and lingered by the gate in the brilliant sunshine, jiggling him in her arms. 'And look at you, stranger!' Her eyes took in the softer, wavier hairstyle, the elegant white blouse with its confetti-like circles of black suede. 'Two kids and still as glamorous as ever. Isn't she, Dan?'

'Too right.' He cocked his head and squinted at her. 'Could yer just move over there to your left an inch or two? Stop! Right there, with the sun behind yer.'

A bemused Oriel fingered her double strand of beads, waiting for some compliment, but he just stood there – then gave a theatrical sniff and said, 'That's better. The sun was in me eyes.'

'Oh, he's a ratbag!' All laughing, Melinda lashed out with her free hand. 'After you've been so worried about him! He needs his backside singeing. Shouldn't joke, I'm really lucky to still have him.'

She spent a brief moment telling Oriel about the dreadful fires, pointing out the blackened patches on the landscape, those parts merely singed imitating autumn colours. 'Well, come in, Orrie, and have a cuppa. You'll stay for tea?'

'There's only an hour and a half before the last train goes back to Melbourne,' warned Daniel.

'Time enough for tea!' scolded his wife. 'We'll have it early. You will stay, won't yer?'

'Thank you.' Oriel picked up her bag and followed Melinda into the house, Daniel behind her, his effect on her as electric as ever. What foolishness had deceived her into thinking she could bar him from her life just by distance? How could her heart be thumping at such a rate and yet her words be so evenly delivered? 'I've brought one or two things. I didn't want to land myself on you if you hadn't had time to get anything in.' She dumped them on the table, earning Melinda's gratitude. 'Can I just visit your necessary before I get any more liquid down me?'

'You know where it is.'

Leaving the baby with her friend Oriel exited through the back door. When she returned only a few minutes later Daniel was no longer present. The effect was devastating. Melinda saw her friend's eyes tour the room expectantly. 'Dan's had to go out to see a mate – couldn't get out of here fast enough. Don't think he fancies the idea of sitting listening to two women clucking all afternoon. I tried to make him see how rude it is of him to walk out after you've been so worried about us and took the trouble of coming up here to make sure we were safe, brought us all these lovely things, but he wouldn't have a bar of it. Blokes! Still, we'll have a better time without him, won't we? Sit down and tell me all your news!'

When a subdued Oriel arrived home at half past nine Clive had fed their daughter and was just about to go and run her bath water. 'Oh, here's your mum come and caught us out! We wanted to stay up late to see you, didn't we, Jen?'

'Mummy bath me,' said the nineteen-month-old child.

Exhausted, Oriel laid the sleeping Dorrie on a chair, barely able to cope with the effort of speaking. 'I think we'll forget about the bath tonight.'

Clive frowned. 'Nothing's happened to your friends, has it?'

'No, they're all fine.' She rested one buttock on the chair arm.

'Told you they would be – she doesn't sound too happy about it, does she?' Clive joked to his daughter.

'I'm just so worn out.' Oriel rubbed her forehead. Daniel, Daniel, why couldn't you have stayed?

'I told her not to go straight after that long trip, didn't I?' Clive asked Jennifer. 'But would she listen?'

'Come on then, Snugglepot.' Oriel bent and kissed her little dark-haired girl. 'Let's get you put to bed and I can sit down.'

'Don't I get one of those?'

Dealing him a light kiss she got on with her task.

Later, after reading Jennifer a few pages of *The*

Gumnut Babies and tucking her in bed, and the baby in his cot, she slumped exhausted in an armchair. 'Oh, my legs. I haven't even got the energy to put a record on.'

Her husband had recuperated somewhat. 'What do you want, Gladys Moncrieff?' When she said she didn't mind he took a large record out of its paper sleeve and placed it on the turntable, then went to relax in a chair. 'It's too late for me to go anywhere now. I'll make do with Gladys tonight.'

'What d'you think about getting a wireless?' Her query held little enthusiasm, designed only to take her mind off other things. 'I've seen a nice one for ninety pounds.'

'Ninety quid? Phew! I'll bet they'll be down to a third of that in a couple o' years when they're not so new-fangled. Same happened when I got my car.'

'I just thought it might be a change from the gramophone, seeing as I'm in the house most of the time.'

'Well, whose fault is that? I offer to take you out but you won't come.' It was uttered with a laugh but there was criticism behind it.

'I didn't mean you won't take me out.' Oriel was sullen. 'I don't particularly want to go out after I've been looking after the children and the house all day.'

'I'm glad somebody gets some attention round here,' he said cheerfully. 'Oh, get a wireless if you like. It would be rather good – but why does everything you want have to be so expensive?'

Oriel knew that he considered her to be shallow and ostentatious for surrounding herself with such luxurious items, when all she was really trying to do was create an oasis that would take her mind off the cruelty and sordidness of the world, and her own unhappy marriage.

The dialogue fizzled out. He picked up a newspaper and held it right in front of him. Oriel could not see him picking his nose but knew from experience that he was doing so from the way the pages trembled.

Irritated, she said in an effort to distract him, 'I think I might go to the art gallery next week.'

The paper came down revealing a suspicious face. 'What's made you suddenly want to go there?'

She noticed to her disgust that he was still raking his nostril. 'No particular reason. I just feel like going.'

The distaste must have shown in her expression for, realizing what he was doing, he pulled out his handkerchief and wiped his fingers. 'Yes, but you've never shown any inclination to go all the time we've been married.'

She frowned. Gladys was singing the same line over and over. Seeing that Clive was not about to correct it she heaved herself from the chair and went to examine the gramophone. 'This record's cracked.'

'Jenny's been using it as a plate for her doll. You were talking about the art gallery.'

She sighed and put on another record. 'I just saw a poster, when I was waiting for the train, advertising an exhibition of local artists. I thought it might be enjoyable, that's all.'

He turned his mouth down and went back to the paper. 'You go if you want to.'

As the tune came to its end he folded the newspaper, put it aside and went to put on another record. 'Do you want a cup of tea?' Noticing that she was about to get up he said, 'No, sit there, I'll make it.' And he went into the kitchen.

In his absence she leaned over to grasp the newspaper and in the glow of the standard lamp behind her chair, took to browsing. Amongst the other items she came across an advertisement for the exhibition, and was instantly supplied with the reason for his suspicion. Along with other contributors, a certain Errol Windross would be hanging his display of war paintings. She sighed, half amused, half infuriated. Did he seriously think that she was going there to take up with Errol again after all these years – a man who had long been consigned to history?

Apparently he did, for he was to raise the subject again later in the evening, asking, 'Do you want me to come to this art exhibition with you?'

'Oh, I don't know if I can be bothered to go now.' She sounded weary.

'That was a quick change of mind.' His eyes held mistrust.

She realized that her answer had given credence to his hunch about her meeting Errol, but angry though she was at him she did not respond.

'I think I might go to bed in a while.' He took out a cigarette. Oriel did not join him; she had given up the habit some years ago.

'I'll go in the bathroom first, then.' She took the cups to the kitchen, visited the bathroom then changed into her nightclothes and lay there waiting for him to come to her, dreading the advances he was sure to make, unable to refuse without good reason, hoping he would be too tired.

But when he slipped into bed beside her and his movements told her he was not too tired she resigned herself to lying there beneath him, asking herself what sort of a fool she was to put up with this.

Oh, Daniel. Daniel.

As ever it was Dorothy to whom she turned for solace, pouring out her woes on an impromptu visit after a trip to buy a radio licence.

'I almost didn't call in,' she told her friend in tongue-in-cheek manner as both sat down in easy chairs to coffee, whilst Jennifer and Dorothy's younger son nibbled biscuits under the table, the baby asleep in his pram. 'It was either come to see you or run off with Errol Windross and I chose you – I hope you're flattered.'

'Errol?' The brown eyes opened wide.

Oriel pretended nonchalance. 'Oh yes, didn't you hear? He's got an exhibition at –'

'Oh, I saw that!'

'Yes, so did Clive and when little old innocent here mentioned she wouldn't mind going to the art gallery for a change he as much as accused me of having an illicit liaison. Honestly!' She dropped her theatrical air and sipped her coffee. 'He really gets my goat. I didn't even know Errol was there!'

Dorothy gave a sympathetic laugh. 'Clive doesn't get any better with age, does he?'

'Does Cuddy think you're going off with every man who comes to the house? Mine does! He makes me sick – and it's not just that, it's his blasted nose-picking. He thinks I can't see what he's doing behind that newspaper but I can hear his wrist going click, click click as he rakes around.'

'Ugh, how revolting!' Dorothy almost collapsed in disgusted laughter. 'You'll have to ask him if he has a miner's licence.'

'He wouldn't care. Sometimes he doesn't even bother to hide behind the paper when he does it – I mean, it's tantamount to an act of contempt for the person you're with, isn't it? At least I do it in private.' She chuckled, as did her friend.

'Does he still go out and leave you on your own every night?'

'Yes, thank goodness. I wish he'd leave me for good.' She responded to her friend's look of disbelief. 'I do!'

Dorothy made an admittance that her own marriage was not all it seemed. 'I've often wondered what it would be like if Cuddy died, tried to imagine how I'd feel if he had an accident and didn't come home. Once he was late and I really thought he'd been knocked off his bicycle or something. I was ever so relieved when he finally came in.' She nibbled a thumbnail. 'That was a long time ago, though.'

'Yes, I've gone down that road too,' said Oriel darkly. 'Would you ever think of leaving him?'

'I did try.' Dorothy gave a tearful little laugh at her friend's shock over this sudden disclosure, and hugged herself, rubbing her upper arms. 'Don't say anything, will you?'

'Oh, Dot, I wish you'd spoken up before if you were so unhappy! Here's me going on – how long ago was it?'

'After I'd had Tim.' This was her second child. 'I went to Mother's but Cuddy came to take me back.'

To date, Oriel had been too steeped in her own troubles to ponder that Cuthbert might have dominated his wife by any other means than his will, but now she detected a sinister note to Dorothy's words.

Remembering the livid bruise and her friend's attempts to make light of it she breathed, 'He hits you, doesn't he?' Why had she not noticed before?

Dorothy gave a shameful nod, then without any drama started to cry, just sat there with tears rolling down her cheeks.

Oriel realized that this was the first time she had seen her friend weep, that it was always she who leaned on Dorothy, never the other way around. She erupted. 'Just wait till I get my hands on him!'

Dorothy held up one hand, the other holding a hand-kerchief to her nose. 'Oh no, don't! I beg you, Oriel, please don't say a word. You'll only make it worse.' She blew her nose, then mopped away all trace of tears. 'It doesn't happen very often. He's all right if I do as he wants.'

'But you shouldn't have to live like that! Does he hit the children?' Oriel was already contemplating going to the authorities.

'No, just me.'

'The shit – sorry! Oh, Dot, why not just leave him?'

Dorothy leaned on her knees and shrugged. 'He's always so apologetic after he's done it. I still have feelings for him. He's a good father. I couldn't take the children from him, and I couldn't go without them. Besides, where would I go? Not Mother's – she's no idea that he does it, I only told her that we row. But we don't row, I daren't row with him, daren't even offer an opinion. I can't go anywhere else. How would I live? I've no money of my own.'

'I can give you some!'

Dorothy shook her head. 'No! No, thanks for the offer, but I've made my bed.' She gazed at the carpet.

Oriel felt guilty and selfish. 'My problems are nothing beside yours. The money's no obstacle. It's cowardice that's my *bête noire*.' How could she be so cruel to a man whom everyone loved? Everyone except herself. 'I don't know why he doesn't leave me. He can't be happy. I wish he'd meet someone else and just go. But there's not much likelihood of that happening.'

'Looks like we're both stuck in the same boat, doesn't it?' Negating the seriousness of her previous revelation Dorothy sat upright, donned a jolly air and hoisted her coffee cup. 'Cheers, sailor!'

Oriel gave a tight smile, but was slow to raise her own cup, for what seemed like some kind of perverted joke to her friend was a genuine nightmare to her. She did not want to be in this boat, for there seemed imminent danger that it would capsize.

16

Throughout the next two years Oriel clung to that sinking craft, with only Jennifer and Dorrie to act as lifebuoys, helplessly awaiting the monumental wave that was bound one day to swamp them.

Perversity lending a hand, she had begun to take out her frustration on the very ones she loved most – her children, though it was Dorrie who received the brunt of her ire, for he was more like his father than ever. At three years old he was into everything, and everything he did got on Oriel's nerves. Shouldering enormous guilt, she tried desperately to fight her irritable impulse, compared herself unfavourably to her own mother who had dedicated her life to her child. Yet the moment he misbehaved again she could not help but lash out at him verbally, all noble gesture vanished.

For all Oriel might scold her little son she was very protective of him when in her father's presence for she knew what real violence Nat was capable of towards boys. Never once had he raised a finger to either child but to see him treat the two so differently seemed to Oriel as if he had taken a flail and used it upon her heart.

Waiting now for her parents to arrive for a long summer holiday in Melbourne, she knew it would start the minute he got through the door – and so it did.

Tanned and smiling, Nat entered the hall and immediately swept Jennifer up in his arms for a cuddle before anyone else, making great play of examining his grand-daughter. 'Our little Jenny Wren!' Those who despised Nat would be amazed that such a taciturn fellow as this could project so much charm. The little girl's dress had become rucked up to display her navel and catching sight of it, he stuck his finger into the hollow and exclaimed, 'Aw, you've been shot!' Then, chuckling, he put her on her feet and embraced his elder daughter whilst Bright followed suit.

'Hello, Dorrie, aren't you married yet?' Though not so cruel as to ignore the little boy completely Nat merely patted the child's head as he continued on to the living room with everyone else. 'How yer goin', Clive?' He shook hands with his son-in-law. 'By, I could do with a cup o' tea!'

Oriel went to put the kettle on, then returned to chat whilst waiting for it to boil.

Jennifer was organizing her grandparents, as was her wont. 'You sit there, Grandad. You sit there, Vicky –'

'I don't want to sit there!'

'You have to!'

'Stop barguing,' little Dorrie told his sister, who ignored him.

'No, you're not allowed to sit there, Nanna! You have to sit here in the special chair.'

'Oh, do I? Sorry! I'd better do as I'm told then.' Bright took off her hat and flimsy gloves, handing them over at her granddaughter's demand. 'Oh, it's good to be here.'

Dorrie swung on the arm of the chair, happy to see her. 'I've got two nannas. Nanna Widdowes and Nanna Prince.'

'That's right!' His grandmother petted him, then turned to her daughter. 'I can't get over how Brighton's changed. Where's all the green gone?' Hundreds of acres of farmland were now covered in housing, and the only open spaces were the parks. 'As for Melbourne –' She shook her head in disbelief.

Her daughter agreed. During the ten years she had been in Australia she had seen the metropolis creep further and further outwards from its arc around the bay. What had once been country towns were now part of its suburbs, and contrary to the increasing flow of immigrants from the old country there was less and less Englishness about the place.

'There're still as many strikes as ever, though,' complained Oriel. Despite the Prime Minister's obsession with industrial extremists his confrontational stance had only exacerbated matters. Throughout the year the ever-present union unrest had reached a climax, characterized by national violence on the waterfront, in which armed police had shot and wounded strikers. The optimism of the post-war years was beginning to fade, the electorate demanding political solution. The Bruce-Page government may have been returned, but only just. 'I thought Labor might get in this time – Jennifer, take your feet off the furniture.'

'I don't reckon they'd do much to solve this massive overseas debt if they did get in,' proffered Nat.

Bright had read of this in the papers but admitted she did not really understand it. 'I thought we'd been having bumper export crops?'

Nat was patient. 'We have, but so has everywhere else. Prices are at rock bottom. I'm glad I'm not in farming.' Seeing his investments dwindle in value he had converted them to cash some time ago.

Bright apologized for her ignorance. 'Oh well, whatever's going on I still think it's sad that Melbourne isn't the capital any more. People here must be very put out.' Government House had moved to Canberra the previous year.

Oriel gave a wan nod, but in the silence that followed her mind was once more consumed with her own miserable state and not the one of Victoria.

Nat was feeling uncomfortable. Dorrie had come to hover by his chair. He could almost feel his breath – could certainly feel his gaze. After trying to concentrate on the two girls playing with dolls at his feet, he was forced to study the child enquiringly.

Gaining the attention he sought, Dorrie asked, 'Am I your little Jenny Wren as well?'

'Don't be daft, you're a lad.' Nat laughed, though not unkindly.

Clive wanted to kill him. 'Away, Dorrie, let's go get that tin of biscuits.' Tense of feature, he went to the kitchen, shouting to his wife, 'Kettle's boiling!'

Oriel was furious at her father too and went to make the tea, Jennifer and Vicky galloping after her in imitation of ponies.

'Why doesn't Grandad Nat like me?' Dorrie enquired of his mother.

'He does!' Oriel tried to sound cheerful as she set the teacups on a tray. 'He's just grumpy. That's what we'll have to call him – Grandad Grumpy! Here, pick what sort of biscuits to put on the plate. Not you, Jennifer, let Dorrie do it.'

In the others' absence Bright quietly remonstrated with her husband.

'I didn't mean owt,' he defended himself. 'All I was saying was I can't call him by a lass's name.' Nat genuinely did not realize that he was making this distinction between his grandchildren.

Bright knew this, but warned him all the same, 'Well, just take care what you say and remember, he's only three years old.'

When the tea and biscuits arrived, to make up for his previous slip, Nat asked Dorrie, 'Are you coming to town this afternoon, see Father Christmas with us?'

With his grandson's wary nod, the girls came scrambling on to Nat's knee. 'Can we go up and down in the lift?' begged four-year-old Jennifer.

'You can do anything you want,' promised her grandfather. 'If you let me have me cup o' tea first.' They left him in peace and returned to their dolls.

Munching a biscuit, Dorrie sat on the carpet and continued to watch his grandfather with wary eyes, his normally talkative nature subdued. Excluded from the conversation that, from his viewpoint, seemed to be taking place miles above his head, he noticed how differently his mother behaved in his grandfather's presence.

'We noticed a lot of For Sale signs on our way here.' Bright sipped her tea. 'Your father says there's a recession coming.'

Clive thought otherwise. 'Business is booming at Myers, and everywhere else for that matter.' All his friends had wireless sets and refrigerators and every other household appliance.

'It might be,' replied his father-in-law, 'but I'll bet most of 'em are buying on credit. I've seen all this happen before. You have this massive building spree and prices go through t'roof, then the next minute you can't get rid of stuff – have to sell it at next to nowt. Read t'newspapers, all the signs are there.'

'Well, there's a lot of unemployment, I'll grant you,' said Clive. 'But –'

'Too much borrowing.' Nat gulped his tea, savouring the taste it left in his mouth. 'You can't go on for ever. There's only so much money around.'

'It's all right for those with ready cash,' replied his son-in-law pointedly. 'But some of us have to borrow.' It was his intention to take out a loan to buy a replacement car, for after eight years the leather seats were all dried and cracked by the sun, the paintwork robbed of its lustre.

'Well, if you need anything come to me,' said Nat. 'Mark my words, there's going to be an awful big headache coming.'

'Can't see it myself.' Clive had never felt so well off. Materially at least.

To prevent further argument, Oriel asked her father, 'What's the latest news from home?'

Nat tried to recall the contents of Spud's last letter.

'My old business is still going strong, apparently. Just as well – Spud's had to take his son-in-law in with him. He hasn't worked since that General Strike they had two years ago.'

Bright chipped in, 'He wants to buy those rented houses off your father.'

'Wants 'em for next to nowt, though.'

Bright used his own argument. 'But you said it wasn't worth keeping your money in property. You might as well take what he's offering and cut your losses.'

Nat did not like anyone to get the better of him. 'Trust a bloody pom,' he muttered, no hint of irony in his Yorkshire accent.

'Look, Daddy!' Vicky held up a golliwog belonging to her niece. 'Can I have one o' these?'

'Aye, we'll buy you one this afternoon,' said Nat.

'We'll ask Father Christmas if he'll bring you one,' corrected his wife firmly.

'Have yer seen this, have yer?' Jennifer was brandishing another toy.

Oriel corrected her daughter. 'It's not yer it's yoooou!' She gave a helpless look at her mother. 'I don't know! She spoke so nicely before she started that kindergarten – watch where you're going, stupid!' This was directed at her son, who in his rush to display his own toys had bumped into the sofa and hurt himself. She felt her mother's disapproval, but it could not match the contempt she felt for herself. Seizing the tearful child she kissed him better, then tried to tickle him into laughter. With her fingers probing his ribs Dorrie broke into tearful giggles, and from his shaking body emerged not only laughter but staccato noises from his rear. 'Oh pardon me!' exclaimed his mother in mock horror. Then to her parents: 'The laughing fartalier.'

'Really!' Bright laughed. 'Using language like that – and you dare correct your daughter for her speech!'

Smiling, Oriel set the child on his feet and drank the

last of her tea. 'Well, who's going to help me make lunch? Don't all shout at once.'

'I'll come.' Bright collected the teacups.

Not wishing to be left with his father-in-law, Clive rose too. 'Come on, Dorrie! Let's go and dig up some worms for our fishing expedition. We won't be long,' he told his wife, and gave her a kiss in passing.

Oriel sighed as her son tripped in his dash. 'For heaven's sake!' Bending, she set him on his feet again before going on her way to the kitchen.

Her mother followed, cups in hand. 'He's a little monkey is Dorrie, isn't he? I suppose he gets a bit of a handful at times.'

Oriel knew that this was a comment on her displays of short temper, and wanted to shout, it's not Dorrie who's the problem! Can't you see? I'm angry because I'm condemned to spend my life with a man who drives me up the wall, knowing I can never escape unless I let you down, and I'm taking it out on my son.

'It must be difficult when they're so close together in age,' tendered Bright. 'It might be an idea to wait for a while before you have any more.'

'What makes you think I want any more?' The comment emerged on a disparaging laugh. Yet it was not the thought of bearing children that repelled her but the process that created them. Even the image of Clive on top of her made her feel sick.

All at once, in the middle of peeling potatoes, she came to a decision: if she could stop the physical side of her marriage then things might not be so hard to bear. She would no longer submit to the demands that so revolted her. Then perhaps, she dreamed, he would grow tired of this inhuman treatment and abandon her. At least then she would not have to confess to her mother that she was the one who had let her down. She had tried, she really had.

*   *   *

At first, that afternoon's decision inflicted little extra pressure on an already fraught relationship. Clive was accustomed to being rejected for one reason or another. Be that as it may, after three months had passed with no physical contact between them he felt entitled to object, was more confused than ever by his eccentric wife, could not understand what he had done to spawn this treatment. Even in the grip of depression Oriel had never been one to lower her standards of grooming, but faced with this unhappy state of affairs Clive began to neglect his own appearance, and at the weekend would dispense with his work suit in favour of more casual attire, and even declined to shave. Realizing that her determination to survive this marriage had imposed yet another toll, she began to dread being seen with this scruffy companion, hated having people assume they were a couple. They might live together, sleep together, but they weren't a couple.

Why could others not see this? Perhaps, she thought as she waved with artificial cheer to a neighbour from the car this Sunday afternoon, perhaps I've become too adept at pretence. She lifted Dorrie from her knee to wave to another as the open tourer wheeled into the street where they lived after its weekly visit to Clive's parents. The afternoon had been passed in the usual series of events: they had eaten dinner, Clive had fallen asleep, she had been left to talk to George and Daphne when she did not feel like talking at all but falling into permanent slumber.

Noting this taciturnity, Clive offered a laugh of sarcasm as he drove. 'You look as if you've enjoyed yourself. I suppose you're as fed up of going to Mum and Dad's every Sunday as you are of me.' When she did not respond he suggested, 'We could just go every other week if you want, and maybe take the kids for a drive to the bush instead.'

'If you like,' came the dull reply.

But in their lacklustre marriage, every other week became every other month. Oriel did not care. For the more she was confronted by the sight of his parents, one at either side of the fireplace like two Toby jugs, she saw an image of herself and Clive in twenty years' time and it made her want to die. She could not stand another twenty years – another twenty minutes.

Sensing that he was in danger of being cast overboard, Clive set up a desperate battle to keep her, uttered endearances, offered what he thought she wanted to hear, and when these failed to work he employed pathos, his fearful words drifting across the gap between them in the bed that night. 'You don't want me to go, do you?'

If only she had the courage to speak the truth. But, ever the coward, all she could think of were the people who would be hurt if she said yes – her parents, his parents, and most of all the children. She answered in the negative but was otherwise silent.

His voice was thoughtful. 'No . . . your mother always said you were very loyal.'

Oriel grimaced in the darkness. She might have guessed he would use her mother, knew that she could never bear to upset her. She recalled now the piece of emotional blackmail he had employed before introducing her to his own mother all those years ago. He had used this tactic throughout their entire marriage, always making out that she had a heart of stone simply because she refused to enunciate her feelings, would not share with him the thoughts that were inside her. Oh he's a lovely bloke, people said, you're so lucky – indeed she herself was guilty of this. She had actually said to Dorothy that he was too good for her. How lacking in self-esteem could one get? Then she frowned as his last words finally made an impact. 'When did she say that?'

'Oh, years ago. When we had that spot of trouble. She told me it was all because your father abandoned you before you were born, that you were mixed up about men.'

Oriel was furious at her mother's disloyalty. It had to be my fault! It couldn't have just been that Clive and I aren't right for each other, it had to be that I'm crazy like her! How could Mother have betrayed me so? One would have thought that she of all people would have understood. There had been only one man for her – even if people had thought she was mad her love for him was unshakable and she could never accept a consolation prize. So why could she not understand that Oriel felt this way too? All right, she had made the error of mistaking pity for love and she had tried her best to be responsible but should one mistake be allowed to ruin one's entire life?

In the dark silence, she thought again of all the people whose feelings she had been trying to protect by remaining here, and one by one they eliminated themselves from her list: her parents had no care for her emotions, they had gone the way they wanted to go; she thought of his parents, the Toby jugs, bored to death with each other. The very image sent her into a pit of blackness. The children: there was no easy answer here, they would be hurt. Only now did she begin to understand her mother's decision to come to Australia with her father all those years ago without a thought for her daughter – or so it had seemed to Oriel at the time. How much anguish Bright must have suffered then, but in the end one had to put one's own survival first. For to stay was to die and what good would she be to the children then?

At that point, Oriel decided that her first loyalty must be to herself. It sounded too grand a proclamation when she did not even know which direction she was going to take but the certainty was that she must stop putting other people's feelings first. Clive would roar with laughter at that! When had she ever thought of anyone but herself? he'd demand. She could hear him saying it, though the dark room was silent. If I hadn't put others first d'you think I'd still be here now? she'd respond. But no, she wouldn't. She wouldn't reply at all. Let him think that she was cold and unemotional and selfish. She didn't care. Freedom tweaked at her fingertips. No longer did her mind scream, I wish I were dead, but, I wish I were alive.

'I told your mum, I always thought you were the best thing that ever happened to me,' murmured Clive.

Oriel closed her eyes and issued a mental scream. Resolution demolished, she turned away into the night.

17

Faced with no chance of escape, other than to perform the unthinkable and walk out herself Oriel groped for anything that might keep her afloat. Taking a leaf from her mother's book she started to keep a journal, but what was there to write? The truth leaped out from those blank pages: you are on your own in life. There is only you.

Whilst she proceeded to endure this stifling existence, life for others was in turmoil. A letter from Melinda brought news that Daniel and the timber workers had gone on strike – indeed, every trade unionist in the country seemed to be at war with Prime Minister Bruce. Daniel's job had always been well paid, and once recovered from the hardships of the Mallee his wife had managed to build a comfortable nest for her family. Today, however, her letter was filled with resentment that Daniel had been asked to work longer hours for less pay. She wondered how long they could hold out for justice – and asked when Oriel and her family would be coming to visit. It had been so long since their last meeting, and she fervently needed a shoulder to cry on.

At first, Oriel had tried her hardest not to go, knew that when she set eyes on Daniel the futile desires would once again be stirred. In keeping with this attempt, her reply to Melinda explained that Dorrie was ill, though she would visit soon if she could. It also contained the offer of financial help should Melinda so require it.

Four months were to pass before another letter came. The workers were still in deadlock. Scab labour had been used to transport the timber from the mills. Amid the pessimism there was a momentary note of amusement to

Melinda's letter as she told of how the strikers had greased the rails to prevent the train getting through – like a centipede trying to climb an icy-pole, was her simile – but eventually the employers had triumphed. There was now talk of evicting strikers' families from mill houses. Melinda was safe enough there but she did not know where the next penny was coming from. It was this desperation in her letter which finally propelled Oriel into a course of action she had been trying to avoid. Filling a basket with anything that might prove useful she left the children with her mother-in-law and took the train to Yarra Junction.

Oh, the crushing disappointment when, at the very moment she entered, Daniel jumped to his feet and said he had to go out and look for odd jobs. Heart and mind in perpetual war, Oriel wondered how she managed to sit there and listen to Melinda's grumblings about him, could have screamed at her friend that she would swap places with her any day, poverty or no, but old friendship forbade any such comment. When Oriel went home, Melinda's gratitude ringing in her ears, she felt worse than ever and thereupon decided she must write to her mother and arrange to take a holiday in Queensland, or go insane.

Just prior to the intended winter sojourn with her parents, however, the Victorian timber strikers finally voted to go back to work, thus ending six months of hardship for her friends. Once again, with hopeful heart, Oriel travelled up to Yarra Junction to give succour, and once again was chagrined not to see Daniel.

'He's grabbing all the overtime he can,' explained Melinda when her friend asked after his whereabouts. 'It's gonna take us ages to get back on our feet. Still, he's always been a hard worker, despite what I sometimes say about him. He doesn't seem to mind. Clive still in work? Good – wouldn't like to swap for a while would yer?' And she laughed.

Leaving behind her unhappy marriage, Oriel embarked on her holiday in Queensland where the sunshine and lush vegetation acted as palliative. Even in winter her mother's garden was engorged with flame and magenta.

As ever her parents were glad to see her and, wrapped up in their grandchildren, seemed not to care that Clive had been too busy at work to accompany his wife. As at every reunion, Oriel noticed a great difference in her sister's appearance and remarked over how tall she had grown. There were slight changes in her parents too, both a few pounds heavier, a few more lines upon each face. Fit and tanned from his coastal jaunts, Nat was a picture of health, though Oriel was concerned that Bright looked somewhat drawn and when her mother momentarily disappeared into the bedroom she asked after her health.

Nat replied that she was fine in general. 'She just gets her old trouble from time to time,' he murmured.

On her way back Bright overheard and laughed. 'There's nothing to concern yourself with. I don't dive under the table any more.' The odd thoughts and violent images still occasionally flashed through her mind but after all these years she had learned to cope with them. 'I didn't bother sending your birthday present when I heard you were coming.'

It had been her daughter's birthday the previous week. 'You can open it now if you want.'

Oriel showed eagerness to do so, the children crowding round.

'Shove up, nuisance,' Jennifer told her brother, and at her mother's reproval said, 'Grandad says it.'

'That doesn't make it right.' Oriel presented mock severity. 'Your brother's name is Dorrie.' Without Clive to burden her she felt almost light-hearted. 'Thirty-three.' She bit her lip as she took off the wrapping. 'Poor old devil.'

'Nay, you're nobbut a lass – this one'll be fifty next

year, you know.' Nat indicated his wife, who swiped at him.

'I'm not forty-nine yet! He always has to let folk know I'm four months older than him. Do you like it?' Bright watched Oriel try on the nasturtium jumper, which fitted over her hips and had a scarf collar with fringing at the ends. 'I bought it the last time I was in Melbourne,' she admitted. 'You can't get anything up here.'

Oriel said it was beautiful and went to find a mirror in which to admire herself, deciding to keep the garment on.

Nat was appraising his granddaughter. 'Jenny's looking posh an' all.'

'D'you like my shoes, Grandad?' she asked him.

'I do, they're lovely. I'm told you've got a birthday coming up soon an' all. How old will you be?'

Jennifer said she would be five. Her cousin Victoria announced she would be ten in September and proceeded to tell the other children and her sister of the duties she performed around the house.

'I'm nearly four,' piped up Dorrie.

'Are you? Stop fiddling with that ornament – because you'll break it! Be told.' Lips tight with exasperation, Nat turned back to his granddaughter. 'So are you having a party, Jenny Wren?'

Jennifer replied that she would and there followed conversation about which friends would be invited. After listening a while, Bright said she would put the kettle on.

'Stay there!' Nat ordered her. 'I'll do it, you can't be doing too much at your age.' He went off to the kitchen, leaving the females to talk. A moment later, Dorrie sauntered in. Without paying him much attention, Nat pottered around, lifting cups and saucers out of the cupboards.

'Can I help?' asked his grandson.

'No, it's done now.' Nat waited for the kettle to boil.

The little boy stood beside him, hands gripping the edge of the workbench, his head barely level with it.

'I help my mummy,' offered Dorrie.

The man did not seem inclined to chat. 'Aye well, as I said, it's done now.'

A long silence followed, during which Dorrie wandered up and down the kitchen trailing his hand over its fittings. As ever, Nat felt awkward and did not know why, could not think of anything to say.

'I like your cooker,' said Dorrie. 'It's lovely.'

His grandfather could not help a twinge of mirth. 'Thank you very much.'

'You're welcome,' said the little boy to Nat's further amusement.

'Right well, make yourself useful and go ask your grandma if she wants a sandwich to go with her cup o' tea.'

Dorrie scampered off and returned with Oriel. 'I'll do them. Mother's just taken Jenny down the garden.'

'No, I'll do 'em! You can stand and talk to me, though.' Nat began to spread butter over slices of bread. 'What d'you want on 'em – and don't say that awful brown stuff,' he warned Dorrie. 'It's like spreading – well, I won't say in front of a lady.' He threw a curious glance at Oriel. 'Is there owt bothering you?'

Immediately she was on the defensive, playing with the scarf of her jumper. 'Why do you ask?'

'Well, you've got odd shoes on.'

She looked down in horror. 'Oh my God! I must have been like it all day. How come I didn't feel the difference?'

'Well, they are quite similar,' joked her father. One shoe was brown, the other navy.

After a moment's laughter they fell to silence whilst he continued to make the sandwiches, then he lifted his head and looked through the window to see black specks floating through the air and on to the line of washing. 'Oh, for God's sake, not again!'

'Is Aunty Thora coming?' enquired an innocent voice.

Bemused, Nat and Oriel both looked down at Dorrie, then the child's mother burst out laughing. 'That's what I always say when Clive's sister comes to visit.'

Nat had to smile too and explained to his grandson that he was only grumbling about farmers burning off their cane. He finished laying slices of ham on the bread. 'Now then, is there anything else you want on this?'

Oriel asked for some tomato. Her son put his finger on his chin as if in deep thought. 'Er, I'd like zelaba.'

The father looked enquiringly at his daughter. 'Don't ask me,' said Oriel.

Feeling playful towards his grandson, Nat made up a word of his own. 'We haven't got zelaba, how about some ossicant?'

Dorrie extended the silliness. 'And poobra.'

'I wouldn't have thought ossicant would go very well with poobra,' pointed out Oriel.

Then all three set to chuckling, Nat making an observation to his daughter: 'This'n's a right comedian, isn't he?'

Pleased that her father was granting Dorrie more attention now, Oriel gave a fond smile. 'He keeps us amused.'

This buoyant mood was to continue throughout the holiday. Accepting his grandson as a personality and not just an encumbrance, Nat included him in all activities, decreeing that they would have their own orchestra and each person would represent a section – Bright would be strings, Oriel woodwind and so on and so forth – Dorrie would be drums and each time the conductor, Nat, pointed at him, he would make as much sound as he could, which of course he did, and after great cacophony everything finally collapsed in laughter. The musical interlude might have sounded like a disaster but in truth was a great success, for at the end of the holiday Oriel could tell by the way her father spoke to her son that the little boy was firmly entrenched in his grandfather's affections.

'I hope you'll come again soon,' Nat told not just his

beloved Jenny Wren but his grandson too, endowing each with his own brand of affection. 'It's easier if you come here. Saves me having to get somebody to look after t'hoss.'

Dorrie turned to his mother for confirmation. 'When can we come and see Grandad Grumpy again?'

'Eh, meladdo, if that's what you call me you needn't bother.' But Nat showed he was joking by ruffling the child's hair.

Whilst Bright was kissing each of her grandchildren goodbye, Nat embraced his daughter, constantly patting her back as if trying to make reparation for the previous neglect of her son. 'He's a grand little chap,' he muttered gruffly into her shoulder. 'I'll miss him – you too.'

Oriel was glad that her parents assumed her tears to be just an indication of her sadness at parting, when in fact they flowed more from a sense of dread at going home.

Winter turned to spring and still Clive maintained his pathetic attempts to keep her, grinding her further into despair. The crumbling state of her marriage was echoed throughout the country. In October Prime Minister Bruce was finally and savagely rejected by the electorate and Australia had a new Labor Prime Minister, James Scullin. Alas, the damage already done could not easily be remedied, both in the state of the country and in Oriel's marriage.

Christmas was a mere six weeks away and still she had not left him, though separation loomed ever near. With every hour her dilemma intensified. She had been feeling physically and mentally ill for weeks. Each day after he went to work, her children to school, she would flop on to the sofa and sit and stare until it was time for them to come home again. Her entire day was black. Every morning upon rising she was presented with this colour and did not know how she would ever manage to wade through it. She could not eat. Her clothes hung on her. She was so depressed that even though he was the cause of that depression she even looked forward to his coming home just to have another adult there.

Naturally Clive noticed her despondency, how could he not? He probably felt the same way too. Why then would he not give in and find someone else? Daily, each was administering to the other a personal brand of poison and neither was prepared to be the first to call a halt.

Belatedly, Oriel came to recognize that through her own suffering she was causing others to suffer too, knew that if she did not do something about this awful dilemma now she would keep putting it off until ... who knew what would happen? There was no kindness in delay. She must end it now – tonight. He would be hurt and rejected, yes, but he would recover. She could not continue to wait and hope that someone else would make the move for her. She must face the truth, for it was of her own making.

With fresh determination she began that day to clear out cupboards, ready for her departure, sorting out unwanted possessions, sentiment overcome by a ruthless need to purge, until the entire house had been cleansed.

An automaton, she went to collect the children, mindless of their chatter as they skipped happily beside her. Upon a change of clothing, she gave them tea and sat dejectedly whilst they ate it, trying to think of how to tell them, determined that she would. But not yet.

When their father came in a few hours later he was carrying a bouquet, which he presented with a look of hope. The dismay must have shown in her visage for his own face reflected it. 'Can't I even bring my wife flowers?'

Oriel gave what she hoped was a smile but knew in her heart that it was a grimace. How could she smile, the way she felt? She took the flowers and without even unwrapping them stuck them in a vase of water. Say it.

Say it! But there was no way to tell him whilst the children were there. At least until they went to bed she had an excuse not to make her announcement, though the interval was not a time of relaxation. Tension mounting, she grabbed a book to deliver their bedtime story, eyes flicking up between each turn of page to consult the clock. Reaching the end, she could no longer bear the suspense and said, 'I think we'll have you two in bed now.' They opened their mouths to whine. 'Bed!' She shooed them from the room.

Drawn of feature, Clive glanced at her from his chair by the fire as she returned from the children's room and flopped on to a seat. 'Have they been a nuisance too?'

If you know you're a nuisance why don't you just bloody go? begged Oriel silently. 'No, it's just me.' She kneaded her brow. Say it, coward. 'I've got a bit of a headache.'

'Must be all that thinking you do.' He rose to put a log on the fire. The spring nights were still cold. Noticing that he was about to incinerate a woodlouse he carefully picked it from the log and put it back into the bucket.

Oriel's sense of purpose disintegrated. How could one possibly tell a man whose kindness extended to a woodlouse that one could not bear to be in his presence a moment longer? Hence, by the time they retired the subject of her release had still not been broached.

Though still in the same bed they slept as far away from each other as possible now, sleep being rather a misnomer, both coping with the night as best they could.

Daybreak came. Oriel groped for the clock and peered at it, but the curtains disallowed sufficient light to infiltrate the room and she put it down and lay there for what seemed like half an hour. If she did not tell him this morning she would have to struggle through another entire day before having a second chance. Fearing that if she lay here another minute her body would rot into the mattress, she rose swiftly, put on a dressing gown and moved to the window to draw back the curtain. Now she was able to read the clock. It was only five thirty. There was neither sound nor movement from Clive, but Oriel could tell that he had been awake as long as she had, lying there silently dying. She took a deep breath and said without turning, 'I can't go on like this.'

A look of fear passed over his face – the look of a man who knows he is to receive the *coup de grâce* – but he denied it to the end. 'What d'you mean?'

Oriel's bleary eyes stared out of the window. 'Us.' Us? There was no us. Never had been. 'I just can't face any more.'

He caught his breath. 'You mean you want a divorce?'

'Yes.' And from that point Oriel began to regain life.

'God, what a time to choose!' Clive rolled out of bed and paced the room, hand on head. 'How can I go to work as if nothing's happened?'

She did not answer and did not care. Released, she felt wonderful and terrible at the same time, for the children still had to be told – and others. She could not wait for him to be out of the house so she could spread her glad tidings.

Dazed, he fought for words. 'I suppose I'll have to be the one to leave.'

'You don't have to go right this minute.'

'That's kind of you.' Clive glanced frantically at the clock. 'We'll have to talk about this tonight. I haven't time to give it full attention now.'

I don't see that there's much to talk about, thought Oriel but said as she left the room, 'I'll go and make breakfast.'

Clive could not stomach any food, gulping only a mouthful of tea before going off to work early.

It was only then that a great wave of relief surged over Oriel. Half an hour ago she had felt close to death, now had come resurrection. Surely the worst part was over. Sipping her tea, she decided not to tell the children yet, for they would obviously be upset and want to stay off school and she had other things to do.

Awoken later, they came in to breakfast not knowing that anything was wrong, only that their mother was unusually happy for so early an hour. After taking them to school, she had a cup of coffee and sat down to think about how she would ever explain this to her mother. But her mother was a long way away and they had not arranged to see each other this summer, the journey being what it was.

Deciding to postpone it, she went off instead to give Dorothy her news.

Her friend's first reaction was that Oriel must be joking – she was beaming widely as she made the announcement. But then why go to the bother of playing a joke at this time of morning?

'Well, what a bombshell. Divorce! What d'you plan to do now? Will you be leaving or –'

'No, he's said he'll go. If I can afford to keep the house on I will. I don't want to disrupt the kids any more than I have to.'

'Have you told them yet?'

A shake of head. 'I'm dreading it.'

'Well, any way I can help you,' Dorothy reached out and patted her friend's hand, 'you only have to ask. It's a big step setting out on your own.'

Oriel shrugged. 'Not really. I got to the stage where I thought, why am I so worried about being lonely? I couldn't be any lonelier than I am now. I'll have to go.' She rose. 'I've made an appointment to see a solicitor.' Not wishing to compromise her privacy by selecting one in Brighton, she had sought a more anonymous, if more expensive, practice in the city. 'I hope Clive hasn't chosen the same one – it'd be just my luck.'

Leaving Dorothy, she travelled by green electric tram to the city, avoiding the area around Myers for fear of being seen.

The solicitor asked what grounds she sought for dissolution. Oriel looked flummoxed. 'Does he have other women? Does he beat you?'

'No, he's a nice man.' The moment it emerged she realized how stupid it sounded, but had no wish to vilify Clive. She was hurting him enough.

There was a slightly derisive edge to the man's smile. 'Mrs Widdowes, "nice" hardly constitutes reasonable grounds for divorce. You'll have to come up with something better than that or we'd be laughed out of court.'

Confounded by legal rigmarole, Oriel went home, determined to be rid of him, whether it was legal or not. During her journey, she made the decision to tell the children when they came in from school, for she did not want Clive as an audience when she spoke intimately to them.

That afternoon, having collected them from school she gave them tea, then told them as a special treat they could help her mix the Christmas pudding.

It was whilst they were weighing all the ingredients – plus some of Dorrie's imaginary ones – that she said casually, 'By the way, Daddy will be going to live somewhere else soon.'

Jennifer was grappling with the wooden spoon and the thick mixture. 'Will we go with him?'

Oriel tried to sound cheerful. 'No, but you'll still see him.'

'Doesn't he want to live with us any more?' asked Dorrie through a mouthful of currants. Perhaps he was to blame for his father leaving – had not Grandad always said that boys were a bad lot?

'Well –' Oriel fought for explanation. 'It's just that Mummy doesn't want him to live here.'

Jennifer dropped the spoon and started to cry. Little Dorrie, grave of face, looked on whilst his mother put her arms round his sister, studying Oriel in an odd way as if he were trying to read what was in his mother's mind. Within minutes he too was crying, but after a great deal of reassurance from Oriel that they would still see their father the children were coaxed back into mixing the Christmas pudding, too young to understand the real implication of all this.

Clive was annoyed that she had divulged the situation without his knowledge. 'You treat them as if they're just yours,' he accused her, after the children had been put to bed. 'You always have. You act as if I never had anything to do with their conception – come to think of it I didn't! You even made that decision by yourself, as if my opinion was worthless.'

Oriel did not argue, but considered his words. By her decision not to leave him all those years ago, in thinking that it was the right thing to do, she had only succeeded in creating more hurt for him, for everyone. Her attempts to survive this unhappy marriage had made her appear selfish in his eyes. If only he had not put up such a fight to keep her.

Clive had obviously been doing some thinking through the day. 'Why should I be the one to leave? It isn't me who wants a divorce, for God's sake.'

'I suppose I'll have to go then,' sighed Oriel, without stating the obvious that it was her money which had bought this house and many of the things in it.

He had apparently hoped that having to abandon all this material wealth would be just too big a wrench for her. When this did not work he muttered sullenly, 'No, I'll go. I don't want to uproot the kids. I'll get meself a little house somewhere. I won't need to take much with me. All this furniture would look out of place in the sort of house I'll be able to afford. You'll have to give me time to find somewhere, though.'

She returned a dull nod. After the thrill of this morning's disclosures there was anticlimax now.

'I suppose they'll all come sniffing round once I've gone.'

By they, Oriel knew that Clive alluded to her many supposed admirers. She did not respond.

Paradoxically, they both climbed into the same bed that night, lying there like two lumps of wood, staring at the ceiling.

Eventually he said, 'I don't know what I've done.'

'You haven't done anything.' You've just been yourself, she added privately. Why let him remain in ignorance, demanded her conscience? Why let him believe that you're the only one at fault? But much as she detested him, much as she had wanted to kill him throughout their marriage, Oriel was not deliberately cruel, could not grind her heel into his wound.

'Have you told your mother yet?'

'No.'

'No, I don't suppose you would have.' He sighed heavily. 'But I'll have a few words for that father of yours when I see him, tell him how he's ruined my marriage.'

Oriel's voice held impatience. 'It's got nothing to do with anyone else.'

'Well, I think it has. I agree with your mother. Him running off and leaving you has made you cold and hard – well, you've never shown me any affection, anyway.' He gave a bitter laugh. 'I don't know if it's reserved for anyone else.'

Oriel sighed, but refused to enter an argument.

'You won't be happy till you're dead,' he mumbled, then turned away from her.

Neither of them slept. The following morning Clive moved into the adjacent bedroom, which he continued to use for the next couple of nights.

Relief turned to pressure. A week and then a fortnight passed, and Clive had given no sign of moving out or even hinting that he had found another place to live.

Eventually, however, Oriel's coldness towards him made him announce, 'It's obvious you want rid of me so

I'll go and stay at my mother's till I find somewhere else.'

She did not correct him.

'I'll be back to see the children, take them out – I'll take you too, if you like.'

Oriel wanted to shout, for Christ's sake I can't stand the bloody sight of you! But ever the coward she answered, 'If you want.'

'I still love you, you know.'

She turned away, despairing that he would ever leave, but leave he eventually did the following day.

Had Oriel guessed upon watching the door close behind him that his intention was to visit her several times in the week that followed, she would not have allowed herself to experience such relief. It became obvious that even if they were living apart he still regarded her as his wife – his property, thought Oriel darkly. She realized then that she had never regarded him as her husband, hated even referring to him as such. A husband was more than a bedfellow, more even than the father of one's children. Alas, at thirty-three years of age she despaired that she would ever find that other half of her soul, for it had already been captured by someone else.

Having further matters to discuss with her solicitor, she telephoned to make an appointment, then made another trip into the city. Far too early, she browsed around the shops, catching an occasional glimpse of her own reflection, an emaciated, lonely figure in a white cloche hat, the contours of the pale blue dress showing every jutting bone.

She wandered at leisurely pace up Lonsdale Street. The pavements were full of men. Unemployed men loafing on corners, old men, young men, middle-aged men, all drawing close scrutiny from Oriel, who found them all wanting. So absorbed was she in her examination that she paid little heed to her passage through the shoppers until she collided with a hard body with hands that grasped her upper arms and a face that bestowed admiration. Apologizing, she allowed herself to linger, feeling the heat of those hands on her arms, the warmth of his smile, the question in his eyes. Then, denial in her own eye, she tore herself away and continued up the street. Above the noise of traffic a clanging sound made her turn. An old tramp festooned with billycans overtook her. At odds with the hot summer day he wore an army greatcoat, the smell from his unwashed body travelling in a slipstream behind him. Oriel moved across the pavement.

It was then that she saw Daniel coming towards her and her heart turned a somersault as he saw her too, waved and donated the warm smile that she held so dear. But upon his approach she saw that he looked unwell, appeared drained and thin. His clothes were hanging on him, his trousers ruched up by a belt that was fastened two notches tighter than normal. Despite these observations Oriel was overjoyed to see him and spoke in cheery tone as they came to meet before the stained-glass window of the Shamrock Hotel.

'What're you doing in the city, Mr Maguire? I hope you're not looking for work?' Though the timber strike had long been over its repercussions were still being felt; there was now a lot of unemployment in that industry, as everywhere else.

His expression had deceived her. 'Nah, I'm one of the lucky ones. Still got me job at Powelltown. Just taken time off to go to the hospital for some tests on me head.' He waved aside her exclamation of concern. 'They couldn't find anything wrong. I've been getting a few more headaches than usual and I thought it might be the bit o' shrapnel going walkabout. It has moved, they say, but only a fraction. Made me feel like a complete bludger.' He grinned. 'I was just off for smoke-o before going back to work. Shout yer a cuppa if yer fancy coming and telling me all your latest news.'

She took a deep breath, inhaling beer fumes from the hotel. 'There's plenty to tell – I'm divorcing Clive.'

Daniel's face altered. He was shocked, yes, but there was something more in his eyes than that. Oriel thought she detected a gleam of pleasure, but he covered it up with a solemn commiseration. 'Strewth, when did this happen?'

'A few weeks ago.' She stood aside for a Chinese man and his European wife to pass. 'I've come in to see the solicitor again – there's something I forgot to ask last time. I went to see him the day I broke the news.' She gave an embarrassed laugh. 'A bit quick off the mark, I know, but now I've taken the plunge I want to get it all over with as quickly as possible.' She looked at her watch. 'I'm not seeing him for three-quarters of an hour. Shall we go for that cup of tea?'

During their brief search for a watering hole nothing more was said about the divorce, and after several interruptions by the waitress it was difficult to pick up the subject again. In the cushioned alcove of the basement tearoom with its intimate dimly lit atmosphere, Oriel desperately wanted to talk about her relief and exhilaration at being free but was afraid of being thought callous. She felt so wonderful and warm at seeing this beloved face.

Halfway through a cigarette, Daniel sipped his tea and replaced the cup in the saucer. 'So, how's Clive taking it?'

Oriel matched his movements. The tea was hot and she licked her lips. 'He's been very understanding.' Why on earth had she said that? He didn't understand at all, that was the reason she was leaving him. She had said it because she did not want to appear hard before Daniel, cared what he thought about her. 'But he's devastated. Keeps asking what he's done.'

'And what has he done?' The viridescent eyes studied her.

'Nothing. He's a good kind man who'd make anyone else a good husband.'

'But not you. I reckoned all along he wasn't the one

428

for you.' He never took his eyes off her, even whilst he pulled on his cigarette.

Oriel looked flabbergasted. 'How?'

Daniel slightly averted his face so as not to blow smoke into hers. ''Cause I am.'

She was totally confused. He couldn't possibly mean what she thought he meant.

'The one for you.' He confirmed her own desires. 'I've always loved yer, Kooka. Did you never guess?'

Oriel's heart came into her mouth, her face was white, she found it hard to breathe, could not believe what she was hearing.

He gave a mirthless chuckle, stubbed out the cigarette and rubbed his tanned hands over his face. 'That's really set the cat among the chooks, hasn't it?'

Around them, waitresses moved back and forth with steaming trays, clattering crockery, tinkling spoons. Oriel heard none of it. Still totally stunned, she made lame utterance. 'But . . . what about Mel?'

His face was in turn joyous then anguished. 'I love her too but not in the way I feel about you. I think I loved you from the minute I set eyes on yer, trying to look all bossy in yer big hat, the day I came to be a father to Alice – that's who I really came back for. When I saw you, felt what I felt then, I should've turned right round and gone back out that gate without saying what I'd come for – if I'd had any sense. But instead I stayed to do the right thing by Mel. That's all our marriage was about, on my part at least. Doing the right thing.'

'Mine too,' she breathed. 'But by doing that, prolonging matters that should have been ended years ago, it's not just him I've hurt but lots of people. It's right what they say about the road to hell being paved with good intentions.'

Daniel frowned. 'I thought that was the road to Sydney.' Then he was serious again. 'Yeah, I know what yer mean. Oh, I did, I do, have feelings for her. She's been a good wife in most respects. I'm sure I don't deserve her and I know she doesn't deserve what I'm gonna do to her now. I want to marry you, Oriel.'

Oriel's pulse grew even more rapid. Why did her own joy have to be founded on another's pain? Her heart went out to Melinda and her children. 'Oh God, what have I started?'

'It's not just because o' you, Kooka.' He pushed the cups aside, reached out and grasped her hand. She returned his grip, aching to hold him against her. 'Things've been pretty desperate for a long time between us. She knows but won't face it.'

'Like him.' Oriel nodded.

'I've been baching at the mill for years, well yer know that. She wanted me to build a place for us up there but I always made excuses. The marriage wouldn't've lasted this long if I'd had to live with her all the time. I knew I'd been right when I had to stay at home for six months during the strike. We ended up going crook at each other half the time. The only reason I come home on a weekend is to see the kids.' His face was overwhelmed with despair. 'I don't know how I'm gonna leave them. It'll rip me guts out.'

Oriel clung to his hand. This was all moving incredibly fast. Only hours ago she had resigned herself to being alone, sworn that she would never marry again.

'But there's no way they can come with me,' he continued, 'and I can't stay there. I'm just wasting away. I have to face it. I can't have them and you too.' He fixed her with an anguished smile, then blurted out a laugh. 'I'm taking a hell of a lot for granted, aren't I?'

Oriel shook her head and gazed deep into his eyes. 'I've always loved you too.' She looked guilty. 'I know it's an awful thing to say but whenever I visited Melinda it was really you I wanted to see.'

'And I always made a point of keeping out of the way as much as I could because I couldn't bear to see yer and not to have yer. All those hunting trips, they were just to get me away 'cause I knew if I stayed something would happen between us and I couldn't hurt Mel like that.'

'But you can now.' Oriel did not intend cruelty and hated seeing him flinch.

He rubbed at her knuckles with his nutbrown thumbs. 'I have to, I've no choice.' His expression changed. 'Yes, I do have a choice, an' I'm making it.'

She found the whole situation amazing. 'I never imagined . . . I mean, you looked so happy. I thought I was the only one who was hiding my feelings. D'you think Mel noticed?'

Daniel shook his head. 'She's not that perceptive.'

Oriel felt disgusted at herself. How could she do this to her good friend, not to mention the children?

'What about him, was he suspicious?'

'Oh, all the time,' replied Oriel evenly. 'But then that's just part of his character. He only sees the bad in people, never the good – where I'm concerned anyway. He always thought I was having an affair with everyman. I wasn't.' She gave a reassuring smile, then turned sombre again. 'I'd never have done that.'

Daniel nodded, then fell silent for a while before asking, 'Where's this solicitor of yours?'

'Spring Street.' Oriel snatched a look at her watch, then threw him a desperate glance. 'And I've only got five minutes to get there. I'll have to dash.' It was obvious she did not want to leave.

'I'll come with yer.' After paying the bill Daniel took repossession of her hand. As luck would have it, shortly after they emerged into the sunlight, a tram appeared. Together they ran and jumped aboard one of its open-sided cars, not bothering to sit down but standing close together, bodies occasionally bumping as the tram made its way up the street. When they alighted moments later, Daniel was still holding her hand, loath to release it even when they arrived at their destination, and said he would wait across the road by the Houses of Parliament until she came out.

Oriel gave her representative the news that she had met someone else and even though this meant admitting unfaithfulness it was the legal ground that she had needed. She asked where she stood in regard to money.

The solicitor wore a knowing smile that said he did not believe she had only just met this person in the space of a few weeks, but merely asked, 'Have you any money of your own?'

'All the money in the account formerly belonged to me. It was part of an inheritance, but it's in joint names now.'

'I'd change it over to your name if you can,' he suggested. 'Before your husband does the same. Things could get nasty.'

Oriel gave a curt nod, angry at him for referring to Clive as her husband. With her mind on the man outside, she was able only to think of a few more questions before thanking him for his time and rising to leave.

Before opening the door for her, the man asked, 'Mrs Widdowes, you are prepared for the fact that the admission of adultery will make you a social outcast?'

The terrible indictment made her jump – she had never even kissed Daniel but then she supposed adulterous was what their relationship now was. 'I don't care.' Her expression caused the solicitor to nod, open the door for her, and wish her luck.

When she emerged from the darkness of the office her unfocused gaze toured the area outside Parliament House and saw only a group of figures, none of whom was Daniel, dashing back across the road from taking lunch in the old world excellence of the Windsor Hotel. At first she panicked at the thought that he had been snatched from her before she had ever tasted his lips. She began to walk along the street, wide eyes searching, and in seconds he was there beside her, taking repossession of her hand and drawing a look of vast relief. Now she realized why she had always been averse to holding Clive's hand. It was such an intimate act: told the world that you and this person were one.

'Just needed a bit o' shade.' He smiled warmly. 'Where to now?'

Oriel gave a happy shrug. 'Oh anywhere, I don't care – let's go in those gardens over there.'

Still linked together, they moved slowly along the footpath. An immaculately dressed woman emerged from a building just at the time of their passing. Unaware that he was in the vicinity of a high-class brothel, Daniel touched his hat. The woman gave him a cool smile, glanced at Oriel, then minced off in the opposite direction.

The sun beat down, the tiny turned-up brim of Oriel's cloche hat affording no shade. Face cast down towards her snakeskin shoes, she underwent a period of deep thought, then began, 'Melinda told me you changed towards her after you got the piece of shrapnel in your head.'

He smiled down at her, playing with her fingers. 'She likes to blame everything on that, but really . . .'

'She said you weren't the same when you came back from the war.'

'Was anybody?' He made to cross the road.

'I don't know. I've never been to war.'

'And pray to God yer never will. It's not the little scrap o' metal that's changed me, it's the things I've seen. And I don't just mean the blood and guts and the stink and the brutality.'

'Where did you get wounded, Gallipoli?'

'No, I was there first but then I got transferred later to Belgium. Passchendaele.' Daniel was quiet for a while, seeing the expectation in her eyes and appraising her ability to bear what he was about to divulge. He remained silent for a long time, then as they veered off the footpath into the quieter surroundings of the gardens, finally said,

'Yer know what the hardest part was? They were such cheerful, gritty little blighters. Sometimes I wished they had've sworn and yelled at me so I wouldn't have liked 'em so much, cursed me for not having any anaesthetic for them nor even a cup of water. A cup o' ruddy water. Not much to expect when yer dying, is it? But they knew there wasn't that much to go round. Everybody was in the same mess, couldn't drink the local stuff, yer see. I'm not saying they were all angels – you'd get the odd one or two who'd kick up a stink – but in general they never complained, never wanted to be any trouble.'

The scent of sun-warmed roses cloyed the air, but Daniel's mind was in another place. 'They lay on that beach hour after hour under boiling sun and freezing cold nights 'cause we couldn't get to 'em for the shellfire. And the perishing flies! When yer used to them in a country like this yer don't give much thought to what strife they can cause till yer see 'em crawling over ripped flesh. By the time we finally got 'em loaded on to hospital ships their wounds had turned gangrenous. Christ, the stink.'

Gripping Oriel's fingers, he took a deep breath, his words emerging not in flowing sequence but in unconnected snippets as the memories jumped into his mind. 'Hospital ships? Huh! That's a laugh, cattle ships more like. We had to pick out all the rotten ones to go to the operating room first – and I mean rotten – stinking, putrid. Arms and legs. That's what's most vivid. Loads of arms and legs in a basket. Have y'ever smelled anything that's gone orf, like a dead roo by the side of the road, or anything? Well, multiply that a thousand times and yer might just get the picture. But nobody who wasn't there can really imagine it.

'A lot of 'em didn't make it to hospital. Even if they did it wasn't safe there. Some had to lie on tarpaulins in the open. A putrid writhing carpet of 'em. I don't think that's any way to treat brave fellas, do you? A lot of us got really mad about it. If we'd got hold of the bloke who was responsible for planning it all –' He shook his head. 'No protection whatsoever. I happened to be there just after a shell had hit a pile of these wounded fellas. What a shambles. Limbs all over the place. I didn't know where to start. And they never grumbled, went on cracking hardy, thinking you were doing yer best for 'em.'

He gulped. 'I once went out to collect some wounded and I came across this bloke who'd been shot in the throat. How long he'd been out there in the sun I don't know. He couldn't speak but he kept cupping his hands to his mouth and his eyes kept begging me to give him a drink. I didn't have one. But the pleading in those eyes – a bit like yours, big and blue, he was only a young kid – the pleading in them just got to me. I did the best I could for him then promised to come back with some water even though I knew he wouldn't last more than a few minutes. Took some doing but I managed to get back to him with the water. He was dead o' course. His big blue eyes still looking at me. I see them every night.'

Daniel's own troubled eyes stared straight ahead as he wandered through the gardens, in and out of shade. Oriel hung on his sentences as if they were barbed wire. To all intents and purposes everyone else had disappeared from the world.

'The day I copped it I was trying to rescue this little digger who'd got too close to a shellburst. I sat in the middle of a bloody nightmare, bombs exploding all around me, with me hands trying to push his flesh and lard back inside him. Like sago pudding it was, great thick globules of blubber – yer wonder where it all comes from, he was such a little bloke. Then he couldn't stand it any more. He started to squirm like a maggot on the end of a line. Begged me to shoot him. Training? What training? Nothing can prepare yer for that. On and on he went, saying I was cruel, if I had any heart I'd put him out of his misery.'

He looked at her but it was a different Daniel to the one

she had been with a moment ago – a demented anxious creature. 'I'm not cruel, Oriel, I'm not.'

'I know.' She gripped his arm.

'You said I was. When I told yer I was going hunting yer said, cruel devil. I'm not cruel. I'm not.'

'I know!' Oriel had never been faced with such a crisis, did not know how to help him.

'Yer really hurt me when yer said that. When a bloke's got little kids to feed and not much dough he doesn't tend to give much priority to possums.'

Tears pricked her eyes. How her impulsive words must have wounded him if he had been carrying them in his head for so many years.

He gave a shuddering sigh and returned to his tale. 'Yer wouldn't think a man with that kind of injury could last so long, but he did. And I had to sit there in the mud alongside him and pretend I was doing something for him when all I had was a bloody field dressing, and listen to him pleading and squirming till it was safe to get him away. Well, we thought it was safe. That's when I copped mine. I just remember the scream of a shell. The bloke with me said, you're hit, mate! Didn't hardly feel it till he told me, then I don't remember nothing else. But I remember him. I remember him all right.'

Oriel brushed at her eyes, too stunned to comment on his divulgences.

Faced with her silence he went on, 'It's . . . it's like yer own brother dying a thousand times over. It was to me, anyway. Some o' me cobbers didn't bat an eyelid. If it affected them like it did me they hid it well. To see all these big-hearted young fellas who went off to fight for the glory of the Empire ending up as a basket of maggot-ridden arms and legs. Even when they were treated like scum by some o' the pommie officers – they didn't like us yer see, thought the Canadians were the dog's whatsits but we were just rabble 'cause a lot of us wouldn't salute 'em – but the diggers laughed it off. Don't know how they stayed so cheerful. I got sick of it, I can tell you. Sick of seeing me mates laughing one day and blown apart the next. I'd seen photos of their girlfriends and mothers and sisters, knew them all by name, read their letters when I didn't have any of me own. Then imagine this, yer've coped with all that, yer've got through it and yer come home and everybody else is going about their business as normal and some bloody idiot comes up to yer and asks what it was like to see all these wounded men. And yer say oh, it was a bit of a lark really and they look at yer as if yer nuts. So, yer see, if I flare up with people it's not the bit of shrapnel in me head that's the cause, it's the stupidity of them that makes me angry – they had no idea, no idea at all. I can't believe the lack of imagination some of 'em have.

'The sheer needless waste and the cruelty of it. They say it was the war to end all wars but it'll happen again and again and again, and young blokes'll still line up to volunteer for King and Country. I've come to the conclusion that people need war. What else would they find to light up their dull lives, to fill their newspapers, to sell their guns? The world'd collapse if there wasn't a war in some place or another.'

Oriel was solemn. 'So you wouldn't volunteer if you had your chance again?'

'Bloody oath!' He shook his head, apologized for the language, then sighed. 'Ah, I dunno. What choice have yer got when yer mother needs yer? It was a rough old trot for sure, but if it taught me one thing it's that Australia should be a nation in its own right, not just the appendix of another. I was proud o' being part o' the Empire once but after that lot I think we earned our colours.'

Her mind was in turmoil, filled with gruesome images. 'Is it silly to ask if you still believe in God? I mean I know you never go to church but neither do I.'

'That's a big one. Yeah . . . yeah, I probably do. Can't

really help it, being a lifelong Catholic an' that. Though I don't know what kind o' bloke He is to let that happen.'

Oriel shared this view. 'That's what I find so hard to understand. I look at the awful things people do to each other and I think, is this all there is? Surely there has to be something more. If there isn't then what's the point to any of it? Why does He let it happen?'

'If I knew that –'

'When you talk to the other men –'

'Oh, blokes aren't big talkers, yer know. Tends to strip yer naked, an' I've never thought a naked bloke was a pretty sight. At least now yer've got a better idea of why poor Jim's the way he is, why he doesn't want to see anybody. Get a bit that way meself. Yeah, I think all us diggers're likely candidates for the giggle house.'

Oriel said she found it hard to understand why some men were more affected than others if they had all gone through the same. Norman, for instance, seemed on a pretty even keel.

Daniel cracked a grin. 'Yer've got to have half a brain to go mad. Nah, well, we all cope with it in different ways. Shove it out o' sight – don't think I go round talking about it to everybody.'

'But surely you must've told Mel?'

'Oh yeah ... at least I've tried, but it's not really the type o' conversation she goes in for. There's some things I can never tell – even to you.' He noticed that she was pale. 'And you thought I told yer the worst of it. Cripes, listen to us – Stiffy and Mo! That's enough for today. Let's talk about something more cheerful.'

He made a remarkable effort to resurrect the character whom he normally presented to the world, even going so far as to crack a joke. 'Listen to me – I'm supposed to be back at work. The boss'll kill us. Oh well, I'll tell him the doc had a hard time finding me brain. Come on, we'd better make our way back. Think I can remember where I parked the car.'

Oriel was content to wander back into town, down towards the busy shopping valleys, holding hands with him, proud for folk to see them together and to think Daniel was her husband – which he was. She smiled up into his dear face. Never had she felt so much at home, so totally loved.

Daniel took out a cigarette then belatedly offered one to her. She declined, laughing as he found his matchbox filled with dead ones. Spotting a crippled veteran balanced on a trolley nearby, his empty trouser legs fastened up with safety pins, Daniel moved up to him and in easy manner asked, 'Got a light, dig?'

Oriel adored his beloved face as he stooped low over the match, noted his nod of gratitude and his, 'Thanks, mate,' as he dropped a coin into the tin mug as inconspicuously as he could.

He took an inhalation of smoke, looked confused, then manoeuvred her round to face him, whilst shoppers milled around them on the wide pavement. 'I'm gonna have to go home and tell her.'

She nodded. 'I'll have to tell him. He's staying at his mother's but he'll no doubt be around later with some excuse, pretending I can't do without him.'

Daniel looked concerned. 'Will yer be right?'

She nodded. 'I will if I know you'll be coming back.'

He rubbed his palms over her shoulders affectionately. 'It might take a few days. I'll have to give up me job and look for another in the city. But don't worry, I won't let yer down, Kooka. It'll come good. Should I ring y'at your house?'

She thought on this a moment. 'Best not. I don't know whether he'll pick up the phone. I could leave a message with Dorothy, then you can telephone her when you're on your way. Here, I'll give you her number – but only ring through the day. I don't want to cause any trouble for her.'

Tucking the scrap of paper into his pocket he kissed

her then, a firm but not passionate kiss on the lips. 'I can't believe this is happening, can you?'

She gave a tearful laugh. 'No! Only this morning I'd envisaged myself a lonely old woman . . .' Her sentence trailed away. Now it was Melinda who was going to be lonely. She did not have to voice her fears.

'I know, I know.' He gripped her upper arms. 'After all I've just told yer, it's the worst thing I've ever had to do.'

'I feel so guilty, Daniel.'

'Don't. I feel guilty enough for both of us. But even if you change yer mind I've decided I'm leaving her anyway. I have to. It's not fair on anyone to continue like this, I'm taking my frustration out on the kids.'

Oriel nodded in recognition. 'It was unfair of me to let it go on for so long. If only I wasn't such a coward. D'you know, for the first time I understand how my mother felt about Father. She had more sense than I did. She knew he was the only one for her and wasn't prepared to accept second best – not that I'm saying Clive is inferior in any way, I did love him once, but even then it wasn't in the way I love you. I can't believe I've found this happiness. I'm afraid that if I let you go now I'll lose you again.'

'Wherever you are, however long it takes I'll find yer,' promised Daniel. Both showed reluctance to part. 'And you haven't given me an answer – about marrying me.'

She sagged and gave laughing affirmative.

They hugged again, then Oriel was forced to break away. 'I'll have to be back for the kids coming home from school.'

'Want a lift? The car's about stonkered but –'

'No, better not. I'll have to explain to them first before they see us together.'

'You can bring them to live with us,' came the immediate offer.

'If he'll let me.'

Daniel shoved the cigarette in his mouth and looked at her, an unspoken question in his eyes.

'But even if he won't,' she added, 'I'll have to come. I love them dearly. Besides you they're the most important people in the world to me, but there's nothing else I can do.'

'God bless yer, Kooka.' He finally allowed her fingertips to slip from his and uttered a gentle word of parting. 'Ooroo.'

18

On her way to the railway station, Oriel did as she was advised by her solicitor and visited the main branch of her bank to alter the account details. Ordinarily, she would use the local branch but the sooner this was done the better. The teller accepted the bank book off her and gave her a receipt saying they would return it the next day to save her waiting.

She arrived home to find Clive mowing the front lawn. Initially her heart fell as, at the sight of her, he smiled and brought the mower to a halt. But as irritating as his frequent visits had become this one was opportune and she decided to take full advantage of it – if she could summon the courage. They reached the front door together. Clive removed his grass-covered shoes on the porch and made to follow her into the house. 'I took the afternoon off, felt a bit bilious this morning but it'd gone by lunchtime so I thought I'd come and mow your front yard. Don't worry, I won't expect anything in return. I'll just wait for the kids to come home then I'll go.'

She crossed the hall and made for the lounge where, feeling his doglike presence behind her, she turned to look at him. This was going to be like kicking a puppy. Unexpectedly for both of them, she broke down and sobbed. He came to her but she recoiled and he did not press his attentions but looked on with sympathy as she fell on to the sofa and heaved.

'If you want me to stay tonight I could telephone Mum and Dad to say I won't be back.'

How devious can you get, screamed Oriel's mind. He had caught her in her most vulnerable moment and used it to his own devices. But she was too mentally exhausted to resist. 'If you like,' she muttered tearfully, 'but you can sleep in the spare room again.'

Wearing a rather triumphant smile, she thought, he came to sit down beside her on the sofa and patted her knee as her tears subsided. 'What happened to us, Oriel? We used to have some good times, didn't we? Especially in bed.' He gave a warm chuckle.

Were we ever in the same bed? demanded Oriel silently. Revolted by his touch she pulled away as far as the arm of the sofa would allow. It was sufficient. He withdrew his hand.

She braced herself. 'I have to talk to you.'

He seemed to welcome this. 'Maybe we should have talked more often.'

As ever he had received the wrong signal. 'No, it's too late for that,' she answered tersely, and asked herself, is it me who's giving out all the wrong messages or is he just stupid? What did it take to communicate with this man when all Daniel had to do was read her mind? That wasn't quite true. Clive could read her mind as well, but disliking what he saw was fighting it in the only manner that he knew.

'Oh.' His face fell.

He thought I'd come to my senses, thought Oriel. He really can't believe that I want to leave him. 'The other day when I told you there was no one else,' she began cautiously, 'well, there wasn't then ... but there is now.'

The boyish face retained its composed expression but she knew him well enough to tell he was mortally wounded. He rose and moved across the room to another chair, facing her. 'Do I know him?'

Oriel hesitated, balling her handkerchief. 'Yes.'

'It's Errol Whatsisname, isn't it?'

She prevented herself from laughing. 'No, of course not.'

'Well, are you going to tell me who he is or do I have to keep guessing?'

'It's Daniel.'

The announcement was a total surprise. 'Melinda's husband?'

Did he have to remind her? 'Yes.'

He shook his head in total disbelief. 'And what does she think to all this?'

'Daniel hasn't told her yet.'

'Ah!' Clive gave a nasty nod. 'This bloke wants his cake and eat it. He won't leave her, you know. How long's it been going on?'

'Nothing's been going on. We only met by chance today.'

'Don't give me that!'

'It's true.'

'I don't believe you! All those trips you made on your own to Yarra Junction – you were probably sleeping with him then.'

'Oh yes, with his wife and four children in the same house,' said Oriel wearily. 'I haven't slept with him. I didn't even know how he felt about me until I bumped into him today.'

Clive's temper increased, his pride hurt. 'It's bloody ridiculous! You don't go off with somebody just like that. He must've given you an indication before this. All those times you visited –'

'He wasn't there most of the time. He was staying out of the way on purpose.'

'And what kind of friend are you who pretends to go and see Melinda when all the time it's her husband you're after?'

She allowed him to berate her. There was nothing she could offer in the way of defence.

'Well, aren't you going to argue with me?' Her lack of response seemed to add to his ire. 'So what's happening then? Where're the pair of you going to live? Don't think

444

you're bringing him here. That's not fair while I'm stuck at my mother's in a poky little room.'

Oriel was astounded that he could even contemplate this. 'I wouldn't do that!'

'No?' He obviously didn't believe her. 'Why should he have everything I've worked for?'

She noted that Clive's initial fears were for material possessions, not for her or his children. 'You can come back here if you want to,' she said wearily.

He ceased carping. 'D'you mean just for tonight or for good?'

'For as long as you want. You're right, it's not fair that you've had to do without all your things.' She noticed a spark of hope in his eye and uttered an inner gasp. My God! How could he even think she would have him back after what she'd just told him. 'As I said before, you'll have to sleep in the spare room. Now that you know there's no chance of us getting back together I don't mind you being here.' Surely I can't put it any plainer than that, thought Oriel.

'Think you've got it all planned, don't you? What happens if I say to the lawyers I don't want a divorce?'

'You can't force me to live with you.'

'No, but I can make it bloody hard for you! There's never been anything like this in my family. Mum'll be devastated. What am I going to tell people?' His demand was pitiful. 'They've just seen me move all my suitcases out now they'll see me moving them back in.'

'Who gives a damn what people think? It's really nothing to do with anyone else. They'll probably have more to say when they see me moving my things out.' At his look of shock she underwent another period of inner rage – what did she have to do to get through to him that it really was over?

'What about the kids?'

Oriel shrugged helplessly. 'We'll have to do what's best for them.' She composed herself, rising to look in the mirror and dab at her blotchy face. 'They'll be leaving school soon. I'll have to go and meet them.'

'I'll take you in the car. When you say "what's best for them" I assume you mean they should stay with their mother.'

She had envisaged this. 'How would you look after them if you're at work all day? You can see them any time you want.'

Another retort from Clive. 'How would you like it if the boot was on the other foot and you were only allowed to see your children every weekend and somebody else was being mother to them the rest of the week?'

Oriel tried to remain calm. 'Do you really think I haven't put myself in your shoes a thousand times? I don't want to hurt you but I have to go, Clive, and that means the children will have to come too.'

He looked tormented. 'If it were just you, I'd let you stay here and move out myself, but he's taking everything I've got as it is. I can't let him take my house too, for God's sake.'

'Of course you can't and Daniel's not the sort to take it.'

The reply was heated. 'I don't want him taking my children either but it doesn't look as if I've any bloody choice in the matter!'

'He's got children of his own –'

'Then why doesn't he stop with them?' raged Clive.

'He can't. He can't stay where he is and neither can I. But whatever happens, you're still their father.'

After a moment, he gave a sigh of resignation and suggested gruffly, 'Can we tell them together this time?'

She could barely control her frustration. He was still acting as if they were a couple – they had never been a couple – but she was too exhausted to resist. 'If you like,' came her dull reply.

The children were delighted to see both parents come to meet them in the car. Their happiness was not to last, however, as on arriving home they were told gently that their father was moving back in and their mother would be moving out shortly and they would be going with her.

Jennifer was confused. Since Mother had told them that their father would be going to live somewhere else little had changed apart from his disappearance from the breakfast table. Otherwise they had seen as much of him as they had always done. But the information that she herself would be leaving her home brought apprehension. 'Where are we going? Will I be able to go to the same school?'

Oriel crouched in a pose of reassurance. 'I'm not sure where yet.' She would have to make a start on that. 'But you'll still see your friends, and Daddy.'

Dorrie did not understand either, just knew that he did not like this funny feeling inside him. To disguise his anxiety he said, 'Can I have a Vegemite sandwich?'

Oriel laughed softly and patted him. 'Of course – but come and wash your hands first.'

After that, everything proceeded as it always had. The children were fed and bathed, were read a story by their mother and were put to bed. With nothing further to discuss, Clive went out and left her as he had always done.

Oriel seized the newspaper, intent on finding a new home. There were three columns of houses for sale but only half a dozen properties to let. Five of these were in St Kilda and Toorak – far too expensive to contemplate. The only other was a cottage in Parkville, on the northerly side of the city. Lacking option, she wrote down the details, spent an hour or so listening to the wireless, then went to bed, but lay awake for a long time imagining herself in Daniel's arms. Shortly after midnight, she heard the door to the spare bedroom click. Somewhat more relaxed, she turned off the lamp and fell asleep carrying Daniel with her.

*   *   *

Jennifer was reluctant to attend school the next morning but Oriel jollied her into going, feeling it was best for the children to retain some form of normality. Besides, Clive had telephoned work to say he was still unwell. If she kept the children off school she would have to stay here to look after them and she did not want to be in the house with him. Upon wrapping their favourite playlunch and putting it into their satchels, she said goodbye to Clive but did not inform him that she would not be back immediately. As far as she was concerned now that the divorce was in motion she was not beholden to him any more. They were no longer man and wife – if they ever had been. After depositing the children at school she went to enlist Dorothy's help in finding a property to let in Brighton.

Her friend was baffled. 'But I thought you were staying where you were?'

'That was before I met Daniel.' Oriel perched on the edge of the sofa.

Dorothy frowned, but not for too long. 'You mean, you and him are –'

She nodded happily. 'I can't believe it. It's all –'

'*You* can't believe it?' Dorothy flopped into the chair opposite her, laughing. 'Ye gods, how on earth did this happen?'

Oriel shook her head, obviously still amazed by it too. 'I don't know. It's as if someone engineered it but I swear that marriage was the last thing on my mind two days ago.'

'Marriage!' Dorothy was confounded. 'You haven't even got a divorce yet.'

'I know. It was bad enough before, having to wait to be free, but now it's going to seem like a lifetime.'

'You always had a soft spot for Daniel, didn't you?' said her friend, eyeing her. When Oriel bit her lip she added, 'Oh, don't worry, it wouldn't have been obvious to most people. You just got this little smile on your face when you told me what he was like after you'd first met him. Then you never mentioned his name again – even after you'd been staying at Melinda's on holiday you never mentioned him once unless I happened to ask.'

Oriel looked rueful. 'And here's me thinking I'm being clever. I might as well have been open about it. Clive thinks I've been having an affair with Daniel for the last ten years anyway. He won't believe it just happened on the spur of the moment, that we were both walking along the same street and bumped into each other and within half an hour Daniel had proposed. It's not quite the stuff of reality, is it?'

'No, but it's awfully romantic,' sighed Dorothy, looking rather wistful. 'Golly, aren't you brave?'

'Melinda wouldn't think so.' Oriel's red lips formed a cryptic smile. 'To her I'll be a cruel home-wrecking bitch. And maybe I am.' She gripped her knees.

Her friend supported her. 'They can't have been right for each other in the first place.'

'Who knows? I thought Clive was the right person for me once – until I lived with him. Then I realized the truth in the old saying, marry in haste and repent at leisure.'

Dorothy shrank. 'Oh don't, you're making me feel guilty for introducing you to him.'

'You didn't force me into wedlock with him though, did you? I hate to admit it now but I think I married him because all my friends were getting married and I didn't want to be left out, and I picked the first man who didn't reject me. And if I'm honest it was to spite my father as well, choosing someone who was the complete opposite of him. My mother thinks I'm still looking for a father, apparently.' She sighed and told Dorothy about Clive's disclosure. 'I feel really hurt. How could Mother say that behind my back? And she's wrong. I certainly don't look upon Daniel that way. Far from it.'

Having seen a photograph, Dorothy agreed that he was very attractive. 'He's got a lovely smile.'

'Yes, he has. It's not just that though, it's – oh, it's hard to define, but it's something in his eyes that tells me he knows everything about me. We're like two halves of the same person. Even when I thought I loved Clive it felt nothing like this. Sometimes I got the feeling he didn't have an earthly idea what I was talking about. Daniel and I might not agree on everything but when he speaks and when I speak there's no ambiguity, each of us knows precisely what the other means. When I'm with him I feel like I'm inside him – oh, what airy-fairy stuff for this time of the morning!'

Oriel jumped up. 'I'll have to go, I've got a house to look at in Parkville. I know it's miles away but it was the only one in the paper I could afford. It'll mean a lot of travelling back and forth to school but I can always move back when something more suitable comes up. That's where I need your help, in finding somewhere in Brighton.' Dorothy said she would go out now and look. Oriel issued profuse thanks. 'The thing is, I need to move in tomorrow.'

'Tomorrow!' Dorothy grabbed her bag.

'Well, Daniel could call at any time – I gave him your telephone number by the way. Hope you don't mind? Anyway, I'll have to dash. Can I meet you back here in an hour or so?'

After travelling to the city, making quick inspection of the house in Parkville – which was grubby and rundown and a bit cramped for a family of four, but at least readily available and the rent cheap – Oriel returned to Dorothy's in the hope that her friend had had more luck.

Alas, she was informed that none of the houses to let in Brighton was available at such short notice. Thanking her, Oriel used Dorothy's telephone to reserve the house in Parkville. 'At least I'm a long way from Clive,' she grinned at her friend.

With lots to do she did not tarry. When she arrived home around eleven Clive was in the hall on the telephone listening to someone who was obviously doing all the talking.

When the other person drew breath he said, 'Excuse me, she's just come in if you want to speak to her.' Handing over the receiver he announced, 'It's Melinda,' before stalking off to the lounge.

Reluctantly, Oriel lifted the receiver to her ear. 'Hello.'

'Just a minute! Alan, stop doing that.' There was a short series of frustrated gasps, then Melinda spoke from a public telephone. 'Oriel, please, don't do this to us. I'm begging you, not just for myself but for the children. They're hardly more than babies and they love their daddy. You're ripping this family apart.'

Oriel could only say, 'Mel, I'm so sorry. I didn't mean it to happen.'

'Then don't let it! All you have to do is say no. Please. If he isn't getting any encouragement he'll stay, I know he will. You don't know him, Oriel. You've only met him a handful of times, you can't possibly know what he's like to live with. He's just going through a bad patch, he thinks you'll solve everything but you won't. You can't love him any more than I do.'

Oriel faltered. 'I know it's not what you want to hear but I can only say I'm sorry.'

There was a muttered response which she did not catch, then the line went dead. Trembling from shock, she put down the receiver and was about to wander off when the telephone rang again, sending her heart into palpitations.

Fearing it was Melinda again she let it ring a few times before picking it up and issuing a cautious hello.

It was Dorothy. 'Can you talk?'

'Not really.'

'All right, I'll do all the talking. Daniel's just rung. He wants to meet you in the city on Saturday at noon under the clocks.' It was Wednesday today. 'He's going to ring back for an answer in an hour. What do I say?'

It might be Dorothy who spoke but in Oriel's mind her

451

voice was obscured by Melinda's pleading accusation. *They're hardly more than babies and they love their daddy . . . All you have to do is say no.*

'Hello! Are you there?'

She inhaled. 'Yes.'

'You mean yes you can meet him?'

Oriel stammered, 'No. Yes! I don't know – Dorothy, I'll have to ring you back.' Her mind was a whirlpool.

'What's wrong?'

'Everything.'

'Well, remember I'm here.'

'You don't know how much I appreciate that, Ratty. Thanks, I'll ring you later.'

Her stomach was rumbling, but food was the last thing on Oriel's mind. Seeking privacy, she wandered ghostlike into the dining room and sat to gaze at her reflection in the polished wood, but was not allowed to be alone for long.

Clive appeared in the doorway, suspicion in his eyes. 'Who was that, Rudolf Valentino?'

'No, it was Dot.' With things to organize, Oriel had intended to remain in the house but found that she could not stand to be in his company. She ejected herself from the chair. 'I'm going out.'

'Where?'

'That's for me to know.' But she did not know at all – had no idea where her brisk march would take her, only hoped it would help to clear her mind.

It was to no avail. After an hour under the blazing sun, Mel's accusation nagging at her conscience, she was forced to see the futility of this and decided to go home. Happily, when she got there the house was empty. The telephone was ringing too. It was Dorothy again. 'Sorry, when you didn't ring back I rang you but I got hold of Clive and he gave me the third degree.'

Oriel lowered herself on to a wooden chair. 'I had to go out. I can't think in this place.'

'Daniel rang again. I explained I hadn't been able to get an answer from you so he said he'd wait under the clocks anyway.'

Oriel nodded to herself. 'I couldn't say before when Clive was here. Mel rang me.'

'Oh Lord, I'll bet that was tricky.'

'I know you don't like her, Dot, but it was really awful.'

'I'm sure it was.' The tone was genuine.

'No, she wasn't nasty as you'd expect her to be, quite the opposite. She begged me not to take him.'

'Well, she would know how to manipulate you, you've been friends a long time.'

Oriel cringed.

At the other end of the line Dorothy felt the vibration. 'Sorry, I'm not being very helpful, am I?'

Oriel's fingers gripped the receiver. 'I don't know if I can go. I just keep thinking of his children.'

'Ah.' Dorothy gave quiet acknowledgement.

'I can't get them out of my mind. Just when I've found him. I can only have Daniel if I destroy his family. I don't know if I can do it.' But what was the point of life without him?

'Well . . . I'm sure you'll do the right thing,' said her friend.

When Clive returned Oriel suspected nothing, not having the slightest interest where he had been. However, he came out into the backyard where Oriel, seeking therapy, was wrenching out weeds.

'If you're wondering where I was, the bank manager rang and asked me to go in for a chat. Seems he had a call from the branch in town. They were a little concerned that you'd requested our account to be transferred to your name only. So was I. I kicked up a bit of a stink. So, now you'll be pleased to know that neither of us can get any money out unless the other one signs too. Serves you right for trying to cheat me.'

Oriel flung aside a shard of Chinese pottery and stood up. How can I be cheating you out of what's mine, she thought angrily, but uttered through gritted teeth, 'I was advised to do it by my solicitor. We'll see about this.'

Storming for the washhouse she changed her shoes, rinsed the dirt from her hands and went to her bedroom. After a quick application of lipstick she grabbed her bag, then went directly to the bank where she approached the nearest free teller, producing the receipt she had been given. 'I left my bank book with you yesterday and now I want it back!'

Unnerved by the customer's tone, the inexperienced young man left the counter and approached an older member of staff. Both stared at Oriel whilst obviously discussing her. She seethed.

The stupid-looking youth came back to the counter. 'Sorry, madam, I can't hand the book over. This account's been temporarily frozen.'

'You've no right! That's my money!'

Heads turned. The youth tried to be helpful and traced a finger over the names on the inner cover of the book. 'Well, it's a joint account, you see. You can have it if your husband signs too.'

She erupted. 'It's not his bloody money, it's mine!'

The young fellow's mouth fell slack, making him appear even more idiotic. 'I'm sorry but it's in joint names. I can't give you any money without your husband's consent.'

Oriel was trembling with rage. Her voice rose an octave. 'I demand that you give me my money!'

People were staring, muttering, smirking, but she was oblivious to them. The cashier appeared to be at a loss as to what to do. He was saved by the senior teller, who elbowed him aside and said in pacific tone to Oriel, 'I'm sure we can sort matters out, madam, if you would just care to come into the manager's office.'

'Indeed I will!' Face like thunder, Oriel marched

towards the indicated door, preceded by the unctuous teller and his minion.

The manager, a cadaverous man, was polite. 'Take a seat, Mrs –'

'Mrs Widdowes.' The teller beat Oriel to an answer, and quickly outlined the problem, laying the bank book in front of his superior.

'Ah yes.' Remembering the telephone call he had made earlier, the manager's dark, sunken eyes consulted the book and, noting that a substantial amount was involved, tried to pacify the irate customer. 'Well I don't see any difficulty here, Mrs Widdowes. Certainly we can let you withdraw any amount that you require.'

For one brief moment Oriel's temper calmed.

'Whenever it is convenient for your husband to come and sign the –'

'It's not his bloody money!' Her voice rose to a bellow.

'Would you like a cup of coffee?' tendered the moronic-looking boy, as if he were going to wet his pants.

'No I would not!' Oriel glared at the three imbeciles, who seemed mesmerized by her rage. 'All I want is what's rightfully mine! I've been banking here for ten years!'

'Have you really?' The senior teller feigned interest in order to try to calm the virago and exchanged impressed looks with his companions.

'Needless to say I'll be taking my custom elsewhere once this is sorted out!'

The manager's voice was uneven but he retained his air of control. 'We'd still need your husband's signature.'

Oriel shot from her chair causing the trio to flinch. It was futile to remain here. She was only going to make herself more and more angry. Before she reached the door, however, she remembered something. She still had an account in her maiden name, the one she'd used before her marriage. There wasn't much in it – fifty pounds she discovered on rummaging in her bag and triumphantly producing the book – but the act would serve as small revenge.

'Well, I won't need his signature for this! You can close it, now.' She almost threw the book at the manager.

'Certainly, madam.' He remained polite. 'Mr Bettridge, would you finalize this account and bring the money back to my office. Mrs Widdowes, are you sure you wouldn't like –'

'No thank you!' Stiff-backed, Oriel sat down in an attitude that said she had no wish to converse either. When the money was brought in and counted out before her she stuffed it into her handbag and without comment left the bank.

Upon being presented with her outraged tale of what had occurred in the bank Clive looked sheepish but stood his ground.

'The damned cheek of it!' spat Oriel. 'It can't be legal. Well, I'm going to ring my solicitor right now.'

Upon telephoning, she discovered that the bank was in order in requesting both signatures. The only consolation was that Clive could withdraw nothing either without her permission. If she had received better advice then she would not be in this mess but it was too late now. Slamming down the telephone she went back to demand of Clive, 'What am I supposed to live on?'

He was waspish. 'Hasn't that Daniel got any money?'

'That's got nothing to do with it!'

'Yes it bloody has! I haven't worked my arse off for nine years in order for him to walk in and grab the lot.'

Oriel wanted to shout, don't be so bloody stupid! You think we bought all this on the pittance you earn? But she had hurt him enough by leaving him and so kept the retort to herself.

He reverted to his pathetic stance. 'It's not fair. I haven't done anything wrong.'

Her snakeskin shoes paced the carpet. Oh no, good old

Clive couldn't possibly have done anything wrong, could he?

Faced with her silence he demanded, 'When are you going to live with him then?'

She stopped pacing and looked subdued. 'I'm not sure if I am now. I keep thinking of his kids. He's asked me to meet him but, I don't know –' Her voice trailed away.

'I think you should at least go and talk to him.' Clive gave a bitter laugh. 'Huh! Listen to me, telling my wife to go and meet another man. But this business needs sorting out. It can't go on like this.'

Oriel performed another silent scream – I am not your bloody wife! I never have been and I never will be, and even if Daniel weren't involved do you think I'd have you back?

But he was right about one thing: it could not go on. Even as she voiced her reluctance to hurt Daniel's children she knew in her heart what her path would be.

Looking at the clock, she saw that it was almost time to go and pick up the children. Refusing the lift he offered, she departed.

Instead of coming straight home, she asked Jennifer and Dorrie if they would like to go and play with Dorothy's children for a while, giving herself the opportunity for more heart-pouring.

Upon hearing the latest fiasco, her friend as ever was sympathetic. 'That's not right! What are you going to live on if Clive won't sign?'

Oriel looked out of the window, watching the children playing in the garden. 'I don't give a damn if he won't sign now. I won't go grovelling to the bank to get what's rightfully mine and I certainly won't be seen dead with him.' She came back to sit with her friend.

'Once your divorce comes about I expect he'll have to give you some money,' opined Dorothy.

'Probably – but how long will that take? Clive's deter-mined to drag things out. And why should he have more than his fair share? I mean I know he's entitled to what he earned but most of that money came from Miss Bytheway, not to mention what I've already invested in the house. And I've got the children to look after. Fifty pounds! That's all I've got in the world. What a good job I kept that account open or I wouldn't have had any money for bills or even food.'

'So you closed it?'

'You're damned right! I wouldn't deposit so much as a fart in that bloody bank now.'

Dorothy couldn't help laughing. 'I'm sure they'll be pleased about that.'

Oriel barked a quick laugh too, but was soon eaten away by anger again. 'God, I've never been so humiliated.'

'You should live with my husband,' replied the other with a telling look in her eye.

Oriel was repentant. 'Oh, he hasn't hit you again, has he? Is there anything I can do? Why don't you take the plunge with me?'

'I'll be all right, I usually am.' Dorothy noticed that her friend was tugging bad-temperedly at her clothes. 'Don't tell me you've caught fleas into the bargain?'

'It's this blasted money holster,' complained Oriel, and lifted her blouse to adjust it. 'They're not made for women.'

Dorothy howled. 'You're not meant to wear it across your chest! It's a wonder you haven't cut your circulation off. You're meant to sling it over your shoulder.'

'Are you sure? I did it like that first but it kept slipping off – and I'm taking no chances of that greedy little rat getting his hands on it. It's all I have. Did I tell you he's been going through my bag? He's paranoid that Daniel's going to come and take everything he's worked for. *He's* worked for, mind. I haven't done any of it. Oh no, he was the one who sewed the curtains and the clothes and the chair covers and organized the children for school and washed the sheets when they peed the bed. Oh no, I haven't done any of it.' She patted her chest where the money lay. 'Well, he isn't getting his paws on this. It goes everywhere with – oh, hello, Cuddy!' She broke off as Dorothy's husband came in.

'Oriel.' Cuthbert gave a curt greeting and remained surly as he addressed his wife in punctilious fashion. 'I'm sorry to interrupt your tête-à-tête but I was taken ill at work. I must have developed Clive's complaint – though not the whole of it, I trust.'

Dorothy bit her lip and hurried to tend him. 'Oh dear, come and sit down. Can I get you anything?'

'Yes, you can get rid of this woman from my house.'

Realizing that he was referring to her Oriel gasped, 'I beg your pardon?'

'Your husband's told me all about your callous disregard for him. I must say I always thought he was a saint to have put up with you all these years. I have never had very much respect for you, Oriel, and could never imagine what pleasure my wife derived from your company, but now you have sunk far below my previous estimation. I have to inform you that you are no longer welcome here.'

'Cuddy, Oriel's my friend,' beseeched Dorothy.

'Be quiet,' she was ordered by her husband, and obeyed. 'Will you please go?'

'Gladly.' Oriel picked up her handbag. 'I've no wish to be in the same room as a wife-beater.' Seeing Dorothy cower under her husband's furious glare, she tilted her chin at Cuthbert and issued forcefully, 'And if you so much as touch my friend once more I'll have the law on you!' She turned to leave, adding more gently, 'I'll see you some other time, Dorothy.'

'No, you will not,' came the terse reply. 'I do not wish my wife to associate with such a woman. You will not try to contact her again.'

Not wishing to exacerbate her friend's maltreatment, Oriel simply threw a quick look at Dorothy who was standing behind her husband and was reassured by the wink that came in return. Without another word being exchanged, she collected her children from the garden, and left.

Still trembling from the contempt she had received, it was a relief to find her own house empty again. Giving Jennifer and Dorrie tea, she joined them at the table to nibble on a slice of bread and butter that felt like carpet as it made its way down her throat. The cup of tea was too hot. Unable to settle, she got up and opened a drawer of the sideboard with the intention of looking through some personal papers which she had gathered together earlier, but found they had already been disturbed. Momentarily forgetting the children's presence, she erupted, filling the air with expletives. Just what had he thought to find?

She was not to be allowed to ask this until much later, long after the children had been put to bed. Forced to sit and listen to the wireless, she tapped her foot with burgeoning impatience, seething over Clive's audacity. By the time he came in she was ready to kill him.

'Find anything of interest amongst my belongings, did you?' she demanded as he came through the doorway of the lounge. The moment the comment had left her lips she knew she had played into his hands. One glance at his face showed a man on the verge of explosion and she had provided the detonator.

'You bloody rotten bitch!' He went berserk. The transition from pathetic martyr to cuckolded husband was astounding to behold as he ranted and raged and swore, spittle flying everywhere. 'You sit there accusing me! It isn't me who's done anything wrong. I've never looked at another woman, never! I've done everything I possibly could for you. I've never knocked you around – maybe you would've thought more about me if I had!'

Idiot, thought Oriel, but sat perfectly still and made no accusation of his shortcomings for she recognized the final act of a defeated cornered animal and was too afraid to push him further into that corner.

'I've been sat out there for ages looking at that rope the kids use for swinging on the tree – I'm not bloody kidding!' he screamed at her. 'And you've driven me to it. Wait till that Daniel finds out what a cold hard bitch you are! And if he shows his face around here I'll bloody kill him!' Looking wildly around him he seized the nearest thing to hand – a book – and threw it at her.

She cringed to protect herself as the tome bounced off her stomach to the floor and Clive stormed out of the room – but she tensed for another attack as the sound of his fists reverberated against the double doors, punching them wide open and rocking them in their hinges as he barged back in to spit at her, 'I hope you both rot in hell for what you've done to me!'

She sat there for a moment, wide-eyed and listening as the pounding passage to his room terminated in a slam. Only then did she hear the sound of her daughter weeping. She sighed, and was about to go tend the child when her four-year-old son appeared in the doorway to stare at her.

'It's all right,' she told him with certainty in her voice. 'Your father's all right.' For she knew that for all his self-pitying hysterics Clive would emerge from this trauma the same as he had always been, would go on living and doing the same old things year in year out, like the dog who turns around and around before he lies down to sleep, not knowing why he does it, only that he must.

'Jenny's crying.' Tongue curled round his upper lip, Dorrie played with his pyjama trousers. It was terribly hot, his hair was clinging to his brow.

Oriel was sweating too though hers was as much from fear as from the heat. 'I know. I'll go and see her. Come back to bed.' She put her hand on the little boy's shoulder and steered him down the hall to his darkened bedroom next to the pantry.

'Why is Daddy shouting?'

'He's –' She pushed her hair behind one ear. 'He's angry with Mummy because she has to go and live somewhere else.'

The drowsy face looked up at her. 'Are we coming to live somewhere else too?'

'Yes. Remember I told you? Well, we'll be going tomorrow.'

'Is Daddy angry with me and Jenny as well?'

'No! He loves you. None of this is your fault.' Oriel bent down to pick up her son, cuddled his heated body, and installed him in bed before going to comfort her daughter, to whom she gave the same explanation that none of this was their fault.

To alleviate their discomfort she turned on the fan, then sat between their two beds, singing to them. After soothing them back to sleep, she crept from the darkened room, crept to the linen cupboard, took out a blanket and went to the dining room, keeping her ears alert for another attack. But there was no sound from Clive's room. Her own bedroom door had no lock but the dining room did. Feeling safer here she turned the key, lay down on the sofa, covered herself with the blanket, and tried to sleep.

19

In the morning she prepared to leave, creeping about the house like a thief as she collected as many clothes and belongings as she could. Only then did she get the children out of bed and give them breakfast.

It was in the kitchen that she found the letter. Unable to witness the departure of his wife and children, a sleepless Clive had sneaked from his bed in the early hours and before leaving the house had composed a rambling damnation of her behaviour throughout their marriage.

Whilst her children ate, Oriel read it dispassionately, then folded it up and scribbled on the back of it. 'I hope you find the person you deserve.' He'll probably take that to mean that he deserves someone better than me, she thought – interpret the phrase as a vindication of his own behaviour, whilst in reality it meant that she hoped he would find someone who was as lacking in intuition and imagination as he was. A person who was willing to spend the next twenty, thirty or even fifty years with a man who was content to get up at the same time every day, eat the same breakfast, go to work at the same job, rush to catch the six o'clock swill, come home to a meal on the table, abandon her in favour of his cronies, then come home to bed in the hope of sexual gratification. That person was not Oriel. She was not sure what she wanted from life, only what she did not want and she did not want him. She wanted to awake to a feeling of anticipation, not to the terrible quandary of how she was ever going to get through another day. There was nothing wrong with him. There was nothing wrong with her. They were just different, and that difference had been slowly killing them both. Why could he not see that?

She played with her wedding ring, wanting desperately to remove it and with it all trace of her marriage, but how would that look when she had two children? For their sake she left it on.

'Finished, Mummy!'

She turned to smile at her son and daughter. 'Clean plates? Good-o. Well, run and collect a few of your favourite toys and books – just a few. I won't be able to carry much, but you can get the rest later. I'll take them to the new house and they'll be there waiting for you when I pick you up from school.'

Jennifer and Dorrie ran off to rummage through their toy cupboard. Simultaneously, the front door knocker sounded. Oriel jumped, then left the washing up and went through the hall to answer it, her face dropping at the sight of Melinda and her children. She hesitated before holding wide the door, 'Mel . . . come in.'

'No thanks,' was the icy reply. 'I just come here so's my children could see the woman who's taking their father away.'

Oriel's expression crumpled. Her eyes toured the row of solemn little faces, hardly daring to linger upon Alice, who had always shown such admiration of her 'aunt', and who now beheld her with fear and accusation.

'Have you no conscience?' Melinda's voice tremored, but her expression remained firm. 'How d'yer think we're gonna live with no wage coming in? How we gonna pay the bills, buy food? How can you do it? Not just to them but to me? My best friend – at least I thought so! I always looked up to you for the way you took me in and looked after me when I had Alice, never believed what your father said that y'only took me in to spite him 'cause he walked out on you and your mum – but I believe it now. You use people to your own ends, Oriel. You been coming into my home just so's you could steal my husband.'

Oriel's grip tightened on the edge of the door. 'You can't steal people, Mel. They're not possessions.'

'Shut up! I'll have my say.' Melinda fought back tears of rage.

Oriel was close to tears too. 'Mel, I am truly sorry for what's happened.'

'Then don't let it happen! There's time yet. Dan's working his last shift at the mill but he could always tell 'em he's changed his mind. Just leave him alone and stay with your own husband. I reckon Clive'll feel the same way as I do. He'll forgive you and be glad just to have yer back, as I will Dan.'

Oriel's temper flared. 'I haven't left Clive for Daniel! I'd already started divorce proceedings. It was sheer luck that we bumped into each other.'

'Lucky for who? Certainly not these children! And what about yer own, eh?'

Oriel's mind was reeling. She nipped her brow. 'That was the wrong choice of word. I meant to say coincidence.'

'All right, I'll take you at yer word. You'd finished with Clive, you were feeling vulnerable, you were scared of being on yer own, I know I would be – I bloody am! Then you met Dan and you thought he could look after you. I can forgive that. He's a lovely man, makes everybody feel as if he cares about them – but I mean everybody, Oriel, not just you, you're nothing special. Who d'yer think he's been sleeping with the last two days? If yer think he's been saving himself for you yer wrong.'

Oriel showed no emotion, pushing the other to frustration.

'You don't know him!' yelled Melinda.

'I do.'

It was the certainty in Oriel's voice that led Melinda to the realization that her marriage was over. She stood there facing the other woman for long seconds, then said tersely, 'Well, yer'd better make sure he gets another bloody job then. He's still got four kids to feed!' Grabbing two small hands, she led her brood away.

Oriel watched her stalk down the path to the battered car and withdraw from it the painting that Nat had given her years ago, watched as she hurled it over the garden gate with a cry of futile retaliation. 'See how yer like them apples!'

Leaving it where it lay, Oriel shut the door and collapsed against it, trembling, then opened her eyes to see her own children standing before her, their arms full of toys and books, bewilderment on their faces.

Collecting her senses, she tried to look cheerful. 'Don't worry about all that row, it's just something silly. Now, what would you like for playlunch?' A falsely animated discussion followed, during which Oriel enlisted their help in preparing the sandwiches. How she could conjure so many jokes she did not know, was only glad that they worked. By the time they reached school she had been able to calm the youngsters and they went through the gates with no complaint.

After leaving them, she took a bus into town where she collected the keys to her new home. As the name might suggest, Parkville boasted wide open spaces, Royal Park on one side, the university grounds on the other, with many desirable residences amongst its rolling green acres – but Oriel's cottage was not one of them. Situated in a pocket of working-class housing, it formed part of a terrace, and was surrounded by wood yards, industrial sites and a steam laundry.

Evidence of petunias amongst the weeds in the tiny front garden told that it had once been a pretty little house, as did the iron lacework around its front verandah. Now, rust and flaking paint prevailed. Having come prepared for cleaning, with cloths and disinfectant, Oriel was nevertheless horrified at the size of the task before her. Why had she not noticed it yesterday? Every room stank of urine and sweat. It would never be in a fit state for the children tonight. Her chore was further delayed by the fact that there was no hot water, but luckily the gas had not been turned off, and in the time it took to boil a kettle she was rushing about cleaning and scrubbing and swearing as the cuffs of her gingham smock kept catching on doorknobs almost ripping the seams.

'Bloody buggering knob!' After the umpteenth time of being dragged backwards she lashed out at the door with her foot, chipping even more paint off it, before tearing and ripping the smock from her back and hurling it at the wall. After the display of rage she took three deep breaths, scolded herself into some sort of order, and launched herself back into her task.

Alas, despite taking nearly every layer of skin off her fingertips with copious amounts of bleach and scourer, almost asphyxiating herself into the bargain, the house still reeked.

It was by now midday but Oriel had not thought to bring anything with her to eat. Famished and exhausted, she was about to go out and buy something when a knock came at the door. Frowning, she answered it to find her friend on the doorstep.

'Oh thanks be to God – the cavalry!'

'I can't stay long!' Humping a basket, Dorothy rushed inside, looking furtive. 'Cuddy'll kill me if he finds out. Oh, I'm really sorry about yesterday, Oriel! I wouldn't have had it happen for the world. He told me I hadn't to see you again – that was even before he knew about Daniel – but I took no notice, thinking he's out all day at work and wouldn't find out. Trust him to get sick!'

'Oh well. Just so long as he didn't take it out on you after I left.' Happy to see her friend, Oriel shrugged and ran a hand over her dark waves, then glimpsed the barest hint of agitation in Dorothy's face before the other turned away. 'He didn't, did he?' She caught at her friend's sleeve, eyes quizzing her face. Though Dorothy denied there had been violence Oriel knew she was lying. 'Oh, he did, the bloody wretch! I could kill him! Oh, what can I do – or have I done enough?'

'It wasn't your fault!' Dorothy tried to make light of yesterday's violence. 'Somebody else had upset him at work. He just gets . . . frustrated.' When her friend begged her not to put up with this appalling treatment she refused to budge. 'I'm all right, honestly! It's you we have to worry about at the moment.' Seeing that Oriel was holding a hat, she asked, 'Were you going out?'

Oriel sighed. 'Yes, you just caught me. I was going to find something to eat.'

'I can save you the trouble.' Dorothy began to unload the contents of her bag, amongst them a flask of tea. 'I wasn't sure if you had a stove so I brought tea and sandwiches – there's a quarter of tea, bread, butter, milk, sugar and some Vegemite too.'

'Oh, you little beauty! I'm almost fainting with hunger. I have got a stove – and I found an old kettle – but it's not much to speak of.' Oriel disposed of her hat, bit into a sandwich and watched the other pour two cups of tea. 'I've had a disastrous morning. First Melinda turned up on my doorstep –'

'Crikey Moses!'

'I'll tell you about that in a minute – then I've been trying to get rid of this dreadful stink and nothing will shift it.'

Dorothy flared her nostrils and bit into her sandwich. 'I think the floorboards are impregnated. You'd better be careful, there might be bugs. Get some tins and shove the bed legs into them with a bit of kerosene.'

'I haven't even got a bed yet. And there's a thousand and one other things I've got to do.'

'Well, you don't have to do them on your own.' Still munching, Dorothy rolled up her sleeves. 'That's what I've come for. It's the least I can do after what Cuddy said.'

'Bless you.' Oriel embraced the other with her eyes. Under Cuthbert's rule Dorothy had become more matronly than ever, in her grey dress looking fifty rather than the same age as her companion. In the space of ten years the majestic young woman had been displaced by a downtrodden housewife. But Oriel had never felt so affectionate towards her friend as now. 'Instead of you helping me, it should be the other way around.'

'I'm just glad that one of us is happy,' said Dorothy, totally caught up in her friend's romance. 'Anyway, you were saying you need to buy a bed.'

Oriel nodded. 'Amongst other things. I'll just buy the one, I can have the children's beds moved in tomorrow, but then there's linen, cutlery – all the things I've collected over ten years and now I'm having to set up house all over again.'

'Why don't you bring some of them from home? Clive won't need all of them.'

'Well, I might later, but I just need some essentials.' Oriel crammed the last of the sandwich into her mouth and during the rest of their lunchbreak she told Dorothy about Melinda.

Afterwards, feeling conspicuous and embarrassed at her dishevelled appearance, she went out to buy the items of furniture she required, leaving Dorothy to continue cleaning.

Upon alighting from the tram in Elizabeth Street near the post office, who should she see coming towards her but Thora. Expecting to invite further malice, she braced herself, but as the other came nearer still wearing her smile of greeting she guessed that her sister-in-law must be unaware of the impending divorce – Clive was probably too ashamed to broadcast it. Thus, Oriel was nudged into mischief. As Thora slowed down, preparing to talk – had even opened her mouth – Oriel took great delight in marching straight past her without so much as a greeting. The look of offence on her sister-in-law's face was small revenge for past hurts but it would have to do, for she doubted there would be further opportunity.

It was ironic that in such a big city she was to see two people she knew in a matter of minutes. This one was more difficult to avoid. Even though Daphne had her back turned and was looking into a shop window there was no way Oriel could ignore all the many kindnesses she had received from Clive's mother over the years. She tapped her on the shoulder and said hello. Daphne turned, smiling, and said hello too, no hint that she knew about Daniel. They engaged in chit-chat for a moment. No mention was made of Clive's brief stay at his mother's house.

Then Daphne asked, 'Is Clive going fishing on Sunday?'

'I don't know.' How the hell should I know? thought Oriel. His movements are none of my concern. Hadn't the fool told his mother that they were going to be divorced? She got the suspicion that Daphne assumed that just because he had gone back to the marital home everything was sorted out. And Clive had obviously let her think that. Well, if that was how he wanted to play it was none of Oriel's concern now. The mother would side with her son and that was how it should be. She curried no sympathy nor did she expect it. But she would have liked to have said thank you for the good years, for the way you welcomed me into your family, I'm sorry you're going to be hurt, I truly am. But all she said to Daphne was, 'Oh well, I'd better be going.' It was all so very polite. So very English. Taking her leave, she was never to see Clive's mother again.

Mulling over the previous enactment as she walked along the busy street, she realized that Clive was not alone in his reticence. Did she not find it impossible to break the news to her own mother? How could she imagine it would be any easier for him?

Shortly, other things were to preoccupy Oriel. Selecting a bedroom suite for twelve pounds ten shillings, instead of the seventeen guinea one she would have preferred, she also chose a sofa for five pounds twelve and six, a cheap table for one pound six and three, four chairs at nine shillings each, a rug for seven and six, plus a dozen sundry items. Having been fortunate enough to purchase all her requirements at the one department store, she asked that those things she could not carry be delivered this afternoon or tomorrow morning at the latest.

She watched the bill being drawn up and added, 'I'll pay by cash once the goods are delivered.' All these things would deduct a sizeable amount from her fifty pounds but there was no choice: her cheque book was now useless.

'Very well, madam.' The counter clerk performed his addition, then asked, 'Could I have your husband's name, please?' She frowned and asked why this was necessary. The clerk remained polite. 'I have to put it on the bill.'

'You can put my name on the bill.'

'I'm afraid that won't be sufficient, madam.'

Oriel felt her temper rising. 'May I enquire why, when it's I who am paying the bill – a considerable bill, might I point out to you.'

The clerk was about to argue his case, when Oriel snapped, 'I don't have a husband!'

'My apologies, madam, you are a widow?'

The reply was taut. 'No, I am separated.'

The clerk's whole attitude altered, no longer bestowing the courtesy of a title. 'I'm afraid my superior would frown on this.'

Oriel fumed. 'Very well! See what your superior thinks when I take my custom elsewhere.' With as much dignity as she could muster she stalked out.

But she was to find that it was the same at the next shop and all this arguing was taking time she could not spare. In the end she was forced to accept the humiliation and rather than grovel she lied, saying she was recently widowed, and the items she had ordered were loaded for immediate delivery.

Upon her return she found that Dorothy had completed

most of the chores which was just as well, for within the hour a furniture van rolled up with the bedroom suite, table and chairs, sofa, bedding and a box of pots and pans, giving the friends another frantic period of work before having to make the lengthy trip to pick up the children. After a quick gulp of tea from the flask, the dishevelled women left the house together. Dorothy made little comment about the immediate vicinity but Oriel knew what she was thinking.

'Not much garden, is there?' There was a strip three feet wide beneath the front window.

Dorothy was cheerful. 'You don't need a garden, you've got the park and the zoo –'

'And horses somewhere, by the smell of it,' said Oriel.

'And you're only five minutes from town,' finished the other. 'There are a lot worse places than this.'

Having witnessed the housing her father's tenants had had to endure, Oriel knew this to be right. It was just such a comedown from her own lovely home. 'Let's hope Jenny and Dorrie agree with you.'

Catching the same train, they travelled all the way together. Not until the school disgorged its seething mass of elves did Dorothy take her leave. 'Good luck, old pal. I don't know when I'll be able to call on you again but I'm sure you won't need me when you've got Daniel.' She smiled and left, carrying her friend's eternal thanks.

Oriel and her children made the thirty-minute journey back to the city and Parkville, where she introduced them to their new residence.

The house might be a lot more habitable than it had been that morning, but it was incommensurate with Jennifer and Dorrie's idea of home.

'Where's all the furniture?' The little girl wrinkled her nose as her mother showed her through the rooms. All that was to be seen in the living room was a small hearth rug on bare boards, a sofa, a pine table and four chairs; a bed, a wardrobe and a dressing table in another room, and a food safe in the tiny insalubrious-looking kitchen.

'I haven't had time to get much yet. Here!' Oriel handed out glasses of lukewarm milk and Vegemite sandwiches, which cut down on the questions for a time, but after these were consumed and the light was beginning to fade, plunging the house into gloom Dorrie said, 'When are we going home? I want my daddy.'

He looked as if he were going to cry. His mother picked him up and cuddled him, breaking into chant. '"Ching Chang Chinaman bought a penny doll. Washed it, dressed it, called it Pretty Poll. Sent for the doctor, the doctor couldn't come. Because he had a pimple on his –"'

'Bum bum, bum!' yelled the two children, laughing.

'Come on, get your nighties on and I'll read you some stories before bedtime.' Their mother visited the little pile of books and toys then, sitting on the sofa, she beckoned them to her. Perhaps now was the time to tell them that Uncle Daniel would be living with them. But try as she might it was hard to broach.

'Aren't we having a bath?' Jennifer watched her mother assist Dorrie with his pyjama bottoms and comb his hair.

'Not tonight.' Oriel did not want to tell them there was no bath. 'I don't care if you pong.' Planting smacking kisses on their cheeks, she took a child under each arm. Then, in the yellow glow of gaslight, read them a favourite tale before guiding them through the dingy passageway and tucking them up on the new bed with its fresh sheets, the one she had bought for herself and Daniel.

They were afraid to go to sleep and so she had to climb in with them, intending only to stay a while but with the exacting day and the comfort of their small bodies she fell into a doze and when she awoke it was to pitch-darkness. Unwilling to get up and undress in case she disturbed the children, she closed her eyes and went back to sleep.

Upon rising at first light, all were covered in red bumps. Pretending these were mosquito bites, Oriel tried to soothe the itching as best she could with cold cream, then gave the children breakfast. With no refrigerator the milk was most unpalatable and when she tried to make toast a cockroach scuttled from the stove, making her yell out.

'Do I have to sleep with him tonight as well?' sulked Jennifer. 'He kicks.'

'No, I'll arrange for your own beds to be brought round this afternoon,' her mother told her, which met with little enthusiasm.

With packs of sandwiches, they left the house at seven thirty, catching a tram to the city, then the train to North Brighton. Oriel wondered how long she would be able to keep this up. Apart from costing precious funds it was a fifteen-mile round trip twice a day. But until the situation grew desperate, she could not bring herself to rob the children of their school friends too.

There were plenty of chores to tackle when she got home. None of the removal firms she contacted was able to transport the beds that afternoon and so she arranged for it to be done the next day. Then, no sooner was she entrenched in more washing and cleaning than it was time to set off to collect the children from school.

Jennifer was tearful upon realizing that they would once again have to endure the austerity of the cottage. 'I don't like living here. I want to go home.'

Her little brother was just as bad. 'We've nothing to play with.' When his mother reminded him of the toys he had brought with him he explained, 'Yes, but we played with those yesterday.'

Oriel swallowed her frustration. 'Well, we'll go and fetch some more tomorrow. Please be good and eat your tea, there's nothing I can do at the moment. Maybe tomorrow we'll find some children for you to play with in the park.' She had still not told them about Daniel.

Whilst they ate, she wandered to the window and stared idly up and down the street. An ambulance was parked across the road. She looked on as a man came out of a

474

house carrying a small child, and she continued to watch until the doors of the ambulance had been closed and it was driven away.

After eating their tea Jennifer and Dorrie persisted in whingeing. Oriel did her best to entertain them but eventually, fearful of losing her temper, she packed them off to bed.

The next morning she was greeted with the sound of their whines about breakfast and finally snapped. 'Look! I don't want to be here either but we have to put up with it for the time being – now eat!'

She wheeled away to the window, frowning as the sound of quiet weeping punctuated the miserable atmosphere. There was another van parked across the road where the ambulance had been yesterday. Its driver was just in the process of returning some equipment to it. With a jolt of recognition, Oriel watched him replace the instruments in his van. She had seen them once before when her own house had been fumigated after the outbreak of influenza. Her skin crawled – there was disease only yards away! Telling Jennifer to stop snivelling, she hurried outside and accosted the man, asking for information as to the nature of the disease within.

'Dunno, missus, I'm only here to do me job.'

She nodded and was about to return to her children when the householder came out and announced bitterly, 'It's meningitis!' At Oriel's blushing expression he added, 'That's what you were asking about, isn't it? And you can tell the rest of the sticky beaks my boy's dead!'

Oriel's heart went out to him, but there was terror for her own brood too. Uttering her sympathy she rushed inside and shut the door, leaning on it as if in a vain attempt to bar disease. Jennifer was still snivelling though the tears were forced. 'I want to go home!'

Oriel sank on to a chair, her heart plummeting too. Looking around that decrepit room and listening to her children whimper and scratch, she asked herself how she

475

could be so selfish as to inflict this life on them, expose them to the risk of that awful disease. The poor little things had asked for none of this. The very thought of parting, even temporarily, induced the most agonizing sickness but Oriel knew in her heart she must restore them to safety until she could provide somewhere better for them to live. With a great shuddering sigh, she put her head in her hands, not looking at them as she spoke. 'I'll take you home if you want to go.'

Jennifer cheered immediately. 'Goody!'

'But Mummy can't live there with you.'

'Oh, why not?'

Oriel agonized, shamed by the memory of how hard her mother had fought to keep her, imagining how livid her father would be and what a hypocrite she herself was after all the names she had called him for deserting her in babyhood. No, you're not deserting them, she told herself, you'll get them back when you've the financial means.

Trying not to cry, she answered, 'Because ... because, I just don't want to live with Daddy. I love you both.' Lifting her eyes, she looked into the two little enquiring faces then looked away quickly, but it was too late, the tears began to flow. 'And I'll come for you as soon as I –' She broke off, unable to continue.

The children wept too. Scooping them up, Oriel hugged and kissed them fiercely, one in either arm and continued to sob until the tears ran dry. Then, mopping all their faces, she sniffed and said, 'I'll come and see you as often as I can, and as soon as I've found a better house for us to stay in I'll come and fetch you to live with me again.'

'When will that be?' Jennifer contorted her head, trying to wipe her eyes on the short sleeve of her summer dress.

'Not long,' Oriel assured her, reminding herself to cancel the transportation of their beds. 'Now, come on, I'll take you home.'

'Aren't we going to school?'

'Not today, it's Saturday.' Upon all being properly attired, she hurried them from the house, hoping that their father would not yet have left for work.

Before Oriel had entered, Clive had been sitting alone, nursing his sense of bereavement. The look on his face when his estranged wife and children came into the house was one of dull suspicion. Whilst he returned the little ones' greetings, Oriel acted with brevity. 'I've had to bring them home for a week or two. The house I'm renting isn't fit for them to live in.' His only response was a dumb stare. 'I wasn't sure if you'd be at work.'

He finally responded to her. 'I'm not going back till Monday. Just as well, isn't it?'

Jennifer wrapped her anxiety in a mundane request. 'Could we have a biscuit?' At her mother's reply both children ran off, competing to see who could get to the tin first.

'I know it's going to be difficult,' continued Oriel when they'd gone. She took a deep breath. 'But if I still come and collect them from school on an afternoon and get them ready for bed on a night all you have to do is see to them on a morning.'

'And what about the school holidays?' asked Clive. The children would be off from Christmas to the end of January.

'Maybe your mother could help.' Daphne only lived a couple of stops away on the train. 'I'll come and get them when I'm able.'

Clive responded with customary sarcasm. 'Yes, children do cramp your style a bit, don't they? But don't worry, I've nobody to impress.'

'Neither have I!' Oriel felt nauseated by her suppressed rage. 'Don't you understand, I'm doing this for their sake?'

'Well, I didn't think you were doing it for mine.'

'That place isn't fit for rats.' And that's what I feel like, thought Oriel. The rat deserting the sinking ship. 'But I'm looking out for somewhere else nearer their school. I'll come and get them whenever I can.'

He nodded. 'They'll be fine with me. I'm sure Mum'll jump at the chance to take care of them.' She's a good mother, his tone seemed to imply.

Oriel chewed the inside of her cheek. 'We'll have to sell this place. I can't afford to buy a house of my own otherwise.'

'If that's a hint for me to let you and Daniel move in —'

'Of course not.' She tried to hang on to her temper. 'I'm just saying, as you're the one who lives here it'll be up to you to show the real estate agents round.' He said he would see to it. 'Thanks. I should think it might take a while, three months or so.'

Other thoughts and responsibilities kept leaping into her head. 'I know you think all this is my father's fault but I'd ask you not to write and say anything. I'd like to break the news myself.' When he nodded, she cast a tortured gaze in the direction of the kitchen, and said, 'I may have to come back to collect some things later. I'll just go and say goodbye, then I'll be off.' Managing to hold back her tears this time, she took leave of her son and daughter, telling them she would be back to visit in a few days. On her way out she pulled off her wedding ring and put it into her bag, before returning to the dilapidated cottage. Only then did she break down, howling and wailing like a demented beast, rocking back and forth, her whole body racked by agonized sobs until her misery finally erupted in a violent gush of vomit.

Thus, the joy of meeting Daniel that noon was tarnished, for he too had endured this heartbreak. She read it in his eyes long before he saw her, eyes that gazed emptily at the busy lunchtime traffic as he waited for her under the clocks. Upon her quiet greeting, he spun and immediately took her in his arms, gripping her as though his life depended on it, and Oriel responded in similar fashion.

Without another word, she took his hand and led him to the place that was to be their home, and here they fell into each other's arms, half insane with passion, unleashing the human and spiritual need that both had repressed for so long. Thereafter, sublime in their union, they lay entwined beneath the flaking ceiling, embraced each other with their eyes, gave tender kisses, stroked and soothed and loved – but there was pain too, dreadful agony, as Daniel spoke of the wrench of leaving his children and Oriel revealed that she, too, had suffered thus.

'I can't tell my parents,' she wept into his bare shoulder. 'I know I'll have to tell them some time but not right now. I just don't know what to say. All the things I threw at my father for abandoning me when I was a baby and here I am abandoning my own children.' Her body shook.

'But you'll get them back.' Equally distraught, he smoothed the hair from her wet cheeks, but in his mind was the permanent image of his own children's faces as he had said goodbye. 'Things'll never be the same with mine. I left their mother everything I had, the car, money, everything, so they wouldn't suffer materially but it'll make no difference to how they feel.'

Such misery could not continue. Tears abated, Oriel wiped her face on the sheet and sighed. 'My mother thought I was mad when I wanted to leave him years ago. Her opinion was everything to me. It never occurred to me that she could be wrong. But I still can't bring myself to write and tell her.'

He used his thumb to wipe away one of the tears she had missed. 'Is there any chance of her coming down from Queensland and taking you by surprise?'

'I hope not, I said we wouldn't be going for a holiday this summer and she said she didn't know if she had the energy to come down to Vic. She won't know unless Clive writes and tells her. I asked him not to. If I keep answering her letters and sending photos of the children she won't be any the wiser.'

'Any strife from Clive's family?'

'No.' She recalled the polite scene with Daphne in town. 'Just a few funny looks from my neighbours, but I couldn't give a damn what they or anyone else might say. I think I've served my sentence. People like us, we have no hope of gaining their understanding. We haven't lost our children in an earthquake or a flood, we've left them deliberately. At least you have a choice, they say. Well it must be very nice to be so practically minded, to know just where your feet are going to land before you've even taken a step. Most people don't consciously set out to hurt others, it's a matter of accident. It's easy to condemn when you're not involved. I'm as guilty of that as the next person. I hope I'll be a bit less quick to judge now before I have the facts – and if he's so bloody perfect why aren't I still living with him?'

She laughed then and hugged him. 'Oh, sorry for going on like this. I'm just letting off steam. It's usually poor Dorothy who hears my woes. Doubt whether I'll see very much of her now. I feel rather guilty that I've escaped and she'll be stuck with Cuthbert for the rest of her life. He hits her, you know. But try as I might I can't persuade her to leave.'

After a moment she asked softly, 'Did you know Mel came to see me?'

Daniel nodded. 'Not till she came back, though. Sorry.' He stroked her arm thoughtfully. 'It's like the bloody Eureka Stockade up there. She'll fight me over the divorce, says if she can't have me then nobody else will.' As if to deny this, he kissed her.

Oriel savoured the mouth she had desired for so long, imbibed deeply of his spirit, then drew away and sighed 'I can't help feeling we're going to pay dearly for this.'

'Didn't you know? We're going straight to Hell.'

She asked if his parents knew. He laughed, the vibrations passing through her own body. 'I can't win. They haven't spoken to me for years because I married a Protestant and now they won't own me 'cause I'm living in sin with a woman who's married to somebody else!' He snorted and tightened his embrace on her. 'Ah, who cares? There's plenty of other things to worry us – like me having to find a job, and I won't find one by lying here.' Delivering a quick kiss, he scissored his legs and jumped out of bed.

Sublime of face, Oriel looked on as he wandered naked to where he had dropped his clothes on the floor, enjoying the opportunity to study his male form, neither abashed nor guilty. 'I suppose I should get a job too. I've used most of the fifty pounds I had saved.' She told him all about the episode in the bank and everything else that had happened since Wednesday. 'I've just been spending all my time cleaning this place. I can't understand how there could be any bugs left but I still wake up with bites.'

'They'll be living behind the wallpaper. I'll have a go at stripping it off later.' By this time he was dressed and perched on the bed. 'Ah well, she'll be right. Fancy a cuppa tea?' He pressed her back on to the mattress. 'Stay there, I'll make it.'

'I can't, I feel decadent.'

'Oh yeah, real Sodom and Gomorrah stuff. Don't worry, I've got plenty lined up for you this arvo. After we've had this cuppa you can come and help me find a job.'

The light-hearted mood that accompanied their departure had evaporated by the time they got home several hours later. After registering at the Government Employment Bureau, Daniel had toured numerous timber yards and sawmills, but none had any vacancies.

'Be buggered,' he told her as they relaxed on the sofa,

removing from her feet her high-heeled shoes, and rubbing her blisters. 'It doesn't have to be a timber mill. I'll take anything. I'll go out again tomorrow.'

Between kisses, she reminded him that tomorrow was Sunday. 'I'd like to go and see Jen and Dorrie. I haven't explained about you yet.'

Daniel admitted this would be difficult and said he would stay at home out of the way.

In the event it was academic for when she arrived in North Brighton it was to find that Clive had taken the children out himself. Oriel returned home, forced to content herself with the knowledge that she would be collecting them from school the next day, and spent the remainder of the afternoon helping Daniel strip off wallpaper.

Monday brought little joy on the work front, an entire day's search of the city producing nothing more than aching feet. Plucked from the security of her comfortable lifestyle, Oriel now began to notice the inordinate amount of men loafing against verandah posts and around billiard rooms, and came to realize the seriousness of the unemployment situation that had hitherto been merely a statistic. The declining export figures that she had always skipped over in the newspaper now took on grave meaning. Her father had been proved right, though it was possibly much worse than he had forecast. The country was in the grip of depression.

The children were pleased to see her, though, when she collected them from school. Their father had given reminder that Mother would be coming to meet them and take them home. However, Oriel could tell from their excited chatter that they took this to mean she would be staying.

'I can only stay till Daddy gets in,' she explained gently, whilst giving them tea. 'I haven't found another house for us yet – but maybe next week.'

'Will Uncle Daniel be coming to live there too?' asked

Dorrie, pushing a small toy car up and down the tablecloth.

Oriel was shocked and angry with Clive for divulging this, but tried not to show it. 'Well – yes, he is actually.'

'Daddy told Nanna Widdowes you left us and ran off with Uncle Daniel,' accused Jennifer. 'I don't want him to live with us. I hate him.'

Oriel wanted to weep. 'But you liked him before.' Daniel had always been popular with her children.

The little girl was insistent. 'He took you away. I hate him.' Her teeth mutilated a slice of cake, spilling crumbs everywhere.

'He hasn't taken me away! Even if I can't live with you at the moment, I'm still your mummy.' Receiving no response, Oriel's miserable eyes moved to her son. Dorrie said nothing, didn't even look at her but kept on playing with the toy car. Normally he would not have been allowed to do this but guilt demanded Oriel not to rebuke him. 'Uncle Daniel's not trying to take your daddy's place. Even if he wasn't coming to live with us Mummy wouldn't be able to come back and live here.'

'Can I get down now?' asked Dorrie. When his mother gave permission, he said, 'I'm going to make you a cake,' and running to his toy box he took out anything that could be used as a mixing bowl and utensils. 'First we put in some flour, then some, er, margarine, then some water, eggs, then some intelligent chocolate.'

Oriel leaned on her elbow, supporting her chin with her palm, trying to make her smile appear genuine.

'You're not supposed to put your elbows on the table,' warned Jennifer.

'Sorry – listen, it'll soon be Christmas, what present would you like?'

'A car,' came Dorrie's immediate request.

'A doll's pram,' said Jennifer, then looked worried. 'If we move house how will Father Christmas know where we are?'

Her mother said he knew where everyone lived. 'Just to make sure we'll write him a letter.' She organized the children with paper and crayons, then sat back to watch as her little son, unable to write anything other than his name, drew a picture. Later, she gave them an early bath and read them stories until their father got home, at which point she took on a slightly agitated air, kissed each good-bye, gathered together their letters and said she would post them on her way home.

That night, reading Jennifer's note with Daniel at her side, she displayed sorrow over the little girl's request. 'She wants Father Christmas to take you back to Aunt Melinda.'

He rubbed her knee. 'Mine are the same. You're the Poison Queen as far as Alice goes. What about the little bloke?'

Oriel sighed and told him Dorrie had been inscrutable. 'Usually he's quite open – intuitive too; he knew my father wasn't fond of him.' Daniel had been aware of that prob-lem all along and Oriel had also told him of the break-through in that area last winter. 'But I just don't know what he makes of all this.'

'Poor little fella.' The tanned face softened. 'He's just managed to establish himself in his grandad's heart and now some bloke comes and steals his mother. He must've been knocked rotten by it – they all must.' He heaved a sigh. 'But, as they'd be quick enough to tell us, we've chosen.'

Oriel laid her head against his shoulder. 'I think mine'll come round. They always liked you, and they're only little.' This thought brought fresh tears. After wiping her eyes she added, 'I told Clive I'd go early on Saturday and have them while he's at work. Will you come with me?' He said he would. 'We'll have another look for houses too. I don't know what possessed me to rent this place. I was just so desperate. Before you came I felt as if I was going mad, I feel so guilty.' She covered her mouth with a hand.

Daniel removed it and lowered his lips to hers, speaking in a warm, convincing tone. 'Don't worry, Kook, everything'll be all right in the end.'

20

Throughout the rest of that week, which saw Oriel rushing to and from Brighton every evening, Daniel searched for work but to no avail. Determined to go out again on Monday, he accompanied Oriel to her weekend meeting with the children, waiting at the end of the street whilst she brought them to him. Despite Jennifer's previous objections she was to put these aside when she saw the cut-out doll and its wardrobe of clothes that Daniel had brought her, and treated him as she always had done, with affection. Dorrie was more guarded. Though he accepted the cardboard glider, whenever Daniel spoke to him he answered only in monosyllables and was much less talkative than usual with his mother.

In general, though, the day was a success and before returning the children to their father Oriel told them she hoped that before too long they would all have a new house to live in.

However, after several repetitions over the following weeks, this promise began to sound false. There was still no house to rent in Brighton – even if there had been it was doubtful they would be able to afford it, for Daniel's search for employment continued to be fruitless. To save money, Oriel had dragged her old bicycle out of the shed and though it now took a lot longer to make her daily visits to collect the children it was worth the effort just to see them.

'I'd have loved to have had somewhere else by Christmas,' she moped. 'It'll be murder knowing –' Catching sight of Daniel's face she bit her tongue and stroked him.

'Well, I don't have to tell you. What're we going to do about presents for the children?'

Daniel had not wanted to think about this. 'Don't concern yerself about mine, I'll make something.' He felt bad enough having to pay maintenance out of the money Oriel had brought with her. It was no good asking any of his relatives for help, they were as poor as he and anyway, most of them had snubbed him.

'I promised Jenny a doll's pram and Dorrie a car before I knew we'd be strapped for cash. I'd hate to let them down.'

'You don't have to.'

She was glad he understood. Her children had never been used to going without. 'It'd be money better saved though. I could kick myself now for blueing all that cash at the beginning.' With the purchase of the furniture and other unnecessary acquisitions the fifty pounds had been whittled down to less than twenty-five and Christmas was going to take a big chunk out of that. 'Oh, what am I talking about – Clive will surely agree to the children's gifts coming out of the bank account. Though I doubt he'll want to fork out for presents for my parents and Vicky. I'll have to buy for them. If I don't they'll know something's wrong.'

A lesser man would have pointed out that all their financial problems could have been solved by one simple cry for help to her parents, but Daniel knew Oriel as well as he knew himself. It was not mere pride that stopped her from revealing her dilemma but the sheer anguish that such a revelation would provoke. He watched her sympathetically.

Oriel had drifted away into her vivid imagination, experiencing the looks of horror on her parents' faces when they discovered how she had failed them. The stigma of divorce was bad enough, but what would be the extent of her mother's shock when she learned that Oriel had abandoned Jennifer and Dorrie – albeit temporarily? Bright worshipped her grandchildren. Oriel worshipped her mother. She had come to care for her father's feelings too. How would Nat react after all the contempt she had poured upon him in the past for his own desertion? And so, though it was true that a confession could solve their monetary problem it was far outweighed by her feelings of guilt and shame. She would leave it as long as she could – perhaps next week the house might be sold – but she knew that the longer she left it the harder it would become.

Returning to the present, Oriel sighed. Whilst her financial needs might be overridden by other problems the money would have to come from somewhere. 'Should we sit down with pen and paper and see how long our cash is going to last?'

Together they went over their expenditure, most of which went on the rent of fifteen shillings per week and the maintenance for Daniel's children, a similar sum. Taking the gloomiest prediction that they might have to remain here for three months until her house was sold, they agreed that if they were frugal their cash would just about hold out.

'But I think we have to face it, Kooka,' he told her. 'I might end up having to go and grovel for me job back at Powelltown – if it's still open to me. It'll mean living apart all week, but what else can I do?'

Oriel recognized the necessity, but held on to him tightly. 'Oh God, I don't know what I'll do without you!'

'Rather that than the susso. Anyhow,' Daniel returned the hug, 'I'll give it till after Christmas.'

Cards and gifts arrived from Queensland, plus a glorious ten-pound note that was meant to be shared with Clive.

'We know you like stylish things,' wrote Bright, 'and we can't buy anything like that up here so we thought you could get yourselves something nice with this money.'

A beaming Oriel used two shillings of the bonus

immediately by treating Daniel to a picture show. Yet, notwithstanding the delight over this, the clandestine visit from Dorothy and the support of Daniel's friend Norm, the festive season was not so festive for the errant lovers. After delivering their gifts to their respective children – and in doing so being forced to endure the company of estranged spouses – each tried to pretend that it was not Christmas at all, but despite the fact they had each other, the closedown of the city spelled a nightmare for them, the final straw coming when a group of destitute youngsters gathered outside their front door to sing carols. By the second line, both of them had tears streaming down their faces and, unable to confront the carollers, they turned off the gaslamp in the pretence of not being home. It was a poor ruse, for the light had been visible from the street. There came another fervent rattle of the letter box, then a voice shouted through it, 'Yer lousy bastards, we know yer in there!'

Oriel and Daniel fell into hysterics and were compelled to hand over precious coppers, if only in appreciation of this spark of light in an otherwise dark Christmas. But never had either of them been so glad when it was over.

Another decade was born. During that first month of 1930 Daniel was a regular participant in the ever-increasing queues for work. Though his efforts met with perpetual failure this did not deter him from repeating the exercise day after day. This morning was yet another such day. Before leaving Oriel he asked what she intended to do with her morning. She would not see so much of her children now that they had just gone back to school after the summer holiday.

'Well, I thought I'd do a spot of burglary.' Determined to start the year as she meant to go on, Oriel had decided to visit her old home and collect a few more belongings, her sewing machine amongst them, in an attempt to make this place more habitable. She had also entertained the idea of planting vegetables in the back yard.

'Clive be at work, will he?'

'Yes, there shouldn't be any trouble – though why I feel guilty at taking my own things I don't know!'

'D'yer reckon he'll have any old kero tins in his shed? I want to make a billy cart for Angus' birthday, might as well start collecting them now. Only if yer can carry them without busting a gut, mind. 'Sgonna be another hot one today.'

Oriel said she did not mind having a lot to carry. 'It'll give me an excuse to use public transport. I've got calluses on my bottom from cycling thirty miles every day.'

He frowned. 'Sounds serious – gimme a look.' Rebuked, he laughed and kissed her.

They left the house together, parting at the gate, for Daniel was going to visit a local timberyard as he did every morning before going elsewhere, just to make sure that no vacancy had occurred overnight. The woman who lived next door was about to come out at the same time, but saw them kissing and slammed the door with a disgusted comment. How the people around here had found out that she and Daniel were not married to each other Oriel could not guess, but did not care. Loath to tear her lips away, she dealt him a last kiss and went on to the city where she took a train to North Brighton.

All was quiet here – in fact the house seemed dead. Her eyes fell on a small pair of shoes under one of the chairs. Sadness welled up inside her. Fighting it, she rushed out to the shed and, dodging the huntsman spiders that lurked there, eventually found one kerosene tin, which she put outside the front door to collect on her way out. On her return she found a letter from her mother propped on the hall table. Clive had left it unopened though it was addressed to both of them – how considerate. She ripped it open. Her mother gave thanks for the gifts she had sent. The news from Queensland was bright and cheery, though it did little to encourage optimism, especially upon reading her mother's offer of a holiday.

How could she go? The children would give away her secret immediately – and even if she did not take them there would be interrogation. Interrogation that she did not have the strength to resist. She would have to lie – it was easier in a letter – tell her mother that she could not take the children from school – perhaps next year – and hang on to the hope that her parents would not decide to come down to Melbourne.

After taking half an hour to compose a reply, she put this in her pocket ready to post on the way home, then set to cleaning the kitchen and the bathroom, ran the vacuum cleaner over the carpets and polished the furniture to impress prospective buyers – though none had yet come forth. Puffing with fatigue and frustration she washed her hands then made a foray into the bedroom they had once shared and went to a cupboard to remove some of her own belongings. The smell of staleness pervaded everything and there were items of clothing lying on the carpet. Eager to escape, she did not touch these.

It was as she went towards the door that she saw the lone stocking lying amongst the soiled shirts and handkerchiefs. She bent to examine it, holding it distastefully between her fingertips. There was a hole in the toe, the reason it had been discarded. It was a colour she herself would not have worn, nor would it have fitted his mother. Oriel gasped in both amusement and outrage. 'The two-faced –' After he had accused her of bringing Daniel to live here, something she would not have done, he had not wasted any time in bringing his own floozie into her house.

With a dismissive snort she let it drop and went to collect what else she had come for. As she buzzed about gathering utensils, the odd ornament and book, she noticed a bare nail sticking out of the wall where once had hung a commemorative plate of Queen Victoria's Coronation given to them by Grandmother Widdowes. She frowned, but not for long. He had taken it down and hidden it in fear that on her expeditions his estranged wife might spirit it away. Oriel could have laughed. As if she wanted his family heirloom! She had left behind far more precious things than this – the ruby glass centrepiece for one. Never had it entered her head that he would claim it as his own, but he had thought it of her. There would be no crass retaliation. Oriel could not have supported the ornamental glass along with all the other things, even had she wanted to. Having collected everything she had come for, she departed, looking like a pack horse beneath the weight of the sewing machine and the shopping bag of knick-knacks and the kerosene tin.

Oriel had been tempted to call on Dorothy, but had been dissuaded by the notion that Cuthbert could be there. Now it was out of the question, for she had barely walked ten yards and her arms felt as if they were being dragged from their sockets. Instead, she managed to hobble to the nearest bus stop and waited under the boiling sun.

A stray brown and white cow trotted down the road, weaving on and off the pavement, in and out of the trees, trying to avoid capture by the local ranger. Oriel watched its wild-eyed passage, smelled its dung-streaked flanks as it thudded past her, and felt sorry for the animal, inwardly cheering it on. It was still managing to evade its captor when the bus came. Perspiration soaking her dress, she struggled on board and capsized gratefully into her seat, wondering how she was going to cope at the other end.

During the journey she half listened to the two women behind her gossiping, whilst still trying to decide what to do about her parents.

'That's a nice hat she's wearing, isn't it?'

'Yes, it isn't very often you see young people in hats these days, is it?'

'No, they hardly wear any clothes, never mind hats!' The women shared laughter. Oriel gave a faint smile too but was soon once again concerned with her problem.

'Did you hear about that woman from – I can't remember what street she lives in but it's near Mrs McKenzie – anyhow, she's run off and left her children. I know! Isn't it dreadful? Never seem to stick with things these days, do they? What sort of a mother deserts her kids? There was no warning. One minute she's there and the next she's run away with some chap. Can't understand anyone like that, can you? Why do they go and have kids if they fancy the fellas so much?'

It gives us something to do while we're waiting for the next bloke to come along, thought Oriel satirically, gazing out of the window as the bus sailed by a public house where stood a man with a placard condemning those who entered to eternal damnation.

'Oh, I can't understand any mother who could do that. Apparently, she's gone orf with somebody else's husband too – and he's got four little children.'

Oriel suddenly realized they were talking about her. Ears pricked and lips compressed, she was to hear all manner of inaccurate details before the bus reached the city, some of which made her gasp out loud and at one point she turned around to glare. Unaware that she was the subject of their gossip the women merely stared back at her until she looked away, then lowered their voices so she could no longer hear. But her imagination provided the content, and when she finally alighted from the bus she was absolutely furious and glared once again at the women before lumbering off towards home, the sewing machine banging against her legs and her heart thudding with indignation.

With no one in whom to confide – for Daniel was still out searching for work – she spent a couple of hours fuming before it was time again to go and collect the children. Her anger had in no way abated.

Dragging her bicycle to the gate, she launched herself upon the congested city, stopping only to despatch the letter to her mother that she had been unable to post earlier. Then, dodging cars and trams, she cycled on to Princes Bridge and towards Brighton.

It was probably the rage that caused her to wobble, to veer out into the road and in front of a truck. Alarmed to receive the severe rebuke of its horn, she wobbled even more, panicked and all of a sudden found her front tyre had dropped into a tram line. The harsh jolt catapulted her over the handlebars – displaying peach silk camiknickers as she thudded on to the road, at the mercy of the traffic that came from behind. Robbed of all sense, it was miraculous that the impetus caused her to roll towards the gutter and the truck missed her head by inches – though it crushed her bicycle to a useless mangled heap.

Stunned, Oriel lifted her face from the hard road, saw the threatening wheels, heard the honking of horns, and with great effort tottered to the safety of the pavement, her half-conscious brain filled with brilliant swirling lights. The truck driver jumped down from his cab to descend upon her, cursing, but when he saw her bleeding forehead his attitude changed somewhat and he took a step back as passers-by crowded round, one of them offering Oriel a handkerchief to apply to the graze.

Eyes dazed, she held out her hand to receive it and noticed that her white gloves were filthy. Pressing the handkerchief to her brow, she surveyed the wreck of her bicycle, her whole body throbbing. 'I've got to go and pick up my children from school,' she murmured. 'How will I get there?'

'You can't go yet, the police and ambulance've been called,' a voice explained.

'I don't need an ambulance.' Oriel tried to dissociate herself from the scene but was gently detained. 'I must go!'

Despite all complaints, she was forced to wait in the heat, half choked by exhaust fumes, until the ambulance arrived. This took an age, for by now the bridge was thoroughly congested, the traffic backed up right past the railway station and along Swanston Street. All she could think of was that she would be late to pick up her children. A look at her wristwatch served to reassure her, there was plenty of time yet. Nevertheless, she swayed impatiently from foot to foot, trying to avoid the curious stares of the onlookers. Impervious to the chaos overhead, the brown Yarra continued its gentle meandering flow.

When the ambulance finally got through and two men jumped out to tend her, Oriel insisted that she was perfectly all right and, after an examination of her superficial wounds they got back into their vehicle and drove away. But there was still the police to contend with. Whilst one officer in a white pith helmet attempted to get the traffic moving again, the other grilled her, those unaware of the reason for the hold-up honking their horns. Oriel was made aware by the glower of hot impatient faces that all of this was her fault but all she could think about was the seconds that were ticking away. Between questions, she stole another look at her watch – and her heart stopped upon seeing that it showed exactly the same time as it had ages ago. The jolt must have broken it. Panicking, she told the police officer that she really must go or her children would think they had been abandoned – if they did not already think it.

Finally, with a warning that she had only just escaped prosecution for her reckless driving, she was allowed to go. With her bicycle unridable, she was forced to hurry back over the bridge to the station. A look at the clock caused more panic – she had been delayed almost an hour!

Luck appeared to have changed sides, for she was to catch a train within three minutes, but there were still another thirty to endure before she arrived at North Brighton. By the time she reached the school, having run all the way from the station, she was sweating profusely and in danger of passing out.

The schoolyard was deserted. Not one child was in sight. Frantic, Oriel raced through the doors and along the corridor, peering into each classroom on the way, but the only person she encountered was a cleaner. Almost delirious now with worry, she asked the puzzled woman if she had seen two children, a boy and a girl, but received only a smiling negative.

They must have grown tired of waiting and gone home alone – that was the only answer. What if they had been knocked down on the busy main road?

Head throbbing, Oriel made her way there, sick with exhaustion and fear, to be met by a furious Clive in the hall.

'Mummy, you're naughty!' Jennifer ran to scold her, her little face distorted by a sulk.

'I'm sorry!' Overwhelmed by relief Oriel gathered the child into her arms, extending her apology to the little boy who hovered nearby. 'I got delayed.'

'You've bumped your head,' observed Dorrie.

Oriel did not want to tell them of her near fatal experience, they had enough to worry about. 'Yes, well, I –'

She did not have time to voice her invented excuse, for Clive stepped in. 'Go and get into the car,' he told the children sharply.

When he used this tone there was no arguing. Jennifer and her brother went outside to where the car was parked. The instant they had gone their father turned on Oriel.

'Their headmistress telephoned me at work to say no one had come to collect them! I've had to drive all this way –'

'I'm sorry!' Oriel tried to explain. 'I had an –'

'I don't want to know! Look, this has got to stop. You're messing everyone around. You either want them or you don't!'

'Of course I want them! If you'd let me ex–'

'Well, you have a funny way of showing it! They were in tears when I arrived. I can't keep doing this or I'll get the sack and there are plenty of others who'd jump into my shoes. Now, we're off round to my mother's for tea.' He began to move to the door, Oriel having to move after him. 'If you can't manage to pick them up on time you needn't bother at all.'

'Are you saying you won't allow me to see them?' Her words tasted like vomit.

'I'm saying that as it's so hard for you to keep your promise to them my mother will be picking them up from school in future. I'm sure she won't mind. When you've made up your mind what you want perhaps you'll let me know. Until then you can come when it's convenient to me – Saturday would be best.'

He was at the door and waiting to lock it.

She took a hurried couple of steps on to the porch. 'I'm still taking them to live with me as soon as I get somewhere!'

'We'll see.' Clive locked the door and, with Oriel after him, strode down the path, wrenched the engine to life and got into the car. The children scrambled to kneel up on the back seat as it moved away.

'I couldn't help it, I had an accident!' she managed to blurt at last, but her words were lost as the car drove away, two little faces staring at her over the turned down hood.

Unprepared to receive her devastating news and appearance when he returned from his futile search for work, Daniel felt as if all the world were conspiring to rob them of happiness as he held the sobbing Oriel to his breast and tried to comfort her. His feet, his entire body ached, his mind too. Faced with constant rejection he had looked forward all day to coming home, sitting down to a quiet supper and his lover's sweet embrace, but here he was again faced with more troubles. He felt he would go mad, but could not afford to do so, for Oriel was close to collapse herself.

After calming her, brushing aside her apologies that there was no supper ready for him, he made her have something to eat, then afterwards said they would go out tomorrow and look for a house in Brighton whether they could afford it or not and before she knew it, it would be Saturday and she would see her children again.

Their concerted efforts to find somewhere met with good results, in part. They managed to find a house in North Brighton that would be vacant in three months, by which time they should be in a better position to afford the rent. In this hope they put down a holding deposit of five pounds.

Her confidence only half boosted, Oriel awaited her Saturday visit to the children with trepidation, but it eventuated that Clive was in better mood that morning and she was permitted to take Jennifer and Dorrie out without any hitches. Still, it was a dreadful wrench to hand them back, knowing it would be another week before she would see them again, and that feeling was reciprocated in their eyes.

Deprived of her children, except for that one precious day of the week, Oriel began to wilt. It was February now and still Daniel was no closer to finding employment. Hating the thought of being parted from her, but hating even more to see what the loss of her children was doing to her – for he knew all too well how that felt – he told her of his decision: he would go and ask for his old job back at the mill.

Tearfully, she watched him count out the coppers and silver in his pocket, too bereft to accompany him to the station, feeling only half awake. The temperature had been in the nineties for three days and nights, preventing adequate sleep. Her dress had been on a mere fifteen minutes and already it was drenched. 'When will I see you?'

He took her in his arms and sighed, nuzzling her face with his. 'Not till Saturday, I'm afraid. I know, it's gonna be murder, I'll be thinking about you all the time. I'll beg a lift home off somebody rather than waste money on the rattler.' It was far too hot to retain this embrace for long. Dealing her a passionate kiss, he donned his hat, shuffled it into position and took a long hard look at her before saying, 'Ooroo.'

Oriel could hardly bear to wave him off and after closing the door she broke down in tears. What on earth was she going to find to take her mind off things? Why, you idiot, she accused herself, instead of sitting here moping, why don't you show some gumption and find a job yourself?

Having dispensed with newspapers in order to save money, she was forced to visit the city library to peruse the situations vacant columns. This entailed a wait, for others were of like mind. But her impatient foot-tapping was worthwhile and after scribbling down three or four suitable positions, she marched out of the library, purpose and determination in her step.

When she reached the first address on her list there was a lengthy queue that stretched right out of the building. Declining to stand in the boiling sun, Oriel decided to return later and went on to the next office building. Here she found another queue. This one being slightly shorter, she joined it and waited, and waited, and waited, her mind filled with thoughts of her children and Daniel.

An hour later she was sitting at a desk being interviewed by an impatient-looking man. In this heat, everyone wore a similar expression. Without even taking down her name, he asked if she had any experience in the secretarial field.

'Oh yes,' came the confident reply.

'And am I to be allowed to see your references?' The man sounded as hotly impatient as he looked. Oriel replied that she had not known she would need references, but she could get them for him in a matter of weeks.

'That's no good to me! Have you seen the queue out there?'

She was offended. 'But I've always held a very responsible position.'

'Who were you with last?'

The look on his face sapped her confidence, transporting her back to the time she had made her application to be a nurse, the awful rejection she had felt at being turned down. 'I worked for my father – he had his own business.'

'Sorry, you're wasting my time.' With a flick of his hand, the man dismissed her.

Face burning, Oriel rushed past the waiting applicants and out into the sunshine, feeling stupid and helpless and angry. After buying a cup of tea and a muffin and using that twenty minutes to compose herself, she found enough courage to visit the third address on her list.

But it was the same answer here. Consigning her list to a rubbish bin she went home, thoroughly disillusioned.

When she entered the house, however, she was hit by a rush of joy and flung herself into Daniel's arms. 'Oh, you're home!'

He laughed, swept her off her feet and pressed the length of his hot body against hers as they enjoyed a fervid kiss, but then held her from him, his face becoming weary and despondent as her own had been a moment ago.

She guessed. 'The rats, they wouldn't give you your job back!'

'There was no job – no mill. It closed down at the end of the last shift. Wouldn't it rot yer socks? I tried all the others up there, but with two hundred blokes in competition . . .' He shrugged, enfolded her in his arms and rocked her. 'Looks like the old susso for me, china.'

She moaned and planted lots of kisses all over his face. 'I've been out trying to find work myself but there were hundreds for the same job and I didn't have any references, but I'll go out tomorrow and try again.'

He gave a subdued nod, then remembered. 'Here, brought you a pressie. Been carrying it in a bag of ice.'

'Ooh, Violet Crumble!' She beamed at this small luxury before taking a bite then holding it out to Daniel.

He shook his head. 'Know it's a bit extravagant but what the hell? You don't get much enjoyment.' He fell upon the sofa. 'I called in to see the kids on me way back.' Lowering his head to his hands, he rubbed his face in an attitude of despair. Knowing how he must be feeling, that he had a big suppurating hole where his gut used to be, Oriel put the chocolate aside and came to him. They sat there for a long time, trying to knead the pain from each other.

Daniel recovered, a spark of life in his eye. ''Sfunny yer know, I don't feel quite so bad over chucking the job up last year, knowing I'd have lost it anyway.'

'Why has it closed down?'

'Same as everywhere else. No demand for the goods. If you can do the same job with cheap foreign pine yer not gonna pay through the nose for good hardwood.'

'So all the men from there will be coming to the city.'

'No point is there? Aren't you gonna eat yer chocolate before it melts?'

'It's given me toothache. I'd better not eat it all at once or I'll end up with a mouthful of black pegs, then you won't want me any more.'

'Course I would!' He cocked his head and looked thoughtful. 'On second thoughts, no I wouldn't.' He laughed, Oriel laughed too, both marvelling at how they could do so. How could one be so desperately sad and yet so blissfully happy at the same time?

Daniel returned to his former topic. 'I spoke to some o' the blokes – the ones that'd speak to me, anyhow.' He had faced a lot of ostracism for leaving his wife and children. 'A couple of 'em are talking about going prospecting. Whad'yer think about me havin' a go at that before I resort to the susso?'

Oriel looked dubious. 'I hope you have better luck than Father did.' Her mother had told her about his adventures in the Yukon. 'He never found a speck, and that was when there was a gold rush on.'

Daniel nodded. 'That's what I thought, but I'd have given it a go if you'd wanted. Righto,' he rubbed sweaty palms over his moleskinned knees. 'I'll do what I have to do.'

Knowing how she herself would feel at having to accept charity, Oriel was desperate to take that woebegone expression off his face, and blurted, 'Let's just give it a few more days! I'll get up at the crack of dawn tomorrow and be first in the queue – no, there's no need for you to go trailing out again. Have a rest. I insist.'

'You can insist all yer like, I can't have you going out looking for work while I lie in bed.'

'But you said yourself there are no jobs for men.'

'Then I'll go apply to the susso. I'm not loafing around while –'

'Well, all right, go look for a job if you must but not the sustenance. Please,' she begged him. 'I might have some good news when I come back.'

Coming to an agreement, they both set about making dinner. Thankfully, around that time there was a drastic drop in temperature of twenty degrees and they were able to open the windows again to admit the southerly breeze. It was wonderful to be able to cuddle up in bed without their bodies sticking together.

In the afterglow of love, Oriel snuggled lazily into her beloved's arms. 'Don't suppose there's any need to set the alarm.' They were always both awake by the crack of dawn, their turmoiled minds preventing further rest. She peered through slitted eyes at the shelf on the far wall. 'You've moved that clock, I can only see the top half of it without lifting my head up.'

His voice was drowsy. 'Would it be more convenient if I insert it under your eyelids?'

She giggled and nudged him, then nestled into his arms and both fell asleep.

When morning came, Oriel performed her usual toilet as best she could without a bathroom, dressed in a two-piece suit and, adding a dash of powder and lipstick to her face, she prepared to leave. Daniel said he would wash the breakfast dishes before going out to look for work. He followed her to the door, kissed her and was about to close it when at the last minute she turned back.

'Oh, I'm forgetting my bag!'

He went to get it for her and after kissing her once again, closed the door.

The door opened again. 'I thought I had a pen!' Oriel re-entered looking harassed.

'Here!' Laughing, he found the item on the mantelpiece. 'Crikey, you're making more farewell appearances than Nellie Melba – will yer just go!'

Snatching the pen off him she left the house, intending to join the first queue she came across, and when this turned out to be for vacancies at a clothing factory she did not balk but tagged on at the end. Even as she joined it there were others behind her.

'Gawd, look at her,' muttered a voice to her rear. 'Clothes like that and she's pinching our jobs.'

Flushing with anger and embarrassment, Oriel was about to sidle away, when an inner voice told her to stay put. She was as much in need of the work as they were.

For half an hour she shifted her weight from hip to hip, squinting at the glare of sunlight on glass and metal, shuffling inch by inch, closer to salvation, forced to listen to derogatory comments from the girls behind her. Finally, when she felt that her aching calves were about to snap, she found herself third in line and tensed in readiness for her interview.

The female interviewer took one look at her. 'I don't think you're exactly what we're after, dear.'

Oriel could have screamed. 'I'll do anything!'

The interviewer allowed her a few more seconds and tried to see her left hand but it was below the level of the desk. 'Are you married?'

Oriel thought of Daniel. 'Yes.'

There was a tut. 'I'd have thought one of the others could have told you and saved you queuing – we're not hiring married women.' The woman looked at Oriel's smart outfit. 'We can't give jobs to housewives wanting pin money when there are single girls needing to make a living.'

'But my husband's out of work!'

The woman showed hesitation at casting her out without a chance. 'I suppose it's silly to ask if you've done this kind of work before?'

'I can learn.'

'Sorry, dear, there're plenty of experienced girls waiting out there.' And that was that.

No matter how many queues she joined that morning, Oriel was to be constantly rejected. Feet throbbing, worn-out and close to tears, she made for home, wondering if Daniel had had any more luck. Along the way, placards told how unemployment had risen to twenty per cent – as if she needed telling. There was slight hesitation by a newspaper stand. Her beloved would probably not be there when she got home, a newspaper would take her mind off the emptiness. Delving into her purse, she was about to part with precious pence – then was stopped by a flash of inspiration. What an idiot! Instead of wasting time in queues she could have been earning a living from home, writing for the newspaper.

Rushing there, she found the house empty, but her longing for Daniel was soon put aside whilst she decided what form her composition should take. Nibbling the end of her pen, she decided to put her own experiences to good use and began to scribble an opinion of how married women were treated in the workplace. In the hour that followed she had produced an article and had time to go back into the city and deliver it to the newspaper office before Daniel got home.

As both had feared, he had had no luck, but Oriel's enthusiasm over her venture persuaded him not to resort to charity just yet. All that they could do now was to sit back and wait.

During the week that followed she ran to meet the postman every day, and every day was to be disappointed. However, on Friday, when Daniel had gone out hunting for work and she herself had been about to go to the market, she was finally rewarded by a whole bundle of letters. Excitedly she sifted through them, discarding those that were bills. Finding an envelope that looked promising, she tore it open there and then. It was from the newspaper! Her mouth turned up in apprehension as her eyes read:

> Dear Mrs Widdowes,
> Thank you for your most interesting submission
> . . . it is with regret that we cannot accept it for publication due to a marked similarity to the recently published article submitted by a regular correspondent. We will however be happy to hear from you in the future if you have an original idea to air.
> Yours . . .

Oriel was devastated, felt utterly useless and near to breaking point. Crumpling the letter and trying not to cry, she stared for a while into thin air, picturing Daniel's face when she told him. He had been so confident of her success, had been duped by her stupid enthusiasm. Now she had failed him, failed everyone.

Her intestines made a sound like a bottle rolling down a concrete path, nudging her mind from its crippling despondence. Dragging herself from the chair, she went to collect some coins from the ever-dwindling cache in the dressing table drawer, donned hat and gloves and plodded off to the market.

Her journey took her past yet another queue. The people in this line were from all walks of life, some trying to avert their faces from the street in case a passerby should see how low they had fallen, others wearing the tattered clothing and the doleful air of the habitual charity seeker. How soon would it be before she or Daniel was standing here? Their calculated budget had been thrown out of gear by the five-pound deposit on the house, funds were perilously low. Oriel faltered in her tracks, agonizing over her next move. The thought that came to her was appalling, but if it meant sparing Daniel this gross indignity then she would do it. So deciding, she diverted her path and headed for Myers.

Clive was most put out by the appearance of his estranged wife at his workplace. Mouth pursed, he escorted her to a private corner to hear what she had to say.

Oriel detested having to perform what she saw as grovelling but with as much dignity as she could muster said, 'I need your signature so I can get some money out of the account.'

'Couldn't it have waited till you came to pick up the children?'

She was insistent. 'No, I need the money to live on and I've bills to pay.'

'How much?'

Oriel pondered. Better to withdraw enough to save her having to ask again. 'Twenty pounds.'

'Twen–! Some bill!'

She tried not to display anger, though inside she boiled at having to explain why she needed her own money, especially in the knowledge that he had had a woman in her house. But any truculence might deprive her of her access to the children. She could not risk that. 'It's simply to save me having to ask again.' You think I really want to be seen in the street with you? she silently demanded.

'Well, I can't come now, you'll have to meet me on my lunchbreak.' Clive was already going back to his work. 'I'll see you outside in half an hour.'

Oriel emerged from the department store, wrung her gloved hands and wondered what to do. A fully loaded tram sailed by, its flanks laden with parasites. She turned and followed its path, and for thirty minutes paced the streets, noting how Melbourne had evolved over the last ten years, lovely old buildings being pulled down to make way for more skyscrapers, traffic lights, ugly modern wall lamps alongside the elegant drooping standards of old, her eyes latching on to anything that might take her mind off the test of endurance that lay ahead.

Eventually Clive came out and walked briskly alongside her to the bank. Head lowered, Oriel tried to inject a gap between them so that people would not know they were together. Once in the bank, both scribbled their signatures, Clive acting as if this were his death warrant, and saying that he himself did not need any cash, he could make do on his wages. 'There you are, I don't suppose you'll have any more need of me so I'll go and get my lunch.'

Oriel folded the money into her bag and walked home, trying to think how to confess to Daniel what she had just done.

Her worries were for nothing. 'She'll be right, Kooka. You don't have to explain to me, I understand.' In manner most kind, he took her face in his hands.

Blue eyes swam with anxiety. 'I just felt so wretched after getting your hopes up about the newspaper article.'

'Aw! Yer poor little thing, and it was such a good piece – didn't they say so? Maybe –' Her expression forestalled his question. She would not risk submitting another article just to have it rejected. 'Aw well, never mind. Come 'n' sit down and let me take your shoes off. I shouldn't be wearing them anyway.' He grinned and squeezed her. 'Look what a nice dinner I've made yer.'

Oriel looked at the table set with two plates of bread, ham, tomato and cheese, and wanted to cry. 'Oh, you shouldn't've waited for me, you must be starving.'

'Nah! Come on, sit down and tell me all about it.'

After the meal and a cup of tea Daniel heaved a sigh. 'Well, it's no use me sitting here, I'll have to go and throw meself on the Government's mercy.'

Oriel gasped. 'But that's the reason I went grovelling to him, so you wouldn't have to do that!'

'I can't keep on asking you to pay for my kids, darl.'

'And I can't have my husband standing in line for charity when I've plenty of money here – look!' She leaned over and grabbed her bag, took out the notes and flourished them at him.

'Then I'd be accepting your charity.'

'Maguire! Don't be so bloody proud.' She pushed herself from the table and came around to cradle his head in her arms. 'I love you, what's mine is yours, it's not charity. Please, please, just take it.'

Daniel stared at the money for long moments, wrestling with his pride. 'Folk'll say I'm living off a woman.'

'I don't care!'

'I do.' Faced with two choices – to live off the Government or live off Oriel – he did not know which was the most shameful. But in the end he gave a silent nod, and Oriel uttered a sigh of relief.

When he rose shortly afterwards and said he had better be off, she showed confusion. 'I still have to go out,' he told her. 'If there's a job to be found out there, I'll find it. I won't let yer down.'

Weary of foot, she sighed but nevertheless said she would accompany him, shoving the money into her bag. 'And here's me thinking we could spend the afternoon in romantic interlude.'

He looked disapproving. 'I couldn't waste me time like

that! Well, not the entire afternoon, anyhow.' Grinning, he escorted her into the city.

Whilst Daniel investigated every factory, every yard, read every postcard in every window, Oriel waited in the shade of a verandah. At the end of the afternoon he had found nothing – as both had privately guessed. Hooking one of her arms through his, the other through the handle of her bag, a hot and weary Oriel plodded beside him towards home, whispering that she would make him feel better when they arrived.

He turned to embrace her in his grin as they stepped to the edge of the kerb and made to cross the road. Eyes diverted, he did not see the young cyclist who, in one fluid and much-practised movement came sweeping past them, hooked his arm through the handle of this well-dressed woman's bag and before Oriel could even open her mouth had ripped it from her possession, swerved away and was pedalling furiously off down the road.

Oriel came to life, screamed and pointed. 'He's got our cash!' Heads turned at her frantic cry but no one gave chase except Daniel who pelted off down the road after the cyclist, arms and legs moving like pistons, heart pumping and face straining with determination.

Oriel ran after him for a time, but with her high-heeled shoes an obstacle to speed she got nowhere, was forced to stop and stand there watching as Daniel, his legs no match for wheels, fell further and further behind his quarry. Losing his initial burst of steam, he petered first to a trot then to a halt, whence he threw down his hat in a last burst of frustration as the cyclist swerved into an alley and out of sight with a triumphant flick of his head, taking their money with him.

21

Beware of Bootleg Criminals, Keep Victoria Free From Crime and Corruption. Vote No to Prohibition. Daniel gave an ironic laugh as similar posters entreated him and Oriel wherever their futile search for work took them.

'I can't afford the grog anyway! Don't know why I even bothered to vote.' The fact that he and the majority of the Victorian electorate had recently voted against prohibition did not make beer any easier to come by for those with no funds to spare. He had barely been able to afford a gift for his daughter's birthday. 'Shouldn't grumble. At least we're not starving.'

The robbery had been a crushing experience, yet the lovers refused to be cowed, bolstering each other with the opinion that they were still better off than most in their position.

Oriel sympathized for the loss of his pleasure. 'Yes, it's rather fortunate that I've never been one to find gratification in food or drink. All my pleasures come from up here,' she tapped her head, 'or down there. There's nowhere in between.'

'Yeah, I had noticed.' Daniel grinned at her through the sunshine.

'Do you think I'm awful?' Her eyes sought reassurance. 'I've never known any other woman say they like it. I often wonder if it's something to do with my grandmother being – well, you know, in the blood so to speak.'

Daniel smiled at her innocence. 'I reckon girls like your granny don't do it for pleasure but out o' necessity.'

She gave a thoughtful nod. 'Yes, I understand her a bit

better now. It must have been dreadful for a fourteen-year-old to bring up a baby. I certainly don't despise her now – not that I'd do it myself.' She smiled. 'Even if we were starving. I'd rather steal, I think.'

Daniel said she might have to. Whilst it was true that they had not yet reached crisis point, for they still had some money in the dressing table drawer, this would not last for ever.

The three months they had predicted it would take to see an end to their troubles became four, then five. Though Oriel sneaked through her old home collecting things to sell, the proceeds did little more than help to keep their heads above water. It was useless now to think they could afford to rent the house in North Brighton and the deposit they had left on it was forfeit.

Whilst Oriel waited in vain for her divorce to come to court the For Sale sign outside her house began to lean to one side, being joined by the forest that had sprung up all over the city. There had been one offer but that had been so derogatory that Clive had refused it. With winter approaching it was unlikely that there would be any more until the warmer weather arrived. Oriel detested the thought of having to ask him for more money. When she had told him of the robbery he had shown no sympathy, only disgust. She had always found difficulty in asking anyone for help and when that person was someone she detested the task became anathema.

Less extravagant these days – her one luxury a weekly soak at the public slipper baths – Oriel learned to make do and mend, played barber, reduced her food bill to shillings instead of pounds and patched clothing. With his army experience behind him, Daniel could sew and darn and knit too. With such joint talents they would make ends meet. If there were the occasional bout of melancholy, it was not the dispossession that induced it, but the self-imposed exile from their children, which was as raw as ever it had been. Despite the fulfilment they had found in each other there was terrible guilt to be endured.

The meetings with Jennifer and Dorrie were becoming increasingly strained. At first there had been the zoo and the Glaciarium and Luna Park, but now with no money to spare she resorted to taking them for walks on the racecourse or the beach, which cost nothing, the only remaining extravagance being a chocolate nut sundae and a look round the toyshops before bringing them here to a place she knew they detested.

Daniel was wonderful, playing games with them when she herself was at a loss. But Oriel knew this was not fair to them, nor to him – there were days when he could not even bear to visit his own children it was so painful, this in itself incurring yet another slice of Melinda's wrath.

There might be no work, but Oriel never seemed to be idle. Every odd ball of wool she had pillaged from her old home was utilized to make Dorrie a Fair Isle jumper. Using her sewing machine, she made Jennifer a winter outfit from one of her own dresses, and a hat to match. Proud of her industry, she handed all of these over at their next meeting.

The little girl accepted her outfit, but was not overly enthusiastic.

'She's not too keen on the idea of going out today,' explained her father, getting ready for work.

Oriel bristled, feeling it was just Clive's way at getting back at her, but managed to sound cheerful in her response. 'Oh, we'll have a lovely time! I thought you loved our chocolate nut sundaes? Of course you do! Run along and get your coats.' She waited for her children to leave the room then turned to Clive, her face annoyed.

He forestalled her with a curt flick of his hand. 'It's nothing to do with me. Neither of them was very happy when they got home from seeing you last week. Jenny says she doesn't want to go out with you because she knows you're only going to leave her again. Dorrie's started wetting the bed.'

Oriel sighed in dismay. 'Are there sheets to be washed now? I'll do them before I go out, then.'

'I suppose it'll save my mother from having to do them,' he made cool observation, before leaving for work.

Throughout the meeting with her mother, even when they were enjoying their usual jaunt around town, Jennifer remained anxious, her mood infecting Dorrie too. Though broken-hearted herself, Oriel tried to jolly them with extra treats that she could little afford.

'Tell me what you're reading at school!' she asked as they were on their way to meet Daniel in the park. Her daughter shrugged and said she didn't know. Oriel laughed. 'You must know.' Jennifer had been reading well until now.

This having no success, Oriel changed tack. 'It'll be your birthday in a month or so. Would you like a party and invite your school friends?' The little girl shook her head, drawing a sound of astonishment. 'Why ever not?'

'I don't want them to know I haven't got a mummy.'

Oriel sagged, her heart shrivelling. 'You have got a mummy!' Leading them to a less busy section of town, she lowered herself to their level, wrapped her arms around both children, hugging them together, trying her best not to cry. People were looking. 'Just because I don't live with you doesn't mean I'm not your mummy. But we can't live together until we've sold the house and bought a new one.'

Dorrie pushed his mother away. 'We have to go home now.'

Oriel did not force her attention on him. 'Don't you want to come back with me and see Uncle Daniel?'

He was adamant, mouth sulky. 'No, I want to go home and see my daddy.'

'Daddy won't be there,' Oriel told him, then saw the panic in his eyes – he feared that his father was going to leave him just as his mother had! She was quick to reassure. 'He's gone to work, he'll be back later. But I can take you home if you really want to go.' Both children said they did.

At her mother's tearful reaction, Jennifer thought she should put forth her reason. 'I have to help Daddy with the housework, you see, because he hasn't got a mummy now.'

Recognizing that explanation was urgently required, Oriel struggled for words that such young children could understand. Hitherto, she had always left them with the parting words that she would see them next week, but realized now that they must have no inkling of how long this time span was. Faced with her hesitancy, Dorrie jumped in first.

'Are we really coming to live with you?'

'Yes, of course!' Oriel stroked his hair as they walked to the station. 'I'm sorry it's taking so long, but I've told you we have to wait until we get some money. Don't you think I want you to come and live with me?'

Dorrie was unable to voice his fear – if his mother didn't want Daddy maybe she didn't want him either. 'Doesn't Daddy want us to live with him?'

'Yes!' Oriel wondered if her children could have chosen a more public spot in which to air their grievances. 'That's the trouble, each of us wants you to live with us, but that's not possible. Even though Daddy wants you he's agreed that you'll live with me when I can find somewhere nice for us. But things are difficult at the moment. Wait until we get home and I'll try and explain it all to you.'

Having to field many more questions throughout the thirty-minute journey, she was relieved finally to arrive at the house in North Brighton. Here, she made them comfortable with drinks and biscuits then, after taking a few sips of her own tea, kneeled on the carpet nearby in order to be level with their faces.

'Would you –' She broke off and cleared her throat, then steeled herself to begin again. 'Would you rather live with Daddy all the time?'

Both children thought about this, then shook their heads. Somewhat relieved, Oriel nodded.

'But I don't like it when you only come to see us once in a while,' announced her daughter. 'It makes me sad.'

Oriel turned to Dorrie and asked if he felt that way too. He gave a solemn nod.

'It makes me sad too,' admitted their mother, and allowed herself to cry as endorsement of this. The children wept also and did not push her away when she hugged them. She wiped their eyes and her own, then continued as the two grave little faces looked on. 'I'm sorry you're hurt. But sometimes grown-ups can't help hurting children. They don't mean to, it just happens.'

'Why did Daddy say nasty things about you to Nanna Widdowes?' Her son pulled at the fringing on a cushion.

Oriel tried not to blacken Clive in their eyes though she herself detested him. 'Sometimes when people are hurt they say things they don't mean.'

'Don't you love Daddy?' asked a teary-eyed Jennifer.

Oriel did not know what to say. 'The important thing is that I love you, both of you – and Daddy does too. We want you to be happy . . . and you're not happy at the moment, are you?' Both shook their heads. She kissed and stroked them. 'You said it made you sad when I only come once a week . . . would it be better if we didn't see each other at all until I've found a new house for us to live in?' It would be such a sacrifice – carried the risk that they would forget her – but it couldn't continue like this. The visits had become as challenging for her as they were to the children. Putting an end to these disruptions might be the kindest thing to do.

'How long will that be?' asked Jennifer.

Oriel was honest. 'I really don't know. Nobody wants to buy this house and until I sell it I won't have the money to buy another one. But if you change your mind and want to come and visit me then all you have to do is to tell Daddy.'

The children agreed that they were willing to wait and Oriel delivered loving kisses, emphasizing that she would come back the moment she had more to offer them – and of course she would be present on Jennifer's birthday. When Clive came home he was informed of their decision and was quick to give agreement.

But as he went with her to the door, the tots out of earshot, he made additional comment on the plan: 'I'm glad you've decided to stop messing them around.'

'You make it sound as if I've been doing it deliberately! I would've had somewhere else to live by now if the money hadn't been stolen.' Why did he persist in holding her to blame for that?

His reply was derogatory. 'Yes well, if you looked after that as well as you looked after the children I'm not surprised it got stolen – and I'm telling you this!' He precluded any objection. 'If you walk out on them now, you don't come back.'

Her flesh crawled. 'But I've told them –'

'I mean it. You can't keep playing with people's lives like this and expect them just to take it.'

Oriel was angry but did not raise her voice in case the children overheard. 'I've told them I'll come back for them and I will! Don't you dare tell them otherwise.'

'I wouldn't dream of it, they've been hurt enough. No, I think they'll just get over you on their own, grow sick of the way you've messed them about and come to recognize that they're better off with somebody who has regard for their feelings. Anyway, I've said my piece. Goodbye!'

On this empty note the afternoon ended. Short of barging in and abducting them there was nothing much Oriel could do except to wait and come to get them when she was better armed – and she was determined to do so. Lacking any other option, she went home to weep upon Daniel's loving breast.

Whilst Oriel and her lover continued to exist like automatons, the Depression worsened. The year saw a mass exodus from Melbourne, hundreds of thousands of men and whole families took to the road in old cars and trucks, wagons, bicycles and on foot looking for work in other areas. But there were still queues everywhere: queues for job vacancies, queues for the dole, queues for the soup kitchens – even outside the pubs that had started to give free meals, much to the disgust of the temperance movement. There were barefoot kids with billy carts collecting bottles on the beach, infants crying with hunger, young factory workers congregating on street corners. Yet still in the back streets there were those who would risk their last coppers on a game of two-up.

With winter upon them the Defence Department opened its warehouses. Khaki greatcoats and tunics were dyed black and given to the poor who wore them as a badge of adversity. The Prime Minister, James Scullin, turned to British experts for help in guiding Australia out of depression, thereby incurring the scorn of others in his party who accused him of deserting Labor's creed by inviting British lords to run the country.

Acting out of charity and also in need of something to restore his manhood, Daniel travelled up to Powelltown and helped to cut firewood for the destitute of the city – but some had no hearth in which to burn it. Around Melbourne's inner suburbs houses fell vacant and into disrepair when the tenants could not pay their rent, and were eventually demolished to make way for factories. With each bulldozing the shanty town that had sprung up on Dudley Flats took in new inhabitants who erected yet more makeshift shacks of corrugated iron, kerosene tins, cardboard and anything else they could get their hands on, whilst the rest of the world went on as normal, with tales of rape and murder sandwiched between the more important sport results and the society pages.

From Bright's recent letter, the Depression seemed not to be affecting her and Nat at all. The only mention of it was in a comment about the queues of unemployed men that Bright had seen during a shopping trip to Bundaberg. 'But I suppose you'll see more of it down there,' she opined to her daughter, the irony of which was not lost on Oriel. If only Mother could see her haggling for payment over items that had once graced the family home . . . But if it had been difficult to contemplate a confession six months ago, it was downright impossible now. Some days, the pressure of guilt, sadness and confusion was unbearable.

Funds dwindled, as did the visits from Dorothy. Oriel had not seen her since Easter three months ago. Daniel's friend Norm was their only source of friendship now. He too had been unemployed for months since his workplace had closed down, though being a bachelor he was luckier than his pal with no one to support but himself. Even so, he had been forced to turn to the sustenance handouts in order to maintain the room he rented in Carlton. On his friend's latest visit, Daniel revealed that they may have to make this sacrifice too, telling Norm that he did not know whether they would be able to pay the rent for much longer.

There came immediate offer from Norm. 'Yer can share my room with me!'

Seeing an end to the intimacy she shared with Daniel, her only comfort, Oriel stuttered, 'Oh, Norm, we couldn't dream of it!' And she nudged Daniel with her knee just in case he should be about to agree.

However, as the winter dragged on and their money evaporated to a little pile of coins, the day finally came when they were faced with a choice of paying the rent or Daniel's maintenance payment to his estranged wife, and naturally it had to be the latter. The first week was not so bad. His knock unanswered, the rent collector went away. By the following week his knocking became more persistent and, in the knowledge that they would soon be evicted if they did not do something, Daniel said they must seriously consider taking Norm up on his offer.

Oriel fell into despondence as she watched him leave the house with the intent of seeking shelter from his friend – but luck must have been smiling on them that day, for he was to return with the joyous news that he and Norm had managed to get jobs with the council, who were providing relief work by laying new roads in the city.

'Bloody ripper, eh?' He swung her round. 'Won't be for long but at least it's something. Another thing, I been talking to Norm.' He grinned as her face fell. 'Don't worry, I haven't booked us in at the Normie No-nose Temperance Palace – but he says there's a vacant room in the same building. I think we oughta take it.'

Oriel agreed to this compromise. 'But how will we afford to move all our stuff?'

'Norm's borrowing a van.'

'We can't go without paying the rent!' It was not only the dishonesty that made her cringe. 'People will see us.'

'Not in the dark they won't. He's coming late tonight – now just get packing!'

Oriel felt like a criminal, creeping back and forth to the van in the dead of night, carrying boxes and chairs and all manner of other belongings, terrified that someone was going to spot the shadowy figures and call the police. Thankfully, with only a few large items, the mission was quickly accomplished and she was soon on her way to Carlton and her new home.

In the dinge of low wattage, the room was less than welcoming, its linoleum stained with heaven-knew-what and no shade upon the feeble globe, but Oriel was too tired and grateful to object. After installing the furniture, she and Daniel thanked Norm and fell into bed, encouraging each other that tomorrow would make it seem more like home.

Morning light did little to improve their surroundings. The room was dark and airless, the sashes of its bay window jammed shut. The large building was shared with dozens of strangers, their footsteps audible at all times of day and night, up and down the staircase, the stench of their cooking impregnating Oriel's clothes. There was a copper in the back yard for the communal laundry, and only an open fire on which to cook their meals. Conversant now with how her father's tenants must have felt, Oriel regretted her own negligence – but she was used to making the best of things by now, and quickly set to work making it habitable.

Should any emergency arise concerning her offspring, a note was dispatched to Clive, telling him where she had gone. There was no reply, though her request that he forward any mail was heeded. She sent the same news to Dorothy, and though she did receive a pretty little card in return, there was no visit from her friend. She was glad in a way, having no wish for Dorothy to see her in such poverty.

Daniel, too, had people to inform though he made the cynical comment to Oriel that with the roadwork almost completed and no replacement in store, they might not be able to afford even this luxurious palace for long.

It was good for Daniel to have his friend nearby. She herself grew to enjoy Norm's company, and even made tentative acquaintance of the other residents. There were two little girls across the hall, delightful well-mannered children who would often engage her in conversation. With her own daughter unappreciative, Oriel decided to use her talents on those more deserving. Unpicking another of her old dresses, she ran up a couple of small frocks for her new friends. It was wonderful to see their faces as they paraded before their mother, and in response the woman invited her new neighbours in for dinner, such as it might be. Though Oriel grew very fond of the youngsters, they could never make up for the loss of her own children. How much longer could their absence be tolerated?

Loath to spend any more time than she had to indoors whilst Daniel and Norm were out looking for work, she continued her own search. Factories, shops, offices, laundries, hotels – all were explored. Her daily expeditions had become almost automatic. By the time she got home on a night she could hardly remember where she had been, the breadth of her travels only evident from the worn-out shoe leather.

Today, she plodded along the driveway of yet another clothing factory and made the usual wan request, anticipating refusal.

'We want outworkers.' Noting her air of confusion, the man in the enquiry office looked at her over his glasses. 'Have you got a sewing machine?'

Oriel's heart started to race, the spirit of wretchedness immediately dispatched by an eager response as she told him that she had. The man handed over a large bundle of pieces and instructed her how to sew them together.

'Bring them back the day after tomorrow at noon and you'll get another lot if your work's up to standard.'

Oriel was euphoric! Holding the precious bundle tightly to her breast she almost ran home to start work immediately on the pieces.

When a tired-looking Daniel returned later, bringing Norm in to share tea, he was amazed at her enterprise, and gave hearty congratulations, picking up one of the finished garments to inspect it, then passed it to his friend.

'Growse! Not sure it'll fit me, but.' Norm held the woman's garment against himself, mincing up and down, his little button nose in the air.

Daniel grabbed him and pretended to waltz. Though grinning, Oriel dared not take her eyes from her work for fear of ruining it.

Daniel gave Norm a kiss then pushed him away. 'D'yer think you'll get them finished in time?'

Without taking her hand off the machine, its needle racing, Oriel puffed at a strand of hair that was irritating her face. 'If I don't there'll be no more work. I'll finish them even if I have to stay up all night.'

'No need for that. Norm'll take over when you get tired.' At his friend's objection Daniel looked over Oriel's shoulder as the machine clattered and whirred. She felt his warm breath on her head. 'Give us a look at what yer doing. Yeah, I can do that! Half a tick while I get us something to eat then I'll give it a bash.'

And so it was with his help that Oriel was able to hand over the finished garments on time, thus begetting a new source of income which, whilst only a pittance in reward for all the muscle-aching labour, was nevertheless like manna from Heaven.

Proud of her own and Daniel's abilities to keep their heads above water, she was therefore outraged when not long afterwards a solicitor's letter came to say that the errant husband was not granting his wife enough maintenance and Melinda had been obliged to fall back on charity. Payment must be increased forthwith.

'There's always something, isn't there? They give it to you with one hand and take it away with the other. I knew it was too good to be true! That . . . bloody bitch.' She tossed the letter aside, and apologized to Norm for her temper. He made no contribution – Oriel noticed that he never did where Melinda was concerned – but gave a brief gesture and slipped away to his own room.

Daniel despaired of how he was going to raise more

money. 'There's nothing else for it,' he told her. 'I'll have to apply for the susso.'

In the face of legal action, Oriel saw that there could be no argument but, having heard of the high-handed manner of the Ladies Benevolent Society, to whom the Government had handed responsibility for doling out sustenance, she assumed that Daniel would be going instead to the newly formed reactionary body where Norm received his support.

'Aw Christ, I'm not going there! 'Srun by bloody Commies. I didn't go through a war to see the country ruined by them. No, Norm might not care who pays for his beer but I'd rather throw meself on the tender mercies of the Gorgons.'

Aware of the stigma attached to such decision, the stringent home interviews applicants were forced to endure, Oriel detested the idea, but with no other solution she offered to be here for Daniel when the representative made her assessment.

The moment she answered the door to the interviewer it was obvious there was going to be difficulty. The woman was of the type that both she and Daniel abhorred, a do-gooder, with that benevolent kind of smile that said of course I will help you, you poor unfortunate souls, but at the same time I am going to ensure that you are fully aware what a charitable person I am.

After accepting the offer of tea and asking several questions of Daniel, the woman turned to his partner, notepad at the ready. 'And do you work, Mrs Maguire?'

'Oh, I'm not –' Oriel bit her tongue but too late. At the woman's questioning stare she looked desperately at Daniel, who explained the situation.

'I see!' Between queries, the woman had been scrutinizing the room for the last ten minutes, and now began to pace it, investigating the contents of the alcove cupboard without asking leave to do so. 'That puts a very different perspective on matters. Little wonder you're finding it difficult to support your wife and children and this lady as well.'

To cover his anger Daniel went over to the mantelpiece and picked up the cigarette that he had purchased that morning and had been hoping to save until tonight. His angry ignition of a match filled the air with sulphur.

Watching its tip glow, the woman added for Oriel's benefit, 'May I just offer a little hint on your housekeeping methods, my dear?' A supercilious beam accompanied this. 'You would greatly increase your budget if your man gave up the dreaded weed. Does he drink as well?'

Furious, but unwilling to spoil Daniel's chances of payment, Oriel shook her head. To witness his humiliation was far, far worse than her own.

The woman finished her examination of the room and came to sit down again, asking who was caring for Oriel's husband and children and other intimate questions about her marriage, all of which were answered through gritted teeth. Having gathered all the information she required, the woman smiled kindly upon them both, sitting with knees tight together like a prim schoolgirl. 'With such little children to consider, could I not impose upon you to return to your respective spouses? It would be far kinder to all, you know.'

Daniel's face was hard as he pulled on the cigarette. A muscle twitched in his jaw. 'There's no chance of that.'

The woman sighed and rose. 'If I cannot instil good sense then I can at least make sure your dependants do not suffer. We will provide sustenance.'

'Oh, you've spoiled it – I was just considering hanging meself.'

Ignoring Daniel's remark, she told him where to collect his handout and finally departed, leaving both to choke on their anger, Daniel feeling dirty and reviled.

*   *   *

If she had hoped this ordeal would at least result in gaining peace from one source, she was wrong. As winter gave way to the spring rains Melinda, still unsatisfied with the money she was getting from Daniel, turned up at their apartment.

'Is he in?' Straight of face, her cool blue eyes went past Oriel into the room beyond.

'If you mean Daniel, then no, he's out looking for work.' Impatient to return to the pile of sewing and her machine, Oriel declined to invite the other in.

'Tut! All this way for nothing, wasting my petrol – well, you can tell him he might think he's getting away with a few extra bob a week but if I don't get any more I'm going to court and tell 'em he's not man enough to support his wife and children! Do you know I've had to get a job to make up the money he doesn't gimme?'

Oriel lost her temper then, sick of this carping. 'And why shouldn't you bloody work? Everybody else has to make some sort of effort to provide for their children – or do you expect to be looked after all your life?'

'Huh! That's easy for you to say with all the money you've got.'

'Money, money, money! That's all that matters to you, isn't it?'

'I'd like to see how long you'd last without it!' Melinda pursed her lips.

'Are you blind?' Oriel cast her arm around the room. 'Does it look as if we're living in luxury? I've been surviving on next to nothing for months, making do like the rest of the population.'

Melinda almost gagged on her scorn. 'Making do? With two men at your beck and call – one looking after your children and the other scurrying about like a poodle after your every whim while totally neglecting his own family!'

'For God's sake! Does your stupidity know no bounds? Can't you get it through that thick avaricious head –' Oriel hated arguing, detested the way it made her feel afterwards, but she was sick of having to tolerate all this drivel. 'Do you think I sent my children back to their father by choice?'

'Of course you've got a choice!' scoffed Melinda.

'I'd do anything to have them back living with me.' Even to think of them was agony.

'Oh, I'm well aware you're capable of anything! Yer think I believe a word you say any more? You couldn't wait to dump those children – both of yer.'

'And who's looking after yours?' demanded Oriel.

Melinda ignored her. 'And Daniel's even worse than you are! What sorta bloke is he who leaves his wife and kids with nothing?'

At the injustice of this accusation Oriel felt her arteries were going to explode. 'You won't let him alone, will you? He left you everything he had –'

'Huh! A great deal that was!'

'He sends you all his susso every week and I see none of it, not one penny.'

The other's face was mean. 'And why should you? You're not his wife, you don't have to look after his kids! You've got plenty of your own, and Daniel knows it! What sort of a bloke sponges off a woman?'

'And what sort of a woman takes everything a man has?' yelled Oriel. 'I'm surprised you didn't ask for the shirt off his back too! You're even intent on taking what little pride he has left.' But she could see that her argument was wasted on her erstwhile friend. No longer was she eaten up with guilt, she was glad she had taken Daniel from one who only saw him as a provider, one who was shallow and greedy and vindictive. A thought had never entered Melinda's head that did not concern money or the lack of it. Fury robbing her of words, Oriel resorted to vulgarity. 'Oh, just shut up and give your arse a chance!' And she slammed the door in her opponent's face – though the last word was left to Melinda who delivered a curse and a hefty kick to the wood before leaving. Whence, Oriel broke down in tears of anger and frustration.

22

The scent of spring danced upon the air but the mood of winter prevailed. Gone were the weekly dips at the city baths, replaced by Norm's zinc tub. Frugal as they might be, and even with Oriel earning from her outwork, the money they received was insufficient for their needs. Once again they were looking at the fact that they would be unable to pay their rent, for taking precedence over this were the birthday gifts that had to be provided for Daniel's son Alan and her own little boy. Almost as bad, was the quandary of how to deliver the latter's. Though utterly humiliated at having to do so, Oriel thought it best to seek leave from her estranged spouse before going to visit her son.

Clive showed the usual lack of enthusiasm when she turned up at Myers. At least you've kept your job, she wanted to shout at him, but as ever remained dispassionate to his goading, first enquiring if there had been anyone to view the house lately. A negative response did not surprise her. Asking after the children, she was told that they had been upset at first but had now grown accustomed to life without their mother.

'D'you think it'll disrupt them if I come for Dorrie's birthday?' she asked. 'I want to bring him a present but not if it's going to make things worse.'

He was aloof. 'I don't think that's a good idea – but I suppose you'll do what you want to do, you always have.'

Oriel noted that the way he phrased it absolved himself of any deliberate ban. 'If you really think it would upset them I won't come.' She hung her head, unable to look at him. 'If I bring Dorrie's present here will you give it to him?' Upon his affirmation, she left.

Intending to walk home, she headed along Elizabeth Street, eyes lowered in despondence. A woman's feet appeared in her path. Without lifting her head she sidestepped, the woman sidestepped too, and when Oriel repeated the evasive action so did she, making it into a kind of dance. Oriel raised her angry face to demand what the other thought she was playing at – then saw that it was Dorothy and the bad temper was wiped away as she greeted her old friend warmly.

'Ratty! How lovely to see you. I would've called but I didn't want to cause trouble for you.'

Dorothy said how nice it was to see her too, though there was some hint of reserve in her greeting. 'You're looking well.' She didn't mean it. Oriel looked skinny as a rake – and what had happened to the glamour Dorothy had so admired? The high heels had been replaced by flat shoes, and the outfit was uncoordinated. Still, she would probably be quite hard up in her position. 'Have you time for a cup of tea? My treat,' she added quickly.

Chatting as they went, the two friends went to find a tearoom where, over honeyed crumpets, Dorothy asked, 'So, how are Jennifer and Dorrie?'

'Oh fine!' Then Oriel lost her verve and formed a cynical grimace. 'No, not fine really. I haven't seen them for ages.'

Dorothy admitted, 'Yes, Cuddy did tell me.'

Her companion was tart. 'I suppose he got Clive's version. Well, for the record, I came to an arrangement that I wouldn't see them until I could provide us all with a home.'

She told Dorothy of all the trauma that had occurred since last they had met. Her friend showed incredulity. The Depression had hardly altered her own lifestyle – it was difficult to imagine what Oriel must be suffering. 'I don't know how I haven't gone mad. God knows when I'll see them again – but I will.' She rushed her cup to her lips.

Dorothy used her little finger to flick a sticky crumb from the corner of her mouth. 'I saw that old lady, the one who used to be your neighbour, last week and she was telling me you've only had one lot to view your house.'

Oriel placed the cup in its saucer and sighed. 'Yes. I wouldn't have guessed it would take this long. It's been almost a year.'

'Ye Gods, doesn't time fly! So are you still living in Carlton? I presumed you did when sending your birthday card.'

Oriel gave an appreciative smile. 'Oh yes, thanks for that! Yes, if we can afford the rent we'll be stuck there until the divorce is heard. Don't ask me when that will be. That blasted solicitor – did you know you can use any name you choose as long as it's not intended to deceive? No, well neither did I and he didn't think it would be important to me. I only found out a few months ago. I've been stuck with Mrs Widdowes all this time when I had no need to be.' She remembered all the humiliations she had suffered because of this. 'I've always hated it. Oriel Widdowes – it sounds like someone's saying oriel windows with a cold!' She mirrored Dorothy's smile. 'It's funny, I'll be Maguire again after I marry Daniel – he's still out of work by the way.'

'Oh, you're still together then?' A look of relief flooded Dorothy's face and she clutched her breast. 'When you just kept saying we and never mentioned his name until now, I hardly dared ask!'

'Yes, of course. Who did you think I was living with?' The eyes beneath the dark fringe were puzzled.

In her relief Dorothy jabbered, 'It was just that I heard you'd split up and when you wrote and told me you'd moved and didn't mention him – well, I didn't like to mention him either in case I hurt your feelings. I'm so glad for you!'

Annoyance spread over Oriel's face. 'Who told you that?'

'Oh, it was just something Cuddy heard.'

'Maybe his wishful thinking,' muttered Oriel. 'He can't use me like a punchbag as he does his wife so he makes things up.' She saw the other's cheeks flush with offence. 'I'm sorry, Dot, but this is the second lot of idiotic gossip I've heard and it's getting me ruddy angry! I'm sitting on a bus minding my own business when I'm treated to the biggest load of rubbish I've ever heard in my life – about me! And this was from women I'd never even seen before! The next one to open their mouth gets a pie in the face.'

Misled by this remark, and unfamiliar with the true depth of her friend's suffering, Dorothy turned impish. 'I heard other bits of highly improbable gossip too. Apparently Clive's got Daniel a job at Myers and you're all living in the same house. Yes, really!' She laughed in sympathy. 'I'll put Cuddy right about you splitting up when I get home – oh no, I can't or he'll know I've seen you. Anyway, I already told him it probably wasn't true.'

'Probably?' Oriel thought perhaps there was a hint of jealousy in Dorothy's attitude now; resentment that her friend had found happiness with a man whilst she remained trapped in her own violent marriage.

The other's face dropped. 'Well, no, I said –'

'What do people think I am?' raged Oriel, drawing looks from the other diners. 'Did they imagine I was just having a quick fling and then it's on to the next man? I adore him, he's the only man I've ever truly loved, I'd die without him, and we're going to get married as soon as people will let us – although as far as I'm concerned that man is already my husband and always has been so you can tell that to whoever you like.' Gathering her skirts, she made to leave the teashop, face set in a mask of annoyance.

'Goodbye, Dot, perhaps we'll meet in happier times.'

In retrospect it had been mean and crass to wreak her frustration on the only friend she had, but Oriel no longer had the energy to care. Dorrie's birthday came and went. Desperate to see both children she used precious funds on the train fare to Brighton and hid around a corner to watch as they left school in the company of their grandmother. The experience was so upsetting that it did not bear repetition – even if she could have afforded to do so.

A month went by, Christmas was less than a fortnight away and they had still paid no rent. Letters came, demanding settlement, Daniel ripped them up. Another was about to be consigned to the bin too when he noted that it was from a different legal firm and quickly opened it.

After a moment, his face brightened. 'Now isn't that a turn-up? Melinda wants a divorce.' He handed it over for Oriel to read, and gave a laugh of recognition. 'She must have another fella.'

Though Oriel was pleased, the tone of her voice conveyed otherwise as she read the legal document. 'On the grounds of your desertion and adultery.'

'Hey, isn't this what we wanted? Don't knock our one bit o' progress.' He put his arms around her, chivvying her into better mood. 'Come on, sooky, crack yer face – yer'll be havin' me thinkin' yer've changed yer mind.'

Oriel returned his enthusiastic hug then, scolding him. 'Don't you ever say that again! Here – take this and go buy a bottle of beer to celebrate. Go on! We can't pay the rent anyway so what does a few pence matter?'

Within days, they were regretting this extravagance, for when Oriel returned her finished garments to the factory she was told that there was nothing to collect.

The supply of outwork continued to be sporadic. Faced with the long hours of idleness, she began to slide into apathy. Had she not had her beloved to urge her on she felt that she might just drift away into insanity, but Daniel was firm, in spite of his own traumas, refusing to be subjugated, bolstering her with the hope that around the corner, over the hill, there might be someone who would buy her house and in a few months they may be out of this mess. Scavenging through the council tips, he found a pad of unused paper, and ripping off the dirty outer covers brought it home and thrust it at her, urging her to write down all that had happened to them over the past year, put down her thoughts, her feelings, her ideas – anything to get the frustration out of her system. Her obedient response proved beneficial, the journal serving to occupy her until the next batch of work came along.

To preserve his masculinity, Daniel had taken to working for the meagre sustenance payment and, today, he and Norm were out assisting with the construction of a Shrine of Remembrance to their fallen comrades. Yet again, Oriel had delivered the latest batch of garments to the factory, only to find that there was none for her to collect. Discouraged, she went home and made herself a cup of tea. There were sheets to be washed. She should really be taking advantage of the hot weather but unable to fight the torpor she continued to sit there gazing into space for a long time, until she felt the blackness threaten to swamp her. Daniel's voice nagging her conscience, she heaved her leaden body from the chair and went to prepare the copper in the yard, then, collecting Norm's sheets she left them to soak with her own.

It was when she went back later to give the linen a pounding that she met the strange-looking character in the hall and jumped in shock.

The tramp apologized for frightening her. His voice was at odds with the long grey hair and beard – he was obviously younger than he looked. Recovering her equilibrium, Oriel said it was quite all right, proceeded into the yard and, injecting all her weight into the effort, she pounded the sheets in the copper. Her back to the door, she could nonetheless tell that the eccentric character had followed her and was watching her every move. Uncomfortable and perspiring from her efforts, she turned and said she had no paid work to offer him, but he was welcome to some soup in return for his assistance with these sheets.

Discarding his swag and jacket, the man rolled up his shirt sleeves and came forth with outstretched hands. Oriel looked at them, fearing that her laundry was going to be even dirtier after it had been washed, but surprisingly his fingers were not all that grubby – though he smelled dreadful. There was no mangle at hand. Dashing the sweat from her brow with the back of her hand, she took one end of the sheet and he held the other, twisting it until all the soapy water gushed out. After a couple of rinsings and similar manglings, they hung it over a line. The chore was repeated with the other sheets and afterwards Oriel took the swagman indoors, groping her way through the hall, her eyes almost blinded in the transition from sunlight to darkness.

Blinking several times, she cut some bread and doled out the thin soup, hoping there would be enough left for her husband and Norm – it had had to suffice them for three days already.

'We've been eating it cold in this weather. It's too hot for a fire and that's the only way we can cook – but it's really nice.'

The tramp did not appear to mind and draping his jacket over the back of his chair, sat down and tucked in hungrily. Allergic to his body odour, Oriel moved as far away as possible and affected to go about her business though there was little to do, and she kept her eye on him lest he attempt to steal anything. She wondered what tragedy had led him to this life and pictured herself and

Daniel, unable to pay the rent, in the same position.

After he had finished eating, had dabbed his moustache with a handkerchief and thanked her kindly, she expected him to go, but he sat there savouring the taste in his mouth, his eyes on her. The expression in them made her suddenly afraid – whatever had she been thinking of inviting this odd character into her home?

Unnerved, she made a hint that he should leave. 'Well, my husband will be home soon.' She prayed that Daniel would come home for lunch. Often he did not.

He made no move, merely nodding. Time passed. With growing unease Oriel nibbled her thumbnail and glanced at the door, wondering whether she could get to it before the tramp. He seemed to sense this, the look in his eyes daring her to make a move. Blood pumping, she was still looking at the door when it opened and to her great relief in walked Daniel and his friend. As she released her trapped breath the tramp stood and presented his face to the two men. Before she had time to explain to Daniel he had taken a step forward and thumped the swagman in the chest.

'You old bastard! Bit early for Father Christmas to call, isn't it?'

Behind the abundant beard Jimmy Magee grinned and allowed himself to be manhandled by the two friends, surrendering to their affectionate punching and name-calling whilst Oriel, clearly dumbfounded, waited for explanation. It was even more mystifying to see that a dog had entered with them.

'Yer great drongo!' cried Daniel. 'Don't yer know who it is?'

'Sorry about that, missus.' Amusement in his dark eyes, Jimmy came forward and bent his weathered face close for her inspection. Only then did she recognize the pointed features beneath the whiskers, that sardonic expression he had used on her all those years ago, and she offered a smile in return whilst shaking him by the hand.

'Oh, you had me going for a minute – you devil! It's so nice to see you again! Well, I'd offer you some refreshment but you've already had it.' Grinning, she told Daniel and Norm about their friend's assistance with the laundry.

'Hope he's left us some soup,' opined Daniel, peering at the pan. Oriel said there was enough for all and went to serve it, asking the men to sit at the table for they were cluttering the room. She served only a small portion to herself, in order to offer Jimmy the last drop in the bottom of the pan which he accepted.

Only now, as she carried bowls to the table, did she enquire about the dog. 'If you don't mind me asking, what's that doing here?'

Daniel stroked the greyhound's panting head. 'We found him.' He threw an impudent grin at Norm. 'Well sort of.' Pouring the animal some water, he told Oriel that he had in fact untied it from outside a shop whilst its owner was inside, and intended to look through the lost and found column of tomorrow's newspaper. 'Thought there might be a good reward – he's a lovely animal.'

She bit her lips at this audacity. 'And what if no one claims it – how are we going to feed him?'

Daniel patted the dog's ribs. 'Doesn't look as if he eats much. Don't worry, I picked me mark. Lady who owns him obviously thinks the world of him judging how she kissed him before she went into the shop. Won't be with us for long.' He sat down.

Oriel hoped he was right, and also wondered how long Jimmy intended to stay. With four people and a dog the room was feeling distinctly overcrowded – and Jimmy's odour seemed to have manifested a presence all of its own.

Daniel finished his soup, sat back and took a deep breath. 'Jim, it's great to see yer, mate, but Christ, you bloody stink.'

Jimmy looked slightly hurt. 'Sorry, think it's me jacket.' Abandoning his seat he picked up the garment and tested it with his nostrils. 'I'll put it outside.'

'Better tie it up then or it'll have run away when yer go back for it,' contributed Norm. 'Tin bath in me room if yer wanna dip.'

Still showing a mark of offence, Jimmy accepted and, pulling a clean shirt and pants out of his swag he left the room.

Daniel let out a breath and started wafting the air. 'I don't smell that bad, do I?'

Oriel pretended to have passed out, then came to life, laughing. 'No, yours is good honest sweat, he must have been saving his for posterity.' Whilst feeling sorry for Jimmy she went to open the door to allow some fresh air in, being careful not to be quite so obvious when their friend returned smelling somewhat sweeter.

Throughout the afternoon, news was exchanged, Jimmy telling Daniel that he had already heard on the bush telegraph about his broken marriage and his new address, and Daniel having to put him right on misinformed snippets of gossip. Towards the time that would usually be reserved for tea, the visitor produced cigarettes and bottles of beer from his swag. After bringing in the clean sheets and replacing them on the bed, Oriel accepted a glass and was happy to sit for a while chatting, but then when Daniel invited his friend to stay the night and Jimmy accepted, she finished her last drop of beer and said, 'I'll leave you boys alone, I'm sure you don't want me earwigging. I'll just go out and get some extra food in.' Though just how, she did not know.

Jimmy caught her surreptitiously examining the contents of her purse. 'I'll only stay if I pay me way.' He handed her a collection of silver coins.

Noting her hesitancy, Daniel urged her silently to take it and knowing how his friend was so easily insulted, she did. The dog vied with her at the door. Recognizing his problem, she took him with her to the shop, leaving the men to enjoy their beer.

But it turned out that Jimmy had brought much better than this, as Oriel was to find out when she came home and began to prepare another meal. Upon learning that neither of his pals had worked for almost a year he told them that only a few days ago on his journey here from the Dandenongs he had learned of a vacancy at a timberyard in Ferntree Gully.

'Matter o' fact, a mate offered it to me. He's got the old gut-rot – looks as if he's on the way out. Been keeping the job up as long as he can but he's just about had it now. Said I might give it a go if I get short o' cash.'

'Might?' Daniel laughed in outrage. Norm, too, bared the gap in his teeth.

The bearded mouth grinned back. 'Ah well, you know me. Never can tell what frame o' mind I'll be in from one day to the next.' Asked how he got by, Jimmy said he cost very little to keep. 'If I'd known what strife you were in I would've put yer name forward but anyhow, I don't think he'll have given it to anybody else. Go up there tomorrow and tell him you've come in place of me. He's a good bloke, he'll see yer right. Sorry, there's only one job, Norm, but you haven't got a wife and kids.'

'Rub it in, won't yer?' Norm looked away and played with the little button of flesh that passed for a nose.

'Keep me ears open for yer, though.'

Having suffered so many disappointments, Oriel put all thoughts of the job from her mind and served the cold evening meal which had to be shared with the greyhound. The conversation proceeded after tea, taking in the state of the country, the mounting unemployment figures and industrial violence. It was unthinkable but Australia seemed on the verge of armed warfare between the classes. Even the Government faced a split from internecine squabbles.

'Yer can blame this bugger,' joked Daniel, pointing at

Norm. 'He voted Labor in.' Always a republican, he was nevertheless quite moderate and did not have contempt for the bosses – someone had to run the show – but he did hate communists and believed it was this section that was driving the country towards ruin. 'If Scullin can't keep his own mob in order how can he run the country?'

'Only voted for 'em to get rid o' Bruce.' Norm had no steadfast views on politics. He glanced at the dog, who lay in anxious pose by the door. 'Reckon it wouldn't matter who was in, still be in a mess. Right about Scullin, but – Phar Lap'd make a better Prime Minister. Only good thing he did was appoint a genuine Aussie as Governor-General.'

Daniel took a drink of beer. 'Sir Isaac Isaacs – his father was an imaginative bastard, wasn't he?'

Norm yawned and stretched. 'Jeez, I'm feeling tired. Reckon I'll take me leave – good to see yer, Jim. Thanks for the grub.' Nudging the dog out of his way, he left.

'Tired my arse,' Daniel snorted and gave the dog a pat of encouragement. 'He's got a sheila somewhere. Used to have the pleasure of his company every night but for the last couple o' weeks he's been real toey – reckons we don't know he's creeping off after dark. Never mind, more beer for us.' He held his glass out to Jimmy.

Oriel made to retire at eleven, bequeathing Daniel a chance to enjoy the company of his own sex without a female constraining their speech. 'I'll plug my ears with cottonwool, then you can say what you like.'

As she rose, so too did the dog and she led him out into the yard to relieve himself, bringing him back moments later and commanding him to lie in a corner. Whilst she undressed the men turned their backs, but she had long ago dispensed with any bashfulness and cared not if Jimmy should catch a glimpse of naked flesh before she climbed into bed. Relaxed from the beer, she closed her eyes and listened to the low drone of their voices for a while, before drifting off to sleep. It was the early hours before Daniel crept in beside her, Jimmy spreading his swag on the floor next to the hearth.

In the morning after breakfast the swagman left, wishing his friend luck with the job.

Not long after seeing him off, Daniel left too. Not daring to entertain hope, for this had been dashed too often for confidence, Oriel accompanied him as far as she could, taking the dog with her, before going to see if there was any work for her at the factory. Fortunately there was and she spent the rest of the day stitching, and wondering if her beloved had succeeded in getting his free ride on a goods train, or whether as had happened to so many he had been ejected by an unsympathetic policeman and had had to make his way on foot. Concentrating on her sewing, she only stopped to let the dog out into the yard, then worked right through until late afternoon, when she paused for fifteen minutes to snatch a cup of tea and a wad of bread, again sharing it with her canine lodger. Resuming her task, she rattled on until it grew dark and she had to get up to turn the light on, working on until ten. Then, her shoulder muscles feeling as if they had been pierced by red-hot needles, she abandoned the machine, stretched painfully, and had just made another pot of tea when the dog barked and Daniel entered. By the look on his face she knew he had been unsuccessful, had seen that look too many times to bother asking. Instead she hugged him tenderly, then made him sit down, asked if he wanted something to eat and when he shook his head she handed him a cup of tea.

He took a grateful sip, staring at the dog for a long time, before saying, 'Well, don't suppose we'll see much o' Norm now.'

Oriel frowned and asked what he meant.

'Must've set off last night. By the time I got there he'd beaten me to it.' His voice held a type of weariness she had not heard before.

'You mean he's stolen the job?' She could not believe such treachery. 'Surely he wouldn't do that to a mate. How d'you know it was him?'

Daniel stretched out in the chair, his expression remaining fixed. 'I asked the bloke outright. Norm didn't show his face but I know he was there.'

Oriel uttered a sound of disgust. 'I can't believe – I mean he knows we haven't paid the rent in weeks – and you've got children to feed!' She began to rave, asking what kind of man could do this to his friend? 'He hasn't even got a wife, for God's sake!'

'He has now – or soon will have when he can get me out of the way.' Daniel summoned amusement. Seeing she was never going to guess, he explained. 'Told you he's been sneaking off to see a woman, didn't I? Don't you think it's a bit odd that Mel's just asked for a divorce?'

She gasped at the audacity, and could not bring herself to join Daniel's merriment, calling Norm every name she could think of, the dog keeping well out of her way. 'I knew my first instincts were right! You can never trust anyone with a gap between their teeth.' Clasping a handful of hair, she beheld Daniel with confusion. 'I thought you'd be angrier than this. He's betrayed you.'

'Think we've all done things we're not proud of,' he reminded her. 'These are bad times. I'd have done the same in his position.'

'No you wouldn't.'

It was late. Daniel was worn out, his voice became impatient. 'All right, I can't pretend I'm happy at not getting the job but at least if he's looking after Mel then she's sweet and that makes it easier for me to see the kids – now can we drop the bloody thing and go to bed?' He planted the cup on the table slopping tea everywhere and started to rip off his clothes.

Meekly, Oriel took the dog out into the yard, then came back to join Daniel in bed.

'I'm sorry,' she whispered, when they had lain there for some moments without speaking.

With a groan, he pulled her into a fierce embrace. 'It's not your fault. Don't think I'm mad at you. I love you.' After a moment of soothing her with kisses, he rolled over on to his back and gave a huge sigh. 'For Jesus Christ's sake, will it never bloody end?'

Though both had been expecting it, the manner of their eviction came as a shock. Oriel was bent over her sewing machine, stitching for all she was worth, Daniel had just come in from an afternoon's labour on the Shrine and was crouched over a bowl washing the dust from his naked upper half, the dog was stretched out along the hearth asleep, when the door opened and two men came in.

'You've got five minutes to get out!' The speaker was a surly fellow with unusually short legs, beady eyes and big ears. Ignoring the barking dog, he stood his ground.

Oriel saw that Daniel was about to tackle him and shouted for him to desist, for the man who accompanied him was a brute. 'No! Daniel, just let's gather our things and go.' She made to pack up her machine.

'Leave everything as it is! That and the furniture can go to cover the rent you owe.'

'We don't owe that bloody much!' Throwing down his towel, Daniel strode forth. The speaker's larger accomplice took a step to meet him and, presented with the open door, the dog made a bolt for freedom, taking with it any chance of claiming a reward. Words of frustration poured from Daniel's mouth but the advantage this gave him was only slight.

'You can take what you can carry,' relented the man. 'You've now got three minutes.'

As Daniel reluctantly caved in with a harsh expletive and started to dress, a hot and bothered Oriel rushed to gather what she could, mainly clothes and other transportable items, shoving them into carrier bags and knotting them in blankets. Daniel too grabbed as much as possible, cramming the bag with everything from metal to paper, any item that might prove essential. At the noise, other residents of the house had come into the hall to stare, some craning their necks over the top of the balustrade, all pouring derogatory comments upon the evictors. The mother of the two little girls for whom Oriel had made the dresses shouted and condemned her oppressors but it did no good. Within minutes she and Daniel were standing on the pavement in burning sunshine.

'You can stay in our room for tonight.' The woman had followed them out, shading her eyes with an arm. 'There's not much space but –'

'No they can't!' The big-eared man intervened. 'I'm not having them sneaking back in there. I want them out altogether.'

'You can't tell me who I can and can't have in my room!' retorted the woman.

'Shut up!' Seeing her open her mouth he repeated himself. 'I said shut up!' So violent was his emission, so vicious his face, that she shrank. 'Get inside unless you want to be next!' He was like a rabid koala.

Oriel issued hasty thanks as her would-be helper retreated indoors. Then, with a look at the intransigent expressions of the two men, she and Daniel wandered away. Never could she imagine her father being as vicious as this with his tenants.

'At least it's not bloody raining,' muttered Daniel as they ambled aimlessly along the road. In fact it was uncomfortably hot. Seeing she was having difficulty carrying her bags he divested her of one of them, adding it to his own load.

Oriel did not ask what they were going to do – why should Daniel know any more than she did?

However, he gave his prescription. 'We'll have to find

somewhere to sleep tonight. How much money we got?' When told a few shillings, he added, 'Not enough for a room then. Let's hope it stays warm and we can sleep in a park or something. Come on, we'll head across the city. Yer never know, I might even find a job. How're your feet standing up?' She said they were all right. 'Well, if yer get tired just tell me.'

Hitching a free ride on trams wherever they could go, they crossed the city and spent an hour or so just wandering the streets looking for work. Oriel's mind was in conflict. On the one hand she was afraid of the future – could not even see a future – yet at the same time the thought of having no material possessions to bind her was strangely liberating.

They sat for a while on the city beach, staring at the sea for answer. Then, as the sun descended, Oriel sat upright and began to rummage in one of the carriers. 'Now, let me see. We've got a knife . . . a piece of rope, there's the sea . . . but no pills, I'm afraid.' She presented a cheery face. 'Never mind, a choice of three isn't bad – which would you like?'

'I'm more of yer skyscraper man meself. When I go out it'll be in style. Haven't got the energy for suicide today, though.'

Oriel wrinkled her nose. 'No, I can't be bothered either. Come on, let's go to the market.' She told him that at close of business there was usually condemned fruit to be had – it would serve as their tea.

Weighed down by their few possessions, they hobbled across the shifting sand towards the road, calf muscles aching. In the streets above the beach a group of young women in bathing costumes got in their way, giggling and laughing at the collision. Oriel glared over her shoulder and uttered a sound of disgust at their incongruous attire, speaking loud enough for them to hear. 'My God it's a public highway! Doesn't anyone have any manners today?' How she hated these flighty, carefree creatures who had no inkling of the burdens others had to bear.

Upon reaching the market, they stood watching with a crowd of others whilst the stall owners tipped crates of unsold fruit into deep pits, most of it perfectly sound, this disgusting waste making Oriel even angrier. The market inspector came forth bearing a bottle of phenol. In the time it took him to remove the top, hungry people had jumped into the pits, collecting as much fruit as they could before it was destroyed. Daniel emerged triumphant, his pockets bulging with apples and oranges. These, their evening meal, were eaten in a garden which was later to be their sleeping place. Using the stuffed carrier bags as pillows, they cuddled up together and closed their eyes. It was a long night.

Overcome by troubles, sleep was periodic, giving them much time to think. Whilst Oriel merely pondered on the coming Christmas, fretting over her children, Daniel worried over these things too but at the same time tried to construct a solution.

Warm breath on her face as they snuggled close together, he murmured, 'There's no point hanging round here. We'll both go mad just wandering round in circles. We'll go and stay with Jimmy. Do us good to get out in the bush.' He felt her chest rise, and stilled her objection before it emerged. 'Yeah, I know we haven't the fare, we'll just make our way to the railway yards and jump a rattler. Don't know if he'll be there but it's worth a go.' It was not yet dawn. 'Too early to get anything to eat yet but if I lie here much longer I think I'll seize up.' Groaning, he threw aside the blanket, rose and pulled Oriel up after him. Around them in the darkness others were stirring. Daniel gathered their belongings together. 'Come on, we'll go the beach 'n' see if we can find some dead marines, bring us a few extra pennies.'

Even as early as they were, others had beat them to most of the empty beer bottles. They could hear them clinking inside the sacks that were being dragged along the sand. But there were still less obvious treasures to be found. Through the dinge, a pier beacon outlined shadowy figures all shuffling along the shore, probing with bare toes. Points of light sparkled upon the inky sea, its smell tweaking their nostrils. Oriel put down her possessions and took off her shoes – she wore no stockings, could not afford them now. Keeping an eye on their belongings, she and Daniel began to mimic the others, combing the sand with eyes and toes. A lone, sullen child observed them, then moved away, trailing his sack before they could steal its contents. If Oriel had only known it, she was enacting the movements of her father almost forty years earlier.

Espying a packet of cigaretttes, she pounced and finding that it had two inside hoisted it triumphantly.

Daniel groaned. 'Just my luck when I've given up smoking. Got a match?'

It had been issued ironically but to his delight she was to find a box half an hour later and rattled it at him, both mentally recalling the day they had first met. He said it would probably contain all dead ones but no, he was able to light up a cigarette and inhaled as if he had been granted a taste of heaven. During the next half an hour, they were to find three shillings in loose change, a magazine and a ring.

'Well, if this isn't a good omen!' announced Daniel. 'Come here, let's slip it on yer finger. Now we're engaged.'

Oriel laughed and peered through the gloom, trying to examine the ring, her smile suddenly faltering. 'Oh, I think I read somewhere that an opal is bad luck unless it happens to be your birthstone.'

'You are joking?' He almost choked on his amusement. 'How can we have any worse luck than we've had?' Having succeeded in making her laugh, Daniel flourished the magazine. 'We've got three bob and something to wipe our bums on, what more d'yer want out o' life?' He kissed her, then, still smiling, he looked around him.

The sun was coming up now and through the grey light he saw that the patrol had begun to abandon its search. 'Come on, if that lot're going there can't be another brass razoo to be found, let's go have brekkie.'

Her spine aching, Oriel attached herself to his arm and, leaving the beach like a ploughed field, they went to find a café. Soon, though, after they had finished their bacon sandwiches, Daniel was to see her slipping back towards melancholy.

'Buck up, Kooka.' His greenish eyes offered encouragement. 'Gotta look at it like an adventure. With no house or chattels to tie us down we can go anywhere we want.'

She nodded and smiled, but it was a sad effort.

'We don't have to go to Jimmy's if you don't want.'

'No, that's fine with me.' Oriel needed to get right away from Melbourne, away from her troubles, if only it weren't so much effort.

After finishing breakfast, she went with Daniel to the railway yards and waited for a train that was heading east. As usual, they were not alone. When the locomotive shunted into action people rose as if from nowhere and began to run alongside it, jumping into the goods wagons. Oriel jumped in too and fell back against Daniel in an attitude of relief then sat back to wait. Waiting, waiting – was there nothing else to life?

The train chugged away from Melbourne, out through the suburbs, climbing up into hillier country, amongst verdant hills and fern-filled gorges. Soon the foliage became so dense that it was impossible to see anything else but this and the sky. Gazing sleepily from her wagon, head bumping up and down on Daniel's shoulder, Oriel felt totally enveloped in greenery, extended her hand to grasp at encroaching ferns that brushed the sides of the wagon.

Eyes on the passing signs, Daniel watched for a suitable place to alight and, as the locomotive slowed right down to indicate another country town, he jumped on to the tracks and caught the bags which Oriel threw down to him, and then held out his arms for her.

After they left the train there was still a long way to travel on foot, first along a road and then a steep narrow incline through thick undergrowth. It was hot but at least there was shade. Birdsong replaced the noise of the city. Their shoulders brushed the overhanging branches, drawing forth perfume. Daniel had never been here before and voiced the hope that he was following Jimmy's instructions correctly. To ease the journey, he told her more about Magee's life, that he was from a quite wealthy family but after the war had been unable to stand their shocked embarrassment over his whimpering episodes under the table, their horrified disbelief at his fits of black rage, their pathetic inability to understand why he behaved the way he did, and had totally cut himself off from them – and indeed from the rest of the world – much to their relief. Copying other tortured souls, he had built his home of logs and flattened kerosene tins and lived quite comfortably – though Daniel only had his word for this, having not seen it himself.

Assuming it to be a ramshackle affair, Oriel was therefore taken aback when, after arduous miles, they finally emerged from the ferny undergrowth into a clearing and found a well-constructed cabin.

A knock at the door produced the hermit's bearded face. He was surprised to see them, muttering, 'You must've been walking in my footsteps, I've only just got back myself.' His smile was less broad than a few days ago but he seemed genuine in his invitation for the couple to enter.

Inside was even more of a shock – he had some very nice pieces of furniture, obviously inherited from his family. Dumping her possessions, Oriel took the seat that was offered, Daniel beside her, both looking around in admiration.

Having exhausted his news a few days ago, Jimmy had little to offer in the way of conversation. The atmosphere was friendly but awkward. Daniel soon filled the hiatus.

'Expect you wonder what I'm doing here instead of being at that timberyard job you told me about – well, Norm got there first.'

Jimmy looked dark. 'The bastard.'

Daniel formed a wry smile. 'Then Oriel and me got evicted –'

'Aw well, you can have my bed for as long as you want it,' muttered Jimmy as he went to fetch his guests something to eat. 'And there's plenty o' tucker here.'

The words were friendly but Daniel sensed a hint of reserve, saying hurriedly, 'We're not here to put the bite on yer mate! Only came for a visit, be gone in a couple o' days, we need to be back in Melbourne for Christmas.' He encompassed Oriel in his explanation and she nodded, trying to smile whilst feeling hollow.

Later, tucked up beside Daniel in the cosy bed, with no one else's footsteps thudding up and down the stairs, no voices, no traffic, only Jimmy lying quietly on his swag nearby, Oriel began to feel more at peace.

In the morning, she and Daniel agreed not to make one mention of their troubles and after a refreshing plunge in their friend's water tank, spent the day lazing in the sunshine, recouping their energy. Jimmy caught a rabbit which was devoured with relish in the evening. His belly fuller than it had been for weeks, Daniel said he was in danger of falling asleep and to avoid this made an attempt to repair his boots, using the tools and leather his friend lent him. Whilst he did this, Oriel tried to hold a conversation with Jimmy, but he seemed not to be in the mood for it tonight and buried his hirsute face in a book.

She fell silent, rubbing her mosquito-bitten arms, feeling she should be doing something, making some effort to get her children back. Her emotions ebbed and flowed, one minute at rest, the next in torment. Unable to be still, her roving gaze caught sight of a violin tucked away in a corner. 'Is that what you used to play in the quartet, Jimmy?'

Without looking up from the book, the heavily bearded face delivered a nod.

'I'd like to hear it.'

He continued to read. 'Never play in public now.'

'We're not public, are we, Daniel?'

'I should've said I don't play at all.'

Oriel failed to pick up the warning note of impatience in his voice. 'Oh we don't mind if you're out of practice.' She gave an entreating smile. 'Go on – please, I need cheering up.'

All at once he had tossed the book to the other side of the room and his face was speaking directly into hers. 'I said, I don't play!'

For seconds he pinned her with his hard, black eyes. Oriel shrank under his glare, assailed by the dreadful conviction that everyone in the world was against her now. Daniel's hands paused on the leather boot but he did nothing more than look on in quiet concern.

'Can't you take no for an answer?' yelled Jimmy. 'This is my home, I built it to get away from people like you, asking your stupid bloody questions! Nag, nag, nag! I didn't ask you to come here bringing all your troubles. What am I supposed to be, Jesus Christ? I just want to be left alone!' He hurled himself away from her frightened face and, lifting the edge of a piece of lino that clothed the floor he pulled out a note and threw it at Daniel. 'Here! Take that and rent yourself a place of your own where she can gabble as much as she likes. You can stay here tonight but tomorrow I want you gone.'

Daniel made no comment that it was a ten-pound note, did not ask where on earth his friend had got it, just put it into his pocket and watched Jimmy heft his swag and depart. In the resounding silence, he looked at Oriel, who sat in the same position, too shocked to weep. He went to her, held her. She did not move, just sat there transfixed.

'He's just sick, darlin',' said Daniel softly.

Aren't we all? thought Oriel, feeling as if there would be no tomorrow.

'Come on, we'll go to bed. He won't be back.' And Daniel helped her undress, treating her tenderly, not as a lover but as a little child – though once she was in bed and he beside her, this attitude was folded away with his clothes and he made love to her with passion.

Much later, in the small hours, Oriel was awoken by a noise. Clawing her way out of sleep, she rolled on to her back and listened. Outside the cabin, Jimmy Magee was crying, the stillness of the night invaded by his anguished weeping. So violent were his sobs that from time to time he would heave and retch and shiver, sounding to the horrified witness as if he were about to disgorge his very core. The depth of his emotion, the utter wretchedness of the sound, incised her heart and she too began to weep. Not wishing to disturb her beloved, but desperately needing comfort, she edged her heated body closer to his, and found that he was not there.

It was not Jimmy Magee whose misery rent the night, but Daniel.

23

In the morning they left and, with no further glimpse of Jimmy, travelled back to the city the same way they had come. The clanking sootiness of the railway yards, the grey cloak that typified the area around Victoria Dock, were in stark contrast to the viridian climes they had just departed, but armed with the ten pounds they could at least put a roof over their heads. Shortly after they alighted from the wagon and hopped across the lines, they were to find a ground-floor room in a large red brick terrace. Notwithstanding the drabness of the suburb, this room was superior to the one from which they had been evicted, being furnished with a bed, chairs, table and a cooker – though owning few utensils Oriel was for ever trailing across the hall to ask the resident landlady for the loan of some necessity.

In three days' time it would be Christmas. Wandering round the crowded city, ostensibly looking for work whilst her beloved was otherwise engaged in his own search, Oriel thought of Dorothy and the ungrateful way she had behaved towards her. There and then she decided to telephone her friend and make her apologies. Uncaring whether Cuthbert might answer, she sought out a kiosk and made her call.

Luckily it was Dorothy who answered, brushing aside Oriel's apology straightaway and insisting that it was her fault for being so blasé about the other's problem, saying also that she might come to visit and pull their traditional New Year's wishbone if she could get away once the Christmas rush was over. Inwardly sighing over Dorothy's inability to understand the full depth of her trauma, Oriel nevertheless informed her of the new address before wishing her a happy Christmas and hanging up.

Oblivious to the Christmas shoppers who milled around her, she stared at the telephone for some moments, yearning to ring her children, picturing them at Christmases past, their excited rush to open presents, their gleeful tearing of paper. She was still trying to make her decision when someone's impatient gesture caught her attention and she was forced to leave the telephone kiosk.

Home was in easy walking distance, though the journey was not a pleasant one in this heat. When she arrived, grubby and perspiring, Daniel was already there. Obviously his own search for work had been unsuccessful again, for he remained at the table when she entered, slumped in weary manner, hands covering his face.

She sighed and laid her hand on his shoulder. 'No luck?'

He gave a miserable shake of head and sighed. 'No – I only got a bloody job, that's all.' He leaped from the table with a devilish laugh. 'Fair dinkum – I've got a bloody job! Aw darlin'!' And he lifted her off her feet to swing her round, delighting in the way her face showed the sort of expression that he had not seen in weeks. 'A proper job, no temporary stuff – the dinky-di article.' After Oriel had covered his face in kisses, he set her down and told her all about his luck in visiting the sawmill just ten minutes after another less fortunate chap had severed his arm and had been taken to hospital. 'Feel sorry for him, yeah, but I wasn't gonna knock it back! Start tomorrow, then get Christmas off – not bad eh? Pays well, too. Now we can afford to buy pressies for the kids.' Eyes glittering, he could not contain his excitement.

Neither could Oriel, who said they would go out that afternoon and buy some. 'I'll go and deliver mine tomorrow while you're at work – and I'm damned if I'm asking Clive's permission this time. I'll just turn up at the house.' Though the thought of seeing Jennifer and Dorrie was rather daunting. What would their reaction be?

Having not considered that the children would have broken up for the summer holidays, Oriel arrived at the house in time for them coming home from school, but found it empty. Of course! She damned her stupidity, they would be at their grandmother's until Clive came home from work. Bitterly disappointed, she left the gifts in a bag with a note for Clive, then stared around at her old home. It was strange being here after all this time – as if she had never lived here at all. Wondering whether any mail had come for her she was presented with a worrying thought: Clive would still be forwarding her letters to the old address – had any slipped through during the short interim since her eviction?

Checking the hall table on her way out she found a pile of letters and sifted through them. Finding one from her mother, she saw that Clive had already redirected it to her old address in Carlton, and sighed in relief that he had neglected to post it. Ripping it open there and then, she read: 'Dear Oriel and Clive, don't die from shock, but we've decided to pay you a long-needed visit.'

'Oh God!' She covered her mouth and read on, heart thudding. All that she had dreaded was about to come to reality. Her parents would get here on Christmas Eve. They would arrive in the expectation of a loving reunion and find only lies, deceit and a daughter who was living in sin.

Faced with this awful dilemma, Oriel rushed to the station and caught a train home but found no answer here, for Daniel was still at work and she had to endure nerve-racking hours before being able to share the news with him.

After a passionate hug and the query over how he had fared in his new job, she broke away. 'Before you get too pleased with yourself I think I ought to tell you the bad news – Mother and Father are coming down to Melbourne.'

The tanned face shared her look of dismay. 'Oh, bloody Nora – for Christmas?'

She nodded and distorted her mouth. 'I'm so stupid! I should have written and told them months ago. Why am I such a coward? Oh well, it's no good going over old ground. There's only one thing for it, I'll have to intercept them before they arrive at the house or Clive will stick his two pennorth in – though I doubt even he could make things worse. What a bloody mess.' She clamped her face between her palms, feeling sick at the mere thought of telling them.

Daniel was practical. 'Better arrange something with him. 'Sno good you waiting at the station, you might miss 'em.'

Oriel affected to bang her head against the wall in a display of frustration. 'Oh God, I can't face having to talk to him – still, you're right. I'll go out after tea and give him a ring.'

Later, she knocked on the door across the hall and asked the landlady if she would be allowed to use her telephone.

At this request, the woman's heavily made-up face adopted a grimace that turned the skin of her cheeks into crazy paving. She did not mind lending the occasional utensil but her generosity had recently been stretched by this new tenant. 'Sorry, dear, I find if I let people do that they take advantage and I end up paying for the call. There's one just down the street, though.'

Oriel returned to inform Daniel, who offered to go with her but knowing what a hard day he must have had she ordered him to remain in his chair, and went out alone.

The heat was unabated. Somehow, the soot-engrimed buildings made it appear even hotter.

The telephone box was indeed not far away. Acquiring

the number, Oriel listened to it burring at the other end of the line, wondering whether she would be able to hear the speaker properly, for a steam train was passing over a nearby railway bridge. The ringing stopped, Oriel pressed her ear to the receiver in readiness for the hello – and was shocked to hear a child's voice answer.

'Hell –' Her voice faltered, heart bleeding. 'Hello, Dorrie, is that you? Shouldn't you be in bed?' How wonderful it was to hear him, but how sad too.

The little voice responded. 'I'm allowed to stay up later now – who is it?'

She laughed. 'It's Mummy.'

'Mummy Jean or our other mummy?'

Oriel felt a knife thrust into her bowel, ramming right up through her heart and into her mouth. Her hands gripped the receiver as if glued there. Dorrie was chattering away but totally overwhelmed by horror she did not hear the rest of his words, only those two. The little boy stopped talking and waited for an answer. She tried to speak but nothing emerged. Dorrie's father took command of the phone and made a series of hellos. After a moment of puzzled silence she heard a click. The line had been broken. Drained of colour, she lowered the receiver and rested it in the cradle, then turned and walked away as if in a trance.

When she got home Daniel studied her. 'Are you all right?'

'What – oh, yes!' Oriel summoned life, wiping the sweat from her brow. 'Clive wasn't in.' She could not voice the dreadful news for fear of crying, and there had been too many tears. 'It doesn't matter, anyway. I know what day they're arriving. If I have to wait for every single train, I will.' Adopting nonchalance, she flopped into the chair beside his and leaned her head back against the fusty moquette. *Mummy Jean*.

Relaxing in similar pose, Daniel studied her. Neither of them was the same person he or she had been a year ago, their laughter interspersed by long bouts of solemnity such as he witnessed now, but he knew her well enough to detect an underlying reason for her preoccupation. She did not want to worry him. It was no use grilling her, she would deny it to the end.

'D'yer want me to come with yer, Kooks? Should be at work, but if you need me –'

'What, and get the sack two days after you've started? No thanks!' She smiled but was soon looking thoughtful again. 'No, I have to do this alone.'

'Course you do.' Concerned at her mood, and still wanting to be helpful, Daniel tried the opposite tack. 'I been thinking, I'm not gonna be very popular with your mum and dad when you break the news. You'll probably have to bring them here and there's things you'll wanna say to them. Might be an idea for me to get out o' the way for a day or so and come back on Christmas Night. By then yer should have it sorted out.'

'There's no need. You've been evicted from your home once –'

'No, I don't mind – if yer think you can do without me. Thought o' going up to take the kids' presents on Christmas Eve if I can get away from work soon enough to catch the train. No point me being here if you're not. There'll be no train back but I can get a lift off somebody – but don't go worrying if I can't get back the same night. Might have to bunk at a pal's. Buy a nice piece o' meat and I'll definitely be back to share it with yer Christmas Night. Yer never know, yer mum 'n' dad might come too.'

Mummy Jean. Oriel shoved the voice from her head and agreed to his proposal. 'I don't know what I'm going to do without you, though – God, what a Christmas this is going to be. Even worse than the last.'

'Won't our Oriel be surprised when we tell her we've come on an aeroplane!' Bright had recovered from her

557

initial fear on takeoff and now felt brave enough to look out over the clouds. She had not divulged her mode of travel in her letter, wanting to make this grand announcement in person.

'She will that.' It had taken little for Nat to persuade his wife to adopt this daring form of transport. She hated the gruelling journey by rail or road, and ever since watching the warplanes take off from her bedroom window in York had expressed an interest in flying. 'I wish we'd been able to do it sooner.' The passenger route had not been in existence for long.

'Never mind, I'm really enjoying it now, aren't you, Vicky?' The child sat between them. 'Your father's such an adventurer.'

'I don't know about adventurer,' said Nat, though feeling rather smug at his own bravery. 'But why take days when you can get there by teatime?'

Bright forgave his exaggeration – they had had to make the journey by rail down to Brisbane, but certainly the onward trip to Melbourne would be drastically reduced, their only stop Sydney. 'Unbelievable,' she sighed. 'I feel like Father Christmas on his magic sleigh.' They came bearing many gifts.

'There is no Father Christmas.' Vicky had outgrown the pretence.

'You might not believe in him but there are people who do,' warned her mother. 'Don't spoil it for the little ones.'

'Aye, I'm looking forward to seeing their faces when they open these.' Nat twitched his mouth.

His wife noted with satisfaction that he used the plural. 'I wonder what Dorrie will have up his sleeve this time?'

'Aye, he's a right comedian.' There was affection in Nat's praise.

Bright smiled. 'You really got to know each other last time, didn't you? He's a lovely little chap.'

'Don't think I'm weakening! I'm only getting well in

with him so he'll let me play with this train set we've bought him.'

Bright delivered a scolding grin over Vicky's head. 'Aw, come on, admit it, you've got a soft spot for him.'

'Aye well, mebbe you're right.' He looked grudging, then gave her a genuine smile. 'I just hope I'll feel the same by the time he's ten. I still say there's nowt so obnoxious as a ten-year-old boy – except maybe an eleven-year-old boy.'

His wife berated him, then handed round a bag of toffees and the conversation petered out, replaced by the drone of the engine.

Afraid that her parents might arrive early, Oriel had been waiting at Spencer Street Station since after lunch in tremendous heat, watching the interstate trains come in, watching them go out. Now, by late afternoon the muscles in the back of her neck felt as if they were on fire. Her shoulders had begun to droop, not merely from the hours of waiting, nor from missing Daniel, but from the weight of all her problems which seemed to increase by the second.

Mummy Jean. Tears came to her eyes as she put herself in her children's place, feeling helpless, knowing she was a useless mother, and above all fearing her parents' reaction. Where on earth had they got to?

From Essendon Aerodrome, Nat and his family had gone to the nearest railway station and made the rest of their journey across Melbourne by train to Flinders Street Station then, via a city rank, completed the last festively decorated stretch by taxi. Grumbling over the cost, he was now hefting the suitcases through fading light down the path of his daughter's house.

Ahead of him with Vicky at her side, Bright frowned at the For Sale sign. 'Oriel never told me they were selling.' She proceeded to the house, catching a movement at the window where two small faces had appeared.

Hearing the click of the gate Jennifer and Dorrie had hoped for a glimpse of Father Christmas but instead saw their grandparents and before Bright could reach the door the two children came bounding out.

'It's Nanna and Grandad Grumpy!' Dorrie leaped around like a sprite.

'Now then, Dorrie!' Encumbered by luggage, Nat merely gave vocal greeting, but for once put the boy before his sister. 'Have you got some zelaba for tea?'

His memory short, the five-year-old wrinkled his nose that was peeling from sunburn, and giggled. 'Silly old bugger.'

Nat affected shock but was highly amused. 'I beg yer pardon!'

Still rather in awe of this man, Dorrie hastily explained to show he was not really being rude. 'That's what Daddy calls you.'

'Does he, beGod? I'll have words for him. Hello, Jenny Wren! Pretty as ever.'

Bright chuckled and stooped to deliver hugs and kisses to both children, then raised herself to greet Clive who stood in the doorway. Normally he would have divested her of her bags but today he offered only confusion.

With Nat at her side now, Bright laughed. 'Do we have to take our shoes off first?'

'Sorry!' Clive stepped aside and watched his in-laws deposit their bags in the hall. 'You, er . . . you've come to see the children obviously.'

She remained smiling. 'Didn't you get my letter?'

Things fell into place then. Clive lifted his chin in recognition. 'I wondered why you kept sending them here. She still hasn't told you, has she?'

'Told us what?' Nat had begun to wonder why they were being kept in the hall.

At that precise moment a woman appeared in the living-room doorway and smiled at them in pleasant manner.

'She's left us,' said Clive.

As Bright gasped and looked distraught, Nat remained cynical. 'I wonder why.'

Clive saw that he was looking at the woman. 'Hang on, she left me for another man!'

'You mean to say, she left the children with you?' Nat's voice was hollow, his mind suddenly wrought with the image of his own mother's back as she walked away from him.

Receiving a nod, Bright almost collapsed and tears filled her eyes. 'Oh, God, how could she!'

Nat felt as if he were going to vomit, was furious both at his daughter and his son-in-law. 'Is it too much to ask that you let my wife sit down?'

Clive became solicitous then, escorting Bright into the living room with a demonic-looking Nat and three confused children taking up the rear. 'Jennifer, why don't you two take Victoria to play with your toys?'

Dorrie clung and whined. 'I want to stay with you.'

His father reassured both children. 'I'll be here, I just want to talk to Nanna and Grandad alone. You can talk to them later.'

'Are you going to talk about Mummy?' Dorrie chewed his upper lip with his teeth.

'Never mind – Jenny, take your brother, you can come back in a minute.'

Dorrie studied his grandmother, who was blowing her nose and trying to regain her composure. Her attitude worried him. 'Have you seen Mummy?' But she was spared having to answer, for his sister intervened, grabbing his hand and leading him away, Vicky following.

When they had scampered off, the woman uttered her first words. 'Can I get anybody a cup of tea?'

Accepting the offer, Nat watched her go. 'Well, she seems pretty much at home here.'

'Don't think you're coming into my home and running down my friends!' warned the younger man. 'You leave

Jean alone. It's your daughter who's to blame. You don't know any of it, do you? Well, sit and have your cup of tea and listen to this!'

As a skin of tannin formed on the untouched teacups, he told the calcified listeners of Oriel's affair with Daniel, how she had not only messed his life about but the children's too, had not been to see them in months. 'She went to live with him a year ago, said she was trying to find a place where she could take the children but so far that hasn't materialized, and I'm not sure I'd let them go now. They're happy enough here.' He saw the change of expression on their faces and sought to divert any further unpleasantness. 'Anyway, I've got her latest address if you want it.' He made as if to get this.

'Don't worry, we won't be off there.' Dark of face, Nat rose. 'Come on.' He summoned his wife. 'We'll have to go find an hotel.'

Feeling more than her fifty years, Bright rose reluctantly and studied Clive with compassion. 'I'm so sorry.'

Her son-in-law had always liked her. 'It's not your fault,' he told her, then looked pointedly at her husband.

Nat delayed his exit to challenge the younger man. 'If you've summat to say –'

Bright knew what was coming and tried to avoid it by interrupting. 'Clive, I'll leave the children's presents!' But her voice was ignored.

After a year Clive had recovered from the initial fury at being cuckolded, but there was a residue of deep bitterness and now he directed it towards his father-in-law. 'It's a good job you weren't standing there when it first happened or you would've got a damned sight more than a cup of tea. Do you think that just because you decided to come back into Oriel's life when she was eighteen you wiped away all the harm you did her? She'll never be like normal people. She thinks that Daniel's going to solve her problems but she's wrong, she'll get fed up of him just like she got fed up of me. She's going to spend her

562

whole life skipping from man to man and all because she's looking for the father she never had in childhood –'

Nat erupted. 'Don't talk bloody rubbish! You're trying to cover up your own shortcomings by blaming me.'

'I'm not the only one that thinks it.' Clive looked at his mother-in-law for confirmation.

Bright wanted to disappear into the carpet. 'Clive, I asked you not to –'

Nat uttered no words, but the look of betrayal in his eyes said everything. He turned and walked out, calling for Vicky and seizing his cases on the way, with Bright running behind.

'Nat! Nat, wait!' She tried to catch up. Darkness had fallen and she stumbled. 'I never meant –'

'Not now.' Mind spinning, he strode down the path, stopped dead and looked up and down the darkened street, cursing himself for not considering what he was going to do for transport. 'Go back and ask him to ring for a taxi – a local one; I don't want to be stood here all night.'

'But –'

'Don't worry, I'll wait.' His expression was taut. Not for twelve years had she seen such a face. 'But if I go back in there I'll do for somebody.'

'How could she do such a thing?' Bright hugged herself, was almost in tears again as she thought of her grand-children who might be lost to her.

Spotting Vicky running down the path to catch them up, he sighed. 'Just bloody go.'

At that same juncture, Oriel came upon the scene. Frantic that she must somehow have missed her parents getting off the train from Albury, she had, half an hour ago, decided the only thing for it was to brave their shocked contempt and meet them at the house in North Brighton where they must surely be.

She saw her father and the little figure beside him as she hurried up the street, and her gait faltered. Waiting for his wife to come back Nat lit a cigarette. She saw his tensed expression in the matchflame as she approached. As he lifted his face and shook out the match he saw her too, paused in his action for a second, then threw the dead match on the ground.

Oriel came hesitantly towards him. Vicky cried out and reached up for a hug, which her sister delivered but afterwards gave her entire attention to her father, wide blue eyes holding his face. 'He's told you, hasn't he?'

Nat gave a curt nod and looked around impatiently to see where his wife had got to. After phoning for a taxi Bright had tarried to say a proper farewell to her grand-children and to ask her son-in-law why he had been so spiteful, but now, as the taxi appeared in the street, she emerged and came down the path. Nat hailed the cab and as it pulled up he shoved Vicky inside, holding the door open for his wife. Bright got straight in, with Nat after her. Oriel thought her mother had not seen her at first but when she shouted out, the older woman turned pain-filled eyes from the dark interior of the car and asked, 'How could you?'

That was all. Her father slammed the door and the taxi pulled away. With hollow heart, Oriel watched it disappear into the darkness until all that was left was the whirr of cicadas. Totally destroyed, she made her own way home.

It had been difficult to find an hotel at this time of year. Tempers were barely controlled as Nat drove round and round before eventually finding a vacancy at one which had few comforts and inefficient staff. After a tense sup-per, Bright put Vicky to bed, then came to sit beside her husband, stroking his hand whilst he sat gazing bleakly at the wall.

Nothing was said for a while, until finally he asked without looking at her, 'Is that what you really think? That I'm to blame for all of this?'

'No!' She tightened her grip on him.

His face was unmoved. 'You told him you did.'

'I didn't! I was just trying to make him feel better after she'd been going to lea–' Bright suddenly remembered that he knew none of this, but too late.

'Go on.' He had dealt her a sharp glance but now turned his cold blue eyes away.

She sighed and rubbed the arm of his expertly tailored suit. After all these years under the Queensland sun, Nat still loved the opportunity to dress up. Aborting several attempts, she finally blurted, 'Oriel wanted to leave him after they'd only been married a short while. It was that time she came up to see us on her own before Jenny was born. I talked her out of it, thought it was just a flash in the pan. If I'd known she'd been harbouring it all these years –'

'So you told Clive it was all my fault.'

'No!' Her face was burning. 'Well, I just said I thought it could be because she hadn't had a father around when she was little and she was mixed up – but I didn't intend any blame towards you! I've always said –'

'I know what you've always said.' Nat was cool. 'But you told him different.'

'It was just to make him feel better! Nat, I love you, I wouldn't blame you for all this. Oriel's a grown woman. It's no one's fault but her own – oh, how could she leave those children?'

'Just like her father left her.'

Realizing she had said the wrong thing again Bright dug her nails into her forehead wanting to scream. 'What if Clive won't let us see them any more? What if he gets married again?' The thought produced more tears. 'I'll never forgive her!'

Nat gave her a sideways look, then stood abruptly. 'I'm off to bed.'

*   *   *

Oriel had gone to bed too. Afraid of the darkness without Daniel, she had opened the half-bottle of whisky in an attempt to be able to sleep. It had been meant as a gift, a rather extravagant gift, for him. She did not usually drink the stuff herself but now, her altruism quashed by the shock of parental hostility, she filled her glass, tilting it at her mouth and shivering as it burned its way down. The glass was refilled – how difficult it was to achieve unconsciousness, thoughts and voices swirling round her head – but the more she drank the worse her pain became.

She woke to crapulence, the sound of Christmas bells and the call of festive greeting from one resident to another on the stairs. Though it was tempting to curl up into a ball, she dragged herself out of the mould-spotted bed and went to wash and change, should her beloved come home early and find a drunkard.

He did not come. She waited all day in her best dress, thinking of Daniel with his children, wondering if she would ever see her own again, wondering where he had slept last night, wondering was that his footstep in the hall, wondering, wondering. Pressure had been building up inside her head for days, her brain crammed with thoughts and voices – *Mummy Jean* – surely there could be no room for more but, yes, now her mother's face accused her, her father's too. She tried to fight them – what did they know of her tragedy? Hidden away in paradise the Depression had touched neither of them. Yet, their faces and accusations continued to haunt her, pushing her further and further towards the abyss. She was a rotten daughter, a rotten mother, a rotten wife.

Fighting panic, she sprang up and busied herself with the evening repast, turned on the oven and installed the joint of Christmas pork. Soon, the smell of it was wafting through the house, but still Daniel did not come.

After a night's sleep, Nat's anger had burned itself out. He had still not forgiven his wife, but, in recognition that Christmas would be totally ruined for his younger daughter, had suggested they try to maintain the festive spirit for Vicky's sake. Bright had agreed and, before breakfast, made the tentative appeal that they ring Clive and ask if she could join Jennifer and Dorrie in the opening of their presents. Their son-in-law kindly acceded, saying that the child could also stay the night in order to allow them to go and see Oriel.

Still Nat had refused to do this. Back at the hotel, he and Bright had picked at a lukewarm Christmas lunch, but demurred the offer to join in party games and retired to their room. Nat collapsed on the sofa and remained in this position for some time, nostrils taut at the sound of the people downstairs enjoying themselves when all he wanted was peace. It wasn't fair that this should happen at his time of life.

Finally, he broached the subject, the tone of his voice and the look on his face showing he had been thinking of nothing else all day. 'I always said he wasn't right for her.'

Pale of feature, mouth turned down, Bright nodded. 'And I always said I'd never desert Oriel whatever she'd done. Didn't take much to shatter that resolution, did it? Once a Maguire always a Maguire. God, I wish I'd listened to you and persuaded her not to marry him – but I genuinely thought she loved him. And I always found him so nice.'

'Isn't it strange how so-called nice people can be such little shits?' Nat lit a cigarette.

Though hating the bitterness, she interpreted his meaning. 'You never know someone until you live with them. I suppose she wouldn't have left him without good reason, would she?'

He shook his head. What had been his mother's reason when she had left him?

'Often it's difficult for outsiders to see those reasons. I've been thinking about it all day, about the way people thought I was mad when I refused to marry anyone but you. Maybe she feels that way about Daniel. Maybe she's always loved him and didn't dare say. I can understand that – though I still for the life of me can't understand why she had to leave Jennifer and Dorrie. I asked their father if we'd still be able to see them. He seemed vague.'

'He needn't think he's keeping me from my grandbairns.' Nat took a long drag.

'Didn't Oriel look ghastly?'

Her husband closed his eyes and nodded.

'I feel awful now, treating her like that. I was just so mad.' She watched him for a moment, then asked, 'Can you forgive me for putting forth my stupid theory to Clive?'

After a moment's hesitance, he patted her knee. 'Maybe it's not so daft.' For too long he had been laying the blame at his mother's door. She had left him. He had left Oriel. She had her reasons, he had his and Oriel would no doubt have hers. It was impossible to tell what another was feeling, even when suffering an identical crisis. Everyone coped in a different fashion. He had matured enough to see that. But now the circle must be broken. The grudge against his mother was too deeply engrained to be removed, but it was at his fingertips to prevent the same thing happening to Dorrie. He puffed out his cheeks, eyes staring into midair. 'Still, we won't find out if we don't give her a chance to put her side of the story, will we? I wish I'd got her address off him now.' He laid the smouldering cigarette in an ashtray and rose. 'I think I'll give him a ring.'

He stood for a while with the receiver to his ear, but the call went unanswered.

Hovering nearby, Bright explained. 'Clive said he was taking the children round to his mother's for tea. Dorothy might know. I hope so. I just keep seeing Oriel's face when I said my last words to her.' Tears came again along with a sense of urgency. 'Can you ring? I don't think I'll be able to get my words out.'

Nat picked up the telephone again, and waited.

Oriel was still alone. The whisky bottle had come out again. It was empty now and it had not helped. *Mummy Jean, Mummy Jean, Mummy Jean* – Daniel, where are you? My babies, my babies.

She fell on to the bed, squirming her face into the musty pillow, trying to escape the voices. Alcohol and despair fuddled her senses. Above the landlady's cackling merriment came the throbbing of her own blood as it pulsed through her arteries, swishing, thudding, her mind seemed on the verge of explosion, as if someone were trying to cram a mattress into a cushion case that was far, far too small and threatened to burst at the seams. Her own words came back to haunt her – we're going to pay dearly for this happiness – and the seams began to give way. In the certainty that everything was lost she staggered from the bed, across the hall and out into the night, dropping the bottle on her way.

Her fingerprints were barely cold upon the glass when Daniel came through the door, grimaced at the sound of drunken singing from his landlady then accidentally kicked the bottle and sent it spinning across the linoleum. Cursing the drunk who had abandoned it he went to pick it up and took it into his room.

The door was slightly ajar. 'Sorry, I'm late, darlin'! Oh, Christ I've had a helluva –'

He broke off upon entering. The light was on but Oriel was not here. There was an awful smell of burning too. Opening the oven he gasped at the cloud of heat that came out and shut the door quickly on the burnt ember inside. Hearing a female voice just outside his door he thought it must be her and went cheerfully to answer it. 'What the hell d'you call this for Christmas dinner?'

Bright donated a barely polite smile, her husband saying abruptly, 'We've come to see our Oriel.'

The grin faded. 'Oh – she isn't here. Can't be far away, though. Come in.' Daniel stepped aside, then suddenly thought to explain, 'Sorry, I've been away. She did meet you at the station last night?'

Removing his hat, Nat shook his head. 'We came by aeroplane. We did see her briefly but – well, we were a bit angry and we didn't give her time to say owt. Clive had already told us, you see.' Faced with the austerity of the room he turned to his wife, both looked askance. 'She's been living here for a year?'

Daniel seemed half amused at their shock. 'Oh, nowhere so good as this! No, we've only been here a couple o' days.' He asked them to sit down then told them briefly of the eviction.

Perched on the edge of the battered chair, Bright was horrified. 'We had no idea! Dorothy never mentioned – we telephoned her to get your address, you see, because Clive wasn't in.'

'Yer would've been sent on a wild goose chase anyway. Clive's only got our old address.' In the tense interval he started to become concerned. Oriel was still not home. 'Said yer didn't have time to say much to her – what exactly did you say?'

Nat looked guilty then. So too did Bright. 'We were so angry,' she said. 'How could she leave her children, Daniel?'

His pleasant expression became hard. 'And how could I leave mine? That's what yer wanna know, isn't it?'

'It's a fair question to put to the man who's taken our daughter from her family,' said Nat. 'I mean, we don't know what your intentions are. You might leave her tomorrow for all we know.'

'And what about Melinda?' asked Bright.

Daniel contained his anger by scratching furiously at his neck. 'I'll tell you something now – not that I feel the need to! It's just for Oriel's sake. I've never touched another woman while I've been married to Melinda. Never. I must admit I've enjoyed looking at a few, but to me if a man really loves his wife those things remain in his head and if they don't then he doesn't really love her. I know blokes who think it's perfectly okay to have other women on the side just so long as they're taking home the bread-and-butter and their wives don't find out. Well, I'm not one of 'em. They can argue till they're blue in the face that a quick how's-yer-father isn't a betrayal but to me it is. So if yer think that's all it is between me and Oriel yer can forget it. I've loved her for years, and I will till the day I die.'

He rubbed his head, which was throbbing. Mrs Prince was embarrassed but that would not stop him. They had obviously upset Oriel by what they had said and now he would demand they listen to him. 'I'm not shrugging off any blame. I have betrayed Melinda and I won't give any excuses because I don't care how people want to judge me. Until they've been through the same situation they don't know how they'd react – I never foresaw this happening to me in a million years. I love my kids, it ripped my guts out seeing them cry when I left. But I had to be with Oriel. I know I'm a terrible father. I don't need you or anybody else to scream that at me to make it sink in, but I reckon I just wasn't born to be good and noble and responsible as my accusers seem to be. I don't know what you people think it was like to make that decision. D'yer imagine I just waved 'em merrily goodbye?'

'No, of course not.' Bright's voice was soft.

'And you're hardly the best judge,' Daniel accused Nat. 'Oriel told me you two never met till she was an adult so you should know exactly what I'm talking about. I hate meself for doing it and Oriel feels the same but we couldn't live without each other. We just couldn't. Everybody's different, it isn't right for people to judge. It's just not bloody right. Okay, I could've stayed till they were grown up – in theory at least – so could Oriel, but would the kids've been any more well-disposed towards us knowing that we were only staying for their sakes? It'd be as if we were blaming them for being born. Whatever happens I'm still their father – and Oriel only took hers back to Clive because he made it so bloody awkward for her to get at her own money and provide a nice home for them. She thought she was being selfish making 'em live in a place like this.'

Bright exchanged a harassed look with her husband. 'He didn't tell us that.'

'No, and I bet he didn't tell you she travelled fifteen miles a day back and forth to collect them from school, nearly killing herself in the process, until he stopped her! Soon as her house is sold and everything's sorted out we're having them to live with us. It's just this divorce business dragging on and on. I've got a job now, I'm working hard to make it happen. It's gonna be all right.' His anger suddenly turned to anxiety. 'Something's wrong. Oriel should be here.' He racked his throbbing brain for where she might be.

Nat sighed and looked at his wife, then his eye caught the empty whisky bottle that Daniel had put aside on discovering his cremated dinner. 'Somebody's been knocking it back.'

'Well, it's not me!'

'I didn't say it was.'

'I found it in the hall. Oriel can't stand . . . can't stand litter.' Panic flickered in Daniel's eye. He knew. He just knew. Racing from the house he stopped dead and looked up and down the darkened street, a man demented. Nat came out after him. 'What's up?'

'We've got to find her!' The tone of Daniel's voice conveyed the seriousness of this.

When he set off at a run both Nat and Bright pursued him through the darkness, wondering if he knew where he was going.

They did not have far to run. Daniel saw the outline of a figure sitting on the parapet of the railway bridge and gave a strangled shout as he rushed to interrupt her. 'Oriel!'

'Don't frighten her, she might fall!' urged Nat still pursuing.

The figure did not turn but merely swayed in the warm night air as the three came running towards her. Daniel reached her first, clambered up and grabbed her around the waist with one arm to prevent her falling on to the track whilst his other hand tried to prise her fingers off the sooty brickwork, but it was as if they were welded there. 'Oriel! It's all right! I'm here!'

Voices came through her tortured mind. Daniel's voice. Seeing him, relief flooded her dazed eyes but she could not let go, her fingers having gripped too long. If she let go now she would be lost.

'We've got you, lass, you won't fall!' Nat had climbed up too and was trying to lift her fingers one by one but each time he managed to get one loose her grip intensified. 'For goodness' sake, you're like a little limpet – just let go. What you doing up here?'

'Holding God's hand,' murmured his daughter. 'Can't let go. Don't want to jump.'

He groaned in despair. 'Oh Christ, she's had a right skinful.'

Daniel sighed and, with accusation in his voice, told him, 'No, she's just reached the end of her tether.' With coaxing words he finally managed to prise her bloodless fingers from the bridge and pulled her backwards into the safety of his arms, cupping the back of her head to his chest, kissing and stroking the face that stank of whisky. 'Oh Oriel, darlin', sweetheart, what were yer thinking of?' he begged her.

'You didn't come back,' came her slurred murmur.

He hugged her even more tightly. 'Didn't I say I might be late? I had to walk part o' the way, got here as soon as I could. And why were you standing up there? Don't yer know the trains don't run on Christmas Day? Aw Jeez, you silly little –' He broke off to kiss her.

Oriel lay against him, suddenly aware of the other concerned faces. 'I'm sorry . . . I'm a rotten daughter.'

'Oh, lass, why didn't you come to us?' asked her distraught breathless father.

'She did.' Bright sobbed and put her arms round the embracing couple. 'I'm sorry! I'm so sorry I didn't listen.'

'A rotten mother,' slurred Oriel.

'No, no!'

'Never done anything for anybody, just hurt people. My babies.' Her mouth crumpled.

Nat swore and frowned, trying to retain his manhood though the tears stung his eyes. 'Oriel, don't worry about anything else. We'll get you out of that place and buy you a decent house so you can have the children to live with you and Daniel. Don't worry, we'll get them back. We'll get them back. Away, lad,' he said to Daniel. 'Let's get her home.'

The final hours of Christmas Night were spent in the bosom of people who loved her. Whilst Oriel drifted in and out of sleep others were discussing her future.

Bright recognized that it was not just the drink talking, her daughter was on the verge of mental collapse, but she refused to let her be hospitalized. 'I'm not having her go through that. We can look after her ourselves. Daniel, she can stay with us while you're at work.'

He thanked her, his eyes never leaving the face on the pillow.

'I suppose it's inevitable this happened,' she opined. 'With her mother as mad as a bloody hatter.'

'You're not mad, lass,' said Nat. 'Just a bit puddled.'

She thought of something else. 'We can't let Clive know or he'll never let her have the children back.'

Nat spoke to Daniel, keeping his voice low so as not

to waken Oriel. 'I meant what I said before about buying a place for you to live in so's she can get the kids back. I don't want to tread on any toes but if you feel about her as strongly as you say you do then I don't think you'd deny her that.'

Daniel shook his head. 'Wouldn't deny her anything.'

'Good. Can't do anything till after Boxing Day but I reckon what with the housing market being the way it is we could have one in a week. Like me wife says, she can come and stay at our hotel – not tonight but you can bring her tomorrow. It's a bit of a dump, we'll get somewhere better after Christmas. Will you accept some money to keep you going while we get sorted out? Buy her a new frock or summat?'

Daniel said he would.

Nat dipped into his wallet and handed over most of what was in it. 'I can get some more when t'bank opens. If you need owt don't be afraid to ask. Most of it'll be Oriel's when we go, it's more important she has benefit of it now. I can't understand why she didn't ask earlier if you were in such trouble. I know she's never liked asking for help but, bloody hell, we are her parents.'

'She would've had to tell yer why she wanted it and she couldn't bring herself to hurt yer,' explained Daniel, looking tenderly upon his loved one. 'That's been half her trouble.'

'I suppose we didn't make it any easier,' acknowledged Bright.

Daniel told them about her efforts to keep the children with her, but things had just got out of hand. 'We just didn't know it'd last this long. Looks like it'll go on a lot longer for most poor buggers.'

Nat raised his eyebrows at the degree of suffering he had witnessed in the city. 'Doesn't really hit you till it happens to your own.'

After a thoughtful silence, he turned his head to look at Bright, whose face looked slightly yellow under this poor globe. 'Well, I suppose we'd better be going, give this lad some peace, and we have to go over to meladdo's and pick Vicky up tomorrow.' Rising along with his wife, he took a look at the bed on which his daughter lay deep in sleep. 'She must be worn out.'

Daniel nodded, feeling overcome by weariness himself. 'She's had a lot to cope with.' He left them suddenly and stooped to rummage in a carrier. 'Here, take this with you. It'll explain a lot more than I can. Managed to rescue it before we were evicted.'

Bright took the wad of crumpled paper that was her daughter's journal and began to leaf through it, sampling its contents with grim fascination before putting it under her arm to take home.

Nat arranged for Daniel to bring Oriel to the hotel tomorrow noon, then, eyes averted, gave one last instruction. 'When t'lass wakes up tell her . . . erm, we love her and that, yer know.' He half turned as if to go. 'And when she sees us tomorrow, she'll have her bairns back.'

'It was a bit rash of you to promise that,' scolded Bright as they made their way out of the grimy suburb and into the bright illuminations of the city to find a taxi. 'You'll only make her worse if Clive won't wear it.'

Nat stopped to light a cigarette, then walked on. 'He will when I've finished with him.'

'Oh, you're not going to –'

'No – though I'm not saying I wouldn't like to kick his head in. What I meant was, everybody has their price.'

Bright worried that any attempt at bribery might make Clive dig his heels in further. 'Oh, I don't think he's the type that can be bought.'

'Everybody can be bought – even your Pope.'

Walking briskly at his side, his wife scoffed. 'You're telling me if we offered His Holiness a million pounds to kill someone he'd do it?'

'No, but if I said to him, you shake my hand I'll give you a million pounds to donate to a good cause –'

'That's not the same!'

'Course it is. He's allowing himself to be bought, and if I word my request correctly Clive can be bought as well – here y'are, there's a taxi!' And hailing it he escorted her back to their hotel.

Bright did not intend to read all of her daughter's journal that night, but once she had begun found it too enthralling to stop until she reached the end, and insisted on keeping Nat awake too by reading out certain passages. Both were moved to tears.

After wiping her eyes and before lying down she tapped the bundle of papers, a spark of determination in her eye. 'This deserves to be published. Once Christmas is over I'm going to take it to a newspaper office and show it to the editor – I'm sure he'll agree to serialize it. God, the poor souls, haven't they had a terrible time of it?' She turned off the lamp and lay down beside her husband and was silent for a moment. Then, her sigh rent the darkness. 'Oh, I hope we can get them back.'

The next morning when his in-laws came round to collect Vicky, Clive bowed to his father-in-law's request that they have a private chat, and listened without interruption to what Nat had to say, before making his reply.

'So let me get this right – you're offering to let me keep this house in return for giving up my children?'

'I'm not asking you to give them up, just to let them live with their mother. She won't stop you from seeing them.'

'Oh, that's very generous of her. What makes you think I wouldn't be allowed to keep this house anyway? It was Oriel who deserted me and the children. I should think any judge would frown on that – not to mention her adultery.'

'That was something else I wanted to discuss.' Fighting

the urge to smack Clive's face for his snide remarks, Nat remained calm. 'Have you thought seriously what having to admit adultery would do to Oriel? How it would make her look to the rest of the world?'

'Oh, don't tell me!' laughed his son-in-law. 'You want me to take the blame.'

'Well, you have got a woman living here and I doubt she just irons your shirts.' Nat tried to be amiable. 'Come on, Clive, it's nowt to a bloke –'

'Why should I care about her feelings? She didn't care about mine.'

'I don't think that's true but never mind – what about your kids? Don't you care that people are going to point at them and say their mother committed adultery?'

Clive scoffed. 'Even if I took the blame it wouldn't alter that fact!'

'Nay, it wouldn't.' Nat offered no defence, but looked his opponent directly in the eye.

Clive stared back. 'You've never liked me, have you?'

'Nothing personal, I just didn't think you were right for her. That being said, I think you're a good father –'

'And you'd know?'

'I know you want what's best for 'em. They haven't seen their mam for a while. Apart from any other arrangement we might come to I'd like to take them to see her today.'

Clive prevaricated. 'Oh, I don't know about that, I was going to –'

'It's not much to ask. It is Christmas, lass is missing 'em.'

'And that's my fault?'

'Aw, look, stop pissing me about, Clive!' Nat couldn't keep up the niceties. 'I haven't got time. Let's get this sorted out. You can have the house and five hund–'

'You'll let me have my own house?' There came ridicule.

'Five hundred!'

'You're not buying my kids!'

'I'm not asking to buy 'em! I'm paying you to stand up in court and spare their mother, and I want them to be happy!'

'They are happy! They like Jean.'

'Ask 'em then! Let's have 'em in here and ask 'em who they want to live with. If they say they want to live with you and see their mother at weekends I'll abide by that.' But I hope to God they don't, thought Nat, for I can't let Oriel down. Not again.

Clive maintained his determined stance for a moment, then went to the door and called the children in.

When Oriel had awoken she thought it had all been a terrible nightmare, until Daniel had taken her in his arms and related gently what had happened. Even now, being driven in a taxi to her parents' hotel she could not credit last night's scene with reality. Her head still felt crammed with cottonwool, her thoughts befuddled even by the simplest of acts such as fastening a row of buttons on her dress, which Daniel had had to do for her. It was not simply the aftereffects of the whisky. She was very, very sick.

But she would get better now. Blessed with Daniel and the knowledge that her parents had forgiven her and still loved her, she would get better.

Seated on the back seat of the taxi beside her, Daniel gripped her fingers, kneading them, delivering solace. So fragile, she looked, so lost – never had he loved her more than this moment, wanted to cry at the sight of her. He had not passed on the entirety of Nat's message. Oriel had no inkling that she was going to the hotel to meet not just her parents but her children as well. For if he had told her and Nat had been unsuccessful . . . God knew what it would do to her.

Trying to cheer her, he related what had happened when he had arrived to deliver the gifts to his own children – Norm's comical look of horror at being discovered with Melinda. Oriel tried to match his grin, but soon her anxious mind had drifted somewhere else.

The taxi pulled up outside the shabby façade of the hotel in Brighton, Daniel helped Oriel out and paid the driver, then escorted her inside.

The woman at the desk, a dilatory creature who drank from a glass while addressing them, said that the occupants of room 14 were out at present. Daniel said they were expecting him and he would wait. He was in the act of shepherding his befuddled companion to a chair when another taxi pulled up outside. His alert gaze scoured the vehicle, and his heart plummeted in disappointment. Nat and Bright were alone. Thank God he had not told Oriel about the children.

She had seen her parents getting out of the taxi and went nervously to greet them.

It was as he went with her that Daniel saw another small head start to emerge after those of the adults, heard Oriel's joyful intake of breath as she ran to the door, hurling it open and throwing herself at her children. Rushing after her, his anxious eyes went to Nat for confirmation, which was delivered in one simple nod. Relaxing, he allowed himself to smile, sharing the joy of his beloved, whilst his heart was filled with envy and sadness for a loss that would never be healed.

The Longing

Jane Asher

'Topical, emotion-charged . . . grips from the very first page'

Daily Mail

Michael and Juliet Evans are thirty-something, happily married and successful. Just one thing casts a shadow over their comfortable existence: the baby they long for has not, so far, materialised. So instead of decorating the nursery and visiting Mothercare, they resort to a world of private clinics and medical jargon, their hopes and fears rekindled by a young doctor with the power to transform their lives.

The waiting game has begun. But as the pressure builds, Juliet begins to lose her grip on reality. A different, more powerful longing takes hold, and her family and friends watch with agonising suspense while she struggles on the edge of darkness - until something happens that will twist all their lives again . . .

'A writer who does convey real emotional power . . . Like all really good novels, (*The Longing*) is true . . . in the way that its characters seem real and the world in which they move is one we recognise. Even better, its power increases as it goes on, drawing you further into its plot, gripping more tightly with every page . . . if Jane Asher were not already famous, this book would make her so'

Daily Express

0 00 649050 6

LaVyrle Spencer

That Camden Summer

The heart has a mind of its own . . .

Roberta Jewett, independent and free-thinking, has divorced her pilandering husband and arrives in Camden, Maine with her three daughters, full of hope for a fresh start in the town where she was born. But it is 1916, and a woman divorced is a woman shunned, especially if she has a full-time job and drives a Model T Ford.

Condemned by her mother, harassed by her lecherous brother-in-law, and scorned by the townsfolk, Roberta defies them all and perseveres in creating a happy home for her daughters. Only one man, widower Gabriel Farley, treats her with respect and, as their friendship deepens, the chemistry between them becomes hard to ignore. But they are both held back by unhappy memories and only a brutal act of violence forces them to acknowledge the love that has grown between them; a love which, in the face of the cruel hypocrisy and prejudice of their neighbours, will be put to the ultimate test . . .

0 00 649715 2

The Girl Now Leaving

Betty Burton

Lu Wilmott grows up in the Portsmouth slums of the 1920s. Stricken by diphtheria, she is sent to the Hampshire countryside to recover, and in this idyll she discovers a robust fighting spirit, new and challenging friends, and the first stirrings of sexual attraction.

But, faced with little choice, she follows her mother and aunts into the city's infamous staymaking trade, where young girls and old women endure conditions so appalling that Lu comes to realize that things must change. And she can be the instrument of that change.

Her journey to maturity, from proud but shy child to energetic woman, encompasses love, deep friendship, and a growing political awareness as the Spanish Civil War casts its influence over Europe. Above all, Lu is a survivor – and one to be reckoned with.

'Betty Burton constructs the world from the female point of view . . . carefully considered, subtle, and observant'
Sunday Times

ISBN 0 00 649631 8

Time Shall Reap

Doris Davidson

In 1915, when young Elspeth Grey, ill and heavily pregnant, becomes destitute in a strange city, she casts herself upon the mercy of Helen Watson, a compassionate woman she once met briefly on a train. Helen and her husband, themselves expecting a baby, gladly give the girl a home. Sadly, however, after Elspeth's son is born, Helen loses her infant, and in her traumatized state, transposes the two births in her mind. With the neighbours also believing that little John is Helen's baby, Elspeth gradually finds herself deprived of her child as well as of the man she loved.

Elspeth is given a second chance in life with marriage to David, a soldier badly scarred by the war. But the tangle of secrets overshadowing Elspeth's youth causes misunderstandings that lead eventually to tragedy. Only when the full truth becomes clear can she and her family find happiness and freedom from guilt . . .

0 00 647323 7

Fallen Skies

Philippa Gregory

'It is both uncompromising and brave'
ELIZABETH BUCHAN, *Daily Telegraph*

Lily Valance wants to forget the war. She's determined to enjoy the world of the 1920s, with its music, singing, laughter and pleasure. When she meets Captain Stephen Winters, a decorated hero back from the Front, she's drawn to his wealth and status. In Lily, he sees his salvation – from the past, from the nightmares, from the guilt at surviving where so many were lost.

But it's a dream that cannot last. Lily has no intention of leaving her singing career. The hidden tensions behind the respectable facade of the Winters household come to a head. Stephen's nightmares merge ever closer with reality and the truth of what took place in the mud and darkness brings him and all who love him to a terrible reckoning . . .

'Superbly crafted . . . a fine book.'   *Daily Mail*

ISBN 0 00 647336 9

Lady of Hay

Barbara Erskine

'Barbara Erskine can make us feel the cold, smell the filth, and experience some of the fear of the power of evil men . . . The author's story telling talent is undeniable'   *The Times*

Jo Clifford, successful journalist, is all set to debunk the idea of past-life regression in her next magazine series. But when she herself submits to a simple hypnotic session, she suddenly finds herself reliving the experiences of Matilda, Lady of Hay, the wife of a baron at the time of King John.

As she learns of Matilda's unhappy marriage, her love for the handsome Richard de Clare and the brutal threats of death at the hands of King John, it becomes clear that Jo's past and present are hopelessly entwined and that, eight hundred years on, a story of secret passion and unspeakable treachery is about to begin again . . .

'Fascinating, absorbing, original - and hypnotic'
                                                           She

0 00 649780 2